Notebook Mysteries

Notebook Mysteries

Books
1 - 2 - 3

KIMBERLY MULLINS

To my family-it has been a grand adventure.
To Claudia, for being there and supporting me.

NOTEBOOK MYSTERIES ~ THE BEGINNING

MARY AND ELLIS

Notebook Mysteries

Mary
and
Ellis

KIMBERLY MULLINS

CHAPTER 1

1866 GERMANY

*M*ary Herwig boarded her ship, carrying all of her belongings in her carpetbag. She waited patiently in the line at the entrance point to the ship. Once aboard, she moved to the rail, silently saying one last goodbye to the country where she had been born and raised.

She would never again return to Germany. There was no family left there, her parents and grandparents had passed away and her brothers had migrated to America ten years before. She was only ten when they left for a new life.

After Mama and Papa died, she received a letter from the United States. The sight of Hans' name prompted her to open it quickly. She cried happy tears when she read that they wanted her with them. The war in the states was over; it was safe to travel.

That letter was her talisman guiding her into the US. She didn't stop to think, she immediately put her bakery and home up for sale. Both sold quickly, and the money would allow her to open a bakery in Chicago. She had been planning this move for the last ten years, ever since her brothers had left, saving every letter from them. She knew where her future would be.

The trip was without problems. She was a good sailor and had made lots of flatbread to balance the times of seasickness. This allowed her to have something in her stomach when the ship rolled. Plenty of people were sick over the side of the ship, a fate she hoped to avoid. By the end of the voyage, she was five pounds lighter than when she had boarded.

Mary followed the mass of people off the ship and into the long lines for entering the United States of America. She patiently waited in line to show her paperwork and pass the screening. Everything about her was clean, having listened to her brother's instructions and washed up thoroughly before exiting the ship.

She glanced around at those surrounding her, trying to determine what would cause her to fail the inspection. The lines were long, and she had seen families removed for coughing. She breathed deeply and tried to keep herself calm. *Please don't cough,* she thought to herself. *I just need to do this one thing to get into the country and be with my family.*

She hoped the process wouldn't take too long. As the line finally moved, she picked up her bag of belongings. The exit wasn't visible from her spot, but she knew who was waiting for her there.

When it was finally her turn; she moved up to talk to the frowning man who stood between her and her new life. "Papers?" he asked.

She handed him her paperwork and waited patiently. He stood between her and the United States, she must pass the inspection. He handed the papers back to her and said, "On your way, that way." He waved for her to move past his station.

She wanted to run but forced herself to move slowly from the room. The guard at the door opened it for her. Taking a deep breath, she stepped through and heard a voice calling her name. Her eyes found him immediately; it was one of her brothers, Ernst. She ran to him, not noticing the heavy bag bouncing off her legs.

"Mary! Mary, is it really you?" Ernst asked wondrously standing a foot away from her

"Yes," she said, choking back tears. "It is me."

He grabbed her in a bear hug and didn't let go for a few moments. He finally drew back and observed, "You are grown."

"That happens," she said wryly

"It has been too long, little girl."

"Yes," she said softly.

He cleared his throat, trying not to show how emotional he was at seeing her. "I have the train ticket for home for tomorrow morning. I thought you might like one night on land that does not move."

"You're right. It would be nice to be still for a night." *A bath would also be amazing*, she thought. "Have you been to New York City before this?"

"I have," he confirmed. "We came through here also. I will show you around after dinner. Now, I will take you to the hotel. Is this all you have with you?" he asked, taking the bag from her.

"Yes. Thank you. That would be wonderful."

They made their way to the cab he had waiting. He handed the bag to the driver and helped her into the carriage, climbing in beside her.

On the way to the hotel, they talked about family, how old everyone was, and what everyone did in America. They both waited on the big question about Mama and Papa until all the family was together.

The next morning, Mary felt refreshed and ready for the next part of the trip: Chicago, by way of Buffalo. They had a long trip in third class. Mary felt any other class was frivolous, and she didn't want to waste her money on such things. They would arrive in Chicago just the same as the other classes would. She was prepared for the weeklong trip with several books and a notebook full of her business plans.

After a long week, they pulled into the station. She stepped off the train, with Ernst behind her carrying her bag. Loud, deep voices called her name. "Mary!" She turned and was engulfed in hugs from her brothers. Ernst, not wanting to be left out of anything, joined them.

She stepped back to look at each of them and said, "Otto, Hans, Paul, and Ernst." *They look much the same,* she thought.

Hans, being the oldest, took over and said in English, "Mary, we are so happy to welcome you. We have missed you."

"I am so glad to be here," she said, sniffing loudly.

"You are with us now," he said gruffly. "Your English is much improved." He remembered the little girl trying to learn the English words when the brothers were preparing to leave the old country.

"I have been working on it," she said. "I knew I would be with you one day."

Hans teared up and said in a shaky voice, "I am glad. Only English is spoken outside of the German areas. You must be prepared."

He looked at his brothers and said, "We need to get everyone back to the house." It had been decided that Mary would be staying with Hans and his family.

She nodded, feeling like she needed two baths. "That would be wonderful."

His eyes teared up again as he looked at her. *She looks just like Mama,* he thought.

"What is it?" she asked in a concerned tone, noticing his tears.

"Nothing. I am just glad you are here," he said, wiping his face quickly.

They located the wagons and climbed in. "May I ride up

front?" asked Mary. She wanted to see everything as they drove through Chicago to Hans's house.

"Yes," Hans said and helped her into the seat beside the driver.

She turned and said, "Such a big place."

"Yes, and growing constantly. You will find a large number of Germans here," said Hans.

"That will be nice." *The familiar accent is comforting*, she thought as she sat back on the seat, hugging her bag to her.

They pulled up to a large house on a nice street. Mary looked around and asked, "Where are we?" *This is too grand for their family*, she thought.

The brothers laughed and Paul said, "Hans's house."

She looked at the home, marveling at the size. It seemed quite big to her eyes, but in reality, it was an average house in a middle-class area. "So big," she said.

"For the family, you will see," said Hans as he swung her down to the ground. The brothers grinned as they followed her up the stoop and into the house. Hans had seven children, all boys who needed the room to run around.

As she entered, the first thing she heard was, *CRASH!* And then, "Hey! Leave my stuff alone!" and "That's not yours, it's mine!"

"Boys!" A woman's voice called out. "A little lower, please." The woman walked out of the kitchen and was drying her hands on her apron. "Oh! You're here! Boys! Mary is here!"

Mary stood with Hans and the other brothers as the boys ran down the stairs to greet her. Some pushing the others on their way down.

"So many," she said to Hans. "Does everyone have so many?" she asked and looked around at her brothers for confirmation.

"Hans has the most," said Ernst.

Hans grinned. "I wrote you about them. There's seven in all."

Hans's wife walked over and said, "I am Katie. Welcome." She gave Mary a tight hug.

"Thank you," said Mary, hugging her back. She was glad to be with family again. She had missed her brothers and wanted to know their families.

Katie took over and directed, "Boys, introduce yourselves, then go outside for a while."

They grumbled some, but each gave their name and hugged her before heading outside.

Mary's head was spinning trying to remember each one. The last one came up and Hans said, "This is Frederick, our oldest. He has been looking forward to meeting you." Hans nudged the boy, who appeared to be about fourteen.

"Yes, Frederick, you wanted to ask me something?" Mary prompted him.

"I would like to work in your bakery," he blurted out quickly.

Katie hastened to assure her, "He is a talented baker and wants to learn from you."

Mary looked at him consideringly and said, "I will need a baker's assistant. You can show me what skills you have while I am getting my bakery organized."

He grinned widely and said, "Thank you."

Katie looked down at him and said, "That will be later. For now, go out and play with your brothers."

Frederick smiled happily and said, "Thanks again," and ran out the door.

Katie looked at Hans and said, "Take her bag to her room." She turned to Mary and said, "We moved the boys in with each other."

"Oh, I don't want to put anyone out," she protested.

"They will be fine; they need to spend more time trying to get along without fighting. Now, up you go. You will want a bath and a rest before this evening."

Mary looked around at her brothers, bewildered by this take-charge person.

They all grinned at her, as they knew Hans's wife would be in charge once they got to his house.

Mary stopped before she hurried upstairs and glanced at all of her four brothers in one place. "Will I see you all later with your families?"

Katie answered for them. "Of course. We have the whole family coming over tonight."

"Everyone?" she asked, excited to see them all together.

"Yes, will it be too much for you? I can ask them to come another day."

"Another day? I have been waiting ten years to meet everyone."

Katie nodded. She was happy that Mary was finally with the family.

Mary looked at her brothers one last time and said, "I will see you all later."

The brothers called as they left, "Bye, sister. See you this evening."

Hans followed them up and placed her bag in her room. He kissed her on the cheek and headed back downstairs.

Katie showed her the bedroom and the water closet. "An inside water closet," said Mary in a wonderous tone as she looked around. *We didn't have this in Germany.*

Katie smiled gently. "Yes, Hans wanted the water closet installed before you got here. He worked day and night to make sure it was perfect."

Mary teared up and said, "Really? Just for me?"

"Yes, of course. He loves you. We all love you. He would do anything for you."

Mary started crying and Katie said bracingly, "Now, stop that! This is a happy day."

"I know. I wish Mama and Papa could have been here with us," she said, wiping her tears with the back of her hand.

"Yes, well. We do, too, but here we are. Come now. Get undressed and hand me your clothes; I will get them washed. Do you have something else to change into?" Katie looked at her, judging her size to see if Mary could fit any of her dresses.

"Yes, I have a dress I can wear," Mary said proudly.

"You go on now and, when you are done, come back here and lie down. I will keep the boys downstairs and allow you some quiet time."

Mary hugged her quickly and then moved to the water closet. She took a bath and washed her hair before lying down. It should dry before the evening meal. The windows were open, allowing in a nice cool breeze. *I will just lie down a moment,* she thought, drifting off.

"Wake up, Mary," said Katie.

She opened her eyes slowly and asked, "Mama?"

"No, Mary, it is Katie," she said gently, brushing Mary's hair off her face.

Mary shook her head to clear it and said, "Yes, that's right."

"Everyone will be arriving soon," she said softly. "Why don't you get straightened up and meet us downstairs."

"Yes," said Mary. She was both excited and nervous at the same time.

"We will be downstairs when you are ready," Katie said and left the room, closing the door behind her.

Mary got up slowly and walked over to the dresser to get her brush. Her hair had dried, and it hung in long blond waves down her back. She walked over to her bag and found it empty; she looked around for her clothes but didn't see them. She noticed a closet and opened it. Her one good dress was hanging there, freshly pressed.

So nice, she thought. *I am going to like having sisters.*

She dressed and pulled her hair into a low bun and put on

her dress. The powder blue of the dress matched her eyes. Her mother had been talented with the needle and had fashioned this dress during the last months of her life. It was made from the same fabric that made up her mother's wedding dress.

She hesitated briefly as she opened the door. *Stop being such a ninny. This is your family.* She took a deep breath and headed downstairs.

She needn't have worried. As she made her way down, her brothers and their families immediately pulled her into the room. Any nerves she had were driven away by family all talking at one time.

Hans watched for a moment from his chair, puffing on his pipe. After a few more moments, he said to the group surrounding her, "Let her breathe."

At that moment, Katie walked in and said, "Dinner is ready."

As they made their way to the dining room, a fight almost broke out when each brother tried to escort her in. Mary giggled, enjoying having them around.

Once she sat, Hans asked, "What are your plans?"

He knew that she was always a planner and that she had been running the bakery in Germany for more than ten years.

"I want to open a bakery," she said simply.

"Did you get a good price for the bakery and the house?" he asked. All conversation stopped as she answered. The brothers had agreed that they would help get her started if she needed it.

"Yes. I have it with me. It should be enough to get me started. I thought I would begin baking here and handing out some pastries locally."

Katie mulled that over and said, "That is a good idea. You might also think about taking some to the local businesses."

Paul said, "I know someone who can show you properties in different areas to give you an idea of the size and location you might want."

"Who are you thinking of?" asked Hans.

"Ellis Evans. He is an engineer, but he also works as an inspector. He will know the buildings that might work." He looked over at Mary. "If you are okay with that, I will notify him."

"That would be wonderful," she said, grateful for the support.

Hans said, "We should get you to the bank, the money needs to be somewhere safe."

She nodded, but inside she was unsure about the bank. The money was sewn into her undergarments to keep it safe. It would take some convincing to let someone else manage it.

The dinner ended and the brothers wanted some alone time with Mary. The women and children stayed in the main sitting room while the others moved into the study.

After everyone sat down, Hans asked gently, "Mary, tell us about Mama and her last few weeks."

She took a deep breath and tried to stay unemotional as she shared. "It was hard. I was running the bakery and watching out for her. She got sicker and sicker. After a while, I had to hire a girl to help out. Then, when it looked like it was the end, a few weeks before she died, I shut down the bakery and stayed with her."

"Was she in pain?" asked Hans hoarsely.

She looked around and realized they were all missing their mama. "No," she lied. "She was peaceful, and she said to make sure her boys remembered her."

The brothers were openly crying.

The truth was her last hours were harsh; she was in extreme pain, Mary thought to herself. She also didn't mention the morphine that she had administered to allow her to die. That would be between her and God. She would eventually have to answer for what she did.

CHAPTER 2

*E*llis Evans was outside the restaurant, listening to his best friend and brother in spirit Cole Tilden talk about his latest case. He looked around absentmindedly and saw a young woman with lovely blond hair walking nearby.

"Are you listening?" Cole asked in an exasperated voice

He turned away reluctantly from the girl and said, "Yes, I just saw someone."

Cole started telling him about his latest case with Pinkerton and noticed his attention had wandered again.

When Cole could not get Ellis's attention back, he asked, "Who're you watching?"

Ellis wasn't listening; he was looking around for the girl he had seen. He saw a flash of blonde hair again and started in that direction.

Cole put a hand on his arm and reminded him, "Ellis, we're supposed to be going to lunch, remember?"

"Oh, yes," he said and turned reluctantly to enter the restaurant with Cole.

They entered and were sat at a center table. "Besides aren't you supposed to be still hung up on Abbey?" Cole asked.

Ellis focused on Cole and said, "Yes. Well, I haven't heard from her since she left."

"But you haven't gone out with anyone since then," he observed.

"I haven't met anyone I felt as strongly about as I did with Abbey," Ellis said simply.

Did, thought Cole.

He and Ellis had both been a little in love with Abbey, a lovely girl with thick auburn hair. She left the country quickly and wanted both Cole and Ellis with her. They wanted her to pick between them, but she wouldn't choose and left. That was the last time they had seen her.

Cole didn't mention to Ellis that he was trying to find her. He used his Pinkerton contacts since joining the company to help him. He assumed she was continuing to do what she was good at: being a thief. She had always been good with her hands and there had been a string of jewel robberies in the areas where she was known to frequent. She didn't seem to be on Pinkerton's radar as yet. He was worried it would be just a matter of time.

CHAPTER 3

*E*rnst held the door open for Mary to enter the bank. He followed her closely into the lobby. She turned back to him and said, "Ernst, you don't have to go everywhere with me."

"Hans says I go. I go," he said simply.

She argued further, "Don't you have to work on your furniture?" Ernst had a small shop where he sold custom furniture. He just stared at her. She finally gave up and said, "Very well, but let me talk to the man who sets up accounts." She didn't want to disclose her savings to anyone she didn't trust.

He nodded, understanding this was her business, and followed her in. They made their way to the waiting area. A clerk came over and asked Ernst, "What can we do for you?"

Mary spoke up and said, "I would like to talk about opening an account."

He looked surprised at her statement and took a long look at her. "We have an account manager who will see you now."

Mary nodded and walked with Ernst to follow the clerk over to the manager's desk. She thought, *He looks young for a bank manager.* The clerk leaned over and spoke into his ear. He looked over at Mary in surprise.

"Would you like to sit down?" He indicated the two chairs in front of his desk. He didn't offer to shake hands and Mary was glad. They appeared to be wet.

"Yes, thank you," Mary said. She and Ernst sat down.

She watched the manager closely. His hands were wet, and he appeared to be sweating. He also kept looking over her shoulder. She finally turned around to see what held his attention and saw a clock nearby. *Did he have another appointment?* she wondered.

"Your name?" he asked.

"Mary Herwig," she replied. "What is your name?"

He said quickly, "David Kerns. You would like to open a new account?"

"I would," she said firmly, Hans had convinced her to consider using the bank to manage her money.

He pulled out some papers and said, "You will need to complete these."

Mary ignored the papers and said firmly, "I want to talk about your bank security first."

"Our security?" he asked, the last syllable went up, showing his distress.

"Yes. If I am to put my life savings here, I want to know it is protected."

He looked desperate as he said, "We have a large safe in the back and we have guards in the front."

She looked behind her and saw that the guards were not there. She turned and asked him, "Where are they now?"

"Who?" he asked, looking everywhere but at her.

"The guards are not where you said they should be," Ernst said, looking toward the door.

"They might be on break," Kerns said weakly.

"Break? At the same time? Is that a good idea?" she asked.

At that moment, three men came in wearing cloths over their mouths and noses, carrying guns. "Everyone down! Now!"

Ernst pulled Mary to the floor. They made eye contact and waited.

One of the robbers walked directly over to Kerns's desk and said, "You, up and over to the safe."

Mr. Kerns didn't hesitate and jumped up to do what they asked. Mary watched them closely as he went to the safe. The other men stayed with their guns trained on the tellers and people in the bank. When they got what they wanted, they ran out.

Everyone stood up slowly, discussing the robbery.

Mary watched Mr. Kerns and noticed he appeared to be calmer than when she had first gotten there. She squinted at him and thought, *He is involved in this.*

"I think we'll be shutting down to deal with this," Kerns said to Mary and Ernst. "You will come back to talk to me?"

She nodded but knew she would not be using this bank again.

They waited for the police to be notified and had to be interviewed.

Mary and Ernst were released and, as they were leaving, Ernst said, "That was exciting."

"Yes. Yes, it was."

They headed home to tell the family about the events they were involved in that day.

CHAPTER 4

$\mathcal{P}$aul had set up her appointment with Ellis Evans. He was to meet her at the house the next morning.

When he arrived, Katie called up and said, "Mary, Ellis is here for you."

She called down, "I am on my way."

Mary started downstairs and saw a young man waiting. He was tall and slim with light brown hair. The glasses he wore made him look rather studious. As she reached the bottom step, she noticed he was staring at her rather intently.

He started abruptly and said, "I've seen you before."

"I do not think I have seen you," she said, looking closely at him. When he didn't continue, she prompted, "You were going to show me some shop locations."

That reminded him why he was there. "Yes, let's go. I have several to show you."

They headed out to the cab he had waiting. He helped her in, and he gave the driver the addresses.

She looked at each space carefully and put questions to him. "Where would the ovens go? I will need space for multiple workstations and a front room for the counter."

He listened intently to what she would need and thought about the locations he had picked out. "I think I have a few more that might work. Can we go out again tomorrow?" he asked.

She noticed it was getting late and she had a family dinner that evening. She had a plan for employment that would involve the family, and she wanted to run it by them. She looked closely at Ellis as he was taking notes. *His brown hair could use a brush,* she thought. He was so intelligent, but very little social skills. There was something about him that fascinated her, so much that she would like to know about him.

"Ellis?"

"Yes," he said, absently looking down at his list.

"Ellis," she said again.

He looked into her eyes and gave her his full attention. The direct gaze flustered her a bit.

"You were saying?" he asked.

"Was I?" she asked and shook herself. "Yes, I wanted to know if you would like to come to dinner with the family tonight."

"I don't want to interfere with your family time."

"You will not be." She laughed. "It is just the family with lots of food and conversation."

Ellis hadn't had family around for a long time. He hesitated only a moment before agreeing. "I would love that."

"Wonderful." She broke their eye contact. "Come by the house at 6:30 tonight."

"I will be there," he promised.

CHAPTER 5

"So, you're going over to eat dinner with the family?" asked Cole thoughtfully. He was sitting in a chair in Ellis's small apartment kitchen.

"Yes," he said, trying to work the iron to press his shirt. He wanted to look nice for Mary.

Cole watched him iron in more wrinkles than he was removing. He watched for as long as he could and finally said, "Sit down, you're not doing it right." Once Cole took over, he commented quietly, "You haven't mentioned Abbey since you caught sight of Mary."

Ellis sat on the chair Cole had vacated and said, "That time seems so long ago."

"It was," agreed Cole. *Why can't I stop thinking about her?* he thought.

"Cole, there's something about Mary. When I look into her eyes, I see things for my life I didn't think I would have. A family of my own."

"Ellis, we'll always be family," said Cole.

"I know, but this is different."

Cole understood. He had thought the same thing. "How does

she feel about you?" he asked.

"I don't know," Ellis said simply.

"Well, man, should you find out?"

"Yes, I should, and I will," he promised. "Will you be okay on your own?"

Cole smiled and said, "Yes. I have a lady friend I'm meeting for dinner and then the theatre. I want to hear more about Mary later."

Ellis grinned. "Yes." He finished dressing, brushed his hair, and made his way to Mary's brother's house. He was there on the dot at 6:30pm and knocked briskly on the door. It swung open and a tall German man was standing in the doorway. "Hans?" he asked.

"Ja, you must be Ellis? You are helping our Mary find her bakery."

"I am."

"You come in. All of the family is here, and the house is very noisy," Hans said proudly.

A boy called from the stair, "Papa, come up. I want to show you something."

"Would you mind if I leave you?" Hans asked.

"No, of course not." Ellis noticed all the people in the sitting room, and he hesitated before going in. It was a little over-whelming and the smell of food pulled him toward the kitchen instead. He headed that way without stopping and pushed the door open. Mary stood beside the kitchen table, stirring a spoon in a large mixing bowl. He didn't notice the other ladies in the room.

She smiled at him and thought, *He is rather sweet.* "Are you lost?" she teased.

"No. It's just busy out there," he said, indicating behind him.

"It is just family," she commented.

"Is it like this all the time?" he asked.

"Mostly," she confirmed.

He suddenly smiled and said, "I think I would like that in my home also."

She smiled to herself as she finished mixing the glaze for the strudel and asked, "Would you like a small piece?"

"I would," he said and walked over to the kitchen table.

She cut a small piece of strudel and glazed it before handing it to him. "Careful now, it is hot."

He took it carefully and blew on it before taking a bite. He closed his eyes and enjoyed the flavors. "I could marry you just for your baking," he said without thinking. His eyes widened when he realized what he had said.

She grinned and teased, "I may have to take you up on that."

He turned red, but teased back, "Only if you promise to make this every day for me."

"We will have to see about that," she said, looking into his eyes.

They stood there gazing at each other until Hans came in and cleared his throat. "We have dinner on the table."

They looked around in surprise and saw they were alone in the kitchen. "On our way," said Mary, covering her baking with clothes. Ellis offered her his arm. She took it and gave him a soft smile. They joined everyone in the dining room and sat next to each other. Extra tables had been set up to take the overflow.

Ellis was surprised at how relaxed and included he felt. Both Mary and his friend Paul kept him included in the conversation. He hadn't experienced that in years.

During dinner, Mary had a request for the family. She stood up and said, "I would like to have the bakery be part of the family. I would like the children to learn the baking skill and each spends time as a paid employee."

The parents looked at each other and her. Everyone started talking at once.

"We love the idea!"

"Such an important skill."

Katie said, "Mary, I think everyone likes the idea."

"Good, I will need a list of anyone older than ten who can start once I choose a location."

After dinner, Ellis caught Mary by the hand and found a quiet place in the hallway. "Can we walk together tonight?" he asked.

"That depends," she said, wondering how he would react to her request.

"Depends?" he questioned.

"Yes. I think someone is stealing money from the bank."

Ellis looked a little confused at the change of topic and asked, "Why do you think that?"

"We were in First Bank when it was robbed; the manager was acting very nervous."

"That doesn't seem out of the ordinary during a robbery," he reasoned.

"No, you don't understand, he was nervous before the robbers arrived. I think he also arranged for the guards to not be in place at the time of the robbery."

"What do you want to do?" he asked.

"I want to change into men's clothes and head over to a nearby gambling establishment and see if he is there."

"And if he is?"

"I don't know," she said honestly. "I think he is involved in something he can't get himself out of."

"Why not," said Ellis with a shrug. "I'll meet you in the back."

"Okay."

He said his goodbyes and headed down the front stoop. He ducked around to the back door and waited. It wasn't long before it opened, and a young gentleman came down the stairs. He paused on the steps and looked around.

Ellis realized it was Mary. He called softly, "I'm here." She looked over and went down to meet him.

"Ready?" she asked.

"Yes. Are you okay with walking or do we need a carriage?"

"I am fine. I walked daily at home in Germany, and I do the same here each morning."

They headed into town to the gambling establishment. As they reached it, he said, "Pull down your hat." She did as he suggested, and they entered.

The gambling tables were past the restaurant and in the back. The man guarding the door asked them for a password, which Ellis answered quickly. Mary made a mental note to ask him about that.

They entered the room; it was full of people and cigarette smoke. "Do you see him?" asked Ellis in a low voice.

Mary looked around and saw Kerns. "Poker table toward the back," she said in a similar tone.

"Lead the way," Ellis said.

They started toward the table and Mary thought to look at the other tables as they passed, so it didn't look like she was targeting that one table.

There was an empty seat and she nodded toward it. The dealer said, "You can join. The initial bid is two dollars."

She pulled out the two dollars and placed them on the table as the cards were dealt. She kept an eye on Kerns and saw that he was a terrible player. *It is no wonder that he is in such debt*, she thought to herself. She played and won the first hand, then the second. It was time to pull out, she nodded at Ellis and picked up her winnings from the table.

She decided to pick a fight with Kerns. She turned to him "I think you stole my money," she said in a loud voice.

"No! I didn't do anything!" He looked confused at the accusation.

"I think you did, and I think you should step outside." She leaned toward him in a threatening manner and said, "If you don't, I will discuss this with the house manager." She needed to get him out of there.

The pit boss moved over to them and said, "We don't think Mr. Kerns wants to go with you."

"Oh, I think he does," she countered.

He glowered at Mary intimidatingly. "You either stay and play or you go out without Mr. Kerns."

Ellis stepped up. "Do we have a problem?"

The pit boss realized he would not be able to intimidate this man. He knew Kerns would be back and finally told them, "Fine, you can go."

They got Kerns outside. He turned toward them and said indignantly, "I didn't take your money."

They pulled him down the street and into an alley. Mary whipped off her hat.

"It's you. You were the woman at the bank with all of the questions," he said, confused.

Mary responded, "What I think is that you have been losing money to those people and they are using that to have you steal from the bank."

He tried to bluster but realized he was caught. "Yes, that's it exactly," he admitted.

"Mr. Kerns, you are the worst player I have ever seen. Why do you go back?" she asked.

"Well, at first, I was winning every game; then my luck turned, and I couldn't win anything. The debt kept piling up, but I thought if I just kept playing then I could make it up," he said helplessly.

"Mr. Kerns, it's a setup," said Ellis. "These places do that initially, so they catch you. They probably targeted you because where you work."

Kerns covered his face with his hands and sank down against the wall. "There's no way out. I owe too much money."

"Have they been putting pressure on you again after the bank robbery?" she asked.

"Yes," he said helplessly.

"Do you have family in town?" Ellis asked, thinking about the next steps.

"No. I moved here when the bank promoted me."

"Where are they?" Mary asked.

"Ohio."

"First thing we need to do is get you out of town and away from the bank," stated Ellis firmly.

Kerns looked at them pleadingly. "I need to go back in."

"No. You have a problem. You should stay away from those places," Mary said, trying to reason with him.

"But I can't leave my job."

"They will kill you if you stay here," stated Ellis bluntly.

That shocked him into silence. "How do I pay for a move like that? I don't have any money."

"My winnings," Mary said calmly

"Will you give them to me?" Kerns asked. "I'll buy the ticket."

She looked at him and said, "No, I do not think so. We will purchase the ticket for you, and you will leave."

"Okay, okay. Meet me at the bank tomorrow."

"We will," she said as she looked at Ellis and he nodded. She looked back at Kerns. "Will you be able to get home okay?"

"Yes. I'll go straight there," he promised.

They helped him to his feet and watched him head away from the gambling establishment.

Mary reached for Ellis's hand. He put his in hers and pulled her close. "That was a nice thing you did there."

"I just can't stand to see someone bullied," she said.

He leaned his head down and kissed her gently. She returned it and sank into him.

When it was over, he said, "We never did get our walk. Would you walk to the park with me?"

"Yes," she murmured. They walked and talked about their lives before their meeting and about where they would like to be in the future.

CHAPTER 6

The next day, Ellis and Mary stopped by the train station and picked up Kerns's ticket to Ohio. They made their way to the bank. He wasn't at his desk and they inquired of his clerk, "Do you know where Mr. Kerns is?" Mary inquired. "I had an appointment with him."

The clerk looked uninterested and said, "He hasn't been here this morning."

"Do you know his home address?"

"I'm not supposed to say." He shook his head and said, "Oh, what do I care? He's on Brighton Street, Apartment 12."

They headed over there and knocked on the door. When no one answered, Ellis, pulled out a lockpick and opened it. She watched, admiring his skill.

When he noticed her interest, he grinned at her. "I'll tell you later," he promised.

She nodded.

He opened the door and the smell overwhelmed them. "Don't go in," he cautioned. He knew that smell. "We need the police. Now! I'll wait here and you go get them."

As she ran off, he noticed a kid of about twelve hanging out down the hallway. "Hey, did you see anyone go into this apartment?"

"No, I just came out when I heard you at the door," he said.

"Can you take a note over to the Pinkerton's office for me?"

"What's in it for me?" the boy asked, leaning against the wall, willing to negotiate.

"How about a dollar?" Ellis suggested.

The boy's eyes lit up and he nodded. Ellis cautioned him as he walked over. "Fifty cents now and fifty cents when you return."

"That's fair," he said. "What am I taking?"

"A note. Make sure you go straight there."

"I will," he assured him. He wanted the fifty cents.

Ellis wrote out the note and handed him the money. "Hurry, please."

He took the money and nodded quickly, running off in the same direction Mary had.

CHAPTER 7

Mary ran as fast as she could and found the local policeman walking his beat. They both ran back to the apartment, Ellis was waiting in the hallway. She and Ellis stayed in the hall wall and he went in. He came out quickly and said, "Definitely dead. I'll need to notify the station. Don't leave!" he ordered.

They assured him they would be there when he returned.

It didn't take long for several more uniforms and a medical officer to show up.

They talked at length with the police officers and gave them all the information they had about Mr. Kerns.

The police officer said, "Our detectives would like to speak with you."

Ellis and Mary looked at each other. Mary looked back and said, "If we can help."

While the police were moving the body out of the apartment, Mary and Ellis were taken to the station. They were put into a room with a table and chairs. A man entered and said, "I'm Detective Donaldson."

"I am Mary Herwig, and this is Ellis Evans."

"How do you know Mr. Kerns?" Donaldson asked, opening his notebook.

"I met him at the bank," she said.

"What were you doing at his apartment?"

Mary said, "He is involved with gamblers and helped organize the bank robbery the other day."

Detective Donaldson looked flummoxed at this. "What makes you think that?"

She told him about Kerns's gambling losses, the missing guards, and his behavior in the bank before the robbery.

"That's a nice story, but is there any evidence of this?"

There was a knock on the door. It opened and a man Mary didn't know stood there. She was surprised when Ellis said, "I sent my friend a note and asked him to do me a favor."

Cole stepped in, went up to Mary, and said, "My name is Cole Tilden. It's very nice to finally meet you."

"Young man, what are you doing here?" Donaldson asked.

"I am with Pinkerton," he explained.

"I don't think this is a Pinkerton matter."

"No, no, it isn't, but Ellis asked me to locate two people." He looked behind him and called out, "Bring them in."

The officers brought in two men. They didn't look happy to be there.

"Who are these men?" Donaldson asked.

"They're the guards who were supposed to be on duty the day of the robbery, but were missing during it," said Cole. "Talk," he commanded and nudged one of the men.

The man glared at Cole and said, "We were paid to take a long break the day of the robbery."

"By whom?" asked Donaldson.

"Kerns," he admitted.

"Okay, take them to the next room," said Donaldson. He decided Mary and Ellis knew something and said, "Give me all the details."

After they finished, the detective said, "Keep a low profile until we get these men."

"We will," they promised. Cole, Ellis, and Mary exited the station together. Cole laughed suddenly and said, "I can't wait to get to know you, Mary." He hugged her.

They all three laughed as they made their way down the street.

A few days later, they heard several people had been picked up for the robbery. The murder of Mr. Kerns would eventually be linked to them.

CHAPTER 8

*E*llis was out with Mary again later that week, looking for bakery locations. "Mary, I think I have the perfect place for you."

She accompanied him to the location and waited until he opened the door for her. When she walked in, she immediately knew it was the one she wanted. She went to Ellis and hugged him tightly. "This is the perfect one for me," she confirmed.

"Mary, I think you are the perfect one for me. Will you marry me?"

"I thought you would never ask. Yes"

He pulled her to him and kissed her for a long moment. "There is another building I would like to show you."

She frowned.

He asked, "Trust me?"

"Yes," she said softly.

They made their way to Hans's street and went to stand in front of a house just down from his. "I found this for us." They stood looking at the four-story house with dreams of their future together.

"Can we go in?" she asked.

"Together?" he asked and held out his hand to her.

She took it and they went in - excited to begin their lives together.

35

NOTEBOOK MYSTERIES ~ EMMA (BOOK 1)

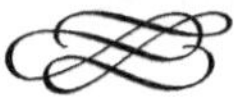

EMMA

Notebook Mysteries

KIMBERLY MULLINS

PROLOGUE

here to start, the Narrator thought as she sat drumming her right fingers against her lips. *Where to start*, she thought again, glancing around the brightly lit room, looking for inspiration. The room she chose to start her writing project was in the attic space of the old Victorian she and her family called home. The house faced east, the room's dormers caught the bright morning light, and it washed across the writing desk where she sat. She chose the early morning hours to work on her book because she liked the feel of the sun on her face and the peace it gave her.

The room was large and furnished with an old dark brown leather chair stationed next to a lighter brown antique desk on the east wall. Located across the room from the desk was a tall white dresser with brass handles, two white iron twin beds covered with patchwork quilts, and aged lace throws. The floor was whitewashed and a large colorful area rug lay under the beds.

It was a place where she could be away from the noise within the house. Her family was usually in high spirits about something or another and could be quite loud. *Family,* she thought with an exasperated shake of her head. *I'll have to get to them soon enough.*

She moved her hand from her lips to where the pencil laid on the desk, absently rolling it back and forth, while she continued to concentrate on her book plans.

A shuffling of shoes on the steps caught her attention, and her mouth quirked up in a quick smile. She looked toward the door and saw her dear-one walking into the room.

Dear-one was a tall, slim man—so tall that he had to duck under the doorway to enter the attic. He wore his usual brown suit with a pressed shirt and vest. His face rested in an absent-minded expression as he carried a battered brown box under his left arm and (of course) an open book in his right hand.

He dropped the box onto her desk, startling her, and then settled himself into the leather chair nearest her. He relaxed back, put his feet up on the edge of the desk, and continued to read. He hadn't glanced at her the entire time, but that wasn't unusual.

He didn't look up until she tapped his battered brown leather shoe.

"Where should I start?" she inquired, tilting her head toward her writing paper and typewriter.

The reader of this might wonder why the Narrator chose not to inquire about the box. Well, Dear-one was always moving things about and working on projects; it got tiresome asking what was in one box or another, so she just nudged it out of the way.

He acknowledged the question by lowering his book, brushing a thick brown curl back off his forehead, and then, finally meeting her eyes with his, stated rather brusquely, "Well, at the beginning, of course. Where it all started."

She glanced down at her desk, again nudging the brown box so she could glance at her notes. *The beginning,* she thought. She reflected on how life as an investigator had begun. The long and varied career with many highs and lows, that affected everyone who came into contact with it. She did not know it would eventually lead to this point and writing a book, but she wouldn't have changed it for the world. "But the details of it. How to remember everything?" she fretted aloud.

Dear-one didn't look up from his reading this time when he said, "Look in the box. Something in there might help." She didn't notice a sparkle in his eyes, as he kept them averted toward his book.

She glanced at him suspiciously, stood up, and folded back the lid. She realized what was in it almost immediately and knocked the heavy desk chair back as she moved closer. She sighed into a long smile. Looking at him, she said, "The notebooks, where did you find them?"

He glanced up and, with a smile, said, "I had them put away. I thought you might want to keep them to look at one day."

Her eyes filled with tears as memories began flooding her senses. She pushed back the tears and, with a deep breath, started pulling items from the box. As she kept removing notebooks, she was taken aback by the sheer number of them. They were small black scribble books that fit easily into a pocket, full of years' worth of data, detailing the life of an adventurer. "So many," she murmured, "so many adventures."

Dear-one agreed quietly. "A lifetime's worth, to be sure."

He had suggested the beginning. *I might as well start there*, she thought. She dug until she found the oldest notebook and the earliest case. The black leather crumbled a bit as she handled it, but the papers inside were not damaged.

She took one in her hand. "I'll call it Case 1, The Office."

He interrupted again to say, "Love, there is another case to discuss, a very important one," he reminded her. "It should be the first one."

She knew the case of which he spoke, and finally agreed with a nod of her head. "Yes, you are quite right. I should start there."

She started organizing the notebooks into piles, stacked by date. Though, for this case, she could almost go from memory. She opened that first notebook and saw the title. She picked up her pencil to start the work.

CHAPTER 1

1871 CHICAGO, LATE NIGHT

"Wake up, Dora, Sister," Papa said as he nudged their shoulders. He reached over to turn up the gas lamp above the side table.

The two girls had been asleep for hours and were groggy.

Dora yawned as she opened her eyes and saw Papa standing over them. Intuitively she knew something wasn't right and immediately asked, "Papa? What's wrong?"

Sister woke up, rubbing her sleep-filled eyes, laid silent and watchful. She was waiting to hear how Papa would answer Dora's question.

"No questions now, you must get dressed," he said as he handed each of the girls their dresses and sat on the edge of the bed.

The girls quickly scooted to the side where Papa was sitting and they started pulling their dresses over their night shifts.

He knelt in front of them to help each button the front of their dresses.

They watched Papa silently and noticed his hands shaking. His hands never shook. Sister's hand reached out for Dora's, they held tight to each other, staying silent, waiting for Papa's next direction. Dora and Sister were little girls of eight and six and would do anything their beloved papa asked of them.

It was very dark and quiet in the house as their papa gathered them together to walk downstairs. Holding each other's hands, the girls followed him down the staircase to the first floor. As they moved closer to the front door, they became aware of the noise outside.

Papa turned to the girls and squatted down in front of them, taking each of their small hands in his, and said gently, "Girls you must listen to me, something is happening outside. We are going to go out, but I need you to stay on the stoop and be as quiet as possible. Can you do that?" He didn't wait for an answer as he handed them their shoes. "Dora put on your shoes and help Sister with hers."

"Yes, Papa," Dora said as she sat down to slip on her shoes and helped Sister with hers. As they sat waiting for Papa to take them outside, Dora just couldn't stop herself from asking, "Papa, what is happening?" She started to look around the foyer, feeling something or someone was missing, she realized Mama was not there. "Papa, where is Mama?" Sister continued to let Dora speak for her as she sat there holding onto Dora's hand.

Papa, not wanting to answer a question he did not know the answer to, went silent for a long moment in the dark house. He stood up without answering and went to the door. He just couldn't make himself open it; he felt somehow that the motion of opening the door would force him to admit something he didn't want to happen, had happened. He reached out hesitantly toward the brass doorknob and finally opened it. He turned back to the girls, took their hands in his, and brought them out onto the stoop. They stayed together holding hands with Dora leaning against Papa's leg.

Chaos greeted them as they stood and stared out. Their senses were overwhelmed with the sounds of distress coming from neighbors, friends, and family scattered throughout the street. There was the smell of smoke in the air and the general disorder of the people lent an almost surreal look to the night. It appeared that all the neighbors had come outside in a hurry and most were still in their night clothes. If it wasn't scary, it would be funny. Even Mr. Smith, the local preacher, who normally was very dignified with nary a hair out of place, was in the streets in a long dressing gown and a stocking cap that barely contained his wiry black hair.

People continued to flood into the streets from the surrounding houses. "Fire!" shouted someone and a constant cry of "The fire will get us all!" came from the crowds that had formed. The crowds could smell the smoke and see the flames as the fire spread through the city and above the building tops. The fire was actually at a greater distance from their neighborhood than it appeared, but the panic-stricken people couldn't process that fact.

Dora, not sure of what would happen next, sat down on the top step of the stoop and started to cry in response to all the confusion, saying quietly, "I want Mama." Sister continued to stand next to Dora, quietly patting her head and silently taking in the confusion that surrounded them.

Papa, who had not moved from the stoop since exiting the house, seemed to visibly shake off the feeling of unease that gripped him. He gathered up his thoughts and spoke loudly and directly to the crowd gathered in the street around him. "Friends, neighbors, and family," he nodded to each group. "Please be aware the wind direction doesn't appear to be driving the fire this way," he said in a calm but stern voice. "We must stay calm and keep watch on any changes in wind patterns. Those with small children, please return to your homes. Those who can help will need to start forming groups to organize shelter and food for survivors. If you can help, please join me over by my stoop."

That statement and his apparent leadership calmed the

people down; it gave them purpose and direction. The groups started to disperse and families with small children went into their homes. As the volunteers came to the stoop to help, Papa assigned group leads and started them working on compiling lists of available food, resources, and shelter locations.

Papa went to where his girls were still sitting quietly. He sat between them, pulling each of them close to him, and said softly, "It will make me happy if you would go to Uncle Hans' house to get some rest."

Dora looked up from Papa's chest with tear-drenched eyes and asked one last time, "Papa, where is Mama?"

Papa could never lie to his girls and this time Papa did not evade the question. "I think she might have gotten trapped by the fire at or around the bakery. We do not know more than that," he said honestly, trying to hold things together for his girls.

Sister watched his face and seemed satisfied. Dora's eyes threaten to overflow with tears, but she held them back as she said, "Yes, Papa, we will go to Uncle Hans' house."

Papa motioned to Frederick to come up the stoop for the girls. Frederick was the oldest son of Hans and the oldest cousin in the family. He was a very nice-looking, slim young man with thick brown hair and a lovely smile. Papa was happy to see that Frederick was already teasing smiles out of his younger cousins as he moved them to his house to get some rest.

Mama's brothers, Hans, Paul, Ernst, and Otto approached Papa about sending a small group of two into the area where Mama's bakery was located. Papa agreed and started to shrug into his jacket in preparation to leave with them. Otto stopped him by placing a hand on his arm and said to Papa in a rumbling German voice, "Ellis, it is best for Sister and Dora that you remain here."

Hans agreed and added, "Also the neighborhood will be looking to you for direction."

Papa wanted to argue, but he looked around at the people still in the streets, and then his gaze went to Hans' house. He knew they were right and he reluctantly agreed to wait. They all agreed that Paul and Otto would head out toward the business district and hopefully to Mama.

~

It was hours later when the brothers came back. They were sweaty and covered in soot. The two brothers that had stayed behind, ran up to them with water and wet rags. The four brothers hugged each other; glad they were back together.

Paul and Otto took the water and wet rags gladly, the night was hot and the fire had made it almost unbearable. Otto sighed, knowing he could not delay any longer, and said, "Let's find Ellis." The brothers nodded at each other and looked for Papa.

He was directing survivors into the established shelters when he spotted the four brothers coming toward him. He went quickly over to meet them.

The first to speak was Otto, he looked Ellis directly in the eyes as he spoke, "Ellis, the area is flooded with people that are evacuating. Paul and I could not get through and we were advised by the Pinkerton detectives, that the area will continue to burn overnight."

This statement seemed to affect the brothers and Papa at the same time. The men all appeared defeated with their heads hung low.

"There is still a chance," Papa whispered brokenly, "a chance she is among the evacuated or the injured." As Papa spoke, he glanced down the shadowed street. The brothers made eye contact with each other and shook their heads silently. Paul and Otto had gotten close enough to the area to determine it was badly damaged by the fire and that very few people would be coming out alive.

Papa wasn't ready to accept that Mama might have been taken from them. He looked searchingly in the direction of the bakery. He squinted his eyes trying to see a greater distance. A familiar figure appeared to be coming toward them. "No," he said and shook his head to clear it. He looked again and she was still there. He started smiling and broke away from the brothers at a run, toward the image. Hans started to go after him, but Otto said, "No, let him be." The brothers watched Papa but did not interfere.

He kept running to her image, but the closer he got the more transparent she became. Finally, as he slowed down, he saw that she was smiling a sad smile and waving. Her image faded into the night before Papa could reach her. At that moment Papa knew that it had been Mama saying a last goodbye. The grief washed over him as he sank to his knees, crying.

Mama's brothers came to him, pulled him up, and hugged him close. Papa let his emotions take over for a few moments and he cried into Otto's shoulder. The brothers watched with tears streaming down their faces.

When Papa was calmer, he looked back at Hans' house. "The girls," he said, as he straightened and pulled away from Otto. "I must be here for them." The brothers nodded in agreement as they patted him on the shoulder and rubbed their own eyes.

Mama would still be unaccounted for as the hours went by and the fire was slowly extinguished. Her normal working hours started at 3am, but she had gone in early to prepare a special order that was to be picked up the next morning. The German pastry she was famous for was Chocolate Leaves with Asbach Uralt-Poached Pears and Grapefruit-Lemon Quark Mousse which required hours of preparation and baking time.

Papa kept muttering, "That dessert, if she hadn't needed to be in extra early, she would still be alive." Dora and Sister heard

Papa's comments that night. Both Dora and Sister would revisit that memory one day.

The date was 1871 and the time was close to midnight. The news would filter in slowly through the rest of the night with details about what and who had been lost. The fire spread quickly through the business area of Chicago where the bakery was located. It was a fast and destructive fire because the building materials at the time were mostly wood topped with highly flammable tar or shingle roofs. The city had also been in a drought condition that allowed the city to burn for three long days. The flying embers scared residents into believing that they were at risk of losing everything.

The fire would eventually destroy approximately 2.2 square miles, displacing 100,000 people and killing three hundred. Papa had been right about people needing help and needing everyone to provide a helping hand. Many people without homes would take shelter in parts of the city where the fire had not taken hold.

Their fears had been realized, Mama was one of the three hundred that had perished in the fire. The girls stayed with their aunts, uncles, and cousins while Papa and Mama's four brothers made their way through the barricades that were set up by the Pinkerton Detectives to protect residents from the still burning city.

They wetted blankets in horse troughs on the way to the area and draped them over their shoulders. They were able to make their way through the still-smoldering buildings to reach Mama's bakery. The men did not see the absolute destruction of the business district; they had a purpose, to find Mama.

As they entered the structure that used to be the bakery, they saw that the front area, where customers would buy from the display cases, did not survive the fire. The walls were gone and the cabinets were reduced to black rubble. They entered the kitchen and were surprised to find it was largely intact due to the stone walls and cement floor Papa had required them to have. *Still not enough to protect her,* thought Papa, *not enough, I'll have to do better.*

Mama's blonde hair was seen first by Hans. "Here! She is here!" he called out. Her appearance was a surprise, she had not been burnt at all. For a moment it gave the brothers hope that she still might be alive. Papa knew that she was not.

In later visits, Papa would notice the structural concerns that led to Mama's death. For now, though his only thoughts were to retrieve her. She was lodged under a large support beam that had fallen from the ceiling of the kitchen. Papa pushed the emotion back and helped Mama's brothers work throughout the morning to dig her body out.

None of the brothers or Papa spoke while trying to free her. The men burned their hands, paying little attention as they removed the beam. Once her body was uncovered, they stood in silent prayer before moving her. They placed a white sheet over her, crossed themselves, whispered their final prayers, and carried her back to her home.

Notifications were made to the police, but there was no investigation, the cause of death was listed as an accidental death due to the fire.

Additionally, they reported there was one staff member that had gone missing. He was a kitchen helper that was always by Mama's side. The police presumed him dead when a body could not be located.

There wasn't time to grieve, due to all the cleanup and work of rebuilding. Papa sat down and spoke honestly to Sister and Dora about what had happened to Mama. While they moved forward and stayed busy, Dora seemed the most affected by the tragic event and Papa could hear her crying at night. He did what he could to help the girls all the while thinking that if Mary hadn't had that special order, she would have been safe with them.

Sister, Dora, and Papa were surrounded by Mama's family, friends, and customers at the funeral. Everyone seemed to be wearing black, mourning the dead and trying to figure out how to move forward. It was a dark and grim period of Chicago's history.

Time would start to heal wounds and life would start to move forward again quickly. The family agreed that Frederick, also known as Cousin, had the drive and talent to run the bakery business. The family pitched in with labor, materials, and time, to get it going again. They renamed the bakery "Cousin's" with Ellis' approval.

Until the bakery was functional again, Cousin and other family members would work out of the kitchen in Dora and Emma's house. There, they could watch the girls, keep the family together and keep the bakery going. Mama had already started training both of them, so they were helpful to Cousin and would continue learning at the same time.

As the cleanup began, so did plans for the rebuild of the great city. Chicago would rebuild while the bricks were still smoking, nothing would hold the people back from the rebuilding.

Papa, a structural engineer by trade, would also help to lead investigations into the fire. He would help to determine that one of the root causes was that the city was at risk from fires due to the current building codes. Added to that was the lack of fire water available to firefighters.

Papa would be at the forefront of new codes and building standards for Chicago and would be in demand from other cities to help with their codes. Chicago would rise out of the ashes, moving forward at a fast pace, but with safe design.

CHAPTER 2

CHICAGO 1881 PRESENT DAY

$\mathscr{H}$e was watching her window, located on the third story of the house, waiting for the lamp to illuminate and tell him that Emma had started her day. He stayed in the shadows waiting for that light.

Emma woke early that morning, long before the sun could start its morning trek across the sky. She stretched out her arms and yawned broadly on the bed before throwing off the covers. She laid there for a bit before she sat up and moved to the side of the bed. She stood and winced as her feet touched the wood floor, it was early spring in Chicago and the early mornings could still be cold. She lit the gas lamp above her side table, the illumination allowing her to see around the room in the early morning hours. Her night dress was warm but did not protect her feet from the cold. She sat back on the bed and pulled on heavy wool socks she kept on her nightstand. She ran across the room to stoke the wood in the fireplace. Once it was going, she stood there for a moment enjoying the radiant heat, rubbing her hands, and thinking about her day ahead.

When she felt warmer, she went about her morning ablutions, using the wash basin and pitcher located in her room to wash before dressing. She quickly used the lavatory, located down the hall, and returned to her room to change into her bakery uniform. She traded her wool socks for long black stockings and stayed as close to the fireplace as she could while dressing.

Finally dressed, she took a moment to look at herself in the tall standing mirror. She had made some revisions to the basic white uniform that was required by Cousin for working in the bakery. Most of the girls there wore long white skirts that covered their boots. Emma had fashioned her full skirt into a split skirt and shortened it so that the hem just touched the top of her high black boots. The uniform top consisted of a white button-up shirt with puffed-up sleeves and included additional buttons to attach an apron. She would carry her apron and bakers' hat with her to the bakery. Emma generally shocked people with her fashion-forward approach, but she didn't let anyone else's attitudes affect or change how she presented herself. She considered herself an advanced and independent woman of sixteen who did not follow the rules of fashion to the letter.

As she finished getting ready, she piled her white-blonde hair onto her head in a high pony tail and perched her red hat on top. She carefully inserted her hat pin, grabbed her bag and she headed quietly downstairs through the dark house. *It's always odd,* she thought to herself, *how much a house can change when the voices that normally shook the rafters were quiet.* She paused for a moment and thought, *I think I prefer the noise.* She smiled slightly and continued to the kitchen.

She pushed open the swinging door to the kitchen and found her breakfast on the large round oak kitchen table. There was a note that accompanied it, *Sister, do not forget your lunch and be sure to eat breakfast. Love you.* Dora always made sure that Emma had some fruit, bread, and a bag of treats waiting. She grabbed some butter from the ice box to add to her bread. She added the butter and was already gobbling it down while she put on her red-lined coat and exited the house. She had a couple of miles to walk to get to the bakery to help with the early shift.

As she walked, she finished her breakfast and pulled out her omnipresent black notebook and pen. She took down her observations as she walked, *It was cold, the city streets were dark and families were not yet stirring.*

Her white figure glowed in the dark as she moved through the streets. The moon was full and illuminated the path. Emma didn't notice the shadow that would accompany her to the bakery.

Her watcher, still in shadows, had long learned that Emma's skills at observations made his task difficult. He had to keep a long-distance between them, so she would not detect him following her. He started for a moment when he saw someone approaching Emma. He sank back into the shadows as he realized it was Tony, the same boy who was always around her. He was her constant companion, especially in the mornings.

As usual, she felt more than saw Tony take her right arm and put it into his elbow. She glanced over, smiled up at him, and teased, "You have nothing better to do than walking me to the bakery on my work days?"

"Nope, I need to be there anyway and you are on my way," he said cheerfully.

Emma knew this to be untrue, Tony lived close to the bakery and had to walk extra steps to be with her in the mornings. She didn't remind him of this instead, she absently handed him an apple and a sweet roll from the bag Dora had sent.

He took the offered food and covered his grin with a bite. *Slowly but surely, she's getting used to me. My next step is to ask her to the dance. I have long-term ideas about my and Emma's future, she just doesn't know it yet*, he thought wryly.

They went along companionably, enjoying the quiet of the early morning and each other's company.

"So, what's on your schedule today? Though I think I know at least one of the items," Emma teased him.

"Deliveries. Bakery in the morning and the afternoon, different courier jobs."

"And…" she said, encouraging Tony.

"And the Museum," he filled in. "They have some amazing exhibits this week. Did I tell you the Curator asked me for my opinion on some of the new paintings?"

"Really Tony? That is wonderful." Emma knew Tony loved the Museum and could either be found there or at the library looking at art books. His goal was to eventually work at the Museum.

"What about your plans?" asked Tony.

"Well, not as exciting as yours. I'm sure that my bakery list will have rye rolls, pies, and maybe some special desserts," sighed Emma, resigned to her current job.

Emma worked several mornings a week at the family bakery. It was the same bakery that Emma's mama first started when the family emigrated from Germany. It was located in the business district of Chicago. *Though if Cousin has his way, they will have locations all over Chicago*, Emma thought.

Mama's bakery had been heavily damaged during the fire of '71 and had to be rebuilt. When Mama's brothers were inspecting the damaged bakery with Papa, they realized that many of the businesses around their shop would not open again. The family pulled their resources to buy the extra space and expanded into one of the largest bakeries in the area.

Papa was not involved in the day-to-day running of the bakery but was present every day during the rebuild. He was there to make sure the rebuild was to a high building standard and that not just the kitchen would survive the next fire, but the whole building. He also took a special interest in the anchoring of the support beams and the types of materials being used. A preventable loss like the one that killed Mama, wouldn't happen again.

On the day of the new bakery opening, a plaque was put into place that read: *Mary Evan's Bakery first established in 1865.* Papa had vowed that this bakery would stand and Mama would be remembered for it. The family was all in attendance when the plaque was unveiled. Emma and Dora were very proud of what their Mama had started.

The family believed that the bakery would hold them together and be an extension of them. All members were involved in the day-to-day running of it; from the baking to the cleaning, and the accounting. All of the children were required to put in time to help out and learn the trade. Not all of the children would be bakers, but they would have an appreciation for hard work and family-led businesses.

As Emma and Tony approached the door, Tony stopped to chat with the other delivery drivers and Emma headed inside to start her work day.

The watcher stayed in the shadows until Emma left his line of site. He knew her schedule and would be back about the time she would be leaving.

Emma loved the smell of baking bread and other pastries as she opened the back door and stepped into the kitchen. In that moment, memories of Mama would flood her senses. She hesitated only briefly because everyone started to yell about the draft coming into the room. She pushed the heavy door shut with her shoulder and went to her workstation. She found her task list there from Cousin and read the first thing on it. *Rye bread, of course,* she thought, rolling her eyes as she continued to review the list.

The kitchen was busy with everyone arriving and setting up their stations for the day. It was a large room that contained a row of seven ovens against the wall and individual work benches lined up in 3 by 2 rows. The room was already full of bakers that morning and working ovens made the room nice and warm.

Hellos came from all corners, she waved generally to the other bakers. She slipped off her coat, hat and buttoned on her apron, tying it at the back. As she slipped on her baker's hat, she noticed it was just 4:15am and it was time to start her day. After she hung her hat and coat up in the closet, she glanced at her list again, started putting together the ingredients for the dough to make the pastries and pie shells, and rye bread. She placed them in a jumble on her workstation and started separating them for her first order of the day.

She started with the rye bread and went to work on rolling out bread for buns and loaves, making small talk with the other bakers. The action of working the dough made her think of a quote she had read: In the Early American Cookery, The Good Housekeeper, 1841 the author says, "There are three things which must be exactly right, in order to have good bread, the quality of the yeast, the lightness or fermentation of the dough, and the heat of the oven. No precise rules can be given to ascertain these points. It requires observation, reflection, and a quick, nice judgment, to decide when all are right. The woman who always has good home-baked bread on the table shows herself to have good sense and good management." What Emma always took from that quote was the "observation, reflection and a quick, nice judgement." That defined how Emma looked at all things in life.

It had become easier to make bread. She thought to herself, *Yeast, what a marvel.* Yeast was invented in 1868 by the Fleischmann brothers and baking powder was invented in 1869, which was a blend of monocalcium phosphate, sodium bicarbonate, and starch and tallow breads to rise without starters. In 1873 flour was improved with a flour mill that efficiently separates wheat germ and bran from the white endosperm, making cakes and pies so much easier to make.

Rye rolls were made each day and sold out by lunchtime. As more and more households had two working parents, bread had to be bought rather than made.

"How are you today, Emma?" asked Chloe, one of the few employees that was not a cousin or a family member. Chloe was getting to an age where she would be making a decision to either continue working at the bakery or to be married. She had a long-term idea that might allow both and sent a long sideways glance towards Cousin.

"I'm good," Emma answered as she continued to work on her rolls. She noticed Chloe's eyes drifting time and time again to Cousin. Emma smiled to herself and kept working.

The bakery was a happy place, a place full of gossip about the neighborhood, family, and all sorts of things. Emma knew she would have to remember what was being said and share it with Dora later.

Cousin worked the bread and chattered on about his weekend, "...she is a pretty girl and we had a good time. I may have to ask her out again." Cousin stood tall with broad shoulders, thick brown hair, and gray eyes. Both of his parents had come from Germany.

Two of Emma's female cousins, working at stations near him, smiled, knowing he liked to play the field and thought of nothing permanent but the bakery. He would eventually marry, but it would be a while before he would make time for the bakery and a family. He had plans to make this business grow and he didn't want anything or anyone to slow him down.

As the conversation continued, so did the baking. The bread and pies were being pulled out of the ovens and the shelves were filled for the morning deliveries and the breakfast rush.

Emma was especially interested in the delivery boys that were there early each morning. She watched as they piled in through the back door. They showed up in the early hours, as the sun was coming up, to pick up orders consisting of bread, cakes, pies, and other assorted desserts, ready to be delivered that day. Tony got to the bakery earlier than other delivery drivers because he accompanied Emma in. He usually waited for his friend Tim, before coming into the kitchen.

As they came into the bakery together, Tony's dark brown eyes searched until he found Emma. He shot her a wide grin and tipped his bowler hat toward her. Emma nodded back and sent back a similar grin. Tim sent an absent wave her way and made his way to the boxed cakes, pies, and bread.

The delivery boys were dressed typically in long pants, shirts, and slouchy jackets. The hats they wore were different types, some soft felt hats pulled over their eyes and others in dressier bowlers. They would slouch in and grumble as they picked up their deliveries. Cousin would slip each a berliner and a grin to get them moving.

Emma knew many of the delivery boys but had grown up with Tony and Tim. Tony Marella was Italian and had straight light brown hair, dark brown eyes, and a lanky build. He was sure that he would be a businessman one day and make his family proud. Tony had a lovely family with a mom, dad, and three brothers. His dad had a plumbing business with two of Tony's brothers. Their business consisted mainly of new construction for gas and water lines.

Tim Flannigan was the quieter soul, big as a mighty oak tree. He was a good foot taller than Tony and his arms were busting out of his sleeves. He had thick red hair and blue eyes, a true Irishman. Tim lived with his aunt and uncle; his parents had also perished in the fire of '71. His life had been saved because he was staying with friends the night of the fire. He was also a few years older than Tony and Emma and was already attending night school to get his accounting degree.

Tim had lived at the boarding house for a time after the fire, prior to his aunt and uncle moving to Chicago to take care of him. Tony came over to Emma and Dora's house to visit him each day. They became very close friends during that time. The boys also started taking mathematics and engineering classes with Papa and Emma. They both excelled academically.

Emma gazed wistfully toward the wagons parked outside the bakery. She envied the boy's ability to leave the shop and run around the Chicago streets making deliveries, having adventures. They always seemed to be having much more fun than Emma.

Tim had caught the look and tilted his head thoughtfully. He shook his head as if to clear it. *I'll have to think about how*, he muttered thoughtfully.

"Emma," said Cousin brusquely, but with a slight smile. "Stop daydreaming and get those pies in the oven." That snapped Emma and Tim out of their thoughts.

"Yes, Cousin," said Emma, and immediately did as she was told. She had completed the rolls and had moved to work on the final preparation for the pies. She had trimmed the remaining dough that was on the edge of the pie and added an intricate decorative twist. She finished it with an egg wash on them to make them shine before putting them in the oven. She then started on Almond-Cherry Soufflés with warm Chocolate sauce.

"Emma," called out Cousin. "I have a change to your list this morning."

"A change?" Emma asked as she paused, holding the items she had gathered for the next dessert on her list.

"Yes," said Cousin, "we have a special request for your Mama's specialty, Chocolate Leaves with Asbach Uralt-Poached Pears and Grapefruit Lemmon Quark Mousse. They want it this week, so next time you are here we need to add that to your usual list. Leave me a list of items you will need."

"I will," she said to Cousin. She thought to herself, *That's odd. Mama was known for this dessert, but it had not been ordered outside the family since the fire. She was the only person on staff that had the experience to make it properly.* She started her list of ingredients that would need to be compiled and put it on Cousin's desk.

While Emma continued to work, she took careful notice of the time the delivery drivers were leaving. She pulled out her black leather notebook and wrote down as many notes about the boys as she could remember, cataloging the information for a later review. How they were dressed in trousers, un-pressed jackets, and button-up shirts. How they wore their caps and hats. The delivery boys were a bit disreputable, but that made them even more interesting.

As Tony was walking back and forth to the wagons, he saw her scribbling and smiled. "Getting it all down?" he teased Emma in a low voice.

She glanced up and returned the smile. "Trying to," she whispered, glancing around again for Cousin.

The delivery drivers would pick up cakes, pies, and breads for early morning orders and bring back the additional orders for that evening or the next day. Once deliveries were completed, they moved on to other types of deliveries, papers, lumber, etc. They had free rein in the city and could go anywhere on their own. Cousin allowed the boys to keep the wagons and horses for their afternoon deliveries and in trade, they fed the horses and kept their stables clean.

Emma wanted to have adventures, she wanted to see more than the bakery and the boarding house. There was no way that would happen if she did not find a way to get out. She would always have her love of baking, but she knew that her future involved activities outside of the bakery.

I had to find a way to go on deliveries with the boys and see more of the city, she thought. Emma had seen quite a bit of Chicago already but wanted to see more. There was a time after the fire that Papa would not let Emma or Dora out of his sight, so that meant the girls were taken on many of his structural engineering jobs and could navigate the city at an early age.

Emma finished out her morning and headed home for lunch and afternoon studies.

Her watcher had stayed nearby and was there when she exited the bakery to head home. Her path changed very little, so he stayed back so as not to be detected. He was ever vigilant about knowing where she was and what she was doing.

Emma continued her walk home, brushing off her white skirt and shirt as she went. She carried her coat because the day had warmed. There was a swagger in her step and her red hat perched jauntily on her head. The ever-present notebook was taken out, allowing her to make observations as she walked.

As she continued down the street, she heard a voice call her name from down the street, "Hey Emma," and turned toward it.

Her watcher took a step toward Emma until he saw her reaction to the person calling her. He immediately recognized the delivery driver Tim and he stepped back into the shadows.

Tim pulled his delivery wagon next to the curb near Emma.

"Hey Tim, did you finish early today?" asked Emma.

"Nah, not yet, want a ride home? I'm headed in that direction," Tim indicated with a nod.

"That would be nice," Emma said and took his hand to climb up on the wagon. "Anything interesting on the route today?" she inquired as they started toward home.

Tim shook his head. "No, not unusual, but we did see several Stubing department store deliveries come in today. We also had some orders for the train station."

Emma liked to hear about people traveling. "Did you see the passengers?" she asked eagerly, inching up in the wagon seat.

"Yes, some. Mostly we go into the back of the station, but this time they let us deliver berliners to the train engineers. We also got to see inside the train," he said lightly.

Tim thought Emma was going to pull herself off of the seat with excitement. She had a million questions about the train. "How did the train run? Did you see the engine? Was it loud? Did you get to ride on it?" and many more. They talked more about the train and what Tim had seen as they made their way to Emma's house. He pulled the horses to a stop and hopped down to assist her off of the wagon.

"Is Dora home?" he asked innocently as he swung her down, looking everywhere but at her.

Emma hid a smile by placing a hand over her lips as if to

wipe something off and said, "Why yes, you might check with her to see if she would like any deliveries this week."

Emma knew that Dora didn't usually order, but Tim obviously wanted to see her, so she told a small fib to help him out. Emma accompanied Tim up the stoop into the house. They entered the kitchen by cutting through the dining room off of the foyer.

Dora had the house opened up with the sun streaming in all of the windows. The kitchen was particularly bright due to the additional windows she had Papa install over the sink. The afternoon sun lit up Dora's naturally brown hair with highlights.

Dora sat at the kitchen table making notes in her household journal. She had the same head for detail that Emma had, but applied it to the household accounts. She took the time for her journal between lunch and dinner. She looked up, as she heard the door open, expecting her helper Amy, Emma, or one of the boarders. She was startled to see both Tim and Emma in her doorway.

Emma spoke first since both Tim and Dora were busy trying to not look at each other. Both Dora and Tim were red-faced and the conversation appeared to be at a stop.

"Dora, Tim wanted to check in with you about an order you might need," she looked encouragingly from Dora to Tim.

When neither would talk, Emma just kept talking about anything she could think of. When she started a conversation about seeing tigers in the streets that morning and there was no reaction, she realized that they were not listening.

Emma got exasperated when it looked like Tim was turning to leave without saying a word to Dora. Emma stopped him, placing a hand on his arm, and said, "Oh for heaven's sake, Dora, Tim says there is a dance this weekend and would like you to go."

Tim looked astonished at this, since he had said no such

thing, but went along anyway. "Definitely, there is a church social this weekend. Would you like to go," Tim gulped, "with me?"

Dora had no way out and really didn't want one. She looked directly at him for the first time, smiled slowly, and said, "Tim, I would love to go with you."

Tim grinned a grin so wide it threatened to split his face. He started backing up and hit the wall, which caused the picture next to him to bounce. He mumbled that he would be by at 8pm on Saturday to pick her up and barely missed hitting the doorway on his way out. Emma and Dora heard a loud "wahoo" from the front of the house.

When they heard the front door open and close both girls dissolved into giggles. "I thought he would never get it out," said Emma.

"No," said Dora, "it would have taken twenty years." She sobered abruptly and asked Emma in a worried tone, "What will I wear?"

Emma had pulled out her notebook and was reviewing it when she heard Dora's concerned comment. "Weren't you planning your pink dress?" Emma inquired.

"Well, that was before I was going with someone," said Dora wryly.

"We can put something together," she reassured her. She started drumming her fingers on her lips and said, "I have a lace overlay that might work. Lay the dress on my bed that you are thinking of and we can make some alterations this evening."

"Okay, but nothing too daring," she said with a wink, "and thanks."

"No problem. Well, I'll leave you to your work," Emma said. "I told Papa I would be in class this afternoon." With that last comment, Emma headed to her father's study, leaving Dora with her thoughts of Tim.

Both Emma and Dora were home-schooled by their father.

Dora had moved away from engineering into mathematics. She was eighteen now and decided that mathematics was the skill she would need for reviewing her accounting books and expenditures. Emma continued to work on civil and structural engineering. Papa used her as his assistant for real-life application of code enforcement on buildings.

As lessons wrapped up with Papa, Emma applied herself to the lacework drape for Dora's dress. Dora had laid out her blue dress as her choice for the dance. *It would look lovely with her blue eyes,* thought Emma.

Dinner that night was another noisy affair that Dora and Amy ran with quiet precision. As dinner came to a close, the groups separated. The kids worked on homework at the dining room table and the adults sat quietly talking in the family room. Papa would share his time between helping with homework in the dining room and conversations in the family room.

Dora worked at a little table near the sofa, reviewing her books for the week, while Emma worked with Miss May, adding details to the lacework for Dora's dress. The other adults in the room were either reading or speaking in quiet conversation.

Papa had heard about Dora's invitation from Tim. "As I understand it Dora, Tim was so excited he got three blocks away before he remembered he had a wagon with him," Papa teased her.

Dora took the ribbing good-naturedly, pleased that Tim was excited as she was about the dance. She looked over her books and daydreamed a bit about Tim and their possible future.

Emma saw that Dora was embarrassed and did not join in with Papa's teasing. She kept herself busy with the lace pattern she was working on for Dora's dress. Emma had used her skill in engineering to start drawings and patterns for the intricate lacework that she and Miss May designed. She would have to apply herself to the project to have it completed by Saturday evening. Miss May would help her with the final attachment of the lace to the dress. Miss May and Miss Marjorie chatted next to Emma while she worked the lace. The evening came to a quiet close with the gas lights being turned out and families heading up to their rooms.

CHAPTER 3

The next morning at the boarding house, Emma woke with a start and then realized that it was not her early day. She sank back slowly on the bed, stretched out with her hands above her head, and curled her toes. Emma was off for the day and she could already hear other boarders on the stairs, getting ready to start their days.

She took some time getting dressed that morning in a divided skirt that was similar to the style of the ones she wore at the bakery, but this one was a vibrant red. The skirt also had a black band at the waist and a layer of lace showing just at the bottom. Her outfit was completed with a high-necked white lace shirt and a longish red jacket. Red was her favorite color and she wore it whenever she could.

She stood in front of her mirror, pulled her hair into a pony-tail, and grabbed her rounded modified bowler hat. It was also red and had a similar black band to that of her skirt. She reached for her black lace-up boots, put them on, and laced them up before heading downstairs.

"Sister," called Dora, hearing Emma's boots on the stairs, "kitchen first."

"All right," said Emma with a good-natured groan, she headed to the kitchen, slipping off her hat and placing it out of the way in a closet off the foyer. She had been hoping to sneak out, but that was impossible in this house.

Breakfast first. She knew the drill and off to the kitchen she went. She knew what Dora expected her to do, so she breezed through the dining room, grabbed plates from the pantry, and twirled around the large brown table as she set it up for breakfast. She entered the kitchen in her usual dramatic fashion.

Dora had whipped up a jelly cake early that morning. She was busy cutting it into the thin slices for the breakfast table when Emma entered the kitchen.

"Good morning, Dora, Amy," said Emma fairly singing the greeting. Both Dora and Amy looked toward the door and smiled.

"Good morning, Sister," said Dora. "Did you sleep well?"

Emma nodded and said, "Very," as she grabbed a biscuit.

Dora glanced at the clock and asked, "Sleep in a bit?" Dora and Amy had been up early to start breakfast preparations.

Emma nodded and said, "Yeah," her mouth already full of biscuit and jam.

Dora glanced down at Emma's divided skirt. "Lose the bottom of your skirt?" she teased her.

Emma gave Dora an exaggerated frown and then they both smiled at each other. Dora and Amy continued their preparations for breakfast, Emma pitched in to help as they piled up the food on platters and placed them on the kitchen table, to be moved into the dining room.

The kitchen and the rest of the house were Dora's domain. Emma knew who was boss and did what she was told.

Dora and Emma were 2 years apart, but closer than most sisters due to the loss of their Mama at such young ages. The sisters were ½ German (from Mama's side) and ½ Welsh/English (from Papa's side). Dora had more of the German build with a very lovely full figure and was a very pretty lady. Emma favored her father's family and was slight in build. Both girls had lovely hair, Dora's thick and light brown and Emma's thick white-blonde hair with Dora having blue eyes and Emma having brown. Both of the girls favored their mother in looks.

Mama and Papa met when she first immigrated to America. She had been looking for a good solid building to start her business and had been told Papa was the best person to help her with building inspections. They hit it off from the start and the story goes that Papa proposed in the first two weeks of their meeting. Mama evidently felt the same way because she said, "Yes." Prior to the fire of '71 Papa, Mama, Emma, and Dora were the only people to live in the big house. Papa was a successful structural engineer and had saved his money to help his family have a comfortable life. The house had many unused bedrooms and was four stories high. Mama had teased Papa about wanting to fill all of the rooms with children. Sadly, that wouldn't be the case now.

On the first floor, there was a large entryway that led to the stairs. Additionally, on the first floor, there was a large kitchen, dining room, study, and sitting room. The second floor contained five bedrooms and the third floor had an additional five bedrooms. The fourth-floor attic was the highest space in the house and was mostly used when Mama was alive for projects and sewing.

After the fire, so many people were homeless and needed help. Papa opened their home to family and friends, needing a place to stay while their homes were rebuilt. What had started as friends and family needing a place to stay, would eventually lead to their house being turned into a boarding house business run by the family. Boarding houses were a popular trend to house the many visitors and people that had moved to help rebuild Chicago. They provided lodging and meals for a price.

Papa always had a long view of the future for his girls. He was aware that before 1860, any money made by a woman through a wage, investment by gift, or inheritance, automatically became the property of her husband once she was married. The current laws also made the identity of the wife effectively-- legally absorbed into that of the husband. This would make the couple one person under the law.

Papa and Mama had never wanted that for their daughters, they wanted free-thinking women who could make their own way in the world. They had always kept their money from their respective businesses separate in case something was to happen to one or both of them. Papa heard that the legislatures were working on the Married Women's Property Act to help protect women's rights, but that was years away at this time.

The boarding house provided an income for the girls' future as well as the added benefit of helping them stay busy and not have time to dwell on the loss of their Mama.

Once the boarding house moved toward being a permanent business, Dora's talent for organization became apparent. She talked Papa into letting her take over running the boarding house. He had the same thought in mind and it didn't take much convincing.

Papa and Emma had been worried about Dora since Mama had passed away. She had not been excited about anything until she took over the running of the boarding house. Dora liked the people around them and the energy that came with them. Having children in the house and the kitchen made her happy.

Initially, Dora did both cooking and the boarding house management with help from Emma. Though she was young, she proved she could run it as a successful business. As it became more successful, Dora was able to hire Amy to help with cooking, serving, and general housework. Larger events, such as Christmas, required additional help to be brought in for cleaning and serving.

Dora went into her new role with ease, her demeanor changed from a quiet one to one where she clearly enjoyed being in charge. *Looking back, she would have been a great general of troops*, Emma thought with a smile.

As usual, Emma had pulled out her small black notebook and was scribbling in it. "What are you writing this time?" asked Amy. Amy Brown was a small woman but had a core of lead under her skin. Her size and general appearance made her look much younger than she actually was. Amy was in her mid-20s with a light frame, small bones, and curly red hair. She did not live at the boarding house, but rather she lived with her brother and his family nearby. She was unmarried and did not seem concerned about her single status. She was a hard worker and was always ready to help with whatever task was offered.

Emma replied with a shrug, "Observations of this or that, what I'm going to do today, and things I need to work on." Emma didn't want to overshare before she was sure what her observations could mean.

Dora loaded up trays and said directly to both Amy and Emma, "Well, Emma put that down for now, both of you help load up the table with breakfast."

Emma closed the notebook with a clap and put it into her skirt pocket. The trays were loaded with berliners, eggs, sausages, bacon, fresh-baked bread, assorted jams, and jellies. As they moved the food to the dining room table, the fragrant smells wafted upstairs. Boarders started appearing before Dora could ring the breakfast bell.

The current boarders included two older ladies, Miss

Marjorie, and Miss May, as well as two families with small children. In the general confusion of the table, Emma sat in her favorite spot between Miss Marjorie and Miss May.

Miss Marjorie gave the appearance of a fragile elderly woman of 80, but she was actually a criminal of the first degree with a spine of steel. She and her husband were professional bank robbers. They had gotten caught on their last job and had been sent to prison. Miss Marjorie was the only one to make it out the last time. She was philosophical about what had happened to her husband and said they had a grand, adventurous life together.

Papa had been friends with Marjorie and her husband in the past. Emma wasn't sure how long Papa had known each other but knew that their friendship went far back.

Miss Marjorie would be among the first of many "specialists" that Papa would bring into the boarding house after Emma's "incident" occurred. The specialty that Papa wanted Emma to learn from Miss Marjorie was not safe cracking, but her other talent, throwing knives. They had been working together, developing Emma's skills, for the past few years. Emma was as good as or better than Miss Marjorie.

Miss Marjorie looked over at Emma and asked, "Will we be practicing today?"

"Yes," Emma nodded, her mouth full of pastry and sausage. She swallowed and wiped her mouth with her napkin saying, "Let's meet outside after breakfast."

Miss Marjorie agreed with a nod. Emma didn't see her, but she looked over at Miss May and winked. Miss May nodded discretely.

Dora cleared her throat at Emma after hearing her plans for the morning.

"Oh, and after I help in the kitchen," Emma said hurriedly.

Dora nodded approvingly.

Miss May jumped in, not wanting to be left out, "We also

need to work on that lace this evening, we have a deadline next week for some lace overlays."

Emma smiled warmly at Miss May and covered her hand with hers. Emma said, "I'm looking forward to it." Miss May's cheeks got red and she smiled warmly back at her.

Miss May could work lace in the most beautiful styles and was much in demand. She didn't have any children of her own and wanted to pass on the lace craft to Emma. Emma had a talent for working lace and was already selling her designs to local shops to give dresses a finishing touch. She was another one of Papa's specialists, her specialty was as an escape artist. There wasn't a binding of any type; cuffs, ropes, chains, and locks, that she couldn't get out of. Her lacework kept her fingers nimble just in case her skills were needed.

Emma cleared the table and everyone went off to start their day, Dora gave her a sideways look and nodded toward the kitchen. Dora and Emma finished clearing the table while Amy started washing the dishes. After they finished, Dora sat down and said resigned, "Okay, I don't like gossip, but if everyone else knows what is going on, then so will I."

Emma shared the gossip she had picked up the previous morning at Cousins; Cousin's new lady friend, Chloe's side looks, and all of the other information that floated around the bakery.

After breakfast cleanup was completed, Emma met Miss Marjorie outside in the backyard. It was fenced in and a had grassy area that was well taken care of, as well as garden areas full of flowers and vegetables.

The yard was used for many activities, Emma worked with her knives there, as well as training with her specialist in self-defense.

She carried the targets out to the fence. The targets were made of plywood sheeting, marked with a human body drawn roughly on them. Miss Marjorie and Emma arranged the time for the day's lessons to start early, after breakfast. They had deliberately chosen times that the boarding house kids would be at school, so no harm could come to them.

"It is important to practice and know where the knife is going at all times. You want to wound your aggressor, but you need to know how to throw it lethally also," Miss Marjorie said each time they worked together.

Emma had two separate knives; balanced and unbalanced. Her preference was the balanced knife, one that could be thrown by the blade or by the handle.

"It is also important," Miss Marjorie said, "to know how to throw both types of knives in case you get into a situation where you have to use one you are unfamiliar with."

Miss Marjorie went on to explain that this type of throwing knife was commonly made out of a single piece of steel or other material, without handles, unlike other types of knives. The knife has two sections, the blade which is the sharpened half of the knife, and the grip which is not sharpened. The purpose of the grip is to allow the knife to be safely handled by the user and also to balance the weight of the blade.

Emma worked at it until she could throw over and underhanded. She had a natural talent for throwing knives and knew that this skill would be useful to her.

"Emma, we need to work on concealed knives and how to access them without hurting yourself," stated Miss Marjorie.

The Narrator is interrupted by Dear-one as he is reading over her shoulder. "You should mention the scars."

"Oh, yes," said the Narrator.

To continue with the story…

Emma learned to work with the knives through daily practice sessions with Miss Marjorie. During those sessions, she had a couple of accidental cuts, one on her upper arms and one across the back of her hand. Both had healed but had left scars, the one on the back of her hand would be a constant reminder to keep her mind on the task at hand.

"Emma," Miss Marjorie said, "we have something for you."

"You do?" inquired Emma with a tilt of her head.

"Emma, you have learned so much about knives, but I need to share some secrets with you. One, you must always carry two knives with you. Those knives could one day save your life. Two, you must not let anyone, even close friends, know where you keep them," Miss Marjorie lectured.

Emma listened very closely, Miss Marjorie had led an adventurous life and knew that she was following in her path.

Miss Marjorie continued, "May and I have talked about where the second knife could be hidden." She pulled a small box from under her shawl and opened it, it was a small knife, about 6 inches long, with a leather sheath and a tie. "This will fit best around your upper thigh. We will cut a slit in your skirt pockets that will also allow you to easily access it. Let me show you how to put it on." Emma pulled up her skirt so that Miss Marjorie could place the sheath on her leg. Emma let the skirt drop and Miss Marjorie reached over and quickly tore a hole in Emma's skirt pocket to show her how to access it.

"Should we place it on the inside of my leg, in case I am checked for knives?" asked Emma, worried that she might get in a situation where they would take the second knife from her.

Miss Marjorie thought about that for a moment before she said, "Since you are a woman, I really don't expect they will think you are clever enough to have a clutch piece on you." She continued with a warning, "You will need to practice pulling it out and not cutting yourself."

"May?" Miss Marjorie prodded gently, looking over Emma's shoulder.

"Yes," Miss May said breathlessly, "I have it right here." Emma turned around when she heard the other woman's voice.

"You startled me!" Emma said with a laugh. Miss May had not come out at the same time as Miss Marjorie and Emma.

"This is for you," Miss May said before handing Emma a hatbox.

Emma let out an excited squeak as she pulled off the box top. There she saw the beautiful black felt bowler hat with a dashing red lace ribbon and a red feather. Emma slowly took it out of the box and was careful to not crush the hat or the beautiful red feather.

Miss Marjorie said sharply, "Emma hand that to me, you must be careful, this is a special hat." Emma handed the hat gingerly to Miss Marjorie.

Miss Marjorie pulled the "hatpin" out of the hat. The "hatpin" was actually a very lethal-looking knife with a black handle. Miss Marjorie threw it and hit the center of the target.

"That is no simple hat pin," Emma said as she went to retrieve it.

"No," said Miss Marjorie as Emma returned and handed her the knife. She continued, "I had Mark, my knife smith, balance it for you. I also asked May to put a compartment where the hatpin should go, so that you can have this with you always. You must treat it carefully." The feather was actually attached to the hat and the knife had a special holder to protect Emma from being cut.

Emma nodded, "I'll be careful."

Emma noticed the intricate red lacework that accented the base of the hat, she immediately recognized Miss May's work. She went to her and gave her a long hug. Miss May teared up as she hugged her back.

Miss Marjorie cleared her throat, she wanted to get back to business. "Now," Miss Marjorie said, "we need to work on removing the knife from the hat and throwing it in one smooth motion."

Emma nodded and stayed serious and intent on the instructions she was being given. Emma put the hat on her head and started practicing pulling the knife out and throwing it in one smooth motion. It took a bit of practice, but she managed to get to her targets.

Miss Marjorie commented, "You will have to continue to practice with both knives, but remember their location should stay a secret until they need to be used."

"Thank you, Miss Marjorie," said Emma and hugged her.

"Well," she said patting Emma's shoulder, "we would do anything for you dear."

After knife throwing, Emma spent the rest of the morning working with Papa on math equations and engineering designs for his company. Emma worked on Papa's draft table in the study, updating changes to the current building project drawings.

After they were updated, there were clean-up duties and lunch to help with. Boarders usually were already off to work and school so lunch was usually just family, Miss May and Miss Marjorie.

Papa noticed Emma's new hat perched on a nearby table. Emma saw the direction of his considering gaze and said in a rushed tone, "Papa, Miss May, and Miss Marjorie made that for me."

Papa looked to the ladies at the table. "That is a lovely hat, ladies, and a very thoughtful gift," said Papa. Both ladies blushed at the compliment.

"Emma," said Miss Marjorie, "you must not leave it out." She squinted her eyes as she made the warning.

"That's right," said Emma, "I don't want it to get damaged." She picked it up carefully and took it up to her bedroom and placed it in a box under her bed. She had shown Dora the hat and the secret. Dora would be the only person to know about the knife in the hat, but no one would know where she would hide her second knife.

Emma's afternoon included reading and working on several lace designs. The day slowly wound down with the familiar routine of getting dinner on the table. Boarders filled in and conversation flowed about the day's events.

Miss May looked over at Emma. "We need to work on those new designs tonight and complete Dora's overlay."

Emma nodded and smiled. She enjoyed the lacework and wanted to show her some of the ideas she had drawn up earlier that day. The evening wrapped up with Emma working patterns and lace with Miss May. The intricate patterns were laced together and prepared to be delivered to the seamstress.

CHAPTER 4

The next morning Emma wanted to discuss something with Papa. She went down to his lab and work area located in the basement of the boarding house. "Papa," Emma called, watching him sitting at his work table. He had several types of concrete in front of him that he was analyzing for defects.

When Papa was working on a project, he did not hear anything around him.

Emma walked over to him and tried again, this time tapping his arm.

"What!" Papa said, in a startled voice. He almost fell off his chair, trying to see who was behind him.

"Nothing Papa," Emma said with a grin and brushed his hair off his forehead. "You got tied up in your work again."

He grabbed her in a bear hug. "Don't do that again," he said with a chuckle. "What is it I can do for you? Is it time for lessons already?" he asked as he continued to look absently down at the concrete and other papers on his workbench.

"Well," Emma said, "I have a favor to ask."

"A favor you say?" asked Papa and looked at her thoughtfully.

Though she was a gifted student, who could look at a building and calculate the angles without the aid of an instrument to measure, Papa knew she preferred to be outside where things were happening. He had an idea of where this conversation was going. When Tim had dropped Emma off yesterday, he had stopped by and brought up the idea of Emma going on deliveries with him. Papa and Tim had worked out a plan that would allow Emma to go on when she felt she was ready. Papa had not expected the request to be so sudden. He took a deep breath as she began.

"Papa," Emma started rubbing her hands together nervously, "I would like to work with the delivery boys when I'm not at the bakery or helping out around here."

He took a moment to really explain what this might mean. "Sister…After the incident." His eyes welled up with tears.

"I know Papa, but you also know that I have worked with the specialists you brought in and I know how to protect myself," she said as she looked him steadily in the eyes. She did not show any emotion and refused to let the past event affect her future plans.

The event Papa was referencing was when Emma was about 10 years old. She had started working the morning shift at the bakery and usually walked home alone prior to having lunch at the boarding house. The walk was normally uneventful, but that day she had taken a slightly different path to see some different neighborhoods. When she tried to remember details from that day, it only came in flashes. She remembered her notebook, something hard-hitting her head, and a man who was on the smallish side, but very strong.

She had not known how to defend herself and was almost beaten to death that morning. She was saved by someone that had interrupted the beating, forcing the attacker to run off. He got her back to the boarding house, left her on the doorstep, and knocked on the door prior to leaving. Tony and Tim were there for lessons with Papa and had answered the door to discover Emma laying on the stoop. As they moved her into the house, they heard her continually asking for her notebook. She was nearly unconscious, but she still wanted that book.

They never found out who had saved her that day and the notebook was never found. Papa had looked and put out feelers but was unable to find who had beaten her up or the person who had rescued her.

Emma woke asking for her notebook, but she didn't know why she felt such urgency about it. Her memory continued to be a concern, the doctor indicated this was normal and she may never recover her memory of that day.

Papa let Emma take time to recover. Dora, Tony, and Papa kept her company, reading to her and making her laugh again. They knew when they found her attempting to walk around her bed by herself that there would be no holding her back.

Papa set plans into motion to start protecting Emma as soon as possible. He wanted to protect her, but he didn't want her to lose her sense of adventure that was so much part of who she was.

Papa's plan involved building a group of specialists that would teach Emma and Dora how to protect themselves. The first of these specialists to move in soon after the event had occurred was Papa's friend Danny Madden. Danny's particular specialty was self-defense methods. He believed in the importance of physical fitness and self-defense. They worked on kickboxing, parasol defense, shin-kicking, and jump kicking.

Emma had excelled at kickboxing and had started wearing special pointed boots in her training. She learned that her elbows and knees could deter most would-be villains. For the more serious attacks, her split skirt would help her utilize her kickboxing skills. Dora participated in the self-defense with Danny, but over time decided that her plans would not require Papa's other specialist training.

~

"Papa, you know I can take care of myself," said Emma, bringing them both out of the past.

"I know Sister, I would not want to come up against you in a fight," he teased lightly, but still looked concerned. He was also thinking, *Though it had been six years, we have not found the man who attacked her.*

"Papa," she tried again, "you know Tim and Tony will look out for me." They were as close as brothers and let her tag around with them. Nobody messed with them and they kept out of trouble. Papa knew both boys well and knew he could trust them.

Papa said, "Ja, this is good." Though Papa was English he had picked up the German expressions from their extended family. "If you get them to agree, you stay with them and you give me a hug." He smiled at Emma and she grinned back, hugging him.

"Emma," he said, "you must always wear the pointed boots."

"I will Papa," she said and turned to go back upstairs. Before she got very far, he grabbed Emma lightly by her ponytail, gave it a quick tug, and let her go on her way.

Papa called after her as she ascended the stairs, "Oh, by the way, we will be doing some math tonight." She groaned but knew there would be a compromise. "One more thing, you must have breakfast first."

"On my way now," said Emma racing up the stairs.

Papa smiled as he watched his daughter leave the basement. He had some lingering fears, but he knew she had the training to take care of herself and Tim and Tony would keep an eye on her. Papa went back to his work, settled on his decision.

The breakfast ritual had started again and the families were filling in chairs around the laden table. No one missed breakfast at the boarding house.

Emma went into the kitchen and asked Dora, "Dora, what can I take to the table?"

Dora and Amy started handing Emma trays of eggs and sausages. They followed her in with trays of pastry, toast, and biscuits.

As they made one more trip to the kitchen to retrieve pitchers of milk and orange juice, Emma said to Dora, "I don't have time to sit to eat, I'm going to help with the deliveries for Cousins today."

Dora looked up at this news, she was concerned, but she knew there would be no holding Emma back. "Papa agreed?" Dora asked casually, continuing to gather the pitchers on the table.

Emma groaned a bit. "Yes Mama," she teased. "Papa approves. Do you?"

Dora looked at Emma and said with a serious expression on her face, "You are not my daughter but you are my sister and best friend. Take care of yourself out there. Will you be with Tim and Tony?"

"Yes. Want me to take a note to Tim?" she asked cheekily.

"Oh, you," she said and swatted Emma on her behind. "Take something with you to eat." She turned and picked up the milk and orange juice pitchers to move to the dining room.

Emma followed her and made a quick bacon and egg sandwich before dashing up the stairs. She finished eating her sandwich before making it to the second floor. She made her way to the small spare room to the left, off of the main hallway. The small room had become a storage location for things left behind by previous boarders.

Emma opened the door and entered the room. She moved the piled-up boxes out of her way as she made her way to the dresser located on the far side of the small room. She searched through the dresser drawers until she found a pair of men's pants, a white shirt, and a well-worn newsboy cap. She dressed and pulled her long white-blonde hair into a tight braid and coiled it inside of the cap.

Emma wanted to see if the disguise worked on people who knew her. She remembered Miss Marjorie's advice and slipped out of the pants to look closely at the pockets. She slit the pocket seam in the right pocket to allow access to the knife she had secured to her thigh. She practiced pulling it out and putting it back into place. She glanced at her pointed shoes. *Not exactly boyish,* she thought but her pants would cover most of the top part of them. She also thought that maybe a compartment in her shoe for a sharp knife would be helpful. She would have to talk to Miss Marjorie about that.

Emma walked into the kitchen and saw Dora was already there, kneading dough for rolls at the table. She barely spared Emma a glance when she asked quizzically, "Sister what is that you're wearing?"

"You recognized me?" Dora raised an eyebrow at the question. Emma was disappointed that she hadn't fooled her.

"Yes, now what are you planning?" asked Dora. Emma told her the plan and how she would ask Tony and Tim to look out for her. Dora nodded and said, "If Papa is good, then I am also, but be careful. Tell Tim I'll have his hide if anything happens to you."

"His hide, huh? Is that all you want?" Emma teased, bringing a blush to Dora's face.

Dora made a dash for her around the table but Emma was too fast.

The two sisters squared off across the table and Dora was the first to stop. "Sister don't stay out too late. Here, take a lunch with you since you won't be at Cousins today." She handed her the bag she had packed, it contained roast beef on a hard roll. "Also, there's a berliner in there for a snack this morning."

"Can I have one for Tim and Tony?" Emma wheedled.

Dora held out her hand to retrieve the bag, she graciously gave into the request and put the extra berliners in the bag for Emma.

Dora walked around the table and handed Emma the full bag. As Emma absently took it from Dora, her mind already on other things, Dora took the opportunity to pop Emma on the behind.

"Hey," yelped Emma, jumping a bit. The boy's pants provided little to no padding between Dora's hand and her behind.

"You deserved it," she wagged her finger at Emma but had a sparkle in her eyes.

"Yes," said Emma with a cheeky grin "and I'll continue to do so." She headed out at a jog and waved to the boarders still sitting in the dining room talking. Emma bounded down the front stoop, taking the steps two at a time and she remembered that the delivery boys rarely had clean faces. She bent down at the base of the stoop where some flowers were planted and rubbed some dirt on her face and hands. *No reason to go further with putting dirt on my arms and legs since they won't be seen*, she thought.

How to approach Tim, she thought for a moment and started to drum per fingers against her lips, until she remembered that her hands were dirty. *Well*, she thought, *the best way is to be myself and be direct*. She knew he was around the bakery, off and on during the day, so she headed that way on foot.

Her watcher had a habit of sleeping at times when Emma was supposed to be home. She was a contrary girl though and just as he nodded off, he heard her boots scraping on the concrete. He woke quickly and shook his head to clear it. *Okay*, he mumbled to himself, *we are on the move.* There was something different about Emma, *Boy clothes today? Interesting.*

She headed toward the bakery and was about halfway there when she saw Tim on his wagon.

"Hey Tim," she called when she saw him, but he kept the wagon moving. He did raise a hand and wave her way absently but did not direct his gaze toward her. She knew he did not recognize her so she ran up to the side of the wagon. "Tim, I have a favor to ask of you," she said in a hurried manner as she jogged beside him.

That voice made him pull the wagon over to a stop and he turned toward her. Quick as a whip he grabbed Emma's hat off of her head. "Well, well, playing a bit of dress-up?" he mocked and he bounced back into the wagon seat, still holding her hat. He tilted his head and gave her a wide grin, the type that takes up the whole face and crinkles up the skin around his eyes.

He had expected to see Emma at some point today. Emma's papa had sent a note to let him know she would be asking about being a delivery driver and that she had his permission. He had not expected her to be dressed as a boy. *Though*, he thought, *it made things much safer and a lot less trouble.*

"What's up, little bit?" asked Tim.

Emma had thought about how to ask him but spoiled the plan by rushing into the question, "I need a favor. Can I hang out with the delivery drivers and help on the routes?"

He pretended he needed a moment to think about her question. "I'm not sure Emma, we go into some rough neighborhoods," he said cautiously.

"I could stay with you or with Tony," she wheedled. "I just want some adventure and not be stuck inside all day."

He understood, he wouldn't want to be stuck inside all day either. "Okay," he said, knowing her papa trusted him and that she could handle herself. Tim and Tony were aware that Emma's papa had made sure Dora and Emma practiced self-defense and both knew some nasty tricks to get out of tight spots. "Just don't give yourself away to the other guys, well except for Tony, and stick close," he said with a serious expression on his face. Tim and Tony could be overprotective since the incident.

"Also," Tim continued, "we have an opening. Rudy's family moved and we could use the help. You'll make the lowest pay since you're the new guy."

She nodded and exclaimed, "That's great." And since she didn't expect to get paid, any amount would be nice.

"Though you might want to try walking a bit differently. You walk like a girl," he remarked, tossing her hat back at her.

Emma nabbed the hat midair and replied smartly, "Well, that's what I am."

"Well, if you want to be taken for a boy, just keep your hips from swaying and keep the talking to a minimum," he suggested.

As she was attempting to climb into the wagon, he dashed her dreams of working deliveries today.

"Not today, meet me at the Bakery, first thing Monday morning and practice walking like a boy until that time," Tim said.

"Can't I come on your afternoon deliveries today?" she asked in a disappointed voice. "I have berliners and I can give you one if you let me go." She shook the bag at him as a bribe.

He had already spotted the bag and deftly snapped it from her hand.

"Well, I have the bag now and you definitely can't start today. Once I finish my morning deliveries, my afternoon deliveries involve heavy lifting," he said. He also wanted to tell Tony what

Emma was up to. Tony was his best friend and he knew that he had special feelings for Emma, even though she chose to ignore those feelings.

"Okay, but can I have my sandwich?" asked Emma.

"Yes, I can do that," said Tim as he reached into the bag, retrieved her sandwich, and tossed it to her.

"Thanks," said Emma turning to head back home feelings both parts excited at the job and a bit disappointed she couldn't start today.

As Emma walked off, Tim made a clicking sound to move the horse and wagon on to their next delivery.

CHAPTER 5

Tony came to the boarding house for dinner that night. She noticed he looked more serious than she had ever seen him look. He sat by Emma at dinner and didn't say much, but did eat his fill of Dora's cooking. Papa had a good idea of why he was there and let the matter stay between them.

Just as dinner was being cleared off the table by Amy, Emma, and Dora; Tony said quietly, placing his hand on Emma's, "I'd like to talk with you."

Emma glanced at Dora questioningly, Dora nodded.

Emma and Tony were best friends and occasional partners in crime. She looked up at him and said, "Okay." It wasn't a surprise that he wanted to talk, she figured Tim had informed him about her plans. "Walk around the block?" she suggested.

"Yes," Tony said. He was much quieter than usual with her. His head hung a bit forward with his silky brown hair falling into his eyes as they exited the boarding house.

Once they were outside, they began the walk silently, side-by-side, not touching. "Emma," Tony started, looking down the street in front of them, and for once in her life, Emma did not interrupt him. Tony was surprised that Emma had not already interrupted and had paused expecting it. He took a deep breath to start again, "Emma, I know your Papa, Dora and Tim have all said it's okay for you to start working deliveries with us, but will it be safe for you?"

Because she did know Tony, she let him talk. She continued to keep her gaze averted toward the houses down the block. She could see more than just the street ahead of her, she could see her future starting to form. "Tony, it's time. Time for me to have an adventure and see all of Chicago and then, eventually the world. You know that." She paused for a moment, continuing to look down the street in front of them. "Tell me something, if I hadn't been hurt would you still be so protective of me?"

He stopped her, put his hand on her arm, and turned her toward him. He reached out and tilted her chin to look him in the eye, "I honestly don't know. I think not. I want every dream you have to come true, but Emma, I can't forget that day and carrying your broken body into your house," his voice broke for a moment, laying his forehead on hers.

"I know," she said earnestly, "and you were amazing, coming every day to sit with me; reading and talking to me when I was going out of my head from boredom. Tony," she paused and grabbed his hand, "you know I can handle myself." That event changed how she saw herself and how she wanted to be seen. She saw her previous self as weak. She was a much stronger person now and wanted him to see her that way.

"Yes," Tony said, having participated in some training exercises with her, he was aware of how well she could fight. He thought to himself, *She had changed so much after that event. The adventurer was still there but there was a new strength there as well.*

"Emma," he said passionately, "I want you to enjoy your life and become the person you are meant to be. You are sixteen now, but I want to know you at eighteen, twenty-five, forty-five, sixty-five…."

This made her laugh. That was Tony, planning, and planning. At 16 she wasn't ready to find out if she was in his plans, but for now, she wanted him as her friend, her best friend.

"You will be careful." It was more of a statement than a question.

"Yes," said Emma.

As they had turned toward Emma's home, they continued walking side by side. Tony threw an arm around her shoulder and squeezed.

"Besides," teased Emma, "won't I see you first thing Monday morning, prior to my first delivery day?" She bumped against him with her hip. He had always acted like it was just chance, running into her and walking with her to the bakery.

"I'll be there as usual to walk you that morning," Tony said, admitting for the first time that he did plan to join her. "To be clear, it's not to protect you, but to keep me safe." With that statement, they laughed until they reached her stoop.

"See you," Tony said and watched her walk into the boarding house. He thought about Emma all the way home.

"See you," Emma said softly and then closed the door. Her thoughts were on Tony and next week.

CHAPTER 6

Saturday came around faster than Emma had expected. She had laid her yellow and white dress with green trim on the bed. Dora walked into Emma's bedroom twirling around to show off her bright blue gown with a beautiful lace overlay. Emma clapped and smiled delightedly that her sister was so happy.

"Oh, Emma, the dress looks brand new. Thank you so much for adding the lace for me. What do you think? How do I look?" she asked excitedly, turning toward the mirror patting her upswept hair.

"I think Tim will love it," Emma teased answering the unspoken question. Dora turned a delightful shade of red but did not contradict Emma's statement.

"Sister, Dora, your ride has arrived," called Amy from downstairs.

Dora opened the door and turned back to Emma. "Sister are you ready to go?" asked Dora, distracted, and thinking about Tim.

Emma looked at her a bit puzzled. She had not put on her dress as yet. She decided to give Dora a break. "Almost, I'll meet you downstairs," she said gently. She knew how important the dance was to both Tim and Dora.

Dora turned back to the mirror to put the finishing touches on her hair before she exited and headed downstairs to meet Tim.

Tim heard something on the stairs, he looked up and everything seemed frozen in place for a moment. As Dora stepped on the last step to the foyer Tim said, "Dora you look beautiful." It was the most personal statement that Tim had ever made to her.

"Thank you," she said, glowing with the complement, "and you look very handsome."

"Great," he said, "Let's go." He grabbed her by the hand and started pulling her toward the door. He had completely forgotten about everything except Dora.

Dora dug in her heels as he tried to pull her along. "Tim, we have to wait for Sister," she reminded him.

He shook his head as if to clear it. "Oh, that's right," he said as he glanced down and realized he still had her hand. Instead of dropping it he tugged her toward him and gave her their first kiss. It was sweet and strong, just like Tim.

Dora's world tilted and her eyes closed, as she enjoyed the moment.

Emma was coming down the stairs in her standard rush and realized she might be interrupting something. She stopped and leaned against the banister. "Hi Tim, do I get one of those also?" she teased.

Tim turned red but did snag her arm for a kiss on the cheek once she reached the landing.

The three smiled at each other. "Is Papa coming with us?" asked Emma.

"No," Dora said. "Papa has a late meeting, Tim's family will meet us there."

"Emma," Tim said innocently, "Tony asked if he could ride over with us tonight. I told him it was okay."

Emma nodded and said with a smile, "That will be nice."

Tim turned around and smiled to himself. Tony would be happy with that response.

Tim helped Dora up on the buggy seat of the wagon. They had a box sitting on the sidewalk to help with the difficult dresses and getting into the wagons. Tim went around and swung Emma into the back of it. He had cleaned it out and laid a blanket down for comfort. As they started toward the dance, Tony came running up behind them. Tim didn't stop and Tony ran to jump into the back with Emma.

"Hey," he said nodding to Tim and Dora. "Hey, Emma." He bounced a bit as he sat down next to her.

"Hey yourself Tony. What's up? Did you work today?" asked Emma, she was always interested in what the boys were up to.

"Yes, I got some extra deliveries for the Curator at the Museum," answered Tony.

"Anything interesting in the delivery package?" she continued questioning him.

"Yes," he nodded, "it was some new sketches from a local artist. The Curator was there and let me watch while he unpackaged them." They continued to discuss the Museum until they arrived at the dance.

It was the End of Spring Dance at their church. It was colorful and lively with a band and lots of people. As they entered the crowded room, Emma glanced around seeing refreshment tables set up along the walls, chairs set up for people to rest between dances, and finally a dance floor and a band.

Emma and Dora had taken over the German chocolate cake for the dessert table, earlier in the day. As Tim and Tony helped Emma and Dora off with their coats, Emma already was eyeing the other refreshments.

Emma danced with Tony and Tim. *That is, when Tim could be pried away from Dora, Emma thought, smiling slightly.*

She looked around and noticed Chloe was watching Cousin dance with multiple partners. She went over to her and asked in a whisper, "What are you doing? Go dance with him."

"Nope," she said, "that's not the way I'll get him to notice me. I have another idea." She went up to the band and asked to set in for the next song. She had never done this before and Emma noticed that Cousin's eyes had followed her graceful figure to the bandstand. He was talking to another girl but waved her off as he continued to watch Chloe.

Cousin was curious when she pointed to a small case she was carrying. The band leader had indicated yes with a nod of his head and offered her a hand up to the stage. Chloe took it and stood with the band, she opened the case and pulled out a violin and bow.

Cousin continued to watch her as she tested the bow and tightened the strings on the violin. She put it up to her chin and nodded to the bandleader. She drew the bow across and began a lively jig that the rest of the band joined in with.

It was entertaining and had Cousin's full attention. He started clapping his hands, realizing he was enjoying himself for the first time that night. He thought, *Hmm, I might have an interest in violins.* He took a harder look at Chloe.

Emma watched Chloe in amazement and shook her head. Emma went on with her night, mostly she watched the other dancers, walked around with Tony, and listened to him describe various things at the Museum while they ate many of the delicious desserts. They both gave a small wave as they spotted Tim and Dora with Tim's aunt and uncle.

After the dance ended, the four gathered back together and located the wagon to head home. It was a quiet night and all four just let the comfortable silence linger. They stopped at the boarding house and Tony helped Emma down from the back of the wagon. They said their goodbyes and Emma headed up the stoop. Tony watched until she went in and turned to say goodnight to Tim and Dora. He raised his hand but realized they couldn't see anything but each other. He let his arm drop slowly and turned toward home with a spring in his step and a whistle on his lips.

Tim and Dora sat a bit longer before getting out of the wagon. They continued looking into each other's eyes. Dora was the first to speak. "Well, I should go in," said Dora.

That got Tim moving and he jumped down from the wagon and walked around to her side and said, "Let me help you down." He twirled her around to the sidewalk.

"Tim, I had a wonderful time," murmured Dora still locked in Tim's arms.

"Me too," said Tim, not letting her go. "Dora, would you like to go to church with me tomorrow," Tim asked and as she was about to nod, he continued, "and to the park for a picnic next Saturday and then…"

He would have kept going but Dora touched his hand with hers and said, "Tim, I would love to go anywhere you would like to go."

Tim started grinning, he squeezed his arms around her and kissed her until her knees shook. He walked her to the door and kissed her again. Stepping back from her, he smashed his hat back onto his head and started down the steps of the stoop two at a time.

When he hit the last step, he turned to the right and was on his way home when Dora called, "Tim?"

He looked up at her grinning and asked, "Yes?"

"Tim, you live that way," Dora said gently, indicating to the left with her hand.

He glanced both left and right and realized she was right. With the correction made he turned left and started toward home again.

"Tim?" she called again.

He looked up at her again and inquired, "Yes Dora?"

"You forgot your wagon," she commented with a small giggle.

His face turned a bit red and he looked around for the wagon. Once he found it, he made his way over, climbed up on the seat, picked up the reigns, and turned to say to Dora, "All good now?" He waited for her nod and then headed toward home.

Dora continued to laugh softly at his antics as she went in.

As she closed the door in the house, she leaned on it and looked dreamily up toward the landing on the staircase. She noticed Emma was waiting for her. She hurried upstairs to talk to Emma. The girls got together and shared secrets into the night.

CHAPTER 7

First thing Monday morning, before the day broke, Emma started towards the bakery. The only difference was this time she was dressed like a delivery boy. Tony met her on the walk as usual with a casual greeting.

Her watcher saw the two boys and realize one was Tony. He couldn't hear them but he saw that when Tony pulled off the other boy's hat, a bright blonde braid came flowing down her back. It was Emma. *So off on an adventure,* he thought. *It would make his job harder but he would follow.*

She practiced walking like a boy on the way to the bakery. Tony swatted Emma on the butt with her hat and gave it back to her to put on before the other boys saw her.

"Emma," Tony said, "stay in the back entrance near the wagons. I'm sure the cousins will know you faster than I did."

She nodded, thinking she should let Cousin know that she would be working deliveries for a while. She would go see him later that day.

The other boys started getting there. Emma didn't make eye contact and pulled her hat lower over her eyes. She stood next to Tim's wagon and waited for him.

Dear-one commented, "They knew from the beginning."

"Who knew what?" the Narrator asked, distracted when she realized that he was reading over her shoulder.

"They knew you were a girl and who you were. They just didn't let on," he said.

"Hmm," she said, "that puts a few things into perspective." She grinned at Dear one.

Dear one just raised an eyebrow at her and said, "You will have to tell me what you mean."

"Maybe later," she said, getting back to her writing.

Back at the bakery…

As the other boys arrived, they parked their wagons and headed in for their deliveries. They normally contained pies, cakes, assorted breads, and other small pastries. These were brought out and carefully placed into the wagons. The bakery had several horses drawn wagons, with special lockboxes for the baked goods. Other local deliveries would be made via pull wagons or bags.

Tim and Tony were part of the group of wagon drivers. Emma wanted to be assigned to one of the delivery wagons because they go deeper into the city and she wanted to see as much as possible.

Tim exited the bakery with the first load of bread, cakes, and pies. He motioned for Emma to help load them into the lockbox on the wagon. She climbed up on the back and he handed over the items to put in the box. It took several trips before they could be on their way. After the final items were placed in the box and it was locked, she jumped down to the ground to move to the front. She reached to climb up to the buggy seat when Tony walked over.

He pulled down Emma's hat playfully over her eyes and gave her a crooked grin. He said as Tim walked up, "Tim you and…"

"EJ," Emma filled in. EJ being short for Emma Jane.

"Okay, you and *EJ* have a good day," he said. He looked at Tim with narrow eyes.

Tim nodded to the silent question.

Tony nodded and headed back to his wagon, it was time to get the teams moving. Emma pulled out her notebook to document the day and the movement of people in the early morning.

Tim looked over at Emma and her ever-present black notebook. He couldn't remember when he first saw her using it, it had always been a part of her. The presence of that book did remind him of a bad day, about six years ago when he and Tony found her hurt on the stoop and all she could ask for was that notebook. She would continue to ask for it as she convalesced. They had never found it.

Tim had a list of the morning deliveries, most were routine, but there might be an addition to the schedule. "Emma mark off each delivery as we make them," Tim said as he handed her the list and Emma did as directed. As they started their deliveries Tim directed her to jump down and take them to the appropriate door.

When they pulled into a nicer area where all the homes were made of stone. Tim said, "Remember, you must go to the back door of these homes. The help will take the deliveries."

"I will," she nodded knowing the neighborhood. She had actually been in the front doors of many of the nice homes in this area, when Papa had worked as an engineering consultant, updating the design requirements after the fire.

Tim handed down their orders of bread, pies, and a cake. She would have to make two trips. She made her way around the back of the building and used her elbow to ring the back bell. The door opened quickly revealing a tall imposing housekeeper.

"Well, do you have something for Mr. Black?" she asked briskly. She was a woman who had things to get done and this little slip of a girl, dressed as a boy, was slowing her down.

"Yes, of course, your pies and cakes and assorted breads," Emma said as she was allowed into the kitchen to place the order on a large rectangle table. She inhaled the wonderful smells and noted the colors of the kitchen. Black and white checked floors, white counters, and cabinets and silver trays being prepared for the family's breakfast.

Emma quickly put the items down and made a second trip for the rest of the order. She placed it with the other baked goods on the kitchen table. "Well, on your way now, scoot," the housekeeper said to Emma, nudging her toward the door. The housekeeper's mind was on her schedule for the day.

"You there," Emma could hear her tell the maids and footmen in the kitchen, "get these pies, cakes, and breads put away." They went scurrying to carry out their task.

Emma headed out trying to keep all of the details in her head to write down later. She jumped back into the wagon next to Tim, without any help. She was already adopting more boyish mannerisms.

Tim noticed and the right side of his mouth quirked up, but he didn't say anything. The more boy-like she behaves, the safer she will be.

Emma didn't mind the work, she was so excited to be out and about. She thought, *There are so many people moving around, even in the early hours of the day. People on horses and trolley cars, on their way to work, or just starting their days at home. Milk trucks trudging along slowly but surely on their routes.*

She took everything in on that first day; how the day changed, how the quiet streets began to fill up with people, horses, buggies, and wagons. The noise started when the construction workers arrived for work on the different buildings. In Chicago, the rebuilding had been continuous since the fire. The buildings were going higher than anywhere else in the country. She could not wait to see the city from the new high views.

She was documenting the people she saw on the street corners. It was interesting that the neighborhoods seemed to dictate the types of clothes people wore. The people living in the nicer neighborhoods had quieter classy clothes, the working areas had more rough clothes, and the gaming areas were a bit more disreputable and were flashier.

Tim interrupted her observation, "Emma where are we on the list?"

She had the list in her hand and read off the next two delivery locations.

"Got to keep our priories straight Emma. We need to keep on schedule and it's your responsibility to not let me miss a delivery," he reminded her.

"Oh, I won't miss one, I promise," she said and applied herself industrially to making sure the list stayed up-to-date. As she updated the list, she kept looking around making observations, and writing as fast as she could. Emma also added some notes to the delivery pages to help with identifying locations so that she could be more helpful on the next trip.

As Emma continued her observations, she noticed the maids in the nicer neighborhoods had milk delivered to their doors and in poorer ones, families carried pitchers to be filled by the driver on the trucks. A few hours into their deliveries they started seeing businesses opening their doors and children being sent on their way to school.

Tim had indicated their routes had added more deliveries into working-class areas as women began working outside the home.

"Why is that?" asked Emma.

Tim answered, "The ladies no longer have time for baking days, so the families' weekly bread and desserts are coming from us now."

As the morning wound down, Emma wanted to talk about everything she had seen.

Tim cautioned, "Emma, I love you are happy to be working with me, but remember you will only be on the wagon a few days a week."

"I know," she muttered. "I just like being out and seeing so many things and people." She continued to talk about her day a smile lit up her face and Tim couldn't help but smile back.

Curiosity finally got the best of Tim. "What are you writing so often?" he asked, waving his hand toward the black notebook in her hand.

"Just what's happening around us," she said. Her face took on a more serious look as she continued, "I just don't want to miss something that might be important."

Over the next few weeks, Emma's schedule changed to allow her to spend more time with Tim on the delivery wagon. During that time, she got to know the neighborhoods and the businesses on their route. She continued to document her observations, looking around for patterns in the people and their days.

In the evenings she went over her observations and started grouping the ones that stood out. The first of these was around Stubings, the large department store located on their route. There was something strange about those deliveries, but she couldn't determine what it was. These observations were separated from her general notebook and put into one that would focus just on that observation.

She kept the two notebooks with her during the next week's deliveries. Emma also spent several afternoons after her shift at the bakery, hanging around Stubings making notes on schedules and deliveries. Her Stubing case book was beginning to fill with drawings and observations. She noticed something odd with the wheel height on the wagons being used for deliveries and returns at the Stubings dock.

She started making sketches of the different wheel heights to illustrate the difference based on the weight load of the truck. She was able to approximate the weights that would impact wheel height; how high or low the wagon sat on the wheels. These were documented- which types of trucks would deliver to the store. By doing this she was able to show that trucks leaving Stubings were actually heavier than when they went in.

Patterns were also forming about when different deliveries would occur. She kept separate notes and drawings on what the delivery drivers wore. The behavior of the drivers was recorded for final documentation.

She reviewed her notes after completing a few weeks' worth of observations. She was ready to run the information by Tim to get his input, before taking the next step. She waited until they were on the way to their first delivery before she broached the subject with him.

"Tim," said Emma determinedly, looking directly at him.

"Yes," said Tim absently as he drove the wagon. He appeared to be looking ahead, concentrating on his driving but his mind was actually on the next time he would see Dora.

"You asked about my observations and if anything comes from them?" she stated, she kept her voice flat, not wanting to sound too excited about her findings.

"Yes," he said again, this time slowing down the wagon to a stop as he turned to look at her.

"The location we are at right now, this is where we usually are this time of day?" she asked, indicating Stubings Department store with her hand.

He nodded in confirmation.

"That truck has been here every day this week," she moved

her head to indicate the large truck parked at the dock. "Correct?"

"Is there a point to this?" asked Tim getting a bit exasperated. "We do have work you know."

"I have a point, just a second," she said and continued sharing her findings. "In this area of town delivery trucks come in and out daily to the various department stores, nice men's clothes shops, and restaurants. I started thinking something was off about those trucks and personnel."

He waited more patiently now for the rest, it was becoming interesting. He did have one question, "What made you suspicious of these particular trucks?"

"Well, the suspicious trucks appear to be from the same company, but there are no insignias on the uniforms, the clothes the men are wearing don't match and they were smoking. When I noticed those differences, I started monitoring the trucks," she said simply. "I also noticed something odd with the height of the wagon's wheels when coming and going." She pulled out her notebook and showed him the drawings before continuing. "The wheels on the truck sit lower when the wagons are full. I compared the wheels on their trucks when they went in and when they would leave. The trucks leaving should have more wheels showing; the truck here today, routinely has a heavier load, when leaving."

They were sitting with a clear view of the alley where the deliveries were completed for the store, when Tim commented thoughtfully, "Well, that could be because they had returns to the manufactures."

"I don't think the difference would be that extreme and the truck wouldn't be empty coming into the store," she commented.

"Anything else?" Tim asked, thinking through what she had shown him and rubbing his forehead with his right hand, keeping his left on the horse straps.

"That is it," she said, as she snapped her notebook closed.

Tim looked up at the sky and appeared to be talking to a higher power when he said, "I just wanted to give her a chance to get out of the house and help with deliveries, but no instead we are in the middle of an adventure." He shook his head in an exasperated manner.

He seemed to come to a decision and looked at her with narrowed eyes, he said slowly, "So if you're right, it could be a long-term robbery."

"I think it might be," she said nonchalantly. And then she asked determinedly, "What should we do?"

"No cops," they both said at the same time. They knew that Mayor Harrison was in office and he was corrupt. The local gangsters in the area knew they could get away with anything.

"I have an idea," Tim said and parked the wagon by a nearby café. They jumped down and crossed the street, heading towards the Stubings front entrance.

The store was not opened as yet, but they could see movement inside. Emma tapped lightly on the windows. At first, the personnel inside ignored them but came to the door when they recognized Emma and Tim from the bakery delivery cart. A woman with curly ginger curls piled high on her head and a black dress unlatched the door but did not open it more than a crack. "What's up kids? Do you have some pastry for us this morning?" she asked and smiled at them.

"Is your manager here?" Tim asked, ignoring her question.

"Why? Need a job?" she sent them a bright smile. When Emma and Tim did not respond to her questions she continued, "I am Miss Woods, our offices will be opened later today if you want to apply, though you are a bit young."

"No," Emma said, "we have some important information that your manager might want to know."

Her tone conveyed a seriousness that made Miss Woods cock her head. She seemed to come to a decision when she said,

"Just a moment." She closed the door and latched the lock. They could see her hurrying through the store.

A few moments later a tall distinguished man dressed all in blue with a crisp white shirt walked in an unhurried stride toward the door, followed by Miss Woods. He opened the door wide and asked the kids to come in.

"I'm Mark Jones, Head Manager of Stubings. Miss Woods indicated you need to speak with me about something important. How can I help you?" he asked in a sincere manner, looking both Emma and Tim in the eyes as he spoke.

Tim nodded to Emma to begin. "Mr. Jones, we believe that the delivery men on your dock are not actually delivering anything but are taking merchandise from your store."

Mr. Jones asked a simple question, without any inflection, "Why do you say that?"

Emma continued and took out her black notebook and started, "Well for one thing the uniforms on the delivery drivers do not match the ones normally worn by your delivery drivers, secondly, they were smoking, and finally the wagons are fuller now than when they came in."

"How did you notice the wagons were fuller when leaving the store?" asked Mr. Jones curiously.

Emma referenced the engineering drawings within her notebook. "The truck is sitting lower," she pointed out the measurement on her drawings.

"Hmm," Mr. Jones murmured, "the drawings remind me of someone. Are you, by chance, related to Mr. Evans, the structural engineer?"

"My Papa," said Emma softly.

"Hmm," Mr. Jones murmured contemplatively. He seemed to come to a conclusion and turned to Miss Woods saying in a commanding voice, "Can you get Mr. Taylor?" He turned back to the young people to explain, "He is our Head of Security."

Miss Woods immediately went to find him.

She and a gentleman that Emma assumed was Mr. Taylor arrived with about 10 tough-looking men. The men were looking to him for direction. *They must be the security staff,* thought Emma.

As Emma watched Mr. Jones interact with Mr. Taylor, she noticed that there was something odd about his jacket. It seemed to be a bit larger than he needed in the chest area. She continued to study him when she realized the larger jacket must be covering a gun. She jotted down her observation of the people and their activities.

Mr. Jones looked at both kids and said, "You both best be on your way. I will be in contact soon."

Emma and Tim headed back out the way they came in. They were crossing the street when they saw Mr. Taylor and the tough-looking men swarm out of the back-loading docks. They grabbed the men that were loading the tucks and took the loading manager by the neck, pulling him into the store.

Emma and Tim got a front-row view of the event. "What will happen next?" Emma shot Tim a wide-eyed look.

Tim shrugged, "I'm not sure, I think it depends on if the store wants to keep it quiet or involve the police."

"Should we wait?" she asked.

"No, I don't think so," said Tim, "better to do the right thing and just be about our business."

"But didn't Mr. Jones say we would see him later?" Emma asked, still looking at the store.

"Yeah, but I think he's a bit busy at this point," he said wryly. "Come on," He and Emma climbed back into the wagon to continue with their day.

As they were leaving Tim glanced at Emma, smirked, and said, "So already stirring things up?" He continued with a warning, "I wouldn't mention our involvement in this to anyone." He made a clicking sound at the horses to be on their way.

They pulled the wagon out and began making deliveries on

the road as if nothing had occurred. They had about an hour's worth of deliveries near Stubings. She had hoped they would hear about the outcome from her observations but understood that could be dangerous. If one of the gangs was behind the theft, then it was best that they were not mentioned. They continued on their way with people taking little notice of them.

Emma went back to jotting down other observations of their route. They finished for the day and Tim dropped her off at home on his way to his afternoon deliveries. As she entered the house, she was thinking about that morning's events and how exciting it was to have her first case have a successful conclusion. She had her head down, glancing at her case book when she smelled butter and chocolate. She knew what was cooking in the kitchen and immediately headed toward it.

Inside she found Amy working hard on cleaning up after lunch and Dora in the middle of dessert preparations for that evening. Emma's mouth watered when she saw the ingredients laid out and instantly knew that she was putting together a German Butter Cake with Egg Liquor.

Emma tried to snag some of the cake batter, but Dora was too fast and pulled the bowl away. Emma sent Dora a sorrowful look and soon she relented and let Emma have a spoon to lick. Emma took the proffered spoon and sat down at the table to enjoy it. When she finished, she took it to the sink to wash it off.

"Tell us about your day," said Amy. She was curious about the city, but not curious enough to want to experience it, although she did enjoy Emma's stories.

Emma was very quiet as she moved to the icebox to pull out the ingredients for her lunch. Ice was delivered every 2-3 days to keep the food preserved. She took out the cheese and started building her sandwich. Dora and Amy looked at one another when Emma didn't start regaling them with her day's adventures. Normally Emma would talk them to death with the details of her day. *What had happened to make today different?* Dora wondered to herself.

Emma set the items on the table, put together her sandwich, and placed it on a plate to eat. She put the sandwich items back in the refrigerator and started out of the room. "I'm taking my sandwich upstairs," she said distracted by her thoughts and not answering Amy's question. She was already opening her notebook for review as she went up the staircase.

Amy looked at Dora and Dora shrugged. *I'll have to check in with her later*, thought Dora, and went back to her flavorful dessert.

Meanwhile, Emma was making her way to the desk in her room. She finished her sandwich and started adding closure notes on the case of the Stubing store thieves. It was an exciting case, but she was a little disappointed that she was not involved in the takedown. *Maybe in the future*, she thought. She closed the book on that case for now and put it away.

She pulled out her general black notebook and started reviewing her notes from the previous weeks to see if they could be moved into an individual case book.

Her notebooks documented the ongoing building in all areas of the city and construction work could be heard when the sun came up. Their city was growing so fast, it was a city that would be the tallest in the world. The continual building attracted more people to the city and increased the population.

Neighborhoods have a rhythm to them, she thought as she continued to review the different areas of Chicago they deliver to. The rich residential areas were quiet with the only early morning activity being deliveries of milk, papers, and bakery items. The quiet on the outside of the houses was not indicative of the actual work going on in the downstairs area. Personnel worked hard to ready them for the day. Many of these houses required baked goods to start their day.

The working-class neighborhoods were already familiar to

Emma since her family lived in that area. Many people living there, owned businesses or were professional people. The families had help for their households, some lived in and some did not. The middle class both bought and made bakery items.

They didn't deliver as much to the people of lesser means, most of these ladies made their own bread and if pastries or other treats were wanted; they were of the day-old variety. Cousin sent day-old pies and cakes to these neighborhoods and the money made from these was split between the delivery drivers.

They also had Gamblers row on their route. These streets were as quiet as the other business areas. They weren't street gangs but had business establishments that kept their goings-on hidden from the police. They were also good bakery customers. Cousin figured business was business and if they were paying, he would supply berliners, cakes, and breads. They were nice enough, but Tim took no chances and had Emma stay with the wagon during these deliveries.

She completed her review and snapped her notebook closed. *It's time to work on homework and knife throwing*, she thought as she got changed and went downstairs.

That evening was quiet with the family and boarders scattered downstairs, talking, doing homework, and other things. A knock sounded at the door. "I'll get it," Emma said as she hopped up. She opened the door to a postal delivery man. He handed her two envelopes and asked her to sign for them. She signed for the letters and closed the door. She stayed in the hallway and opened the note that had her name on it. It was from the Stubings store manager they had assisted in preventing the theft that morning. It said simply, "Thank you" and enclosed in the envelope was fifty dollars. She was stunned for a moment and realized Tim's envelope most likely also contained fifty dollars.

"Emma, who was at the door?" Papa called.

"No one, it was nothing," she said absently. Carrying the cards and thinking about the money, she went slowly upstairs. She was working at the bakery tomorrow and would see Tim when he came in to pick up his deliveries. She had kept her word to him about not telling anyone about their adventure. They both felt that it was safer for everyone if they kept quiet. She hid her money and card in the bedpost.

She carried Tim's card to the bakery the next morning, where she worked the early shift. She said goodbye to Tony as he was leaving for his deliveries before she headed inside. She turned back around and called, "Hey Tony."

"Yes?" Tony responded.

"Could you tell Tim to find me when he gets here?" asked Emma.

"Sure," Tony said, curious about why, but since she talked to Tim most days, it really didn't seem to be out of the ordinary.

Tim got the message and came in looking for Emma. He spotted her and went over to her workstation.

"Hi Emma, you wanted to see me?" asked Tim with an easy grin.

"Yes," she nodded her head toward the coat closet. Tim looked questioningly but shrugged and did as she asked.

After they stepped into the closet, she shut the door and handed him his envelope. She said with little emotion, trying to keep the excitement out of her voice, "I got this last night. I opened mine and I think you're going to like it."

He slowly opened the envelope Emma had handed him. The money spilled out into his hand. He teared up for a moment and thought, *This will pay for the rest of my school and allow me to become an accountant.* He was shocked and just stood there, not moving. The moment overtook him and though he looked directly at her, he could see so much more than just that closet at that point.

"Tim," Emma said and touched his hand.

It seemed to wake Tim up and he shook his head. "Yes?" he asked.

"Tim, I can keep the card and you can come by and pick it up this evening at the house," Emma said with a smile.

Tim nodded and said, "Yes, I don't want to be carrying this around today on deliveries." He handed her back the card and money. She tucked it into her dress pocket.

He grabbed her and hugged her fiercely. He left to begin his day, whistling on his way out of the bakery.

Emma went to her workstation to continue her assigned task list.

Tony was curious about the meeting but knew that Tim's heart belonged to Dora. He made a mental note to ask about that meeting at a later date and headed on his way for his morning deliveries.

CHAPTER 8

A few weeks later, Tim and Emma were making their way to the back of one of the social clubs, also commonly known as a gambling house, for a delivery. Emma was sitting in the wagon while Tim carried the pies and cakes to the back door located in the alley. She was making notes and glancing around when she noticed a slight man leaning against the alley wall, smoking. He looked very familiar and she realized why. He was one of the 'delivery drivers' that they had turned in for theft at the department store. He wasn't wearing the same clothes but with his straight black hair and angular face, he was definitely one of the robbers. He had an evil look and a perpetual sneer on his lips.

Emma pulled down her hat and buried her face in her little notebook, hoping she would not be recognized. He glanced over a few times, then flicked his cigarette in her direction before heading inside the club. He deliberately bumped Tim's shoulder as he passed him in the doorway. Tim didn't think much of it and headed back to the wagon.

As he climbed in the back for more pies, Emma leaned

forward and muttered under her breath near his ear, "Tim, let's go."

"What's your rush?" he asked his hands full of pies that were to be taken inside.

"That man who you passed in the doorway," Emma said and nodded her head toward the alley. "That's one of the men we got into trouble a few days ago at the department store."

Tim nodded a small, imperceptible nod at her and said in a low voice, "This is my last delivery and we'll be on our way." Tim carried the pies into the club in a normal manner, not showing the nerves he was feeling.

The time that Tim was in the building seemed to be an eternity to Emma. Tim finally came back out, climbed on the wagon, nonchalantly took the reins, and clicked at the horse to move on. They did not show any of the fear they were feeling as they exited the alley.

~

Her watcher was also in that alley. He tried to be in locations where Emma might be at risk. He saw the man take notice of Emma. *Well,* he thought, *I'll have to keep an eye on that one.*

~

"Did he say anything to you when you went back in?" Emma asked a bit worried.

"No, he just walked past me." He didn't mention the man deliberately bumped into him again when he was exiting. He said briskly, "I'll switch this part of the route with Tony."

Emma cocked her head and said, "No Tim, I think that would call more attention to us. Let's just act as if nothing has occurred."

Tim thought about this and nodded his head slowly in agreement, "Maybe you're right."

They continued on their way to their final stops for the morning. Emma made a note in her notebook to open back up the Stubings Department store case and add the latest observation.

"Emma," Tim's quiet voice drifted to her as Emma continued to write. "I know what kind of things you write, but why? Why do you continue to scribble in that notebook?"

Emma continued to write and didn't look up and said simply, "Mama."

"Your mama?" Tim asked quizzically.

"Yes," she said, "I remember sitting in the bakery early mornings and Mama would tell me that baking, like life, required a person to be hyper-observant. Whether it is the smell of yeast when it is ready to be kneaded or the smell of a cake just about to be done or to recognize what's going on around you that may need your attention."

She continued, "Mama gave me my first little black notebook to start adding my observations and recipes into. When I review the observations, I can visualize details that I may have missed. It helps me correct errors the next time the situation occurs. It also helps me with baking and other things. If you're not paying attention, you could miss something very obvious. Small changes in your daily life could mean big things."

"Or," he commented dryly, "it could mean very little." He chuckled and continued, "So, it's the details of things that interest you." *I'm different than that*, he thought. He could see the details but felt the future could be as important as or more important than the present. He had dreams that moved past the details of this job. He thought about those courses he had used the reward money to sign up for. It would allow him to move up his plans and complete his degree within a year.

As both dreamed, Tim and Emma listened to the clacking of the horse hooves on the road.

Tim mentioned, at the end of the morning, that their last stop would be the Hells. Cousin had sent day-old bakery goods to give out; pies, cakes, bread, and of course berliners. Tim and Emma went to the outskirts of, but did not enter Chicago's "Little Hell". It was a ghetto and lived up to its reputation for violence and gangs. Initially, the Irish immigrants, who lived there, had a hard time getting jobs and fitting in. They preferred to live on their own, but as new immigrants started arriving from Italy they did not mix well and violence was often the result.

Tim knew better than to enter down the main street but instead parked at one of the outreaching apartment buildings. The kids knew to be around the area in case there were some baked goods they could pick up. Some days he wasn't able to come but when he could, they were very appreciative. They knew Tim by name and called, "Tim!" Each trying to jockey for first place in the line. Kids and adults called, "Toss me some bread" and "got any pie left today?" They paid as much as they could, mostly in pennies.

As they finished their day, Emma expected to be dropped off at home or the bakery, depending on Tim's afternoon schedule. But today, Tim indicated it was time to let Emma see the delivery boy's hangout. She had heard about this before but had never been allowed to go. This was a big step for Emma to hang out with the other delivery boys.

Tim pulled over near the alleyway where the hangout was located. The neighbors hadn't minded the kids boarding up part of an alley as a hideout and shelter. They kept the area clean and the hangout could be taken down quickly if needed.

Tim bumped the door open with his hip while balancing a bag of berliners and a lunch bucket. Emma trailed in behind him also carrying her lunch bucket. The other delivery drivers were hanging out and sitting against the wall, on a scarred-up bench, or stools at a small wood table. The boys made a move for the berliners, but Tim being taller than the others, held it above their heads. Tony leaped onto the table and nabbed the bag from Tim, getting the first berliner. This seemed to be a normal occurrence and everyone laughed. Tony tossed the rest of them to the group and jumped back down. He nodded to Emma to join him at the table. She pulled up a stool and sat down.

As the other boys continued to eat, they didn't seem curious about a new face. Emma did notice that they were watching her, but then she realized she was eating her food too neatly. She used her arm to wipe her face. With this act, they ignored her and went about their business.

As they finished up, everyone went on to their afternoon deliveries. Emma stood up and dropped her notebook. She didn't think anything of it when one of the delivery boys picked it up and handed it to her.

Dear one was reading through her book and looked up and said, "Didn't you think it odd at that point that someone was helping Emma with her notebook?"

"They weren't just being polite?" asked the Narrator.

"Boys around other boys are not polite. They knew who and what Emma was," said Dear-one.

"Hmm," said the Narrator.

Since Emma had been taken to the hideout, she thought she might as well ask about accompanying Tim and Tony on their afternoon jobs. "Tim," Emma inquired, "can I tag along?"

Tim hesitated and looked at Tony. Tony did a sharp shake of his head and narrowed his eyes at Tim. Tim answered, "Not today Emma, we're making deliveries to someone who doesn't like surprises. Wait here for us? Then we will take you to the boarding house."

Though she was disappointed, she was okay with waiting

until their afternoon jobs were completed, before heading home. Emma hung out for about an hour reviewing her notes. Some of the boys came and went during that time and acknowledged her with a nod of their heads.

Tim returned to pick her up and dropped her off at the boarding house. Dora was out front sweeping the steps as they pulled up. Tim, grinning a wide grin, left with a wave and a shout-out to Dora.

Dora was smiling as she accompanied Emma back inside. They made their way to the kitchen to discuss Emma's day. She told Dora about the different accents she had heard in the Hells that day and how she was allowed into the boy's hangout place. Dora was appropriately impressed.

Emma finished her descriptions and went upstairs to take a bath to wash off the grime of the day. It was a habit that she enjoyed. She reached out for her towel to dry off and climbed out of the bathtub, her hair escaping the pins holding it out of the water. When she finished and changed into her dressing gown, she laid on the bed and fell asleep. Dora came up to check on her and remind her of her lessons and work with Papa that afternoon. Emma dressed and headed downstairs to begin her late afternoon duties.

That evening, after dinner Emma was sitting with Dora in the kitchen reviewing her notebook. Dora looked at her and asked her in a studied casual voice, "Emma, you and Tim talk a lot?"

"Yes," Emma murmured, not really paying attention to her answers.

And when she didn't continue Dora asked the question in another way and a more determined voice, "When you are talking to Tim, do I ever come up?"

"Yes. No. What?" Emma exclaimed when that one question permeated her thoughts. The question shook her out of her notebook and into the conversation with Dora.

She repeated her question and that got Emma's attention. Emma frowned, not wanting to stop reviewing her observations. She first looked down at her notebook then at Dora. "Dora, when I'm with Tim, what we talk about is between us. I can't share confidences," she softened her tone and reached over to touch Dora's hand, "even for you."

Dora looked down at Emma's hand on hers and sighed saying, "I know, but I just was curious if he thinks about me as much as I think about him."

"That I can answer. Yes, he talks about you all the time and it is all good."

"Is it?" She smiled and said again, coyly, "Is it?"

"Yes, now no more sharing. I need to concentrate on my notes," she scolded Dora.

"I'll work on my books," said Dora as she gave in to Emma's request and opened her accounting books.

Emma concentrated on her notes. The man who may have recognized them at the social club was troubling. *I'll keep the case file open, just in case,* she thought.

Emma continued to review her general notebook and noticed something peculiar about the observations she made while in the business district that day. The same men were turning up at the same corner each morning for the past few weeks. It was not odd to see people out early, but at this time of day, people normally had a purpose; delivering bread, milk, that sort of thing. But these men's purpose for being in that location was unclear.

She marked the note with a star, determined to look into these men and their motives for being at that corner at that time of day.

CHAPTER 9

Over the next few weeks, Emma kept a close eye on that area. She made notes on anything that seemed to be out of the ordinary. She also continued to talk to Tim during deliveries.

Tim was whistling and enjoying the day when Emma broached the subject of Dora. "Tim?" Emma asked, hesitant to get involved in his romantic life.

"Yes?" asked Tim cheerfully, thinking she wanted to discuss deliveries, observations of the day, or both.

"Dora mentioned that she hasn't seen you as much lately," continued Emma.

Tim frowned, "Emma, you know I added more classes to get through with my degree faster."

"I know Tim, but Dora needs some reassurance. You might want to talk to her about any plans that involve her future."

"You know I'm working for our future and once I'm set, I'm going to ask her to marry me."

"I know that," said Emma patiently, "but Dora doesn't. You haven't mentioned your plans to her yet?"

"Well, at first I thought it would be a longer process, but

with our reward money I'm able to move up the timetable," he explained.

"I think it is time for you to have a conversation with Dora and take me out of the middle," Emma recommended.

Tim thought about what she said and commented, "Yes, it's time. Dora should have input into our future. I'll speak with her."

Emma nodded, satisfied with his response, and returned to her observations. They had started deliveries in the business district that morning. She started to notice odd things, such as the men she had seen before (noted in her journals to keep an eye on), appearing and disappearing on that corner near the businesses on the first floor of multistoried buildings. Emma was familiar with the businesses and who worked there. These men did not match the typical profile of a store worker. She also noted the time and the fact the stores were not due to open for a few hours. *Are they coming from the shops or another location?* She thought consideringly and put a star next to that observation for later review.

She started thinking that if something nefarious was happening, they would probably not have used the front doors of the businesses. An investigation of the individual stores and surrounding areas would be necessary. She looked over at Tim, knowing he was preoccupied with thoughts of Dora and kept the new observations to herself.

She looked closer at the men and realized with a start that one of the men was the same one that she had recognized from the department store robbery and in the alley at the social club. She would have to keep a low profile on this, he could be real trouble.

Later that evening Emma was sitting at the kitchen table, marking her observations, when she saw Tim knocking softly at the back door. Emma leaned over and tapped Dora, who was sitting with her back to the door. Shea was reading a book at the kitchen table and looked toward Emma questioningly. Emma indicated the door with her pencil and Dora turned toward it. She saw it was Tim and immediately got up with a smile on her face.

"I think I have another place to be," said Emma as she hurriedly vacated the room.

Tim nodded gratefully toward Emma, but kept his eyes on Dora, "Dora can we talk?"

Tim sounded so serious, that it made Dora anxious. "Of course. Is everything all right? Your aunt or uncle?" she asked anxiously.

"No, no they are fine. I just wanted to let you know why I haven't been around lately. I'm trying to get our future moving forward."

"Our future Tim?" asked Dora, all at once teary and happy.

"Yes, evidently, I have been thinking about our future so much, that I have not talked to you about it," he said in a self-deprecating way.

Dora nodded to him encouragingly to continue.

"Dora, I only see you in my future and I want to marry you. Would you marry me, when I'm done with my accounting degree and I have a job?"

"Tim, I would marry you without a degree or a job. You're what's important. The rest isn't."

"Your answer is?" he asked, his eyes darkening with emotion.

"Is yes!" she shouted, feeling so happy.

Tim grabbed her and spun around, kissing her until they were both dizzy.

They didn't hear the kitchen door open but they did hear a very loud clearing of a throat. They both looked toward the door and a group of people looked on expectantly for news.

"Well?" said Emma impatiently, already grinning.

"I said yes," said Dora turning her red face into Tim's chest.

The group cheered and filed into the room to offer their congratulations to the happy couple.

Papa got to Tim first and shook his hand. "What are we thinking about the timing of this activity?" Papa asked half teasingly.

"We haven't had time to discuss that yet, but I'm working on completing my degree and getting a job first. Maybe next year?" he said as he sent an inquiring glance toward Dora.

She nodded, wiping her eyes.

Papa nodded, embraced his daughter, and smiled broadly at Tim, "Welcome to the family Tim."

Emma broke out some sparkling cider to help celebrate the news of the evening. After a toast, everyone went out of the kitchen to give the couple some time to talk quietly.

Emma went up to her room, smiling at the good news. Once there she pulled out her notebook, she wanted to continue working on marking her observations as immediate or delayed actions that would require more study. She added some questions—why were they there? —waiting for something? someone? were they taking something in versus taking something out? She finished up her notes and got ready for bed thinking it had been a nice day.

CHAPTER 10

*E*mma went downstairs the next morning to help with the breakfast set up. "I wonder if the newspaper has been delivered yet," she mused as she opened the front door and glanced down, "There it is." She scooped it up and started reading on her way to the kitchen.

She took a moment in the dining room to read the paper front to back. Observations sometimes came out of ordinary articles and not just in the crime section. She was reading through the current events section when she came upon something interesting.

Emma heard Dora's voice calling, "Emma."

"Coming. I'm checking on something," Emma called back, still looking at the paper. There was a story that caught her interest. It involved a flower store and the history of the area around the business district where the store was located. The article also detailed information about the mostly abandoned tunnels connecting the basements of the various shops. The tunnels were in place originally to move coal for heating and to move supplies.

It was the kind of article that would have normally been

skimmed, but Emma took a moment to tear it out after she finished the rest of the paper. She tucked it in her pocket, folded it back, and placed it on the table. She needed to think about the article and how it might relate to her observations. She entered the kitchen, ready to help with breakfast.

"Good morning, what were you doing when I called you?" inquired Dora.

Emma saw that Dora and Amy had breakfast ready and waiting to be served. Dora had already started working on a dessert for tonight's dinner.

Emma didn't answer Dora, but quickly ran around the table and hugged her, "Dora I'm so happy for you."

"Me too, now start taking these to the table," said Dora, indicating the breakfast items after returning her hug.

Emma was focused on Dora and had not moved to take the breakfast items into the dining room. She wanted a taste of that batter before anything else.

Emma was staring so intently that Dora finally relented. "If I give you a spoon full, will that get you moving?" asked Dora, shaking her spoon at Emma.

Emma nodded as she grabbed the spoon, licked it clean, and started moving food in for breakfast.

Dora had been so excited about her engagement, that she had gotten a head start on breakfast and filled the time that was left by making her German Apple Cake. She knew that Tim would like it, so she would fix him one for his lunch today.

At breakfast, Papa was opening his paper at the table to read and noticed a hole where an article should have been. He knew who was responsible and looked through the hole at Emma. He folded the paper down onto the table and tilted his head forward to look at her over his glasses and asked the question, "Emma?"

"Yes, Papa?" she responded vaguely, clearly her mind was on other things.

"Emma," he prompted waiting for her to raise her eyes to his.

When she finally did look his way he asked, "You're doing I suppose?" indicating the paper.

"Yes Papa," she said with a guilty voice, she knew he enjoyed his paper at breakfast.

Papa clicked his tongue, shook out the paper, and then went back to reading the articles that were still in place.

Later in the kitchen, Emma was helping Dora and Amy clean up. Dora looked over at her curiously. "All right," said Dora, "what's was so important that you had to tear Papa's paper."

"I'm not sure," Emma said slowly, "it's just something that caught my attention and might be connected to some observations I've made previously." When Emma didn't provide any more answers and went quiet, Dora knew to leave her alone with her thoughts.

Emma wasn't scheduled to work on anything else that day and thought she could talk Papa into letting her start her afternoon work later that evening. She closed her notebook and went to find Papa. She was right, he was working on a project that would need some additional review but she could take the day off if she promised to review the data that evening.

"Yes, Papa," answered Emma.

She went back to the empty dining room and was able to think more clearly about the observations she had made. *The men,* she thought tapping her pencil on her lips, *they were always near the place where businesses were connected through tunnels in their basement and at times when those businesses are not open. Were they utilizing the tunnels somehow and is it connected to the local businesses? Is it possible? But why, what were they after?*

She thought more about the area, *The bank was a couple of blocks off and it seemed like a lot of tunnels to access it. The article had said parts of the tunnel were collapsed, so whatever was happening had to be related to one of the shops or businesses on that road.*

She looked at her list of businesses; flowers, jewelry, café, millinery, department store, and a few closed businesses. Emma made a note to ask Tim about the area tomorrow.

Shoot, she thought, *I won't be working on the delivery wagon tomorrow, I'll be at the bakery. I'll need to go over today.* Emma had been in the tunnels and explored them with Papa when she was younger. She knew how to get in and out without being seen. The café on her route had an accessible tunnel; it was just off the kitchen through the basement. Additionally, the basement door was usually kept open because it was used for food storage and should be able to be utilized without much notice.

She finished her notes, closed her notebook, and thought, *It might be dirty work. She* went to put on her delivery boy clothes and grabbed the portable gas lamp that Papa had made for her. She slipped out the front door, carrying her boots and slipping them on outside. Her watcher slept as she slipped quietly by, making her way uptown.

She scanned the area as she approached the cafe, looking for anything that might be suspicious. Nothing seemed out of the ordinary and the men were no longer visible. She really didn't expect them at this time of day, though she had to be careful once she was in the tunnels.

She looked down at her clothes as she approached the café entrance, *I should probably use the back door,* she thought ruefully, shaking her head. She ducked around the corner into the alley behind the café. There was a backdoor there that opened into the alley. She entered the kitchen hesitantly and tried to stay out of sight, it turned out that she needn't have worried.

The cook saw her lurking around the door and he yelled, "Hey boy, make yourself useful and take those crates downstairs to the basement."

Emma kept her hat pulled down over her forehead, grabbed the crates, and moved toward the basement. She was happily surprised when she realized the crates were empty and would be easy to carry. She picked them up and nudged the door open to the basement with her foot. There was enough light from the kitchen to allow her to see the gas light on the wall about halfway down the stairs. She made her way down carefully and as soon as she reached the lamp, she used her hip to support the crates while she reached up to turn the gas lamp up. This allowed her to see the steps and further down into the basement.

She continued to make her way slowly down, the bit of nerves she had were chased away by the excitement of an adventure. Her steps moved more quickly as she reached the bottom of the stairs.

The basement was dark and there were gas lights scattered throughout, but Emma chose not to use them. She set the crates down on the floor, near the stairs and turned to the right to find the wall with her hands. Once she found it, she felt her way around the room, moving boxes as she made her way around. *There must be an opening,* she thought. Almost ready to give up, she pressed against the wall and found herself falling through a doorway into a tunnel.

Once she picked herself off the floor and dusted her pants off, she pulled out the small gas light that Papa had fashioned out of a pipe and a repository for kerosene. She knew it had limited life, so she was careful to not go too far into the tunnels.

Emma made her way further into the tunnel and she was able to see that the area had been cleaned up and appeared to have been used lately. Emma noted mentally, *The tunnels are too clean, they shouldn't be this clean.* During her exploration with Papa, she had seen debris piled up blocking most of their path.

She worked her way further into the tunnel but didn't want to go too far without a map or some directions. She would also need to get more supplies now that she knew where one of the entrances was located.

She could hear male voices coming up the tunnel toward

her. She quickly extinguished her small lamp and stepped back into the shadows. She was close enough to both see them approaching and hear the men's conversations, without being seen. She quickly pulled her hidden knife in case it was needed. She breathed a small silent sigh of relief when she realized the men were not advancing toward her. She continued to watch them and listened intently to their conversation. *It is the same men I saw on the corner*, she thought.

"That door is opened," one of the men said in disbelief. "How did that happen? That door is heavy. It just won't open by itself."

Emma sucked in her breath when she realized she had come through the door they were referencing. *Careless*, she thought, *I should have known better*. She stayed where she was and listened to them complaining about the rats, their heavy boxes, and general life, as they made their way down the tunnels.

"Must have been rats," said the other man laconically, in response to the first man's question.

The first man would not let the conversation go. "Rats, how big would one have to be to open a door that is that heavy?"

The other man, not really caring about this conversation said, "I've seen very big rats here in these tunnels. Why does it matter? Could we just drop it and get these items delivered?"

At that moment, Emma realized the voices would go faint and then loud. *The men must be going in and out of various businesses*, she thought. She crept closer to make note of the locations where they were taking the different items, taking care to not be seen.

The first man was talking again, "I'll be happy to unload this stuff. How many more trips are there? And why are we so late today?"

"Our contact couldn't get the goods off of the ship until now. At least it isn't hot."

The other man grunted a reply as he set his box down and opened the door with a small pry bar from his pocket. They got through the door with the boxes and it slammed shut behind them. Emma stayed and waited to see if they would return. She didn't have long to wait, they exited one door and entered another, carrying less items out than they carried in.

Ships, Emma thought, *smuggling. It has to be.* She jotted down the locations the men entered: the mercantile, the specialty fabric store, and the jewelry store. Oddly no boxes were being carried into the jewelry store.

Emma thought, *Better to get moving now while they are in the jewelry store.* She made her way back to the café entrance and up the basement stairs to the kitchen. The cook had his back to her and she was able to make it out to the alley without being seen.

She dusted herself off, took her hat, and pounded the dirt out of it on the wall of the alley. She put it back on and tucked her braid into it as she left. She pulled her hat down over her eyes, made her way back to the main street, and continued home

As she hesitated at the bottom of her stoop, she absently noticed the same man who slept in the alleyway on her way to work in the morning. She nodded to him in recognition and made a mental note about the location she had seen him today.

Emma took the stoop steps two at a time, forgetting about the man. She made her way to the kitchen and without saying hello she immediately went to a pile of papers near the door. "Do we still have the newspaper from today?" asked Emma flipping through the papers.

"Well," said Dora as she answered a question not aimed at her. "I might have it put back for some jar storage. What are you looking for?"

"Types of ships coming in and dates," Emma muttered. She found the papers in the pantry, where Dora kept the storage jars. She pulled out her notebook and noted the dates that they were in port. She sat at the table and flipped through her book for dates that the men had been in her area. The dates the men were seen and when the ships in port coincided. She tore out the schedule to add to her notebook.

Dora raised an eyebrow and said, "Going to tell me what is going on?"

"First I'm going to tell Papa, then I'll give you all the details," she promised as she spun around and left the room in a hurry, calling the door to swing wildly.

"Why so fast?" Dora called after Emma, catching the swinging door and holding it open.

"No time to talk now," she said over her shoulder. "I need to talk to Papa."

"I think you've been in those boy's clothes far too long, you're getting too many boyish mannerisms," called Dora ruefully.

"Why thank you, Dora." Emma tilted her hat at her with an impish grin and made her way to the basement.

The stairs were well lit and she could hear Papa talking to himself as he worked at his bench.

"Papa?" Emma called softly, not wanting to disturb his work but she needed his input on her observations.

Papa looked up and said, "Oh, hello Sister, what can I do for you? I thought you were taking the day off today. Did you decide to help with some deliveries?" He noticed Emma was in her delivery clothes.

"Papa, I wasn't working with Tim today. I had some follow-up to do on some observations that I had made during my deliveries." She paused for a moment and pulled out her notebook and clips of paper. "I found this in the paper this morning," she said as she handed the folded-up articles that had been cut out of his paper this morning.

Papa took the articles from Emma and unfolded the crinkled paper. "Hmm..." Papa said and pulled down his glasses on his nose to read the article. He looked at her over his glasses. "So. tell me more," he said, resigned to the fact this daughter would forever be involved in some adventure or another.

Emma fidgeted a bit, and then laid the case out for him. "When I was making deliveries, I noticed several men were hanging out on the same corner at the same time each day. I've seen them at that same location for weeks." She chose not to tell Papa one of the men was also identified in the department store robbery. "There's no reason for them to be in that area in the morning if they don't have a business to open. Then last night while I was reviewing the paper, I saw the articles about the tunnels."

"When you saw the article, you put that together with the men," he finished for her, remembering the many times he and Emma had explored the tunnels under Chicago.

"Papa, I went to the tunnels today," she stopped when she saw his concern. The tunnels were a 60-mile web that wound 40 feet below this city's downtown streets and river bed.

"Papa," she put her hand on his hand and started again, "I was safe, I know the tunnel location I was in. I did not stray far from the area and I kept in the shadows."

"Emma, we've been through the tunnels together but are you sure it's safe? Especially if something is going on? If you got too far, you might be caught in floodwater from the river bed," Papa said, concerned about this new development.

She looked down at her notes and then up again at Papa. "Yes," she said her voice firm now. "I'm not taking any foolish risk. I wouldn't go down during heavy rain."

She looked back down at her notebook and continued with her observations and descriptions of what she saw in the tunnels. "I saw the men taking heavy boxes into the mercantile basement, long tubes that looked like fabric into the clothing store, and finally they didn't seem to be taking anything into the jewelry store."

"What about this other article, the one about the ships?" Papa inquired.

"My observations are that the men tend to appear when the ships are in port from Rio de Janeiro. I believe it's a smuggling operation. The dates for ships from there fit the schedule," she said indicating the article with her finger, "and the tunnels would be a perfect way to move illegal merchandise."

Papa reviewed the notes closely, nodded his head, and said, "You definitely have something here." The river was connected by a large train-size hole that opened up in one of the tunnels that dipped some 14 to 19 feet below the bed of the Chicago River.

"What do we do with this information?" pondered Papa out loud.

"Should I go back to the tunnels to gather more data, before we go to the police?" asked Emma, ready to move forward to the next part of the case.

Papa kept his head down, continuing to review the information, quietly gathering his thoughts. He started, "Emma this is excellent work and you have connected the dots on this case." He paused, thinking that the current police chief for Chicago did not have a good reputation, and taking this to him would only stir up controversy. He started again, "I think what we do Emma is wait…"

"But Papa," Emma interrupted, thinking he did not trust her to continue with the case.

"Let me finish Emma. I want to wait, but I also want to contact a friend at the Pinkerton Detective Agency. They're a private company, who would be able to keep an eye on the situation," Papa said keeping his voice calm, knowing Emma would want to move forward quickly.

When Emma heard the Pinkerton name she stopped breathing for a moment and then in a rush said, "Can we go now?"

"No." Papa chuckled at her eagerness. "I'll need to make sure Cole is in the office and is willing to hear about your observations."

Emma nodded and asked, "Cole?"

"Cole Tilden. I've known him for a while," he said quietly, not sharing how he knew him.

"Okay," she said eagerly, "I'll head up to change and practice my knife throwing until dinner."

"That's fine, Sister," said Papa and shook his head a bit as he watched her run up the steps and exit the basement.

Later that night Emma was sitting with Papa and Dora in the kitchen. Almost all the boarders had retired for the night. Miss May and Miss Marjorie continued to sit together in the lounge talking quietly.

Papa and Emma filled Dora in on the current case. "Papa," inquired Dora, "how do you know an investigator at Pinkerton?"

Papa sat quietly for a moment and then started explaining how he knew Cole, "Well, I actually have known Cole from a long time ago. We grew up together."

Dora and Emma looked at each other. They had heard very little about Papa's life prior to Mama. It was like his life began when he met her.

He continued, "You know that my Mama had died when I was born and my Papa, your Grand Papa, had worked himself to death by the time I was twelve. I ended up on the streets and was living in alleys. I actually met Cole in an alley, he was on his own also. We formed a club, we protected each other and each made sure the other was fed. We were some of the best pick-pockets in the area."

"Papa!" both Dora and Emma exclaimed.

"We had to survive and that was the way we did it. We didn't want to live in the county poor house and the only other option was on the streets. At that time in Chicago, there were many children without parents, on the streets, committing mischief. We were so good in fact that people were starting to notice," Papa explained.

The girls were fascinated and when Papa paused in his story, Dora spoke for both girls when she asked, "What happened?"

"Well, Cole and I were working at the corner of Market and Smith," Papa said catching Emma's eye and winking at her.

"Of all places," Emma said wonderingly at the connection his story had to her observations of mischief at the same location.

"Papa, were you scared?" Emma said, concerned. Even though it was a long time ago, the sisters felt for the little boy with no parents.

"I was," he admitted, "but the best thing that could have happened to me was to get caught."

"Did you get sent to jail?" Emma sat back in her chair, astonished at the information.

"No, no. I didn't know it at the time, but I was being set up to pick a certain person's pocket. It was Mr. Gibler, a local teacher, though I didn't know it at the time since Cole and I didn't attend school," Papa admitted. "He had me by the collar, I thought that was it and I would be sent off to reform school or jail."

He stopped for a second and laughed. "Cole was very protective of me and he rushed over trying to rescue me, instead Mr. Gibler also grabbed Cole by the collar too. For a little guy, he was very strong. Instead of calling the police, he hailed a cab and took us to his home. We weren't punished but we were fed and allowed to get cleaned up. Mr. and Mrs. Gibler made us a deal that if we would follow their rules and attend school then we could stay with them. Cole and I lived with them until we both made the move to college. Mr. Gibler got us work at the local school as janitors and tutored us on the side."

"Papa, why don't we know the Giblers?" Dora asked, curious about the people that helped him.

"They passed away," said Papa simply. "There were older when we met them and I think we were their last chance to have a family."

Dora asked looking into Papa's eyes. "Why don't we know this story and why haven't we met Cole?"

"As we got older and we went off to school our lives just went in different directions. We still care very much for one another. Also, Cole has just moved back into the area to take over the Chicago Pinkerton operations."

That gave the sisters something to think about. "Bed now," Papa said, both girls nodded and they headed upstairs.

It was a little while later, Papa sat in the sitting room, reading when a knock sounded on the front door. He answered the door and a delivery person handed him a note. Papa thanked him, shut the door, and opened the note. After reading it, he turned and looked up the staircase, toward the landing. He saw Dora and Emma peering down at him from the second floor and asked, "Sister, want to come with me tomorrow after making deliveries and meet with Cole to discuss your case?"

Emma's eyes sparkled when she said, "Definitely, yes. I'll have Tim drop me here when we finish in the morning."

Dora smiled at Emma, knowing she was getting something she had always wanted.

"Night, Papa," said the girls quietly. The family made their way to their rooms to get some sleep.

CHAPTER 11

The next day after Emma completed her deliveries, she met Papa at the house. He was waiting in the foyer for her when she arrived. "Hi, Papa, ready to go?" she asked as she jammed her hat on her head and started making her way back to the door.

Papa cleared his throat.

Emma looked back and asked, "Yes, Papa?"

"Maybe you want to go as a young lady and not a ruffian?" he indicated a hand toward her delivery outfit.

"Oh, sure, Papa." Turning toward the stairs, she started up, she would like to look her best the first time she met with the Pinkerton detectives.

"Emma, ten minutes, no longer," Papa warned. "We have a cab coming."

Emma nodded quickly and headed upstairs, taking them two at a time. She changed into her red skirt with the black trim, red jacket, and white shirt with a black tie. She topped off her outfit with her black bowler hat with red trim. Her hidden knives were secured in her hat and on her leg. She shook out her skirt and looked at herself in the long mirror, took a deep breath, and

141

was ready to go. Papa watched him come downstairs and nodded approvingly. He offered her his elbow and they exited the house.

Waiting in front of the house was the hansom cab Papa had called. He helped her in and climbed in next to her. It pulled away and they made good time to the Pinkerton offices. He had them dropped off a few blocks from the office so they could talk ahead of the meeting. "Emma, when we go in, Cole will be there. Just tell him your story. Do you have your notebook?"

"Yes Papa, right here," she said and patted her jacket pocket.

As they passed an alley, Emma was hanging back a few steps behind her papa, when a hand grabbed her and pulled her in. Her first reaction to the assault was to pull her knife. Her "assailant," who was at least a foot taller than Emma, did not expect to be defending against a knife. Before he knew what had happened, she had him pinned to the wall with a long knife under his chin.

Her "assailant" was a tall, skinny kid who was just a bit older than Emma.

"Why did you grab me? You villain!" shouted Emma.

He smiled a crooked grin and tried not to move his head as he said, "You're a bit of a villain yourself." He nodded carefully at the knife stuck in his neck.

"Why are you smiling?" Emma asked gruffly, not removing the knife, still ready to defend herself.

Papa had realized Emma was not with him and doubled back. He found her and her "assailant". He was pinned against the wall with a wicked-looking knife and a furious Emma.

Emma expected Papa to jump in angrily, instead, he leaned one shoulder against the brick wall of the alley and directed a question at the "assailant" completely ignoring Emma's knife. "So, are you learning the business?" He didn't wait for an answer and said to Emma. "This is Cole's son, Jeremy Tilden."

Jeremy waved his fingers at Emma with a smile, keeping his

head very still. Emma slowly backed off, she removed her knife from his neck and replaced it in her hat, allowing Jeremy to straighten up.

"I was just testing you to see if you could defend yourself," he said as he grinned at her and offered her his elbow.

"Uh-huh," she said. She looked at him and then at her father and slipped her arm into Jeremy's.

The trio headed to the large gray stone building on the corner. They started up the stoop together. "Pops is waiting for you," Jeremy said as he shoved the large wooden double doors open with his shoulder. As they opened the door, men were sitting at desks at the entrance. The gentleman at the first desk rolled his eyes at Jeremy and indicated that they could go into Cole's office.

They went through another set of doors down a long hallway. Jeremy jauntily tapped the door and pushed it open. "Pops," he called out, "found them in the streets and had to protect them from the lower elements."

"Protection?" Emma murmured and fingered her hat that she had taken off as they entered the Pinkerton Offices.

Jeremy saw the move and jumped to the side of the desk with his hands raised and a silly grin on his face. "I give, I give," said Jeremy.

Cole immediately came around the desk and gave Papa a bear hug. "Ellis it's been too long," Cole said in a gravelly voice.

"Yes," said Papa a tear in his eye.

Cole cleared his throat and asked, "And who is this lovely lady?"

Papa took over introductions from there and said, "Cole, this is my daughter Emma."

"Emma," Cole said while taking her hands in his. "I've heard about you,"

He looked over to Ellis and said, "I take it Ellis, that this is not a social call?"

"Yes, we have a case you might be interested in," commented Papa. He paused for a moment and then continued, "Well, Emma does."

Cole was about Papa's age with rusty red hair, a gray goatee, was slender as a rail, and wore the typical black Pinkerton suit. He looked like he didn't eat much but did appear to be a cheerful man. Papa trusted him, and so would Emma.

Cole invited them to sit down in the brown leather chairs facing the desk. Jeremy was slouching against the wall, observing everyone.

"Emma," Cole prompted.

Emma pulled out her notebook with notes on the tunnels and started reviewing them out loud. Detailing how people were seen entering and exiting and the crates and tubes and other items she had seen.

When she got to the part about entering the tunnels, Jeremy spoke up, "Do you think you should have been there? Was that a safe decision?"

The group glanced in his direction but mostly ignored the comment. Jeremy shrugged and leaned back against the wall.

Papa added, "The use of those tunnels to move anything other than coal is suspect."

Cole leaned back in his chair contemplating the information that had been provided by Emma and Elis. "Our informants have been making noises of merchandise moving through the area, illegally." He went quiet for a moment, then continued, "We thought initially it might be a small, limited operation but, with this information, I think that we could be looking at a much larger and organized effort. We can put some people over there with the locals that might be involved. For now, we'll need more information."

"Do we need to go to the police?" inquired Ellis. He would trust a decision from Cole.

"No," Cole said, "not now, some issues are going on there as well."

He looked over at Papa and asked, "Ellis have you heard any more about the chief being on the take?"

Emma and Jeremy were startled by this statement. They made eye contact across the room. Jeremy straightened up and paid attention to the next words his father directed at Papa. "We're getting more and more information that criminals are being let go within hours of being taken in. For now, I'll have my people look into it." He glanced at Jeremy and nodded, indicating to him he would be involved.

Papa started to stand up. "Wait," said Cole, "I can't let you get away without making sure we get the families together."

Papa smiled broadly and said, "I agree. You and Jeremy must come for dinner. Do you know when you might be available?"

Cole grinned and said, "We're good most nights, but what about Sunday, after church?"

Papa nodded, "I think we have enough to share. Dinner is about 2:00pm on Sunday, after church. We're looking forward to the visit." With that statement, they all started toward the door. Papa and Cole continued to reminisce as they exited the room. Jeremy and Emma followed at a slower pace behind them.

On their way out, Jeremy grabbed Emma by the sleeve. She looked down at his hand and then up at him as she teased, "Grabbing again? Will I need my knife?"

"No," he said, quickly dropping her sleeve. "I just want to inquire if you'll be at St. Vincent's for the Saturday evening dance."

"Why are you asking?" she asked suspiciously.

"No reason," he said, as he dusted off a nonexistent dust particle from his sleeve.

"I may be there," Emma said slowly, thinking about Tony.

"Well, I may be there also," he said. He followed up with a

rushed statement, "If you're there and I'm there, maybe we could dance or something."

"Or something," Emma said and smiled. "If I'm there and you're there, I'm sure we could dance or something." She whirled away to follow her Papa down the stoop.

Jeremy yelled at her as they started their walk down the street, "Hey Emma, don't forget your hat!" He tossed it to her, she caught it deftly.

"Thank you, Jeremy!" she shouted back, waving at both Cole and Jeremy.

Papa motioned for a hansom cab to take them home. "Papa, do you think they can do something about what I found?"

Papa looked over at Emma, "I think they'll keep an eye out, and when the opportunity strikes, expose what's happening. Keep in mind what Cole said. The police are starting to notice you. You'll have to be cautious about your observations and who you go to. We'll make a list of policemen that can be trusted. And let me know what's going on, in case I need to help."

Emma nodded and stated in a confused manner, "Papa, I only make observations that anyone could make."

"No Emma, you see more than most people. Close your eyes and tell me who is on this road."

Emma liked this game. "A woman is walking a baby in a stroller with a large black hat and a large bag. A businessman with a satchel and a delivery truck being pulled by two gray horses."

"Now open your eyes, everything you listed is exactly what was on the street. Most people can't do that, especially if they're just going through their day. They might notice a few things, but they would miss the details you would pick up. Emma, keep making observations and investigating, just keep a lower profile," Papa warned.

"Yes, Papa."

A cab pulled up, Papa helped Emma in and they headed home. Emma continued to think about what happened at the Pinkerton office. The case is in good hands and she knew that they would keep her involved. She was interested in how they would handle the next steps in the case.

My ultimate goal, she thought, *would be to work at Pinkerton as a detective*. She knew that Pinkerton had never hired a woman as a detective and she would have to prove she was the perfect first one for the job. For now, she would continue to build her skills.

CHAPTER 12

Saturday began quietly. It was an off day for Emma, both at the bakery and the delivery jobs. She slept in, knowing that breakfast on Saturdays was at your own discretion. There was plenty of food in the kitchen for boarders and everyone ate at their own pace. She thought that she could grab a picnic basket and see if Dora would like to go down to the river to take a respite.

That idea got her out of bed with a spring in her step. She got ready for the day and dressed in a brown split skirt, a brown jacket with red trim, and a red shirt. She pulled on her boots, brushed her hair, and braided it so that it fell straight down her back. She left her hat for now and made her way downstairs.

She looked for Dora; she wasn't in her room or the kitchen. Emma waved at Miss May and Miss Marjorie who were enjoying their morning tea in the backyard, sitting on hand-made chairs and taking in the sun of the day.

She found Dora in Papa's study, reading. Emma jumped on the couch next to Dora, startling her and asking, "What are you reading?"

Dora turned the book to show the spine to Emma, it was

Alice's Adventures in Wonderland. It was a literary nonsense genre but Emma loved its adventures. "Do you like it, Dora?" she asked excitedly.

Considering that question Dora looked over to Emma and commented, "It's good but not really for me, I think I prefer romances or mysteries."

"Oh, but what about the Mad Hatter? He was so interesting, or the part in the story about…"

"Sister what can I do for you?" Dora interrupted. She knew that Emma usually had something on her mind.

"Oh, nothing, I just thought we might take a picnic basket to the river and hang out a bit."

Dora thought a moment and said, "That sounds like fun. What about window shopping on our way?"

"Sounds like a plan," said Emma. "Leave at 11:00am? I can put together the basket."

"No," smiled Dora. "I can handle it."

"Thanks, Dora," Emma said in a sing-song voice. "Add something sweet, please?"

Dora nodded her head as Emma raced out of the room. *Off to practice her knife skills*, thought Dora. She called after her, "Eat something please."

Emma nodded and went to the kitchen for fruit and buttered bread. When she finished, she retrieved her hat and an extra knife. She wanted to practice different methods of accessing the knife in her skirt and get smoother at pulling the knife from her hat. The knives hit her target over and over, but she needed a moving target. *Was Tony busy?* She got her knives organized and headed to his apartment.

She knocked on the door and the youngest Marella answered, "Hey Emma."

She glanced down, "Hey back, Enzo."

"Here to see me?" he asked hopefully, standing on his tiptoes, trying to impress her. He knew full well that she was there to see Tony and that he would need ten years and at least six more inches before he could impress her.

"Hey Enzo, move out of the way and let Emma in," called Tony from the living room. As she entered, she could see Tony's two other brothers were lying about the room each reading a newspaper. They were casually dressed and had their shoes off. Tony had scrambled up when he heard her at the door. He ran his hand through his hair and tucked in his shirt while looking around for his shoes.

Tony's dad was sitting comfortably in a large chair, reading the paper, when he looked up and said, "Hi Emma, nice to see you." He gave her a smile very similar to Tony's.

"Hello Mr. Marella," she said with a large grin. Tony's dad had brown hair with grey sprinkled throughout and was extremely charming. It was like seeing Tony twenty years from now. "How is business?"

Tony's dad owned a plumbing and gas fitting firm. During this time running water, sewer connections, and gas for lighting and cooking had become more common in both residential and business buildings.

His demeanor changed at the question. "Busy," he said not looking up to answer her. She found his response odd, he was normally very open about projects he was involved in. Emma sent him a searching glance and started to ask him more questions when Mrs. Marella came out, distracting her from following up.

"Emma," Mrs. Marella called from the kitchen. "Come give me a hug. Do you want something to eat?"

"No, Mrs. Marella, but thank you." Emma hugged Mrs. Marella tightly as she exited the kitchen. She was like a second mom and she always had food to feed guests. "I'm just here to talk to Tony." He came up behind Emma and put an arm across her shoulder.

"What's up Emma?" he asked, as he looked down at her.

"I'm working on my knife throwing today and I'm hoping you have some time this morning because I need someone to help with some targets."

"So," he teased, "you automatically thought of me when you needed a target?"

"Well yes," laughed Emma, "actually I did. You make the best moving target."

Mrs. Marella heard the banter but was not concerned. Emma was good with knives and would not hurt him. She got a bit pensive when she saw them together and she continued to worry that Emma could break Tony's heart.

She had warned him that Emma was very young and could change her mind about things. She felt that he listened. He had said in a serious tone to his mom on the topic of Emma, "I think I just met my forever person too soon. I'm trying to give her space to grow or make any changes."

Mrs. Marella remembered something, "Emma, I hear there are congratulations in order."

Emma knew exactly what she was talking about and grinned when she said, "Yes, Tim and Dora surprised everyone. They're very happy."

"Have Dora come by and see me, I want to hear all about it," said Mrs. Marella.

Before Emma could respond Tony said a bit impatiently, "Mom we have to go."

"Remember we have an early dinner, the dance is tonight," his mother reminded him.

Tony glanced at Emma and said, "Yes Mom, I remember."

This was Tony's chance to have Emma to himself, he had looked forward to this all week.

Emma turned a bit red because she had also been looking forward to dancing with Tony.

Tony's dad threw his jacket and hat at him and said, "On your way." Emma again thought about how he changed when she asked about his job. She would have to ask Tony about it later.

As Tony and Emma descended the stairs they were talking about the news of the day, current games being played, and families. There was never a shortage of conversation between the two. She thought about asking Tony about his dad but decided to keep it light and asked instead, "Did Tim tell you before he proposed to Dora?" she asked interestedly.

"No, I don't think he wanted to share that before he spoke to Dora. It's a big step."

"Yes, they're so steady in their feeling for each other and ready to take the next step." They both got quiet and a bit contemplative as they approached the boarding house.

Tony shook off any deep thoughts he was having and ask, "Backyard?"

She nodded and said, "Yes."

As they went through the house, Tony said, "Just a minute," and ran into the kitchen. Emma heard a shriek and ran toward the sound. She opened the door and saw Dora scolding Tony for scaring her.

"What happened?" asked Emma, entering the kitchen.

"I just came in to give her my congratulations," Tony said innocently and winked at Dora. "Ready?"

Emma opened the door and waved Tony into the backyard.

"What do you want me to do?" he asked.

"Well, I would like you to walk around over by the target. I want to work on hitting your garments rather than you," she said rather innocently looking sideways at him.

Tony looked over at Emma and squinted his eyes in playful consternation, "Now Emma you know I trust you, but this is maybe taking things too far."

He mulled over what she wanted to do and said, "I have an idea that should help you without injuring me. Go grab an old large jacket and some shirts and meet me back here." Emma headed in as Tony went about setting up two boards in a cross pattern.

Emma came out with a large man's jacket, Tony took it and placed it on the crossed wood he had nailed together. He stuffed the sleeves with older shirts. "Let's try this." He stood it up and put a large amount of space between him and the target.

She tried to throw the knife to hit the sleeve of the jacket.

Tony watched her and acknowledged to himself that he could not match her skill with knife throwing. Though he noticed that she hit a little close to the fake arm. "Ouch," he said.

"Oh, you can take it," Emma said as she threw her clutch knife.

"What's the reason for this activity?" he asked curiously.

"Well, I don't want to hurt everyone I throw a knife at, or at least not badly," she said thoughtfully, thinking of her current cases. They worked on throwing knives for a couple of more hours that morning until she was hitting exactly what she was aiming at.

Dora stepped outside and called, "Sister, it's about time. Hey Tony."

Tony smiled and waved back. He noticed the basket. "Something to eat in there?" he asked hopefully.

"Yes," she said. "and Tim," who stuck his head out the back door behind Dora. "Who just happened to show up when I was putting the basket together. Emma are you fine with the boys coming along?" She looked to Emma, ready to tell them no if she didn't agree.

Emma considered the question and saw Tim's hopeful expression. Emma grinned and said, "The more the merrier."

The group got organized with blankets and a picnic basket and exited the house together. They climbed into Tim's wagon, Dora in the front with Tim and Emma in the back with Tony. Tim turned around so he could see both Dora and Emma and asked them, "Where to ladies?"

"I believe there was window shopping, strolling along the boulevard, and a picnic by the river planned for today," said Dora.

Tim nodded, conscious of the fact that he and Tony were the interlopers in the sister's day. "I'll have to drop the wagon off before we get too far."

The wagon was dropped at a safe location and the group was ready to begin their day together. Tim jumped down and went around to help Dora. Tony has also jumped down and assisted Emma out of the back of the wagon.

While they were strolling. Emma glanced around, looking for anomalies around her while Tim, Tony, and Dora were enjoying the day.

Tony noticed where Emma's attention was leading. He tapped her hand that was tucked in his elbow and he shook his head silently at her. She understood what he was referring to and tried to shut down her hyper observation.

Okay, she thought, but she kept an eye on the skinny kid that seemed to be walking too close to people in front of them. She could see him lifting wallets as he went through the crowd. He started to drift back and sidle up to Tony, she grabbed his arm as he reached for the wallet and had him face planted against the wall.

"Hey, what are you doing?" shrieked the kid in surprise.

Tony knew Emma could handle the situation and just stayed close. He spotted a police officer walking his beat and called him over.

The police officer came up and said, "What's going on here?"

The pickpocket, who was still flattened against the wall, decided to take the defensive route, "I wasn't doing nothing and she grabbed me."

Emma looked at him steadily and stated, "Really?" She had taken her small knife out, without anyone noticing, and cut the pickpocket's jacket pocket. He didn't realize what she was up to until multiple wallets fell to the ground.

The policeman looked on astonished, Tony looked resigned.

The policeman grabbed the pickpocket by the collar and scooped up the wallets.

"Those are mine," the pickpocket said indignantly.

"Yours? So, you're Harry Smith, Marty Hochberg, and Phil Mozier?" He didn't wait for a response. "Off to jail for you. Thanks, little girl. What's your name?"

Oops, thought Emma, *I'm supposed to keep a low profile.* She hesitated for a moment and then admitted, "Emma."

The officer nodded, "Emma you did a good thing today. I'll remember this."

Great, she thought, *just what I need,* and nodded to the officer. The officer walked off with the defeated pickpocket.

Tony and Emma had to run to catch up with Dora and Tim. They were so taken with each other that they had not noticed what happened behind them. Emma squinted a bit at Tony as a warning, he understood that it might spoil the day and didn't say anything. He nodded and gave her a slight smile.

The two couples continued to enjoy their sunny walk and easy conversation, as they headed down to the boulevard and river on foot. Tim was carrying the picnic basket and Tony carrying the blankets.

They found a grassy area that overlooked the river and sat down for a nice lunch. After they had eaten, Dora and Tim wandered near the water for quiet conversation. Emma and Tony lay side by side on the blanket looking at the sky. Emma glanced over at Tony with a hand shielding her eyes and said, "Will you be coming to the dance tonight?"

"Yes," he said still looking up at the sky. He wondered why she had asked. Since Tim had started to see Dora, they all rode together to the dances on Saturday night. "Why ask?"

Emma was looking up at the sky again and stayed silent.

Tony leaned over her and asks again, "Why?"

She finally slanted a look at him. "A son of one of Papa's oldest friends is planning on attending. I thought you could meet each other. I think you might have a lot in common."

"Meet me?" Tony was bewildered at the turn in the conversation and the introduction of a new character into their lives. *And what was he to Emma,* he thought to himself. He took a breath and fell back on the blanket, he wanted to reserve judgement until tonight.

They lay quietly until Dora and Tim returned. Tim and Dora put the leftover food into the basket, while Tony and Emma folded the blanket. They headed back to the stable to retrieve the wagon and head home.

Tim said, "I'll see you this evening for the dance. Tony, let's go." He reluctantly dropped Dora's hand to leave.

Tony looked searchingly into Emma's eyes and said, "I'll see you tonight."

She didn't smile but nodded and stared back, before breaking contact.

Dora and Emma watched as Tim and Tony departed in their wagon. She looked at Emma with a worried expression and said, "What did you say to Tony? He looked upset."

Emma shrugged and said a bit defiantly, "I told him Jeremy, Cole Tilden's son, would be at the dance. I've told him, prior to this, that I'm too young to make any decisions about my future. I can have other friends."

Dora touched Emma and stopped her before they entered

the door. "Please don't hurt Tony. If you do, you could be making a mistake that could have long-term repercussions."

"Dora, I just don't have Tony's view of the future. I can see my path as an adventurer but I don't want to get married or have kids."

"Emma, you're sixteen and you'll probably change your mind later. I'm just letting you know that you should be careful with other people's feelings," Dora cautioned.

Emma shook her head to clear it and said, "First, I have one boy that I have trouble with and now I think that adding another boy to the equation is going to help. I'm an idiot."

"No," said Dora, hugging her, "just very young."

CHAPTER 13

They went their separate ways until dinner. Emma had some lace work and went to find Miss May. While she worked on her patterns, she was thinking about Tony's dad. She should have taken the time to talk to Tony about her concerns, instead, she had let herself get emotional about their relationship.

The afternoon wound down to dinner with Emma and Miss May working on lace commissions. Dinner was an independent affair. Dora didn't cook on Saturday nights. The family met in the kitchen for a casual dinner of sandwiches, before the dance.

Emma packed up the Snickerdoodle cookies she made the previous night to bring with them.

The evening was just beginning when the girls went up to change for the dance. Dora put on her green dress with yellow trim, while Emma put on a deep pink dress with a lace overskirt.

"Dora, have you seen Mama's scarf, the red one?" Emma called down the hall.

"Of course, red," teased Dora, knowing that Emma had to

have something red on most of the time. "I think it's in Mama's trunk."

Emma nodded in agreement, "I'll check there."

"Try to hurry," Dora said. "We need to get going soon."

Emma ran quickly to Papa's bedroom to open the trunk located at the end of the bed. She had been through the trunk before but had never gotten to the bottom. She sat down on her knees and opened it. She pulled out blankets made from their baby clothes, a jewelry box, assorted dresses, and finally scarves. She found the scarf she wanted, but as she pulled it out, she found it had gotten caught on something. Gingerly pulling on it, she found it was caught on a 6" X 6" wood box. One small tug caused the scarf to slide out and she placed the box on her lap. Turning it over, looking at all sides, she saw it was plain with no distinguishing marks and appeared to be latched but not locked.

She wondered for a moment if she should ask Papa's permission to open it. Just before she made that decision, she heard Dora calling from downstairs to hurry up. She glanced back down at the box, but decided what was in it could wait until she got home later that evening.

Taking the scarf and box with her, she went to her room. The box was placed under her pillow and she put it out of her mind as she finished getting dressed.

A second shout came from downstairs for Emma to hurry up. Tim and Dora were eager to get going.

As they exited the house, they saw Tony was waiting in the wagon, He jumped down to help the girls. Emma sat on the lockbox in the back of the wagon and Tony sat on the wagon floor. Dora road up with Tim. Emma hummed a bit looking at the sky and trying to not think about that box under her pillow.

They pulled up to the church, and saw that many people had arrived and the musicians were already playing.

"Fun," said Emma, and she jumped down without help.

Dora commented, "Emma."

Emma glanced back at Dora's pointed look and realized that some of her boyish tendencies were still with her.

"I'll be more careful," promised Emma and waited for Tony to catch up. He offered his elbow and they walked into the dance together. As they entered, she glanced around for Jeremy. She made eye contact with him across the room. He looked straight back and did not glance away. He sent her a crooked smile that she had trouble looking away from. As she returned his smile, he slowly made his way over to her and said, "Hello, Emma."

She introduced a reluctant Tony to Jeremy. Jeremy reached out his hand to shake with him. Tony looked at it but did not shake it.

When Tony did not shake it, Jeremy withdrew with a shrug of his shoulder.

"Well, we're at a dance. Emma, would you like to dance?" asked Jeremy. Jeremy was actually looking at Tony when he asked. Tony looked like he wasn't going to let her go but then finally relented.

Jeremy offered Emma his elbow and they proceeded to the dance floor.

Tim came up behind Tony and placed a hand on his shoulder. "Don't worry, it's only one dance. Remember you always said you were in for a long wait with Emma."

"I know," he said a bit shortly.

He started thinking about what his mama had said about her. "Tony, you might want to back off from Emma until she is older."

"But Mama, I like to be around her."

"I know, but she isn't ready to see you as a suiter. It might be time to let her go her own way for a while."

"Mama, I just feel a connection with her that I don't feel with anyone else."

Mama smiled indulgently, "You're like your Papa. He took one look at me and told me that I was for him. It also took me a while to see that same future. If you want her, the best way might be to separate for a time."

~

Tony had disregarded that conversation until now. He began thinking about what Mama had mentioned about a separation.

Meanwhile, Emma and Jeremy danced a lively dance together, Tony waited patiently and claimed the next one. Jeremy and Tony monopolized her time until she was too tired to dance.

Emma was just walking out for some air with Tony when Jeremy came up and greeted them cheerfully. Tony tried to get rid of him but Jeremy didn't take the hint and said, "Oh, I could use some air also."

Tony looked annoyed by the additional third person on his walk but said nothing. The three walked around the little park connected to the church.

Emma thought to herself, *Well this is getting a bit tiresome.*

She ventured into some conversation, trying to involve both boys. "Jeremy is working with his father at Pinkerton detectives." This comment made Jeremy preen a bit.

Jeremy was curious about his competition, "Tony, what do you do?"

"I'm working deliveries mostly around town," said Tony.

"Interesting," he said honestly. "You and Emma work together?"

They both nodded at him.

"What are your future plans?" inquired Jeremy to Tony.

Tony took a moment to answer the question. "I have some

ideas I'm working on. I'm not sure right now what form those will take."

Jeremy nodded understanding about future choices. "I'm working with my dad at Pinkerton. I think that's where my future is."

Emma was quiet, thinking about the opportunities afforded to boys and not to girls. To be anything in this world, a girl would have to be two-to-three times as good as a boy. *That will just make me work harder*, she thought.

Emma looked at the timepiece attached to her dress. "I think if we're going to dance anymore, we must get back into the church." They realized she was right and hurried back. When Jeremy reached for her hand, she glanced back at Tony with a raised brow and he waved them onto the dance floor. Jeremy was a good dancer and his funny nature kept her laughing throughout the dance.

The dance went on and Emma continued to switch off between Tony and Jeremy. All three got along well together, but there was a bit of a struggle when the last dance was announced. Both boys had an arm and took off in opposite directions. At that moment Emma felt like a wishbone about to be torn into. When Jeremy accidentally tore a lace drop on her dress, she said quietly, "Stop. Outside, both of you."

The three moved toward the door and felt her exasperation boil over. "There are plenty of girls to dance with in there and it doesn't have to be just me." She looked over at Jeremy and said, "We just met this week, I think you can find another partner for this dance." She smiled at him to dampen the negativity of her words.

Jeremy nodded and said, "Sure, I'll see you tomorrow," and headed back inside.

"Tomorrow?" Tony inquired.

"Yes. His father is a very close friend of Papas and we're having them over for Sunday dinner after church." Emma could tell he wanted to be invited but she knew she had to have a hard talk with him.

"Tony, don't you think we need some time apart? You can't be happy with just scraps of my time."

Tony took her hand and held it gently looking into her eyes. "Emma I'm happy with whatever time you give me. I get that you're young and I don't want to overwhelm you. You're my best friend," he said simply.

Emma used her free hand to cover their clasped ones. She looked up and said, "Tony the time just isn't right for this. I treasure our friendship above all else and when I'm ready, I'll let you know."

He nodded reluctantly. "Maybe it would be best for me to back off for a bit."

"But Tony, I don't want to see less of you," she said plaintively, just realizing what she was going to lose.

"I think you're right," he said turning away, pulling his hands out of hers. He raised a hand to wipe at his eyes. "I think it would be best if I found other friends to hang around for a while. It will give you space to grow and be yourself without me."

Tears also welled up in her eyes, she didn't foresee losing her best friend tonight. She didn't think she could handle not seeing him. "Tony, please wait," she tried to take hold of his hand.

"No," said Tony, stepping back from her. "This is for the best. But know I'm here anytime you might need me."

That step he took from her felt like an ever-widening gulf. "Tony?"

"Yes Emma?" murmured Tony, wishing to be anywhere but here.

"Can we dance the last dance together?"

He couldn't deny himself or her this last opportunity to be close. He pulled her to him, closer than he had at any dance before this and they swayed to the music drifting out into the garden. She looked up at him as the music was ending and he looked down at her. He started to bend his head toward hers and she held her breath in anticipation. He shook his head to clear it.

"Emma, what we need is space," Tony said in a low voice and turned to leave, exiting through the garden gate.

Emma just started to realize what she had done but could only stand miserably watching him leave.

"Tell Tim I found a way home tonight," Tony called without turning around as he disappeared from her sight, leaving her to stand alone in the garden.

Emma wandered slowly back into the room as the dance was breaking up. Dora waved at her from across the room and approached her quickly. She searched her face and saw that Emma was very pale. "Are you ill?" she asked concerned that Emma might be coming down with something.

Emma stood there, miserable and not wanting to talk about it. "Tim?" Emma said, ignoring Dora's question.

Tim glanced down questioningly.

Emma kept her voice void of emotion and her face blank as she continued, "Tony left early and he said to tell you not to wait for him."

Tim frowned, Tony wouldn't leave Emma for any reason. He would have to go see him after he got the girls home and get the full story. But for now, he had his Dora to be with. He squeezed her hand and she smiled up at him. It had been a fun night with everyone offering them congratulations on their engagement.

As they wandered out toward their wagon, Emma noticed that Dora and Tim were preoccupied with each other, holding hands and staring into each other's eyes.

Emma cleared her throat. "Well, it looks like I'll be driving the wagon home."

Before they could contradict her, she got the wagon ready for the trip home. Dora and Tim sat in the back of the wagon talking softly while she drove home. Once they got there, she waited a moment and then said rather loudly, "I'm going in now."

Emma jumped down without help and slowly walked up the stoop. Tim helped Dora down from the back of the wagon and took the opportunity to give her a quick, intense kiss. There were more kisses, he took a deep breath and allowed his head to clear. He said regretfully, "I'm going to check on Tony and you might want to talk to Emma."

Dora nodded, she had been thinking along the same lines.

Papa and Emma opened the front door for Dora. "Was the dance fun, girls?"

They both nodded.

"Papa, Emma, and I are going to set out some macaroons, would you like some?" Dora asked.

Papa smiled a wide smile and followed them to the kitchen.

Dora was still dreaming about her evening with Tim, but she knew she needed to talk to Emma before she went upstairs.

Papa finished his macaroons and with a wave, he departed to continue his work in his study.

"Sister," Dora said, reaching across the table to gather Emma's hands in hers. "What happened with Tony, tonight?"

Emma felt an emotional response wash over her. Her eyes filled and she had to gulp to get air. "I don't know, I think we may not be friends anymore," she said in a halting tone.

"Oh, Sister," said Dora. She was sympathetic but had to be realistic with Emma. "Sister when you talked about this with me earlier, you were clear that you weren't ready to be with Tony in a romantic way and you were ready to tell him."

"I didn't think that would affect our friendship," she wailed placing her head on her arms and starting to cry harder.

Sister is so very young, thought Dora with a shake of her head. She scooted her chair closer to her and put her arm around her shoulders.

"Sister, in this situation you can't have it both ways. Tony cares a great deal for you and being around you as a friend is going to hurt him."

"It will? I didn't think about that," she said slowly raising her head and showing her tear-drenched eyes to Dora.

"No, but you must think about it now. I would be surprised if we don't see Tony for a while," Dora said firmly.

"So, no visiting him? No seeing his family?" she asked completely stunned that the one conversation had completely changed her life.

"Sister," Dora tried again, forcing Emma to look her in the eyes. "You ask for this space and you're going to have to let him have his as well. Do you understand?"

Emma understood that Dora cared deeply for Tony and did not want Emma to continue to cause him pain. She took a deep shuttering breath to clear her thoughts. "Okay," she said, "I'll give him some space."

"Good," said Dora relieved. "I'm going up to bed." Dora's thoughts shifted to Tim and kept those with her as she went upstairs. Emma went up after her with thoughts of Tony on her mind.

Emma entered her room, still a bit down knowing that she wouldn't be able to talk to her best friend. As she flopped back on the bed with her arms out-flung, her hand encountered a solid object. She looked toward it and noticed the box she found in her mama's trunk peeking out from under her pillow.

Emma thought, not wanting to think about Tony, *Just what I need to keep me distracted.*

She reached out and slid the box toward her on the bed. Sitting up, she placed it on her lap. *Is it important? It might just be a pair of old shears.*

She unlatched the box slowly, the box creaked as it opened and revealed newspaper articles. *Articles,* she murmured to herself and pulled them out carefully. She checked the dates. *These were when Mama was still alive,* she thought.

The articles documented different crimes that had gotten attention about ten years ago. Each seemed to be attributed to an unnamed source. *Curiouser and curiouser,* she thought. She stood up taking the box with her to the desk.

She began to lay the articles out on the desk in date order. Each article alluded to a local crime boss. There were murders, burglaries, and gambling halls. The articles referred to information coming from an inside source, exposing the different crimes.

Emma wondered to herself, *Who was the informant and why were these in Mama's chest? Was it something Mama was curious about? What makes these special enough to cut out and place in a box?* Most of these occurred when Emma was little, in the time prior to the fire.

She moved the box to the side of the desk and opened her drawer to pull out a new black notebook. Opening it quickly, she began to document what the articles might have in common:

- All were in mama's chest
- All were from the Tribune newspaper
- All were within a 2-year time frame, prior to the fire
- All had an unnamed source that implicated a local crime boss (John Harden)
- Same byline, written by the same author.

First thing, Emma thought, *find the author and see if the source is still round.* Emma had a gut feeling Mama was somehow involved in these old articles, *But how?*

She carefully folded back the articles and placed them back in the box and put them in her Mama's bedroom chest. They had not been disturbed all this time. They would be safe until she wanted to review them again.

She did a final review of her new case book and made a note to go to the paper's office tomorrow. She wanted to see if the writer was still on staff and if he would agree to speak with her. It might be a stretch to think the writer might still be there, but she would try.

CHAPTER 14

The next morning, the articles were still on her mind as she started making her way downstairs to the kitchen. She was headed to the bakery, where she was scheduled to work that morning.

As she entered the kitchen, she grabbed her regular breakfast roll and her lunch bag. She also grabbed the last two pieces of pie for the little man that always seemed to be nearby.

She had known for some time that she had had company on her early morning walks. She didn't know why but she felt that there was no threat from him. The presence felt more protective than anything. As they walked, Emma and her shadow, she thought about how to get him the pie.

Do I hand it to him? No, she thought, *that might make him upset. I know, I'll sign the note from a friend.* She took out her notebook as she walked and jotted down the message. She would find a way to make sure he got the pie.

Someone was running near her and she could tell without looking- it wasn't Tony. "Hey Tim," she said in a low voice without looking over.

"Hey, how did you know?" asked Tim sounding disappointed that she knew who he was without looking.

"I just knew," she said in a low voice. Sad that Tony had continued with their agreement of seeing less of one another.

"Emma did you want to talk about it?" asked Tim.

"No," she knew what he was referring to. Outside of Emma, Tim was Tony's closest friend. They continued to walk to the bakery, more quietly than normal.

Her observer noticed the change also. *What had happened?* he thought. Tony always watched out for her in the mornings.

"Tim, got a second to do something for me?" inquired Emma.

"Sure," he said wondering if the favor involved Tony, "working at the bakery today?"

Glancing down at her clothes and then up again, Emma said, "Yes, it's my day here." With a slight smile, she handed him the bag with the pie in it. "When we get to the bakery, could you take this to the alley and give this to the man hanging out there with this note?"

"Why would you want to do that?" Tim asked bewildered.

"Papa told us a story, not long ago, about his childhood and how hungry he could be, living on the streets. I just thought about that little man when I saw that pie this morning," she answered honestly.

Dora had told Tim what Papa had said about his childhood and he understood. He looked at her and then at the pie she was holding out to him, shrugged, and said, "Sure." He took it from her.

She went into the bakery while Tim delivered the pie to her shadow. Her day went on as usual from there.

Today she was working on Spitzbuben, a traditional dessert. She sandwiched two cookies together with a decorative cutout and a layer of jam running between the German cookie layers. She started by making a buttery cookie with a light lemon flavor.

The jam was jarred in the summer so the cookies could be made all year. Once the jam jars were opened and the cookies had come out of the oven, Emma started compiling the cookies and placing them on parchment paper to be placed into the cases in the front and for special orders.

As she compiled them, she thought about how she could meet the writer, if he still was working at the newspaper office. *I'll just have to go to the Tribune newspaper office and ask,* she thought. She mulled this over for a minute. Tim and Tony would know how to get into contact with people at the paper. They both had helped deliver papers in the past.

She finished up at the bakery and headed home to change. It had been a productive morning and she was feeling good. It was also coming up on lunch, so she stopped by the kitchen on the way in. Dora had a sandwich waiting for her. Emma sat down and started eating, tearing at the crusty bread and putting pieces into her mouth.

Dora said, "Chew please," and gave her a glass of milk.

Emma winked at Dora. She handed her an apple to eat as she finished her sandwich.

"What are you doing today? Working with Papa?" asked Dora.

"Oh, shoot," Emma said out loud. "Well, I'm supposed to, but I need to run an errand."

"Papa is out at the new building, you have some time," Dora said helpfully.

"Great," Emma said, relieved. She didn't want to let Papa

down. "I'll be back in about an hour." She didn't want to share information about the articles with Dora, until she knew more about their possible meaning.

"All right," Dora said cautiously. This quieter Emma was a new thing.

Emma headed upstairs to change out of her bakery clothes and into her delivery clothes. The sheath was secured to her leg and her pants pulled on. The loose white shirt went on easily and she inserted her knife inside an opening in her pants pocket and into the sheath. Her braid was wrapped around her head and covered with her cabbie hat.

She hurried, trying to catch Tony and Tim at the clubhouse before their afternoon deliveries started. She pushed the door of the clubhouse open with her shoulder and went in. The other delivery boys didn't take much notice of her, but Tim did. He immediately got up from the table, where he was having lunch with Tony when she entered. Before coming over to her, Tim leaned down and said something to Tony in a low voice.

Emma noticed that Tony was not going to come over to speak with her. She tried to not let the hurt show, pulling her hat down to hide her tear-soaked eyes.

Tim came over and said casually, "Hey, what's up?"

She cleared her throat and leaned in a bit toward Tim and spoke in a low voice. "Tim, I need a contact at the Tribune. I'm following up on a few things."

"What things?" he asked suspiciously. Tim had already been pulled into more than one adventure with Emma.

"Nothing really," she said evasively. "I'm just reviewing something I saw in the paper." She smiled to distract him. A pretty girl could make a young man forget almost anything.

The smile did its job and Tim said, "Speak with Harry Morgan, he works on the dock and knows all of the going's on at the paper."

Emma jotted the information in her notebook. "All right,"

she said and tipped her hat to him. "Off I go." She headed out. Her shadow was with her, she shrugged and went on.

She found the location of the paper and headed to the dock at the back of the building. In the mornings and evenings, wagons would be parked in the area waiting for papers to be loaded. There was little activity this time of day.

"Away with you boy, we don't have any work and papers won't be available until this evening," called a man from the dock. He was a big man with dark, longish hair, a mustache, and heavy around the middle. He waved his hand dismissively toward her.

Emma ignored this direction and moved closer to the dock to inquire, "Are you Harry?"

Harry looked a bit surprised at the voice coming from the boyish figure and looked closely to make an observation. "Well, it's a girl dressed like a boy." He chuckled and said rather loudly, "What can I help you with?"

"Tim Flannigan said you might know someone who used to write on the paper or might still write on the paper."

"That big Irish kid who makes deliveries?" he asked.

"Yes," she said briefly.

Harry looked a bit impatient and then said briskly, "What's the name of the person you are looking for?"

She pulled out her notebook and glanced down at the page where his name was written and commented, "His name is Daniel Cooper. He would have been a writer here about ten years ago."

"Oh, Danny boy. Well, he's still here but he isn't writing much, other than editorials these days. You want to meet him?" he offered.

"Yes," she said eagerly, nodding her head, almost dislodging her cap in the process.

He leaned down, reached out his hand, and pulled her up on the dock, she landed with a bounce. Harry said, "Follow me."

Emma followed him through the large open warehouse doors to a back staircase. As they went past the second floor, she looked at him questioningly and he said, "Up we go." So up they went.

They exited the narrow stairway into a busy room full of desks and cigarette smoke. She coughed a bit as she went by, the reporters didn't glance up as the dockworker accompanied by a raggedy boy crossed the room. They went to the opposite side of the room where an office was closed off from the rest of the room by glass. Harry knocked twice and was able to get a response from inside to enter.

Emma glanced at the wording printed on the door and realized they were heading into the Editor's office. *It appears that the reporter has moved up since the original articles were printed, I wonder if it was the articles that helped with his promotion,* she thought.

The door opened and Emma could see a gentleman at a large desk. He appeared to be in his forties, trim waistline with a full head of brown hair, and a bit of gray in his sideburns. He looked impatient at the intrusion until he saw Emma. His eyes went wide and then he sat back in his chair to look at her consideringly.

"Thought I was seeing a ghost for a moment," he said with a faint smile. "Emma, Mary's daughter, I presume?" He stood up and came around his desk to greet her with his hand extended.

Emma shook hands and commented curiously, "You knew my mama?"

"Yes," he said, looking at her a little too intently. "You do look just like her, but a bit taller. Although," glancing down at her pants, "I don't think I remember ever seeing her in pants."

"Harry, I have it from here." Daniel waved a hand at Harry to vacate the room. "Thanks for bringing her upstairs." With a nod to Daniel, Harry left the room with the door swinging shut behind him.

"Well, Emma what can I do for you?" asked Daniel.

Emma pulled the articles out of her pocket and said, "I was curious about these articles."

He frowned when he saw what she was holding.

She hurriedly continued, "Also they have things in common; they're all of your articles during this time period and about the same groups of criminals. Why would Mama have kept them and how did you know her?"

Daniel avoided the question by starting a conversation about Mama. "I met your mama in the bakery. Her pastries made me fall a little in love with her."

Emma was a bit startled by that remark.

Daniel raised his hand and held it up toward Emma. "Not to worry girl it was all on my side. Your mama only had eyes for your papa. Through I did try to get her attention by hanging out too much at the bakery," he reminisced.

Emma let that information go by and instead started in on more questions about the articles. Daniel had no choice but to address the questions in front of him.

"Emma those articles are old news, news that ended with the fire," he trailed off-looking very sad for a moment. "What's your interest in these after all this time?"

Emma started to explain, "I'm looking at what her role was in these. How was she involved? Was she a source?"

"Emma," he came around his desk and took her hands. "Emma," he began again, "I would rather not go onto this now, maybe sometime in the future. I would like you to keep in touch with me, here's my card. Let me know if you need anything," and with that, he escorted her out.

Emma felt like she was being rushed out, with Daniel providing little to no information about Mama. The act of not sharing actually gave her new information to investigate:

1. Daniel did admit to knowing Mama

2. Daniel said things that happened ten years ago didn't matter, leading Emma to believe Mama probably was involved

in the cases and possibly providing information to Daniel for the articles.

She let herself be walked out of the building and to the docks where Harry was still working. As she went past Harry, he abruptly bumped into her. Daniel glared at him but didn't say anything. Daniel's attention seemed to be on getting rid of Emma as fast as possible.

There was nothing more she could do, so she headed down the side stairs and off of the dock. She put her hand casually into her pockets as she was walking away. Her hand encountered a piece of folded-up paper. She didn't pull it out until she was out of sight of the docks.

As she was leaving, she heard Daniel speak in an angry tone to Harry, "What are you doing standing around. Get back to work."

She waited until she was several blocks away before she pulled out the paper, it had an address on it. It said 234 Smith Street at 8pm and today's date. She knew it well, the location was the downtown library and the date was for this evening. She put the note back into her pocket and patted it with her hand, she would be there.

CHAPTER 15

She was thinking about the meeting that evening with Harry as she was completing her assigned work from Papa later that day. She tried to concentrate on the work but she was nervous. It would be nice to have more information about Mama and her involvement in those articles. She put the thoughts out of her mind and focused on her work and got it finished before the dinner hour.

Dinner was the normal noisy affair with Miss May and Miss Marjorie talking about the past and the kids talking all at once. Emma sat there thinking about her evening meeting. The person she was meeting was a stranger and she thought it best to not go on her own, but Papa was called out of town on a consulting job so he wouldn't be available and Tim was in a night class that evening.

She would like to get Tony to come with her, *but*, she thought, *it was probably too soon to ask him for a favor. Though...I might just wander by Tony's apartment building on the way to the library and if I ran into him accidentally, that would be....* She shook her head. *No, I'm better than that and I won't use Tony in that way.*

She was wearing her blue and red plaid skirt with red trim

and a red shirt. She slipped on her jacket and grabbed her hat. She made sure both of her knives were in place. Emma heard a tap on her door, she called "Come in." She saw it was Dora. "Hey, what's up?"

Dora saw Emma getting ready to go out. "Sister, where are you heading out to this time of night? Isn't it a bit late?"

"Just headed to the library." The path to the library was an easy path from the boarding house.

"Library?" she asked as she sat on the bed with a bounce. "Looking for a new book?" Dora asked curiously.

It was time to tell Dora. "No, I'm going to see if I can find some additional information on a case." She pulled out the articles she had found in Mama's chest. She handed them to Dora while explaining her suspicions and similarities between them. She also explained where she had gone that day and the note placed in her pocket.

"This person who put this in your pocket. What's his name again?"

"Harry. Harry Morgan"

"Sure, but why all the secrecy? Does this really involve Mama?" Dora was interested in anything that might involve Mama.

"I'm not sure," Emma said, "but I would like to know why she kept these and why Daniel doesn't want to talk to me about her. It is obvious that she had something to do with these articles and maybe the outcomes."

"Sister, shouldn't you take someone with you? You don't know this person," said Dora worriedly.

"Well, I thought about Tim but he's in school and Papa's out of town. I think it'll be fine and I'll be out in the open at the library," answered Emma truthfully.

Begrudgingly Dora nodded and sent her on her way.

Unbeknownst to Emma, Dora sent a note via one of the local boys to Tony and explained Emma's situation. She was hoping he would put aside his hurt feelings and show up at the library for Emma. *I did what I could*, she thought, as she put the matter out of her mind and set to work on her food list for the rest of the week.

In the meantime, Emma had started skipping down the stairs on the stoop, heading in the direction of the library.

~

Her watcher had settled into the alley for the night and had not expected to be running around. He sighed and got up to follow.

~

They both caught the cable car to the library. She and her watcher jumped off and walked the final path toward the library.

~

Her watcher stayed outside and kept an eye on people going in and out.

~

Her meeting was scheduled for the non-fiction stacks. She went to a table in the area and sat down. She had the articles and her notebook in her left hand and she tapped her lips with the fingers of her right hand.

It had been about thirty minutes when she heard something behind her. "Don't turn around."

It was Tony. To say she was shocked was an understatement. She didn't turn but murmured, "Why are you here Tony?"

"Dora was concerned about this meeting," he murmured.

"Oh, okay, thanks," she said but thought, *I think.*

"How long are we going to wait for this guy to show up?" Tony questioned.

Emma mumbled out the side of her mouth, "Another twenty minutes, then we're out of here."

"That's fine," he said as grabbed a book from the shelf, and sat at a nearby table. He glanced at the title and laughed out loud, he had inadvertently picked up a book on true crimes. He just shook his head and started to read.

Twenty minutes later… "Time's up," murmured Tony.

Emma nodded, resigned that there would be no additional answers tonight. She sighed and got up to leave with him.

Well, for now, thought Emma, *I'll put these back in the chest and revisit them at a later date.*

They took the long way home walking instead of taking the trolley, there wasn't a lot of talking but there was a companionable silence.

Her Watcher followed at a distance behind.

~

Tony left her at her door without comment. As she watched Tony walk down the stoop of her home, she said softly, "Thank you, Tony."

She didn't think he heard her but he turned his head toward her with a nod.

She softly closed the door and headed upstairs, mulling over the day's learnings. Though she tried to keep her mind on the case, her thoughts kept drifting to Tony. She would have to remember to tell Dora thank you for sending him to the library. She knew she could defend herself but it was nice to know Tony would still look out for her. There might be some hope for them.

At this point in the case, she thought, *if Harry didn't consider it important enough to meet her, maybe she should put it away for a while.* She made some notes in her black book and inserted the articles back inside.

She heard a soft knock on her door. Emma called softly, "Come in."

Dora came in wearing her nightgown and her hair under a bonnet. "Did you meet him? Did he tell you about Mama?"

Emma shook her head regretfully and said, "No, he didn't show up."

"Oh, that's too bad, will you keep looking into the articles?" Dora asked, disappointed.

"For now, I think I will hold off. I will let you know if something changes," promised Emma.

"Thank you, Sister, get to bed," Dora said as she kissed her on the head.

Emma got ready for bed with thoughts of Tony and the case swirling in her head.

CHAPTER 16

A few days later Emma opened the front door to retrieve the newspaper that was lying on the steps that Saturday morning. It was early and Emma had the day off. She picked up the paper and unrolled it. She liked to read through the paper to pick up observations on a different level. She read the articles written from a perspective that was not hers.

The front page was pretty routine and contained mostly political events ongoing in the city. It was the article on the bottom of that page that got her attention. A body had washed up in the river and was found by several children. It had yet to be identified.

Hmm, thought Emma, *interesting.*

She looked at the description carefully. The body sounded familiar, with dark, longish hair, mustache, very tall over 6.4. It matched her own written description in her case book. She tore out the article and folded the paper back up. *Was it Harry?*

She needed to run by the paper office and quietly inquire if Harry was there today. It was still early enough for her to get there before breakfast. She went back upstairs to dress quickly in a black skirt and red blouse. Her hat and knives were checked before she made her way to the kitchen. There she grabbed a toast and eggs sandwich from the kitchen and gave Dora a quick hug as she headed out. She would keep this to herself for now, she didn't want to upset her.

She made her way to the docks. The wagons were getting back from their morning deliveries. A man she didn't recognize was at the dock where Emma had last seen Harry.

She recognized one of the boys unloading papers and walked over to him, "Hey Mike."

"Oh, hey Emma." He looked surprised but happy to see her. His face flushed so much it matched his red hair. A pretty girl could really fluster a young boy.

"Mike," she said in a low voice. "Have you seen Harry for the last few days?"

He tilted his head and said, "Now that you mention it, no. I just figured he was on vacation."

Emma started to write that comment down, when Mike put out a hand to stop her saying, "It is really odd though, Harry had said he would see me the next day." He shrugged and went on unloading his wagon.

Hmmm, murmured Emma thoughtfully. *It might be him, there was no guarantee but the coincidences were piling up. Did this have to do with my questions? I need some real help on this. The problem was that Papa had gone out again on another job and had taken the train for a meeting in New York and would not be back for two weeks.*

Jeremy, she thought, *he's training at Pinkerton. Either he or his dad could make the necessary inquiries.*

She knew that Cole and Jeremy lived close to the Pinkerton's office in a very nice neighborhood. She had been by there many times on her route.

Instead of using the back door, as she would have with deliveries, she went to the front door and knocked. She expected a member of the staff to answer but found herself face-to-face with Jeremy.

"Hey," said Jeremy surprised but happy to see her. "Here to see me?" he teased. He knew that she and Tony weren't talking and thought he might have a chance.

"No, I'm here to see you and your dad," she said in a firm voice and a set face.

Jeremy hid his disappointment and said in a more business-like voice, "Something we can help with? Find us an interesting case?" Emma was proving to be someone who would bring excitement wherever she went.

Without waiting for a response from Emma, Jeremy turned and called out, "Pops."

Cole walked out of the dining room into the open space of the living room. He had his collared shirt unbuttoned and a napkin tucked into the top. He was also carrying a cup of coffee. "You called?" he said to Jeremy a bit sarcastically.

"Yes, Emma is here on a visit. She wants to share some information."

"Oh," said Cole and snatched off his napkin, and tossed it on the table. "Emma welcome, come in, come in." He waved her toward a couple of chairs in the living room. "Would you like some breakfast?"

Emma took a seat but sat on the edge as she answered, "No sir, I have an observation to review with you."

He could see she was serious. Emma wasn't sure how much to share. She started with the article about the body. "I think that the man listed here is Harry Morgan, the gentleman who runs the docks at the local paper." She handed him the article of the man found washed up on the beach.

"Yes, I saw this, this morning," Cole said tapping his hand on the article. "How did you know him, Emma?"

"I was following up on some newspaper articles I found, he volunteered to review them with me." She took a deep breath and continued, "When he didn't show, I thought he had changed his mind and just didn't want to meet me." Emma didn't mention her mama's connection to the articles. "I also went by the docks this morning and found out that Harry had not been around for a few days."

"Who did you speak with?" asked Cole in a business-like manner.

"A friend, Mike Carmichael, he works delivering papers in the mornings," she answered in the same tone.

"You spoke to no one else?" he asked.

"No, I came straight here," she answered.

Cole knew that was something else there but didn't pry further. "Okay," he said, "I'll notify my contacts at the morgue and see if we can confirm that it actually is Harry Morgan."

"Emma," he said looking directly into her eyes, "good job."

She smiled and looked over at Jeremy. He had been silent throughout the story. He sent her a crooked smile.

"Jeremy, could you see Emma home?" Cole asked though he knew the answer.

Jeremy could tell it was not a question and did not hesitate to agree. Plus, he had the added benefit of more time to be alone with her, he liked having her to himself.

As she was leaving, she glanced around the home she had not noticed before. It was a grand multistory house, but you could tell they actually lived there. Books were lying on tables, notebooks lying around. It was a house that made you feel comfortable.

"Thank you, Cole, I appreciate your help in this matter," Emma said in a heartfelt manner.

"No, Emma," he said taking her hands, "thanks for coming directly to me."

As they made their way home, Jeremy kept Emma entertained with detective stories. Emma was laughing at Jeremy's antics but sobered suddenly when he asked casually, "Can I take you to the park this weekend and maybe the dance also?"

Another friend to let down, thought Emma, feeling a bit dejected on the topic of boys. "Jeremy," she started.

He stopped her when he saw her expression. "Okay, I give, wrong moment?"

"For now," she said, relieved he understood without a long conversation. "Thank you, Jeremy," said Emma.

"That's all right, I understand," said Jeremy not feeling let down, because she had not said no.

"We'll let you know if he is indeed Harry Morgan." And with that, he tipped his hat and skipped down the stoop toward home.

A few days later Emma received a note from Jeremy. *Confirmed to be Harry Morgan, will follow up when we get more details.*

He was murdered. She took a moment to realize what that meant. Harry, a man who she had met briefly was not there anymore and a brief conversation with her may have led to his demise. She knew that if she was even remotely responsible, then she would continue to investigate. It was time to pull each article and investigate them one at a time. She pulled out the first of the articles and laid it on her bedroom desk. It detailed an investigation into illegal gambling operations found in a local flower shop.

She made notes on the name of the shop and the location. It was off her route but she did know where it was. She would head there after her shift at the bakery tomorrow.

Should I tell Dora, she thought to herself. *No, I will wait.*

<h1 style="text-align:center">CHAPTER 17</h1>

The next morning, she was reviewing her list at the bakery. She also noticed that the Almond-Cherry Soufflés with Warm German Chocolate Sauce was again on her list. *Odd*, she thought, *that had not been ordered for years but now it is being ordered once a week.* She made a mental note to add that observation to her notebook. She also made a mental note to ask Cousin who was ordering that particular dessert. Putting it out of her mind, she pulled the ingredients together for a German Red Wine cake. The cake came together quickly and went into the oven.

She finished up her list of baked goods, taking a bit longer to put together the special dessert. When her morning was wrapped up, she cleaned up and changed into street clothes prior to leaving. Her street clothes included a black and white checked dress with red trim. She did a quick check for her knives and took her hat with her as she left the bakery.

She went directly to the flower shop listed in the article. She walked around the area, it was a nice, clean location. As she approached the shop, she could see flowers in buckets and containers on the sidewalk. *This must be it,* she thought. The window displays were full of brightly colored flowers and greenery. She took a deep breath to steady herself and she entered the shop. A bell jingled above her head, she glanced back at it and then forward toward the sales desk.

"Hello," she called to a man of about fifty. He had a round stomach and a cheerful expression as he came out of the back carrying flowers in one hand and a vase in the other.

"Oh hi," he called back cheerfully, "do you need some help?"

"No… Yes, I think so," she hesitated and then came to a decision and pulled out the article to show him.

He raised an eyebrow at her. "Okay, so maybe no flowers." He placed the flowers he was carrying in the vase and placed them on a table. He reached over to take the article she had pulled out. He sighed as he read it over and slumped down on a nearby stool. "It's been a while since I thought about this event."

"Is that you in the article?" she asked tentatively.

He was silent for so long that she thought he didn't hear her question. He looked up at her but his eyes appeared to be looking through her. "Yes, this was a lifetime ago. Every day after they took over my business, it felt like parts of my soul were being cut away. Then one day, like today, a pretty blonde lady came into my shop and changed my life. Now another very similar pretty blonde lady comes in…," he focused on her and said, "and you are?"

"I'm Emma and my mama was Mary Evans."

He nodded slowly and said, "Yes, I thought so. I guess you have the right to know. Yes, the article is about me and this shop. I am Karl Murphy."

He stood up and stepped to the shop door. He turned the opened sign to closed and pulled the shades. Emma wasn't threatened by his actions and felt comfortable staying and hearing more.

"Would you like some lemonade and maybe some cookies?" he asked.

"Yes," she said.

He indicated that she should follow him to the kitchen in the back of the shop. He had a small white table with four chairs in the cheerful bright yellow room.

"You did know my mama?" she asked.

"Yes," he said pouring the lemonade and waving her into a chair. He handed her a glass and a cookie, fixed one for himself, and sat down. "Yes," he said again. "I knew her. She had that lovely bakery. I believe it's gotten bigger and has a new name?"

She nodded in confirmation. "The bakery still belongs to the family and one of my cousins has taken over the day-to-day operation. He has lots of expansion plans." She waited for a beat and then started again. "You have more information on Mama?" She was ready to get down to business.

"Yes," he said, sinking into his memories of Mary. "We would sometimes trade flowers for berliners." He savored the thought of a berliner for a moment. "I don't suppose you have any with you?" he asked hopefully and when she shook her head he sighed. "It was a weekly habit, she would come by when she was out making deliveries and stop by to share the news."

"What happened? How did you get involved in that?" Emma asked indicating the article, really wanting to know why Mama kept it. *Was it because they were friends?*

"Oh, that…" he grimaced, indicating that it had not been a good time for him. "A bad element had moved into the area. They started to move on to different businesses. They used threats, and intimidation to get us to do business with them. I was struggling at that time, flowers weren't selling that well and when they offered a business deal to use my storage space, I agreed."

"At first, I didn't realize what I had agreed to. The money seemed good and I tried to go along, but what started as a rental opportunity had turned into a much worse situation. I was alone, I tried to contact my brother for help, but I couldn't reach him. It was just me and I didn't know how to get out of the situation I put myself into."

"Mama was still coming around?" she said trying to determine her Mama's role in this situation.

He continued, "Mary knew something was wrong when she would visit me. The men had started hanging out in the front of the store, bothering the customers and ruining the small amount of business I still had. They had started using my backroom to keep stolen goods and to run gambling operations. I just had no one to turn to, except for Mary. She took me to the side and asked if I had someone that could help, when I said no, she indicated she might know someone."

"Daniel Cooper, the reporter?" she asked, wanting to connect the dots on the case.

"Yes, but I didn't know his name until the articles started coming out."

"Why go to a reporter and not the police?"

"At that time, we didn't trust the police in Chicago. The department was even more corrupt than it is now."

She cut an eye to him on that one, knowing that there still wasn't a lot of trust in the local police.

He continued, "Mary hoped that if they stirred up enough trouble for the police, they would have to intervene and shut down the illegal activities. She was the main contact with Daniel."

"Mama was the source for the articles?" she asked.

"Yes," he confirmed and stopped for a moment to wipe his eyes, his thoughts steeped in memories of her. "She was so special and cared so much about us. She was able to talk to the different store owners and not arouse suspicion by pretending to make deliveries to their shops. They wanted the assistance and were willing to talk to her, once they saw she could help. Some people talked because they already were being infiltrated and being forced to do illegal things. Others talked to her because they were afraid, they might also be drawn in."

"Going by the series of articles, it looks like Mama kept going after your shop was saved."

"Yes, the articles kept coming out. I worried about her but she assured me that Daniel could keep her name out of the paper. She counted on him to keep her and her family safe."

"Did she mention us?" she asked hopefully.

"Yes, she talked about your papa and her special girls all the time."

Emma would have loved to spend the day, hearing about the past but she needed to get moving. "So, what happened, how did it finish for you?"

"Finally, I was cleared of any wrongdoing but the persons responsible for setting up the operations had not been arrested. They went away, but the threat was still around. I almost lost the shop during that time."

"How did you get through it?"

"Well, the articles kept coming out about other businesses nearby and eventually the area seemed to get too hot for the organization to stay alive. Mary took no credit for helping us. She loved the mystery of it all. She also deeply cared for the people whose lives were affected." He continued, "I do know that she made this Daniel Cooper famous. I do remember him. I trusted Mary and she trusted him, so we shared our stories. I have to admit if Daniel had not written them, I don't know where we would have ended up." He trailed off, seeming to be lost in the past again. He looked down for a moment and then came abruptly back into the present.

"And you girlie, what are you doing asking about the past?"

"Mama died when I was very young and this is a way for me to find out more about her," she said simply.

He nodded understanding loss and trying to connect with those lost to the past.

Emma started to leave but turned back with a question, "The leader of the organization, you indicated that the police were able to shut down a number of businesses that they determined were involved. Who was the main person?"

He shook his head. "It was probably John Harden, but we will never know for sure. The organization had so many layers that the main guy was never found. It was like a regenerating organism, cut off its head and another grows in its place."

"Did John Harden leave, after the police got involved?"

"No, I don't think so, I think they just went underground."

A bell went off in Emma's head and she thought, *Underground could it be the same organization or just a new variation of the same thing, this time more hidden and through the tunnels?* "I have to go," she said abruptly.

She stopped herself and said in a kind voice, "Thank you for your time today. I really appreciate it. I'll stop by again soon and maybe we can trade some flowers for berliners."

He smiled and then laughed out loud, delighted at the way the day had turned out. "Yes, girlie you have a deal. Stop by soon and we will have a trade."

He watched her leave and immediately grabbed his jacket. He needed to let certain people know that the smuggling operations were being looked into by outside people. He went out the back way to the alley so he wouldn't be seen by Emma.

CHAPTER 18

$\mathcal{E}$mma stepped up her investigations and started gathering information on which stores were involved in the current smuggling operation. It was fairly obvious if you knew what to look for. She continued sending her notes to Pinkerton for review. New observations were communicated to them in face-to-face meetings every few weeks. This involved links from the stores to the tunnels and suspected businesses involvement. Cole asked her to step back some and keep a low profile while they used the new data to build a file.

As the weeks went by, Emma threw herself into her other cases and stayed out of the smuggling one. Several of these panned out into arrests- pickpockets who frequent the streets during heavy traffic times and gambling establishments. Though the last one had been more accidental with her stumbling into a room full of gambling tables. When she notified Officer McGarity, he immediately shut down the operations and put more people on the streets to watch for pickpockets. Papa had provided his name as someone that could be trusted.

She was doing exactly what Cole asked her not to do, she was being too obvious and getting too much notice.

During that active time, a note was delivered to Emma at the boarding house. It was evening, so everyone was in the sitting room enjoying the conversation. Tim and Dora were on the small sofa with their books in front of them, Tim's for school and Dora's house accounting.

There was a knock on the door and one of the older kids, Joe, had run to open it. There was a moment of quiet and then he yelled, "Emma, there's a letter for you."

A letter? I wasn't expecting anything, she thought to herself as she went into the foyer to take the note.

"Is it from Papa?" asked Dora in a worried voice moving into the foyer to join Emma.

That was also Emma's first thought, that something had happened to Papa. She opened it and read. "No, no. It's a note from the Chief of Police. He wants to see me in his office in the morning. Too bad Papa isn't here to review this with me."

Tim joined Dora and Emma to review the note. Dora said, "I think it would be all right. It is the Police Chief and it's not as if he's a crime boss or something."

Emma's mouth quirked up and she remembered the conversation Cole and Papa had about the current Chief's character.

Dora continued, "The note also indicated that McGarity would be picking you up. Isn't he one of the ones you trust with your cases?"

"Yes," said Emma, tapping the note on her hand and considering what she should do.

"Wait a minute," Tim said, feeling like he should step up. "Shouldn't I go with you?"

"No," Emma said slowly shaking her head to emphasize it. "I can handle it on my own."

Dear-one read over her shoulder and said, "I think you should include the rope story here. You're making it sound like it all just came to her, when in fact she had to work to get those skills."

"Yes, I agree."

Back to the story.

"Emma, we need to talk," said Dora determinedly.

"I agree," said Tim, firmly, placing a hand on Dora's shoulder.

"You have a say also?" scoffed Emma, bristling at people wanting to dictate her comings and goings.

Tim nodded and said in a strong voice, "In this case, with Ellis out of town, I think I do."

Dora nodded at him encouragingly to continue. "I think we need to talk about your continued investigations when multiple people have told you to stop. You're attracting attention, such as this meeting with the Police Chief."

"Dora, let's move into the kitchen, we're attracting some attention," said Emma indicating the boarders in the sitting room that were all but leaning toward their conversation.

Emma, Tim, and Dora went into the kitchen.

"Sister," started Dora as they sat down at the table, "you know we love you, but you are fallible. You let your temper and stubbornness push you into decisions that may be questionable. You have to realize that these decisions could affect more than yourself."

Emma started to interrupt, but Dora cut her off, "Don't you remember when you thought you didn't need Miss May to show you how to get out of the ropes the first time?"

Emma turned bright red. "Not my best moment," she admitted.

"And what happened?" Dora encouraged.

"I wouldn't ask for help and I sat tied up in that chair all morning and then ended up turning it upside down on me," she admitted.

Tim, finally finding humor in their conversation, laughed out loud, "I didn't know about that."

"I didn't think we needed to let anyone know, it would have

embarrassed Emma," shared Dora, "but you are family now," and placed her hand into his.

She focused back on Emma, "I bring it up because the rope story proves that you sometimes need help and you need to ask for it before you get into trouble."

Emma agreed and told her she would try to be more thoughtful. "I still think I should go alone."

Tim looked doubtful but knew he couldn't miss work at that hour and said, "Fine, just make sure you let us know if there's any trouble." He leaned over and kissed her on the cheek to apologize silently for his slightly overbearing manner.

She smiled, showing she understood, and reassured them that she would take no chances.

She thought about the rope story on her way upstairs.

Miss May had tried to give her direction but Emma thought she could do it alone. She couldn't and after she knocked herself down and lay there for an hour struggling, Emma had apologized to Miss May and asked for her help. After she untied Emma, Miss May showed her the trick for getting out of the ropes.

"There are tricks to escaping ropes, many of them involve pretending to not understand what is happening to you." She started to demonstrate by having Emma tie the rope around Miss May's wrist.

"If I'm in a position where I'm being tied up, by putting my elbows here against the ribs," she demonstrated the position. "What I'm doing is creating a false space in my wrist. Under no circumstances put your arms straight out when your hands are being bound, instead, appear submissive as your wrists are tied. Doing this creates a position in the curvature of the wrist, leaving enough space, so when the time for escape presents itself, you can extend your arms, place your hands flat and slide them out." She demonstrated this quickly.

Emma asked, "Can you show me that again?"

Miss May smiled, happy that Emma was paying attention. "Yes"

"Can I do it now?" asked Emma excitedly.

They worked on ropes for hours after and tied Emma up several times a week after that until she became proficient.

Jerking herself out of her memories, Emma started to get ready for bed and thought about her meeting tomorrow. She pulled out her notebooks to distract herself. Emma was making additional notes about fairly obvious crimes that were being overlooked by the local law enforcement. She would keep this to herself for now.

The next morning, after breakfast, Emma heard a knock on the front door. The kids were getting ready for school so she ran to the window overlooking the stoop. She glanced out and saw McGarity there in his dress blues.

Emma pulled open the door to greet him. "I didn't realize we were so formal today," she teased as she pulled a cloth from her hair. She had been using it to hold it back as she helped clean up the boarding house.

McGarity was a young officer, very serious about his job, wanting to show his best side for the Chief. *Letting Emma see me in my suit wasn't bad either,* he thought.

"Let me change, I won't be a moment." She hurried upstairs, forgetting to ask McGarity to sit down or offer him something to drink.

Dora wandered out of the dining room at that time and stumbled into the officer. "Oh, excuse me. Am I under arrest?" She grinned up at him in a teasing manner.

"No miss," he stuttered, taken a bit off guard by a pretty girl. "I'm waiting to take Emma to meet the Chief."

"Yes, yes," murmured Dora. "I did hear something about that."

Emma was tucking in her shirt and tightening her belt as she descended the stairs. She had two pins in her pocket and dashed them into her hair prior to plopping on her dashing red hat. She grabbed her jacket from the coat rack before McGarity could offer to help and slipped it on.

"Ready," she said brightly.

McGarity looked a bit bemused at this very pretty girl, he had only seen her in her baggy and boyish delivery clothes. "Yes," he said and offered her his elbow. "Off we go. Nice to meet you," he said to Dora as they were leaving.

Emma took the offered elbow and the two headed out to McGarity's hired cab. Dora waved them off, still worried about the meeting, but knowing Emma could take care of herself.

The trip was quiet, with only Emma providing the conversation. The closer that they got to the station the quieter McGarity got. Emma was getting a bit nervous and had many questions for him.

"What should I expect when I see the Chief?"

"I'm a bit confused as to why the Chief wants to see you," McGarity wondered aloud. He continued, "Normally, no one sees him but the top brass. Funny thing is, I didn't even know he knew my name until we started working on these cases a few weeks ago."

They pulled to a halt in front of the precinct. "I'll be taking you in, but I'll not be allowed in the Chief's office. Be polite," he advised, "he's a powerful man."

Emma nodded slowly realizing that this meeting may be more involved than a simple thank you. Emma didn't think and jumped out of the cab before McGarity could make it around to help her. McGarity was a bit startled when she didn't wait to be helped down, but she was too preoccupied to notice.

She made her way through the Precinct. Each room filled with blue-coated police officers seemed to quiet as she entered. As she started to ascend the stairs to the upper offices, McGarity was replaced by a higher-level officer. He escorted her up to the third floor where a pair of heavy double doors stood closed. The male secretary inside barely paused to glance at her and told her to take a seat in the chairs in the outer area.

The officer that escorted her upstairs, stayed with her. They sat in complete silence during their wait. Emma wasn't sure if there was someone in the office with the Chief or if she was being kept in the waiting area to intimidate her.

The secretary stood, went to the Chief's door, and went into the office. He came out and spared her a glance, "You may go in now."

Emma and the officer rose. The secretary frowned at the officer and said, "You may stay seated." The officer sat.

Emma walked to the double doors, unsure of how to open them.

"Oh, for goodness sake," the secretary said as he came around the desk to open the door. Once it was opened, he gave Emma a good push into the room.

Emma stumbled a bit as she entered. It was a large office with a large wood desk setting on a nice rug. The wall behind the Chief was all windows. He sat at his desk and did not stand as she entered the room. *Evidently, I don't rate high enough to be allowed to sit. That's okay.* She had heard enough about him to know that she didn't want to be in that room very long.

This man was purported to be corrupt but his appearance was more like that of a kindly grandfather with a round body and soft white hair. Well, that was until she got a good look at his face. He had a set expression that looked like granite to those looking directly at him. His face was square with a large chin. He did not appear to be in the best physical shape, his uniform covering a lot of fat around his middle.

Strange, she thought, *he looks familiar.*

Before she could process this, he spoke, his voice sounding loud in the quiet room, "Girlie, I hear you are causing trouble."

"Trouble?" Emma parroted back to him.

"Yes," he thundered. "You need to keep your eyes and ears on your own business. Let the police handle things."

"But you aren't," she said without thinking.

That response changed his face from granite to an expression of absolute fury. His face started to turn purple, he stood up and leaned forward, planting his hands on his desk. The motion made Emma back up, but only a pace. She didn't want to show that she was intimidated.

He waggled his fingers her way, "I'm warning you that you will not like my response if you don't stay out of business that's not yours."

"Warning me?" she decided to just let her responses fly. "Really?"

Narrator commented, If Emma hadn't been only sixteen, she would have known to not poke the bear or not to aggravate or irritate anyone that can make you sorry.

"I'm just seeing what anyone would see if they looked," she said heatedly. The Chief returned her look as Emma continued, "What about the illegal gambling going on Houston Street? What about that house of ill repute on 4th?"

The Chief had heard enough, slammed his hands on the desk, and said emphatically. "Listen here girly, if you don't think I can bring down retribution on you and your family then you better think twice."

That startled Emma and immediately shut her down. She didn't think her actions could hurt her family; she had only been thinking of herself. Dora had been right; her decisions were going to have an impact on people other than herself.

The chief sat back down at his desk, feeling more in control of the situation, and picked up a pen. "I have been told your family owns several businesses. What if the permits for those got revoked and shut down?" his voice went low and menacing.

Emma realized she had gone too far and schooled her facial expression to look contrite, "I'll keep my observations to myself in the future."

That calmed him down, he sat again and averted his gaze. "Fine then, I think we have nothing more to talk about." He waved his hand indicating she could leave.

The secretary, who seemed to be aware of what was said in the room, muttered in her ear as she passed close to him on her way out, "You'll want to listen to him on this and keep a low profile for a while." With that bit of advice, he turned her over to the waiting officer.

He escorted her back to McGarity. He looked at her questioningly but Emma was quiet during the ride home. He walked her to the door, tipped his hat, and left.

She didn't go in immediately; it was still early in the day. A long walk would clear her head. The walk helped to mull over the threats to the businesses, it worried her and she would do anything for her family. *What to do next*, she thought.

CHAPTER 19

What Emma did over the next few days was to continue to work her schedules at the bakery and on the delivery wagon. She was committed to keeping the low profile the Police Chief had told her to keep. She would do anything to protect her family from his threats.

While she was riding in the delivery wagon with Tim she started thinking about the last time, she had seen Tony's dad, Michael. He seemed to freeze up when she asked about his job. She knew that he owned his own business with his sons, installing and repairing gas and water pipes. She hadn't heard anything from Tony about any financial troubles. She decided to check it out, in a low-key way. Laughing suddenly, she thought, *Well at least I'll get to spend time with one of the Marella's, and this case has an added benefit of not involving the Chief of Police in any way.*

The next morning, she was off from the bakery and the delivery wagon, she took the opportunity to go by Tony's apartment building. Not expecting to be welcomed inside, she waited at the edge of the stoop for Mr. Marella to exit the building. Her boy clothes allowed her to blend in as she followed him to his job. As he descended, she ducked out of sight, behind the side of the stoop, pulling her cap lower over her eyes. She waited a moment and then followed him keeping her distance.

～

Her watcher was unsure of what Emma was up to but would accompany her in case she needed him.

～

This could be a waste of time, she thought, *I may just confirm that he was working at his normal job and just didn't want to talk about it. People have good days and bad days. Maybe that was a bad day for him.*

He entered a building that was under construction. *Well, that makes sense*, thought Emma. She waited a moment and followed him in. Since the covert activity hadn't worked out, she might as well say hello to Mr. Marella since she was here. Workgroups seemed to be leaving the building, she smile as they made their way by her.

She made her way through the long hallway and heard voices toward the back. As she got closer, she realized they were arguing. Mr. Marella was saying to the unnamed man, "I can't continue to hide this, it's too much to ask." His voice sounded strained and not at all like his normal voice.

"You agreed," the unidentified man said loudly.

"Yes, because I didn't want to ruin your son's life. But what about her parents, don't they have a right to know?" Mr. Marella asked in a quieter voice.

"I don't want to talk about that," the unidentified man said flatly.

"Well, you're going to have to talk about it. I can't lie

anymore about what I found," said Mr. Marella in a more heated voice.

She could hear someone pacing in the room. A loud sound, maybe equipment falling, and a scuffling notice caused her to make a quick decision. She drew her knife and entered the room. Mr. Marella saw her and dropped the older rather rotund man he was holding against the wall. The man slid down to the floor and tried to crawl away. He noticed Emma's knife and said holding his hands up, still on his knees, "No trouble here."

"Mr. Marella?" she asked indicating the man on the floor with her knife.

"Let him go," he said in a defeated voice, pulling his fingers through his hair.

"We'll talk about this later," the man said, getting to his feet and shaking his fist in a threatening manner as he left the room. They heard him scurry down the hall and out the front door.

Mr. Marella continued to stare at the door that the man exited. Finally, he turned his gaze toward Emma and said, "What are you doing here?" He was shocked at her appearance and he kept staring at the knife in her hand. She had forgotten that she still had it out and she lowered her arm slowly down to her side.

"Are you all right?" she asked, avoiding his question.

"What?" he asked, clearly having a hard time concentrating.

She repeated the question, "Are you all right? Who was that man?"

"Him?" she nodded, and he finally answered, "My boss on this job, this is his house."

"What were you arguing about?" she asked trying to figure out what Mr. Marella was involved in.

He looked at her, ignoring her question, and repeated his earlier question, "Emma, why are you here?"

"I was worried about you. You looked distracted last time I

saw you," she said feeling at a loss. She was trying to help but it wasn't working out.

"That was quite a long while ago," he stated, thinking of that last visit.

"I know," she said feeling guilty. "I had planned to check in with you earlier."

"Well, you needn't worry. I'm just fine," he said brusquely, not wanting to involve her in this matter.

"But..." she tried to say but was interrupted.

"Emma, I said I was fine. Leave it at that," he said in a harder voice.

"Just one thing," she said. He looked at her in exasperation as she continued. "If you want to talk about this or need some help, please let me know. I do have resources that we might use if needed."

"I will," he said feeling he couldn't involve her in this.

"Promise me," she continued to press him.

He looked at her silently for a long time and finally said, "I promise."

"Good," she said, relieved, knowing he would keep that promise.

"Don't you have somewhere to be?" he asked.

"Yes, yes I do," she and started to turn around to leave.

"Emma," he reached out to touch her shoulder saying, "I appreciate your worrying about me. We miss you."

She just couldn't stand it, she whirled around and hugged him tightly. "I miss you all so much." She left the room in a hurry but not before he could see her tears.

Mr. Marella stood there wishing he could call her back and ask for help, but he was in a position where he could get someone hurt if they found out what he knew. Trying not to think about it, he started working on the gas lighting in the room he was in. His boys were working another job, he was relieved they were not involved in this mess.

A few days later, Mr. Marella wasn't sleeping and he was withdrawing more and more from his family. A difficult decision had to be made and his promise to Emma pushed him to make his way to the bakery where Emma was working. He waited a few blocks down the street for her. She was off in the afternoons and he hoped to catch her when she was on her way home. When he saw her, he called out, "Emma can I speak with you?"

"Mr. Marella, of course," she said surprised to see him so soon.

"Is there somewhere private we can talk?" he asked looking around.

"Papa is in New York this week. We can use the basement lab," she suggested, happy that he had kept his promise and was coming to her.

He nodded and they walked together to the boarding house. He seemed so upset she didn't want to ask him any questions until they got to somewhere private. It was a silent walk.

They made it there and went in the front door, Dora was in the dining room as they passed. Emma motioned to her to stay back, she nodded and stayed where she was. Emma and Mr. Marella made their way down the basement stairs. It was Papa's lab but there was a sitting area where they could have their conversation.

Mr. Marella slumped down into the chair and put his face in his hands. Emma sat across from him and waited patiently for him to start talking.

"Emma, I'm so scared and I need some help to get out of trouble," he said with a tremor in his voice.

"What kind of trouble?" she asked trying to keep the worry out of her voice.

"Bad. Really bad," he said in a strained tone.

She waited for him to continue.

"They're threatening my family and actually tried to take Enzo yesterday," he said.

"Take him?" she asked incredulously.

"Yes," he said simply.

"But why?" she asked, not understanding what he could be involved in that might cause someone to take a child.

"I saw something they didn't want me to see. I was working at the Barrett Street building, the one you followed me to," he said, looking at her. When she nodded, he continued, "The building I am working in made it through the fire of 1871 and now we're rehabbing and updating the gas and water lines."

She nodded again, encouraging him to continue.

"We were making good progress and there was one room that they had told me to limit the piping in one wall. The layout they had in mind was going to cause lots of extra pipe. I was the only one there at that point, I had sent everyone else home and I continued to work on that area. I just thought I could save us some time and check inside the wall to see if it could hold the piping." He took a deep breath and continued, "I started taking down the plaster wall, using smaller holes to check for clearance. Initially, there didn't seem to be any problems, so I increased the size of the upper hole. I saw this material inside, it was rough, I admit I was curious and pulled on it. When I pulled on the cloth to remove it, I found it was caught on something."

She was thinking about that and asked, "Didn't you worry that they told you not to work in that room?"

"Not really," he said candidly, "usually if I can save the client money, they forgive any liberties I may take." He paused for a second, knowing what part of the story was coming up next.

Emma saw his hesitation and encouraged him by saying, "Keep going."

This part seemed to cause him pain to talk about. He frowned heavily and looked at his hands as he continued, "That was when I realized what the cloth was covering. I pulled it out.

It was a girl of about twelve, such a little thing with black hair and brown eyes."

Emma was shocked, she didn't know what he had found but she had not expected to hear about a body. She asked hesitantly, "Did you recognize her?"

"No, I haven't seen her before this. I don't think I could have kept quiet if I knew her. I keep thinking of her parents and what they're going through," he said as he looked up, tears streaming down his face.

"How long do you think she's been there?" she asked thinking about how long bodies could take to decompose.

"Not long. She still looked like she might wake up," he admitted, wiping his eyes with both hands.

"What did you do?" Emma wasn't sure what she would have done in his place.

"I didn't know what to do. I know that I felt dizzy and couldn't catch my breath. I kept telling myself I have to go to the police and show them what I found but ... I don't know how long I stood there; I just couldn't move. That was when the building owner Mr. Simpson and his son came into the room."

He seemed to be reliving the experience and continued, "They were angry that I had not followed their plan. Then I realized that the anger was because I had found her. I could tell from how they were acting that they knew she was in there."

He remembered that conversation so clearly, Mr. Simpson was shouting at him, "What are you doing? You had instructions to not enter this room, much less to start taking down the walls."

"There's a girl in there," he stated, still feeling fuzzy in the head.

Mr. Simpson turned to his son and said, "Harry check the house to see if anyone else is here. Now!" Harry moved quickly through the house, opening and closing doors, checking for anyone that might still be there.

Mr. Simpson kept on shouting questions at him, "Why did you enter a room you were told not to? You know this is a firing offense."

Odd, he thought, *They aren't mentioning the girl.* He tried to talk to Mr. Simpson, "Do you know who that is in the wall?"

"That's none of your concern," Mr. Simpson stated, not sharing any information.

"But shouldn't we go to the police?" Michael asked.

"For what?" Mr. Simpson asked belligerently.

"To tell them that we found her," Michael said lamely.

"No, you won't tell anyone anything. You'll keep working the job and forget what you found."

Michael was so confused but something did get through the fuzziness that had taken him over and he straightened up as he asked, "Did you kill her Mr. Simpson or was it Harry that killed her?"

Mr. Simpson looked nonplussed at that question. "That's my business, not yours."

Michael just shook his head and said more firmly, "No. I'm going to the police."

At that moment, Harry came back into the room with a gun drawn, saying, "I don't think so." He looked over at Mr. Simpson and said, "We're going to have to do something with him."

"No. no. I think we can reach an agreement. Can't we Michael?" Mr. Simpson inquired softly.

Michael just looked at the two without saying anything.

Harry said, "How about if you don't cooperate, we take your youngest from you?"

Whatever fuzziness was still affecting Michael disappeared with that one statement, "Enzo? Why would you want to bring him into this?"

"I didn't, you did. Now if you just repair the holes and follow our instructions about the placement of the lamp and keep your mouth shut, then we won't take him."

"You can't be that evil," Michael said incredulously.

"If you don't follow our instructions then you'll find out how evil we can be."

Michael felt he had no choice. He covered up the holes and told his boys to work other jobs while he finished that one.

He brought himself back into the present with Emma and said, "I can't live with what I've done."

"Where's Enzo now?" she asked thinking about what they would do as she drummed her fingers on her lips.

"He's in school," he said, unsure of what she was thinking.

"First thing is to pick him up and place him somewhere safe," she said planning.

"Yes, but where are you thinking?" Michael said, ready to have someone direct him in this mess.

"Not here at the boarding house. They've seen me now and they may check here. Let's put him with my uncle Otto. He has all those boys and he works early mornings, so he'll be there during the day, to watch out for him."

"Will Otto be all right with that?" Michael asked. He was concerned about involving more people in this.

"Yes." She was sure Otto would help, he loved kids and would do anything to protect them. She continued, "Next, we need to get you to the Pinkerton office. We need to meet with Cole to decide the next steps. Are you in agreement with my plan?"

Michael was amazed by Emma's ideas. "I'm in," he said. "Let's go."

First, they wanted to pick up Enzo at school. Michael told

the principal that the boy was needed for a family emergency. It was the truth, there was an emergency in the family.

Enzo walked up to greet his father and said, "Emma what are you doing here? Papa is something wrong?"

Michael bent down in front of Enzo, looked him in the eyes, and said, "I made a bad decision that I don't want you affected by. In order to protect you, we'll need to put you with Emma's uncle until we straighten it out."

Enzo didn't argue, he could tell Papa was serious and understood that he needed to do as he was told. They took Michael's wagon to Otto's house and made sure that Enzo got safely inside.

Otto was there and awake when they entered. "Emma, what's happening?"

"We have some trouble," she said simply, "and we need to keep Enzo from being taken." She explained that there were people angry at Michael and had threatened Enzo.

"Of course, we'll help." He looked down at Enzo and said, "Go in the kitchen to see Freida." He called out, "Frieda, Enzo is coming back to see you." Otto had known Tony's family for a long time.

She called back, "I'm in the kitchen and I have pastry."

Otto puffed on his pipe and said to Michael and Emma as they watched Enzo run to see Freida, "What now?"

Emma answered for them, "I'm taking Michael to Pinkerton to get some help."

"You can't tell me more?" he asked.

"I shouldn't involve you any more than I have," explained Michael.

Otto nodded and hugged Emma saying, "We will take care of him for you. Now you best be off. "

Michael and Emma took the wagon to the Pinkerton offices. Michael asked with worry in his voice, "Will they help? Should we go straight to the police?"

"I'm not sure the police can be trusted and I know we can trust Pinkerton. They'll involve the police when appropriate," she said reassuringly.

"Good," he said, trusting her. He already felt better, knowing Enzo was safe.

As they made their way to Pinkerton, Emma asked, "What do you want to accomplish here?"

"I want to get the girl back to her parents and I want Mr. Simpson and his son Harry in police custody."

Emma nodded and said in a firm voice, "That sounds right."

They entered the Pinkerton office and she went up to the main front desk where the secretary sat and asked, "Is it possible for us to see Cole?"

"They're out on a big job just now and aren't available until later today," the secretary replied.

Emma looked at Michael and nodded. "Do you want to leave a message?" she asked him.

"Yes, tell him to come to 247 North Street as soon as he gets back. Tell him to bring more men with him."

"I'll tell him," the secretary promised. Mr. Tilden had told him that if Emma came in, she was to get an immediate audience with him. He thought, I *should send someone to let them know Emma needs them.*

They turned and were leaving as Michael asked, "What now?"

"We keep an eye on the house so that they don't move her somewhere else," she said simply.

"Do you think that's necessary? Couldn't the police do that?" he asked, ready for this to be over.

She said quietly, "I have serious concerns about going to the police without Pinkertons' involvement. I'm afraid they may try to blame you. The men involved may try to say you killed her and you were threatening them."

"I hadn't thought of that," said Michael slowly.

"So, we head back and you go back to work as if nothing's happened," she said.

"What if they come in while we are there?" he asked, concerned for her safety.

"Tell them you just panicked and had a change of heart," she suggested.

"What will you be doing?" he asked.

"I'll be inside with you. I'm hoping that the Pinkertons will show up soon," she said.

"What if things go wrong?" he asked.

"Then we react and defend. You use anything that's at your disposal to do that and I'll be there," she said.

"I understand what you're saying. We can do that," he said, liking the plan. He wouldn't abandon that child in the wall again.

They made their way back to the house and started working in the room nearest to where the girl was hidden. It wasn't long before Mr. Simpson and Harry showed up. They entered the house with a slam of the front door. Michael motioned for her to move into another room.

Emma mouthed, "Stay calm."

He nodded and went back to his work. He heard them come up behind him.

Harry shoved Michael's shoulder and said, "What are you still doing here? I thought you wanted out."

"No, I'm okay now. I was just nervous," he said continuing to work on the wall, still not looking at them.

"Nervous?" Harry laughed with a sneer. "You appeared angry, not nervous."

"Yes, well I understand where you're coming from and I'm okay," he said continuing to work, not looking at them.

"Yeah, somehow, I don't believe that. And by the way, I went by your son's school and he was gone. Now, where could he have gotten to?" Harry asked musingly.

Michael tensed up but still didn't turn around.

Mr. Simpson was running out of patience and shouted at Michael, "You turn around and look at me."

He turned slowly toward him, keeping his wrench hidden at his side. His thoughts on what Emma has said about going on the attack. Mr. Simpson had the gun aimed at his chest. Harry didn't have a gun and was waiting for instructions from his father. His gaze focused on Michael.

Michael saw Emma come up behind Mr. Simpson with a large piece of pipe. She raised it to swing at his head. There was a whoosh and bang as the pipe met its mark. He went down in a heap. Michael took the opportunity to take his heavy wrench and bring it down on the arm that held the gun. It slid across the room.

Harry was frozen in place, looking at his dad and the attackers. Suddenly there was the sound of breaking glass and boots coming into the building. Harry decided to take that opportunity to leave the house head first through an open window.

Jeremy led the charge into the house. Emma and Michael were sitting on Mr. Simpson, holding him down.

"Is he…" started Jeremy.

Emma finished for him, "Alive? Yes."

Jeremy waved at two of his men directing them, "Take care of him."

"Jeremy another man got away, out the back," she said quickly as she got up.

"You two after him," Jeremy pointed to two of his men. They left at a run in the direction that Harry went.

The other Pinkerton detectives got Mr. Simpson tied up and placed him in the corner.

Emma went up to Jeremy and whispered in his ear. He went pale but looked at Michael and said, "Can you show me what you found?"

Michael indicated the room next door. Emma followed

them. He started opening the walls; immediately an odor permeated the room. Emma continued to watch as they fully revealed the body of the young girl. There was not a dry eye in the house as they viewed the little girl in a light blue dress, her dark hair covering part of her face.

Jeremy had sent for the police and said, "Emma and Michael, we can take care of the follow-up-if you want to leave."

"Will you need our statements?" he asked.

"No," said Jeremy, "we can say we had a source that turned this in."

"Thank you," said Michael.

Emma said to Jeremy, "Thank you for coming."

"Anything for you," he said sincerely. "Now get, you know you don't want to be found here."

Emma looked at Jeremy and said quietly, "I took this case because I thought it would keep me out of the Police Chief's path."

Jeremy nodded and said, "We need to make sure that he doesn't know your involvement. Get going NOW!"

Michael and Emma left in a hurry on foot and as they turned the corner, they noticed the police arriving. They had parked their wagon in an alley a few blocks down. They retrieved it and headed home.

Jeremy did not disclose their involvement in the case.

The girl's name turned out to be Meghan Sanders, she was twelve years old and had been missing for about two months. The papers reported that she had been snatched on her way home from school. The parents were heartbroken; she was their only child.

Mr. Simpson went to prison for the murder and Harry had not been found.

That case was harder emotionally than she was used to. She hoped that future cases would have a less personal element.

CHAPTER 20

The case with Mr. Marella made Emma want to see Tony. Since they had their fight, she hadn't seen much of him outside of work. She didn't know how much she would miss him. He had been her constant companion and life was empty without him.

Tim had kept her up with Tony's latest activities. He had started to work for a local museum that he frequented. It was his favorite place and he spent most of his spare time outside of deliveries within the walls of that Museum. Tim said Tony was over the moon about it.

That evening she went home with thoughts of Tony on her mind and baked him his favorite Streusel to celebrate.

She got the dessert organized at home, boxed it up, and started in the direction of Tony's apartment. Just outside of it, she ran into his mom. Mrs. Marella appeared to be a bit upset to see Emma so near their house.

Emma tried to start a conversation, "Mrs. Marella, hello, how are you?"

"I'm good," said Mrs. Marella, her face set in angry lines. "Are you just going through the neighborhood?" She hoped the answer was yes, wanting to protect her son beyond all else.

"No," Emma said more quietly than before, sensing she was not wanted. "I just wanted to drop this off for Tony to congratulate him on his new job." She indicated the box she held.

"Emma, do you think that's appropriate now?" Mrs. Marella asked rather shortly.

Emma mumbled a bit now with her head hung down, "Well I just thought..."

"Emma it would be best if you headed on your way," Mrs. Marella said with a glare.

Emma looked down at the box she carried and then back at Mrs. Marella. "Can you give this to Tony?" she asked in a rush and put the box in an unsuspecting Mrs. Marella's arms. She turned and slowly walked away.

Mrs. Marella looked at the box, shrugged, and balanced it with her other packages. She made her way upstairs and had to knock on the door to get help. Enzo opened the door and immediately reached for the box of strudel.

"Pastry," shouted Enzo to the rest of the family.

"That one goes to the kitchen," she called, watching him run off.

Tony was washing some glasses when Enzo charged in with the box. He looked up and said, "Pastry, you mentioned?"

"I think so and it smells really good," said Enzo.

Tony opened the box and found the strudel. "My favorite," he said looking closely at the pastry.

His mom had entered the kitchen and was looking distracted.

"Hey Mom, where did you get the strudel?" Tony asked keeping his voice even.

"I um...just picked it up on the way home," Mrs. Marella murmured.

"Picked up," he said quietly as he stared down at the pastry in the box. The strudel looked very familiar and then he tasted it. "Mom, you saw Emma." He immediately recognized the flavor. "Where?" he demanded.

"Tony, you don't..." Mom tried to stop the conversation.

"Where Mom?" Tony asked determinedly.

"Outside," she said begrudgingly and when he raised an eyebrow at her she continued, "Just now."

"Just now..." he didn't delay in going after Emma. He grabbed his hat and jacket and was out the door as she was calling for him to stop.

"I don't want you going after that girl. She doesn't care about you," she said loudly.

Tony stopped for a moment and turned back toward her and said, "Mom you don't know what kind of a person she really is and how much she loves us. You might want to talk to Dad about what she did to help him and our family."

She watched him leave, turned toward Michael, and said, "What is he talking about?"

"Come, sit, we need to talk." She listened quietly and realized how wrong she was about Emma.

Tony went downstairs as fast as possible, slipping on the last ones, pulling himself up, and going outside. He looked left and then right. He saw her in the distance and started at a dead run toward her.

"Emma!" he called. She didn't turn at first. He called again, "Emma!"

She turned slowly and looked at him hesitantly.

"Why didn't you come into the apartment with the strudel?" Tony asked, looking at her searchingly as he got closer.

"I wasn't sure I would be welcomed but, I wanted to let you know how proud of you I am," she said in a bit of a rush.

"Not welcome. You're always welcome," he looked shocked at her statement.

She looked hurt and confused.

Immediately Tony felt guilty about how he had acted toward her. "I know I've been behaving badly by avoiding you. I'm so sorry for that. My only excuse is that I needed some time to work out how I was feeling," Tony said emotionally.

"Tony," she reached out to him but started to pull her hand back before she made contact. He grabbed the retracting hand and pulled her closer.

"Emma I'm sorry that I made you feel like I didn't want to see you, when the truth is, I wanted to see you every day. I've missed our morning walks. Not to mention your pastries."

She blushed but continued to stay silent.

Tony continued, "Let's go back to where we were as friends."

She had thought about this for a while. "Tony, I don't want to go back."

Tony paled at this statement and gripped her hands tighter.

She winced a bit at the strong grip but she continued, "I want to move forward instead."

When he looked confused, she said, "Tony, I really want to be with you, but we'll have to move slowly."

He was grinning foolishly and said, "Really?" he grabbed her closer and gave her a long leisurely kiss. "Is that slow enough for you?"

"Tony," she said blushing furiously, enjoying every second of the kiss.

He was still grinning. *Progress*, he thought.

They walked back to her house slowly holding hands. They didn't talk much until they got to the stoop.

"I really did enjoy the strudel," he said quietly, looking deeply into her eyes.

"I'm glad. Congratulations on the job, I'd like to hear more about it. "

"Tomorrow night," he promised.

"Come over for dinner and then we can walk and talk after.

We need to catch up with each other." They kissed again and she wandered dreamily up the stairs into the house.

Dora was waiting for her, grabbed her hand, and drug her into the kitchen.

"Tell me everything," she said, having seen Tony leave and the long kiss.

Emma started with how she went over to Tony's and ended up kissing him (twice!) on the way home.

Dora had many questions, "So you are together now?"

Emma said simply, "Yes."

"And what about Tony's new job?" asked Dora.

Emma blinked and then laughed, "We didn't get around to talking about anything but us."

Dora laughed with her, knowing how that felt. "Okay, so where do you go from here?"

"Well, we continue as best friends but also with a special addition."

"Hmm, all right Emma, but what about Tony's mom? She sounds like you may be on the outs with her."

Emma sat for a moment and thought about that problem, "Yes, I'll think of something to help with that."

"Is Tony going to tell her?"

"Yes," she nodded, "we don't want to hide anything."

"When will you see Tony next?"

Emma blushed, "He'll be here tomorrow night for dinner and a walk. That is if you can add another person to the pot?" She waited for an answering nod and continued, "We also discussed attending the fair this weekend."

"Don't be surprised if we start seeing him a bit more," murmured Dora with a smile.

"More?"

"Yes, it turns out that Tim and Tony like to spend time with us," Dora said with a smile.

Tony came over that next night to share his possible future at the Museum. Emma caught Tony up on her cases. They were finding their way to a new future, together.

CHAPTER 21

$\mathcal{E}$verything continued to stay quiet for Emma, both personally and in cases. The days moved forward with Emma continuing to see Tony, work deliveries with Tim, and work in the bakery.

On a delivery day, Tim dropped off Emma at the bakery for her so that she could give Cousin their orders for tomorrow's deliveries. As she went in the backdoor, she saw Tony was already there, putting in his orders for the next day. When he saw her, he sent her a wink.

Cousin saw the wink and spotted Emma. "Emma after your turn in your delivery orders I need to speak with you about a special order for tomorrow."

Tony nodded in her direction and headed out to the Museum for his afternoon job.

"What's up Cousin?" Emma asked, taking off her hat and undoing some of the tight braids in her hair with her fingers. She handed him her delivery orders.

As he was glancing at the delivery orders he said, "We have an order of Chocolate Leaves with Asbach Uralt-Poached Pears and Grapefruit-Lemon Quark Mousse that came in again this afternoon."

Emma squinted at him, "That is getting ordered a lot lately…"

Before she could finish, Cousin interrupted, "And only your Mama and you know how to make it the way this customer likes it."

She grimaced and explained, "I don't mind making it occasionally, but this is happening multiple times a week."

He got to the point quickly, "Will you be able to make it?"

Emma signed and then nodded, "Yes, I can do that. I need to check the supplies for all of the ingredients."

Emma jotted down the ingredients and Cousin reviewed the list. "I have all of this," said Cousin, "but the rose water. I can have some delivered before you start in the morning."

Emma noticed Chloe was frowning at Cousin from her workstation, "What's up with you and Chloe?"

"There is no me and Chloe and I don't want to talk about it," he said defensively and walked off glaring at both Chloe and Emma.

She sidled up to Chloe and whispered, "What happened?"

"If he doesn't want to talk about it then neither do I," Chloe said in a huff and went back to punching the dough she was working on.

Oh well, thought Emma, *not my business.*

Funny, she thought as she was walking home later, *no one orders that particular recipe outside of the holidays. I'll have to think about this development. Was it important or just a coincidence that Mama was at the bakery on the night she died because of that dessert?*

She headed home, taking some shortcuts through the backstreets, and ran up the steps of the boarding house. "I'm home," she called out as she sailed into the house.

"So, I hear," called Dora from the dining room, "Change your shoes and clothes."

"Okay," Emma said resigned to changing, and trudged upstairs to wash up and put on her split skirt and blouse. Dora followed her up to hear about her day.

"Dora," she said as Dora was helping pick up the dirty clothes.

"Yes," she replied.

"Do you remember Mama making that Chocolate Leaves desert? The one with poached pears for a special customer? I remember Papa mentioning something about it the night Mama died."

Dora sank to the bed thinking intently about what Emma had said. "Now that you mention it, yes Papa was so upset he kept mentioning that if she hadn't been at the bakery at that hour, she would still be alive. Why do you ask?"

"No real reason," Emma said truthfully. "I have gotten this special order more often than I would have expected this time of year and was curious about it."

"Well, nothing changes the fact that Mama died in the fire," she said.

"Yes," Emma nodded slowly, feeling like she had found an important puzzle piece but was unsure what puzzle it fits into.

"Sister." Dora waved her hand in front of Emma's face to get her attention. When Emma finally focused on her she said, "Dinner in a few hours and homework."

Emma smiled, "I know, I'll check on the assignments Papa left for me. Where are the ladies this afternoon?"

"I understand there's a new exhibit opening at the Museum that they wanted to see. I think it involved old knives. I'm sure they'll talk to you about it tonight," Dora said over her shoulder as she was exiting the room.

Emma went down to the basement to check on Papa, who was back from his consulting trip. "Papa," Emma said softly

"Sister come over where I can see you. Did you have a grand

adventure today?" Papa knew that Emma was like her Mama and got herself in tangles occasionally.

"What's my homework today?" she asked, hoping to move Papa off that particular topic, which included Mama and her special dessert. She didn't want to upset him with her theories.

Papa didn't mind the change in topic, "I have another type of puzzler for you today. I want you to read this engineering document and let me know what should be included in the structural drawings and what should not. Also, two chapters of reading…"

Emma interrupted, "Can it be a mystery novel?"

He smiled indulgently and said, "Yes, once you complete the task. Oh, and some calculations may stump you, so ask if you need me to help."

"Papa, I won't need help," she said confidently, grabbed the work, and took off at a run up the stairs. She headed to the study to set up her homework.

Papa shook his head at his daughter and was back to work within moments of her exiting the room.

Emma pulled her notes out and started to review the problems Papa had put together for her. He had put in some red herrings to trick her, which she looked at thoughtfully. *There are additional unnecessary calculations that were put in to distract me. There is an easier method to figure the load on the concrete.* She made the correction and the problem came together.

She finished the engineering work, grabbed a book, and plopped herself into a large worn leather chair, near the desk. She opened it eagerly and started to read Jules Verne's Around the World in Eighty Days. It was such fun to climb into other people's skin and live for a bit. *What would it be like to live so freely and go to New York or overseas by yourself?* It was her goal, to be independent and travel, having adventures as she went.

She read for another hour and realized it was time to help with dinner. Dora could always use extra hands. The table, like at breakfast, filled fast with people, and platters of food were emptied as soon as they were placed on it. It was because Dora cooked beautifully and everyone knew it.

Dinner was noisy but Emma was quiet. She sat between Miss May and Miss Marjorie listening to them chattering about their day at the Museum.

"Do you want to come outside with me after dinner?" Emma asked the ladies after a break in the conversation.

"We can practice throwing and tell you about the knives we saw today," Miss Marjorie said to Emma. Miss May and Miss Marjorie grinned at each other, knowing it was not just throwing but they would get to hear of Emma's adventures on the delivery wagon.

Once outside both ladies turned to Emma and Miss Marjorie asked, "Anything to tell us about today?"

Emma teased with a question, delaying the answer a bit, "You want to hear about my day?"

"Yes," again they replied together.

"My day was quiet today," she said thinking about that dessert.

"Quiet?" Miss May asked. "No new cases?"

"I don't think so," she hesitated. "I have some thoughts but I'm not sure what they mean right now."

Miss Marjorie nodded at Miss May and they started in on how the Museum displayed the collection of knives. "I have to say," said Miss Marjorie, "in my younger days that collection would have tempted me."

Miss May looked down when Miss Marjorie made that comment. Emma got worried, "Miss May what's wrong?"

This made Miss May look up and both Miss Marjorie and Emma saw that something was really bothering her.

"Well, I thought that Emma might want something from the Museum," she said a bit defiantly.

"Oh, you got me a token from the gift shop? That was sweet of you," said Emma softly to Miss May.

Miss Marjorie looked confused because they didn't go to the gift shop that day.

Miss May, still in a defiant voice said, "No No, something else."

Emma and Miss Marjorie looked at her questioningly

Miss May reached into her long coat and pulled out a wicked-looking knife with an ornate handle.

Miss Marjorie recognized it immediately, "Oh May, what have you done? That is from the Museum's collection. They are not for sale!" Miss Marjorie looked frantic and for the first time since Emma knew her, seemed a bit helpless.

Emma was already thinking of ways to fix this problem. "Miss May, I think I have someone that can help us return this knife."

Miss May said "But I don't need help. I wanted to give you a nice present to remember me... us by," she said looking over at Miss Marjorie.

Emma took Miss May's hand in one hand and Miss Marjorie's in the other and looked into the woman's eyes, "Certainly you must see that I can't keep something that doesn't belong to me?"

Miss May bristled visibly at this remark and said stiffly, "I don't want to give it back."

Miss Marjorie looked at Emma, they didn't want to wrestle it from her. Someone might get hurt in the process.

They continued to speak softly to her, giving her many reasons to return the knife. It was when they said that Emma could get arrested for knowingly taking stolen merchandise that Miss May finally relented to their pleas and begrudgingly handed it to Emma.

Emma slid the knife under her coat, "I need to get this to a secure location as soon as possible." She headed back inside while the ladies stood outside and quietly discussed what had happened.

She grabbed her hat and headed out to find Tony. He would be at home. She was nervous about going over, she hadn't been there since she and Tony had gotten back together. He had discussed Emma with his Mom, but she wasn't as welcoming as he had hoped.

Emma continued to think about how she would respond to Mrs. Marella if she was home. She wasn't looking forward to that meeting, but she had to talk with Tony about the knife.

Tony was working afternoons at the Museum helping to put together displays. He had an interest in history and art. He was hoping the part-time job would turn into a full-time position.

She made her way to his family's apartment. Raising her hand to knock, she hesitated. Her nerves got the better of her at the thought of facing his mom, and she started to turn to leave. *Stop it, you must be brave!* She finally knocked and the door swung open quickly. Unfortunately, it was Mrs. Marella.

"Hi Mrs. Marella," Emma said awkwardly.

"Emma," she said stiffly. The lines around her mouth hardened when she saw who was at the door.

"Is Tony here?" Emma asked in a hopeful voice.

Mrs. Marella blocked her entry into the apartment.

When Tony realized who his mom was blocking, he scolded her lightly, "Mom," and kissed her cheek. When she still didn't move to let Emma in, he said in a more commanding voice, "Let her in," and then said to lighten the mood, "Please."

Mrs. Marella sighed, and she moved to the side. She would do anything for Tony and nodded. "Please come in," she said.

Emma stepped in and as Tony grabbed her hand, Emma leaned into him and said, "Tony, we need to talk."

She sounded serious and Tony immediately said. "Mom, we need to go out for a little while."

"Fine, just not too far," Mrs. Marella said in a worried voice.

"Sure, Mom," Tony understood she was just worried about him.

They headed downstairs together, holding hands. When they got to the street Tony turned to face her. "What is it, Emma? Is something wrong?"

She looked very worried and a bit strained. She didn't know how to begin, so she just blurted the situation out. "Miss May did something she shouldn't have, and I think you're the only one that can help her."

Tony frowned. He had known Miss May as long as she had. He knew she meant the world to Emma. "You know I'd do anything for you."

She looked around to see if anyone was watching them. "Tony look at this," she opened her coat and revealed the handle of the knife.

"But that …" he started, shocked at what was before him.

"…is from the Museum's collection," she confirmed. "Miss May thought I might want it and she got it for me."

"She just took it?" he asked in disbelief.

"Yes, and now we need to find a way to return it," she said determinedly.

"Wow," he sat down for a moment on the stoop. "I guess this is where I test how important I am to the Curator." He shook his head, thinking how things can change so quickly.

"Tony, I don't want to destroy your future. I can go in and explain, as best I can, what happened and try to keep Miss May out of jail."

"No," he said, "we said that we're together and that means that we want to protect both of our futures."

He thought for a moment and said, "I have an idea, can you meet me here in the morning, early? You have off tomorrow for deliveries and the bakery?"

"No, I have a special order. I have to go in early and should have it completed by 8am. Is that early enough?" she asked hoping there was a way out of this situation.

"Yes, I'll meet you there and we'll go to the Museum

together. I'll keep the knife with me until then," and indicated for her to hand it to him.

She looked around to make sure no one was watching and when it was safe, she reached in her coat, took out the knife, and handed it to him. He put it into his coat for safekeeping.

CHAPTER 22

They met early at the bakery the next morning, joined hands, and headed toward the Museum. They made it there just as it was opening and went straight to the Curator's office.

He looked a bit surprised to see Tony so early in the day, but was curious enough to inquire, "Tony you're early and who's this with you?"

"Mr. Johnson, this is Emma," indicating Emma at his side. "She's my friend. Emma this is Mr. Johnson, he's the Curator of the Museum. Emma and I wanted to speak with you about something important."

"Emma Evans?" he asks curiously.

"Yes," she said confused as to how he knew her name because she had never met him before this.

"I heard quite a bit about you and your adventures, please call me Philip," he said and his eyes lit up with excitement.

"From who? Tony?" asked Emma, curiously.

Tony shook his head and said, "No."

"No, it was from a few other sources," Philip said waving his hand to indicate it was unimportant. "What can I do for you? Is this about a case? Can I help you with it?"

"Well, not exactly a case but there is something we need help with." She looked at Tony and he removed the knife from his jacket and handed it gingerly to her.

Philip recognized it instantly. "Where did you get that? That's in our collection or, it's supposed to be." He took it carefully from Emma to examine.

"Well, there is a story there," she started to discuss Miss May and Miss Marjorie and their visit, the day before. She also briefly reviewed their past history and how they had reformed.

"I truly believe this was only a slip and with no malicious intent," she stressed.

Philip listened and didn't say anything until she finished.

"All of this happened yesterday and no one noticed?" he mulled this over. "Could you have Miss May and Miss Marjorie come to the Museum to meet with me?"

"Oh no," said Emma starting to get upset, and in turn this upset Tony.

Philip noticed their distress and realized that he had not been clear. "No, I don't want to get them in trouble. What I would like is for them to show me how we can improve our security around the exhibits."

"You won't turn them in for the theft?" she asked hoping that she heard right.

Philip smiled suddenly and said, "What theft? I have everything that belongs to the Museum."

Emma felt a wave of relief wash over her and she reached for Tony's hand. He squeezed it and offered her a soft smile.

Tony breathed a silent sigh of relief and said to Philip, "I'm so appreciative of your patience in the matter."

He looked directly into Tony's eyes and said in a very serious voice, "Tony, we value you as an employee and would like to see you move into a full-time role here. Can you come in at your regular time today and we'll discuss your new hours?"

Tony nodded and said, "I would love to discuss a full-time role."

Philip turned his eyes back to Emma, "Emma can you bring Miss May and Miss Marjorie in tomorrow afternoon?"

Emma answered, "Yes I believe so, but I'll have to speak with them."

With that, they stood and started to take their leave. Philip stopped then with a rather intense statement to Emma, "Emma I would like to hear about some of your adventures one day." Emma nodded as they filed out of the office. Both were dazed by the morning's events.

They were quiet as they headed out. They sat down on the steps outside the Museum. "Wow," she said.

Still dazed by what had just happened, Tony said, "Yes, wow. We thought it could be the end of our careers and instead, we seemed to have had a positive outcome."

"Well, it looks like I'll have to have a long talk with Miss May and Miss Marjorie," said Emma.

"It looks like I'll also have to have a long talk, but with Cousin," he said.

She leaned over and kissed him softly on the lips, "Thank you for being there for me today."

"Emma, I'll always be here for you," he said and kissed her again.

After a moment of looking into each other's eyes, he said, "I have to go finish the morning deliveries and come back here."

They went their separate ways, with Emma heading home and Tony to his deliveries.

Emma wanted to let the ladies know as soon as possible that the police would not be coming to take Miss May to jail. She got there and went to the sitting room. This was the lady's regular location at this time of day.

They both looked up as she entered, looking apprehensive. She smiled to show it wasn't bad news. One look at her face and they seemed to relax.

Miss Marjorie said, "Sit with us," and patted the seat between her and Miss May. "Well, are we in trouble?"

Miss May said stuttering, "No, no it should be only me in trouble."

Emma held up her hands to stop further comments, she alleviated their concerns immediately. "No one is in trouble. Tony and I met with Mr. Johnson, the Museum curator." She explained how the meeting went. "He would like to speak to both of you."

The apprehension was back and both ladies began to speak at once. Emma gave them a second to speak. Miss Marjorie went first, "Oh no, we can't. It might be a trap to get us."

Emma tried to get to the point fast, "No, no it isn't. I think they want to find out how you did it and how they can prevent it from happening in the future." With that, she left them to their discussion about security for the Museum.

The idea of the security consulting made her think of a business opportunity. She thought to herself, *I'm going to get with Tim before we go over. I have an idea about how to do this.*

That night Tim, Dora, and Emma sat down to discuss her business idea.

"So, this type of thing would allow people to work for shorter terms? And we could have a specialist available for different positions," Tim said consideringly.

Emma continued with her idea, "Yes, my thoughts are we could have different types of positions. Security to start, shopkeepers that need additional help during the holidays, clerical, and others. I think we could set it up and have a fee that is paid to our business."

Tim was starting to get excited. "Emma, I think this might

work. We would need to take it slow initially and I'll still need to find a position. I will work on developing this idea."

"But what about Miss May and Miss Marjorie now?" inquired Emma.

Tim conceded, "You're right. We'll do this short-term and use it as a test case for future jobs. If you are all right with-it Emma." She nodded that she was. "I'll go over to the Museum with them and help negotiate the position and responsibilities tomorrow."

Tim thought it best to go down to see one of his accounting professors for some advice on the appropriate amount of pay and get an idea of the paperwork and contracts that would be needed. The key would be to have an organized business proposition ready to review with him. He sent a note to Philip asking for a few more days and suggested a more formal meeting.

The day of the meeting came around and as Tim and Emma were eating lunch at the clubhouse, Tim indicated he needed to make one more private delivery before taking her home and picking up Miss May and Miss Marjorie. Tim continued, "Also, Tony wants to accompany us to the meeting, I'll bring him back with me."

"Okay, Tim, I can wait here, it shouldn't be long?" asked Emma, happy that he was working with Miss May's and Miss Marjorie's new job opportunity.

Tim chucked her under the chin. "I won't be long," he said and headed out.

"Fine, I'll review my observations of this morning's activities and wait for you here," she called after him.

Over the next hour the other delivery boys filtered in and out, some in pairs and some one at a time until eventually, Emma was alone.

It was quiet and she was wrapped up in her writing. She heard another person come in but didn't look up. She was sitting at the table with her legs swinging from the stool she was sitting on, enjoying the quiet time.

Bang! The "boy" had slapped both of his palms down in front of her, pressing his chest into her back.

It made her start and the hairs on her arms stood straight up. She tried to say casually, in a gruff voice, "What are you doing?"

And then he said something that Emma hadn't heard since that 'incident' six years ago. He placed his wet lips on her right ear and whispered, "Want to play little girl?"

Emma was well trained in how to respond to an attack, but she took a moment to clear her mind and remove any emotion from her response. By that one statement, he made it clear he knew who she was and had wanted her to know who he was.

She made a distressed sound to distract him, much like she had that night he had grabbed her previously. He was too close to her for her to access her hidden knife and she did not have her hat with her. She would have to use other methods to fight back and this time WIN!

She utilized the tools she had at hand and this time she would know how to respond. Her hand tightened around the sharpened pencil and she didn't hesitate to ram it into his hand. It cut through like a sharp knife.

He hadn't expected the move and screamed in pain. Before he could pull back his arm, she had planned her next move. She elbowed him in the airway of his neck. This sent him backward, holding his injured hand to his neck and falling to the floor coughing loudly.

She turned toward him and realized she knew him. That fact didn't affect her response.

He was up in seconds, he pulled the pencil out of his hand and onto the floor before he started toward her, "You interfering little bitch, you think you can stop me this time? You think that notebook you're always carrying will save you?"

He brought his fist around and she wasn't able to miss the

hit to her face. The hit threw her into the wall of the clubhouse. It shook as she hit it.

He continued in a venomous voice, "You keep showing up in my life, writing in those damn little notebooks. And you keep ruining my plans. This time I'm going to make sure you don't ever interfere again."

With that statement, she knew this time she would spare no mercy. The emotions she had pushed down for so long, boil over. She came off the wall with two steps and a perfectly aimed sides kick. Her pointed boot made immediate contact with his groin. He went down like a stone. The momentum didn't stop and she picked up a stool, slamming it repeatedly across his back until he stopped moving.

Her legs sank to the ground under her. *My knife!* she thought and started to laugh. Reaching into her pocket she held it in front of her in case he woke up. She wouldn't hesitate to use it.

She thought for a moment about who he was. The man laying in front of her was involved with both the department store burglaries and smuggling operations. He was also the man who almost killed her six years ago. *What was his motivation back then?* she thought. *He had said that she kept interfering in his life. Had she seen something that day, so long ago, that interfered with his plans enough that he needed to kill her? Did he have her notebook from back then?*

She thought it best to wait for Tony and Tim to come back and help clean up the mess. She also didn't want him to get away.

Her face was throbbing, her eye was probably going black and her ribs ached, but she still didn't move from her guard duty.

Tony and Tim were walking back in discussing their deliveries and the afternoon meeting when they noticed the room was tossed about. "Emma!" They looked frantically around, first seeing the man on the floor and then finding Emma next to him.

Tony ran over to Emma first, carefully removing the knife from her hand, and examined her face, "What happened? Are you …"

Emma interrupted him with a stutter, "It was him."

Tony didn't need to ask who "him" was. His eyes went darker and his face pale.

Tim saw what was happening and cut him off, "Tony let me tie him up, you take care of Emma."

Tony realized Emma was shaking and pulled her into his arms.

Tim indicated he needed to go the wagons for some rope. There was usually plenty left over from their deliveries. He came back in and tied up the assailant's hands and feet. He looked at Emma and inquired with worry, "Are you okay? Your face is a bit worse for wear."

Emma started to nod and winced as she said, "I'm okay."

"Let me check it," said Tony as he tilted her head back to get a good look. "It's definitely going to be black. You'll need to put some cool clothes or ice on it today. Any other injuries?"

Emma didn't answer and kept staring at her assailant, half expecting him to spring back up. "Is he?" asked Emma, leaving her question hanging in the air.

"Well, I wouldn't have tied him up if he were dead, would I?" Tim teased her gently. "He's still alive. You did a number on him. I'm proud of you."

"He's starting to come around," Tony observed. He went over to the man and picked up his head until he saw his eyes clear, then he pounded it into the ground. "Oops," he said, "out again." He moved back to Emma's side.

"Okay, who do we contact to help with this?" inquired Tim.

Emma said simply, "Papa."

Tim nodded in agreement and took the wagon to get Ellis.

Papa sent immediate word to Cole to help resolve whatever the situation might be.

Papa arrived and the first thing he did was go to her. He didn't look at the attacker, afraid of what he might do. Cole arrived soon after and went directly to the man down on the floor, where he was able to determine him to still be alive.

Cole was talking directly to Tim and Tony, "What happened here? Fight get out of hand?"

Tim and Tony shook their heads. They told him who he was and then who took him down. Cole looked nonplussed for a moment when he realized Emma had done this.

The man groaned and tried to sit up.

Cole to Papa, "Get her and the boys out of here. We'll work this out."

Papa, Emma, Tim, and Tony vacated the premises, loaded into the wagon, and moved out slowly toward home. Tony held Emma all the way there.

They got back to the boarding house at about 3pm, just as people were starting to get home. The group agreed it would be best to go in the back door. Tim suddenly remembered the appointment they had missed and separated from the group to go in the front door. He needed to first speak with Miss May and Miss Marjorie about the delay.

He found them waiting in the sitting room. They were dressed nicely and thought they were about to leave. He quietly explained that there would be a delay because Emma had been in an accident.

They wanted to see her immediately, but he explained she was fine and would need some rest. They should give her some time before asking about what happened. They nodded, not happy with not being included, but they understood.

He sat down and organized a note to be sent to Mr. Johnson at the Museum. He asked for a delay until the next day for their meeting. He also thought to let him know Tony had a personal matter to attend to this afternoon.

While Tim was organizing the business meeting, the family decided to bring Emma in through the kitchen. Papa had made sure only Dora was in the room when they entered. Tony walked in with Emma close to his chest, hiding her face in his shirt.

Dora was shocked by everyone in her kitchen all at once. But once she saw Emma's face, she immediately went to get a cold compress. "Tell me, what happened." She narrowed her eyes at Tim and Tony looking for some answers. Tim had come in quietly from the dining room.

Emma spoke in a muffled voice for them. "Dora it was him, he went after me again."

"But Emma got him this time," Tony said proudly.

Emma described the events and then asked if she couldn't go to her room to lie down. Dora took her arm and started to walk her to her room. Emma stopped, turned back to Tim, and asked, "Tim, can I go out with you tomorrow on deliveries?"

Tim considered this and shook his head, "How about in a few weeks? Just give yourself a chance to recover."

Emma nodded and said, "Sure. Could you see if you could get my notebook from the clubhouse?"

"Sure Emma. I'll go back later tonight," Tim assured her.

Emma and Dora shuffled off upstairs.

Tim, Tony, and Papa sat for a moment. Tim told Tony he had taken care of the Museum notifications. Tony nodded, not concerned about his job at this time, he was where he needed to be.

Tony looked at Papa and asked, "What happens next?"

"I trust Cole. He'll take care of it," stated Papa in a firm voice.

Back at Pinkerton's office

"Hassey what did you find out?" Cole asked his lead investigator.

"The name is Zeke Jones. Looks like a lifetime criminal. He's tied to that gambling club and several burglaries in the area. He must know someone important, he has yet to go to jail here. We did find arrest warrants in New York and New Jersey for him. Looks like he likes to beat up women on a regular basis," said Hassey completing his report.

Cole took a deep breath and released it before stating, "Good, then we don't have to include any of Ellis's family. Let's wrap this up. Take him to the doctor and get him patched up. I'll make notifications to the New York and New Jersey authorities. Let's keep this quiet and move him out as soon as he is stable."

Hassey nodded and was on his way to the doctor that was treating Zeke. He was able to confirm he could be moved. They had him on the way to New York on the early train the next morning.

CHAPTER 23

*E*mma lay back in the tub as she let her aching shoulders get some heat and held a wet rag to her bruised face. She stayed in for a long time. When she finally had enough, she dried off and climbed into bed, her face and her ribs throbbing.

Dora came up with a tray and a towel wrapped around some ice, a few hours later but Emma was fast asleep. She placed the towel on her face and took the tray back downstairs, not wanting to disturb her.

Tim, Tony, and Papa were still in the kitchen. Dinner had come and gone. They had kept information pertaining to the event within their small group. Her absence from dinner wasn't mentioned, it was common knowledge that Emma would miss occasional meals due to the cases she was working on.

They also updated Miss May and Miss Marjorie there had been an accident on Emma's delivery route and she was fine. They asked the ladies to keep it quiet for now. They looked a bit dubious at this explanation but did not interfere.

Later that evening, Emma came down the back stairs to the kitchen and heard the group talking.

Tim said, "What are we going to do to keep Emma safe?"

She started to barge in when she heard that, but the next person to speak was Tony and he said, "I think she did an excellent job of that on her own this afternoon."

Emma surprised everyone when she came in and went directly to Tony, and hugged him. "Thanks, Tony." Tony hugged her tightly back.

Tony stood up and tilted her face to get a good look at the blackened eye, "Feeling better?"

She said quietly, adoring him with her eyes, "Yes."

"Emma," Papa said quietly, "could you stay down here with me for a moment?"

Emma looked over and said simply, "Yes Papa."

That statement had a clearing effect on the room. Tim and Tony found a reason to leave. Tim squeezed Dora's hand as he headed out. Dora excused herself and retired to her room.

That left Emma with Papa. "Emma, come sit by me," he said as he patted the chair beside him.

Emma moved over and sat down, "Papa, I'm okay."

"This isn't about that," said Papa. "I had already planned to have you around for the next few weeks. I have a large code project due and I need to have you here to review and confirm my calculations."

Emma was silent, which was unusual. Papa continued with a smile and a twinkle in his eye and said, "It also has the added benefit of me keeping an eye on you."

Emma paused for a moment and admitted, "I would really like to do that Papa. I think I could use a break and some time at home."

Papa didn't know he was holding his breath until Emma agreed. He breathed out slowly. "All right then," he murmured.

"Emma," he said directly to her, "Meet me in my lab after breakfast in the morning to get started on the drawing review." He knew that she would want to keep busy.

"Yes Papa, I'll be there," Emma responded.

Emma got another towel and some ice out of the icebox to place on her face. She slowly made her way upstairs, keeping her shaking hands on the towel. Once in her room, she laid the towel down and looked at her hands. Emma felt a bit like she was breaking on the inside. She sank to her bed, laid down, and cried herself to sleep. She felt Dora climb in and hold her into the night.

The next morning, she woke up feeling refreshed and shook off any effects she might have been feeling. Dora had already gotten up and started her day.

She sat up slowly and thought to herself, *I beat the devil*. That made her straighten up her shoulders and know that she could move on. This gave her a spring in her step as she washed up, and got dressed in a light blue skirt and a frilly blouse. She started to put on her stockings when she caught a view of herself in the mirror.

Standing, she approached it slowly and leaned forward to get a good look at her jaw and eye, both were black and blue. It was still sore as she touched it hesitantly. *Oh, well*, she thought and continued to put her stocking and boots on to head downstairs.

She noticed her notebook was on the side table, Tim must have brought it over early this morning. Picking it up, she fingered the articles she had placed there. Maybe today was the day to ask Papa about them and why he had kept them. She folded them up and placed them back into her notebook. She headed downstairs with a determined expression.

The sun was not up yet as she made her way down to help with breakfast and met Amy and Dora in the kitchen. Dora was working on making bread.

"Well, you look quite nice today Emma," said Amy.

"Thank you," and noticed Emma's eye. "Are you okay?" asked Amy in a worried voice.

"I am fine, just an accident during my deliveries yesterday," commented Emma. "Thanks for asking."

Dora squinted her eyes at Emma. "Sister, what are your plans for the day?"

"I'm taking a few weeks off at the bakery and deliveries to help Papa finish his project," stated Emma somewhat rigidly.

"But..." started Dora.

Emma interrupted, "I know what you're going to say that I'm being irresponsible. Papa sent word to Cousin and Tim last night, they know not to expect me for a while."

"I know Cousin will miss you," Dora said absently, working her bread, folding it over and over in the flour on the kitchen table. "He mentioned that dessert you make has been ordered again this week."

"That dessert," said Emma in exasperation, "it seems all I do lately is make that dessert. Okay, for Cousin, I'll make it here." She mulled that over while she helped put together the morning meal.

After breakfast, she was still thinking about that dessert when she when downstairs. For some reason, she always thought of the night of the fire when that dessert was ordered. She turned off that thought for now and called to Papa in his study, "I'm here, Papa I'm ready to work."

"Over here." The drawings were set up on the drafting table with a high stool. The drafting table was tilted and several gas lights were being utilized for the close work. She worked diligently through the morning comparing the drawing to the required fire codes. It would be tedious work for the next two weeks, but it kept her occupied and she needed that for now.

CHAPTER 24

*L*ater that week, Cousin sent the request for her to make the dessert for the next day's deliveries. He apologized and would send along the ingredients that evening. There would be a bonus expected for making it that night.

Emma shrugged and said if she could do this at home it would be okay. She asked Dora if she could use the kitchen that evening.

"Sure," replied Dora, "I'll help, that way we can share gossip."

They both worked on the dessert and had it cooling on the kitchen table for delivery the next day. Emma had a note sent to Tim to help her get the special delivery to the customer tomorrow.

The next day, she was working code work for Papa when she noticed it was about time to take the special delivery to the customer. She got ready but did not switch into her boy clothes. She didn't expect to be out very long. Out of habit, when she dressed, she attached her sheath to her thigh and slid the knife in. She also grabbed her hat and made sure the larger knife was secure. She went downstairs to wait for Tim.

As he pulled up, he noticed she was in her girl clothes. "No delivery clothes today? Do you want me to deliver it for you?" he offered, knowing she was probably still sore.

"No, I'm good. It'll be nice to get some air and it's just the one delivery." With that, she handed him the box to place on the seat. She could carry it with them.

Tim had completed all of his deliveries for the bakery and had a few business items to do that afternoon.

"Tim, was Mr. Johnson, at the Museum, all right with the delay? I'm sorry that I caused problems with our new business."

Tim pulled the wagon over, "Emma, that was in no way your fault, and no apologies are necessary. Tony explained what happened to Mr. Johnson." She started to interrupt, worried that someone outside of the family was involved.

Tim assured her, "No worries, Tony says we can trust him."

Emma knew that Tony could read people and if he trusted Mr. Johnson then she trusted him.

"What about Tony missing time on his first full day," she said worriedly. "Tony hasn't mentioned it to me."

"He's just being protective of you. I'm sure if you asked, he will tell you."

"Yes," she said quietly, knowing Tony would do anything for her.

They both fell silent as they started moving again. A few minutes later, a boy ran up next to the wagon with a note for Tim.

He scanned it quickly and said, "Emma I have to leave you with the last delivery of the day. I think I have an interview for an accounting position. It says I need to apply in person, immediately."

She asked, puzzled, "At this very moment? Now?"

"Yes, I haven't had one yet. I guess it happens this way. Listen I really have to get going, I'll need to clean up some," he said as he pulled up to the final delivery location. He tied the reins up and jumped down to help her retrieve the dessert. The delivery was to a local shop, one she didn't think was opened as yet.

"Now, just don't go in. If needed place it on the outside. Agreed?" he asked.

"Yes, it should be fine."

"How will you get back?" he asked, concerned that she might need help.

"I can walk or take the trolley."

"Okay, good," he said satisfied with that answer.

He handed her the large dessert and once he was sure she could carry it, he climbed back on his wagon and waved and said, "See you."

"See you and good luck."

And off they went their separate ways.

Emma walked the next three blocks balancing the dessert.

Her watcher was still around, he was always on top of any deviation to schedule, especially around the gambler's road area. She walked past him. There was no mistaking what she was carrying and who it was for. *Why was she alone? Tim normally accompanied her*, he thought worriedly. He started to trail closer than he ever had, something was up and he had to intervene prior to something happening. It was time now for her to meet her watcher.

The streets were still busy with lunch traffic. She passed the large department store on her left and looked in the windows. The glass in the window was shiny and created a mirror effect. She saw the watcher before she rounded the corner. She tossed the dessert to the ground and was ready for him when his arm came around her pinning her against the alley. She stayed silent and watchful.

"Sister," he whispered. "I'm here to help."

Emma's eyes opened wide when she realized who it was following her. He loosened his grip on her arm but did not let her go.

Immediately images flooded into her mind. Seeing him in the alley by her house, doorways near the bakery, all along her delivery route. It was the little man who seemed to be everywhere and even at the church dance. He was always around but never felt like a threat to her. She started leaving him a basket of food for him in the morning and pie for him to find in the evening.

She didn't feel threatened but questioned why with a raised brow. He grabbed her hand and answered simply, as he fast-walked her down the alley, "Your Mama was my best friend."

She pulled him to a stop and snatched the hat off of his head. More memories flooded her senses. She could see him in front of her as he had been then, a small compact man with reddish hair and a freckled face that would turn red when he talked to Mama.

"Thomas Callahan," she said finally. It came out in a little girl's voice, remembering how nice he had always been.

That man was very different now, his skin scarred from burns. Unfortunately, since the great fire, there were a large number of people walking around with similar scars. But behind all of those scars were the same eyes of the man who adored mama all those years ago.

"I think that you're being set up," Tom said in a worried voice.

"Why?" she said still shocked by Tom's appearance at that moment, not realizing he was still pulling her with him at a fast walk.

"Because of that damn dessert. Trouble flows with it. When I realized it was being ordered on a continuing basis, I knew that HE was around," said Tom hurriedly over his shoulder.

"Who is HE?" asked Emma, finally coming out of the shock of seeing Tom.

He continued his story, not answering her question. They had kept walking quickly using back streets and alleys, but had not gotten out of the area where the social club was located. "I was in the front of the bakery when she was working on that special dessert in the back. I heard something in the kitchen and listened to see if she was okay. Before I knew it…"

Tom was interrupted by a deep gravelly voice from farther down the alley, "And she was okay, at that time, but she wouldn't listen." Tom stopped abruptly with Emma slamming into his back.

Two men stepped out of the shadows and blocked their exit. A man came up behind him but stayed in the shadows.

"Wait," said Emma to the man she could see. "I recognize you. You sometimes pick up that dessert that I make." There was no response from any of the three tall men.

"I knew," said Tom in a hard tone at the shadowed figure. "I knew you were in town again when that dessert started being ordered. I've been looking for you. It's time for you to accept responsibility for what happened to Mary."

"Yes, that damn dessert. I do love it though," the man said as he stepped out of the shadows, revealing his face for the first time. "Too bad we're going to have to get rid of you both, like we got rid of Mary. Maybe, you can give me the recipe before I handle this situation."

Emma recognized John Harden as soon as she saw his face. He was infamous enough to have hand-drawn pictures of him scattered around local police offices. He had also been missing for years and was assumed dead in the big fire.

"Take them both," his two henchmen grabbed her and Tom.

"Bring them to the tunnels. I'll meet you there. I can't afford to be seen with them."

The men holding her and Tom did not know that Emma could defend herself. She had her two knives with her and she did not volunteer the information to them. The men tied up Tom but did not tie her up.

Stupid men, she thought to herself.

Tom had been watching Emma for a long time and knew that she was up to something. He would wait and see if he could help. They were tossed into a covered cab.

Emma's hands were free. She reached up to grab her knife from her hat. The cab was made of a material that could be cut and she would have to be fast. Holding up her fingers to her lips, she made a sign to Tom to keep quiet. Next, she cut Tom's binding around his hands and immediately turned to the side away from the men and cut the carriage fabric with a long arc of her arm. The material gave as Tom and Emma move through it. When they hit the ground, they took off at a run down the street.

The buggy rocked, enough that one of the men said, "What are they trying to do, knock it over?"

The other man looked into the cab and could see a gaping hole. "Shit."

He glanced down the street just as Tom and Emma ducked into an alley. The men gave chase after them and both were thinking, *The boss will not take kindly to the two getting loose.* They ran until they got to the alley where Emma and Tom had disappeared.

One of the henchmen grabbed the other by the arm to stop him and said, "So, I hear New York is a good place for businessmen like us."

The other nodded in agreement and both headed to the train station. They knew better than to stick around and be responsible for this mess. The two men made it safely to the station and onto a train out of town before the boss found out what had occurred.

Tom and Emma kept running until she pulled him to a side street to catch their breaths. Emma thought to herself, *I have enough evidence and an eyewitness to finally bring John Harden and his crew down. I know who we can use to help us.*

Emma looked around and determined that the Tribune offices were the closest to their location. *It will have to be Daniel,* she thought. *If there was one man who could help it would be the person who helped her Mama.* They exited the alley and she indicated he follow her. They quickly ran to the paper's offices. It was after hours so there were only a few people around.

Emma hadn't told Tom where they were headed and he appeared hesitant to enter the paper's office. She pulled on his arm to get him moving and they entered the back entrance. The evening paper had already gone out and the reporters had finished their job for the day. The room was empty leading directly to Daniel's office, they ran for the door and both were startled when Daniel opened it.

"Well, Emma, what a lovely surprise, won't you come in?" He indicated for them to come in with a sweeping motion.

Odd, thought Emma, *he didn't seem to be surprised to see her there.* She was too relieved to think about that for long.

"Sit, sit," he said to both of them. "Tell me why you have come to see me."

Tom seemed shocked and could only stare at Daniel, but Emma attributed that to the excitement of being held captive and the chase.

Emma started describing what had happened to them and how it might be connected to the cases described in the original articles he and Mama worked on.

"So," he said, drumming his fingers on the desk, "you both know everything."

"Yes," Emma said. "I think we can put it together and take it to the Pinkertons."

"Well," he said, a knock on the door stopped him, "my other guest has arrived." He moved from behind the desk to open the door and found the head of the gang that Emma had just been detailing the crimes of. John Harden came into the room.

Emma sat as shocked as Thomas and just opened her mouth but words did not come out.

When Daniel saw her shock he said, "Well I guess this is a lot to take in." He focused his next comment on John, "I told you she would come here."

"Yes, you did," said John laconically. "What do we do with them now? Do we take them to the tunnels and out to the club?"

Emma watched their interaction, realizing that the obvious person in charge was Daniel. Emma mulled over the facts silently and asked herself, *"How long had this been going on? Did Mama know?"*

"Yes, tie both of their hands this time." He looked pointedly at John. "This is Mary's daughter and she's just as clever as she was."

Everyone seemed to be waiting for Daniel to take the lead. Emma tried to make sense of it all and said, "Daniel I don't understand, you were Mama's friend. She was the source of your articles."

Daniel ignored her and looked at the gangster. "Bind their mouths also. I'll go with you to the club basement."

Emma and Tom had their hands bound and their mouths covered as they made their way through the newspaper office to the basement. The tunnels at the paper connected to the ones at the social club. They made their way through in mostly darkness. The men leading the way had vast knowledge of the layout.

Smugglers, thought Emma, connecting even more cases with John and Daniel.

Emma recognized the tunnels they were in and was not surprised it was the social club basement that they were pushed into. John said to his henchmen, "Grab those two chairs and move them over here." They moved the chairs and pushed Emma and Tom into them.

Daniel said briskly, "I've got this."

John gave him a look and said, "Yeah, like last time. Just don't make a mess down here. By the way, what happened to Zeke? I thought you said he would take care of this for us."

Daniel seemed bored with the topic and said laconically, "Complications evidently. Looks like we have a labor problem."

Another connection, thought Emma. *The man who attacked me was attached to this group. Were they connected to both attacks?*

John and his men went upstairs, he paused and leaned on the rail to say, "Daniel, you might want to remove her hat." He pointed at Emma.

Daniel took his advice and before Emma knew what happening he grabbed her hat and sent it flying across the room. "I think I'll take this. I'm aware that's where you keep that lethal knife you like so much."

Daniel had silently removed a pistol from his jacket and had it trained on Emma and Thomas. He kept it on both of them and he removed their mouth bindings.

Emma was watching Daniel closely. She was also working on loosening the ropes on her wrist. *Thank you, Miss May,* she thought.

"Are you going to tell me why you have brought us here?" asked Emma in a soft voice, continuing to work on her ropes.

"Yes," Daniel's deep voice reverberated through the room. "You're turning out to be just like your mother, creating havoc in my businesses. We made such a team her and I. She created an opportunity for me to get rich and I wanted it. I tried to include her in my plans for the future but she disagreed."

"What do you mean disagreed? You discussed this with her?"

"Of course," he said. "By controlling crime and the news at the same time, I would be able to have anything in the world I wanted. I also thought we made a good team and that she could be part of this enterprise. She chose no and she wanted to turn me and John into the authorities. We couldn't let that happen."

Emma frowned, "What do you mean, you couldn't let that happen?"

Tom chose that moment to lose control and yelled, "He killed her and tried to kill me that night." Tom's chair shook as he tried to untie his hands and get to Daniel.

Emma stopped moving when she heard Tom's statement. Emma sent a frantic glance to Tom and he nodded an affirmative.

Daniel didn't react to Tom's statement. He very calmly said, "The fire that night was fortuitous, we were able to use it as a cover-up. We were planning to take care of her eventually, but the fire started and moved our schedule up."

"But why," asked Emma, "why did you take her from us?"

"She was in my way," he said simply. "Your mama knew everything I knew about John's business operation."

"You mean crime organization," corrected Emma.

He acknowledged her with a nod, "Yes, crime organization." His voice started to take on a harder edge, "I tried to explain to her that we could manage from the inside of the organization, to clean it up while being part of it. I could already see that controlling the media would control the narrative the people saw and believed. I would control the narrative and John would move his operations underground."

"Mama saw through that," Emma guessed correctly.

"Yes," Daniel acknowledged regretfully. "I met with John and we made a deal, we two. I would continue to move up at the paper, with him providing the occasional criminal element to use as a patsy. The plans changed after Mary died. We decided I would oversee operations here and he would go to New York to set up shop there."

"Was the fire in the plan?"

"No, no," he said shaking his head, "the fire happening, was just a case of being at the right place at the right time. We were arguing with Mary when we noticed the room was hotter than normal. The beam became dislodged and almost hit us. I took the opportunity the falling beam provided and hit Mary on the back of the head with a rolling pin. We placed her under the beam and the room continued to fill with smoke. We got out just in time."

"Was my mother dead when you left her there? Did you even check?"

"No. She stood in my way and I couldn't allow that."

As he kept freely explaining the details of his business, Emma realized that he didn't plan on keeping them alive. She kept a shocked expression on her face while continuing to work on the ropes and plans to end Daniel's life. She got the ropes loosened enough to remove them. She just had to get to her knife that was strapped to her leg.

Tom chose that moment to provide the distraction she needed and spit at Daniel. As he started to shout at Daniel, Emma slipped out of her ropes. "You were always low, so low. You were never good enough for her. She was a better person than you."

Daniel, who had ignored Tom until now, put his full focus on the man. "Why do you look familiar?" Daniel snatched the hat off of Tom's head. Like with Emma, Tom's ginger hair gave him away.

"You! But, you're dead!"

As Daniel wiped the spit off of his face his calm demeanor seemed to dissolve in front of them. His hands started shaking and his face darkened to an odd purple color. "You a little nobody. You were always with her, like her guardian angel. I couldn't take one step toward her without you there blocking me."

He seemed to be back in another time when Mama was alive and what stood in his way –again was Thomas.

He seemed to forget he had a gun in his hand and dropped it when he grabbed Tom by the throat and started choking him. His eyes were starting to bulge and his face turned purple.

Emma took that moment to slip her hand into her skirt and retrieve her knife from her leg sheath. She called out to Daniel sounding eerily like her mother, "Daniel."

Daniel stopped choking Thomas for a moment and turned expecting to see Mary. She didn't pause and threw it with purpose toward Daniel's chest. He hadn't expected a knife to be thrown his way and stood there looking incredulously at it lodged in his chest. He fell forward onto Tom.

Emma ran over to remove his hands from Tom's neck and pushed Daniel's prone body to the floor. Tom's head was rolling back against the wall. She propped up his head and rubbed his face and neck. He was starting to come around, he looked at her and smiled as she untied him, "It's like being with your mama again."

The first door to open was the one from the tunnel and the Pinkerton detectives flooded into the room with guns drawn. Cole and Jeremy led the charge and stopped abruptly when they saw the body on the floor. Cole glanced wryly at Emma, "I am a bit late to the party again?"

Emma nodded.

She ended up in a bear hug from Jeremy while Cole and his men rushed in. "Emma are you okay?" asked Jeremy.

"Yes, but Tom needs some help," she said, indicating to him with her hand.

Cole called out, "We need a doctor down here." He called out to the group, after checking Daniel's pulse, "This man is dead."

The doctor was brought in and as he checked Tom out,

Emma was thinking, "I don't regret throwing the knife and I'm glad he didn't survive. The world is better off without some people."

At that moment the door at the top of the stairs opened and police in blue flocked down the stairs.

She and Tom tried to explain how they had ended up there, who Daniel was and what he had done. The entire room went quiet when two dark figures showed up at the top of the stairs. One was closely followed by another.

The first man was John Harden, *He had not gotten away,* thought Emma. She was relieved and she thought wryly, *I can finally stop making that dessert.*

More surprisingly though, it was the Police Chief that was escorting John Harden. He looked right at Emma and said, "I told you I would take care of it, girlie." And for the first time, he smiled.

She knew immediately who he favored, he was the police officer relative of the flower shop owner. *Guess I was wrong about him. I had the good guys and the bad guys mixed up. I still have a lot to learn,* she thought.

John Harden was in handcuffs and was waiting for the police officer to remove him from the premises. He looked over at Emma and said softly, "You know I really was only in the room when he killed her. I didn't participate."

"But you were there," Emma said more of a statement than a question.

"Yes. I'm sorry for being involved even a little in the loss of your Mama. I'm not sorry to be out from under Daniel's thumb. If you need anything you come find me."

"Won't that be hard for a long time?"

"Well, you never know."

"No, you don't," she agreed softly.

The Police Chief escorted him back upstairs.

Papa and Dora arrived minutes later; Jeremy had sent out some men to pick them up.

Papa shook his head as if to clear it, "I don't understand. What happened here?" Dora hugged Emma close.

Emma spoke up, "Well to answer that Papa, let me introduce you to my constant shadow," she pointed at Thomas. Papa had never gotten close enough to see the shadow's face. But now…

"Thomas?" Papa said brokenly, seeing Thomas brought back Mary. "You-you have been watching my Emma all along?"

Tom wiped his hands across his eyes and said, "They took Mary away from us, I had to keep Emma safe. She's turning out just like Mary," He smiled as he took in the chaos of the room.

Emma continued the story and went on to tell Papa and Dora about Daniel and John Harden and how they had worked together after Daniel had killed Mama. When Papa heard it had not been the fire but it had been Daniel that killed his Mary, he felt an impotent range knowing Daniel was already dead.

"What about John Harden, what will happen to him?" Papa asked thinking he could expend his rage on the man.

Cole saw Papa's response to the news that John was still available for retribution and wanted to stop it there. "Ellis, he'll be going to prison and will get what is coming to him. I've contacted state officials in the governor's office to send a special council down. This will be taken care of properly," he promised.

Emma could see the information noticeably calmed Papa. His hands unclenched and his mouth settled into a more relaxed line.

Papa and Cole headed upstairs to talk to the Police Chief about her role in the death and how to make sure she didn't get into any trouble.

CHAPTER 25

Tony came to the boarding house as soon as he heard about the events at the social club. Later Tony would tell her that Jeremy sent him to her. Emma hadn't really reacted to the events that had taken place until Tony rushed into the boarding house, almost knocking Papa down as he went straight to Emma. Until that moment all of the events that had happened had not penetrated her calm. But once she was in Tony's arms she started to cry and cry. Papa shooed everyone out of the room and Dora pulled the sliding doors closed on the study to give them privacy.

When the tears had slowed down Tony took out his handkerchief to blot her eyes. "Better now?" he asked quietly. "Did you have the adventure you always wanted?"

Emma nodded. "But it was a little more real than expected."

"What will you do now?" Tony asked.

"Sleep," she mumbled tiredly.

"No, I mean long-term," he said.

"Working at the bakery and delivery driving for now. I have some thoughts for the future, maybe school," she said, leaning against him.

"Any more case work?" he asked.

"I don't think I'll search it out, but if something comes up, then I'll see," she murmured.

Tony nodded looking thoughtful. He had something for her but would give her some time to rest before bringing it up.

Their lives settled back to normal and the days became routine. There was one positive change, Thomas walked next to her and Tony on their way to the bakery each morning. She had gotten him a job helping with the storeroom and a room at the boarding house. He would still be close by if Emma needed him.

She admitted to herself, a few weeks later, that she was getting a bit bored. During their long evening walk she mentioned to Tony she could use something to work on.

He stopped and looked at her consideringly. "I may have something for you to look into."

"Really?" she asked, her voice curious, not upset. "You're not usually wanting me to be involved in a case. What caused the change in attitude?"

"I honestly was scared that you would get hurt, but after your last case, I see that you can handle yourself," he explained.

"Thank you," she said sincerely.

He kissed her softly. She saw a bench up ahead and motioned to it with her hand. He nodded as they reached the bench, and they sat down.

"Okay, what's the case?" she asked, wanting to hear more.

"It's Marco. He says there's something odd going on at a house where he, dad, and David are working."

"Odd in what way?" she asked puzzled.

He shrugged and said, "He isn't sure, just a weird feeling in the house. He thinks they're hiding something."

"I'm not that busy and I am due some days off. Any idea how I can get into the house?" she asked drumming her fingers on her lips.

"Dad and his crew are still working piping if you want to be a general helper," he suggested.

She crinkled her nose at him. "General helper? Is that cleanup duty?"

"Yeah, but Dad is aware of why you're going to be there," he assured her.

She came to a quick decision. "Okay, when do I start?"

"I think Monday will be soon enough," he laughed. They took the weekend to rest and relax.

Emma was getting ready for her dinner with Tony's family on Sunday night to discuss the case. A knock sounded on her bedroom door, she called, "Come in."

Dora entered saying in a firm voice, "Emma, I need to talk with you."

Emma answered without looking over at her, "Dora, I don't have time. I'm going to Tony's for dinner to discuss a new case."

"You're avoiding me," Dora accused.

"No Dora, I'm not," Emma said trying to keep her voice level.

"You're not looking me in the eyes," Dora said watching her closely.

A flash of anger went through her and Emma looked her directly in the eyes saying, "Is that better?"

"You're being obstinate. You know that I want to talk about Mama and what happened with Daniel. Every time I ask about it, you're on your way out or you're too busy."

"Well, I don't want to talk about it," muttered Emma.

"Do you think that's fair?" asked Dora in a shrill voice, letting her emotions come through.

"I don't think anything about this situation was fair," Emma said honestly, hoping to end the conversation there. "Can we talk about this some other time?"

Dora took a deep breath and let it out slowly before saying, "If I give you time, will you finally speak with me?"

Emma didn't want to commit to anything, not yet, and said, "I'll try."

"Fine. Work your case," Dora said abruptly and left the room.

Emma sat heavily on the bed, looking down, wishing she could talk to Dora about what happened. She just wasn't ready. She hated when they fought. There had been times over the years when one sister would slight the other and arguments would ensue. They had always been resolved with one or the other admitting wrong. But who was wrong in this case?

She got up and finished getting ready, wiping a tear away. She shook her head and gathered her bag to head down to pick up the dessert she had made earlier for Tony.

Dora was in the kitchen busy preparing dinner when Emma entered. She didn't look up to see who entered and commented without looking up, "It's in the box over there."

"Thanks for boxing it for me," Emma said softly.

Dora just sent a muffled reply back, continuing to work on the vegetables she was peeling.

Emma wanted to say more and wished they were in a better place. She shrugged, picked up the box, and headed out to get her bike. Tony had said his mom was making spaghetti for dinner and she was looking forward to it.

Emma loved the cold air on her face as she was riding over. Her mind cleared as she made her way to the apartment. Jumping off her bike, she put it on her shoulder and carried the desert by its strings with her other hand. She made her way into the apartment building and when she knocked, Enzo had run to the door to let her in.

"Hi Enzo," said Emma cheerfully.

"Hi Emma, we're having spaghetti tonight," he said importantly.

"I heard that," she remarked wryly.

Tony came up and kissed her on the cheek, "Hi Emma."

"Tony," she murmured back in greeting, looking into his eyes.

"Maybe we'll skip dinner," said Tony, seeing that look.

That thought was interrupted by Michael calling, "Tony bring that girl in here. Dinner's almost ready."

"On our way in," he called back as he took the bike from her and put it in the hall closet.

He saw the box she was carrying and asked, "Dessert? What kind?"

"It's a Bee Sting cake," she answered.

"Well, then we might want to stay for dinner and then we go for a long walk after," he teased.

He took the box in one hand and her hand in the other and walked her to the living room. Marco, Enzo, David, and Michael were on the couches and floor reading the paper.

Marco jumped up when he saw her enter. "Emma, thanks for helping with our job this week."

Tony broke off from the group to take the dessert to the kitchen and returned to Emma's side a moment later.

"I don't mind. I got time off from the bakery and delivery wagon." She looked over at Mr. Marella and said, "Michael, I hear I'm going to be helping out this week."

Michael smiled, "Well, I don't think I'll have you pipefitting but I can keep you busy." He held out his hand to her saying, "It's very good to see you."

She smiled at him, taking his hand in hers. She was happy that he was looking like himself again. She leaned over and kissed him on the cheek. "I'm looking forward to spending time with you all this week."

Mrs. Marella came into the room and smiled genuinely at Emma saying, "Emma the dessert looks amazing." Their relationship had suffered when Emma and Tony stopped seeing each other, but the favor Emma did for Michael showed her that Emma truly loved her family.

Emma went over and hugged her saying, "I'm looking forward to your spaghetti."

"That's good because it is ready. Come over everyone."

Mrs. Marella slipped an arm around Emma's waist and walked to the table with her. As they all sat down, blessings were said and they began eating. The food was wonderful and the conversation light.

After dinner, they moved back into the living room and sat down. Emma pulled out her notebook and turned to look at Michael, Marco, and David saying. "Tell me your concerns with the family."

Michael and David looked at Marco. He shrugged and said, "I don't know, it just doesn't feel right."

She thought about that, tapping her pencil on her notebook, and said, "Okay, let's try this, who lives in the house?"

"Mr. Saunders owns the house and is paying us to upgrade it," said Michael.

"Don't forget about his son James coming back," commented David.

"Coming back?" asked Emma, getting curious about this family.

"Yes, James joined the Union Army and he was reported to have died in 1865 at the end of the war. His father had taken it badly and his wife died soon after they heard the news," David continued.

"It must be nice for him to have James back in his life," said Emma.

"Yes, you would think so," commented David.

She heard the caution in that statement and asked, "Have you seen James and Mr. Saunders talk or interact?"

"Not really. They only talk behind closed doors," commented Michael.

"What has James done for work since he returned?" she asked continuing to take notes.

"He doesn't seem to do much," commented David.

"Now David, I disagree with that," said Michael slowly, "he's often working in the garden when Mr. Saunders isn't there."

"What is he doing in there?" asked Emma.

Michael consider the question for a moment and replied, "I'm not sure but he seems to be working with the individual plants."

"Okay, got it, who else lives in the house?" she asked.

"Abigail, James' wife, Mara their daughter, and Christopher their son," replied Marco.

"Can you tell me about each one?" she asked marking down the different names.

"What kind of things?" asked Michael.

"What do they look like; hair color, height, and ages?"

David started, "Well the son, Christopher has brown eyes, dark brown hair, and is about twelve years old. He's sweet but seems different."

"Different how?" she inquired, curious about any differences they could detect.

"I don't know, a little slow maybe? Cheerful kid though," finished David.

"Yes," said Michael, "he always wants to help bring in supplies and will talk your ear off."

"Next?" she asked.

Michael answered, "Abigail the mom, dark brown hair like Christopher's, though the eyes are different, blue, I think. She is average height, similarly to Doris," indicating Mrs. Marella, "and a similar build. Nice but keeps to herself. Oh, and she takes care of the cooking for the family."

"Is there help for the house?" asked Emma.

"Yes, a maid, Mandy. She's a small woman and kind of plain. Dark blonde hair, she doesn't seem to be able to brush it properly. She looks like she's in her thirties," commented Marco.

"There's a daughter?" asked Emma reviewing her list.

David grinned and said, "You should definitely ask Marco about her. I am sure HE has all the details."

Marco went bright red at the teasing, but answered, "She's about sixteen and she has long, lighter brown hair that curls on the sides of her face..." his voice drifted off and Emma cleared her throat to get his attention. "She's about 5'3, slim build." He finished up the description quickly.

Michael was smiling and shaking his head in response to Marco's description.

"Mr. Saunders?" she prompted the group.

Michael answered. "His name is Walter. He's older but still very much mobile and very intelligent. I am honestly surprised that he stepped down from his job at the Pullman Cars factory as early as he did."

"Whose idea were the changes in the house that you're working on?" Emma asked wondering who was paying the bills for the family.

"They were Mr. Saunders' ideas. He wanted the best for his reunited family," answered Michael.

Marco and David nodded in agreement

"Does everyone get along? Is there any strife?" asked Emma.

Michael looked concerned when he said, "Initially I would have said no. When he had me over for the job, he talked about how happy he was his son had returned. How much he wished his wife had lived long enough to see their son had survived."

"Did something change?" she asked.

"I think you should go in and observe them, get your own impressions," said Michael.

"Agreed," commented Emma, as she closed her notebook and held out her hand to Tony. "Walk me home?"

He smiled at her taking her hand in his. They said their goodbyes and they walked home. He walked her bike with him as they made their way there.

"What do you think?" asked Tony.

She hesitated a moment before answering, "Not much right now. It could be that the family is trying to adjust to being together after a long separation. I keep thinking what if my mama just showed up after we had been told she was dead. I can't imagine the emotions that are going through them at this time."

"Yes." Tony had never experienced loss like Emma's family and the Saunders family have experienced. Tony and Emma were quiet on the way home, lost in their thoughts.

They kissed and parted ways with Tony's saying, "I'll put your bike up. Be sure to meet dad and the boys at our house in the morning."

She nodded and said, "Goodnight." She entered the house, thinking about the case. Dora called to her from the sitting room.

"Hi Dora, up late?" Emma asked trying to not start another fight.

"Not too much, I thought I would wait for you," she answered sounding more like herself.

"Hmmm," Emma murmured as she sat in a chair facing the couch where Dora was sitting.

"So, what is the new case about?" Dora asked, curiously.

Emma went over it briefly.

Dora asked, "What do you think?"

"I'm not sure right now, every case is different. I'll have to be patient and observe," commented Emma.

"Well, you're good at that," Dora said with a quiet voice.

"Yes," Emma said in the same tone.

"Will you be undercover?" Dora asked.

"No, I'll wear work clothes but I'll be a girl on this job and no hiding of anything, including my name," said Emma.

"I'll have your lunch ready for you to take. What time will you be leaving?" Dora asked.

"I confirmed with Michael, since we don't want to disturb

the family, we start at 9am. I'll meet them at Tony's house and ride over with Michael and the boys," Emma said as she stood up and started to leave the room.

Dora stopped her abruptly with a hand on her arm and said, "You know I'm still angry with you about Mama, but," when Emma started to interrupt, she frowned. "I'll give you some time to think before I ask again."

Emma thought a moment and said, "So will you stay angry with me until I talk about what you want to talk about."

"Emma," she sighed deeply. "My anger will eventually turn into disappointment. Disappointment that you won't share something personal with both of us. Will you please think about that?"

"I will." Emma felt suddenly lonely without her sister, even though she was next to her.

"I'm going up now," said Dora. "Will you be coming up soon?"

"In a moment," Emma said sinking back down on the chair, thinking about what Dora had said. *I'm just not yet ready to talk about what happened.*

The next morning rolled around more slowly than most. She lay in bed thinking about her day and not wanting to face Dora downstairs. Her day began later than she was used to, both the bakery and the delivery jobs required a much earlier start time.

She moved to the side of the bed and pulled on her wool socks to protect her feet from the cold floor. Taking a moment, she organized her thoughts for the day. Once she felt settled in her plans she stood and strapped on the knife and pulled on the pants and shirt she had laid out the previous night. Her hair was pulled into a ponytail, she braided it to hold it in place and out of her way.

She changed out her socks, added her boots, and made her way downstairs. As she descended, she noticed the house was louder than she was used to. The children were still home and getting ready to start their days. Breakfast was being moved into the dining room and the breakfast bell rung. People came from their rooms and down the stairs at a fast pace. She managed to get herself a biscuit and sausage as she listened absently to Miss May and Miss Marjorie about their security work at the Museum. When she got her fill and started to help clean off the table. She carried the first platter into the kitchen and saw Dora working rolls at her kitchen table.

"Good morning," said Dora a bit formally.

"Good Morning. Thank you for breakfast. I can help clear, then I have to get going," Emma said ready to help.

"We have it," she said avoiding Emma's gaze. "Don't forget your lunch." She nodded to the table, where it sat.

Emma reached out and took her lunch pail, staring at Dora, wanting to say something, but not knowing what. She finally nodded grabbed a coat and headed out of the back door to begin her day.

It was a nice spring day with a chill in the air. Papa's coat hung on her frame, it was big and comfortable. She ambled along looking forward to her day and saw Tony walking toward her.

"You didn't have to meet me; I was on the way to your house," she called.

"I like to see you and without competing with my family," he teased. He noticed her distant expression and asked, "What's wrong?"

"Dora wants to take about what happened with Thomas and Daniel. I'm just not ready to talk about it yet."

Tony nodded. She hadn't discussed the case with him either. They walked toward his house holding hands and talking about their day.

Enzo must have heard her on the stairs because he yanked open the door as she arrived. "Morning Emma."

"Morning Enzo. Having a good morning?" she asked, always happy to see him.

"Well, it would be if I could skip school," he said sending his Mom a winning smile.

She knew her boys and didn't let them manipulate her. She shook her finger at him saying lightly, "None of that. You're going to school."

"Oh Mom," Enzo groaned.

"Oh Enzo," she mocked back. "Get your books." He nodded and ran off, knowing he wasn't going to win this argument.

Michael came out of his bedroom and was pulling on his coat when he noticed Emma, "Emma good to see you."

"You too," said Emma sincerely.

"Marco and David, get finished with your breakfast, everyone is waiting for you," Mrs. Marella reminded them to get them moving.

"Sure ma, we'll get ready," David's said and tapped Marco, pointing to their room.

"Oh, okay," said Marco with his mouth full and followed his brother out of the dining room.

"Emma they'll be ready soon," Mrs. Marella called as she cleared the table. "Would you like something to eat while you wait? I made pancakes this morning."

That was tempting, thought Emma. She said with a smile, "One would be nice."

Mrs. Marella smiled at her and got her a pancake. She was very happy that Emma was back in their lives and with Tony.

Everyone piled into the living room at the same time. Tony was in a nice suit and everyone else was in work clothes.

"Here are your lunches," said Mrs. Marella, handing out lunch pails to each person. She looked over at Emma saying, "Emma do you have your lunch?"

"Dora took care of me this morning," she said holding up her lunch pail.

They headed outside, she saw that David had gotten the wagon ready and was waiting for them. Tony helped Emma into the back, gave her a kiss goodbye, and said, "See you later."

"Yes, bye," she said.

She watched him walk away and waited. He turned to grin and wave at her. She grinned back. The wagon pulled away giving her a jerk. She noticed Marco was patting his hair down and buttoning his shirt. David was grinning but didn't say anything. Emma smiled and looked around as Michael drove them to the job.

They were slowing down and Emma turned to see where she would be spending her days. She started her observation of the house. *It was a large Victorian-style home, mostly blue and white. The other houses in the neighborhood appeared to be better maintained,* she thought, noticing the sagging porch and missing shingles. *He must not have wanted to work on the house after his son was declared dead and his wife died. What a sad thought, going through the motions of living and not really living.*

The boys jumped down and Michael handed down their tools. Michael looked at Emma and said, "We're working all over the house, so make yourself generally useful; moving trash, cleaning up jobs, and toting materials as needed." Emma nodded knowing that she needed to appear to be a working member of the team.

They carried their lunch pails and tools to the door. As Marco knocked, they heard a sound of scurrying steps that reminded her of Enzo. The door was thrown open and it was a small boy.

This must be Christopher, thought Emma.

Christopher focused on Marco and said loudly, "Marco!"

"Hey Christopher, how are you?"

"I'm good. Do you want breakfast? Can I help you with your work today?" And the questions continued. Marco was extremely patient with him.

Emma noticed the lovely craftsmanship in the house as they walked through the foyer. There were hardwood floors, dark paneling, and a lovely curving staircase.

"We're in the back," indicated Michael, to get them moving.

Emma trailed the group as she glanced around the house and documented as much as she could. "Very clean, polished even." She didn't see the maid that was mentioned earlier. "She might be helping in the kitchen."

She heard something behind her, a swishing of a skirt. She turned and saw a very lovely girl.

"Who are you?" the girl asked.

"Emma," Emma said, trying to determine what the other girl's tone was.

"You're a girl," the girl exclaimed.

This must be Mara, she thought and replied to her question, "Yes."

"And you're working in plumbing and gas pipes?" she continued.

"Yes," she kept her answers short trying to get a read on the girl. She could see why Marco was so taken with her. She was very beautiful.

She surprised Emma with her next statement, "I so want to learn to do something useful."

That was surprising and Emma was about to respond when Michael called her back.

"Have to go," she said to Mara.

"Can we talk sometime about your job?" she asked.

"Sure, that would be nice," replied Emma.

She nodded her head at Mara and headed back to where Michael and the boys were setting up. She saw Christopher was keeping Marco company. He was able to work as Christopher continued to talk.

Mara came in and reminded Christopher that he was

supposed to be with her working on his school work. He went, begrudgingly with her.

"I will see you soon Christopher," promised Marco.

Christopher grinned in response and left with Mara.

"Emma," Michael said, seeing her attention had wandered. "Move those pipes to the next room. We'll be starting there next."

"Okay," said Emma. She put on her gloves and started moving the pile of pipes, they weren't heavy just bulky. She noticed the room they were upgrading was the main sitting room. Michael had commented they had completed the family bedrooms.

The morning went by quickly and she stayed busy moving materials and cleaning up. When they broke for lunch, she was ready for the break but admitted to herself the physical labor felt good and kept her mind off her sister.

They sat out in the garden eating lunch. Michael and Emma sat in chairs at a garden table. Marco and David were sitting on the patio with their backs against the house.

Marco kept looking around and Emma noticed. "I think I saw her in the library," said Emma casually.

"Oh, I think I need to check the gas lines in that room," he said and headed inside.

"Marco," Michael called, "we already completed that room."

"Oh, well then, I'll check to see if they're working properly," he said quickly.

"Careful there," Michael warned him softly.

"I get it, dad," Marco said quietly, understanding they were employees at the house.

Michael nodded and waved him on.

As Marco was leaving, a very attractive older woman in a dark blue dress came out with a pitcher of lemonade. "Would you like something to drink?" she asked the group.

"I would," said, Emma. "Thank you." David also stood up and walked over to get some lemonade.

"How is the sitting room progressing?" Abigail asked.

"It's going well if you would like to review the details with me," said Michael standing up.

"Thank you," and they headed back in to review the improvements.

"She seems nice," Emma commented to David as they left.

"More so than her husband. At least she talks to us. I get the idea the husband would rather we weren't around," David commented softly.

"Why do you say that?" she asked curious about this man she hadn't met.

"He's just not friendly. You'll see when he comes home this afternoon."

"Where's the older Mr. Saunders," asked Emma.

"He's working in his garden, seems to be his favorite place," said David.

"So, he's active?" asked Emma.

He smiled and said, "You need to meet him. We have a few minutes if you want to go back there."

"That would be nice." They made their way to the back of the house and entered the garden area. It was a lovely greenhouse attached to the building. Glass windows surrounded the room. Lush greenery covered the lower windows. They saw an older gentleman that looked to be in good shape.

David said as they approached him, "Mr. Saunders, how are you?"

"David," he said and smiled. "How are you today? Is this a new helper?"

"Yes, this is Emma Evans, she's working with us this week."

"What are you helping with my dear?" asked Mr. Saunders, in a kindly voice.

"I am cleaning up and helping where needed," she replied.

"Sounds interesting," he said with a smile.

"Grandpa!" came a yell from Christopher as he came in running and hugged his grandfather's knees. He rubbed Christopher's hair and tilted his head up saying, "Hi Christopher. How are your studies going?"

Christopher frowned and said, "I hate school."

"But you will try some more for me? Mara is doing her best to help you," he said softly.

"Yes, I know," he said shuffling his feet. "Can I work out here with you?"

"How about this, another hour with Mara, and then you can come out and help me with my planting. Do we have a deal?" he asked.

"Yes sir," he said grudgingly.

"Great. Now get back to Mara and finish your schoolwork."

He grinned up at his grandpa and ran back into the house.

"He's always at full speed. Hates to sit still," commented Walter.

He caught Emma's considering glance and she decided to comment and see his reaction. "I heard about your son returning after being missing, that is such a wonderful thing."

His expression went more serious, he looked down at the plants he was working and he replied, "Yes, yes, it is. Shouldn't you be getting back to work?"

David motioned to Emma for them to leave. Emma nodded and said to Walter, "Yes, it was nice to meet you."

"Hmm," he murmured and went back to his gardening.

Emma and David joined Marco and Michael in the sitting room. They finished piping the room and kept to themselves.

As they were packing up for the day, Emma noticed a man standing in the doorway. *It must be the father.* She started walking toward him, but he turned and moved away without speaking.

She didn't think it too odd, that James seemed withdrawn.

Men back from the war sometimes returned changed and uncommunicative. He had so much to be thankful for, being home and no loss of limbs. In town, many men had returned home, missing arms, and legs and were addicted to morphine trying to control the pain.

She mentally went through notes on people she met today.

- Mara-lovely, wants to be useful, something there between Marco and Mara.
- Christopher-amazing kid, a little different, but amazingly friendly and lovely to be around. Obviously, a favorite of Walter.
- Abigail-mother, quiet but seemed nice and ran the house efficiently.
- James-Father War veteran, withdrawn, more than that -unsure of him at this time.
- Walter- grandfather, a very happy man when involved in garden and grandchildren. Unhappy with questions about his returned son.
- Maid-keeps to herself, cleaning or helping in the kitchen.

She continued to make notes in the wagon on the way home, about the details of the day when Marco said something interesting, "Something odd happened."

"What," asked Emma looking at him.

Marco continued, "I was calling Mara's name over and over and she didn't respond until I was really close."

Emma documented this and continued to write. She looked up as they slowed and realized that they had stopped in front of the boarding house. "Oh, you didn't have to bring me home."

"It is the least we could do, you did good work today," commented Michael.

"See you in the morning?" asked Marco hopefully.

"Definitely, meet you at the apartment in the morning," she said as she hopped down. She was grateful for the help after the long day, she waved them off as she headed into the boarding house.

"Emma," she heard a call from Dora as she entered.

"Yes, I'm here," Emma said absently thinking that she needs to go to the library in town to check for any articles on James' return. It would have made a good human-interest story. She was drumming her fingers on her lips thinking.

Dora came into the foyer and asked, "Long day?"

"Not too and the work was interesting," Emma replied.

"Is there a case there," she asked, curious about the family.

"I am still not sure, but there is definitely an interesting story there. Boy leaves for war and returns as man with family," Emma stated thinking about them.

"Have you seen him?" asked Dora.

"James?" She nodded saying, "Just a glance. The other members of the family are lovely, really nice people. Though I did feel an undercurrent with the grandfather when I asked about James returning."

"Walk me back to the kitchen," Dora suggested.

Emma slipped her hand into her sisters' elbow and accompanied her to the kitchen. Emma laid her head on Dora's shoulder as they walked, glad they could still be close even when they had a disagreement.

When they entered Amy was stirring a wonderful smelling soup. Emma commented, "That smells good Amy." Amy nodded, smiled, and went back to her stirring.

"Dora, I think I need to go to the library after dinner."

"All right, why don't you ask Thomas to go with you, he would probably enjoy riding with you," Dora suggested.

"Instead of following me you mean," she said with a grin.

Dora nodded and turned back to her pastry. She wanted to confront Emma again but promised her she could have some time so she said instead, "He is in the study if you want to ask him."

"I will," said Emma and she walked quickly to find him.

"Hi Thomas," he looked up from his book and smiled, always happy to see Emma.

"Would you like to go to the library with me? You can sit with me on the cable car," she teased lightly.

"Sure, that would be nice. Now?" He sat up ready to go.

"No, we can go after dinner," she said with a chuckle. "I need to get washed up."

"You are carrying some dirt with you," he said noticing her work clothes.

"Agreed," she laughed and she headed upstairs to change and wash up.

After she finished her bath, she put on her red slit skirt and white blouse. The thought of a ponytail gave her a headache, she brushed her hair out and left it down. She headed downstairs to help with dinner. Dora was unhappy with her not talking, but Emma wasn't ready for that conversation. Her energy would be channeled into the current case.

Dinner was prepared and everyone moved into the dining room. Emma was hungry from the physical labor. Miss May and Miss Marjorie tried to get her to talk, but she was distracted and didn't say much. After they helped to clean up, she asked Thomas, "Ready?"

"Yes, let me grab my hat and coat," replied Thomas.

They waved bye to Dora and Amy as they headed out the kitchen door.

They talked quietly as they headed to the cable car and into the library. "I will be over here," she said as she headed toward the area where the older newspapers were kept.

She looked through for the date that she knew James had shown up with his family. She found what she was looking for, the article was smaller than she expected. The article did detail that James had come back home and had not died in the war. What was surprising was what was not in the articles. She noted the writer's name and made up her mind to see him early the next day.

She had a nice walk home with Thomas, hearing about his bakery job and people that he had met that day. When she got home, she put together a note, telling Tony's family she would meet them at the house a bit later the next day.

The next morning, she made her way to the paper. She was unsure of how she felt about going into the building but noticed the editor's office seemed to be occupied. "I guess they have replaced Daniel, things must keep moving forward." Going up to one of the writer's desks and asked about the location of the writer of the article she was researching.

He grunted, not looking up from his typewriter, saying, "He is over there." He waved in the direction with his right hand.

She approached the desk he had indicated and saw he was a young man. She asked him, "Are you the writer that wrote the article about James Saunders returning home?"

"Yes, that was me, did you like it?" he asked hoping that he had a fan in this lovely young lady.

Without answering, she pulled out her notebook and pencil.

"Is this an interview?" he asked with a smile.

"Kind of. The article was so brief, for a personal interest story? Wouldn't a story of this type normally have included information about the family and where the returning person had been living and how they were going to move forward?"

He didn't say anything, instead, he sat back in his chair causing it to squeak loudly. He took off his glasses to clean them, not answering any of her questions.

She continued, "Did you interview the family?"

"I did actually," he finally said as he considered her.

"Mara, Christopher, Abigail, James, and Walter?" she asked, going down her list of people.

"Yes, to each, except James, he wasn't home yet, when I started the interview." Remembering that day, he said with a sudden laugh, "That Christopher is a real pistol."

That made her laugh. "Talked your ear off, did he?"

"Yes." He got very serious when he said, "Okay, yes, I did interview everyone. And Mara and Abigail were very nice but didn't share much except they were glad that they were there."

"Walter?" she asked curiously.

"He was also quiet but seemed very happy to have his family with him."

"Christopher?"

"Well, I actually got a moment alone with him and he told me some things that the others didn't."

Emma waited, sure that this would answer some questions. He paused and looked around. "Let's take a quick walk to the dock." She nodded and followed him. It was empty at that time of day and would give them some privacy.

She watched and waited for him to start again. He continued to talk about Christopher, "He indicated that they weren't from the south at all and had actually been living only a few towns over from Chicago. He also said he had a new name and he liked it better than his last one."

"A different name and place. Did you find out anything else? Weren't you curious?" she asked knowing she would have looked harder into the family.

"I was," he admitted.

"What happened? Something must have because the article didn't reflect any of this information," she commented.

"James returned home and realized that I had been alone with Christopher," he said simply.

"What was his mood? Was he angry?" she asked, curious about James' response.

"I don't think anger is the right word. He appeared more scared or panicked," he said thinking of that day.

Emma thought, *A large number of soldiers returned from the war troubled by the intensity of the fighting. They were fighting helplessness, panic, and dealing with sleep deprivation.* "What happened?" she asked, wrapped up in the story.

"I explained the article and he wanted to see what I had planned to publish." He paused before saying, "That is when he offered me money to limit it."

"Did he say why?" she asked.

"He just said they were trying to form a new family and he didn't want outsiders in their business."

"Did you think he was telling the truth?"

"To a point," he admitted, "but I thought there was something up then. And now."

"But you took the money?" she asked curious about a reporter not following up on an article.

"Yeah, I did, I am not perfect and I could use that money. It was more than I would see in six months here. And who was I hurting by publishing a shorter article?"

"Hmm," she said, taking down what she had learned. Christopher wasn't his real name; they came from Johnsonville. "Did Christopher mention what his dad did for a job there?"

"Yes," he said looking at his notes. "He wasn't working. Abigail was, she worked for an influential family, the Lewison's."

"Thanks for the information," she said closing her notebook.

"Please don't mention my role in this to anyone," he warned softly.

"I won't," she promised. "Thanks for telling me."

As she walked away from the newspaper dock, she got her bike from under the stairs, thinking, *The police chief, I will see if he can call and check some facts out for me.*

She went to the Police station and upstairs to the Chief's office. "Emma," said the secretary. "Welcome."

It was certainly different than the first time I was here, she thought wryly and said out loud, "Does the Chief have time for me?"

"I think he will make time. Let me check for you." He got up and went to the door, knocked, and was called in. He came out a moment later and said, "Emma you can go in now. The Chief will see you."

"Thanks," she said sincerely as she walked past his desk and entered the office.

"Emma," the Chief said standing up and going around the desk to greet her. He took her hand in his and said, "Please, sit."

They sat on his couch and she pulled out the familiar notebook. "Ahh you are here on business," he commented, curious but not upset.

"Yes, I hope you don't mind?" When he indicated for her to continue, she described her current case and asked. "I was hoping you could send a telegram over to the Chief there and asked if he is aware of the family. Abigail worked at the Lewison's when they lived there. I am unsure of the names they were using but, I can give you a description and when they were probably there."

"I can send a telegram," he said. "We should hear something later today or tomorrow morning."

She gave him notes on the family, thanked him, and headed downstairs to the veteran's administration office. The office was nearby, she got her bike and walked it there. She asked the clerk for the service record for James Saunders. Pension records were accessible since 1868. "Can I also get a list of people that were in his regiment?" she asked, thinking she was on to something.

She made her way to the boarding house to get organized to go work at the Saunders' house. When she got there the Police Chief had sent a note over with a telegram enclosed. It confirmed that the description matched the family of Doug Gregg. His wife's name was Martha Gregg when she worked at the Lewison's. That rang a bell and she pulled up her list of people from the regiment, Doug Gregg was on the list. *So, Doug did know James.* Looking further down in the note she saw that the Gregg family had left on good terms, owing no money to anyone.

Okay, now I have the information but when do I communicate it? She sent a note over to Michael at the worksite to tell them she would be there tomorrow.

The next morning, she met Tony about halfway to his apartment, "Meeting me again?" she teased.

"Yes, we missed you yesterday," as he leaned over to kiss her.

"Me too, but I made progress in the case," she said.

"Anything you can share?"

"Not yet, I would like to continue to observe the family before I say anything," she said.

He nodded and said, "I understand."

She met Michael and the boys at the apartment and told them she was still working on the case but was making progress. They nodded, Michael said, "Let's go, David get the wagon ready."

As they walked down, Emma asked Marco, "What room are we in today?"

"We have moved to the dining room," he replied.

"That's a large room," she commented.

"Yes, should take 3-4 days to get the room piped and walls repaired. We have cleaned up the previous room, you can work on some final debris removal and help with wall preparation," Michael commented.

"Okay," she said thinking that would give her time to think about the next steps.

They made their way to the house and knocked on the door. Christopher once again let their crew in. "Emma you're back!"

"I am, I had some stuff to do yesterday," Emma replied.

Once again Christopher accompanied Marco. "Mara made

something special for you," Christopher said, "it is a secret though."

"Really," said Marco, pleased that Mara was thinking of him.

Their group continued to talk and moved into the dining room.

Michael motioned to David and Emma, "You two finish up in the sitting room. David, let Emma know what she needs to do."

David nodded and said, "Will do."

Emma and David went into the room and started picking up debris left from the previous day. After a while, David said, "I will check the texture on the wall, we should be able to paint." Emma nodded and kept working on taking debris piles outside.

She was walking back into the house when she noticed James outside with his face up to the sun, he seemed to be very tired. She was curious about this man. He managed to change his family's life by taking on someone else's identity but did not seem to be there for nefarious reasons. "Mr. Saunders is there something I can help you with?" asked Emma.

"What," he said, distracted. "No no."

"It is a lovely day, isn't it?" she asked trying to get to know this man.

"Yes," he said still holding his face up to the sun.

"I need to head back in now," she said when he didn't talk more.

"Yes," he commented softly.

She headed back in, thinking about this man, so many men came back from the war angry, broken. This man seemed to be more distracted than angry. *Had he hurt his head in some way or maybe this was just his way of coping?*

She continued to make several trips, cleaning up the room while David started painting. When she finished the debris removal, she asked him, "Can I help?"

"Sure, grab a paintbrush and start on that wall. Don't get too close to the windows. I will do the detail work." She nodded, grabbing a brush and dipping it into the paint. They worked on the room and were finished by lunchtime.

"Emma good job," said David, looking over her work. "You should be about to move into the dining room to help out there next." He laughed and said, "You have some paint on your face." He reached over to wipe it off.

"Thanks," she said. "That was fun."

"Your shoulders may bother you a bit tonight, so take a hot bath and soak them," he cautioned.

"I will," she promised, rolling her shoulders.

They grabbed their lunch pails and headed outside. Marco and Michael were there and were waiting for David and Emma before they started their lunch.

Abigail brought out lemonade and Mara carried a platter of cut slices of cake. Emma tried the cake and said, "Hmm-this is really good. Can I get the recipe?"

"Yes," Mara commented happily. "It is a Molasses Cake."

Mara glanced over and asked shyly, "Marco do you like it?"

"I do it is wonderful," he said honestly.

She blushed and said, "Well I am going back in."

"Would you like to stay for a moment and talk?" asked Marco.

"That would be lovely," she said as she sat down next to him with her back to the house. They each enjoyed their cake and the afternoon sun.

Once again Emma noticed James walking around. He appeared to be going toward the greenhouse.

"Mara?" asked Emma, watching him.

"Yes," she said, not looking away from Marco.

"Your father? Is he well?" Emma asked carefully.

That got Mara's attention and she focused her gaze on Emma and asked, "You mean the absent-mindedness?"

"Yes," said Emma.

"When he wants, he can focus, it's just that I think memories of the war can overwhelm him," she said. "Mama said he is very different from when they first married."

"Does he work? Or have something he is interested in?" Emma asked.

"He hasn't held a job in a while, but he loves the dirt and working with plants."

"He must come to that naturally from his father, he seems to also really enjoy gardening."

She averted her gaze and said, "Well yes. I do wish they would work together, but Papa doesn't go in there when grandfather is there." Emma noticed the hesitation and made a mental note of it.

"What else does he focus on?" asked Emma.

"Us," she said simply. "He wants to make sure we are safe and secure."

That sounds right. thought Emma. In this situation, taking another identity may be this way because he needed to protect his family. Securing a new name and life for them.

"Michael when will we be finished in the house?" asked Emma.

"Well, the dining room is the last room; we have the rest of the week and we should be done."

"Okay," said Emma. She wouldn't jeopardize their job but planned on communicating the information to the family soon.

The week went by quickly and the rooms were well lit with gas lights. They were testing the lights and doing a final walk-through with Walter.

Emma said to Michael, "It looks like the job is complete?"

"Yes," he said absently.

"Mr. Saunders," she asked Walter after they completed their final inspection.

"Yes Emma," he commented looking from the lights to her.

"Could I meet with you and your family?" she asked.

"I don't understand, why would you need to meet with us?" asked Walter, bewildered by the request.

Michael and the boys stood silent while Emma talked with Walter.

"I would like to go over some information with you all," stated Emma.

Curious he said, "In the sitting room. I will call the family. Christopher, please go get your father," Walter said to him.

"I will," and he ran off to find him.

The family gathered in the dining room, Michael and his boys made themselves absent, knowing Emma would handle things from here. "Emma we will be outside if you need us," said Michael as they went out the door.

Emma went in and sat down, she pulled out her notebook and started, "You know my name is Emma. My full name is Emma Evans. I work as an investigator occasionally." Emma paused a moment when Abigail gasped. Emma tried to ignore the response and continued, "Someone I know asked me to look into your family," she said formally. When she saw that Walter was going to interrupt, she said quickly, "It wasn't meant to be malicious, they were worried about you. I will continue if that is all right."

Abigail, Mara, and James looked very uncomfortable. She thought it best to lay it out in an abrupt manner and turned to James. "I know that you're are not James but rather Doug Gregg and you are all from Johnsonville." The quiet was deafening in the room as she continued to speak directly to James, "I also believe you assumed the identity so that you could move your family here, to protect them."

James aka Doug looked defeated and the women scared, but oddly Walter didn't seem surprised.

James looked at Walter and said, "You knew?"

"You think I don't know what my own son looks like? Where did you get the picture?" Walter asked in a neutral voice. James, aka Doug, had provided the small handheld painting of James's mom as proof of who he was.

James aka Doug said, "You probably won't believe this but I did know him, we were in the same regiment…"

Emma interrupted him saying, "I can confirm that he was part of your son's regiment." Emma thought about how many men Illinois had contributed to the Union Army. Over 250,000 men had volunteered and several thousand died.

James aka Doug watched her and waited a moment before going on, "I was there when he died in the battle at the Potomac and he asked me to take the picture back to you."

"You chose an odd way to do that," Walter commented, his voice not betraying any emotion.

"Yes, when I got here with my family it was so easy to just be James instead of telling you how he died," he said simply.

"How did he die?" asked Walter hoarsely.

James made an indication with his head for his wife to take the kids out of the room. Emma stayed; they had forgotten she was there.

"So many people died immediately. I was with James and it seemed that everyone was dying around us, we were walking through the blood and brains of our friends. I still can't sleep because of the dreams." He took a deep breath to continue, "James took a bullet in the chest. I did the best I could to help him and carried him to the doctor's tent. He talked all the way down about you and your wife. He went so quiet and when I finally got a doctor to look at him, they told me he was dead. I didn't believe them and I just stayed and stayed until finally, they made me go back to my regiment."

Walter let his emotions take over and he cried. He finally looked up and said to James, "Call your wife and daughter back in."

When they came in James aka Doug said, "I will take my family and myself and clear out."

Abigail said to Walter sincerely, "I am sorry if we hurt you."

Walter said, "No you are not going anywhere."

They looked shocked at his statement and stayed still. "I love having you here with me." He turned to look at Emma and said, "Emma, it was time to have this out, so thank you for that. But I think that this information needs to stay inside my family. Can you keep that secret for me, for us?"

"I can, I am very glad you found each other," said Emma sincerely.

"James," said Walter, showing that he would continue to use the alias. "Would you like to come to the garden with me? I can show you what I am working on."

He looked startled but happy and said, "That would be nice." He followed him out.

Abigail and Mara were hugging and crying. Abigail look at Emma and said, "We are so relieved. James, Doug couldn't work and he just wanted to make sure we had somewhere safe to live."

"I understand. I will leave you and your family to your priva-cy," she said and exited the room.

Emma headed out of the house and saw that Michael and the boys had waited for her. She briefly told them what had happened in the meeting. "Please keep this quiet, this family needs each other," she told them softly.

"We will," said Michael. "Everyone okay with that?" They nodded and he turned around to move the wagon forward.

On their way home, Emma thought about how the case had ended. There were no deaths or fights this time, but a group of people that chose to be with one another. She kept thinking about the family members, growing apart because they didn't share more of themselves with one another.

Dora, she thought as they pulled up to the boarding house. She jumped out, without waiting for assistance and said a quick, "Bye." She took off at a run up the stairs and flew through the door, catching Dora, who was checking the mail in the foyer, unawares.

"What is wrong, has something happened?" Dora asked concerned.

"Yes," Emma said. "So many things. Can we talk?"

"Yes, let's go to the study," said Dora in a worried voice. Dora closed the doors behind them and sat next to Emma.

Emma took Dora's hands in hers looking her deep in the eyes, "I want to say I am sorry that I haven't been more open to talking with you about Mama."

Dora didn't realize that this was about Mama, she took a deep breath and said, "What caused this change?"

Emma told her about the case she was working on and how it ended. "I realized that by not telling you about her I was putting a wall between us. I never wanted that." She went on to describe how Mama's case had come together. She detailed how Daniel had tried to make Mama into being the same kind of people they were and when she resisted and they killed her.

"How?" Dora asked in a shaky voice, wiping her eyes.

"They got to the bakery that night, no one was there. They SAID that they were there to talk to her one more time, but they decided she was a liability. Daniel hit her with a rolling pin and then laid her under a beam that had fallen."

Dora knew the rest. She felt calmer knowing what had happened. "Emma, you try to protect me from the harsh realities of life. I am stronger than that," she said quietly.

"I do know that," Emma said earnestly," but I have one more thing to share."

Dora was wiping her eyes and said, "Oh, what else could there be?"

"When I found out Daniel killed Mama, I made up my mind that I would kill him," she said not breaking eye contact.

"But you killed him to protect Thomas," she said, feeling a little lost.

"Yes, but I would have thrown that knife anyway. I knew how it was going to end," she said simply.

"Oh," said Dora unsure of what to say.

"Dora, I didn't tell you because I didn't want you to think I was a monster," she explained looking down for the first time.

Dora immediately grabbed her shoulder and shook her bit, before looking her in the eye. "No, I know who the Monsters here are, you killed one. You are never to think of yourself that way. Do you hear me?"

"Yes," Emma said, tears thickening her response.

"I love you and I always will, no matter what," stated Dora.

"I worry you feel things more than I do," Emma said.

"I don't think I do. I just show mine more. You have been hurting, holding this in and not being able to talk about it," Dora observed.

"Yes," Emma said quietly.

"We will try to do better?" Dora asked more as a statement of fact than a question.

"We will," Emma said as she laid her head on Dora's shoulder.

NOTEBOOK MYSTERIES ~ BOOK 2

DECISIONS AND POSSIBILITIES

Notebook Mysteries

KIMBERLY MULLINS

CHAPTER 1

1883, CHICAGO - PRESENT DAY

*E*mma looked at herself in the mirror as she smoothed down her white high-necked shirt into her full red split skirt and thought, *Mama would have liked the new rational dress movement, as it allows for a more practical and comfortable fashion. I'm probably one of the few girls who can sit down comfortably because I've never worn a corset. Though you can't really call me a girl at eighteen.* She pulled her long platinum blond hair into a loose bun on her head. The style emphasized her high cheekbones and the dash of freckles on her nose.

She took a final moment to examine her image and swirled to check her skirt for any wrinkles. Her split skirt would be considered too short by most, showing the tops of her black high-heeled boots. She nodded at her image, approving of her clothes selection for the day.

Emma didn't care about looks, though she had them. She gave a bit of an exasperated look at her bun, restraining hair that reached nearly to her waist, and acknowledged it could be hot in the summertime. *A short style would be nice,* she thought, but then she looked again and decided she would just have to put up with it. *Tony probably wouldn't like it short.*

. . .

Narrator commented, "Yes, Tony is still very important to Emma and very much a part of her life. They've been together since she was sixteen and they have remained close."

As Emma did a final examination of her clothes for any flaws, she turned away from the mirror and viewed the room around her. It was her childhood room in the boarding house where she lived with her papa and Dora. Their little family had grown over the past two years with the addition of Tim Flannigan, Dora's husband.

Tim and Dora had been married for a little over a year. She could still remember the wedding, how wonderful the house had felt when full of people, food, and music.

CHAPTER 2

1882, TIM AND DORA'S WEDDING

Mama's family had taken over the event and the house for the week. It was a wonderful, joyous time; aunts, uncles, and children were all over the house. Emma spent months making an intricate lace wedding dress for Dora and she looked radiant in it. It was a wedding where everyone enjoyed themselves and no one wanted the day to end.

Emma had felt Mama's spirit that day, especially when she and Dora were alone together getting ready to head downstairs for the ceremony.

With tears in her eyes, Emma helped Dora slip into her dress. They had completed a final fitting a few weeks before, but knowing Dora would be getting married today made Emma emotional.

"Don't make me cry," cautioned Dora, seeing Emma's eyes fill with tears.

"No, no, I won't," she said as she tried to shake them off. "You look beautiful and so much like Mama."

They hugged tightly.

"Enough of that now," said Dora. "I have things to do today."

With that final comment, both girls, looking beautiful in

their lace dresses, stepped into the hallway to be greeted by Papa. Emma started downstairs with Dora and Papa following behind. The ceremony was being held in the backyard. Chairs had been set up there with an aisle separating the guest and at the far end, an arch where Tim and Dora would say their vows. Emma entered the yard first and could see Tim waiting for Dora. *He didn't appear nervous, he did appear to be a bit impatient to begin his married life,* she thought.

On her walk down the aisle, Emma glanced at each side. Mama's family took up most of the space. Her eyes found Tony, he smiled as she walked by. Next, she saw Cole and Jeremy Tilden. Jeremy winked at her. She grinned back and had to force herself to focus on where she would stand during the wedding.

The music that was playing was lovely. Chloe, Cousin's wife, had formed a small quartet that performed at different events. Her skills as a violin player were well known. The quartet included Chloe and Lee Sandel on violin, Elspeth Hanson on viola, and Katie Yu on cello.

Amy opened the back door and motioned to Chloe's group to begin playing the music for Dora and Papa's entrance. As they started down the aisle, Emma's tears started to form again and this time she let them fall. Two of her favorite people were becoming one that day.

Once the wedding ceremony was over; the chairs and arch were cleared out. Tables were put in their place and a dance floor was arranged. Day turned to evening with plenty of food, drink, and speeches. Papa stood by the front table with his arm around Dora.

"I'd like to tell you about these two people that we all love so much. Dora is so much like her Mama. Both of my girls are," Papa said, including Emma in his speech. "Mary would've loved to have been here to see this joyous day. I thought when she died, that our family had also died, but I was wrong. Our family continued and is only stronger with the addition of Tim."

He turned to Tim and said, "Welcome to the family."

The crowd cheered and Dora had her face buried in Papa's chest.

It was a memory she would cherish.

Papa had sent Dora and Tim on a trip to New York, but when they returned, they didn't seem to remember much of what they'd seen. *They had returned well-rested*, Emma thought with a laugh.

She moved to her desk and sat down for a moment while she reflected on 1881, that busy year she began investigating.

CHAPTER 3

1881 CHICAGO

The cases Emma was involved in over the last two years had involved theft from the Stubing Department store, pickpockets, and smuggling operations involving John Harden. In each case, the clues seemed to be leading in the same direction—to one criminal organization.

The spider web of cases intertwined so that the only way to deconstruct it was to pull the one string holding everything together. Emma thought that string was the head of a local crime organization, but it turned out, it was Mama. Everywhere she turned, Mama was connected. Emma had initially stumbled on the fact that she had been helping a reporter with investigations into illegal activities during the year she died. Mama had inadvertently led the reporter to an opportunity he couldn't pass up, to oversee a large crime organization. That reporter wanted Mama to be part of it, but she had disagreed and he had killed her.

Who was that reporter? Daniel Cooper, local paper editor, and secret crime boss. He believed strongly that, if he could control the news, he could do anything or be anything he wanted. He was right—for a while.

Emma was able to deduce that the cases were probably connected and were somehow tied to her mama. She also knew Daniel had more involvement than he indicated, but Emma never suspected he was the person who murdered her.

The final clues had unraveled when Thomas, Mama's good friend, and coworker at the bakery, identified Daniel as her killer. Since she died, Thomas had always been there in the shadows looking out for Emma. He knew one day he might have to step in to save her. What he didn't expect was for Emma to end up saving his life when Daniel tried to kill him.

On that final day, Emma had ended Daniel's life, though it wasn't something she'd planned, she didn't regret it. She did what she had to, to save them both.

CHAPTER 4

1883, PRESENT DAY CHICAGO

*E*mma pulled herself into the present and opened her desk drawer to find her current case book. She still kept her observations in the black notebooks she always carried with her. As she tried to pull the drawer open, it got stuck and she had to pull forcibly on the handle. When it finally gave way and allowed her access, she knelt to discover what had kept the drawer from opening. It was another notebook, wedged in the back; she reached in and pulled it out.

She sat back on her knees, looking at it for a long moment, and realized which one it was. *It must be a day for memories,* she thought, shaking her head. That notebook, the black cover faded with age, was from another day long ago when she was ten years old and involved her "incident".

The Narrator said, "The incident was when Emma was attacked at the age of ten by a career criminal named Zeke Jones, and it was not the last time he would go after her. He had a personal vendetta against her; he felt she was always taking something from him that he believed was his."

Dear-one commented wryly, "To be fair, she did keep uncovering cases where he was also involved. The Stubing store theft, the smuggling operations involving store owners, and then when he had volunteered to "take care" of Emma for the notorious gangster John Harden."

The Narrator added, "When he did go after her that last time, Emma was ready for him."

Dear-one asked, "What happened to Zeke?"

The Narrator said, "Well, we will get to that later."

Dear one said, "You know you say that a lot."

"I know, but I always plan to go back," commented the Narrator, as she continued to write.

Emma opened the notebook and remembered how it had finally returned to her.

CHAPTER 5

1881, THE "INCIDENT" NOTEBOOK

Jeremy Tilden, a friend, and a Pinkerton detective had come by the house to see Emma a few weeks after her second attack from Zeke and after she had killed Daniel Cooper.

He asked her to take a walk with him. She happily acquiesced. She liked Jeremy and enjoyed his company.

"I have something for you," he said as they walked down the stoop and onto the street.

She stopped and turned to look at him. "You do?"

He pulled out a faded black notebook and handed it over to her. She looked at him quizzically and took it as he continued. "I don't want to upset you—with this." She looked at him and frowned.

Opening it, she realized immediately what it was. It was the notebook from THAT day when she was ten, and before that "incident". She was very curious about what she had written. Due to the extent of her injuries, she had not been able to recall the events of that morning. Vague flashes came to her, but nothing telling her why she had been attacked. She opened the book and quickly flipped through the pages until she found the last entry. That final day materialized in her thoughts as she reviewed the details her younger self had documented. As she read, she realized she had seen something Zeke Jones didn't want her to see. He had been beating a woman in the alley between the buildings. The last part was written a bit hastily.

"Hmm, so I *was* always where he didn't want me," she murmured.

"Looks like," commented Jeremy.

"So, you read it?" she asked laconically, looking up at him.

"Caught," he said, smiling a bit to ease the tension. "We were concerned about what might be in it, so yes—Cole and I reviewed it." Cole Tilden was Jeremy's dad and in charge of the Chicago branch of Pinkerton detectives. He didn't say, but he planned to look into the details of that day for her.

She closed it, slapping it against her hand. She tried to decide what her feelings were *-was it an intrusion of her privacy? Maybe, but it came from a place of caring.* Coming to a silent decision, she placed the notebook in her pocket and said, "I appreciate your concern."

They started their walk again along the sidewalk. Jeremy took the opportunity to start a new conversation. "Going to keep investigating?"

"Yes, but I'm going to take a step back and work on a few other things first."

"Still seeing Tony?" he asked casually.

She smiled slightly and said, "Yes."

"Well, I thought I would ask," he said, running his fingers through his brown curly hair.

"Still friends?" she asked.

"Yes, friends," he replied.

. . .

"Are you wondering what happened to Jeremy? His story will continue to unfold in the book. His path will continue to interact with Emma's," the Narrator said as she shot a long sideways glance to Dear-one.

That particular notebook -- many things had come out of it. . .

CHAPTER 6

1881, JEREMY INVESTIGATES THE NOTEBOOK

Jeremy had been assigned to search Zeke's apartment after he had tried to attack Emma the second time. Once Zeke had been taken into custody, Jeremy had been assigned to catalog his belongings. He was loading a box from the desk when he ran across a familiar black leather notebook. *It's the kind Emma always carries with her,* he thought. He was curious enough to want to find out if it belonged to her. He opened it up and, with a smile, noted the girlish handwriting. A ten-year-old girl's writing could be very fanciful. He had no doubt it belonged to Emma.

Skimming through the pages, he realized what the last entry was. He had been told about Zeke's attack on Emma only after they'd locked him up. It was all he could do to not go after Zeke himself.

When he discussed this with Cole, the emotions churned within him again and his fist tightened. Cole grabbed his arm. "Jeremy, he'll get what is coming to him, I promise you."

"Will he?" asked Jeremy in a gruff voice.

"Yes, but we must leave it with the proper authorities to manage," said Cole.

"What if they don't?" asked Jeremy.

"Then we'll step in," he admitted. "For now, we let the system work."

Jeremy continued to read through the observations and realized Emma was always interested in the details of her surroundings; that made him smile. The following information was detailed in the notebook: *Noise coming from the alley on Morgan street, sounding like a woman screaming. A man with dark hair beating on a slender woman with auburn hair and pale skin.* The writing became disjointed after that and there was an appearance of the pencil being dragged down the page.

Jeremy went down to investigate that particular alley; it was located next to an infamous house of ill-repute. He decided to follow up on the lead and knocked on the front door of that 'house'. It opened immediately and two very large men in dark suits blocked the entrance. *Bodyguards,* he thought. He tried not to be intimidated and commented in a cheerful voice, "Hi, I need to speak to the manager."

"What do you want? We're not open until this evening," snapped the one on the left. Neither man showed any emotion.

Jeremy took a deep breath and tried again. "I'm with Pinkerton detectives and I'm looking for someone who was attacked about six years ago in the alleyway next door."

The guard who had spoken first gave him a considering look and then nodded at the other man. He turned and left the doorway without a word. His companion backed up and waved Jeremy into the foyer. Jeremy followed him in, still standing close to the door. He wasn't winning the staring contest with the bodyguard, choosing instead to look around at the foyer and upstairs. The house catered to things he had no experience with, he was curious about what was behind those closed doors.

At that moment a beautiful woman appeared, he assumed was the manager. She walked slowly down the stairs toward him. Two things surprised Jeremy: how young the manager appeared to be—she couldn't have been much into her thirties—and how perfectly she matched Emma's description.

At least I know I have the right person, he thought to himself.

"Mr. . .?" she asked as she stepped off the last step into the foyer.

"Jeremy Tilden, with Pinkerton detectives," he supplied. "And you are?"

"Clair Spencer. What can I do for you?" she asked a bit formally, keeping her distance.

"I'm investigating an event that occurred here in the alley next door some six years ago."

"Really?" She laughed. "Aren't you a bit late?" Though her lips indicated laughter, it didn't extend to her eyes, they were guarded, showing no emotion.

"New evidence has come to light in the case. Do we have somewhere more private we can talk?" he asked, eyeing her bodyguards.

She looked him over and came to a silent decision to talk to this man about something she would like to have forgotten. She indicated the doors behind him with her hand.

He turned and opened one of them to reveal a library with heavy furniture. A room like that in a house like this was unexpected, but he was glad there was a quiet space to conduct their meeting. Holding open the door for her, he waited while she entered ahead of him, her dress rustled as it brushed past. He pulled the doors shut and joined her on one of the two leather chairs situated across from one another.

"A man named Zeke Jones was seen beating a woman of your description in the alley beside this establishment about six years ago," he began.

This statement finally seemed to break Clair's calm demeanor. She stood up and moved behind the leather chair where she had been sitting. Gripping the back of it so tightly, that her knuckles appeared to be white.

Jeremy noticed her distress and tried to get to the point quickly. "Another attack happened right after that first one, just outside the alley, and led to the serious injury of a young girl."

Clair nodded. "Yes, that was me in the alley," she admitted. "That young girl, she was so brave," she said, an awed look on her face. "She just charged us. I could see her over his shoulder, all that blonde hair. She had a piece of wood and swung it hard at his head. He actually shook after she hit him."

Taking a deep breath, she opened up her fist and set her palms on the back of the chair. "He released me and went after her. Once he let me go, the other girls moved me inside. Last I saw of them, Zeke had her by the ponytail and was going around the corner. I didn't know until later how severe her injuries were. When I could, I found out she had survived and that bum Zeke had gotten away with it again."

"You knew he had done this before?" asked Jeremy gently.

"Yes. I wasn't careful enough and didn't listen to the other girls' warnings. He was good-looking and seemed to like me. I was naïve," she said simply, silently forgiving herself for being so trusting.

"Looks like you got over that." He gestured to their surroundings.

"I was at the right place and time to move up in my career. Why is this coming up now, after all this time?" she asked curiously.

"We finally have Zeke in custody. He went after that young girl, Emma, again," said Jeremy, trying not to show how angry he still was.

"Is she all right?" she asked, looking worried.

He nodded. "She bloodied him this time. He was tied up when we got there."

Finally finding the humor in their situation, she grinned broadly and said, "Met his match, did he?"

"He seemed to hold a grudge against her for a very long time," Jeremy commented.

Growing serious again, she said, "Yeah, he didn't like to let things go. I've been forced to hire bodyguards since that time. You are sure he's finally gone?"

"Yes, he was sent away a few days ago, facing charges in several states."

She let out a long sigh of relief and walked back around the chair to sit down. She looked at him and said, "So, why the visit?"

"To put some closure on the information. I'm looking into things in case Emma wants to investigate in the future."

"When you see her, could you tell her *thank you* for me?" she asked graciously.

"Yes," said Jeremy. "Thank you for making time for me today." They stood and she exited the room ahead of him, making her way gracefully back up the stairs. Jeremy watched her for a long moment and then exited the house.

Later that night, Jeremy discussed the details of the meeting with Cole. He stated with a smile, "I admit, I am curious about Clair Spencer."

"I'm not surprised. She does sound fascinating. What are you thinking?" asked Cole.

"I think a discrete look into her background might be a good idea," commented Jeremy in a serious voice.

"Are you thinking there's something suspicious there?" Cole asked, wondering where he was going with this.

"No, not without more data. But I am wondering about the money. How does someone move up like that and own the business?"

"Hmm," murmured Cole. "Keep it quiet. We don't want to cause her any unnecessary trouble."

Jeremy agreed. "I'll start by looking into the business license for her 'house.'"

"Sounds like a plan. Keep me in the loop." Cole began undoing the top button on his shirt and settling in for the night with a book.

"I will. Toss me my book?" Jeremy requested, ready to relax at the end of a long day.

Cole reached for it on the table beside him and tossed it to him. He asked with a smile, "What's for dinner tonight?"

The next day, Jeremy started looking at City Hall and found that the 'house' where he'd met Clair Spencer was also owned by her. *Surprising,* he thought. *Women don't normally own businesses, especially **that** type of business.* As he dug further, he pulled out records for other businesses and property in the area. He spent the rest of the afternoon looking through a large number of dusty old records, finally finding one attributed to Clair Spence. Possibly a misspelling. *Though,* he thought, *it may have been deliberate.*

Continuing to follow up, he went to City Hall to access the last three census records, looking for Clair Spencer or Spence to determine which one was the accurate name. He found a Clair Spence of about the same age, and it also identified her mother. The first two listed Clair's mother, but the last did not. None contained a listing for a father. He gathered his notes and headed over to the Pinkerton office where he shared the information he'd found with Cole.

"What are your thoughts about the second house? Do you think it's another business like the one I met her in?" Jeremy asked Cole.

"Let's take a look and see." The two personally staked out the house. They watched it closely for two days and noticed very few people ever left. The only people that were seen entering were women. Any men who came to the door were not allowed entry.

Cole stated, "We need to go there at night and check out their activities."

"Tonight?" Jeremy asked.

Cole nodded.

That evening they were in place watching the house as a wagon drew near. Cole nodded at Jeremy to follow behind and see where it stopped. It pulled up behind the house they were watching. Two men jumped down; Jeremy immediately recognized them as the bodyguards from the other 'house'.

They watched silently as the men helped an individual down from the wagon. Given the care they were taking, Jeremy assumed it was a woman. They kept her face and body swaddled in blankets, making it impossible to identify her. "Pops, what's going on in that house?" asked Jeremy in a low voice, bewildered by the events he had witnessed.

"I think it's a battered woman house," said Cole, stroking his goatee consideringly. "Let's clear out. They don't need us to expose their good deeds. They kept the location of the house quiet for a good reason."

"I wonder if the situation with Zeke led her to do this?" mused Jeremy as they left the area and retrieved their buggy a few streets over.

"It might be that or a combination of things," said Cole in a low gravelly voice. They climbed into the buggy and headed toward home.

CHAPTER 7

1881, JEREMY AND EMMA

Several days later, as Emma exited the bakery, she was distracted by the notebook in her hand. She didn't get far when she heard a voice call her name.

She glanced around and saw Jeremy leaning against the wall a few feet from her.

"Jeremy," she said with a laugh. "Just in the neighborhood?"

"No, I'm here to see you," he said cheerfully as he straightened up to his full height, rubbing a hand through his curly hair.

"Okay, walk me home?" she asked.

"Sure," he said. He wanted to delay the reason for his visit so he could enjoy her company.

She looked over curiously and asked, "So, what is the reason for your wanting to see me?"

"I did some follow-up on your notebook," he commented.

Emma stopped for a moment and tilted her head at him. "And?" she said, prompting him.

He let out the breath he didn't know he was holding when he realized Emma was curious and not upset. "I made notes on the last entry," he said, looking at her. "I found the woman you mentioned."

"How did you know it was her?" she inquired curiously.

"Your description of auburn hair and pale skin helped. I also chose to investigate the 'house' to the right of the alley," he reported.

"Hmm," she said noncommittally and started walking again.

He followed up with the details of the attack, the meeting with the lady in question, and her 'house'.

"What was the 'house' like?" asked Emma, extremely interested in mysterious things, and this type of 'house' was definitely that.

"It wasn't what I expected," he admitted, his face turning red.

"Now I really want to know what it looked like," she teased.

Still red and squirming, he answered, "It was nice, with rich colors of browns and blues. Some splashes of gold. I mostly saw the entryway, the massive staircase, and the library."

"What was she like?" asked Emma, enjoying his discomfiture.

"Smart," he said, thinking about Clair. "She seems to be a woman who knows who she is and where she's going. She doesn't apologize for who she is or what she does."

Funny, thought Emma. *He didn't comment on her looks.*

"There is another thing I wanted to share, but I would need a bit more privacy than this," he said, looking around them.

"Home then," she suggested.

He nodded and they headed toward Emma's house. On their way there, they discussed different cases they were working on. As they entered the house, Dora heard Emma and yelled out, "Come into the kitchen!"

"We have company!" Emma yelled back. "I need to meet with him first."

Dora entered the foyer from the kitchen, wiping her hands on her apron. "Hi, Jeremy. Sorry for the yelling."

"That's okay." He grinned, he liked when the house was noisy.

"Would you like something to drink or a snack?" asked Dora warmly.

Jeremy started to say no, but he remembered how wonderful Dora's baked goods were. "Do you have anything sweet?"

"Want me to surprise you?" she asked with a smile.

"Yes, please," he replied quickly.

"I'll have Amy bring you some tea and I'll send a sweet surprise." She looked at Emma and said pointily, "You'll need to eat lunch, so don't fill up on sweets."

Emma saluted and Dora winked at her as she left.

With that, Emma and Jeremy entered the study. "Papa is out of town on a job and won't mind if we use the room. Sit, sit," she said.

He closed the doors and sat down on the couch beside her. "This has to stay quiet; many people could be hurt if the information got out."

She frowned. "Are we still talking about the lady you met at the house, the manager?"

"Yes, her name is Clair Spencer. We were looking into her background as a precaution and found something."

This had Emma on the edge of her seat, but a knock sounded at the door. Emma looked toward it, resigned, and said, "Please, come in."

Amy rolled in a tray with tea and Kuchen, a German pastry. She smiled brightly at Jeremy and left the tea and sweets on the little roll cart near the couch. He scooted closer and asked, "Tea?"

"Please," said Emma. He poured a cup for her and himself and picked out a Kuchen to try.

"Clair Spencer," she encouraged as she took a sip of tea.

Jeremy swallowed the bite in his mouth and continued, "She owns the 'house' she lives and manages, but she also owns another house."

"Is it the same type of place?"

"I asked the same thing," he said wryly. "No, she uses this house as a shelter, to take care of and hide ladies who have been abused by the men in their lives."

She sat a bit stunned; she'd thought he was going to say something illegal. "How does she manage it?"

"We're not sure where the money is coming from, but the main people in that house are there for safety reasons and it is a secret location. Cole and I decided to back off so we didn't inadvertently expose their efforts."

"Jeremy," Emma said thoughtfully. "Could you arrange a meeting for me and Miss Spencer?"

"Yes," he said. He noticed she was drumming her fingers on her lips. "What are you thinking?"

"I'm thinking I would love to meet the lady you have described to me. I'm also thinking of ways we might be able to help her."

"I'll set it up," he promised.

At the front door, they parted with a touch of their hands. She leaned against the door frame and watched him leave. He stopped at the bottom step and turned back to give her one last long, searching glance before he headed off.

Dora came into the foyer and watched as Emma shut the front door. "Did Jeremy leave already? I was hoping to talk to him," she said, sounding disappointed.

"Hm," said Emma, still thinking about Jeremy. Shaking herself out of the mood, she said, "I think we need a team meeting."

"What would be the topic of this meeting," asked Dora, wondering if they had a new case.

"Jeremy told me about a woman who is sheltering a group of abused ladies. "

"What can we do to help?" Dora asked immediately. "Are you thinking food, medical treatment, etc. . ."

"First," she said, "Let me meet with the woman and see what assistance we can offer."

"Yes, that would be the right thing to do."

CHAPTER 8

1881, EMMA'S FIRST MEETING WITH CLAIR

Jeremey set up a lunch for both ladies at a restaurant in an out-of-the-way location. Emma pulled her bike to a stop at its entrance and studied the neighborhood. It had an appearance of quiet elegance, one that was inviting. She climbed off her bike and walked it to the door. A well-dressed gentleman stepped out when he saw her.

"Can I put this somewhere safe?" Emma asked as he approached her.

"Yes, of course. I am Charles, your Host." When the reservation was made, the gentleman had told him they would need to store the bike. "We'll bring it out when you are ready to leave," he said, snapping his fingers at his waitstaff to remove it.

As it was moved, he motioned for her to follow him inside the dark restaurant. A woman was seated at the table they were approaching. *This must be Clair Spencer.* Emma had never met a woman in the sex trade before, she didn't know what she'd expected, but this wasn't it. Taking a moment to observe her, she took in the intricate design of the woman's dress. Her eyes moved up to her hair, it was auburn and pinned up high on her head. Her makeup was also applied with a subtle hand.

Clair was evaluating Emma in much the same manner.

Emma chose not to say anything as she waited for the host to pull out her chair. Taking her seat, she faced the woman. They waited for their host to leave before beginning any conversation. Both ladies were nervous; Emma took a breath and said, "Hello."

"Hello," Clair said back, her tone reserved.

"I'm Emma Evans."

"I figured," Clair said laconically.

"Jeremy mentioned your name is Miss Spencer," Emma said politely.

"Clair, please," she said, in the same tone.

"Very pretty. Please call me Emma."

"Thank you." She nodded graciously.

"I've been wanting to meet you since Jeremy told me about the follow-up from our incident," Emma said as she pulled her notebook from her pocket. It was the original one from the attack on Clair and herself. She felt the need to add the final information before closing the case.

Clair's mouth quirked up at the site of the notebook. "Am I being interviewed?" she teased lightly, slightly softening toward this young girl.

"No, no, I just wanted to add to the facts you shared with Jeremy. He mentioned you remember more than I do from that day," Emma assured her.

"What would you like to know?" Clair asked.

"Do you mind going through it again?" Emma asked gently.

"No, I don't. I understand that you want to know what happened." She took a deep breath and began with how she'd known Zeke and how she ended up in that alley. "He was a regular for me." When Emma frowned because she didn't understand the term, Clair explained, "He would come weekly to spend time with me."

"Was he violent toward you during these 'visits'"?

"Not at first, but after a while, he starting to hit me," Clair said.

"Why did you keep seeing him?" Emma asked.

She explained, "He would apologize and bring me gifts. I let it go on for far too long. He wasn't always violent, so I thought I could handle him."

"What happened to set him off that night?"

"He had been late and this is a business, I had another 'visitor'. When he found out, he entered my room and pulled me out and down the stairs to the alleyway. That is when you saw us."

"What happened then?"

"You were charging at us with your blonde hair flying, brandishing a stick almost as large as you were. You hit him in the back of the head, causing him to drop me and go after you." She finished her story with, "The last I saw of you was Zeke grabbing your hair."

More questions were asked about that day, and Clair shared everything she remembered. Emma closed the notebook, feeling comfortable enough to close the case.

Both ladies remained silent as the waiter approached and set the table with tea and cakes. They began eating the cakes and sipping their tea when Emma broached another topic in a low voice, "I wanted to talk with you about your other house."

Clair's eyes darted about the room, shocked and fearful that someone had heard the comment. Protection was paramount and she would do anything to keep the women that house's secrets.

Emma hastened to assure her in a lower voice, "Don't worry, I'm not going to tell anyone. We—my family and I—want to see if there is something we could help with. Whether that be money or volunteers or food."

Clair smiled, a feeling of relief washing over her. "Money is not an issue at this time. I have some wealthy benefactors who help. We also have all the help we need at the house."

Emma wondered who the wealthy benefactors were.

Clair had done some investigating of her own and knew Emma was a type of detective. One who didn't get a lot of attention, but got a lot done. "What we need is someone to help with moving the women out of town to a safer location so they can start their lives over."

Emma looked intrigued at that response. They sat and talked well into the late afternoon. When they were ready to leave, the two struck up an agreement. When needed, Clair would contact Emma about moving the women to another house or another city.

Before they departed, Clair reached over and touched her hand. "Thank you."

Emma didn't ask what for; she knew she was being thanked for removing Zeke from their lives.

They parted ways, knowing it wouldn't be the last time they would meet.

CHAPTER 9

1881, FIRST MOVES FOR CLAIR

It wasn't long before Emma received her first request from Clair to move one of the women from the house to an out-of-state location. They had confirmed the contact, where she would be moved, and the timing of the event. That evening, she met with her team: Tony, Tim, Dora, and Thomas to figure out the best strategy.

Dora said, "Emma, the best way to do this is to dress as a boy."

Tim nodded. "I would agree with that, and I can help with the move."

Emma smiled broadly and reached over to touch Tim's hand. "Tim, out of anyone, I wouldn't want you. You would be recognized a mile away." She paused and looked toward Thomas saying, "I was thinking of you."

A warm feeling washed over him. "Yes, I can help." He enjoyed being part of the team and actively helping with cases.

Tony commented, "I agree. A small operation is better and safer for both ladies."

The group talked the plan through and organized a detailed note containing information on the prearranged evening.

Thomas would deliver it to Clair. Emma would dress in boy's clothes, meet at the house to pick up and transport the woman to a safe location via train. They would walk together to a cab driven by Thomas. Tim would arrange for a private compartment in the railcar and Dora would make sure there was food for the trip.

Clair sent back her agreement to the plans and asked for a final date.

Arrangements were made for the plan to be put into effect.

On the agreed night, Emma was ready to head over to Clair's house for the pickup. She kissed Tony goodbye and left the boarding house on her bike. It was stashed behind a bush as she approached the back door of the safe house and knocked. The door opened quickly, a hand reached out and took Emma's, pulling her into the kitchen. That hand belonged to Clair and she was dressed similarly to Emma. Grinning a bit, Clair tipped her hat toward her.

Emma stayed serious and asked, "Is she ready?"

"Yes, come this way." Clair sobered and led her to the dining room just off the kitchen. When Emma saw her first transport, she shook her head. The lady was dressed like a lady, her hair coifed high on her head and a blue dress with a bustle attached to the back. "Clair, do you have any help here?"

Clair nodded, catching on to her train of thought. "Yes, Katy McKenna is still here."

"We'll need to have them exchange clothes," she said. "There's no way we won't be noticed with her dressed like that."

The lady in question started pulling pins out of her hair and said, "I'll do what needs to be done."

They helped her change into the maid's plain clothes and pulled her hair into a tight bun. Emma looked the lady in the eye and asked, "Are you ready."

"Yes," the lady responded.

Emma nodded and picked up the carpetbag. "Follow me,

please. Everyone else stay here," she directed. Lights in the house were extinguished and they made their way out to the alley. Thomas and the cab would be waiting, a few blocks down. The night was quiet and they walked arm in arm down the street. Though Emma was prepared for any unexpected events, she was glad that none occurred. They located Thomas waiting in the shadows, he quickly headed over to take the bag from Emma. He helped the lady into the cab and Emma climbed in on her own. They made their way to the train station and into their private compartment.

She opened the door and motioned to the porter. He walked over, Emma kept her hat pulled down and her voice gruff when she asked him, "Could you make sure we are not disturbed. The lady needs her rest."

He looked curious but didn't question her request after she placed the money in his hand. "I will make sure you are not disturbed," he promised.

Emma shut the door slowly behind her and looked toward her traveling partner. She didn't inquire about her name, not wanting to intrude into her privacy. Instead, she took her book out of her coat and made herself comfortable on the bench. It was a relatively quiet trip that took a few days. They stayed in their compartment, talking quietly and eating the food Dora had prepared. The train was met by the lady's brother. The brother and sister hugged tightly; Emma reminded them to keep a low profile. He assured her that the husband wasn't aware of his location and would not know to look for her here. Once assured, Emma headed back to the train station to confirm when her return ticket could be used to head home. She had balked at the expense of a private compartment on the way back, but Clair and the family were adamant. Emma would also have to buy food on the train. The wait was short and the trip home uneventful.

As she exited at the Chicago station, she was dressed once

more in female clothes. Tony waved at her as she descended the stairs and made her way to him. She slid into his arms gratefully, laying her head on his chest.

"Tired?" he murmured in her ear.

"Yes, but I shouldn't be, just sitting and reading for two days. I'm also very glad to be home," she said into his chest.

He kissed her forehead and asked, "Successful trip?"

"Yes," she said simply. "Let's go home."

Emma and her team would continue to quietly transport battered women over the next two years. During that time, Clair and Emma would continue to spend time together and what started as a shared experience would grow into a friendship.

CHAPTER 10

1883, PRESENT DAY

That put a closure to it, she thought as she slid the notebook back into the drawer and closed it.

She continued to get organized for her day and thought, *1881-2 brought so many positive things to their lives.* One of those was the job she was getting ready for this morning. It was part of the temporary employment agency that had been started by her, Dora, and Tim over two years ago.

The business began after a rather accidental burglary that involved their friends Miss May and Miss Marjorie. They were eighty and eighty-two respectively and had been extremely skilled burglars when they were younger. Miss May had additional skills as an escape artist and Miss Marjorie in knife throwing. They were also very close to Emma and had taught her those skills.

While attending an exhibit at the museum, Miss May saw a knife she thought Emma would like; she took it and gave it to her. Emma had explained why she couldn't keep it. Miss May reluctantly gave the knife to Emma and Tony to return.

They met with the curator to explain what had happened and to return the knife. Surprisingly he listened to their story and took them at their word. He seemed more curious about how it happened rather than placing blame on who did it. What interested him was the ladies, who could have taken something from the museum without anyone noticing.

The meeting had given Emma an idea. She approached Tim about a temporary employment agency with Miss Marjorie and Miss May as their first clients. He had taken the idea and developed it, with Emma and Dora as his partners.

Miss Marjorie and Miss May began conducting security surveys for the museum. The ladies couldn't work a full-time schedule but could work part-time for them through the new business. Tim helped set their hours and their pay.

Word had gotten out that temporary jobs were available in the security business; so much so that some Pinkerton detectives applied for side work. The business was strongly security-based in the beginning.

The only sad thing that happened during this time was the original ladies, the reason the business began, had passed away. They had passed together, sitting in the garden, holding hands. Emma missed her two friends.

Emma had moved on from that active year by focusing on completing her education. She'd finished business school and had begun working temporary jobs in various fields. She also tried to stay out of trouble and minded her own business.

Dear-one commented wryly, "Really?"

The Narrator sent a side glance and a slight smile to Dear-one. "Well, I did say try."

CHAPTER 11

1881, BUSINESS SCHOOL

Tim was planning an expansion to their agency as soon as Emma finished business school. The initial delay occurred because the schools in the area only took on male students. Emma had known about the male student issue when she applied. She applied anyway, wanting the schools to accept her based on her qualifications and not her gender. The process continued and with each rejection letter, she persevered and reapplied, stating her qualifications in detail.

"A letter came for you," called Dora.

"Did it?" she asked as she walked quickly to the small table in the foyer. Flipping through the mail, she found the one she was looking for. She pulled it out slowly, pondering whether or not to open it. *This could be the one,* she thought taking a breath and slid her finger into the envelope to open it. It was the same form letter she had gotten so many times, she sighed heavily.

There has to be something I can do, she thought as she laid the letter back down on the small table. Emma had wanted to do this on her own but it looked like help would be needed. *There was one person that could help,* she thought and ran up the stairs to change, trousers would not be acceptable. She came back down to the foyer and added the new rejection to the ones she was carrying. "I'm headed out, I'll be back soon," she called, not waiting for a response. Striding swiftly to the cable car, she jumped on and rode toward the destination where her friend worked.

She entered his office and waited until he looked up from his desk.

When he did look up, he said, "Emma! What a nice surprise."

The large paneled office with a wall of windows belonged to the Chicago Chief of Police. *Funny*, she thought *that wasn't what he said the first time I visited here*. It was a nice change and she really liked him. "Sir, it is good to see you also."

"Why don't you sit?" he asked as he stood.

"Thank you," Emma said as she sat down. She hesitated before asking her question.

"Are you here for a visit or is there something else," he prompted.

"A visit but also this." She handed him her stack of rejections.

"What are these?" he asked curiously looking at the envelopes.

"Rejections for business schools I'd like to attend."

"There appears to be more than one," he observed.

"Yes. I have tried to get in on my own, but it isn't working. I was hoping you could help."

"Hmm and what do you think I can do about this," he asked looking at her sternly. He held it as long as he could before laughing and said, "I'm sure we can work something out. Is there a particular one you would like to attend?"

"Yes, this one," she said, pointing to a specific envelope. "I'd appreciate your help with this."

"I'll take care of it, now tell me what is going on with your family."

They had an enjoyable hour, and as he walked her out, he told her, "I'll look into the school this week."

"Thank you," she said and leaned down to kiss him on the cheek.

He smiled and watched her leave before going back to his work.

The letter arrived from the school that Thursday afternoon. The mail was on the small table in the foyer, she spotted it as soon as she entered the house. The envelope from the business school was on top, she didn't hesitate this time and tore it open. She started shouting, "Dora! Dora!"

Dora ran in and said, "What happened? What's wrong?"

Emma waved the letter in the air and had a wide grin.

"You got in!"

"I got in," she confirmed.

Dora ran over and hugged Emma tightly. She pulled back and asked, "When does class start?"

"I didn't check," she admitted. She looked down at it and Dora peered over her shoulder. "It looks like a few weeks and I have to go in for an interview."

"That sounds ominous, do you think they could still turn you down?" asked Dora.

Emma tapped the letter on her hand and thought about the police chief, her lips turned up into a wide smile. "No, I don't think so." She looked back at the contents of the envelope and saw it included a cost structure for the program. The reward money she earned from her previous investigations would be enough to pay for it.

"When will you go for the interview?" asked Dora.

"Tomorrow," Emma replied.

"Emma, behave yourself," Dora admonished. "You want this to go well."

"When do I ever not behave," she teased.

Dora sent her a look.

Emma said in a more serious tone, "I will do my best."

CHAPTER 12

1881-82, EMMA'S APPOINTMENT AT THE BUSINESS SCHOOL

*E*mma dressed in a conservative manner to meet the dean. This included a dark blue skirt, white blouse, dark blue jacket, and a smallish blue hat with a white ribbon perched on her head. Waiting outside the office, she forced her hands open, they had been clenched tightly, showing her tension. Taking deep breaths, she watched the door where her meeting would take place.

The dean's secretary looked over and waved Emma to the door. Nodding, she stood and walked quickly toward it. She knocked firmly on it and was called in. As the door opened, she got a view of Dean Randolph. He was a tall slim nice-looking man with dark hair, who appeared to be about thirty and very serious.

"Miss Evans?" he asked.

Emma approached his desk and took the seat in front, "Yes, thank you for seeing me today."

"It wasn't like I had a choice," he muttered. He looked up from his desk, into her eyes, and said, "I will be honest with you, this is a MALE business school and we did not want to accept you here."

Emma kept her mouth shut and let him talk.

"But you are here, so we must make the best of it. You will be given a chance but you must make the grades and pay the fees on time. If you cannot do either, you will be expelled. Is that understood?"

"Yes, it is," she said in a civil tone.

"The term starts in two weeks, can you make the payment now?"

"Yes. I have it with me."

He nodded. "Please see our clerk. You will also be expected to pass a series of test that tells us what level you are at academically. Are you prepared to do that today?"

"I am," she said confidently. "Thank you."

She started to stand and stopped when he said, "Miss Evans, I don't like how you went about this, but I understand wanting to improve one's self. Good luck."

"Thank you," she said as she stood and left the room. Emma went to find the clerk to get her forms organized. The journey she was on was very exciting. She wouldn't squander this opportunity –for her or the women that would come after her.

Emma's test showed that she was well educated but she was still a woman. Against all expectations of her teachers and the dean of the school, she excelled in each course and graduated at the top of her class. During that time, she had an appointment with the dean to discuss her career options. The meeting was a formal step all students took as they prepared to leave the school.

Emma wasn't worried about her career options and had other ideas about the direction she wanted to steer the conversation. Sitting in the dean's waiting room, she waited for the appointment time. At precisely 3pm, the secretary motioned to her and said, "You may go in now."

As she entered the office, she saw the dean sitting at a round table with folders piled around him. "Come in; sit down,"

Randolph said, indicating the chair across from him when he noticed her in the doorway. She moved quickly across the room, sat in a chair opposite him, and proceeded to open her notebook. He looked over curiously but didn't question it, he was eager to get on with the interview. Opening the file in front of him, he and stated, "Let's begin. . ."

"I have another idea," she said, as she interrupted him.

"What?" he asked, more distracted than ever, sending her a pained look. He had gotten many reports from Emma's teachers on how she periodically interrupted their lectures with her questions. He had planned this meeting to explain that there were no jobs for women available, but as usual, Emma was disrupting those plans.

"Why not bring more women into the school?" she asked a bit forcefully.

"Well, they don't—" he started but was interrupted again.

"They don't do what, perform as well as a man?" she asked, she felt she could guess the answer.

"No, I wasn't going to say that. What I am saying is that they can't get jobs, so it is a waste of our time," he stated, trying to reason with her.

"So, you're saying if I were able to guarantee employment for women, then you would accept them into your school?" Emma asked as she manipulated the conversation.

"Yes," he said, not realizing what he had agreed to.

"Okay then," she said, wheels already turning in her head. Emma closed her notebook and stood to leave.

"Wait, what about you and your position evaluation?" Dean Randolph asked, bewildered by the direction the meeting had taken.

She turned back toward him and said, "I already have jobs waiting for me. Thanks, though." With that, she was out of the room and on her way home.

The dean sat for an additional moment and slowly closed

her file. *Women,* he thought. He didn't expect to see her again after graduation and was happy the school could be a professional environment again. She brought too much energy to the classrooms and was exhausting to the teachers.

That evening, Emma sat down with Tim to develop a business plan for women to work in the offices within their agency. One of their biggest goals was to provide them with more opportunities outside the home.

Tim organized a survey and sent it to the local engineering firms to see if there would be places for graduating women within those offices. Tim spent the next few weeks setting up meetings with other types of businesses to secure additional future positions. Their contacts were enthusiastic about personnel being more available, men or women. Chicago was building quickly and there didn't seem to be enough people to fill the available positions.

Emma and Tim used the data provided by the survey and interviews they conducted to build a detailed business plan to add more women to the workforce. They then went directly to the dean's office at the business school to speak with him about it. When Dean Randolph saw who was waiting for him, he hesitated before inviting them into his office. He hadn't expected Emma to follow up on the promise he'd inadvertently made.

He finally let them into his office and, within a few moments, sat stunned at the job plan they had put together. The opportunities available to women graduates were described in detail; a list with potential contacts was provided for his review.

"So, you're saying you have jobs for people you don't know?" Randolph asked incredulously.

"No, we're saying we have jobs for qualified women," Emma corrected. "You promised that if I could guarantee jobs, you would add more women to your school," she continued determinedly.

"Well, I—"

"Are you a man of your word?" she demanded.

"I am," he said rather indignantly

Tim interrupted both, saying, "Look, this is getting us nowhere." He gave Emma a look as he continued. "I think that if we can speak a bit more calmly, we'll be able to iron out the details."

"Yes, well, we always seem to end up here, don't we?" the dean said as he offered a conciliatory smile to Emma.

Emma nodded and relaxed back in her chair, realizing he was listening to them.

In calmer tones, the dean started, "I will agree to this only if you understand that the applicants will have to meet our stringent entry requirements."

"Oh, they will," said Emma, thinking of the ladies she could encourage. There were several she knew who would do well in the school but didn't know there were options outside of marriage. There was also Clair's house, the women there need options to help them get back on their feet financially.

Emma reached across the table to shake the dean's hand. He paused only a moment before shaking it. Tim smiled broadly and stuck out his hand to help seal the deal.

"Tim, I have an idea," Emma said as they were leaving the dean's office. "It would involve women who need more choices in their lives."

Tim had an idea of who she was thinking about but was more pragmatic. "Who would pay? Can they afford it?"

"I think Clair would find a way. I will talk to her," commented Emma.

"Would she do it?" Tim asked cautiously.

"I think she might. I'll meet with her. I'll need to contact Jeremy."

Emma thought about her new friend, Clair Spencer. Their relationship had changed from survivors with a shared experience to close friends.

CHAPTER 13

1883, PRESENT DAY

So many success stories, she thought. Their success rate with graduating females was in the 90th percentile, with most assuming temporary or permanent roles. Emma's hope was that more women would begin their education prior to getting married. It would allow them some independence within the relationship.

Emma reached for her clutch knife sheath and pulled her skirt up, strapping it on her upper thigh, always glad to have the extra protection.

As she gathered her hat, gloves, and satchel from her brass bed, she checked the knife always hidden in her hat. She had to be careful with it; the knife was quite big and was kept sharp. With that final check, she pulled the quilt over the bed and headed downstairs for breakfast.

Her plans for the day included office work in the morning and courier work in the afternoon. The office work was part of the temporary employment business she operated with Tim and Dora. The business had fit in perfectly with Emma's professional plans.

She found she liked temporary work; where she could

continue to develop her skills observing people. It also left her open to take on independent investigations with Pinkerton. Cole had added her to cases when he realized that Emma could get women to talk when no one else could.

As of now, she was working at Baker Engineering as a temporary secretary. There was no case involved in this particular job. Like Tim had told her, "Not everything involved a mystery. Some were just jobs."

Her home was still the boarding house, shared with family and boarders. Boarding houses had come out of making room for families needing a place to live as a result of the 1871 fire.

The 1880s were a time when boarding houses were part of the fabric of life. Private boarding houses like theirs normally lodged single individuals or married couples without children. Theirs was different, they took in individuals and married couples, but they also enjoyed having children around. Dora continued to manage the household.

The family was very particular who lived with them and only took in people who would get along with them. A few things had changed, Tim and Dora had converted two bedrooms on the second floor into one for their use. Another two were being kept empty for Emma's future specialist. In the past, her father had used specialists to build Emma's skills in self-defense, knife throwing, and escape. Her idea now was to have other specialists come in, use their skills, and build a team.

Emma headed downstairs to help with breakfast and heard a booming voice coming from the kitchen. She pushed the door open and caught Dora in Tim's arms. It was not an unusual occurrence, especially since they had married the previous year.

Tim was big, with shoulders that could breach a doorway, ginger hair, and the ruddy complexion that generally accompanied Irishmen. He was always the first to the kitchen, just behind Dora; usually trying to get her to blush or to snag a Berliner. The first one was not hard to accomplish; Dora blushed whenever Tim was in the vicinity. He was currently teasing her about having her hair tucked into her handkerchief. ". . .but it's so pretty—why not have it down?"

Her response, "And have it in my baking or my meals?"

Tim had extra time in the mornings because their temporary employment business continued to be successful; enough so that, in the past year, he had quit his accounting job. He was enjoying being an entrepreneur and loved running a company with his wife and her sister.

Emma wagged her finger at them. "You are being a bad influence on Amy."

Amy, Dora's helper, stood by the sink doing dishes and just grinned over her shoulder at them. She had been with them for many years. She was a solid woman with dark hair and a happy disposition. She also seemed very content with her job and her life. The house was such a happy place to live and work.

Tim gave Dora a last lingering kiss and turned to Emma to say in a more conservative tone. "Morning, Emma. We need to talk before you leave today. Business."

"Breakfast first?" Emma asked Tim, glancing at the abundance of food set out and ready to be moved to the dining room table.

"Yes, always, especially if it's my Dora cooking." Tim sent a wink her way and Dora's cheeks heated. Tim thought, *I love I can still turn her cheeks red.*

Moving into her manager role, Dora said, "Okay, everyone grab something to move." Amy and Tim took their assigned trays and moved them to the table.

Emma grabbed a fresh piece of bread and some butter before she started to move her platters. "Emma, there's plenty on the table in the dining room," Dora reminded her with a smile.

Emma smiled and said, "Stolen ones taste the best." She ate the bread quickly and helped move the platters into the dining room. The long oak plank table had seen better days but provided enough spaces for twelve people to eat. It was already covered with food: eggs, bacon, two types of toast, pastries, pancakes, and oatmeal. Dora didn't let anyone go hungry.

The first ones to the table were generally the Irish widow—Molly and her twin sons. Emma thought, *I am sure there were odes written to her with her blazing red hair and Irish temper.* Her twin boys were mischievous and always planning their next adventure. Running into the room, just ahead of their mom, they stopped suddenly when they saw Emma.

"Good morning, Sister," they said together.

"Morning, boys," Emma replied.

Second to the table were Bessie and Harold Allen, a young couple saving their money to eventually buy a home of their own. Harold was able to find work in building design and assisted Papa in his engineering work now that Emma was busier with her other jobs. Bessie worked different jobs through their temp business as a housemaid, store clerk, and was being trained in typing. She was only working to fill the time until she and Harold had a baby.

Next to the table was Papa, who in his absent-minded way walked by Emma and dropped a kiss on her head. He never looked up from his notebook where he recorded notes for his engineering jobs.

And finally, last to the table, carrying butter, jam, and bread, were Dora and Tim.

Breakfast was a frantic affair when the food started to be passed around. It was best to take what you wanted quickly, or it wouldn't be around again. Being polite could leave you hungry. Occasionally, there were new people at the table, but fewer appeared over the years. The current boarders had long been considered family. *Family who pay rent,* Emma thought with a smile. *After all, it is still a business.*

She took a minute to look at the chairs on either side of her, where the two boys were seated. It was where Miss Marjorie and Miss May had once sat. How she missed their company and advice. She shook off any sadness, knowing they'd had a good life and had died together.

Emma could hear Papa going on about something; it was probably codes or engineering, the only topics that got him stirred up. The rest of the group knew this and were patient with him. Other topics introduced included the day's events, politics, or gossip. Everyone ate their fill and started moving from the table to begin their days; the boys off to school and the adults off to work. Emma, Tim, Dora, and Amy cleared the table and moved the now empty trays to the kitchen. The dishes were scraped and Amy started washing with Tim drying.

Once the cleanup was completed, Amy headed upstairs to start her list of tasks for the day. Dora, Tim, and Emma sat down at the kitchen table and began their meeting.

He had out his ledger and started with a tally of employees. "We currently have thirty-five temporary employees, thirty-six counting Emma," he said, nodding at her. "The staffing includes fifteen men and women in sales at Stubing and Marshall Field's department stores. In other engineering offices, we have ten engineers and office help. At the bakery, we have two, but they will need more once the holiday seasons start. At the museum, we have four security staff personnel. And finally, at the Baker Engineering Office, we have two administrative employees, including Emma. Also, we are down to two there because they hired two more of our people permanently."

"We should let the business school know that we have had two more women hired permanently in the office," commented Emma.

"Yes, good idea. That will encourage them to bring in more women to train," noted Tim.

"Tim, Papa mentioned he may need some additional engineering support on the new building he is working on," said Dora, looking over her notes.

"Noted. Thanks, Dora," said Tim, taking down the upcoming job. "I'll be getting the checks ready to distribute. Emma, could you pick them up this afternoon?" he asked. The temporary workers were paid monthly after they received their pay from the various companies.

"I can take them around," said Emma. She worked as a courier in the afternoons and could make time to come by the boarding house.

"Any further concerns at this time?" Tim asked. Emma and Dora shook their heads. "No? Okay, we're finished. Emma, please let me know if anyone has any concerns when you drop off their checks."

"I will," she promised.

As the meeting was coming to a close, a knock sounded at the door. Emma looked up to see Tony coming in through the back door. "Good morning, everyone," he said cheerfully. He leaned in and kissed Emma on the cheek. She turned a deep red.

"Morning, Tony," said Emma softly and gazed into his eyes. He gazed back until Tim cleared his throat loudly.

"Hope I'm not interrupting anything," Tim said wryly.

"No," said Tony with a smile. "Nothing I can't do later." He was there to walk Emma to work—or rather, have Emma walk him to the trolley.

Emma gathered up her hat and bag and got organized to leave. "Don't forget to come by for the checks, Emma," called Tim as she was leaving through the kitchen door.

"I'll be here," she promised and they departed the house.

As they were walking, Tony pushed Emma's bike for her. He looked over and said, "Emma, I wanted to tell you about someone that comes to the museum."

"Yes?" she commented, listening.

"He comes and goes each day at the same time."

"Do you think he's casing the museum, planning a robbery?" Her mind was already working on ways to catch this unnamed person.

"No, no, I don't think so." Knowing where her mind was wandering, he said quickly, "His only interest is the photo exhibit."

"Yes, I know that one, the London scenes are very interesting, He has no interest in the other exhibits?" she asked, curious where this was going.

"Never. He comes in and just stares at the pictures in that one exhibit. I think he also carries a camera." He hesitated briefly, then said, "I think he might be one of the specialists you're looking for."

"Really? Photography?" she said. *It's a relatively new field,* she thought to herself. *It might be interesting. The skill would be important because only professional photographers can operate cameras and develop pictures.*

She directed her next question to Tony, "What are your thoughts? For me to learn the skill from him?" That was how the specialists were usually utilized, as more of a supportive role rather than an actual part of the group. They were usually brought in specifically to teach Emma a new skill.

"No," he said a bit slowly. "I was thinking about your idea to develop new specialists with a hands-on role." He smiled and stated in a wry voice, "That is if he actually takes pictures and doesn't just carry a camera around."

"Probably a good idea to check first," teased Emma, bumping him with her hip. "We have been keeping the rooms at the boarding house opened," she mused. "It would be a good resource for new investigations." She turned the idea over in her head, realizing a camera would make it easier to retrieve evidence. "Hmm. Do you want me to talk to him?"

"Not yet. Let me approach him first."

When they got to their stop, Tony turned to her. "Where are

you today?" he asked, leaning down to press his forehead against hers.

"Still at the business office," she murmured.

"I have some items that should be sent out today if you want to stop by later," Tony said, lifting his head. Emma had several clients near the museum that she moved around documents for. The city was still growing and paperwork had to be moved from engineers to city officials, suppliers, and customers.

She leaned in closer and said, "I'll come by after I pick up the checks from Tim. I have a few to drop off in that area."

He lowered his head to give her a lingering kiss and said, "See you later." He ran off to jump on the trolley, giving her a final wave.

She waved back, hopped on her bike, and rode off to her office job. Emma had been at her current assignment for a few months, which was unusual for a temporary job, but people were needed. As she pedaled on, the wind wove through her hair, pulling at her hairpins. Her papa had gotten her a Kangaroo dwarf safety bike developed by Hillman, Herbert, and Cooper. He had a contact who allowed Emma to get a model early and she used it to get to and from work; it was most useful for her work as a courier. The bike made riding quite easy.

Emma worked in an office building downtown. It was a bit of a ride but allowed her to see the city before many people were out and about. Slowing the bike as she arrived at the office. She hopped off and placed it on her shoulder to carry as she entered the building. The first thing she had to do was store it in a closet downstairs. After she locked the door, she moved upstairs to begin her day.

CHAPTER 14

JAKE

Tony was walking through the museum, inspecting the displays and taking notes on any changes that might be needed. He was also keeping a tally of the numbers of people attending the different exhibits. That number would help determine when the exhibits should be moved or replaced.

One of the exhibits, where that tally continued to be high, was the photography exhibit. It contained a large number of pictures featuring everyday life in London, England. The curator had a contact overseas who found art subjects suitable for display in the museum. Tony continued to refine his skills there and, in addition to management, was also learning how to evaluate art.

Tony continued his survey and entered the London exhibit. Their regular visitor was already there, having come every day since the exhibit opened. He always carried a camera that he held protectively against his chest. Tony had previously told the temporary security staff to keep an eye on him. They had reported that he would come in at the same time every day, viewed the same exhibit, and then left at the same time. He never deviated from this routine.

Tony decided to approach the man and find out if he could actually use that camera. As he got closer, he was able to get a clear view of the visitor. He was a young man, slim, in his twenties, with copper-colored hair. The brown suit he wore was always a bit wrinkled and tattered but appeared to be clean. The photos seemed to fully occupy his time and Tony noticed he also seemed to be talking to himself.

Tony approached him quietly and said, "Excuse me." The young man didn't seem to hear him and didn't look over. Tony started again and tapped his shoulder.

This time, the young man shifted his intense look away from the photographs. He looked over for a moment and then returned to staring at the display.

Tony took the initiative and said, putting his hand out toward him, "I'm Tony Marella and I work here at the museum." The young man didn't shake his hand but instead kept looking at the photographs. Tony slowly let his arm drop, realizing his gesture was not going to be accepted. He wondered if he should have had Emma talk to him. He decided to try once again and reached out to touch his sleeve while saying, "What's your name?"

Without glancing over, the man said, "Jake."

Since Jake had finally said something, Tony thought he should push his luck. "Do you like the photos, Jake?"

That seemed to be the key to getting him to talk. He started seemingly in the middle of a conversation. "If you notice the light on these and how the camera was able to capture the different angles. . ." He kept talking about the photos for more than thirty minutes.

Tony realized he hadn't spoken a word since asking Jake about the exhibit. *There had to be a way out of this conversation. How did I get his attention previously?* He reached out to touch Jake's arm and said, "Jake?" Jake immediately stopped talking and looked away from the photos. "I have to get back to work," he told him gently.

Jake nodded and turned back to look at the pictures while Tony continued his review of other exhibits. Later, as Tony moved on to other things, he realized Jake had gone for the day.

This went on for the next few days. Jake would come in at the same time and Tony would approach him after he'd been there for thirty minutes. He learned that Jake worked as a photographer for the police department in forensics. Tony would need to ask Emma what a photographer in forensics did. "Jake, can you bring in some of your pictures for me to view?" he inquired.

"Okay," he said, happy someone was interested in his favorite topic. "I can bring them in tomorrow."

CHAPTER 15

*D*inner time had rolled around; Tony routinely stayed after to socialize and discuss any cases that might be ongoing. *This was the right time to bring up Jake as a possible specialist,* thought Tony. He described their first meetings to the group and then his focus on photography. Looking over at Emma, he said, "He mentioned he works as a photographer for the police. I think he called it forensics. Do you know what that is?"

Emma looked serious when she answered, "Forensics involves police photographers who are forensic scientists who, like medical examiners, biologists, and chemists, develop and document evidence to help law enforcement solve crimes. After the records are gathered, they can be used to prosecute criminal cases. As cameras are improved upon, I expect they are being used more and more in the field."

"You're saying he has pictures of bodies and such?" That gave Tony a moment of pause. He groaned and said, "Oh, good grief, I asked him to bring in a sample of his work for me to view."

The group sat silently and let that statement sink in for a

moment. Then they all laughed. Tim said, "I guess you'll definitely see his work."

"Yes." Tony looked over at Emma and said a bit pleadingly, "Can you come tomorrow and be with me while I take a look at his photographs?"

Emma paused just long enough to worry him and then said, "Of course I'll be there." She reached over to hug him. "And I would like to evaluate him for a specialist position."

Dora asked, "It will be like an interview?"

"More of a pre-interview," Emma quantified.

CHAPTER 16

The next day, Tony glanced at his watch and realized it was Jake's normal time to visit the museum. At that moment, he saw him enter the main door with a large box, which Tony could only assume was full of pictures. He looked at his watch and smiled. *Right on time.* The guards stopped Jake at the door to evaluate the large box. Jake grew visibly upset over them trying to take it from him. "Stop, it's mine!" He wouldn't release it to them.

Before the situation could worsen, Tony stepped in and said to the guards, "It's all right. Jake is here to see me." The guards stopped their tug-of-war with Jake and nodded at Tony. Jake looked relieved as he took his box and started to follow him to his office. Tony hesitated and turned back toward the guards saying, "Let Emma know my location when she gets here." They nodded in agreement.

They continued to the office. Once they entered, Tony gestured to Jake to place the box on the desk. He was curious about the types of photographs he had brought with him. *Will it be the forensic ones? Can I stomach looking at them?* he thought, wishing Emma was there with him.

As Jake pulled the pictures out of the box and organized them into stacks, Tony braced himself for the worst. Jake looked over and said, "Come see." Tony moved over to the desk and hesitantly picked up the first picture in a pile. He was pleasantly surprised; one pile involved up-close pictures of people. None of these were posed pictures, which is how most pictures were taken during this time period. Another stack contained nature pictures: trees, grass, and flowers. A final stack involved close-ups of different types of objects: eyeglasses, grass, and carpet patterns. Tony was impressed; these were as good as those on exhibit.

He laughed suddenly and Jake gave him an intense look. Tony realized Jake thought he was laughing at his pictures. "Jake, I'm not laughing at you, I promise. I thought these might be forensic pictures and I was nervous to see them."

"Those are never to be shared outside of work. It is not allowed," he stated in a stern voice. He seemed to be mimicking another person, probably a supervisor.

Tony said gently, "Jake, you're right, I should have known better."

He nodded in agreement.

Tony continued, "You really know how to use that camera."

Jake looked unsure and answered literally. "Yes, I was trained in England on the use of it."

Tony smiled, realizing he needed to be clearer. "Do you sell your work?"

"No, I just take the pictures. The ones at work stay at work. I can't sell those."

"No, no, I wouldn't think so," he murmured, still looking at the pictures. "Do you have a lab at work?"

"Yes."

"Do you have one at home?"

"No, too small; smells too bad." Again, Jake sounded like he was quoting someone.

At that moment, Emma came in through the office door in her normal rushed manner. "I see you made it on time," commented Tony wryly over his shoulder.

She came up and hugged him from behind and said, "Got stuck at work."

Jake didn't look up from his pictures; he just let the conversation go on around him. Tony reached out and touched Jake's arm and said, "Jake." This action caused him to look up. "Jake, this is Emma. She also wants to see your pictures."

Jake immediately took an interest in Emma and said eagerly, "You like my pictures?"

"Well," said Emma cautiously, "I haven't seen them yet, but I am excited about being able to view them."

Tony and Emma poured over the photos, asking Jake questions about the locations and the items.

"Do you take these with that camera you carry around?" Emma asked.

"Yes, it is a Twin lens reflex camera from the Marion & Co. Academy. It was developed and sold in London. I was lucky to get one."

Emma continued flipping through the pictures and asked without looking up, "Can we keep these for a few days?"

Jake was very hesitant to let them out of his possession and said, "Well, I am not sure."

She looked up at Jake and said in a firm voice, "Jake, we will keep a close eye on them. We want to evaluate these further."

"All right then," he said a bit begrudgingly.

Emma thought quickly. "We would love for you to come to our boarding house for dinner, tomorrow night."

"Dinner? What time? I eat at 6pm."

Emma wiped a hand over her mouth to hide her smile. "Well 6pm is a bit early, but if you come then, we will be close to dinner."

He looked conflicted at the idea and did not seem to be able to decide without some prodding. Tony took the lead and said, "What time do you get off work tomorrow?"

"5pm. I always get off at 5pm, unless there is an investigation and then I have to work late," he stated in a business-like tone.

"We'll worry about that if it comes up. For now, let's plan on me picking you up from your work tomorrow." Jake frowned and Tony immediately understood the issue.

"Jake, is your hesitation because it's a change to your schedule? If it is, I think you'll enjoy having dinner at the house,"

Jake had focused back on his photos and said, "I can wait for you at my job."

Tony smiled and said, "Okay, where can I meet you?"

"I will be in the basement of the police station."

"I'll be there at 5pm and will take you to meet my friends and have dinner," said Tony. He could already tell he was dismissed as Jake started organizing the pictures in front of him. "Jake, I'll do that if you want to head back to work."

Jake noticed the time and said, "I just have time to view the exhibit before I leave."

"Thanks for bringing these in for us to see," said Emma in a sincere manner. Jake nodded and headed out to the exhibit. Tony knew he would be back on his schedule and back to work on time.

He walked over to the desk where Emma continued to look at the photographs in wonder. "He is an amazing photographer," she said, thinking of how this new technology could be applied to her investigations.

"Yes. What do you think about Jake becoming one of your specialists?" he asked.

"I think I like the idea," she said with a smile. "Let's see what the family thinks." She laid down the pictures, kissed him, and headed out to finish her afternoon jobs.

CHAPTER 17

That night after dinner, the group inspected Jake's pictures and discussed his skills. "I think Jake's skills would benefit us," said Emma. "I have a few jobs he would be helpful on."

"Also," commented Tony, "I think we would be good for Jake."

"What are you thinking, Tony?" Dora inquired softly. "What type of help could we provide him?"

"I think we could help him socially; he doesn't understand social cues at all. He also tends to only talk about what he's interested in." He looked over at Emma and asked, "Did you notice he doesn't make eye contact?"

"I did," she responded. "Do you think it's something we could help with?"

"Yes, in the short time I've been talking to him, I see that interaction with me has made him open up. He also tends to speak very little except about photography." Tony warned, "We need to not overwhelm him when he gets here. If we want to get to know him, we'll have to draw him out."

"A small group dinner, here in the kitchen?" suggested Dora, thinking about how to best meet Jake for the first time.

"Yes, we can help you with getting the boarders fed. Tony can bring Jake in through the kitchen and avoid some of the noise," suggested Emma.

Everyone agreed on the plan.

The next night, the kitchen was quiet with just Amy and Dora working on dinner when Tony knocked on the kitchen door. Dora wiped her hands on her apron and let them in.

"Hey, Tony," she said as he leaned down to kiss her on the cheek. "Who do we have here?" Dora asked, turning her gaze on Jake. She noticed right away that he did not make eye contact with her.

"This is Jake."

"Welcome, Jake. I'm Dora and this is Amy." Amy nodded over her shoulder at him from the stove. "As you can tell, dinner is almost ready. Would you like to sit at the kitchen table and have some bread and butter?"

Jake looked at Tony, then at Dora, and said in a somewhat monotone voice, "Yes, please."

"Have a seat," Dora said and indicated the kitchen table. They sat and watched while dinner was completed. When platters started being pulled out, Tony jumped up to help load them. "We will move these into the dining room and then we'll start our dinner in here after that. Okay?" she asked Jake.

He nodded. He had been told they would eat in the kitchen, so he stayed put.

"Tony, could you call Emma and Tim? They're in the study," requested Dora.

"Sure," he said as he went off to get them.

The boarders were at the table talking about their day and enjoying the food. The family had told them there would be a guest eating in the kitchen.

The family sat with Jake at the kitchen table to eat dinner.

Once the food had been consumed and cleared away, Emma and Dora handed out pie to everyone. Tim decided to ask Jake some questions. "Jake, where do you live? Do you live on your own?"

Jake looked up from his pie and answered, "I live two blocks east of the station and two turns off the main road."

Tim frowned. He knew that area. "Jake, those are very nice houses. Are you sure that's where you live?"

"Yes," stated Jake.

"Do you live with your parents?"

"No, they died," he said simply.

"Oh, Jake, we're sorry," said Dora, immediately feeling for the young man. "Was it long ago?"

"Mom passed about ten years ago and Dad about a year ago. I was in London and then I was allowed to come back home," he commented, looking around.

Emma wondered at the expression and asked, "Did someone tell you that you couldn't come home?"

"Yes. Dad said I was just a nuisance since Mom died and he had no time for me. I came home after he died."

"What were your parents' names? We might know them," she pointed out. Tim, Tony, and Emma had worked delivering to that neighborhood.

"Martha and Daniel Cooper," he stated.

Emma looked sharply at Tony. She had known Daniel lived in that area but had not considered him having a family. She followed up with a question and hoped they were wrong, "Jake, did your dad work at the paper?"

"Yes," he said absently, unaware of the turmoil he was causing. "He was the editor."

Tony looked as shocked as Emma felt. She stood in an agitated manner and indicated for Tony to follow her. Once in the dining room, he said in a low voice, "We should probably talk about this outside."

She nodded and accompanied him out to the front stoop. Once there she sat heavily on the first step, looked up at him, and said, "Tony! Good grief, what now?"

"Emma, I honestly had no idea," he said, throwing up his hands.

"I know, I know, but what do we do? Do we tell him I killed his father?" she asked, bewildered.

"I'm not sure what he knows since Pinkerton and the police chief kept your name out of it," commented Tony.

"But is it right? To not let him know?" She paused a moment. "I don't regret my actions, but I regret that he's alone now." She put her head in her hands. "Before we consider him as a specialist, I think we should have Pinkerton do a background check and confirm who his parents are—or were."

"Agreed," Tony said.

They went back in and found Dora and Tim talking at length with Jake about his job. They seemed to genuinely like him.

"Jake, let's get you home," Tony said.

Jake nodded and stood up to leave.

Dora stood also and approached him. She touched his arm, and said, "We would like to see you again."

"Can I come over tomorrow?" he asked quickly.

That caused Dora to laugh out loud. It was hard not to like him. "Well, let's wait a few days," she commented with a smile.

"So, Thursday," he said, taking everything literally.

"Yes," she said, giving in. "Thursday for dinner. Tony, can you pick him up again at work?"

Tony nodded and sent a worried look to Emma. She nodded it was all right. "We'll be going then," he said to Jake and the group.

Jake spoke up at that time and said, "Nice to meet you Tim, Dora, and Emma."

"You, too," they said almost simultaneously and laughed. Jake smiled back in response before following Tony out.

"Wow," Tim started, "is he Daniel's son?" Dora shook her head in response.

"I just don't know." Emma sat back at the table, looking down at her hands. She looked up at Tim and Dora and said, "I'll send a note over to Cole and ask him to look into this for us. I think until we hear more, we don't offer him a specialist position."

"Yes," Dora said. "I understand we have to wait to confirm his identity, but the main question is what will we do if he is Daniel's son?" Emma pondered that for a moment and Dora gently prodded her. "Emma, can you work with someone related to Daniel?"

She frowned. "If there's a connection, we'll have to see. I'm going to get the note written and over to Cole." That was not something she was ready to face until she had to.

Emma went upstairs and wrote out a detailed note to Cole about Jake, mentioning she would like to stop by after lunch tomorrow to discuss any findings.

CHAPTER 18

The next morning was slow to come around, as Emma spent most of the night thinking about Jake and Daniel. She kept dwelling on the question, *Can I work with Jake knowing that I killed his father?* She tried to push the thought out of her head until she spoke to Cole.

The clocked tinged seven times, it was time for breakfast. She went downstairs the next morning to help and have her regular morning business meeting with Dora and Tim. Breakfast was served and their morning meeting was completed just as Tony knocked at the kitchen door. He was waved in by Emma. A knock on the front door interrupted his good morning greetings. "I'll go check the front door," Tim offered, exiting the kitchen.

Dora caught Tony before they departed and asked, "How was Jake last night when you took him home?"

Tony shrugged. "He was Jake. He talked about different types of cameras and exposures the whole way."

"Did he live where he said he did?" she asked, worried about the young man living alone.

"Yes, it was exactly where he said it was. Staff met him at the door. In my opinion, they weren't very nice to him and they didn't like me dropping him off."

"Do you think he's okay there?" Dora asked worriedly.

"For now, but I think we should look into it," he said, also concerned that it was not the best place for Jake to live.

"I already asked Cole for further information on his background and his current home," commented Emma, still not sure how she felt about Jake being in their lives.

"Good," said Tony. "Ready to go?"

Tim came in from answering the front door with an envelope in his hand. "Emma, this came for you," he said and handed it to her.

Emma opened it and read aloud. "Have data you requested. Please come by at the requested time. Signed Cole." She looked to the group and said, "I'll follow up with Cole and we can meet tonight to discuss how we would like to move forward. Agreed?" The three nodded, and Tony and Emma headed out for the day.

Tony didn't feel the need to discuss Jake on their way to work. Instead, he tried to steal kisses from Emma as they walked. She didn't put up much of a fight, she enjoyed the attention.

Thoughts of Jake pushed their way to the front of her mind as Tony kissed her goodbye. He noticed her preoccupation and said, "You're quiet and look a bit tired." He traced the dark circles under her eyes with the tips of his fingers. "Are you all right?" he asked, worried.

She laid her head against his chest for a moment, then tilted it up to look at him. "I'm okay. I just need some time and information before I can make a decision."

He nodded, knowing she would consider everything. He leaned in and kissed her quickly. "Promise me you'll come to see me later if you want to talk."

"I promise," she said as she stepped back and took her bike

from him. "You're about to miss your ride." He looked over his shoulder, panicked, and started to run toward it. She waved at him as he ran to catch the trolley and laughed when he almost tripped trying to run and look back at her at the same time.

Her current job was located 10-12 blocks from the trolly. She biked over to her current job location and pulled to a stop in the front of the building. The smile she had from watching Tony earlier, lingered on her face.

A boy's voice called, pulling Emma out of her musings. "Emma!" a young boy of about ten ran up to her. She recognized him immediately as Henry, her coworker Lauri's younger brother. A quick observation took in his clothes as cheap but clean, his face and hands washed, and his brown hair unruly. "Emma, I need to talk to you," he said in a rushed tone.

Emma paused, getting ready to lift her bike on her shoulder, and said, "Hey, Henry. What are you doing here? Where's Lauri?" Lauri had begun her position at the office as one of their temp employees and was now a permanent employee of the Baker Building Co.

"Lauri is running late; Ma needed her this morning. She's hoping you can cover for her," he continued.

Emma looked pensive at the idea and said slowly, "Okay, I will, but tell her to hurry." She continued to frown as she watched him run off. Emma knew she could do the work, but her concern about covering for Lauri was that their jobs at the office were kept separate, with no two people working on the same project or material.

The position Emma held at Baker had been on and off for the past six months. The office manager, Mr. Tracy, was very picky about who worked on what projects and didn't encourage socialization between the employees—particularly the female employees. Discussions over projects were only to be undertaken with team leads but not individually by the administrative staff.

Taking her bike into the building, she stored it in the closet before heading to the second floor to start her day. Once in the office, she changed into a more appropriate outfit, replacing her split skirt with a longer one. She folded the skirt and put it away in a bag she kept under her desk.

Emma stood from her chair and headed to Lauri's desk to pull her daily folder. Lauri liked to have her work prepared for the day; Emma was thankful for that. There were several bills to type and file. The work was to have been completed when Lauri first got there.

Jobs for women, especially permanent ones, could be hard to come by and Lauri's mom and brother depended on her income. Emma wanted Lauri to keep her job, so she would cover for her. She started reviewing the invoices in Lauri's file and noticed they were different from the ones she handled. These were the customer invoices and Emma handled were from the vendors.

The numbers seem a bit odd, Emma thought, realizing they were different from the ones on her invoice from this company. "Stop with the observations. I have to get her typing done first," she muttered to herself. Emma sat down at her desk and went to work on the paperwork. She was a fast typist and finished Lauri's work in a short time.

Is there time? she wondered and glanced at the clock. Fifteen minutes was all she had to evaluate the customer/vendor invoices. She pulled her file and found the same invoices to the vendor and compared the two. The invoices indicated the amount of structural steel, cement, and sand. Laying them side by side she saw there was something wrong between the customers' and vendors' numbers for steel and concrete components.

Feet could be heard echoing on the stairs as someone ascended to the second floor. There was just enough time for her to put the completed work into the file and replace it on

Lauri's desk. *I'll have to reason out any discrepancies at another time.*

She moved back to her desk as the door opened, revealing the office manager, Mr. Tracy. His hair was combed over, greased and glistening in the morning light. His suit was too tight on his skinny frame.

Emma had pulled her file out and was inserting paper into the typewriter as he walked past. He didn't say a word as he entered his office, barely glancing her way. The management staff treated the women as furniture, a necessary function but not important enough to acknowledge.

Baker was one of the first offices to allow women, even in a temporary capacity, to begin working in full-time jobs, an opportunity occurring due to the shortage of male typists. The men working in Chicago could make more money in the booming construction industry.

As he retreated to his office, Emma pulled out her notebook and documented the discrepancies she had seen and follow-up questions. She slipped it into her skirt pocket and got back to work. If the notebook was found by anyone other than her, it could not be read. It was written in a modified Pitman shorthand, something she learned in business school and adapted.

Emma heard more people arriving and kept her head down, working on her typing. The women murmured, "Hello," as they entered and the men shuffled quietly to their offices. She was transferring her completed work into individual files when Mr. Tracy stuck his head out of his office and said, "Miss Evans, has Miss Taylor been in yet this morning?"

"Oh, yes, sir. She was here before me and mentioned she completed her morning typing. She stepped out for a few moments but said she would be back soon." That seemed to mollify him and he pulled his head back into his office.

Luckily, Lauri came in about that time. Her eyes darted to Emma, who gave a slight nod.

Mr. Tracy heard her come in and stepped out of his office. "Where have you been, Miss Taylor?"

"Here, Mr. Tracy. I went downstairs to check on today's bills and when they will be sent out in the mail," she replied innocently.

Good cover, thought Emma.

Mr. Tracy frowned but nodded and went back into his office.

Lauri reached behind her and brought out a bag containing her jacket and lunch. She slipped it under her desk as she sat down. She mouthed a silent *Thank you* to Emma.

Emma winked back, indicating it was okay.

Everyone settled in for the day's work and the sound of typewriter covers being removed and the click-clack of typing filled the office. While she continued to type, Emma thought about the possible discrepancies in the paperwork.

In Chicago, the soil was wet and unstable, and the best support was structural steel and well-mixed cement. It was only two invoices, so it could have been a localized mistake. The trouble was, she was never supposed to see them next to each other. There was no way to tell her office manager that there might be a problem without disclosing that she'd seen something she wasn't supposed to see.

The possible discrepancies would need to be investigated, but she was hesitant to involve Lauri because of her family situation. She would have to do this on her own and secretively determine if this was a one-time mistake or indicative of a more intricate criminal activity.

Her work was completed and Emma got ready to leave at noon. The last thing she had to do was file her work and set up her desk for the next day. As she covered her typewriter, she quietly got ready to leave and stepped away to the lavatory to change into her split skirt. She pulled out her notebook and detailed her concerns for the day.

The papers, I need more time to evaluate them. There was an ability to make copies, but that would require the hectograph, gelatin duplicator, or jellygraph. The printing process involved a transfer of an original, prepared with special inks, to a pan of gelatin or a gelatin pad pulled tight on a metal frame. It would also require her to take the papers from the office, and that was something she didn't want to do. The only viable alternative was a camera. It was becoming apparent that, regardless of Jake's parentage, she would need him on the team. His skills would give them the ability to grow. *Jake would come in handy as a specialist in this situation. Pluses and minuses,* she thought ruefully.

She nodded her goodbyes to her friends and stepped out with her bag, heading to the Pinkerton office to meet with Cole.

CHAPTER 19

$\mathcal{E}$mma arrived at the Pinkerton offices and hopped off her bike. Taking a moment before heading in, she admitted her hesitancy in determining the truth about Jake's parentage. Maybe she should just go home and tell them she didn't want him as a specialist. She started to turn and do that.

She stopped and thought, *No, you have to find out and make a decision based on the facts, not emotion.* Straightening her shoulders, she picked up her bike and put it on her shoulder to carry it up the stoop. When she reached the doors, one of the agents recognized her and ran over to help.

"Emma, you should tell us when you get here so we can help," he scolded.

Emma said simply, "No reason I can't do it myself."

He just shook his head as he took the bike from her. "I'll keep this here; Mr. Tilden is waiting for you."

She nodded, distracted by her thoughts, and said, "Thanks for the help." Heading back to Cole's office, she knocked and heard him call, "Come in."

When Cole saw her in the doorway, he said, "Emma, come in and sit down." He walked around his desk toward her in an unhurried manner. He was in the typical Pinkerton black suit, black tie, and white shirt. He indicated the chair in front of the desk and he took the one opposite to hers.

"Did you find anything?" she asked once she'd sat down, committed to hearing the news, good or bad.

"I didn't have to look far," he said as he tapped the thick file on the corner of his desk. "We did a background check on Daniel's family after he passed away. Jake is Daniel's son." He could see she had questions, but he held up a hand to stop her. "Jake hasn't lived with Daniel since he was about ten. He didn't have much patience with the boy and, after the mother died, he had shipped him off to boarding schools in England. Judging by the timing of the move and the distance to his school, we think he blamed Jake for his mother's death."

"But why?" she asked, astonished a ten-year-old boy would've been sent from his home and family.

"There was a fire, I know," he said, seeing her expression. "Another fire. Jake's mother was asleep in the living room and died of smoke inhalation."

"Was Jake home?"

"He was," he acknowledged, "but the statements given by the maid detail that he was in his room when she left the house."

"Could they determine where the fire started?"

"The chemicals in the basement," he said simply. "Someone or something knocked over several chemicals near a lit burner."

"Someone?"

"The maid indicated that Jake was always very careful with them and wouldn't leave a hazardous environment. The basement filled with smoke and covered the first floor."

"Where was the maid? Why didn't she wake up Jake's mom?"

"She had been given the afternoon off."

"Who arranged that?"

"The maid said the request came from the mom."

"But what about Jake? How did he survive?"

"As I understand it, he climbed out of his window and jumped down."

"Was he hurt?"

"Broken leg."

"Poor little boy." Emma sat silent for a moment, then asked, "Are we sure Daniel didn't set the fire himself and kill her?"

Cole shook his head and said, "He was in New York at the time and we have confirmation from several people who were there. "

"So, someone did this. Do you think it was related to his illegal activities?"

"Yes, it's probably related."

She pondered that. "Cole, I was wondering. . . is there something wrong with Jake?"

"Wrong?" he asked, looking a bit puzzled. "I understand he can be a bit absentminded."

"No, it is more than that. He doesn't make eye contact; he talks about certain topics all the time and seems to have a timing issue."

"Timing?"

"Yes, he wants to be on a set schedule all the time."

"No, I can't say I know anything about that, except the police indicated he's very professional at work."

Emma let the topic go and asked, "Cole, we have been thinking about making him one of our specialists."

"I do have notes that he is a gifted photographer."

"Yes, I'm just not sure how to explain to him what happened to his father."

"Emma, it's not necessary for you to explain anything."

"But I killed Daniel," she said starkly.

Cole acknowledged that comment with a nod of his head. "Yes. But no one knows that outside of the police chief and this office. Is it fair to limit his opportunities based on who his father was?"

She hadn't thought about it that way. "You're right. Okay, we'll give him a chance."

"Also, Emma, he's very alone. He's in that big house of Daniel's with no family."

"We'd wondered about that. Tony mentioned the staff is quite cold to him. Dora has already been thinking of having him move into the boarding house."

"That would be a good thing for him," he acknowledged.

"His talent with the camera will be a huge benefit to us." With that comment, she closed her notebook and stood, prepared to leave.

"Emma," Cole said, delaying her exit. "I have a second thing to discuss with you." She sat back down and waited as he reached for another folder on his desk. "It's about the shelter Clair runs." Emma was startled at the topic but listened intently.

"We've had some information that someone is selling the location of the safe house to one of the abusive husbands."

She gasped in shock and asked, "Which one?"

"It appears to be Alison's," he commented. "The note was anonymous but it did give her name and shared that they were concerned for her safety. Have you had any trouble moving the ladies lately?"

"No, but we haven't moved anyone in a few months. We have three ladies in the house, but only one who is probably going to want to move."

"Which one?" he asked.

"Alison," she admitted.

"What about the help?"

"No one new."

Cole had been contributing Pinkerton's services for background checks on personnel wanting to work there. They didn't put anyone in the safe house without a cleared background.

"Has anyone been hanging around who shouldn't be? Deliveries showing up that haven't been ordered. Anything unusual?"

"I'm not sure," she admitted.

"We'll have to check them out."

Emma sat stunned for a minute, then asked, "Do we need to move the women to another safe house?"

"No, but we do need to find out who's selling their location. If there are any moves scheduled before we find out, contact me immediately. Also, I'll have agents do some reconnaissance to see if anything stands out. Don't worry," he said when he saw her expression, "we'll keep a low profile."

"You've given me plenty to think about," she said wryly. "Let me get with the team and evaluate our options for interviewing the women."

"I'll let you know if we find out anything."

She nodded and said, "Thanks, Cole. Tell Jeremy hello for me." She left the office and paused just outside his door and laughed suddenly. "Life is never boring."

CHAPTER 20

At the boarding house that night, dinner had been cleared and residents had moved to the sitting room to relax. Tim, Dora, and Tony sat around the kitchen table at Emma's request. Amy had completed her duties and headed home with a cheerful, "Goodbye."

They all looked at Emma to begin. She paused a moment and then said, "I'm sitting here wondering what to discuss first." Coming to a decision, she started again, placing her hand on Dora's. "I'll begin with Jake since I know he's on your mind."

"He is Daniel's son," Dora guessed, not sure she wanted the answer.

"Yes," stated Emma with no expression in her voice.

As Dora took a breath, Tony and Tim looked at one another. Dora withdrew her hand from Emma's and inquired, "Well, what does that mean? We can't like him or have him live here?" Her tone hardened a bit as she continued, "Emma, you need to face what you did to Daniel and that boy." Emma looked hurt at Dora's tone. Dora's voice softened as she continued, "I don't mean for you to tell him. I don't think he would understand the circumstance—"

Tony interrupted, "Not understand? He's a forensic photographer and is on crime scenes all the time."

"Yes, but this involves an emotional element; at least, we think it might. I just don't think he would understand the circumstances," Dora explained.

"Emma, it comes down to this: can you work with him or not?" Tony asked.

Emma sat pensively for a moment and then broke out in laughter. They looked at her like she had lost her mind. Emma said, with a laugh still in her voice, "We've been so worried about if he should live here that we haven't bothered to ask Jake if he wants to live here and work with us."

The group realized what she was saying and soon the room was filled with laughter.

Tony sobered and said, "Emma?"

She knew what he was asking and responded, "This isn't about me or my feelings. I think my only hesitancy is that someday he might find out and not trust us."

Tim said, "I don't see how he could. The Pinkertons kept it quiet and even the police changed the reports."

"Should we just tell him?" Emma asked.

Dora, feeling protective of Jake, said, "I would like him to get to know us. Also, knowing he's so alone, I'd like to have him here. We could give him something Daniel couldn't or wouldn't. A family."

Tim said in a conciliatory tone, "Let's have him over for dinner this week and approach him about moving into the house as well as helping with future investigations. Is that acceptable to everyone?" They all nodded.

"What's our next topic, Emma?" asked Dora, catching how she had closed the notebook containing Jake's information and opened another.

"It relates to Jake being a specialist on our team." She started to explain the possible discrepancies she'd found on the two sets of invoices at the Baker job.

"That doesn't sound like much to go on," said Tony.

Emma nodded. "Agreed. I need to get a look at more accounts to help me determine if this one is a mistake or an ongoing conspiracy. The other thing that bothers me is that the shortages are on the orders and not on the invoices to the customers."

Tim asked, "How do you plan to move forward on this?" He was worried it might affect their contracts with Baker.

"Jake," she said simply. "I need to discuss using a camera to record the data. Any other way, I would have to take the paperwork out of the office, and I don't want to do that."

Tony said, "If Jake accepts, we can review this with him. Is there any reason we can't take our time with this case?"

"I don't think so. Most of our buildings are in the planning stages," Emma commented.

"Okay, so we wait for Jake on that one?" asked Tim.

She nodded.

Tim cleared his throat and said, "Emma, please let me know before you do anything that could jeopardize our contracts. We have people relying on Baker for a paycheck."

"I understand and I promise to check in with my partners," she glanced at Dora and Tim, "prior to doing anything other than investigating."

Tim seemed satisfied with this response. "Thanks, Emma."

"Was there anything else?" asked Tony, glancing at his watch. Time was going by quickly tonight.

"Well, I have another topic, if everyone can stay a while longer?" Emma asked. She looked around the table for confirmation. When she received a nod from each, she opened her next notebook and started describing her conversation with Cole about Clair's safe house. "He indicated there has been an anonymous report that the location of the house is for sale. Alison is listed as the person of interest."

The room went silent. The safe house was a place battered women took shelter to heal. They stayed for different lengths of time before they decided on where or not to move or stay. If they stayed, they would be entering school or looking for a job. "I was thinking of going to the shelter and interviewing the longer-term residents," Emma said.

"Are you thinking one of the women at the house is involved?" asked Tony.

"Yes, it just feels like an inside person is providing the information."

"Emma, I would like to go with you," said Dora, calmly but firmly.

That statement surprised Tim. "Dora. . ." He started, concerned about her being involved in the business at the house.

"Tim," she said, squeezing his hand and looking deep into his eyes. "I want to see it for myself. I also want to see if there's some additional support I can offer."

"All right," he said, accepting her decision, knowing he could deny her nothing. "How are we going to get you both there safely?"

A knock sounded on the kitchen door from the dining room. "Just a minute." Emma opened the door and saw it was Thomas. "Come in," she indicated.

"I asked Thomas to see us when he got home," she explained. She gave him a quick recap of the activities involved with the shelter.

"I have some ideas on that," Thomas said. "I have been making deliveries in the area for Clair." His face went red at this statement.

Dora looked at Emma questioningly. Emma shrugged at the silent question.

He continued. "Emma and Dora would go unnoticed in my wagon. We could have them lie in the back under a blanket."

That could work. "Dora, we could make some pastries to take over for them," Emma suggested.

"That would be nice, it would be more like a visit than an interrogation," said Dora.

The group pulled together their plans and decided they needed to act the next day. Emma would get a note to Clair to set up a meeting. "I'll firm up the plans in the morning."

"Given we have this scheduled for tomorrow night, let's ask Jake about moving in this weekend," suggested Tim.

"Agreed. But, Tony, could you let Jake know he is welcomed to dinner anytime? In addition, let him know we have a special dinner for him to attend on Saturday night," said Dora.

While Dora was arranging Tony and Jake, Emma was writing out the note for Clair. She signed and folded it before giving it to Thomas to deliver that night. "You don't mind?" she asked him. "I could get Jeremy to deliver it."

"No, no," he said a bit hastily as he took it from her.

She looked at him curiously but didn't say anything.

He said, "I'll wait for a response."

"Thank you, Thomas," Emma said gratefully.

He nodded and headed out.

Emma walked slowly into the kitchen where Tony, Dora, and Tim were talking quietly. "The note is off."

"What was up with Thomas?" asked Tony.

"I'm not sure," she said with a shrug. "He hasn't mentioned anything, but he did color a bit when Clair's name came up."

"I don't think we should be talking about this," said Dora.

"You're right. It's their business, not ours," commented Emma.

"Yes," they all agreed.

"Tim, I am heading up to bed," commented Dora.

Tim realized what she said and jumped up. "Oh! I am a bit

tired," he said eagerly and grabbed her hand to rush her upstairs.

Dora paused on the stairs and called down, "Emma, I need you up early to make the pastries for tomorrow evening,"

Emma called back, "Okay. I'll be up early with you. I'm going to walk Tony out now." She reached out her hand to him. He took it, and they walked to the back door and outside. He'd had enough conversation and pulled her close for a long, sweet kiss. She was shaking a bit when he raised his head. He glanced down at her, wishing they could go to their own room in the boarding house. Pressing his forehead on hers, he said, "I'll see you tomorrow."

"Yes," she said. "Tomorrow."

She returned to the kitchen and up to her room. As she walked upstairs, she saw the light under Tim and Dora's door. For a moment, she was a bit envious that Dora had someone with her through the night. She still had no want of marriage but she would like to experience the closeness that came with that type of relationship. *Does it have to be only in marriage?* She mulled that thought over and headed to her room.

CHAPTER 21

*E*arly the next morning, Emma heard a quiet knock on her door. She called out softly, "I'm up."

Dora stuck her head in and said, "Okay, meet us in the kitchen."

Emma nodded as she laid on the bed and yawned widely. Dora closed the door quietly behind her.

Time to get up, Emma thought as she got dressed and headed downstairs to help with pastry preparation in the kitchen.

As they were finishing the pastries for that night and starting breakfast for the boarding house, Thomas entered the kitchen looking tired. He sat down with a sigh and Amy got him a cup of coffee.

"Pastry?" asked Dora.

He shook his head. "Not just yet, thank you." He looked at Emma. She lifted an eyebrow at him as he reached into his pocket and handed her a piece of folded paper.

As she took it, Dora said to Amy, "Can you see if the towels are dry and bring them in? They've been left out overnight."

"Will do," she said and headed to the backyard to retrieve them.

"Thanks, Dora," Emma said absently as she unfolded the note and started to read. "Clair wants to meet me today." She directed her gaze at Thomas. "Did she have any idea who might be sharing the information?"

He shook his head slowly and said, "She said she hasn't noticed anyone unusual hanging around the house or seen the women leave the house for any reason."

"We have backgrounds on all of the help and they are aware of how important their silence is," she said, tapping her fingers against her lips. "That still leads us back to the women living in the house."

"Yes," agreed Dora

A worried look crossed Thomas' face. "I don't think Clair likes the idea of you questioning the women."

"I know she's protective, but if it isn't the help or someone connected with the house, it must be one of them," Emma mused out loud. "Her note also indicates she wants to meet in the same place we met initially. Thomas, can you confirm with her that I'll be there?"

"I can. I'll stop by on my way to the bakery." He paused for a moment and asked, "Do you want me to take you to the meeting this afternoon?"

"No, I'm working as a courier around that area and I have my bike," she said, absently tapping the letter on her hand. Presenting her case to Clair would be difficult; she would have to show she wasn't deliberately targeting the women. This needed to be handled carefully.

Thomas readied to leave, but Dora stopped him by saying, "Time for some breakfast, Thomas?" She didn't want him going without food; he meant too much to them.

"I'll stay," he said, easing back down in his chair.

Dora smiled at him and said, "Good."

They went back to baking while Thomas watched.

Amy tapped on the kitchen window and he jumped up to

help her with the basket. He asked, "Do you want me to take this to the upstairs closet?"

"Please," said Amy with a smile. He took it upstairs while she moved to the stove to start the eggs and sausage for breakfast.

While the pastries cooled on the table, Emma grabbed some bread and butter to eat and headed upstairs. It was time for her to get changed into her office clothes and head to work. She wanted to arrive a bit earlier than normal to compare invoices. Brushing her hair into a high ponytail, she continued thinking about her day. She was pulling on her boots when a knock sounded on her door. "Come in," she called out.

The door opened and Amy walked in. "Emma, Tony is waiting downstairs."

"Okay, thanks for letting me know. I'm on my way down now," she said as she gathered her notebook and stowed it in her jacket pocket. Slipping on her shoulder bag, she did a final check to confirm it contained her skirt, then headed down.

Tony was in the foyer and looked up when he heard her boots on the stairs. Grinning, he watched her walk down. She returned his smile and increased her pace to get to him. He lifted her off the last step and gave her a deep kiss.

"Wow," she said.

"I missed you," he murmured.

"It was only one night," she reminded him with a laugh in her voice.

"Yes." He said and kissed her again.

When they finally came up for air, Emma said, "I need to get my lunch. I want to go in early today." As she stepped away, she looked at what he was wearing and commented, "You look nice."

Tony glanced down at his attire. He wore a dark brown suit with a burgundy tie. "Several important clients are coming in today to meet a few of our up-and-coming artists. I'm hosting the event."

"That's wonderful," she said sincerely.

"Did you want to stop by after your morning job and eat lunch with me?" he asked hopefully.

"What time is your meeting?" she asked as they walked to the kitchen.

"This morning. I should be done around noon."

"I'll stop by," she promised. She lowered her voice. "I do have to meet with Clair at 3pm."

"Tell me about it once we're on the way," he commented to her in a similar tone of voice.

They stopped by the kitchen to get her lunch. Dora noticed him eyeing the cooling pastry and tossed him one. He caught it deftly. "Do me a favor?" she asked.

"Sure," he grinned, "if I can get another one of these."

She grinned back and tossed him another one, saying, "Remind Jake that we want to see him for dinner. Do you think you could bring him with you when you come over this evening?"

"Sure, it shouldn't be a problem," said Tony after swallowing the final bite of the second pastry.

"Now, on your way, both of you. Didn't you say you wanted to be in early, Emma?" Dora reminded her.

Emma nodded and gestured at Tony to head out.

"Have a good day, both of you. Emma, let me know if our plans for this evening change," Dora said, knowing she would be meeting with Clair.

"I will," she promised.

Tony held out his hand as they exited through the back door. Emma accepted it and squeezed.

As they left, they went to the small building on the side of the house where her bike was located. Tony inquired, "Did you hear from Clair?"

"Yes," she said simply.

"Going to tell me what she said?" he asked as they made the

turn onto the sidewalk toward the trolley.

"She's unhappy with my inquiries and wants to talk this afternoon before anyone is interviewed at the house."

"Do you think you can convince her this is from a reliable source?"

"I certainly hope so. If it is true—and I believe it is—we have a leak. Any future moves could be in jeopardy."

"Emma." He stopped her with his hand. "I know this is your operation, but if you can't convince Clair how dangerous this is, I think you should tell her all future moves are out of the question until it's safe."

Emma nodded slowly. "That's what I have in mind. I certainly love adventure, but I will not knowingly walk myself and someone else into an unsafe situation."

They went quiet for the moment and continued walking toward the trolley stop. As they drew closer, Tony offered, "I can take your lunch with me today."

"Oh, thanks," she said, pulling out her lunch pail and handing it to him.

He leaned down and kissed her. "See you at noon?"

"Definitely," she said while climbing on her bike. "See you then!" she tossed over her shoulder as she rode off.

He watched her depart. He knew she would consider all the facts and not do anything rash. With that thought on his mind, he spotted the trolley and ran off to catch it.

Emma rode on through the city to her office building. Arriving early, she hurried to put her bike up and change out of her split skirt. After her belongings were stored under her desk, she glanced around to make sure no one was there. Once she confirmed she was alone, she made her way over to Lauri's desk to review her daily work folder. Pulling it out, she laid it on the desk and pulled out her notebook to copy down the invoice numbers, materials being ordered, and amounts. She returned the file to its proper location, then moved back to her desk.

Sitting down, she quickly compared her notes with her invoices, adding the information from her files to her notebook.

I'll review these later, she thought. *I won't have time for a detailed evaluation now.* With a snap, the notebook was closed and was stored in her jacket. She would have preferred the actual invoices to compare side by side. *The camera. Follow-up would be necessary with Jake, his talents with it were the key to this case. I hope he accepts our offer.*

The office started to fill with personnel as she put paper into her typewriter. Lauri said a quiet hello as she entered and began her work. Emma watched her from the corner of her eye. When Lauri did not seem to find anything wrong with her daily work folder, Emma went back to her work.

A few hours later, after applying herself diligently, Emma checked her watch and realized the morning had flown by. She closed her files and covered up her typewriter. Standing, she made her way to Mr. Tracy's office and knocked on the door; he opened it quickly. He didn't say anything, knowing what she needed. They walked to the file room, and he pulled out his keys to open the door, watching her carefully as she completed her filing. The door would then be locked until it was needed again. Without saying a word, he headed back to his office. Emma rolled her eyes at Lauri, who hid a smile as she watched. The daily files were set up on her desk for the next day.

"Goodbye," she said to Lauri and headed to change into her split skirt.

After she changed, she retrieved her bike and rode toward the museum. It wasn't close to her office, but the bike allowed her to get there in a short amount of time. She arrived and placed the bike on her shoulder as she climbed the front steps of the museum. As she entered, the guards took it and placed it in the side storage room as usual. The guard pointed to where Tony was speaking to a woman. *A beautiful woman*, she thought to herself. She appeared to be a bit older than him; her dress was very stylish on her trim figure. Emma continued to watch them; curious but not at all jealous.

Tony saw her and gave a nod as he started to wrap up his conversation.

Emma noticed the woman place a hand on his arm to detain him. Tony smiled at her and disengaged himself. He waved the administrative assistant over and said, "Could you accompany Mrs. Smith to her cab?"

The admin nodded and offered her his elbow to escort her out. She paused for a moment and stared directly at Emma. Emma stared back, not understanding her interest. The lady broke the rather intense eye contact and turned a charming smile on the assistant walking her out.

Emma put the matter out of her mind and greeted Tony. He leaned over to kiss her hello. "Want to eat in my office?" he suggested.

She nodded, and they headed there. It was small but had a nice desk and chairs. They sat next to each other and unpacked their lunches.

"How did the event go this morning?" she asked curiously, taking a bite of her sandwich.

"Really well," he said with a serious tone. "There's a lot of interest in our new artist."

"Who is he?" she inquired.

"His name is John Singer Sargent. He is a powerful artist and well known for his portraits. We have one of his landscapes on display. It is entitled: *Street in Venice*."

"Venice? Italy? Can I see it?!" she asked excitedly. Travel fascinated her.

"Let's finish lunch first," he suggested as he nabbed her hand in his. They continued to eat and spoke about her afternoon meeting with Clair.

When they finished, he took her to the room where the

landscape painting hung. It was an exquisite picture, one that made Emma yearn to see Venice for herself.

"We hope this one does well with visitors," commented Tony.

Emma didn't want to take her eyes off of it. *So many places to see,* she thought. They parted and she continued to her courier jobs' delivering drawings to companies located near the restaurant where her meeting was located.

After she completed her deliveries, she made her way to the meeting with Clair. Despite very much liking Clair, Emma wasn't looking forward to the tense meeting. Gritting her teeth and setting her jaw, she entered the restaurant. The manager greeted her at the door and waved at a busboy to take the bike to storage until she needed it again. He said, "I believe your party is already waiting for you, miss." He motioned for her to follow him.

They went in the opposite direction from the dining room to a door located down a long hallway. He opened the door and indicated she should enter. As she made her way into the room, she glanced around and noted it was brightly lit with high windows. Across the room was a small table set up with an afternoon tea service. The manager excused himself and shut the door quietly on his way out.

Clair stood near the table, looking out the window. As she turned to Emma, the girl noted the older woman's strained features.

"Clair." She acknowledged her with a nod and started without any pleasantries, but kept her tone pleasant. "We need to talk openly about the information Pinkerton has provided."

"Yes, that's why I requested a private room," she responded and seemed to relax a bit when Emma didn't sound accusatory. "Why don't we sit down? I ordered tea."

"It looks nice, thank you." She watched as Clair poured it for them. She took the cup and took a sip before starting. "All right, let's talk about what was communicated to me. Cole indicated that the shelter location and women's names are for sale to the highest bidder." Clair's face lost some color, but she nodded. "Cole and I thought about the workers at the house, but all have had background checks and clearances."

"Couldn't it be someone outside the house?" Clair asked, hoping it wasn't one of her women.

"We thought of that, but the information is too specific. They're in contact with one of the husbands of a woman at your house."

"How did Cole find out?" she pressed, still clinging desperately to hope it was from another source.

"There was an anonymous note sent to the Pinkerton office. It indicated they were worried about the lady getting hurt."

"Which one is it and why hasn't the husband come to the house to try to get her?"

"It's Alison who was mention in the note. We don't think money has changed hands yet, so we don't think the address has been shared. One of my concerns is that we haven't been keeping the movements quiet from the other residents. We've only kept the method of movement and final locations quiet. When we schedule her move, they'll probably try to take her."

"You think it's one of my women selling information. Already victims, maybe now victimizing the others," Clair said, reeling with that information.

"I'm not sure; we just need to look at each one and confirm their stories. One may be a plant, put into the house to get the locations of the other women. I've also been thinking, is there anyone who has been avoiding a move?" asked Emma.

"We have two, other than Alison, who has not indicated a desire to move out of the city or haven't made any inquiries about attending school," Clair admitted.

"I'll need both names so I can have Cole look into their backgrounds. Though, we may not be able to find out much, especially if their names have been changed."

"It looks like we may have a traitor in our midst," said Clair, her face hardening at the thought.

They both went silent at that thought. Then Emma continued. "Dora and I had thought to come over tonight and bring pastries. She has wanted to start spending time there, possibly teaching cooking classes and listening to the women who need to talk."

Clair said quietly, "I'd like that, as would the women." She paused. "I know it's important, but we must go about the quietly. I want them to continue to feel protected."

"We also need to evaluate our next moves for changes and different routes. Perhaps by buggy instead of trains. Until we find out who this is, we'll have to be creative or delay them until we can assure their safety."

"It was going so well," Clair said absently.

"Yes. It will be so again; we just have to find who is trying to sabotage us," Emma said vehemently.

"Agreed," she said finally. "You and Dora will be by tonight?"

"Yes, Thomas will bring us dressed as boys."

"Thomas, it will be nice to see him," she said, looking happier.

Again, Emma didn't inquire, allowing their personal lives to remain personal.

"What time will I see you this evening?" Clair asked, wanting to be there when they arrived.

"Our thought is 8pm. We'll bring in the treats and start speaking to the ladies at that time."

"There are three," Clair admitted. "Lily, Ann, and Alison. They have been with us for a while. They don't have a family for support and don't seem capable of living outside the house -- safely. I would assume that, since Alison's husband is involved, we can remove her from the list."

"Yes, I agree. So, it's Lily and Ann we need to look at. I'll get the information to Cole. Can you write down their first and last names? He may be able to track down their histories."

"Will we be able to tell from the background checks who might be involved in this?" Clair asked hopefully.

"Maybe, but I think I should still observe them." Emma paused for a moment, thinking. "Who gets the mail or deliveries?"

"The housekeeper answers the door for all reasons, but I don't think we receive any mail there," said Clair.

"I can confirm that tonight," said Emma.

"Okay, we'll see you there. Oh, tell Thomas he can come in the kitchen to wait for you," Clair said innocently.

"It will be a chilly night; I'm sure he'd like to be inside while we're visiting," commented Emma in the same tone.

They had their tea and cakes as a quiet end to their meeting. Clair and Emma briefly touched hands as they left the room. Emma retrieved her bike from the manager and headed to the boarding house to help with dinner.

Tim was already in the kitchen "helping" Dora with a dessert when she entered. "Hey, Emma," Tim said absently.

"Hey back," she responded.

He arched an eyebrow in a silent question. "Later," she said, glancing at Amy's back. They trusted her, but the women at the shelter needed to know they would not share their private information.

He and Dora nodded and continued to work on dinner. They pulled together to get the food to the table. Tony arrived with Jake as they were starting the evening meal, and he sat in the chair next to Emma. She grabbed Tony's hand under the table and squeezed. He squeezed back and gave her a sweet smile.

After prayers were completed, Dora asked, looking over at Jake, "Did you have a good day?"

"I did. We had some interesting cases, but I can't talk about them," Jake said hurriedly, looking around.

Tim said in a calming tone, "That's okay, we understand. Were you mostly in the office?"

"No, I was out a few times today and then I spent time developing pictures this afternoon," he replied. Dora was glad that Jake had not balked at eating in the dining room that evening. The conversation went on around the table, a noisy but comforting sound.

They finished eating and started to clear the table. Emma told Tony in a low voice that they would meet after dinner in the kitchen.

"Papa, you had mentioned you wanted to show Jake something downstairs this evening," Dora hinted to him.

"Does it involve photography?" Jake asked hopefully.

"No, but it does involve similar chemicals, and you might use your camera to investigate some findings for me," said Papa.

Jake looked interested in this development and accompanied him to the basement. The other boarders moved into the sitting room to settle in for the evening.

Amy, Dora, Tim, Tony, and Emma pitched in to clean up after dinner. As plates were cleaned and the kitchen table scrubbed, Dora said to Amy, "You can go home a bit early, if you like."

"That would be nice," she said happily. "I'm reading a new book and I would love to get home early to finish it." She started out and almost ran into Thomas. Laughing she stepped aside, so he could enter.

"Thank you and good night, Amy," Thomas said with a smile.

"Good night," she said and headed off to her house, thinking about the evening in front of her.

"Thomas, you missed dinner. Would you like me to fix you a plate?" asked Dora.

"That would be nice, thank you," replied Thomas.

Dora was handing Thomas his dinner plate when Tony came back into the room. "Good evening Thomas. I checked and confirmed everyone is in the sitting room."

Tim, Tony, Emma, Thomas, and Dora sat around the table. "Emma, you met with Clair?" Dora prompted.

"Yes, She was unhappy that we might be targeting one of her ladies. But she agreed we could do background checks on them and we can subtly interview them tonight at the shelter."

"Was she okay with me accompanying you?" Dora asked, hoping she could still go.

"Yes, she was happy to hear that you wanted to start coming to the shelter. The ladies need some sort of distraction from their situations," said Emma.

Dora smiled. "Good."

Tony said, "We need to get you both organized and the wagon ready." Emma nodded and indicated for Dora to follow her upstairs.

Tim and Tony took a moment to speak with Thomas. "You'll watch out for them? We want you to come back here if anything looks suspicious."

"I will," promised Thomas and stood up to take his plate to the sink. "Let's go."

The three went to get the wagon. They set up blankets and placed the boxes of pastry in the back. "Thomas, meet them at Stevenson Street in the alley," directed Tim.

"I'll be there," he said as he climbed into the wagon and made a clicking sound to get the horses moving, while Tim and Tony headed back to the boarding house.

Emma and Dora entered the kitchen as Tim and Tony were coming in from outside. Even with all the seriousness of their current project, when Tim saw Dora in her pants and a loose shirt, he let out a low whistle; she turned red, enjoying the attention. "Enough of that now," admonished Emma with a slight smile. She helped Dora tuck her hair into her newsboy cap, it was made of cloth with a rounder puffier design, topped with a button. Giving her a once-over, she approved her look. Emma handled her hat carefully. It was her bowler with a special slot for her long knife.

"If you're ready, Thomas is waiting on Stevenson Street in the alley," Tim said, wanting to get them moving.

Tony had started to worry and stated a bit loudly, "I can go with you."

"No," said Emma, moving to him and hugging him tightly. "Better to keep the group small."

He looked down at her for a long moment and nodded his head in agreement. He squeezed her hand before letting her go.

Tim also took a moment with Dora. He tilted her head back with his fingers to look him in the eyes and said, "Be safe."

"I will," she said softly. They shared a long kiss.

For once, Emma didn't tease her. Giving them their moment, she cleared her throat after a few seconds and said, "Let's go." They exited out of the back door.

"Dora," Emma muttered out the side of her mouth as she noticed how her sister was walking, "don't swing your hips too much. Be a boy." Emma slipped into the boy's skin easily and showed no outward appearance as a female. They took a circuitous path to meet Thomas, making sure no one was following them to where he was waiting patiently.

He saw them approach and said quietly, "Hey, in you go."

Emma and Dora climbed in the back of the wagon with Thomas' help. After he covered them with several blankets, he leaped into the driver's seat and moved the wagon out of the alley in an unhurried manner. He wouldn't be suspicious; he made deliveries to the shelter routinely.

Once he had the wagon out of sight behind the shelter, he uncovered Emma and Dora. Emma exited by jumping down and Dora followed her lead. *I can see why Emma likes these adventures*, Dora thought.

Thomas took the pastry boxes out and handed them to the girls. As the three approached the back door, Clair opened it to let them in. She looked a bit pensive but seemed happy to see them. "Come in, come in."

They went into the kitchen. The housekeeper, Katy, was there and rushed over to hug Emma. "Visit or move?" she asked.

"Visit only, and we brought something with us," she teased, indicating the boxes she carried.

"Oh, Emma, did you bring us something sweet?" asked Katy excitedly.

"We did," she said with a smile and set her boxes down the table. She indicated for Dora to do the same. "And I brought someone to meet you." Emma turned and grabbed Dora by the arm and dragged her over to Katy. "Dora, this is Katy. Katy, this is my sister Dora."

"It is so nice to finally meet you. We have loved the pastries you've sent us," Katy said sincerely.

Dora blushed and said, "I'm glad you enjoyed them."

Clair spoke to Thomas in a low voice and then approached Emma and Dora. "Dora, I'm Clair. It's very nice to meet you. I appreciate you wanting to help our little family." Dora and Clair shook hands, rather formally.

Emma knew she used "our little family" to highlight her protectiveness of the women in the shelter.

Clair said to the housekeeper, "Katy, please take the pastries and put some on a tray for the sitting room. Also, prepare some tea." She then turned to Dora and Emma. "Let's adjourn to the sitting room."

Thomas would stay in the kitchen and read while the women conducted their business. The women living in the shelter knew he was a good person but some were skittish around men. He couldn't blame them, knowing what they had been through.

Before they exited the kitchen, Emma stopped Clair and asked quietly, "Where are the three ladies?"

Almost reluctantly, Clair said, "Alison and Ann are in the sitting room, and Lily is in the study reading."

"I'll start with Lily," said Emma, checking her pocket for her notebook.

"I would like to visit with the ladies in the sitting room," said Dora, breaking the uncomfortable pause that had settled between Emma and Clair.

Clair nodded and accompanied her down the hallway. Emma followed behind but broke off from the group at the study entrance. Clair and Dora continued as Emma took a moment to observe Lily before entering. She was a smallish woman in her late twenties, with thick brown hair and a rather plain dress.

As she walked in, Lily looked up from her book and said in a surprised tone, "Hello, Emma. How are you? What are you doing here this evening?"

"I'm well," Emma commented, sidestepping the question of why she was there. "What are you reading?" she asked.

She gave Emma a brief frown before showing her the spine. Emma read out loud, "*The Count of Monte Cristo*. That's a good book. I love all of the intrigues."

"Me, too," Lily commented, studying it.

Emma let the silence settle around them. It was a tool that could be used to force people to talk. She moved to a chair near the couch where Lily sat. Pulling out her notebook, she started asking questions, "Lily, we were wondering if you had plans for your future outside of the shelter."

She looked a bit panicked at the abrupt question and asked with a nervous tenor in her voice, "Am I being asked to leave?"

"No, no," Emma assured her. "We want to know if you would like us to relocate you to another environment or would you like us to arrange for you to attend business school here. We would like to help you move forward with your life."

That statement didn't seem to mollify her. Standing suddenly, she started to pace in front of the fireplace. Finally, she turned to Emma and asked, "Why are you trying to get rid of me? Did I do something wrong?"

Emma studied her behavior, watching for signs of deception. She had worked on this skill for the past two years with Jeremy as her primary instructor. Prior to this, she'd had a bad experience when someone she trusted turned out to be lying. It almost cost her and a friend's life.

There were specific signs to look for: no eye contact, changes in voice, unusual body language, something sounding off, and being overly defensive. And Lily was hitting all five. Emma made notes without showing any emotion. Lily would stay on her list until she got further information on her background.

Emma decided to back off and end the conversation there. "Lily, think about what you might like to do with your future. It doesn't have to be decided tonight. We just wanted to let you know we are thinking about you." She used the word thinking, knowing it could be taken in two ways.

Lily didn't take that as a threat and seemed to calm down. She crossed back over to her chair and sat down with her book. "Okay, I'll get back to you."

"Okay. There are pastries in the sitting room; my sister brought them to share. You're welcome to join us," Emma said, wanting to end the meeting on a positive note.

"No, I'm good here," she said, holding onto her book tightly and sounding relieved the questions were ending and Emma would be leaving.

She smiled slightly, knowing she wasn't wanted and exited the room. There was enough data on Lily to form some conclusions and she was ready to move on to the next person on her list. She walked down the hall to the sitting room and paused in the doorway to observe the people there. There were four women in addition to Clair and Dora. Emma didn't recognize the two sitting on either side of Clair, but she was able to see new bruising on their young faces. Her heart plummeted a moment, thinking of all the hurt girls out there; they were only helping a small percentage. She shook the thought off and entered the room.

All the ladies have tried the pastry, judging by the empty platter on the table, Emma observed. Dora sat talking quietly to Alison; Ann was in the corner reading. Emma wanted to continue her interviews with both Alison and Ann. Clair glanced up and indicated with a wave of her hand for Emma to enter. She stepped in, and Clair quietly introduced her to the two new women seeking shelter in the house. They didn't say much and she understood they were still too skittish to speak with anyone but Clair.

Emma moved closer to Alison and Dora. She had known Alison for the last month and had had many conversations with her. Emma had a gut feeling that she was ready to move on and her next statement confirmed this. As she sat next to Alison on the small settee, she leaned over and quietly said, "I think I'm ready to leave the shelter. Can we speak for a moment?"

Emma nodded and said in a low voice, "Kitchen?" She had made sure to keep Ann in her line of sight. The other woman had straightened up when Alison had moved toward Emma. She didn't appear to be listening, but in fact, she was. *Interesting*, thought Emma.

She motioned to Dora that she and Alison would be leaving the room. Dora nodded, understanding Emma wanted her to watch for anyone who chose to leave the room while the interviews were ongoing.

Emma stood and indicated that Alison should go ahead of her into the hallway toward the kitchen. As they entered, they saw Thomas was speaking with Katy. Alison hesitated a bit before entering; she seemed to be okay with him but didn't want to get too close.

"Thomas, I think there are some books that might hold your interest in the study," Emma said. "I'm sure Lily wouldn't mind the company." Lily wasn't skittish around Thomas and wouldn't mine him in the room with her.

Thomas got the underlying direction and said, "I'll check it out." He would keep Lily busy so her conversation with Alison was kept private.

Katy, seeing that she needed to give them some space, said, "I think I'll go up to bed. Just have them leave the cups and plates in the sink."

"I'll tell Clair. Goodnight, Katy," said Emma, hugging her.

With the kitchen empty, Alison pulled an address out of her pocket. "I have a distant cousin who would allow me to live with him. This is his address. He has a farm out in the country."

"Can I see it?" Emma asked as she sat down at the kitchen table.

"Yes," said Alison, handing it over.

Emma looked at the address and thought about this cousin. She asked, "What is your relationship like? Why are you sure he would take you in and help with transport?"

"I spent most of my summers there as a child. We grew up together," she said simply.

Emma asked, concerned for her safety, "Has your husband been to the farm or met the cousin?"

"No, he was very jealous of any men and would not even let me invite my family to our wedding," she assured her.

Emma frowned. *That would have deterred me from marrying him, but this isn't about me.*

"My husband had me cut off contact with all of my family as soon as we married. I wasn't even allowed to attend my parents' funerals," she said, suddenly tearful.

"No communication of your cousin or these trips you took as a child?"

"No, he only wanted to discuss him. I went along with it because I thought he loved me," she said, looking lost.

"Have you shared this information with anyone in the shelter?" Emma asked.

That question seemed to help bring her back to the present. "No, I just decided I needed to keep moving forward and that means leaving the safety of this shelter. Do I need to be secretive?"

"I would say not to share any information about your possible move at this time. We want to add a layer of privacy to the moves, even from other women in the shelter."

Alison frowned, not saying anything, and finally nodded.

"Alison," Emma said, touching her hand, "could you write the letter to your cousin, asking if you can go live with his family?"

"Yes, I can do that," she said, happy they were setting things into motion.

"Let Clair know when it's ready to be sent. This is important - don't let anyone see it and keep it on your person at all times. Give it to Clair. She will get it to me to be posted," Emma said, stressing the need for her discretion.

Alison would do as she was asked. She had seen Emma get women out of the shelter to safety; she trusted her. Feeling relieved, she said, "I'm looking forward to the future for the first time in a long time."

"I'm glad." Emma decided she needed to ask Alison some hard questions. "Alison, your husband, tell me about him."

Alison took a deep breath to steady herself before answering.

Emma saw the question disturbed her and continued, "We normally don't ask but, in this case, I need to know everything so we can protect you."

"Charles Lewison." Emma felt a jolt at hearing the name; she immediately knew who that was. She would need to let Cole know as soon as possible. He hadn't been able to find much on the women, since they had hidden their last names.

"He's a very powerful man here. He's also very unstable out of the public eye. He could control his public behavior, but once that bedroom door closed, he changed, became violent. On the outside, I had everything but. . ." She trailed off.

"What finally happened to get you out from under his abuse?"

"I would like to say that I escaped," she said sadly, "but I'm not that strong. I hope I can be one day." She paused before continuing, lost in her memories. "I had help. Our maid, Wendy, came to check on me. When I didn't answer, she realized I must be hurt. She left and came back with her husband; he was able to take the door down. They found me on the floor. Wendy had worked for Clair at her other 'house' and knew we could trust her."

"Where is this maid now? Not still with your husband," Emma asked, suddenly worried.

"No, Wendy has an ability to survive. She and her husband decided it was time to move on," Alison said, wishing she was just as strong as her rescuers.

"Yes, that was probably the best decision," acknowledged Emma.

"How long do you think it will take to get things moving?" Alison asked, ready for the next step, whatever that might be.

"I think I have enough to get things set up. It may take some time to organize," Emma said, jotting down notes in her notebook.

"How long do you think?" she repeated, a little apprehensive.

"An estimation?" asked Emma, still jotting down her notes. "Probably a few weeks, if your cousin agrees," she cautioned, not wanting to be overly optimistic.

Alison was very relieved to have a date to plan for. She nodded, feeling secure that her cousin would be there for her.

Emma sat forward at the table, leaning on her elbows, clasping her hands together. "Alison, I have to stress again, please don't share information with ANYONE. In fact, if anyone is too curious, send a note to Clair or me."

"Who do you mean?" Alison asked, bewildered.

"I mean, *anyone* other than Clair or myself. We want to make sure you're protected."

"Yes, I can do that," Alison said, still curious about this request.

Emma reached out to touch Alison's hand. "We will get you somewhere safe," she promised.

Alison gripped her hand and nodded. She used her other hand to wipe a tear before standing and moving toward the kitchen door. She hesitated a moment and turned around. "Emma, I appreciate everything you and Clair are doing here. I will not allow myself to be placed in this type of position again," she insisted.

Emma watched her leave and had a moment to reflect on their conversation. She completed the documentation in her notebook and thought, *I have requested backgrounds on the ladies from Cole but, without a husband's name, the women are nearly invisible. Also, since these are runaway wives, the husbands might be covering up their disappearances.*

At that moment, the kitchen door swung open to reveal Clair. She hesitated in the doorway a few moments and seemed to come to a decision about something saying, "Emma, did you get what you needed?"

"No, not completely," she admitted. "I have an idea but, without more information, I don't want to accuse anyone."

Clair smiled slightly. "I think I can guess the two you are concerned about: Lily and Ann?"

"Yes." Emma smiled back. They thought along very similar

lines. "They've been here the longest and have not asked for a placement or help moving on."

"You spoke with Lily; do you want some time with Ann?"

She nodded and stated, "Yes, can you ask her to come in here?"

Clair said casually, looking down at her nails. "Thomas mentioned you asked him to go to the study for a book to keep him occupied while you were talking to Alison."

"Yes," she replied just as casually, studying Clair's face. "I was hoping that book would keep him inside the study until I completed my conversations."

Clair continued, "I also noticed that Dora seemed to be keeping a close eye on Ann while you were talking to Alison."

Emma made a point to take a moment and wait for Clair to make eye contact with her. "You caught me. I just want to keep the conversations private with each woman."

"Yes, I understand, and thank you for keeping the interview nonconfrontational. I'll get Ann now," she said as she walked out of the kitchen.

A few moments later, Ann peeked her head in the door, smiled timidly, and asked, "You wanted to see me?"

"Yes, Ann, have a seat."

She sat down and Emma watched her closely, studying her body language for signs that she was lying. There was no eye contact, she observed as Ann sat down at the kitchen table, she kept her eyes lowered demurely toward her hands.

"Ann." When she didn't look up, Emma prompted her again in a firmer voice, "Ann." She finally looked up and looked her straight in the eye. That startled Emma. *Why would such a timid woman make such direct eye contact?*

Emma hid her response as she noted that; she knew the hardest ones to detect were the practiced liars who were aware that lack of eye contact is a tell. *I'll have to watch for more subtle responses—behavior pauses or delays and breathing patterns*, she thought.

Emma began, "We've been talking about your future. You haven't mentioned to Clair if you would like us to start planning for your future outside the shelter."

Ann's gaze remained steady. She delayed speaking for a moment. When she did start talking, her voice came out timid. "Does a decision have to be made now?" Emma noted her tone.

"No, of course not, but we would like to know if you're thinking of staying here in the city and going to school or if we need to look into relocating you to a safer location."

"Why now?" Her eyes had a harder look and her voice a deeper timbre.

"Could you think about it? I can come back to discuss it at a later date."

She lowered her eyes and fell back into her timid voice. "May I go?"

She assumed her timid persona purposefully, Emma thought.

"Yes, and thank you for speaking with me tonight," she said.

Ann kept her head down as she left the room.

Emma immediately opened her notebook to document her conversation and observations. She waited in the kitchen for Dora and Thomas and thought, *I've accomplished what I wanted to this evening.*

Thomas and Dora entered the kitchen with Clair. As the group got organized to leave, Emma communicated Katy's message to Clair. She sent a questioning look at Emma. Emma caught it and said, "I'll talk to you soon."

With that, the group exited. Emma noted Thomas and Clair shared a long look as they were leaving.

Dora and Emma lay quietly in the back of the wagon on the way home. Thomas stopped the cart in the alley they'd started from. Emma and Dora felt the wagon come to a stop and took off the cover. After they jumped down, Emma asked softly to Thomas, "Headed back home?"

He cocked his head and said with a soft smile, "No, I think I'll be out for a while."

She smiled, certain he was returning to see that Clair got home safely. They waved him off and started the walk home. Dora couldn't wait to start questioning her. "Well, which one did it?"

"I've narrowed it down to Ann and Lily," she said, thinking of the three conversations this evening.

"Do you favor one over the other?" Dora asked, trusting Emma's instincts.

"They were both lying, but I think it's Ann informing on the house."

"Why Ann? She seems to be such a mouse of a woman."

"She is pretending to be something she isn't. Her demeanor is a disguise." Emma went on to describe her voice changes and her eye contact.

"Where do we go from here?" Dora asked, knowing they had to tread carefully.

"Data," she said simply. "We'll need to build a file on each lady with as much information as we can find. I'll continue to work with Cole on background checks and keep watch on the shelter. I'll notify Clair of my plans in the next few days."

They fell silent as they made their way around the last corner and entered the house through the kitchen. The light was still on. Dora had expected that Tim would be waiting up for her, but Emma was surprised to also see Tony there.

Dora hugged Tim hello.

Tony came over to Emma and gave her a quick kiss.

"Did it go all right? Any clues as to who might be involved?" he asked, more curious than concerned.

Tim wanted to hear what happened as well, so the group sat at the kitchen table while Emma recapped what she had learned. As she finished, Tim and Dora headed up to bed, leaving her and Tony alone.

Wanting to spend some one-on-one time with him, Emma asked, "Do you want to move to the sitting room. Is it too late for you?"

"That would be nice," said Tony softly.

They moved to the living room, sitting quietly enjoying each other's company, not wanting to discuss their respective work. They stayed together for a while and then he could see she was starting to drift off. He kissed her lightly and said, "Up to bed with you."

"Yes," she mumbled sleepily. "Sorry."

"No need to be. I love being with you, sleepy or not," he teased her.

"See you in the morning," she said as she yawned.

"Definitely."

She walked him to the door and kissed him one more time before he left. With the locks secured, she slowly made her way upstairs.

CHAPTER 22

The morning came around quickly. Emma laid in bed, wishing she didn't have to get up. She rolled to her side, pushed her hair back off her face, and moved to sit on the side of the bed. The note for Thomas to take to Clair had to be written this morning. Standing, she walked over to the dresser and splashed some water on her face before beginning her day.

Once she felt more awake, she quickly dressed and sat down at her desk to jot down the note. *Also,* she thought, tapping the pencil on her notebook, *it might be best to drop by and see Cole and Jeremy and let them know what's happening.* She finished and folded the note, placing it in her pocket as she headed downstairs.

When she entered the kitchen, Thomas was just preparing to go to the bakery. "Do you think you could stop by Clair's and deliver a note for me?"

"I think I could make time to see her this morning," he said with a smile, aware Emma knew he and Clair were seeing each other.

"Great," she said with a laugh, handing him the folded note. "Thanks."

Tony was already there as well. Emma walked over to where he stood near the back door and kissed him hello. Breakfast was in the works and the kitchen was a bit crowded. Dora's leadership took over and she said warningly, "If you're not here to work, then I need you out of my kitchen."

"I have an early appointment," said Emma, scrambling to grab some bread and butter.

"Take an apple with you. Your lunch is packed and it is on the table," Dora directed.

She grabbed both and said, "Thank you."

"Tony, do you want something to take with you?" asked Dora, always wanting to feed her family.

"No, Mom took care of that before I left the house this morning," he said, holding up his lunch bucket with a chuckle. As they left, he asked Emma, "Are we in a hurry this morning?"

"I want to stop by Cole and Jeremy's house before work and see if they have some time to discuss the shelter situation with me."

"Do you mind if I accompany you?" Tony asked.

"No, of course not, but it will be a little out of your way," she warned.

"That's fine." She looked at him and couldn't tell why he might want to go along. She shrugged and retrieved her bike. Tony hailed a cab to take them to Jeremy's house, as it was a bit far to walk and the trolley wasn't close to the area.

The cab stopped at Jeremy's house. Tony helped Emma down and retrieved her bike before paying the driver. He placed it on his shoulder and they climbed the stoop to Jeremy's house.

Emma knocked. The door opened and a nicely dressed woman of about Emma's age with long brown curly hair appeared at the door. "Yes?" she asked.

Emma felt a bit puzzled as to who this woman was and why she was at Jeremy's house so early in the morning. "Is Jeremy here? Or Cole?"

The woman looked at her with a curious expression before calling over her shoulder, "Jeremy, company." She looked back at them and said, "Come in, I'm just on my way out." She called as she headed down the stoop "See you later, Jeremy."

Emma absently frowned at her but kept her questions to herself. Tony noticed the frown and tried not to read into it.

Jeremy appeared in the doorway and waved his guest on her way.

"Emma, good to see you. Tony, welcome. You're both here early this morning. Everything okay?" he asked, looking concerned.

Shaking off her thoughts, she said, "Yes, I wanted to follow up on what we learned at the shelter last night. Do you and Cole have a few minutes?"

"Yes, Pops is out on the back patio. Join us for coffee and some breakfast?" asked Jeremy.

"We ate, but we would love some coffee," said Emma, answering for them both.

They followed Jeremy out to the back patio. Cole was sitting reading the newspaper when they exited the house. "Pops, Emma, and Tony stopped by."

He looked up and immediately stood. "Welcome both of you. Emma, I am assuming this is about the shelter. What did you find out?"

"Pops, let them sit down and have some coffee," Jeremy said with a smile.

"Oh, yes, please sit. Jeremy, pour them some coffee," he directed.

Jeremy poured it and Cole started the conversation. "Emma, can you give us an update?"

Emma pulled out her notebook and Jeremy's mouth quirked up as she started to go over her observations of the behavior of both Ann and Lily.

After she finished, Cole sat back in his chair and pondered

the facts. Finally, he said, "I agree that it is most likely Ann and we should keep the shelter under surveillance. What are your thoughts on what Lily might be involved in?"

"I think she is hiding something. I'm just not sure what it is."

"What is the timeline on this? You mentioned Alison has somewhere to go?"

"Yes. I'm going to get her letter posted in a few days. That should allow us to finalize the timeline for her departure," commented Emma.

"You should use the Pinkerton office for the return address," suggested Jeremy.

Cole nodded. "I agree."

"That's a good idea. Thank you," said Emma, grateful for the suggestion. "Did you need us to work on how to pay for your services?" she asked, knowing the additional men would be expensive.

"No, we care about the women in the shelter. We'll take care of it," said Cole firmly.

"Thank you."

"No thanks are necessary."

Jeremy spoke up, "Pops, I can lead the surveillance effort."

"That's a good idea. Report any suspicious activity, but tell the men it should be subtle. Don't approach, just surveil."

"I'll take care of it."

Tony said, looking at his watch, "Emma, we best be on our way."

"Yes," she said. "Work calls and I started on another case."

"Anything you need help with on that one?" asked Cole.

"Not yet, but I'll let you know," she promised.

They thanked Cole and Jeremy for their time and headed out.

Tony hailed a cab, but Emma declined the ride. "I have my bike and I don't mind the extra time to get over there. Miss you," she said to him, lifting her face to his.

"Miss you, too. I'll see you this evening," he said as he kissed her before climbing into the waiting cab. She jumped on her bike and headed off to her office job for the morning.

Emma got there on time, but not early enough to make any additional notes on the invoices. The office was fairly routine that day, typing contracts and filing. She closed her files as noon approached. She was going to head straight to the restaurant for her meeting with Clair.

When she arrived, her bike was taken and the manager escorted her back to his office, where Clair waited patiently.

"Emma."

"Clair." She nodded at her,

"Sit, please." Clair sat down at the round table; lunch was already set up. She said, "I thought you might be hungry."

"I am," commented Emma. "Thank you." She ate her sandwich quickly while Clair sipped her tea.

Clair said, "So, where are we on this investigation?"

"I believe it's Ann or Lily. At this time, I truly believe it's Ann."

"Of all people, that little mouse of a girl, you think she's behind this?" she asked incredulously.

"I do."

"Why?"

"It was her behavior. She appears to be a practiced liar. We're still investigating Lily, but we do feel it's Ann."

"I'll have to get her out of the shelter and away from my other women," she said, feeling protective.

"No," Emma cautioned. "Not just yet. We want to catch her in the act and find out who's paying her to do this."

"So, how do we go about it?" asked Clair determinedly.

"First, Pinkerton has set up surveillance on the shelter to watch any comings and goings. Any deliveries will be monitored and each person, especially those who come around often, will be checked out."

Clair nodded. "That sounds appropriate."

"Second, we'll wait for a response from Alison's cousin. Let her know we'll need the letter as soon as possible and that we'll post it."

"What then?" asked Clair.

"Well, for that," Emma said, "I have a plan." She went on to describe how to move Alison and catch Ann.

As they were wrapping up, Clair asked, "What about Lily? You said she's lying about the reason for being in the shelter?"

"I do. I don't know why yet, but I'll work on it. Do you know where she was before coming to you?"

"She said her husband beat her up and she did have significant bruising to her face when we took her in."

"How did she arrive at the shelter?"

"You know, that's an odd story. Normally, we're contacted at my business and usually by friends. That's how this operates—a friend of a friend. She just appeared on the doorstep and, once I saw her, we didn't question her motives for being there." She paused a moment, thinking. "I had forgotten about that."

"Did she arrive with anything?"

"Another odd thing. She had a bag with her."

"What was in it?"

"Books," she said simply.

"Books?" Emma frowned heavily. "If you were trying to get away from someone, would you take something like that? What kinds of items do the girls normally have?"

"Normally? The dresses on their backs. Most are lucky to get out alive, much less with belongings."

"Curiouser and curiouser," murmured Emma, drumming her fingers on her lips. "We'll continue to observe her. Any idea of where she was before the shelter?"

"She claimed to not want to talk about it. I believed her then, but I'm unsure now," she admitted.

"I'll investigate her and we'll keep that separate from this case." She closed her book and opened another, asking, "How did Ann get to the shelter?"

"It was one of the girls at my business. She knew her and brought her to us."

"Hmmm. More to think about. Can you give me her name?"

"Yes, but she has moved on, I doubt we will be able to find her for questions."

Emma noted that.

"Emma, one more question, who is paying Pinkerton to do this for us?" Clair knew few things in this life were for free.

"They're not being paid. I found out from Jeremy and Cole that the detectives have volunteered their services."

Clair teared up. To see such a strong woman, struggle with her feelings made Emma also tear up. She cleared her throat, laughed, and said, "We need a lighter topic."

Clair brightened and she wiped the tears from her cheeks. "Well, I do have one. I think you know I've been seeing Thomas."

"Yes," Emma said, not allowing any emotion into her voice.

Clair bristled a bit when she couldn't read her tone. "Well, we don't need your approval, but Thomas would like you to be aware of our friendship."

Emma grinned suddenly and said, "Clair, we love that you and Thomas have found each other. Our only concern ever is that Thomas is happy. You make him happy."

"Oh, well then," said Clair, relieved the family didn't disapprove of their relationship.

Emma checked her watch pin on her blouse and, as she picked up her courier pouch, said, "I have some deliveries to make before heading home."

"Of course. Thanks, Emma, for everything."

"We still have lots to do," Emma commented. "Contact me as soon as you have the letter."

"I will," promised Clair.

And with that, Emma headed out.

CHAPTER 23

It had been an active week with two cases being worked simultaneously. Emma allowed herself to sleep in that Saturday morning. There was a knock on her door, and she called out, "Come in."

Dora entered and jumped on her bed. "Going to get up today?"

"Eventually," Emma said as she stretched. "Did you bring me something to eat?"

"Is that all I am good for?" she teased.

Emma thought for a moment and said, "Well, yes."

Dora slapped her hand lightly to scold her and they both started laughing.

"So, did you bring me something?" Emma repeated.

Dora looked at her wryly and said, "Of course." She stepped outside the door and picked up a tray of goodies and brought it back to the bed.

"Mmm, my favorites," Emma murmured as they lounged on the bed and ate off the tray. They discussed their men and other topics.

"Jake will be here tonight; are you still okay with us inviting him to join our family?" Dora asked.

"Yes, you're right. He'll be a good fit for us, and he doesn't need to know what happened between me and Daniel."

Dora teared up and hugged her tightly. "Get dressed and come downstairs." Gathering the items from the bed, she headed to the door.

Emma called after her, "I will. I think I'm just going to hang around here today and read."

"Is Tony coming over?" Dora asked, pausing at the door.

"No, not until tonight. He's running a special exhibit at the museum today," said Emma, stretching and enjoying her lazy day.

"Will he bring Jake or should I send Tim?"

"Tony told me he would bring him."

Dora knew the family would be asking Jake tonight if he would like to join them as a specialist. She was making a special meal for them to eat together in the kitchen.

The day wound down slowly, and the family started entering for the dinner hour. As the whole group arrived—Tim, Tony, Jake, Papa, Dora, and Emma—they sat down and relaxed around the kitchen table. Tim sat next to Dora, Tony, and Emma across from one another, and Jake had a place next to Papa.

Jake was dominating the conversation with his favorite topic —cameras. He was moving into the types of exposures when Emma nodded at Dora. She was the best with him and the most patient. She reached over and touched his hand. He stopped talking and shifted his gaze to her.

"Jake, we would like to speak with you."

When it seemed she had lost his attention, she tapped his hand to remind him to look her in the eyes.

He stayed quiet and watchful. He seemed very nervous being the center of attention.

Tim took up the conversation from there. "Jake, we—" he

paused, glancing around the table for confirmation and, as he received a nod from each, continued, "—would like you to move in here at the boarding house."

"Really? I can bring my things over tonight!" he exclaimed.

His response caused the group to laugh, and Emma took up the conversation from there. "Jake, we love that you're excited. We also want you to have a role in our investigations."

Jake had been around enough to hear about the different cases she had led. He was very curious and sat still as a statue, waiting for more information.

"We believe your photography could be very important to future investigations. We've seen your pictures and know you're very talented. Also, your knowledge of overall photography will come in handy."

Jake couldn't wait any longer and said loudly, "Yes! I would love to."

"I don't think he needs much convincing," Emma commented wryly to the group, and they laughed in response.

The group broke up for their evening activities.

"I will be in the study," commented Tim.

"I will meet you there soon," said Dora and looked at her menu for the next day.

"Dora?" asked Jake.

Dora looked over and saw Jake in the doorway. "Yes, did you need something?"

"I have a question – about my living here."

"Of course, sit down." He sat and she joined him for a talk.

CHAPTER 24

JAKE'S MOVING DAY

Emma sat with Dora and Tim at the kitchen table, they'd completed their morning business meeting.

"Jake wants to move today," stated Tim.

"He was certainly eager last night," commented Emma. She saw Tony at the back door and waved him into the kitchen.

"Good morning," Tony said to the room. He leaned closer to Emma and said a low, "Good morning."

"Morning Tony. Tim mentioned Jake wants to start his move to the boarding house today," said Emma.

"Did you need some help?" asked Tony. "I can make some time this morning."

"I would appreciate the help. Can you meet me at Jake's house?" asked Tim.

"I'll be there," he promised.

"I'm ready to go," Emma said and stood up, gathering her things to leave.

"See you there," Tony said.

"We have to go," Emma said firmly.

"Bye!" called Emma.

"Bye!" called Dora and watched as they exited. She stood and went over to Tim and said, "Tell Jake we have his room ready and Papa cleared out a room in the basement for his equipment. Also make sure you move more than just his photography equipment," she warned. "He'll also need clothes and other personal items."

"I will," he promised and bent to kiss her. When he continued to linger, she pushed at him and said, "Go on with you."

He kissed her again quickly and said, "I will be back soon, with Jake."

As he turned to leave, she said, "Tim one more thing, Jake mentioned something odd to me."

"What was that?" he asked, pausing at the door.

"He asked if the furniture in the boarding house would start disappearing after he moved in."

"Disappearing?" he asked with a frown.

"Yes — I asked him what he meant and he said that the furniture in his home has been disappearing for the past year."

"When did he mention this?"

"Yesterday when I was confirming that he needs to bring his bed over. He was worried that the same thing would start happening here."

"I'll look around the house to see what is missing," he promised and left the room.

Heading down the stoop, he made his way to his wagon, parked in the front of the house. He climbed up, clicked at the horses, and headed over to Jake's house. *The furniture would have to be inventoried and sold, then the house could be put on the market. It would provide a savings account for Jake's future.*

The neighborhood was quiet as he pulled the wagon to a stop in front of Jake's home. Jumping down, he tethered his horse to a post and made his way up to the front door. He knocked briskly on it and waited. The door opened but it wasn't Jake that greeted him, it was the butler. Tim frowned, his unease didn't stem from him answering the door instead of Jake, but the fact he appeared to be in street clothes. *What's happening here,* he wondered. He didn't voice his concerns, instead, he asked, "Is Jake upstairs?"

"Step in please . . . sir," he said seeming to add the "sir" as an afterthought.

The attitude and clothes worried Tim. He frowned as he stepped into the foyer and looked up the staircase. Not turning, he asked, the butler more forcibly, "**Where is Jake?**"

Something hit him on the head--he turned to the butler and saw him holding a shovel. Tim reached up a hand to touch his head, looking bewildered.

When the hit didn't result in Tim collapsing, the butler screamed and tried to hit him again. This time, Tim saw the shovel coming at him and he intercepted it before it could make contact.

Tim looked at him in disbelief. "Give me that!" Tim wrenched the shovel out of the man's hands. "What do you think you're doing? How would you feel if I hit you with this?" He swung it at him in a threatening manner.

"That's enough," a woman's voice said from behind him. Turning he saw the maid on the stairs, holding a gun on him. She gestured to Tim with her gun and said, "Drop that please."

He did as he was told and she gave further instructions. "Now, I want you to move to that closet behind you."

Tim was considering if he should rush her to get the gun.

Reading his mind, she said, "Don't test me -- I will shoot you."

Tim took her threat seriously and moved to the closet she referenced. He stepped in and heard the door lock behind him. Leaning toward it, he listened, trying to find out their plans. "Get Jake, we're leaving," the maid's voice said.

"But what about the house," The butler whined. "It belongs to us, Daniel owed us for taking care of his wife."

Tim stood very still and thought, *It wasn't an accident, Jake's mom was murdered. Was he supposed to die in that fire? How long would Jake have lasted if Daniel were still alive?*

"We have to let that go, it's more important that we get the money from the bank. He is the only one that can do it."

"What about the big guy?" the butler asked.

"We leave him locked up, no one will be here to get him out," she said simply. "Get Jake."

Tim heard feet on the stairs and he looked at the door. He leaned on it to see if he could break it open. *No help there,* he thought. It was too thick and he had no space to ram it. Bending down, he examined the lock. *She had left the key in it.* He felt around behind him and found some paper. He would put his plan into place as soon as they were out of the foyer.

"Get your things and bring him down, we are leaving now!" the maid commanded loudly.

He heard Jake's voice, it seemed to be getting closer to the foyer.

"I don't want to go!" yelled Jake.

"You'll go," said the butler, his voice sounded strained.

Jake must be putting up a fight, thought Tim. *Good for him.*

"No! No! I won't, I am waiting for Tim. I am moving to the boarding house."

"No, you're not-you're coming with us to the bank!" the butler yelled back.

"Bank? I don't want to go there. You can't make me!" answered Jake. Tim heard a bang, that sounded like someone or something had fallen.

"Yes, it is time to get the money. Get up off the floor!" the maid said, quickly losing the last of her patience.

"Why?" he asked, still argumentative.

"Just shut up Jake," Tim heard the frustration in the woman's voice.

Tim didn't hear a response from Jake.

"Jake what is this I am holding?" the woman asked.

"My camera, hand it to me!" Jake demanded.

The woman's voice continued as if she hadn't heard him, "If you do not cooperate, what will I do with this?"

"You will break it," he said in a low voice. Tim had to strain to hear it.

"So, what are you going to do?" she asked.

"Go to the bank," he said in the same tone.

Tim heard the front door open.

"That is Tim's wagon, is he here?" asked Jake excitedly.

"No, he isn't," the butler said shortly. "Just go."

Tim heard the front door slam. He slid the paper under the closet door and kicked the lock. The key dropped onto the paper, he pulled the paper under the door to him.

He inserted it into the lock and opened the door looking quickly around the foyer. They appeared to be gone. A knock sounded, he went to opened it and saw it was Tony.

"Hey-I'm here …" Tony said and he stopped abruptly when he saw Tim's head. "Is that blood? Are you okay?"

Tim touched his head tentatively, "It's ok for now, the help has taken Jake."

"Taken him!" he said nonplussed. "Why would they take him?"

"Theft. They want his money. They are headed to the bank—probably to clean out his accounts before they leave town. We need to head over there."

Tim stumbled a bit going down the stoop. "Are you sure you're, okay?" Tony asked.

"Yes, we need to get to the bank."

"Let's go," Tony said.

They headed out, climbed on the wagon and Tony took the reins. Quickly making their way there, they pulled the wagon to a stop in front of the bank. They jumped down and rushed up to the entrance, Tony pulled Tim to a stop. "We need to think this through, security should be involved."

Tim continued to move forward, wanting to barge in and get Jake but Tony grabbed his jacket, pulling him to a stop, and said again, "Let's get security involved."

Tim nodded, taking a deep breath to steady himself. They entered and looked around taking in the large tiled room with a staircase leading to a second story. Tony was able to locate the guards nearest to the door. They went quickly to them and explained what was happening. The guard called to his men to join them and said, "Can you tell me where they're located?"

Tim and Tony looked around quickly, and Tim said, "Over there at the second teller's window. The dark hair heavy-set woman with the slim young man. Be careful Jake may not understand what is happening."

"I see him. Stay back we will take care of this." The guards spread out and approached the butler and Jake.

Where is the maid? Tim wondered, looking around. There was no way she wasn't here, she didn't seem to trust the butler to get the project done. He continued to look around and finally saw her speaking with a bank officer. They were in the area with the lockboxes were kept. *The furniture they sold, that must be where they kept the money.*

She hadn't noticed the guards approaching Jake and the butler. They quickly took him into custody and Tony stepped up to speak with Jake to reassure him.

Tim didn't wait for the guards and headed toward the lockboxes alone. He waited outside the room and when she came out with a full bag, he moved into her path. "Going somewhere?"

She seemed shocked he was there and didn't move.

"Is something wrong miss?" the bank officer asked when he noticed she stopped suddenly.

Tony had seen where Tim was and send a guard over to assist him.

The guard asked, "Sir, do you require assistance?"

"You'll want to take custody of her bag, I believe it's from stolen property sales," Tim indicated the bag she carried.

"No," she said pulling the bag to her. "This my money."

The security staff took custody of the bag and said, "Please come with me."

She followed him, clutching the bag close to her.

Back at the boarding house that evening. The family was in the kitchen listening to Tim's story. "What happened then?" Emma asked, wanting to hear all of the details. *How did I miss out on this adventure? I wish I could have been there.*

"They took them into custody," Tim said simply. "Kidnapping, assault, and theft." He didn't mention the additional murder charges that would be applied after an investigation.

"Am I still moving in?" asked Jake.

Laughter rang out through the table. Dora took his hand and said, "Of course, you can stay here tonight."

"We'll try again tomorrow," Tim promised.

Emma said, "We will all come over to help."

CHAPTER 25

About a week later, just after lunch, Jeremy and Emma were on a stakeout of the shelter. Emma was dressed as a boy and leaned against a wall near Jeremy. They both appeared to be relaxing and taking in the sun. Their location was the alley of the apartment building adjacent to the shelter; which allowed them to monitor the incoming and outgoing activities.

Emma was humming a bit when Jeremy started a conversation. "So, Jake has moved into the boarding house?" He had been over for a few family dinners and had the opportunity to meet the young man.

"Yes. Finally." She explained what Tony and Tim had to deal with during the move. "I helped with the inventory, the thieves had sold almost everything on the first floor. The money and Jake's mom's jewels were recovered. It didn't happen as we expected, but he is safe with us now. We all pitched in and got him settled the next day."

"What does he want to do with the house and remaining items?"

"He only cares about his photography things. Dora thinks we

should keep his mom's jewelry for him, in case he wants it later. The house and remaining items are to be put up for sale, soon."

"I am glad he is safe and at the boarding house. His family home is very nice, it should sell fast. Were they able to charge the maid and butler with the murder of Jake's mom?"

"The police used Tim's statement to charge them. The butler confessed and stated that the maid formulated the plan."

"I'm glad. There should be consequences to taking his mother away."

"Yes."

The conversation dwindled and Emma thought she would ask about something that was bothering her. "Who was that girl we saw at your house this week?"

"This past week?" he asked, delaying his answer for a bit.

"Yes," said Emma.

"She's a friend," he said simply.

"A close friend?" she asked, treading carefully.

"Getting there," Jeremy said, looking at her facial expressions. Savannah was only a friend, but he was fascinated by Emma's response to his answers. *Could she be jealous?*

"What is her name and where did you meet?" she asked, not willing to admit to herself why she was so curious.

"Savannah Woods and she works in the theatre. Her parents are actors there. She does the costumes and makeup."

"Really?" Emma asked, pushing down the feeling she had no right to have. "Can I meet her? I would love to see what she does." She started drumming her fingers on her lips, thinking about costumes and makeup.

"It seems I'm always facilitating meetings for you with interesting ladies," he teased.

"That's true," she admitted and teased back. "You do seem to know a lot of interesting ladies. I have an idea that she might help with."

Jeremy noticed a delivery wagon approaching and pulled his

hat down over his eyes. "Emma, we've documented that delivery driver here at least twice a week."

"Same person?" she asked intently.

"Yes," he murmured.

"What's he delivering?"

"Flowers."

"Can you tell where it's from?" she asked, not looking toward the wagon.

"Yes, it says The Flower Shop."

Emma smiled and said, "Well, guess what? I have a person I can contact in that establishment."

Jeremy nodded and asked, "Do you need any help?"

"No, I can handle this one." She glanced at her watch. "I need to wrap it up and get home for dinner. Want to come with me?"

"No," he said surprisingly. "I'm going out."

"To meet Savannah," she teased lightly.

"Yes," he said, watching her.

She hid her feelings as she pulled herself to her feet. "Let me know when I can meet her."

Before she could go, he took her hand and said, "Emma, Cole wants to meet soon and probe our potential suspects."

"Tell him later this week. I need to follow up on the flower vendor first."

"I'll let him know." She noticed his hand lingered on hers before he strolled away.

She rubbed where he had touched her, wishing she could figure out why she had such strong feelings for him. She shook her head. *Let it go, just let it go.* She walked away slowly, making her way home and starting to plan her next day.

*E*mma was thoughtful the next day while preparing for work. *I'll have to pick up some Berliners for my meeting later today.*

Noticing the time, she hurried, knowing Tony would be there soon to pick her up. As she made her way downstairs, she absently touched her hand, remembering yesterday's conversation with Jeremy. Feeling uneasy and disloyal to Tony, she battled with herself on how to handle these new feelings. She stopped at the kitchen door, put a smile on her face, and entered. It was business as usual with Dora and Amy preparing breakfast and Tim conducting business at the table.

"Morning, Tim, Dora, Amy," greeted Emma.

"Morning," called everyone.

Tim looked up from his books and said, "Emma, Jake has something for you this morning."

"He does?" she asked absently while putting together the bread and butter for her breakfast.

"Yes, after you went over your office case with him, he thought he had an idea for a camera that might work."

At that moment, Jake pushed open the door from the

dining room. "Emma, I have this for you." He handed her a box camera. It was smaller than the ones she had seen prior to this.

"Jake, is this yours?" she asked curiously.

"Yes. It is a prototype of a spy camera. I met the inventor, Professor Bolas, while I was at school in London. He said it would be good for law enforcement and gave it to me when I left there."

Emma turned it over in her hands and asked, "Will I be able to use it and bring it back for you to develop the pictures?"

Jake was silent for a long moment, then he said, "I think so. We can practice together."

"Sounds like a plan. Can you show me how to use it this evening?" she asked, happy with his initiative.

"Yes, I can make time," Jake said, glad he could offer support for a case.

"Thank you," Emma said sincerely.

Tim smiled at Dora and she responded by nodding. They were both happy she was taking steps to include Jake in their group.

Jake sat down at the kitchen table to have his breakfast while the rest of the family moved the breakfast platters into the dining room for the boarders. Tim, Emma, Papa, and Dora moved back to the kitchen table to join Jake. Since he had moved into the boarding house, the family had started having more private time for breakfast. Papa went to the basement to work; the rest of the family were all still there when Tim started his business meeting.

As they were wrapping it up, Tony tapped on the kitchen door and Jake let him in. "Morning, Jake," said Tony.

"Morning, Tony," answered Jake pleasantly.

"Morning, everyone," he added, speaking to the entire room. Different hellos and good morning greetings came from the group in the kitchen.

"Just a moment; I'll go get my bag," Emma said to Tony from her position at the table.

"No rush." He bent down and kissed her hello. "I always enjoy the mornings and a treat," he teased and Dora tossed him a pastry in response. Tony sat to talk with them while Emma stood up and went to get her bag. She jogged back downstairs and they said their goodbyes to the family. Tony held the door and they exited through the back door to retrieve her bike.

As they strolled toward the trolley, Emma and Tony shared their plans for the day. He inquired, "How did the surveillance go yesterday?"

She mentioned that it involved Jeremy and went on to comment, "I think we have a new lead. You remember Karl?"

Tony got the reference and asked, "The florist? Is he involved?" He hadn't gone with Emma to meet him, but he knew they were friends.

"No!" She laughed. "But I think his delivery driver might be. I plan to meet him today to ask him some questions."

Tony was quiet for a moment and asked, "So, your surveillance was with Jeremy?" There was no expression in his voice.

She looked at him oddly and said, "Yes, he is in charge of all the surveillance for this case and my shift was with him yesterday."

"Hmm," he said noncommittally.

Emma had to let the conversation go. They didn't have time for this particular topic on a workday. The silence settled around them as they continued to the trolley. As they reached the stop, she went to kiss him and, at the last minute, he turned his head, so she kissed him on the cheek. "See you," she said quietly, knowing something was bothering him.

"Yes," he said and turned to catch the trolley.

In all the times they had walked together, Tony always turned around to give her a wave goodbye, but that day he didn't. *What has changed?* she wondered. Shaking off the feeling that something was wrong, she continued to make her way to the office.

Nothing unusual occurred that morning; the noise of type-writers filled the room. As the noon hour approached, she thought, *Just what I needed, a day with no drama.* The day's folders were put into the file room and her next day's work was organized on her desk. *The camera,* she thought. *I'll bring it in tomorrow.* She would have to be early, though it shouldn't be a problem because she knew the building manager would let her in early. Waving goodbye to everyone, she exited the office.

She rode her bike, enjoying the wind in her hair as she made her way to the bakery for the Berliners she knew would be required for her afternoon meeting. She entered the bakery through the kitchen back door and was immediately yelled at by one of her cousins. "Emma! Are you back with us?"

"No, just picking up something," said Emma. She stopped by Chloe's workstation to chat. "How are things? "

Chloe rubbed her very pregnant belly and said, "We are wonderful." Cousin had finally admitted that he saw a future with her and didn't waste time asking her to marry him. Chloe continued to work at the bakery after they were married and would probably do so until she had the baby.

"How are you and Tony?" asked Chloe.

"Funny you should ask. I'm not sure," Emma admitted.

"Why, what happened?" Chole asked, edging closer and dropping her voice to keep their conversation private.

"That's what's odd. Nothing really," she said in a confused voice.

She didn't get a chance to say more before Cousin spotted her and walked over. He leaned in and kissed her on the cheek and asked, "Anyway I could get you for a dessert?"

"As long as it isn't. . ." she teased, referencing the dessert favored by a local gangster.

"Yes, well, I have banned that one. Too many bad memories," Cousin responded.

"I appreciate that."

"I need an order of German Cinnamon Star Cookies," said Cousin.

"I think I can arrange that. When would you like me to have the order ready?" asked Emma.

"We need them for Tuesday delivery. Thanks, Emma."

"I will make them tonight."

"Perfect. I will send over the ingredients to the boarding house for you. Now, what are you here for?" Cousin asked curiously.

"Can't I just stop by because I miss everyone?" Emma teased.

He gave her a look until she relented. "Okay, I need some Berliners for a meeting today."

"I think we can arrange that." He snapped his finger at a younger cousin to get them for her.

While they were compiling the Berliners, Cousin started discussing family business about his next expansion plans. "Emma, would you like to participate and be a larger partner in our next bakery?"

She tilted her head, thought of her savings, and knew she had no plans for it at this time. "Interesting offer. Can I think about it and get with you later?"

"Yes," he replied.

Chloe ran over as fast as her pregnant body could carry her and hugged her. "Come and have dinner with us soon and bring Tony."

"I will, I promise," she said, hugging her back.

Getting the box from her younger cousin, she hugged her and headed out to the florist shop. Her mind was focused on the task in front of her as she rode around the neighborhood where the shop was located. The delivery wagon was not in the area. It was normally parked on the side of the shop. *He must be out on a delivery*, she thought. *Good.*

She entered the shop and heard the familiar twinkle of bells announcing her entry. The area was filled with flowers and smelled wonderful. As she stood there, waiting for Karl, she thought about how they had met two years ago when she was researching her mama's past. That event brought them together, she was happy they had continued to build their relationship and become close friends. She was wandering around the show-room, admiring the lovely flower arrangements when Karl came out of the back.

He smiled broadly and immediately went over to hug her. "What a nice surprise! I didn't expect you today." He noticed the box in her hands. "And Berliners! Come sit," he said, gesturing to the stool by the counter. "I have to stay up front today. I have a few orders being picked up and my delivery driver is out," he said, confirming Emma's observations.

"I had something to talk to you about, if you have time for me?" she inquired.

"Of course, I have time for you, always. What do you need?" he asked jovially.

"Your delivery driver, how long has he worked for you?" Emma asked in her typical blunt style.

He frowned, surprised at the direction of the conversation. "About six months. Is there a reason you're asking?"

"Would he come in the front or the back when he enters?"

He looked at her in a canny manner and said, "He'll be out for a few hours."

"And?" she prompted.

"He'll come in the front," he admitted. "We should be able to see him when he arrives. So, girly, are we wrapped up in another adventure?" he asked, a twinkle in his eyes, rocking back on his stool with hands-on his rounded belly.

"Yes, we have a suspicion that your delivery driver…?"

"Pete Langston," he supplied.

"Maybe working with someone to carry messages that could lead to a woman being hurt and possibly killed," she stated the facts without emotion.

"Hmm," he murmured thoughtfully.

"You don't appear surprised," she said, gauging his expressions.

"Well, you know good help is hard to find," he admitted laconically.

"Can you tell me what you know about him?" she asked, ready with her pencil and notebook.

"I can tell you what I know. Pete Langston is his name, and he is about twenty years old. He keeps to himself and gets deliveries completed on time," he said simply.

"Does he talk about his personal life?"

He pondered the question and answered, "No, not really. He usually talks about the weather or the required deliveries he has scheduled. He stays out most of the day, doesn't keep money that's not his, and he's on time."

"Does he have parents?" she asked.

"I have never inquired," he said and shrugged.

"Could you inquire for me?"

"It's that important to you?" he asked, reaching over to take her hand in his.

"Yes," she answered, letting emotion into her voice and squeezing his hand.

"Then I think I can do that for you," he said warmly.

"How come I haven't met him before this?" she asked.

"It never came up, and he's usually on deliveries this time of day," he said, shrugging.

She nodded.

"Now, let's have some of these." He eagerly opened the box of Berliners. He ate one and, as he reached for another, asked, "Would you like one?"

"Just one?" she teased and took it out of the box to eat.

He grinned at her as they both took a bite of the sweet snacks. They completed their meeting with an agreement that he would send her a message if he turned up any information. She hugged him and said, "Goodbye."

She was exiting the shop when the delivery driver was coming in. He seemed to pause when he saw her but brushed past in a hurry. She raised an eyebrow at Karl, who nodded as she exited.

CHAPTER 27

That night, dinner had wrapped up and Emma accompanied Jake to the basement workshop. Tony was having a late night at the museum and wouldn't be coming by to see her. She found herself relieved that she wouldn't have to endure a conversation she knew was coming.

Putting him out of her head, she tried to concentrate on what Jake was saying about the proper way to hold the spy camera. "You will need to practice holding it steady and make sure there is plenty of light on the paper," he said.

"So, I hold it very steady and I will need to hold the paper up, maybe tack it on the wall. I'll take it tomorrow and try it out in the morning. I sent a note to Tony to tell him I will be leaving early. Thanks, Jake," she said sincerely.

"When you come back, place the camera in my workspace here," he directed.

"I'll bring it by after my office job," she promised.

That satisfied him and he started talking about film and development. Emma stayed and listened, enjoying the discussion about the technical side of the camera she would be using.

They walked upstairs together, with Emma heading to her room and Jake joining the others in the sitting room.

Emma carried the camera, handling it carefully as she opened her door and entered her room. She sat on her bed, looking down at it as she planned on how to use it in the office in the morning. Standing up, she walked to the desk to lay out some papers to practice taking pictures. *Jake was right; it has to be vertical.* He had explained that to her, but she hadn't realized the challenge this presented. The paper couldn't be tacked up because the holes would be noticeable and lead to questions she didn't want to answer.

She sat in her chair, drumming her fingers on her lips. *Where was that packet of chewy candy?* she thought as she pulled open a drawer on the left side of the desk. She moved stuff around, looking for the packet Papa had gotten her while traveling.

As she searched, she remembered what he had told her about it. Just a few years ago, in 1880, Henry and Frank Fleer experimented with chicle from the sapodilla tree. The Fleer brothers made cubes of the chicle substance and overlaid the cubes with sweet material.

"Ahh, here it is," she said as she found the small, flat packet. She looked at the cube and put it in her mouth and chewed until it got sticky. She grimaced, thinking, *I much prefer my sweets in the form of baked goods.* Pulling it out of her mouth, she tore it into two pieces. The chewed cube stuck to her fingers and did not easily come off. There would be some trouble with splitting one piece when it was already chewed. *I'll probably need to chew a much smaller piece, one at a time.*

She removed as much as she could from her fingers and used the small amount remaining to attached it to the back of a paper on her desk. *Definitely sticky, very little will be fine,* she thought as she attached it to her wall. She set the camera up and move the paper around until she was able to get the optimum range.

Okay, that should be it, she thought as she documented the height of the paper in her notebook and put it back on the desk. She reached up to take the papers down and started to try to remove the sticky material. It wasn't coming off easily. *Water,* she thought, she went to her dresser, poured some into a glass, and pulled a handkerchief out. Wetting the edge, she rubbed it. When she finished, she looked at both sides of the paper and thought, *A little less tomorrow should do it.*

One more thing, she thought. *I have to make the cookies before I go to bed.* She headed back downstairs to make them.

CHAPTER 28

*E*mma had gotten a very early start to the office to get the pictures without being seen. She also admitted to herself that she was again relieved to not have to talk with Tony that morning. *I'll eventually have to have a conversation with him, just not now.*

The building manager was in the hallway and saw her storing her bike. "Early this morning, Emma?"

"Yes, I was hoping you could let me into the office. I have a few things to catch up on," she said.

It wasn't unusual for her to be in early, and he said, "Of course." They walked up together discussing the weather and other pleasantries. after opening the door, he left her there, with a cheerful goodbye.

The office was quiet, and she approached her desk quickly, pulling out the chewing candy and Jake's camera before making her way over to Lauri's desk. There, she found eight vendor invoices in Lauri's folder and moved them back to her desk. She pulled the matching customer invoices from her folder. Small pieces of the cubes were chewed, one at a time, and transferred to the back corners of the invoices. She placed them at the height she had documented the previous night. The sticky candy held and she was able to take pictures of each one. The bright light streaming into the room was important, otherwise, the pictures could turn out too dark.

She glanced at the watch attached to her top and realized she had to hurry to get the papers back into Lauri's file. Flipping them face down, she wetted a small fabric square with water from her drinking bottle and rubbed it lightly on the paper to remove most of the substance. When she finished, she saw that it was still a little sticky and the paper would take a bit to properly dry. She hoped Lauri wouldn't notice.

The camera! she thought after returning the papers to Lauri's folder and hearing feet coming up the stairs. She ran back to her desk, sat down, and moved it to her lap, under the desk. It was the office manager; as usual, he barely spared her a glance as he walked by.

She took a deep breath, put the camera safely away in her bag, and thought, *I hope the pictures come out.* Realizing she was still in her split skirt, she went and changed in the hallway closet. Walking back into the office, she saw Lauri a few steps in front of her. They both sat at their desk and Lauri said a quiet, "Hello."

Emma returned the greeting, watching her discreetly. Lauri pulled out her daily file and, when there were no indications that anything was wrong, Emma pulled out her files to start her work.

A few moments later, when Lauri went to separate her invoices to be typed, she said, "These are a bit sticky, something must have spilled on them." She didn't seem bothered by it; it wasn't out of the ordinary for the raw invoices to have had something spilled on them. She continued, "Oh well, I'm typing them this morning, so it shouldn't matter."

Emma nodded, glad the stickiness didn't appear suspicious. Keeping quiet, she got her work completed and headed home.

Jake had been clear about his requirements, so her first stop was his lab in the basement. She opened the drawer and stored it how she had been shown. She understood the equipment had to be handled carefully.

The pictures should be developed later that evening and she could access them with her papa in the morning. This was her first time using the device and she was nervous about the final product.

Heading upstairs, she heard Dora call, "Hi, Sister, how did it go? Will the pictures turn out?" As she exited the basement into the foyer, she saw Dora waiting for her. "It went well, but I'm unsure of the technology. I hope they come out. If not, I'll try again," she said philosophically.

Tim walked up to them and handed Emma a note. "Cole dropped this by for you today and said they want a group meeting on the findings later this week."

"Hmm, I still have to get information from Karl about the flower delivery driver. I hope to have it in a few days. I'll check in with him tomorrow," she said, thinking about what was still needed before the group meeting.

"Emma, be careful," said Dora, a note of warning in her voice.

"I will. Karl can be trusted."

Dora said, "Come eat before you have to go out again."

Emma linked her arms through hers and headed to the kitchen. Her afternoon duties were fairly routine.

That evening, Jake developed the film and indicated the photos would have to dry overnight prior to any inspection. Emma understood and let him work on their development while she sat in the sitting room with the family and boarders, working on some lace patterns. She completed her work, bid everyone goodnight, and headed to bed.

Very early the next morning, a knock at her door woke her from a deep sleep. "Just a minute," she mumbled as she rolled out of bed and grabbed her robe. Opening the door, she was surprised to find Jake there. "Jake, it's very early. Is something wrong?" she asked, pulling her robe belt tight and pushing her hair out of her face.

He didn't answer the question but instead said, "I have the pictures ready."

She knew she would have to go see them, so she said in a low voice, "All right, let me get some socks on."

He nodded and waited as she headed back to her bed, leaving her door open. She smiled slightly and sat down on the edge to pull on her socks. Standing, she gestured for him to lead the way. They went downstairs and into the quiet kitchen; no one was up yet. There was plenty of light in the room to view the pictures, Jake had turned up all of the gas lamps. She glanced down at them and saw they were surprisingly clear and the data could be read. "Jake, these are perfect. With this evidence, I will be able to move forward with the investigation," she said wonderingly.

Jake didn't smile, but she thought she made him happy. "Can I keep these?" she asked.

"Yes." Though he said yes, she thought he looked a little uncomfortable.

"Jake, I know you normally keep your pictures, but you should think of these like your work photos. You don't keep those, do you?"

"No, no, I don't," he said slowly.

"Well, you're now part of our team and your pictures are part of that work product." The information she presented made sense to him and he seemed to relax.

She gathered them up and said, "I'll take these to my room now and show them to Papa later. See you at breakfast. And, Jake, good work."

He nodded, she helped him turn off the gas lamps and they both headed upstairs.

Entering her room, she sat on the bed, knowing she would be unable to sleep. She turned up her gas lamps and compared the photos with her previously copied information. The findings were consistent; the amounts of structural steel, cement, and sand differed between vendors and customers.

Papa should be up in another hour, she thought, glancing at the clock. Hearing movement on the steps, she quickly got dressed and headed downstairs to help with the early baking. Amy, Emma, and Dora worked together to put together the pastries, biscuits, and bread that would be required for the day. Emma was rolling out the dough and pinching off biscuits to go into the oven when she heard Papa in the dining room. As he entered the kitchen, she said, "Papa, when I'm finished here, I need you to look at something for me."

"Sure, Sister, come into my study when you're ready," commented Papa absently, looking at some notes in his hands.

"Let me get the pictures and I'll meet you there." Emma finished adding the biscuits to the pan and placed them in the oven to bake. "I am on my way to see Papa," Emma commented to Amy and Dora.

Dora nodded and said, "We will keep an eye on them." She and Amy would continue working on the breakfast preparations.

Heading to her room, Emma retrieved the pictures and her notes. She made her way downstairs and laid the photographs on the desk for him to evaluate. She placed the invoices that should match -- together.

He studied the picture groupings and the differences between the two. "Hmm," he said. "There's definitely something up here. The invoice from the vendor is providing iron but the customer is paying for steel. There's a significant cost difference between the two. Steel is a better metal to build with; it's becoming the standard for all skyscrapers. Another thing that worries me is that I don't see additional steel or oak timbers to set the foundation. Without that, the concrete numbers should be much higher. See here," he said, pointing to the customer invoices, "the customer is being charged for additional steel to support the foundation but the purchase from the vendor shows a deficit in both areas."

"Papa, this is dangerous. Those buildings could collapse over time and the buildings here are partly for the less fortunate," she said, worried.

"When you and Tim chose the Baker Agency as the first location for women to be in the workplace and met with Josh Baker, did he appear to be an honest man?" Papa asked.

"We met with his assistant, but yes, he has a good reputation in the business. I can't imagine he would condone this. Papa, haven't you worked with him in the past?" asked Emma.

"Not directly, more through third parties like your office. Do you ever see him in the agency?" Papa asked.

"He doesn't come into the office. It's handled by the office manager," she said and went on to explain the separate filing systems.

"You don't ever reconcile the invoices?" Papa asked with a frown.

"No. We just type them up, multiple ones from vendors and one to the customer. One copy for the files and one to be mailed. Other secretaries place them in envelopes for mailing."

"Separate systems and separate books. How did he think he was going to get away with this? Did he think no one would notice?" Papa asked incredulously.

"I believe he thinks the women doing the work are too simple to understand what they are typing," explained Emma.

"Well, you proved him wrong," he said, proud of his smart daughter.

"Any recommendations for where we go from here?" she asked, trusting his decision on these matters.

"I'm thinking about that. We need a meeting with Mr. Baker.

I think it's time, and we have enough evidence to show him," commented Papa.

"You'll set it up?"

"I will," he said, still reviewing the invoices.

"I'll let Tim and Dora know."

He nodded and looked over at her, "Tell them to keep this quiet."

"I will," she said and headed to the kitchen to let her partners know the case status.

Papa got the note to Mr. Baker organized and off that morning. The meeting was set up immediately after lunch that day.

Emma went about her normal schedule and made her way home to meet him. They took a cab to the office, she stepped down and had to arch her neck to see to the top. "His office is in there?"

"Yes, it is one of the tallest buildings that has been built. Baker's many engineering offices are helping to raise the city of Chicago to new heights."

Emma believed Mr. Baker was an honest man, but she would have to be observant of his behavior during their meeting. There was a guard in the foyer. She recognized him from Pinkerton; the security world was a small one. He was dressed in the typical black suit with a black tie and white shirt. He gave her a wink when she waved. Papa didn't need directions, so they entered the stairs and Emma realized they would be going to the tenth floor.

When they exited the stairway and onto their floor, Papa was breathing a bit ragged from the walk and had to lean on the wall to catch his breath.

"Papa, are you all right?" Emma asked, concerned. It wasn't just his breathing; his color seemed off.

"I'm fine, Emma, just a bit winded. We're not all as young as you are," he said with a smile.

She would have to keep an eye on him. As Papa got his

breath back, his color returned and they headed toward the large carved doors at the end of the hall. They led to a large office space that had wood floors and intricate rugs. A male secretary saw them and waved them over to him. As they approached the desk, the secretary said warmly to Papa, "Ellis, so good to see you. Mr. Baker will be with you soon."

"How do you know the secretary?" Emma asked in a low voice as they moved to low chairs near the wall.

In the same tone, Papa answered, "He makes the initial contacts with the engineers and sets up meetings for Mr. Baker's engineering offices."

They only waited a few moments. Mr. Baker came out to meet them and, immediately, she liked his personal touch. She studied his appearance, his hair was black with streaks of grey throughout, and appeared to be in his early to middle 30s. He was also a man with an interesting face. He would have been classically handsome, but it looked like his nose had been through a few fights.

"I'm Ellis Evans and this is Emma, my daughter, who I sent you a note about this morning. I believe she has some information that will interest you."

He looked at her appraisingly and nodded. "Okay. Let's go into my office and hear what you have to say."

She didn't see anything that told her he was dishonest; his manner was open, his eye contact strong, and his voice steady. *All good things*, she thought but would reserve her final judgment until later.

They went in and sat down on the long brown couch, with Mr. Baker sitting in a dark chair across from them. He directed his question at Emma. "You want to tell me why you're here today?"

Emma took out her notebook and started, "Mr. Baker—"

"Please, call me Josh," he interrupted.

"Okay, Josh." She started going over the discrepancies she had found in the office.

When she paused, Josh looked at her in an almost curious manner and asked, "These are rather big accusations. Do you have something to back this up?"

She was relieved she didn't have just her notebook to make her case and said, "Yes, I do." She reached into her long jacket pocket and pulled out the photos she had taken of the invoices and laid them out side by side on the low table in front of him.

He sat a bit stunned at the photographic evidence. He hadn't expected anything other than conjecture. As he looked at the photos, he had to admit they contained incontrovertible proof that building supplies were being substituted without approval. He murmured, "It's funny. I gave that role to Tracey because I thought I could trust him. Prior to taking him on, I had heard things about his previous job, but I thought he deserved another chance. What to do. . ." His voice trailed off. Looking Emma in the eyes, he asked, "Emma, do you believe the engineers assigned to the office are involved?"

She gave some thought to that question before answering. "I don't think so. They are involved in the proposals and development of material costs. The office manager usually works on the initial invoice to the vendors and places the orders and then the engineers confirm the amount billed to the customer."

"Very tricky. I'll bet there are two different logbooks in his office. Do the secretaries have business training? Accounting included?"

"Yes, all of the secretaries in the offices are either temporary or permanent persons who came from the local business school. Accounting classes are required as part of our training," she said quickly.

"We'll need to restructure the office for a few weeks with new management," he said, thinking about how this would work.

Her eyes widened, suddenly worried she had inadvertently put their company in jeopardy. "Everyone will keep their jobs?"

"Yes, as long as no one else is involved in the deceit," he stated matter-of-factly.

"When will you move forward, Mr. Baker?" asked Papa.

"Call me Josh," he said absently. "Tomorrow morning. I can't let this continue." He looked at Emma and warned, "Don't do anything out of the ordinary or say anything to anyone."

"I would like to notify my partners; Tim and Dora," she stated.

"That is fine, just no one else. Is there someone in the office you would recommend over the others to help coordinate the investigation?" he asked, pondering his next moves.

One person came to mine and Emma said, "Yes, Lauri Wheeler is the best secretary in the office and would be my first choice."

"I'll trust you and will talk to Miss Wheeler. I need to bring in another person to help coordinate the efforts from the outside. I will, of course, immediately talk to my lawyers about freezing any accounts the current manager has open."

That evening, Emma told Dora about the case and to keep it quiet until after Mr. Baker confirmed it was okay. "Where is Tim?" she asked.

"He was called out to one of our businesses. He will be home late," said Dora, not offering more information. Emma watched her but didn't ask further questions. Tim stayed out late and Emma figured she would talk to them in the morning.

The next day, Dora mentioned Tim was out early on business. Emma wanted to get to the office early and didn't have time to question her. She couldn't think of anything but the office on her way in. Once she got to her desk, she sat tense, waiting for the office hours to start. She would have felt better if she had been able to discuss the situation with Tim and Dora, it just hadn't worked out that way.

Trying to behave in a normal manner, she pulled out her invoices to start typing. The office began filling with the secretaries, engineers, and the office manager. That was when things changed. Men in nice suits flooded into the office. Josh and surprisingly Tim, dressed in what appeared to be his wedding suit, went immediately to the manager's office. They were accompanied by two police officers and several discreetly dressed men.

Tim managed a subtle nod at Emma before pausing at the door. "I know most of you," he said, directing his speech to the office workers and engineers. He smiled at those around the room who knew him. "For those, I do not know, I am Tim Flannigan, and I am here with the owner of the firm, Mr. Baker. Please, stay at your desks and await further direction." He followed Josh into the manager's office.

Everyone seemed to turn into stone, staring at the manager's door. It seemed to be an eternity before the men returned, and the police officer had the office manager secured in cuffs. He looked defeated as they escorted him out.

Josh stopped by Tim and whispered in his ear. Tim nodded and said to the group, "This is the owner of Baker, Mr. Josh Baker."

Josh started with a reassuring smile to the employees, taking a moment to look each in the eye. "I would like to assure everyone that they still have their jobs." He gave them a minute to digest what he said before continuing. "This is in no way a reflection of your work in this office. We have found an accounting discrepancy that will take a while to straighten out. I would like you to work with Tim in the following weeks. He has graciously agreed to lead the audit for me. I also want to speak with Lauri Wheeler?" he asked, searching for her.

Lauri felt like her heart was going to beat right out of her chest, but she motioned to him with her hand. "Yes, sir, right here."

He looked at her appraisingly and said, "Your experience and leadership here in the office has been communicated to me and you have been selected to assist Tim with the audit. At the end of this, we will determine the final permanent positions of staffing for this firm." He looked away from her and said, "Tim, I'll leave you here to begin."

Josh approached Lauri and clasped her hands in his. "We'll speak soon." And with that, he was gone.

Lauri looked a bit shellshocked. Emma went up to her and asked, "Are you okay?"

"Why me?" she asked, bewildered at the events that had occurred that morning.

"Why not you? You are amazing at your job and they would be lucky to have you. Now, deep breath and be yourself," Emma told her.

Tim called over, "Lauri, come into the office so we can talk. Everyone else, continue with your normal duties." Tim and Lauri entered the office manager's office and shut the door.

Lauri couldn't wait any longer to start asking questions. "Tim, what's happening? Why did the police take the office manager away?"

Tim walked over to the desk and tapped the two identical books sitting on its surface. "This is the reason."

She looked at him questioningly and said, "I don't understand."

He sat on the corner of the desk and said, "You know how all of the invoices for customers and vendors are kept separate?"

"Yes," she said, frowning.

"The owner found out about the filing system and reviewed some of the invoices together. The office manager was keeping the two files separate so he could buy substandard materials and pocket the extra money. He recorded all the information in these two books. We took a chance there would be a written record here," Tim stated in a business-like manner.

"Oh, my goodness," she said, taking a deep breath and sat down on the office chair.

"Yes. These cons are limited. We didn't want to spook him, so we moved in fast. Josh has drafted a letter of explanation to go out to the customers explaining that there will be a probe into all of their projects. At this time, we do not know if the suppliers were involved or it was just the office manager. This must be kept quiet until we can figure it out. We—me and you—will work together to build one file with the proper invoices and project files. You will need to evaluate your staffing and let me know if we can get this done in a few weeks. We've been allowed to bring in more temporary help if we see a need for it," he said as he looked at her expectantly.

"This will also take weekends and evenings," she said quietly, thinking of staffing.

"Yes. You'll need to announce everyone's new job responsibilities," he said as he straightened up, away from the desk. "Let's get started. Please show me the filing system and how they are separated."

"Yes, please follow me." They headed out of the office to the file room, Lauri waved to Emma. "Emma, come with us and help pull files to start the process."

"Yes, of course." She closed the file in front of her and followed them.

As they explained the separate systems in place, Tim rubbed his forehead and said, "We'll need to pull each file and compare the differences in each one. Pull identical files for the same companies, enough for seven people to work on. Lauri, include yourself in the process."

They pulled the files and distributed them to the office employees for them to compile and organize.

Tim commented to Lauri as she started to exit the file room, "Lauri, come to the office, we have one more task." He paused before joining her and called, "Fred and Robert, I need you to come to the office for a discussion."

They entered and Tim indicated for them to sit down in the two chairs facing the desk. Tim was seated behind it, with Lauri standing next to him. The two men sat down. Fred was an experienced engineer in his thirties; Robert was in his late twenties and had trained under Fred. They both looked nervous but waited patiently for Tim to start the conversation.

"Fred and Robert, we don't think you were involved in the office manager's scam." They seemed to visibly relax at this statement. Seeing this reaction, he continued, "We would like you to stay here at Baker and help us through this mess and help us form a stronger, honest company."

Fred spoke up. "You can count on us. We really didn't know what was going on."

"I appreciate you telling me that. What I need for you to do is pull all the project files listing all the materials and highlight the ones that should have been ordered and then get with the secretaries. They will be pulling all the information into one file. I will be reconciling all the missing funds. Lauri here is your temporary office manager." They looked at one another, Tim saw and commented a bit stiffly, "Will this be an issue?"

"No, no," they said in unison.

Robert said, "Just different, that's all." He looked at Lauri and said, "I'm looking forward to working with you as our office manager."

"Thank you," she said warmly. "Let's get back to work."

They smiled back, relieved they still had jobs and headed out of the office to gather the requested files.

She walked out of the office and went over to Emma's desk. "Can you stay a full day today?"

"Yes, I'm okay for today." Emma had expected something like this. The people she normally transported documents for had been notified she would be unavailable for a while.

Lauri started by handing out the files to each secretary and said, "Has everyone gotten their duplicate files?" They nodded. "Now open each file. We want you to put the two invoices together first and then we'll be looking for differences between the two. As you pull these together, the engineers will need to review the original project files with the paperwork to see which matches the original design."

One of the secretaries spoke up. "But that will take some time."

"Yes, it will, because it takes many invoices to make a building. We want to provide data to show how much money has been stolen. If anyone has a problem with this project, please see me privately in the manager's office and we can arrange for a temp to take your place," she said in a firm voice.

The secretary who asked the question looked over at another secretary with a worried expression. She realized they were lucky to still have jobs and stopped asking questions. They got to work. It was tedious but necessary.

They all worked diligently and lunch was brought into the office as a surprise. Dora and Thomas opened the door and came in with many boxes. Emma got up and helped clear a large table near the front of the office. The food was set out and everyone started to eat.

Dora asked Emma, "Where's Tim?"

"Office," she said, taking a bite of her sandwich and nodded her head toward his closed door.

"I'll take a plate into him," she said as she gathered his food. Dora knocked softly and got a call to come in. Before the door closed, Emma heard Tim say, "Dora!"

The staff enjoyed their meal of sandwiches and fruit. Dora had also included some cookies.

Work continued that afternoon with the newly organized files being collected at the end of the day. Tim would be the one to do a final evaluation to determine the total differences for each company. Any instances of overcharging or inconsistent accounting would be cataloged.

Everyone started to get ready to leave and Lauri said, "You all did good work today. Given our progress, I think it will take a few weeks to reconcile the paperwork. At that time, we'll reorganize the office. I'll see everyone tomorrow."

Tim came out of the office and said, "Emma, Lauri, if you will wait for me, a cab has been arranged."

"Thanks, but I'm on my way out now," said Lauri. She smiled as she left for the day.

Emma went into the office and dropped onto the couch with a sigh. She looked around and said, "I've never been allowed in here before."

As he cleaned up his desk, Tim said in a tired voice, "I would rather be working from the boarding house."

"Are you okay with doing this on top of our business?" she asked concerned about him.

"Yes, it's for a very important client and it involves us adding more employees to our business. All the temporary hires for this operation will come from us," he explained.

"That's good," stated Emma.

They locked up the file room; they'd had the locks replaced for the whole office earlier in the day. He pulled the main door shut and made sure the lock clicked into place before they left. They were both quiet on the way home in the cab. Dora and Papa met them at the door. Dora took Tim's hat and walked with him into the study, with Emma and Papa following behind.

"Long day, Tim?" asked Papa.

"Yes, as Emma can attest. We only made a small dent in the files. It looks like this has been going on for some time. I'm not sure how long at this point. I'll have to continue working long hours for a while."

"You can do it, Tim," said Dora in a supportive voice.

"Yes, I know I can. I just have to get used to the schedule," he said taking her hand.

"We can hire a secretary to help with our business until the project is over," suggested Dora.

They heard the front door open and shuffling feet. Dora knew who it was and called, "Jake, we're in here."

He came to the door and saw it was the family and asked, "Hello. Are we in here tonight?"

"No, we're just talking about Tim and Emma's day at the office," said Dora.

"Is dinner soon?" he asked. That made them laugh.

"Soon. Come to the kitchen and I'll get you a snack," she said as Jake happily followed while she asked about his day.

Thomas was not at dinner that night. Emma knew where he was and wasn't worried. He and Clair continued to spend as much time together as they could.

Later that evening, Thomas came in the kitchen door as the family sat around the table talking. "Hi, Thomas, would you like something to eat?" asked Dora.

He smiled and said, "I had dinner earlier with a friend." He turned to Emma and handed her a letter. "This is the letter you are waiting for. Alison said you could read it before sending it out."

Relieved this would start the process of getting her out of the shelter and to a safe location, she told the group as she read it, "This is good. She's kept it simple. Mentions she's missed him and missed getting to know his family. She asks that she be allowed to live with them. She covered briefly that her health was at risk in her current environment. Finally, she mentions that it must be kept quiet and details would follow if he agrees. There are some personal touches."

She turned to Thomas. "This is good to send." Before she sealed the envelope, she put a note inside for them to send all replies to the Pinkerton address. She closed it up and looked at her family and said, "We should know the timing soon." They nodded.

"I'll drop it by the post office on my way to work in the morning," Thomas commented.

With that final issue resolved, a very tired Emma and Tim turned in early.

CHAPTER 29

The next few weeks were a blur for Emma and Tim as they continued working at both the office and their other jobs. During this time, Tony and Emma didn't see each other, and she was grateful for that. There was a showdown coming up between them that she wasn't ready for.

Dora was aware that Emma was leaving early each morning to avoid seeing Tony. Unfortunately, Dora didn't have the same option and rolled her eyes when a knock sounded at the door. *I'm going to get Emma for this,* she thought as she straightened her shoulders and went to answer it. Calling to Amy, "Would you mind setting the table."

She understood that Dora wanted time alone with Tony and left the room.

Dora opened the door and waved him in. "She's not here, is she?" he asked.

"No," she confirmed, going back to the table to continue kneading her bread.

There were too many emotions for him to process; Anger, frustration, and finally pain. He slammed his hand on the table, startling Dora.

"Sorry," he said looking down at the table.

"No need to be, she can be frustrating. She has behaved this way with me, the more I pushed, the more she turned away."

"So, your advice is for me is just to wait until she is ready? How fair is that?"

"It isn't," she agreed. "I think she'll finally stop this behavior after their investigation is completed. There won't be an excuse for her to conveniently hide behind."

"She won't have forever," he said quietly.

"I know and Tony – she knows."

He stood to leave, looking a little lost. Dora watched him and wondered if she should say something to Emma. The answer to that came that evening when Tim and Emma were so tired, they could barely stay away to eat. Dora was infinitely patient with them both, holding their dinner and helping them to bed when they were too tired to move.

As the project wound down weeks later, Lauri, Tim, and Emma were reviewing the last of the files. He closed the final one on the desk, stood up, and went to collapse on the couch, saying, "That's it. It appears this was a simple scheme; it doesn't appear the vendors are involved. I believe this was a short-term event and, once the building materials were at the site, he would have cashed out and disappeared."

"Tim, what happened to all of the money?" Lauri asked curiously, knowing he was in contact with Mr. Baker.

Tim leaned back further on the couch. "Josh's lawyers seized his accounts based on the photographic evidence. The money was found in his and several of his family members' accounts. The police have kept them in custody on a variety of charges to do with fraud."

The assignment was ending soon and he was relieved. Their company had made a lot of extra money these last few weeks, but he would rather be with Dora and their business. "Lauri, how have you liked being an office manager over the past few weeks?" he asked quietly.

"I enjoyed it. I was nervous at first, but I think I was pretty good at it," she said, thinking this was when she'd learn she would be returned to the secretarial pool.

"You were very good," he confirmed. "Emma and I are recommending that you take over as the office manager here, permanently." They both smiled at her.

She sat stunned for a moment, not believing what she was hearing. Positions like this were never offered to women. "Are you sure?" she asked, her eyes darting from one to the other. She was very scared they were going to tell her it was all a mistake.

"Yes, we're sure. You're the most qualified person for the position," stated Emma warmly.

"Wow," said Lauri, not knowing what to say.

"Would you like the position?" Tim asked simply.

"Yes, yes I would," she answered immediately.

"There's still a lot of cleanup to do," he warned her. "Josh will be meeting with the building owners to assure them that changes have been made and there will be transparency in all future projects. I'll also be helping him with money recovery."

"I can handle it," she said confidently.

Tim already knew that, but he was happy to hear she was ready for the challenge.

They headed out to make the final announcements to the staff. Lauri took the lead and started, "We'll be going back to normal staffing starting tomorrow. We would like to thank the temporary workers brought in for this project, as we couldn't have gotten through the work without you. We wish you well in your future endeavors." She looked at each one with a smile.

She turned her gaze on the staff who had been with them prior to the scam being exposed. The engineers and secretaries were listening intently. "We are happy to say that we plan to be here for a long time and want you to stay with us. Our work-flow will be modified and I'll have an office meeting tomorrow to discuss the changes. Our thanks to all for the long hours. We know we took time away from your families, and we appreciate your hard work."

Tim cleared his voice and said, "I am heading out, and Lauri is now your official office manager."

The room broke out with congratulations. Tim waited a moment before continuing. "Everyone here will be receiving a bonus for all the extra work put in. It will be in your next paycheck."

The workers erupted with laughter and the palpable tension vanished.

Emma and Tim were taking a cab home when she said, "Tim, that was very nice of Josh to provide bonuses to the team."

"Yes," he said. "I thought so also. He asked me to give you this." He took an envelope out of his jacket pocket, handing it to her.

Emma looked at him questionably and opened the envelope. Inside was a check for $1000, listed as a finder's fee in the memo section.

Tim smiled and said, "Yeah, mine was the same. This will go to the bank and allow us to do things we never thought we could do. What will you do with yours?"

"First, I am going to faint. Goodness!" She waved the envelope at her suddenly flushed face. "I am thinking about a few things."

Tim nodded, agreeing it would be a good idea to invest the money.

Part of it would go to the Bakery, she thought.

They both settled back to let the cab take them home, very happy they could go back to their normal schedules and see loved ones.

Tim looked over at Emma and was hesitant to start this

conversation. "Emma, now that we've gotten this case wrapped up, you need to talk to Tony. He's feeling left out of this part of your life. He's pretty raw."

"I know," she said quietly. "I'm just not sure what to do about it."

CHAPTER 30

$\mathcal{E}$mma made a decision that night to finally talk with Tony. The time he got off was approaching, she took her bike and made her way to the museum. She rode to the wall just before the museum steps, jumped off, and prepared to pick up the bike when she heard his voice. "No, I can't." He laughed at something his companion said. "I would love to accompany you, but I need to talk to Emma first." The woman continued speaking in a low tone. Emma decided it was time to let herself be seen and walked around the wall to the steps.

She couldn't tell who was more surprised, Tony or his companion. Emma assumed a pleasant expression and said, "Mrs. Smith, Tony. Tony, I thought I would walk you home."

He gave her an odd look but said, "That would be nice." He turned to Mrs. Smith and said, "I'll see you at the museum gala."

"Yes, you will. Nice to see you again, Emma." She gave her a nod and walked to her waiting cab.

"Hi," she said hesitantly.

"Hi, are you back now?" he asked shortly, looking her in the eyes.

"Back?" she asked, bewildered by the turn of conversation. "Back from where?"

"Your case, Em. I haven't seen you in weeks. I come by the house in the morning, and you're already gone. I come by in the evening, and you're not there or you're already in bed."

She bowed her head for a moment, then lifted it to look him in the eyes. "Yes, that would be accurate. I got wrapped up in my case and it became my priority."

"Here's the thing, Emma, on this list of priorities, where do I fall?" he asked, still not showing much emotion.

She didn't have an answer for that and stayed silent.

He continued. "I need someone who's there for me and I'm just now realizing that I made an agreement with you that didn't allow me any say in how our future would play out." He took a calming breath and said, "I'm finally realizing that to grow and change, I need to move on."

Emma hadn't realized they were going to have this play out here. "I think you're right. You've been building a nice career here and have a new set of people you're socializing with." His cheeks turned red at that comment. Leaning her bike against the stairs, she walked toward him, taking his hands in hers. "Tony, we just made a big commitment too early. We thought, because our friendship was so strong, that it would lead to a similar future. I think we're going in different directions."

He sat down on the steps and said, "I didn't think we would be here again. I didn't think I would change so much."

"Me either," she said as she sat next to him and put her head on his shoulder. He put his arm around her and pulled her close. "Tony, you're my best friend, but we have never had a passion that pushed any boundaries."

"Yes. I thought it would come later," he murmured into her hair.

"Where do we go from here?" she asked.

"We stay friends, but we move on in our personal lives." He paused briefly before asking, "Will you go out with Jeremy?"

He knows me so well, she thought and said out loud, "I'm not sure. Maybe. Will you go out with Mrs. Smith?" She had seen the way the widow watched Tony.

He turned red and said, "Her name is Peggy. I think so. She wants to."

Emma laughed suddenly, feeling something had been lifted off of her. "Tony, we will stay best friends. You can always come to me with anything. You'll always be an important part of my life."

"You're so important to me and always will be," he said, pulling her close for a long moment.

They sat for a while. "Walk me home?" she asked.

"Will you still bring me strudel?" he asked, some humor showing in his voice.

"Yes, yes, I will always bring you strudel." She leaned over and gave him a sweet kiss.

They stood and headed home, realizing that, after tonight, things would be different.

CHAPTER 31

$\mathcal{A}$ letter was delivered to the Pinkerton office the following week. Jeremy saw the return address and took it directly to Cole, who directed him to open the letter and find out if the cousin was receptive to Alison moving in with his family. Jeremy did so and saw it was a cheerful but worried affirmative. He said, "We are a go."

Cole said, "Good, then it's time to set up a group meeting. Notify everyone."

It's time to make a plan, and Emma will want to be in the middle of it, Jeremy thought with a smile.

He sent notes to everyone involved in the case to meet at Pinkerton's the following night. He received confirmation back from all. Their group was larger on this case: it involved the Pinkerton detectives who had volunteered their time, Emma, Dora, Tim, Thomas, and Clair.

The next evening, Jeremy looked around the full conference room and saw everyone had arrived. Emma approached him and asked, "Ready to start?"

"Yes," he responded. He cleared his throat and raised his voice to be heard over the noise. "Everyone, let's take a seat and start evaluating the information we have from the stakeouts. I'll list the vendor and let the operations part of the stakeout detail any information found on the type of people making deliveries to the shelter." He looked to his left and said, "Dan? You have information about the person who delivers the milk?"

Dan, a Pinkerton detective, looked at Emma. "The milkman turned out to be related to Emma."

She looked startled and asked, "Does Otto work that route?"

"Yes," responded Dan with a smile.

"Yes, he's my uncle and can be removed from the list," she said firmly.

Jeremy agreed and moved on to the next suspect. "Next is the grocery men. Jonathan has that information."

Jonathan, a Pinkerton detective, spoke up and said, "No one consistent, and there appears to be no pattern to the deliveries; different days and different times."

Jeremy prompted him, "You also looked into the mailman?"

"Yes, though it is a consistent person and on a daily route, we found no deliveries to the ladies at the shelter. Katy confirmed that he rarely stops there and, if he does, she keeps the mail and gives it to Clair."

Clair confirmed, "Yes, we don't have the address listed anywhere, so any mail is usually picked up by me and disposed of at my residence."

Jonathan had one more report. "There is Thomas, who also has access at different hours."

Clair looked a bit panicked that Thomas might get into trouble but relaxed when she heard Jeremy's next statement. "Thomas is part of the team, so he will be taken off the list."

Clair exhaled a breath she didn't know she was holding, and Thomas squeezed her hand and smiled.

Jeremy moved down his list to the flower deliveries. "The one constant delivery was the flowers; it was always the same person. Emma, can you take it from there?" Jeremy asked, glancing at her.

"Yes, I recognized the delivery name on the wagon and I followed up. A friend of mine runs that particular flower shop. I met with him and asked him to get some information for me. He was able to get me an address and a full name. They didn't think we would check it out and it turns out he also has the same last name as Ann. I think Clair can continue here," she said, looking over at her.

Clair nodded. "Emma asked me how the flowers were handled at the shelter and I confirmed with Katy that Ann is the only one who has taken over unboxing them and putting them in vases. She would also take care of debris by taking it to the outside trash location."

Jonathan assumed the conversation. "Once we realized she would move the trash out, we watched the delivery driver. He would make the delivery and then be back in the area about a half-hour later. He was seen walking around and would pilfer the trash."

Cole now spoke directly to Jeremy and Emma. "What's the plan? How do we use this?"

"Our idea," Jeremy said, seeing Emma nod in encouragement, "is to use the communication system to our advantage."

Emma added, "Our safety net here is that I think she hasn't disclosed the location until she gets paid. This is what we have planned..."

The group listened and contributed to the plan to get Alison safely out of the shelter. The date was settled upon and her cousin was notified by telegram.

CHAPTER 32

$\mathcal{A}$ week later, when all plans were in place, Clair was in the kitchen at the shelter talking quietly to the house-keeper about Alison.

"Katy, Alison is sick with a headache and is in her room. She needs quiet and no people visiting. We want her well enough to move tomorrow night by train. Emma will be taking her and keeping the operations small."

Ann was just outside of the kitchen, listening in. *I'll have to get the word out about the date of the move today. Pete should be here with flowers this afternoon.* She immediately went to her room to jot down the information about Alison's departure time, persons moving her, and type of transportation. She folded the note and put it in her pocket.

As usual, she volunteered to move the flowers and organized the boxes for disposal. She took the empty boxes and placed them in the trash outside, near the back door. Her brother would check the flower box and deliver the message. She was satisfied no one knew it was her selling the information about the other women in the shelter. Emma had questioned her earlier but nothing had come of it.

The next night couldn't come fast enough for her. The payday would allow her and her brother to get a new start in a new town.

The night of the scheduled move, everyone was in the sitting room and Alison was still in her room, resting. Clair had excused herself from the group and went to the hallway. Ann could hear Clair talking to someone she assumed was Emma. She smirked, sure that she was smarter than all of them. She moved closer to the door, looked in the crack, and noticed Alison was dressed as a man. She thought, *They're not so smart. I can tell it's her because her long dark hair is visible under the hat. He'll get her whether she is dressed like a man or woman.*

They moved out of her sight, and Ann heard the back door open. She assumed Emma and Alison were leaving. *Alison's husband should have her soon, and we will have our money.* She sat back in her chair, smiling and feeling great about the future.

The two figures dressed as boys exited the shelter, planning to make their way to the train station. Keeping watch for anyone around them, they headed up the alley and down the street.

A man stepped out of the shadows to follow them. He had a gun in one hand and immediately reached out with his other to grab Alison by her hair. When it came off in his hands, he froze, uncertain about what was happening.

Emma took advantage of his confusion and pivoted back on her left foot, kicking out her right leg at a 45-degree angle hitting the hand holding the gun. It flew out of his hand and skidded on the ground out of sight. At that moment, he saw he had the wrong person and went into a fit of rage. Blinded to all rational thought, he reached for Emma, eager to punish her for keeping him from Alison. She responded by taking hold of his arm and twisting it behind his back, then placed her knife at his throat.

"I think we can take it from here," said Jeremy, stepping out of the shadows. He was holding the gun that had been knocked out of the attacker's hand.

"One more thing," she said as she kneed the man in the back, forcing him on the ground. She kept it there while Jeremy tied his hands.

"Where is she?" he screamed desperately.

"Where you won't find her." Emma lowered her face to his and said in a low voice, "You won't have to worry about where she is. You'll be gone for a long time."

Jeremy gestured to one of his Pinkerton detectives and said, "Take him in. We have him for sure on assault." The husband struggled as he was being moved. "Oh, and give me that," Jeremy said, taking the wig from his loosened grip.

"You don't know who I am!" he screamed.

"Oh, we know, Mr. Lewison. We just don't care," an agent said as they dragged him toward a waiting cab.

Jeremy turned to Emma and Dora, who had walked up to stand beside Emma. "Let's meet in the shelter. Dora, good work pretending to be Emma."

"Thanks." She grinned, pulling her hat off and fluffing her hair. "Anything for my sister."

"Nice hair," Emma teased Jeremy.

He smoothed the hair on the wig down and said with a smile, "Thanks. I'll get it back to Savannah."

The triumphant group went back into the shelter where everyone waited around the dining room table. Cole was at the front, Karl sat to the left of Pete, and Ann sat across from them next to Clair. Tim was at the far end of the table and several Pinkerton detectives stood around the room. Lily was also in the room, looking confused.

Emma immediately noticed Karl and went over to kiss him on the cheek. "Thanks for bringing in Pete," she said in a loud voice so Pete could hear.

Pete's confused face turned red at the comment. He turned

to Karl and said, "I thought we were here to bring in a special flower order." He studiously avoided his sister's hard gaze.

Dora went to sit by Tim. "Did it go okay?" he asked.

"Yes, it was exciting," she said.

Tim looked worried, she smoothed his brow and reassured him, "Don't worry, this is just the one time. It was a bit *too* exciting for me." He smiled and pulled her close as they waited expectantly for the bad guys to be revealed.

"Emma, do you want to start?" Cole asked expectantly.

"Yes," she said and moved to the front of the table with Jeremy and Cole. "Please, everyone, sit. We appreciate you being here for the case closure."

"Case? What case?" asked Lily. "Why am I here?"

Emma glanced at Lily and said wryly, "Not to worry, we'll get to you soon enough."

Lily let that sink in and realized she still might be in trouble. She tried to make herself small in her chair.

Emma turned her attention to Ann and said in a conversational tone. "Ann, I understand you have a real interest in flowers and like to set them up after they are delivered." It was more of a statement than a question.

Ann, feeling she was being somehow cornered, weakly said, "Yes, I set them up in the sitting and the dining room." She waved her hand toward the arrangement located in the center of the table.

"They are nice," Emma agreed. She turned her gaze toward Karl. "You do provide beautiful flowers." He smiled in response, and she let her gaze slide to Pete. "Pete, nice to meet you. I know Pete is your first name. What would be your last name?"

He didn't answer and looked down at his hands. "Ann," Emma said, shifting her glance over to her, "would you happen to know Pete's last name?"

Ann's true nature seemed to come out and she said coldly, "I don't know what you're talking about." She could feel the money slipping from her hands; her plans were all coming apart in front of her.

"Hmm, okay, let's make this easy," Emma said. "Your last name is Langston. You are Ann Langston and you are Pete Langston. We know you are brother and sister. We also know you were using the flower boxes to move messages back and forth."

They still looked defiant as she continued. "What? You don't believe me?" She pulled four pieces of paper out of her notebook and unfolded each to read out loud to the group. "The move is scheduled for Tuesday this week, will send times and location in the next note. Oh, and here is the time Alison will be moved." She paused and looked up at Ann, then Pete. "We got you. What do you have to say for yourselves?"

Pete, the less confident of the two, started talking and Ann tried repeatedly to stop him, but he continued. "I started delivering flowers to the shelter six months ago and I noticed Alison Lewison was on the stairs during one of my deliveries. I told my sister who I'd seen and she saw an opportunity to make some money."

Ann finally got a word in and directed her disgust at Pete. "You idiot, there's no way they could have the messages unless you. . . you didn't take the notes with you?" she asked incredulously.

Pete put his head down on the table and wouldn't answer his sister.

Clair stepped in. "By selling Alison's location to a known abuser, you may have killed her and put the other ladies here at risk."

"So?" said Ann belligerently. "Why should we care about her? We wanted the money."

Clair had had enough. "Money? Seriously, you had your brother beat you up so I would take you in, and it was about money? We strive to protect these women and you undermine everything we stand for. You disgust me." She left the room without looking back.

"I think we have enough," Cole said to Jeremy. "Let's take them in."

"What are we being charged with?" Ann asked, still defiant.

"How about facilitation of assault?" answered Jeremy.

That seemed to take her down a peg as agents escorted her and her brother out of the room.

"Lily, don't you go anywhere," Emma warned, noticing her trying to slink out. "Thomas," she called. "Can you bring in those books?" He came in and set them near Emma.

"Those are mine. What are you doing with them?" Lily asked.

Cole took it from there. "Interesting thing about these books, they're all listed on police reports as missing. All were taken during various social events in the last year. So, you say these are yours, Lily?"

"Well, uh. . . uh. . ." Lily was floundering, not knowing how to answer.

"Hmm, let me see." Cole opened each book. "Yes, I can confirm these are first editions and their value is quite high. That will get you significant jail time."

Emma asked, "Were you even beaten up, or was it a setup like Ann's?"

That seemed to finally make Lily open up. "Yes, I was," she said defiantly. "I was working as a maid at the parties you mentioned and my partner would take things to sell. I knew the books were important, but he didn't believe me. He just started hitting me until I couldn't stand because I stole the wrong items."

Clair had walked back in and heard Lily. She understood mistakes and said, "Cole, can we work something out?"

He nodded. "If you tell me your partner's name and where

he's selling the merchandise, I'll see what I can do for you. You will also need to return the books."

Lily looked at Clair and said, "Thank you for helping me even though I deceived you. When I get through this mess, I would like to help out here, if you will have me."

Clair could never turn away from her women. "I'll be here," she said.

Lily stood and, ready to face the consequences of her actions, asked, "Do we leave now?"

"Yes," said Cole quietly. "We'll interview you and see what can be worked out."

Clair hugged Emma and Dora as they prepared to leave in a cab Cole had called for them. They met it a few blocks down the street, not wanting to bring any additional attention to the shelter.

Emma commented, "That was an exciting evening; two cases closed."

Dora said, "I can see why you enjoy this, the unexpectedness of it all."

Emma settled back in the seat. "Yes, but it's more than that. It's the puzzle. Putting the pieces together and seeing if they fit. In these two cases, they fit."

Dora asked, "And Alison?"

"Taken by Papa over land in a wagon. I got a telegram confirming that Alison is safe and he is on his way back," answered Emma.

Tim asked, "Will they charge Lily?"

Emma considered that. "No, I think they'll make a deal with her and we'll probably see her back there at some point."

CHAPTER 33

A few months later, after everything had settled down, Emma was getting a bit bored with no cases to work on. Dora called to her as she was walking down the stairs for breakfast. "Emma, you have a note; it was delivered earlier."

She offered her thanks and made her way into the foyer. She looked over at the stack of letters sitting on the small table, flipping through them until she found the one addressed to her. Opening it, she read it silently.

Dora walked up and hugged her from behind, laying her head on her shoulder. "Who's it from?"

Emma answered absently, "It's from Cole. He has a case he would like my help on."

Dora released her and looked over her shoulder at the note. "When does he want you?" She was thinking about Emma's current temp jobs.

"It says he'd like to meet this afternoon. I'll let you and Tim know if I need coverage," Emma said, excited about the prospect of a new case. She went back upstairs to finish getting ready for her day.

That afternoon, she rode her bike over to the Pinkerton

office. She tapped on Cole's door and was called in. "Good afternoon, I got your message," she said.

"Emma, thanks for coming in. Have a seat," he said, pulling out a case file and studying the information in it. "I'd like you to work as an investigator on a case for us."

She sat down in the chair in front of his desk and asked curiously, "Why me?" She had worked many cases, but this was the first she was asked to take the lead.

He looked up from the file. "It involves a woman whom I believe you already know, Millicent Carlyle Landon."

"Yes, I've known her since I was a kid. Is she all right?" asked Emma, concerned.

"That's what we're being hired to find out. Her grandfather Benjamin Carlyle has requested our services."

"Why did he feel a need to call us?"

"He believes Millicent may have made a mistake in getting married. She's cut off all contact with him and has requested her inheritance be given over in larger advances."

"That is troubling. As I remember, she was very social, though she could be a bit scatterbrained," commented Emma.

"Yes, and Mr. Carlyle has inquired on his own but isn't making any progress, so he contacted us. He asked specifically for you to help out on the case."

"I remember Mr. Carlyle. He's a very nice man. We met them when Papa was helping with his home here and in New York. You say he doesn't live in Chicago anymore?"

"He moved a few years ago and now is at an age where he can't travel easily."

Dear one commented, "So, she just headed to New York?"

Narrator said, "Well, there was a lot of discussion with the family if she should go alone. Emma did point out she had already made several trips by train by herself."

. . .

Tim volunteered to take her to the train station. He was placing her bag in his wagon as Papa and Dora walked her down the stoop. "You will be extra safe," said Dora. "I don't know what I would do without you."

Emma reasoned with her, saying, "It's just a trip to New York. You and Tim have been there without any problems."

"I know, but I was with Tim," she explained.

Papa interrupted Dora and said, "Sister will be fine. She's ready for this step."

Emma hugged him tightly and said, "Thanks, Papa. Now, enough worrying. I need to be on my way."

Before she moved to the wagon, Dora reached up to touch Emma's cheek. Emma clasped that hand tightly to her and said, "I'll be fine." She smiled at her and turned to climb into the wagon. Tim leaped up beside her and clicked at the horses to get them moving.

Papa and Dora waved as they drove away.

When they got there, Tim reminded her, "Be extra cautious and don't stray too far from your private compartment."

"I will. Thank you, Tim." She leaned over and kissed him on the cheek before jumping down. He handed her the carpetbag and clicked at the horses to move forward.

Emma noticed a group of older ladies whispering and watching her. She realized they'd seen her kiss Tim goodbye— all while dressed as a boy—and it gave her a good laugh. She turned around to the still whispering women, winked, and threw them a kiss. That seemed to scandalize them and they whispered furiously to one another.

Emma was laughing as she strode off and climbed the steps to the train. She walked down the long hall to her private compartment. It was expensive, but it would keep her protected from unwanted visitors. She also made sure she spoke to the porter and slipped him a tip to keep people away from her room.

Settling in, she unpacked her books for a good long read. While the train prepared to pull out, she glanced at the titles on her lap. These included: *The Adventures of Huckleberry Finn, The Strange Case of Dr. Jekyll and Mr. Hyde,* and *A Study in Scarlet.* Choosing *A Study in Scarlet* to begin, she opened it to the first chapter to start reading.

Her trip would take about a week and would include two different trains. One from Chicago to Buffalo, New York, via New York, Chicago, & St. Louis Railroad Company, commonly known as the Nickel Plate Road (NKP), and a transfer in Buffalo to New Jersey. The final leg to New York City would be a carriage. It had been arranged with her client to take her over the bridge and into the city.

Tony was still on her mind, even though they had been broken up for the past few months. It was his comment about Jeremy she kept dwelling on. *Was Jeremy more than a friend to her?* She put her head back on the seat and finally admitted to herself that she had stayed with Tony because she didn't want to lose him as a friend. He was her best friend, but not the person she was in love with.

Another thing he'd mentioned, that she should have checked in with him when she took on new cases. That bothered her. *Does a relationship give a man that kind of power over me, to have to check in before taking a job? I don't think I'm relationship material, but Jeremy. . .* She sat there thinking about him, letting the book rest in her lap.

A sudden knock startled her and caused her to check for her two knives before approaching the door. She cracked it open and was flummoxed by the person in front of her. She opened the door wide. "Jeremy, what are you doing here?"

The porter was in the hall and looked over, worried he had

let Jeremy knock on the door. Emma nodded to him. "It's okay, I know him."

As he leaned in, she grabbed him by the sleeve and pulled him the rest of the way into her compartment. "Well?" she asked, bewildered by his appearance. Jeremy smiled in that way that always made her knees melt and didn't say anything. She frowned and said gruffly. "Sit down already. Talk."

"I'm going to New York City," he said, still smiling.

"That, I figured out," she said wryly.

"Pops has a custody pickup that needed to be done and I volunteered," he said, hoping she was happy he was there.

"And?" she prompted.

"And I always wanted to go back to New York City," he said. He'd been born there and had lived there with Cole when he was little.

"And?" she prompted again.

"And you were going, so I thought I would tag along," he said, letting his voice trail off, wondering if he had made a mistake.

"Are you here to provide some type of protection for me?" Her voice grew strained. She had thought they had gotten past this in their relationship.

He decided to take another direction and answered, "No, I was just hoping for some company and, if anyone is protecting anyone, it's you protecting me."

That made her laugh. He always made her laugh. She stopped with her questioning.

"Did I see Tim drop you off? Was Tony busy?" he asked curiously. He was interested in all things involving Emma.

"Yes," she said, quietly. "We're done. Tony needs someone who will be there for him, and that it isn't me. We will continue to be best friends, but no more."

Jeremy wanted to grin and shout, but he knew she would not appreciate it, so he kept a sober look on his face.

"Let's talk about something else," she suggested.

"All right, how about your case?" he asked.

Emma started thinking about what data she could share. She pulled out her notebook and unfolded the telegram she had tucked into it. She read it out loud: "From, Benjamin Carlyle. Emma, I need to speak with you in person about Millicent. I am worried that she has gotten into trouble. Send me a telegram with your travel dates and I will have your train met."

She finished reading and said, "The gentlemen who sent the note is an old family friend and his granddaughter, Millicent, just married at the beginning of the summer. She has somewhat disappeared from the social scene but does turn up at the dressmaker occasionally. I don't know the husband well, but I did meet him at their wedding. He's in his thirties and the grandfather believed he would be a stabilizing influence on her."

She paused for a moment and then continued. "The more I think about it, the more I realize I haven't seen Millie since the wedding. I initially questioned if there was an actual case here, something to investigate? Cole and I decided it was worth visiting Mr. Carlyle to get further information before I start an investigation in Chicago."

"Interesting. You say you knew her previously?" he asked, brushing back his brown curls off his forehead and settled onto the seat next to her.

"Yes, I wasn't able to see her before I left, but she's usually a little silly and not serious. She might be accidentally involved in something, however unlikely," she answered.

"You said you know her husband?" he asked.

"I know of him—successful businessman, nice looking, and kind of quiet. We were acquaintances. We went to some of the same events, but I wouldn't say we were friends. I did speak with him at his and Millicent's wedding."

❧

The wedding

"Emma," she heard Millicent call. She had been admiring the wedding cake, wondering if it tasted as good as it looked. Looking over she saw the bride and groom. "Come meet my new husband, Donald Landon." Emma walked toward the couple, they were resplendent in their finery.

"Donald this is Emma, she made my dress."

"It is nice to meet you. It is beautiful work," he complimented her. He reached out his hand to take Millicent's and said, "We must see to our other guest."

"That's a lovely ring," Emma commented, noticing the distinctive design on the gold band that included a ruby stone on his right hand,

He looked down at it briefly and said in a quiet voice, "Thank you. It is the only thing I have from my father."

"Congratulations again," she said as they walked off.

Present day-Emma and Jeremy

"What about you? Who are you picking up?" she asked.

"My pickup? Sam Cummings. He's a known counterfeiter and was caught making money in Chicago and was sent to New York to testify in a case against the Whyos Gang. He's also agreed to provide information in our counterfeiting case in exchange for leniency."

"Counterfeiting, that sounds interesting. What kind?" She leaned toward him, wanting all the details.

"Mostly paper money. He's been doing this for a while, but he started getting greedy and was printing way too much and got caught. It also turns out his bosses in the gang were not aware of the amount. He jumped at the chance to help us; he knew what would happen if they got to him first."

They continued discussing the cases and then shared dinner

from Emma and Jeremy's bags. The days flowed into one another, with the majority of time being spent together, only sleeping in separate compartments. They read, talked, and generally enjoyed each other's company.

The train switch from Buffalo to the New Jersey line was easy and they ended up sharing a compartment. That leg of the trip took just a day to complete.

"Could you step out for a moment?" she asked, indicating for him to exit so she could change clothes.

He grinned and said, "Well, I can stay if you need help with any buttons."

"Oh, you! Out!" she said and pointed to the door. After it closed behind him, she turned the lock and pulled out her red split skirt, high-necked black blouse, and a long black jacket. She unpacked her hat and confirmed her knives were in place. She was tying her boots when she heard a knock. She reached up to release it and said, "You can come in, Jeremy."

He sat down next to his bag and enjoyed Emma's company a while longer as they waited for their final stop. As they were descending the train steps Emma asked over her shoulder, "Do you have transportation waiting?"

"I don't. Could I get a lift?" he asked hopefully, casually waving off the man who was there to pick him up.

"Hmm, do you need to confirm with that gentleman first?" she asked, hiding a smile with her hand, having seen his gesture.

He turned red, realizing he had been caught. "Yes, I'll be right back." He paid off the carriage and went back to accompany Emma to hers.

Emma started to climb up on her own. "Emma," he murmured, "may I help you?"

She realized she was acting like a boy and smiled at him. She turned to him and said sweetly, "Please." He grinned and lifted her into the cab.

The driver turned to them and said, "The trip will take a few hours and we'll be stopping to give the horses water. The cab has been arranged by Mr. Carlyle, so no directions to that location are necessary."

"We'll have one additional stop that will require an address. Jeremy," Emma prompted, "where do you need to be let off?"

He unfolded the address and gave it to the driver, who nodded and said, "That shouldn't be a problem. It's on our way."

Their ride was pleasant; they talked quietly, enjoying the view and each other's company. As they reached Jeremy's stop, he went to climb out and Emma stopped him with a touch of her hand. "If you have time, would you like to see some of the city with me before we head home?"

He tilted his head and said, "That would be great. My job should be coming together soon and then I'm headed home on the same train as you. I'll drop you a note." She nodded and waved goodbye as she told the driver he could head to the Carlyle residence.

As they drew up in front of the imposing townhouse, she took in the red brick structure that stretched down most of the block. The driver indicated she should enter through the kitchen door. The discretion didn't bother Emma, and she made her way around to the back. She knocked on the door and the maid who answered looked a bit surprised. Emma introduced herself. "Hello, I'm Emma Evans. I'm to stay here and meet with Mr. Carlyle."

The maid blinked and said in a solemn tone, "Oh, they didn't tell me you were so young." She motioned for Emma to follow her and showed her to her room. "Mr. Carlyle will expect you to be down in thirty minutes for lunch." The maid pointed out the water closet and said she would bring fresh water for washing to the room.

Emma cleaned up with a washrag but would not be able to wash her hair prior to lunch. Brushing it, she took time to re-braid it before changing into a dark blue walking suit with a button-up jacket and high neck red shirt. The clothes were the ones she wore routinely to her office positions.

Once dressed and refreshed, she headed down at the time indicated by the housekeeper for lunch. She slowly descended the grand staircase that wrapped around into the foyer. A footman stepped out as she neared the bottom of the steps and said, "Please, follow me to the dining room." Emma did so, admiring the elegant wallpaper, sumptuous rugs, and paintings hung on the walls.

As they entered the dining room, Mr. Carlyle stayed seated. Emma was able to see why she had traveled to see him here; he could not travel to see her. Mr. Carlyle was in a wheelchair and was very pale.

"Mr. Carlyle. . ." she started.

"Emma, come here," he said with a very friendly smile.

She walked to him. "Hello, Mr. Carlyle," she said, taking his hand in hers.

"Thank you for responding so quickly to my request. Now, please, sit down. We will eat first and then discuss why I have brought you all this way."

He indicated for the butler to pull out her chair. She smiled and sat down. They ate their meal, keeping the conversation light, discussing families and what was happening in Chicago and New York.

As the meal came to a close, he waved to a male servant to move him into the study. He looked over his shoulder and said, "Please, join me, Emma."

She nodded and followed him. The study was imposing, with full bookshelves and a large dark desk, settees, and chairs. Light colors of blue and white were used to accent the room. Emma would have loved to inquire about the books, but knew she wasn't there for that.

He tapped the settee arm, and she responded by sitting down. "My granddaughter, as you know, married Mr. Landon about six months ago. Since that time, they have cut off almost all communication with me." He waved a hand. "I do get the occasional note, but no visits and no telegrams. I am concerned about Millie; this isn't like her. She is normally full of information and will talk your ear off."

"Well," Emma mentioned, "there may be a reason. She's newly married and they may want some quiet time together."

"You are right and, if it were just that, I would leave it alone. But it is also the money. They have already run through her annual allowance (this was just March) and Millie will be able to access her inheritance when she turns twenty, which will be later this year."

Emma nodded slowly and asked, "Would you mind if I took notes?" He nodded and she pulled out her notebook.

He continued. "I have our business manager coming over this afternoon to discuss the money that has been requested."

Emma thought, *Money could be the key to the investigation.* As she completed her notes, the butler entered to announce Mr. Beeker was there to meet with them.

A rather average-looking man with hardly any hair walked into the room. "Geoff, please come in. Emma has arrived and I have been going over my concerns with her."

He followed Mr. Carlyle's direction and moved over to the settee to join them. He set the books he was carrying down on the table in front of them.

"Emma, this is Geoff Beeker. He is our financial manager. Geoff, this is Emma Evans, a family friend, and the private investigator Pinkerton sent."

Emma thought she saw a movement of an eyebrow, and maybe his eyes widened slightly when he was introduced to her. He covered well, and the signs were only detected briefly.

"It is nice to meet you, Emma." He nodded his head toward her and looked at Mr. Carlyle. "Shall I get started?"

"Yes, please do begin. Emma, you may continue to take notes," stated Mr. Carlyle graciously.

Geoff opened the books. "Millicent's spending has been somewhat erratic as of late; normal spending on dresses and such, but now also a new person is getting paid out of her finances, a house staffer named Roger Smith. I have enquired about his actual position, but I do not get satisfactory answers."

"What has she said in response to your inquiries?" Emma asked him directly.

"She has indicated to me that her household staff had to be let go, that they no longer performed the services she needed. She also indicated this Mr. Smith was now head of the household and would run the household accounts with significantly fewer people."

"What!" Mr. Carlyle roared, showing a different side to his character that Emma hadn't seen before and causing her to jump a bit.

"Yes, this occurred just after the couple got back from their wedding trip," Mr. Beeker answered.

"Why wasn't I informed?" Mr. Carlyle asked sternly.

The tone didn't seem to bother Mr. Beeker, and he answered in a calm, controlled manner. "Sir, you mentioned that this was her time to grow up and take a hand in her finances. Also, I would have expected some financial spending from her new husband, but there hasn't been anything on the accounts." He directed his next statement at Emma. "One of our biggest concerns is that the wedding dates moved up her inheritance date from twenty-five to twenty and that date is only three months from now."

Emma was busy documenting the information in her notebook: *Millie has not been in touch with her grandfather, out of the ordinary; Millie was married in last few months; household help let go since wedding; a new mysterious person on the payroll; inheritance coming up in three months.* She closed her notebook and said, "I know where I can start. I can track down the help who was let go."

"Also, look into this Mr. Smith, please," Mr. Carlyle requested.

"Also, Mr. Smith," she agreed, nodding at him. "Mr. Beeker, you mentioned her normal spending is for dresses. I also think I can start there; I work for them occasionally providing lacework."

Mr. Carlyle looked satisfied and said, "Well, that sounds like a good start. I would like to set up a weekly telegram with updates from you. Mr. Beeker will send your fee each time the telegram is received. Will that work?"

Emma nodded and said, "Sir, I'll do my best for you."

Mr. Carlyle smiled. "Okay then, dinner is at 8pm. I will not be available tonight, but I will see you for a final dinner tomorrow."

"Thank you, sir. I'll get started as soon as I return to Chicago," promised Emma.

He had returned to his role as the gracious host and asked, "Did you want to see any of the city while you are here?"

"Yes," Emma said. "I want to see everything. If it's okay, I have a friend I would like to meet in the morning. My train is scheduled to leave the following day."

"That will be quite all right. You may use my carriage," he offered.

"Thank you, sir," she responded sincerely. She looked over at Mr. Beeker and said, "Mr. Beeker, it was nice to meet you."

"You also. Good evening, Mr. Carlyle, Miss Evans," Mr. Beeker said as he exited the room.

Emma said, "Goodnight," and headed to the foyer. She saw the butler and asked, "Can you get a note to the Warren hotel for me?"

"Yes, miss, I can do that for you."

She opened her notebook and hastily wrote the time and address to meet. Handing him the note, she said, "Thank you."

"You're welcome."

She went up to her room to take a bath, wash her hair, and rest. Her dinner was delivered to her room that evening. The maid put the tray on the desk and said, "Miss you received a note." She handed it to her and left the room, quietly closing the door behind her.

Emma opened it and smiled broadly. Dropping back on the bed she thought, *Tomorrow will be a good day.*

CHAPTER 34

The next morning, as she was eating breakfast, the maid mentioned the carriage would be available when she needed it. Emma finished and went back upstairs to change into a green traveling suit with a longer jacket and a high-necked lace shirt with lace around the hem to match. Picking up a stylish hat, she pulled out her hat pin/knife and examined it in the light. All of her hats had been modified to allow her to carry various sizes of knives. Sliding it into the special slot, she pinned the hat in place and made her way downstairs.

As she reached the foyer, she noticed a very familiar lanky man with curly brown hair on the far side of the room. "Jeremy, I'm so glad you were able to come over this morning," she said as she rushed over to kiss him on the cheek.

As she stood on her tiptoes, he took the opportunity to adjust the kiss from his cheek to his lips. The kiss could not be defined as sweet; it was more of a slow drop. He pulled back and said, "Well, good morning to you also." She gave him a slow smile in response and held out her hand to take his. They headed outside to retrieve their carriage.

He helped her in and, when asked for directions, they said they wanted to see as much of New York as they could. They started off, and the first thing Emma noticed was the road was made of a different type of material from the ones used in Chicago, which were usually masonry blocks or cobbled stones. She asked the driver, "Sir, excuse me."

"Yes?" he asked, not turning around.

"What are the roads made of here? They have a smooth black look to them," she inquired.

The driver looked around and said, "It's a new substance called asphalt. It was installed about. . ." he took a moment to scratch his beard and think before he continued, "about 1877 when Battery Park and Fifth Avenue were completed. The benefit is that it makes the ride much smoother." That was confirmed a few minutes later when the carriage moved from the asphalt onto stones and blocks.

They rode past the wealthy district, marveling at the ladies' detailed dresses, the well-dressed men in hats and nice suits. As they passed an older man wearing a top hat and a monocle, Jeremy tapped Emma's shoulder to point him out. The man noticed their attention and tipped his hat as they passed. They gave him a big smile and a wave in response.

Next was Navarro Flats, a massive apartment structure on Central Park South at Seventh Avenue. It was an amazing sight to see where so many people lived in one place. They rode along to the Hoffman House Hotel, and she leaned over to say to Jeremy in a low voice, "I hear they have a bar. I'd like to see it."

He wanted to see it also. They asked the driver to stop and then climbed down from the carriage. They entered the lobby of the hotel. It was a grand place, elegant with large paintings dominating the walls, the floors covered with colorful rugs and couches anchoring them. As they made their way to the bar, he whispered to her, "You won't be allowed in, but I think you'll be able to sneak a peek."

She nodded and grinned at him in response. He walked in front of her and she was able to stand in the doorway and get a view of the nude paintings hanging on the walls.

"Sir, do you have a reservation?" said a tall man in a suit, blocking their path. "Women are not allowed here," he added, looking down his nose at her.

"No, no, we don't want to come in. We just wanted to check on the time," said Jeremy.

They turned and walked away slowly down the hall and started laughing as they turned the corner and exited the hotel. They found their driver and continued their tour of the western side of the city.

One of the locations they wanted to see was Madison Square, a genteel neighborhood. The attraction wasn't the buildings in the area; it was a statue. Well, part of a statue—the arm and hand holding a torch. It was the new Statue of Liberty that had been given to the United States by France. Her hand, holding the torch, had been on display in Madison Square Park in New York City from 1876 to now. *The World* newspaper had been advertising to get enough money donated to have a pedestal built for it. They stood marveling at its size and shape, knowing it was only a small piece of the entire structure.

They continued their tour by way of the new structure being built over the Hudson River. It would eventually call it the Brooklyn Bridge; it was a massive structure to behold already with the supports in place. It would be another two years before it was usable for traversing from Brooklyn to New York City, but it would be a marvel when complete.

She looked around at the skyscrapers starting to take shape and thought for a moment of how much impact Papa had. He continued to design and consult on buildings in Chicago and here. The design differences between the two cities were startling. Chicago balanced the visual with the practical commercial design, producing large, square palazzo-styled buildings, hosting shops and restaurants on the ground level, and containing rentable offices on the upper floors. In contrast, New York's skyscrapers were frequently narrower towers which, being more eclectic in style, were often criticized for their lack of elegance.

Their driver let them off in the shopping district so Emma and Jeremy could stroll through different stores, trying candies and other small items. Emma picked up a scarf and lace appliqués for Dora. As she moved on to the next store, the sidewalk grew busy and crowded with children. Something brushed against her pocket and, without thinking, Emma grabbed the arm of the pickpocket, twisted it behind his back, and pushed him into an alley. Jeremy followed closely behind and leaned on the wall to watch the interaction.

"Hand it over," she said, holding out her hand to the blond ten-year-old.

"I didn't do nothing," he said petulantly.

"I'm pretty sure you do plenty," said Emma.

"Let me go," he said gruffly as he continued to wrestle with her, trying to dislodge his arm.

She held him firmly and said, "First, you hand over my purse."

The young thief hesitated only briefly, then used his other hand to hand over the bag.

Emma dropped his arm but did keep a hand on his sleeve. "You know, you're not very good at this particular skill; I wasn't even paying attention and could detect your fingers lifting my purse."

"How would you know?" he said, looking her over dismissively.

"How?" she asked wryly and opened up her hand to show the boy the items she had lifted from his pocket.

"Hey! Those are mine. How did you do that?" he asked incredulously.

Jeremey straightened up from the wall, walked over to them, and said, "She is a *good* pickpocket. You should take her advice and find another occupation." As he looked, he noticed this didn't appear to be a regular street kid; he had clean clothes and nicer shoes. Bending down in front of him, he asked kindly, "Where are your parents?" When he didn't answer, Jeremy leaned closer and tilted the boy's head up. "Where?"

He squirmed a bit and finally said, "Working."

"And where are you supposed to be?" prompted Emma, handing him back the items she'd taken

"School," he acknowledged, sliding his belongings back into his pocket. He continued to look down, clearly guilty.

"Why aren't you there instead of here? This is a dangerous business you're trying to get into. These people don't play and won't like you trying to take their profit," stated Emma.

"I don't like school," he snapped.

That got Emma's attention. "Why not, little man?"

"It's boring. Math is okay, but the reading is so boring."

Emma and Jeremy laughed at that, and Jeremy said, "So, a life of crime begins with a boring book? "

Emma's mind was working, and she drummed her fingers on her lips. She asked, "What's your name?"

"Mark Sutherland," he stated simply.

"If I send you some books guaranteed to keep you interested, will you read them and write me what you think about them?"

That seemed to catch his interest. "What kind of books?" he asked topic.

She listed a few she knew would be interesting. "*The Adventures of Huckleberry Finn, Treasure Island,* and *Around the World in 80 Days.*" She watched his eyes light up at the titles.

"How do I know you won't just disappear and not send them?" he asked suspiciously.

Emma pulled out her notebook, wrote her address, and her name. She asked for his. After she documented the information and tore out the sheet to give him, she said, "If you'll hold off from any more pickpocketing and missing school for at least three weeks, I'll send you the three books as soon as I get back home to Chicago."

"And if you don't send them?" he asked.

"Then our contract is broken," she said simply.

He tilted his head and said slowly, "That's a deal," and stuck out his hand to shake hers.

She covered up her smile with her other hand as she shook. He was released and looked like he would run off when Jeremy asked, "Off to school?"

He looked a bit guilty but said, "Yes, a deal is a deal." He ran off.

"Do you think he will stick to the agreement?" asked Jeremy.

"I think so," she said, feeling they had made a small difference. "I'll send the books when I get home," she promised.

They made their way to the cab and had the driver take the long way back to the house, by way of the bay. It was noisy and dirty but very interesting to see. It made her smile, and she turned to Jeremy to say, "This is one of my wishes, to travel and see more than just Chicago. This is a good first step."

"I'm glad I was with you for this first trip," he whispered as he pulled her close to him. He started a smile that slowly worked its way across his whole face. He continued to hold her until they reached their final stop. Hopping down, he reached up to assist her. As he swung her around, he said, "I'll meet you here in the morning, and we'll have that pick up at the police station before going to the train." Jeremy knew Mr. Carlyle wanted to have a final dinner with her that evening. Leaning down to kiss her, he said, "Goodbye," and climbed back into the cab to head to his hotel.

Emma's evening meal involved a final conversation with Mr. Carlyle and a promise of a telegram the following week. He said a quiet goodnight and they parted to go to their separate bedrooms.

She woke early the next morning and got organized to begin her day. Pulling out her notebook, she made final notes on Mr. Carlyle's case. Lastly, she made a separate note to send the books back to Mark.

Closing the carpetbag, she did a final look around the room. *That's it,* she thought. A knock sounded on the door. "Yes? Come in," she called.

The young brown-haired maid came into the room and said, "Miss, breakfast is ready, and you have a gentleman waiting for you in the foyer."

"Thank you, I'm coming down now," she said, taking her bag in hand and following the maid.

"Oh, and Mr. Carlyle said your gentleman is invited for breakfast," the maid commented as they walked toward the stairs. "I will leave you here," she said and hastened to other duties on that floor.

Glancing toward the foyer, she spotted Jeremy waiting. "Good morning," he called up to her.

"Good morning. Do we have time for breakfast?" she asked as she reached the final step and lowered her carpetbag and hatbox down to the base of the stairs.

"Yes, we don't have to pick up that item for another hour," he said, looking at his watch.

"Good, Mr. Carlyle invited you to eat," she said cheerfully.

"Nice," he said. "I can always eat. Is your bag okay here?"

"I think so. They'll move it if it gets in the way."

They went to the dining room to eat and were told Mr. Carlyle wouldn't be joining them. Their breakfast was an enjoyable meal. Afterward, they made their way to the police station in a cab Jeremy had hired. During the trip over, he told her that, when they went in, she would wait in the outer offices while he took custody of the counterfeiter.

Within the station, Emma was waiting and observing the comings and goings of the officers when she overheard some policemen discussing the Whyos gang. *Hmm,* she thought, *Jeremy mentioned the counterfeiter was a member of that gang.*

She listened in as the police discussed their history. Formed from the remnants of several defunct Five Points outfits, the Whyos were one of the most dominant New York street gangs from the 1860s to now. The group had started as a loose collection of petty thugs, pickpockets, and murderers but, by the 1880s, they had graduated to more high-class crimes like counterfeiting, prostitution, and racketeering.

She thought it odd that they went in through the front door of the station for Jeremy's pickup. *Shouldn't this have been a more secretive operation?* she asked herself. Then, she surmised, *I've never been involved in a prisoner transport, so maybe this is how it is normally handled.* All things considered, Jeremy was in control of the situation.

She watched as he appeared, leading a man in handcuffs. Jeremy took off his jacket and draped it over the man's hands to hide them. The counterfeiter also had a hat pulled low on his face. They would have to be extremely careful transporting him and would be accompanied by police officers to the train station. He nodded to her, and they exited the station to a waiting carriage. Surprisingly, the train trip was uneventful as they traveled from New Jersey to Buffalo. She sat across from the counterfeiter, trying to take in his clothes and mannerisms. There was nothing about him that indicated he was a criminal.

The final move to the Buffalo train was handled quietly, and they made their way to their separate compartments. Entering her room, Emma removed her hat and turned to throw it on the seat when she detected movement out of the corner of her eye. Someone grabbed her by the neck and pulled her back to him. Letting him think she was scared, she made a distressed sound, planning her next move. The train started forward, and she used the momentum to push him back into the far wall. He had not expected her to fight back and loosened his grip, allowing her to break free.

Why am I always being grabbed by men? she thought as she swung around to kick him in the face. She bloodied his nose and stepped back to retrieve her hat knife from the seat.

He took a moment to use the back of his hand to wipe the blood from his nose. He was very angry but in control of himself. She also realized he held a gun in his other hand.

"Gun beats knife. Drop it," he snarled at her.

She could see he meant what he said and dropped the blade onto the carpeted floor.

"Move over here and sit down," he ordered, motioning to the seat. "You're going to get that policeman in here with us," he directed.

She didn't say anything, she just continued to look at him. A sudden knock at the door startled her and, as she glanced over, her attacker was suddenly close to her ear. "Tell him to come in, understand?" he whispered.

"Emma?" called Jeremy.

"Yes," she answered. "Just a second, Tony."

The man waved at her to tell him to come in and positioned himself by the door.

"Tony, you can come in now." She knew Jeremy would understand her warning.

Seconds later, he burst in, but what was surprising was that Jeremy was accompanied by the counterfeiter. She didn't have a chance to think. They were on the man, trying to get his gun away. The room was small, and Emma had to climb up on the chair to keep from being crushed. She took the opportunity to remove her hidden knife from her thigh sheath and jammed it into the attacker's shoulder. That stopped him long enough to allow them to wrestle the gun away. Jeremy held it on him while Emma yanked her knife out of his shoulder. Jeremy looked at him consideringly and said, "Mr. Johnny Dolan, I assume?"

Emma knew immediately who he was talking about and kept a close eye on him. He held a hand on his cut shoulder to stop the blood flow, he looked at them and down at his shoes.

Planning, Emma thought. *I know what he is going to do.* "Jeremy, you should take his shoes."

Dolan looked at her, surprised.

"His shoes?" Jeremy asked, nonplussed.

"Yes, I believe there's something special about them. And don't let him take them off himself," she added.

Dolan's looks turned from surprised to exasperated. They got the shoes off safely and handed them to Emma.

"There is this." She tripped the mechanism, and blades popped out.

"That would have been unexpected. How did you know?" the counterfeiter asked, looking at her in amazement.

"Funny thing, I had a similar idea a few years ago and I heard about a certain someone who wore this type of shoe. I decided it was just too dangerous. Though, I wouldn't mind keeping these for the design," she said hopefully.

Jeremy shook his head no, and she shrugged. She pulled out her notebook to sketch the mechanism, before handing them to him for safekeeping.

The counterfeiter, introduced to her as Fred Snider, Lieutenant in the local New York City police department, moved Dolan to the other room to be held until they reached the next stop. Once he was secure, Jeremy returned to explain things to Emma.

She started with the question, "So, where's the actual counterfeiter?"

"He's in Chicago testifying before the court. He was moved a few weeks ago to a safe house," he explained.

Emma smiled. "It was a setup; the talkative policeman at the station, the daylight movement. All to get Dolan."

"Yes," he acknowledged. "We weren't sure he would go after us, but there was a chance. We didn't expect him to go after you."

"As usual, he thought the woman would be the weak point," she said wryly.

"Well, he didn't know you," he said with a smile.

They continued to talk quietly until the next stop. Jeremy said, "I need to get them off here." As they exited the train, she noticed many policemen surrounding the station. They took Dolan into custody and placed him in a wagon to move him back to New York. Lieutenant Snider would stay with him as an escort. The men waiting gave Dolan a funny look when they realized he wore no shoes.

Emma and Jeremy both settled back into her room. "Well, that was exciting."

"Yes, it was, wasn't it?" He grinned.

She grinned back. They were such similar people. "Want a sandwich?" she asked. Jeremy had ordered a basket of food from the hotel, it was waiting for them when they arrived at the train.

"What were you going to do with the shoes?" he asked as he ate his lunch, watching her sketch.

"Study them to see if there is a safer way to contain knives in my shoes. I thought I might get with Papa about the design," said Emma thoughtfully, taking a bite of her sandwich.

He just smiled. She was always planning. He continued to ask about her case with Mr. Carlyle, and they spent a pleasant and quiet rest of the trip home.

CHAPTER 35

The morning they arrived in Chicago, she met her arranged cab and asked Jeremy if he needed to be taken anywhere. He indicated he had transportation and they separated with a soft kiss.

The cab dropped her off at the boarding house and she bounded up the stairs, happy to be home. She slammed the door open as she entered and ran to the kitchen. Dora met her there with a hug.

"How was your trip? Any problems?"

"Not a one," Emma said, pulling off her hat and undoing her hair. She ran her hands through it, the strands had gotten a bit matted due to the humid air they were experiencing this summer.

Dora noticed and said, "Well, you head up for a bath and hair washing. We can talk about it after you rest."

Emma agreed and headed upstairs with her carpetbag, all her energy gone. After five days of train rides, she wanted nothing more than to take a long hot bath. She lit the gas lamps in the room and wondered if they would have electric lights soon. The demonstration she had been present for in 1878 involved devices with 2,000 candlepower and was created by a spark of current across two carbon rods. *It would be exciting if the technology evolved enough to allow for lighting in residential homes.*

She drew her bath and washed her hair before lying down for a nap. It would still be damp at dinner, but at least it would be clean.

So nice to sleep somewhere that isn't moving, she thought drowsily as she fell asleep.

Dora came in a long while later and nudged her shoulder, saying, "Sister, time to get up."

Emma stretched, yawned, and asked, "Time already?"

"Just about," Dora acknowledged.

Emma patted the bed. "Climb in with me."

Dora hesitated only briefly to remove her shoes and climbed into the warm bed next to her sister. "Ready to tell me about the trip?" she inquired, laying close.

"Yes. Jeremy was there," Emma said softly.

That startled Dora. "In New York?"

"Yes, but also on the train with me," said Emma, looking intently at the ceiling. "Separate rooms, of course," she added, slanting a gaze at her.

"Of course," said Dora with a laugh. "So, tell me, why was he there?"

Emma went on to discuss Jeremy's reason for the trip and the outcome on the way home.

"Well, that is certainly exciting. Did you get to see some of the city? I would hope more than I did," she teased her.

"I did see much more than you did," Emma said with another laugh. "I bought you a few things." She reached over to her side table, next to her, to retrieve the gifts and handed them over to Dora.

"I love these," she said, looking at each one. "So, Jeremy, what's happening there?" inquired Dora curiously.

"I don't know, but I'm enjoying being with him. You know, Dora, I feel different when I am around him," said Emma.

"How so?" she asked curiously.

"When I was with Tony, I always had to be reminded to be in the moment with him. Otherwise, I was always looking for cases, making observations, and never really relaxing and enjoying our time together. With Jeremy, I was able to sit back and focus on us," she stated wonderingly.

"That is different for you," she acknowledged. "Did you enjoy it?"

"I did," she admitted. "I almost forgot to mention Mark Sutherland."

"What, another gentleman?" Dora asked incredulously.

"No, not quite." She went on to describe how she had met him and her promise.

"It sounds fun and something Papa will approve of. What books will you start with?" she asked, curious about the little boy in New York.

"I was thinking *The Adventures of Huckleberry Finn, Treasure Island,* and *Around the World in 80 Days.* I need to write him a letter. Could you ask Tim to take them to the post office today?"

"So quick. You mentioned three weeks of school first?"

"Well more than two will have passed by the time the books reach him. I don't want him to back out of our contract."

"I will leave you to write your letter," she said as she rolled off the bed. "When you're done, can you come help with tonight's dessert?" Dora inquired, turning back to her before she exited the room.

"I can," she promised. Watching Dora close the door, she stretched broadly and rolled to the side of the bed. She got up to refresh herself with a damp rag and ran a brush through her still-damp hair. She sat at the desk to write the letter before getting dressed.

Dear Mark,

This letter is to begin what I hope is a long conversation about adventures and books. As part of our agreement, here are the books I promised. I want to hear any questions from you about the characters and their adventures. I trust you will hold up your side of the agreement and send me a letter back, confirming you are attending school. I look forward to hearing from you.

Sincerely yours,

Emma.

She folded it and got dressed. Taking it with her to the study, she looked around for the books she wanted. The books were located, she bundled them with brown paper and tied the package with twine. She took the letter and books to the kitchen, where she knew Tim would be working.

Tim was exactly where she thought he would be. She leaned over to give him a quick kiss hello on the cheek. "Welcome back, Emma," he said, absently looking up from his books.

"Thanks, Tim. I'm glad to be home," Emma stated with feeling.

"Are those the books I need to get out today?" he inquired, nodding at the brown package.

"Yes," she acknowledged.

"Great, let me get on my way, I wouldn't want to delay anyone's education," he said wryly as he headed out.

"What do you want me working on?" Emma asked Dora.

"Cheesecake, the ingredients are laid out for you," Dora stated. Amy caught her eye and gave her a wink. Emma started working on it.

She completed the cake and placed it in the oven. It was getting close to dinner, and she wanted to run up to her room to clean up. People's voices could be heard through the door on their way to dinner, she hurried to finish dressing and left the room. She ran into the twins, Taylor and Franklin on the stairs.

"Emma, you're back!" they exclaimed.

"Yes, I am," she said and accompanied them downstairs to the dining room.

"Can you tell us about your trip?" Franklin asked.

"Not just yet, but maybe at dinner. Now, help me set the table," she requested.

Taylor and Franklin started pulling out the plates and glasses while Emma got the silverware. Everyone pitched in to move the platters and, as dinner started, Emma let the conversation flow around her. They were all asking the same questions and wanted details of the train trip and New York City. She took time to describe how the train ride was long and the sleeper compartments were wonderfully comfortable. "New York is like Chicago, very noisy and busy. I did get to see some marvelous buildings that I know Papa had helped build." She smiled fondly at him. He sent her a similar smile.

The twins demanded to know about the Hudson River and the new bridge they had heard about. She tried to remember what she had seen and heard. "It was so big, growing out of the water. I would like to see it when it's completed." She looked over at Jake and said, "I may have to borrow your camera on my next trip."

He nodded, "We can work on that."

The women wanted to know about fashion, particularly hats and bustles. Emma confirmed both were bigger. Dinner drew to a close and Emma, Dora, Tim, Jake, and Papa moved into the kitchen to help Amy with the dishes.

Once done, Papa mentioned he would be in the study and looked over at Jake. "Would you like to come with me?"

Jake looked a little conflicted when he said, "I think I would like to hear about the new case, but I can come to sit with you after."

Papa nodded and headed to his study.

Emma pulled out her notebook and started detailing the oddities of the case: money being spent by Millie, limited communication from her to the grandfather, household help being let go. "I think there's something odd there, but I'm not sure it's sinister or dangerous."

Jake asked, "Any photography work on this job?"

Emma mulled that over and said, "Not just now, but I think we can utilize it later in the case."

Jake nodded and sat back to listen to the details.

Dora asked, "What's the first step?"

"Well, first will probably be evaluating the information with Cole, since this is a Pinkerton case," she said.

Tim said, "If we want to be used again, we will need to follow their rules. Agreed?"

Everyone nodded, understanding how important this job was to them.

Emma stated, "I'm thinking I need to locate the household staff who were let go. They may have some observations for me."

Dora said, "I can help with that. Millie's previous cook always had a weakness for Cousin's bread. I'm sure that wherever she ended up, she is still getting it delivered."

Emma made a note to go to the bakery for the information and said, "I can do that in the morning. I will drop by there first."

"The interview with Cole should be your priority," reminded Tim.

"Yes, I'll go right after the bakery. Hopefully, he has time for me. Also, Millie's current man of business is John Darko. Do you know him?"

"I know of him. He has a reputation as an honest man of business. I can look more into him just to be sure," said Tim, making a note in his logbook.

"Another thing, her husband's man of business, we need to find out who that is and see where the money is going," said Emma.

"I can do that," commented Tim.

"Now for Millie, I need some one-on-one with her. Dora, has Mrs. Simpson asked for any assistance for her shop? Or any lace orders?" she asked.

Dora flipped through her logbook and said, "Now that you mention it, there is some sort of cotillion coming up and she did request some temporary help starting this week."

Emma looked at Tim and asked, "Can I be spared a few weeks from the office work?"

He nodded and said, "Your replacement is doing well enough to stay if you're ready to move on."

"I think I am, though if more auditing is needed in other offices, I can make some time," she offered.

They ended the meeting and Emma went upstairs to read and relax as the evening wound down. She slept well that night and awoke refreshed to begin her day. After she got up, she washed her face and got dressed, leaving before the sun lit the sky. The weather was cold that morning, she shivered and sank into her long coat as she rode her bike to the bakery.

Coasting her bike into the back area of the bakery, she hopped off and parked it close to the back door. The smells wafted over to her. *Yum, a wonderful way to start my morning.*

Cousin spotted her as soon as she came in and gave her a big hug. "Hi, Emma, here to work?" he teased. She was one of his most requested bakers and, if he could get her to make something special, it would be a good day.

"I can be," she teased back. "But I also need some information about someone who orders a specialty bread from you."

"I can help with that; my customer list is in the office. Do you want help looking?" he asked, already making his way back to his baking station.

"No, I can do it," she said with a smile, seeing that Cousin was already rolling out the dough to make bread. With the smell of yeast in the air, she made her way to the office and opened the door. It was as neat as he was in life, everything in its place. The wooden file box sat on the desk. He had the files set up by types of baked goods. Dora had provided the cook's first and last name and specialty bread, she pulled out her notebook and looked for the matching card. She found the card she wanted almost immediately and realized that Mille's previous cook had an order due to be delivered that day. Making note of the address in her notebook, she exited the office and asked, "Cousin, can I make this delivery for you today?"

He glanced over and said, with a gleam in his eyes, "Maybe, but you'll have to work for me this morning. I have a large pastry order and some staff are out sick."

She smiled wryly. Having known he would trap her into baking this morning, she had prepared to stay. "I can stay until 10am," she promised.

"You can use your old workstation. The daily list is there," he said, waving his hand toward it. Emma removed her coat and borrowed an apron to cover her clothes. She looked at the card and saw Berliners, Bratapfels, and several cakes. She got to work and enjoyed temporarily being back.

"How is Chloe?" she asked Cousin, curious why she hadn't seen her that morning.

"Good, just tired. The baby's due any day and she's home resting," he replied.

Emma nodded and continued to work and fill her orders. By 10am, she was tired but happy; she occasionally missed working at the bakery. Cousin gave her the bread order and, with a big hug of thanks, she left to begin the first step of the case. Heading out the back door, she put the bread in her tote and rode over to the Pinkerton office.

Once there, she hopped off the bike and placed it on her shoulder to climb the entrance stairs. A Pinkerton detective met her at the door and, instead of a lecture, he just rolled his eyes at her as he took it. He said over his shoulder, "Mr. Tilden is busy with a client just now if you would like to wait."

"I can wait," she called back.

"I think Jeremy is in his office," he said innocently.

"Really," she murmured. "Maybe I'll go there first." With that, she turned and headed in that direction. She knocked, entered his office, and saw a relaxed Jeremy with his feet up on his desk, reading a file.

He looked up, expecting to see one of the Pinkerton employees, and realized it was Emma. He tried to stand but didn't seem to remember his feet were still on the desk and fell backward in his chair. "Hello, Emma," he said with as much dignity as he could muster as he straightened up and got a firm footing on the floor.

She laughed out loud at his antics and said, "Hello, Jeremy."

He let the dignity go and started laughing with her. "Are you here to see Cole?"

She nodded, walked over to his side of the desk, and leaned back against it. It put her in arm's reach of Jeremy. "My team recommended I keep Cole in the loop since this is a Pinkerton case."

"Probably for the best," he acknowledged. "Pops should be available soon. Come here, let's talk about something important."

"And what would that be?" she asked coyly and held off for just a moment and then allowed herself to be pulled into his lap.

"Us?" he asked, sounding distracted.

"Is there an us?" She murmured the question into his neck.

He tilted her head back and said, "I think so," and gave her a slow, wonderfully long kiss. He was lifting his head to add to their conversation when the door opened and Cole strode in.

"Emma, I'm sorry if I kept you waiting." He stopped abruptly when he saw them. "I hope I'm not interrupting anything," he said wryly.

"Well, I found something to keep me busy," she said, slanting a gaze at Jeremy.

"So, I see." Cole chuckled. "Emma, come to my office. Jeremy, I think you have things to do?" He looked at him pointedly, and he reluctantly relinquished Emma.

"Yes, Pops," Jeremy said, wishing she could stay longer.

She waved goodbye to Jeremy and followed Cole back to his office. They sat on his couch, and Emma covered the information provided by Mr. Carlyle and his instructions.

"A weekly telegraph, I think we can handle that," he said.

"I've met with my team and we have some leads." He nodded for her to continue. She covered: the help, money manager, and seamstress.

"That sounds like a solid start. I would say let me know of any significant changes in the case and confirm with me before any undercover work," he cautioned.

"I will," she promised. "My priority is to build the background information first, prior to the first contact."

"Do you expect to make contact with Millie this weekend?"

"I'm hoping to."

"Okay, let's regroup on Monday and see what the next step will be."

"Agreed," she said, closing her notebook and prepared to stand.

Cole stopped her by saying, "Emma, thanks for the help on the transport from Chicago."

"No thanks are necessary, I enjoyed it," she said with a smile.

"Yes, I can see you did," he murmured.

"I'll be on my way."

"Thank you for coming in," he said as he watched her go. *If Jeremy had any sense, he would grab hold of her and never let go.*

As she exited the office, the Pinkerton detective who had stored her bike brought it out and carried it down the stairs for her. She thanked him as she hopped on to head to her first lead in the case. The maid lived in one of the more expensive districts and the paved roads made for a smooth ride. The address indicated it was a single-family home about three blocks up. She slowed to a stop, climbed off the bike, and parked it near the kitchen door. The bag that held the bread was slung over her shoulder, she removed it and tapped lightly on the door. A small older woman answered the door, her gray curls escaping the white bonnet on her head. "Hello," she greeted in a singsong voice.

"Hello," Emma replied. "I have your bread order from Cousin's." She showed her the bread she was carrying.

"Oh, how wonderful. Thank you for bringing it by. I just love their bread. Come in, please," she said, taking it and placing it on the table.

"Thank you. Would you mind if I stay and speak with you for a moment, Miss Grisham?" asked Emma, pulling out her notebook.

"Do I know you?" she asked, taking time to look hard at her.

"I don't know if you remember me, but I did stay at Millie's house one weekend years ago," Emma said, hoping to stir a memory.

"When you were a girl," she finished for her. "You were much younger and didn't eat much while you were with us, as I recall."

"That would be me, Emma Evans. Please, call me Emma."

"Call me Genny."

"Genny. . ." Emma started.

Before Emma could answer, Genny asked her rather abruptly, "Are you here about Miss Carlyle?"

"Yes," she said surprised. "I'm inquiring for her grandfather. He's very concerned, especially when he heard you and the other staff were no longer in place."

"Yes," she said, looking down at the table. "So much happened at once. We were so happy about the marriage, we were hoping the couple would start a family soon. That wasn't what happened and as soon as Mr. Landon moved in, the staff started to disappear. We were told the help that left had stolen items or they were untrustworthy. After a while, it just seemed they wanted us all gone. Roger himself wanted me out, about ran me out of the house. Sadly, I haven't heard from anyone I worked with." She looked dejected and said, "I didn't want to leave, but the situation wasn't working. We tried to talk to Miss Carlyle directly, but she deferred only to that Roger person."

"Roger?" Emma inquired.

"Roger Smith. He showed up right after the wedding and took over the running of the house. We never saw Mr. Landon once he showed up; he was the only person allowed to see him. Miss Carlyle never left her room except to shop, and Mr. Landon was always locked in the library on business."

"Do you feel that Mrs. Landon is in danger?"

"I never saw anything, but we were cut off from any contact with her, so I can't be sure."

"Are there any other household staff members who might have more information?"

"Yes," she said hesitantly. "Susan Baker, her personal maid, was with her every day, but she is out of the country, visiting family. Roger told me." Emma wrote it all down in her notebook.

Emma took a moment to evaluate her notes. *If Millie was married in the last few months, where is her new husband and why has no one seen him? I need more information on Roger -- where did he come from?*

She closed her notebook and thanked Genny for her time. As she made her way home on her bike, she mulled over the information.

The next step, she thought to herself, *is to make contact with Millie.*

Emma worked temporary jobs making lace at a local fancy dress establishment. More affluent women were able to get dresses made for each season and kept up with new styles coming in from Paris. Emma was known locally for her lace-work, a skill she had learned from Miss May. It was time-consuming work and she only accepted a few jobs a year due to the intricate natures of the patterns.

She stopped by the shop. It was quiet when she entered, and she waited in the salon. The owner walked out of her office and saw her. She immediately went to hug her and said, "Emma, how are you? I haven't seen enough of you lately."

"I know, I've been busy. Dora mentioned you need me for some work over the next few weeks?" asked Emma.

"Yes, with the big event coming up, we need some detailed lacework."

"I think I can arrange that," she said. "But can you also do me a favor?"

The owner looked curious and said, "Of course."

"Can you tell me if Millicent Carlyle-Landon has one of the appointments this weekend?" Emma asked innocently.

The owner went to her appointment book and flipped a few pages before saying, "Yes, she has an appointment on Saturday."

"Would you mind assigning me to work with her?"

"That works well for me. She has picked an intricate lace overlay for a few of her dresses," replied Ms. Simpson.

"Please confirm with Millie and let her know I'll be available this Saturday afternoon for her dress design session," requested Emma.

"I will." She had known Emma long enough to not ask any additional questions.

"Can I see the dresses she is interested in? So, I can start the design work?" Emma asked.

Mrs. Simpson pulled out the custom drawing boards for Emma to evaluate. Emma looked up from her notes and said, "I'll put together some ideas to recommend to her this weekend." Before she exited the shop, she thanked Mrs. Simpson for her help and headed home.

Upon reaching the boarding house, after a quick hello to Dora, Tim, and Amy, Emma moved to the sitting room. She pulled out her lace design books to begin sketching several types of overlays that would go well with the dresses Millie was interested in.

After dinner that night, she filled in the team on what she had learned from the housekeeper and detailed her upcoming Saturday seamstress appointment.

Tim nodded. "Good work, Emma. I also spoke with John Darko. He's still handling Millie's accounts and hasn't seen any inappropriate spending from her or the household."

Emma was taking notes. "Did he say anything about the change in staff?"

"Just that he indicated the money to pay them had been shifted to Mr. Smith." Emma started to question that, but Tim continued, "And before you ask, I did inquire about Mr. Alto. He refused to see me, and his secretary indicated he no longer has Mr. Landon as a client. He was rather rude about it."

"Hmm, several suspicious items with Mr. Landon. One, no one has seen him since the wedding and, two, his money is unaccounted for," said Emma.

"Sounds like the beginning of a puzzle, the corner pieces starting to fall into place. I think we wait for Emma's meeting with Millie?" suggested Tim.

"Yes," the team agreed.

CHAPTER 36

Saturday morning, Emma completed the details on her lace designs and got ready for her appointment with Millie. It was not something she was looking forward to. Millie had never really liked her, she had only contacted her when she wanted something. She inhaled and exhaled, trying to calm herself, and went downstairs.

She called from the foyer, "I am going out now."

Steps could be heard running in from the kitchen. Dora hugged her quickly and said, "Don't let her get to you."

"I won't," she promised and headed to the salon, taking the trolley downtown. As soon as she entered, she saw Millie and realized almost instantly there was something different about her. Standing in the doorway, she paused to make her observations. Her mannerisms, manner, even the tone of her clothes bespoke a more subdued woman than she remembered. Yet, in her eyes, there seemed to be something of the girl still there.

Emma decided it was time to make herself seen. "Mrs. Landon, how nice to see you again," she called.

Millie ran over to hug her. Emma stood very still in her embrace; they'd never had this type of relationship previously.

While she hugged Emma, she said, "Millie, not Mrs. Landon. I was so thrilled to hear you were available for my lacework."

Mrs. Simpson noticed Emma and Mrs. Landon were ready for the appointment; she motioned to her assistants to set up the drawings in the large salon.

"Mrs. Landon, Emma, let's get settled in the salon," directed Mrs. Simpson. "Emma, let me take your coat." Emma handed it to her, she gave it to her assistant to hang up.

They moved into the salon and sat down on the plush sofas; the assistants brought out easels to display each dress design. Emma pulled out her design notebook to begin the consultation, she started by showing her the designs. "We have used the lace as you see on the first two drawings of a tea gown, confections that had lace drape over the bodice and again on the edges. The other drawing is a fitted day dress, with lace relegated to the sleeves and a limited bustle."

Millie's response was positive, but not like the orders previously when she wanted to keep adding embellishments to the gowns. This time, she accepted the sketches as is.

"When can I expect my first fitting and a viewing of the lace appliques?" asked Millie.

Mary, the head seamstress, had joined them and stated, "In about three weeks, we'll have pinned muslin designs for an initial fitting."

"The lacework will take an additional month," added Emma. Millie looked a bit pensive about the timing but didn't comment further.

"Would you like some tea, Emma?" asked Millie.

Emma nodded and Mrs. Simpson left them to attend to her next customer. The tea was brought in and the door closed to allow them some privacy.

Emma decided to ask some direct questions. "Millie, how are you doing?"

Millie seemed to struggle a bit with that answer and then finally replied, "I'm fine."

"I only met your husband once at your wedding," she began.

Millie interrupted with a giggle, sounding a bit more like her old self, and said, "He travels, you know."

"Yes, and I understand you've gotten new staff for the house?" asked Emma, watching her closely.

She glanced a bit coolly at Emma. "I think that is *my* business."

Emma understood immediately she should back off that line of questioning. Instead, she asked in a light, conversational tone, "Have you spoken to your grandfather lately?"

"No, I do owe him a letter. I've just been so busy," she admitted.

Emma made mental notes for the first telegram to send to Mr. Carlyle.

Millie seemed calmer as she finished her tea. Emma let the conversation move back to fashion and parties. As the appointment came to a close, Millie hugged Emma again and promised, "I will see you soon." She collected her things and exited the shop. Emma watched from the window as the two men waiting by her private cab immediately straightened to assist her.

Turning slowly away from the window, Emma retrieved her design book and stood.

"That seemed to go well," Mrs. Simpson said, as she entered the room.

"Yes," Emma commented. They reviewed the lace designs proposed and she formally accepted the job, with a promise of an initial deliverable for four weeks from that day.

Placing her drawing book into her shoulder bag, she made her way home, walking instead of taking the trolley. The afternoon had cooled off considerably, but she didn't notice, her mind occupied with Millie. "Is there a case here?" she asked herself. "Or just a worried grandfather?"

Arriving at the boarding house, she hesitated before going in. She sat outside on the stoop, making notes about what she had learned. Millie's behavior was different, but that may be attributed to getting married and growing up. There was also her agitation when she asked her about the staffing changes. Emma needed firsthand knowledge of who was working in that house to determine if Millie was safe.

She completed her notes, making her way inside. Taking off her hat as she entered, she placed it in the closet, then headed through the foyer and dining room to enter the kitchen. Dora and Amy were putting together a stew that already had the kitchen smelling of herbs and meat.

"Hi, Dora, Amy," greeted Emma.

Dora absently cut a piece of bread and added butter before handing it to her. "Is everything okay?"

"After dinner," she mumbled as she ate. Dora nodded and continued preparations.

That night, with their smaller group, Emma said, "I think we've done what we can without knowing what's happening inside Millie's house. I need to meet with Cole and discuss going undercover."

"Has something happened?" asked Dora.

"No, at least, not yet," she replied. She went on to describe her meeting with Millie and her plans to follow up. "It was more than just her words that bothered me; it was the absolute change in her demeanor. It might be her husband's influence. I do remember finding him a little standoffish at the wedding, but I thought that would change with time. I'm also worried that Millie is nineteen and, when she turns twenty, she's expected to receive her full inheritance from her grandfather. I need to get into the house to see what is going on there." She paused a moment, thinking, and asked the group, "How do I do that? Large homes like Millie's need all types of help, but if this Roger is limiting the number of servants, how do I get in?"

Dora spoke up. "They're probably using Moore Services. They're the main supplier of household help here in town. If they're not allowing people to stay permanently, there may be a temporary position open. I know the owner and I'm pretty sure we can work something out."

"Wonderful. Can you get with her soon?" asked Emma.

She pulled out her calendar and said, "I'll make it a priority."

Tim commented, "Won't Millie know you by sight and make an undercover job difficult?"

"Not if I get with Savannah. She'll have some ideas to hide my identity. I also need to review my plans with Cole. I plan to catch them both after church tomorrow," said Emma. Emma and Savannah had gotten to know each other when Emma borrowed the wig for her undercover work at the shelter.

"Emma, invite them to Sunday lunch and we can talk after," Dora suggested.

The group agreed and retired to the sitting room. Emma worked on her lace, Tim and Dora tackled their books, and the others sat and talked quietly.

CHAPTER 37

After church on Sunday, Emma waited for Cole and Jeremy just outside the main doors. "Jeremy," she called when she saw him exit with Cole.

"Emma, how are you?" asked Cole. Jeremy held out his hand as she approached. She took it and let him pull her in close.

"I'm good. We were hoping," nodding to where Papa, Dora, and Tim were standing, "that you both might join us for lunch."

"I think that can be arranged," answered Cole. Jeremy gave an enthusiastic, "Yes."

Cole smiled broadly and said, "We'll need to drop by the house to change clothes and then will be over directly."

"Wonderful. See you both there," Emma said.

"Definitely," Jeremy said as he leaned down to give her a soft kiss goodbye.

Emma and her family got their wagon and headed back home. Once inside, she joined Dora to help with lunch. Amy had Saturdays and Sundays off to be with her family, and the family dinners could be quite large with additional guests.

Sunday lunch consisted of baked chicken, potatoes, and assorted vegetables. The bread had been freshly baked the day before and was cut for the table. Emma was working on the finishing touches for dessert. She finished it and put it on the side counter for later.

As lunch was being pulled together, Emma heard a knock at the front door. Tim, sitting at the table, said, "I'll get it." He headed out of the kitchen.

Emma and Dora could hear Tim and Papa in the front of the house, greeting their guest. *Conversations are always lively with this group*, thought Emma.

Jeremy stole his way into the kitchen and winked at Dora as he snuck up behind Emma. She had seen him out of the corner of her eye and was not surprised when he wrapped his arms around her. She turned and said lightly, "Hello, Jeremy."

"Can't surprise you, can I?" he asked playfully. She just smiled at him in response. "After lunch, want to take a walk, maybe go to the park?"

"Hmmm," she pretended to think and finally said, "Yes. Now, out of the kitchen. You're too distracting."

"I am? Good. Dora, everything smells wonderful," he said on his way to the door.

"Thanks, Jeremy. Lunch will be soon. Get with Tim and help him set the table. When you're done with that, come back for the platters," Dora said in her commanding voice.

Jeremy nodded and went to do her bidding.

Lunch was indeed wonderful and everyone had their fill. As it was cleared away, Cole asked, "Can we close the doors for our meeting?"

Papa and Jake excused themselves while Tim pulled the pocket doors closed behind them.

Cole started, "Well, Emma, I would assume you're ready for some undercover work?"

"Yes." She briefed him on the information they'd learned.

Cole sat back in his chair and said to the group, "Good work and thorough. Emma, the position you were speaking of, you're sure it will be available?"

Dora answered for her. "Yes, I was able to get a confirmation from my contact for an assistant cook position focusing on household baking. She'll pick up her uniform and card on Monday and then meet the house manager."

"What about Millie, won't she recognize you?" asked Jeremy.

She looked at him and said, "My thought was that Savannah could help out with a wig, I have some glasses and perhaps some makeup."

Jeremy nodded and said, "She enjoyed helping with the shelter case. I think she would feel the same about this one."

"Great," said Cole. "Just one thing. I rarely send one person in undercover. We normally have a backup in case of emergency." Emma started to talk, but Cole continued without allowing the interruption and looked directly at her. "Emma this isn't a comment on your skills. It is procedure."

Emma stopped and realized she shouldn't take offense. If she wanted to work a Pinkerton case, she had to follow their rules. "You're right. I'll follow the appropriate procedure."

Cole looked satisfied with that answer.

"Pops, I think I have an idea. Emma, does the house have a garden in the back?" asked Jeremy. Some of the bigger houses had intricate gardens.

"Yes, it's very large and very detailed," answered Emma.

Cole understood what Jeremy was saying and commented "Yes, I see. We could replace the gardener with you for the time Emma is in the house." He looked at her and asked, "Would that work for you?"

Emma nodded in agreement and said to Cole, "Papa and I have the house plans in the study. We would like to show them to you and Jeremy." Cole, Emma, and Jeremy moved to join Papa in the study.

The doors were pulled closed. Papa had laid the blueprints

on the desk. As they studied them, Emma began pointing out the major rooms in the house. "The study, located on the second floor, has a secret room and a staircase leading to the basement," Emma said, pointing to the west wall. Papa handed her a pencil and she drew in the location. "There's also a dumbwaiter in that room with access to the kitchen and basement."

Cole looked at the drawing consideringly and said, "Emma, how do you know about this? Have you been in the house?"

"That's an odd story," said Emma. She looked at Papa, and he nodded encouragingly for her to continue. "Millie and I weren't friends when we were younger. We knew each other, but we didn't have a lot in common. Honestly, I think she felt she was above us because Papa had worked for her family. It was surprising when she sent me an invitation to spend the weekend with her."

"Why did you go?" asked Jeremy.

She shrugged and said, "I accepted because I was curious about why she wanted me to visit, and it had the added benefit of allowing me to see the inside of her house."

"Did she show you this secret passage?" asked Cole.

"No," she said, tilting her head, thinking about that weekend. "No, we were playing at hiding and finding. In this case, Millie was hiding and I was looking for her. Honestly, I went into every room in that house, looked through all closets and under the beds. I still couldn't find her."

"How did you finally find her and uncover the location of the secret staircase?" asked Jeremy curiously.

"It was her laughing," she said simply. "She finally came out and showed me how smart she was for hiding there."

"I'm surprised that she showed you," said Papa.

"I was also," she acknowledged.

"Did you have a chance to go back after that weekend?" asked Cole.

"No, her parents passed away soon after that and she moved

to her grandfather's house. Once she married, the house passed to her and Mr. Landon."

The group discussed the final plans and their meeting drew to a close. Cole stayed after to spend some time talking to Papa.

Jeremy looked over at Emma and put out his hand. "Walk?" he suggested.

"Yes," she said softly taking his hand.

As they made their way down the street, he suggested, "We might want to see if Savannah is available this afternoon to confirm she can help with your disguise."

"Agreed," she said. "Though I will miss our alone time."

"Well," he pulled her close for a kiss and murmured, "we can work on that also."

They were laughing and enjoying each other's company when they ran for the trolley. They talked and held hands all the way to Savannah's apartment in the theatre district. On the way there, Emma said to Jeremy, "Will she be mad we're together?"

"Savannah and I, we're just pals. She's interested in one of the stagehands working backstage on her current show," said Jeremy with a laugh.

Emma smiled and relaxed, enjoying their trip. They hopped off the trolley and made their way to Savannah's apartment.

She answered on the first knock and said sincerely, "Jeremy, Emma, hello and welcome. This is a nice surprise. Come in."

"Thank you. We have a favor to ask," Jeremy said as they made their way into the sitting room.

Savannah watched and realized something had changed between the two. She smiled, knowing this is what he had always wanted. "Is there a case I can help with?" she asked intuitively.

Emma grinned and said to Jeremy, "I like her." She went on to describe the case and what types of changes might be needed to her appearance.

Savannah mulled it over and said consideringly, "A wig for

sure. You mentioned you have glasses? Some makeup can be used to change the look of your lips. You mentioned this is for an assistant cook position?"

"Yes."

"Well, for that, you might need some acting lessons," she commented.

"Acting lessons?" Emma questioned.

"Have you ever observed the staff in a house, the type Millie has?"

"No, not really," she admitted.

"They would not meet their employers' eyes for one thing. For another, they try to stay invisible."

"That works for me. I'll remember to do both."

"And only speak when spoken to and only in hushed tones."

Emma pulled out her notebook to take notes. "I'll study these. Thanks for the advice."

"Okay, let's go to my room and I'll get the wigs out." She gestured for Emma to follow her. Jeremy stayed in the sitting room with a book he'd picked up when they entered.

"We need something dark, maybe reddish." Savannah pulled out the shorter wig. "It will be like the shelter case, but this one will have more pins since it won't be as temporary as the last one." She pulled the wig onto Emma's head and asked, "Will you be able to do this on your own?"

"I think so. If not, I can get Dora to help," she commented.

Savannah explained the makeup as she applied it to her face. The different layers caused her lips to look thinner and her cheeks fuller. Emma looked in the mirror in amazement; she didn't recognize her reflection.

"Let's show Jeremy," she suggested.

They walked into the sitting room and for a moment, he didn't know it was Emma. He said in an incredulous voice, "That's perfect."

"Let's go back and put the items into a bag for you to take home," said Savannah.

Emma took off the wig and used a wet rag to wipe off the makeup. "Promise we will get together for dinner soon?"

Savannah said, "I'm looking forward to it."

Jeremy winked at Savanna and thanked her.

They parted ways, promising to give her all the details once the case was over.

"We still have time to take a cab over to the park," he said hopefully as they left the building.

"That would be nice."

They hailed a cab and headed there. Sitting together, they enjoyed each other's company. Jeremy dropped Emma off at the boarding house in time for dinner. She asked him in, but he had to complete some office work before starting his undercover position with her the next day. They kissed goodbye and Emma headed inside.

She picked up her lacework and went in to sit with the family and boarders. The lacework would take up her evenings for a while. Working diligently, she was able to complete some of the scallops for the tea dresses and started working on the more complicated overlays.

CHAPTER 38

The next morning, Emma readied herself for the day; she put on a plain gray dress and moved to her makeup table. The wig was next. She sat down, pinned up her hair, and pulled the wig over it. Next, she applied her makeup and slid on the ugly wire frame glasses. Taking a good look at herself, she thought, *What a picture you make.*

Gathering up the things she might need, she slid her notebook into her skirt pocket and stowed her knife into its thigh sheath. The clock dinged, reminding her that she had to get going before any of the boarders noticed her. She headed downstairs and slowly opened the door to the kitchen.

Dora saw her in the doorway and waved her in. "Amy is getting the wash, so we have a moment. Eat some breakfast and you can leave out the back door."

"Thank you," Emma said as she ate. "Well, what do you think?"

"I wouldn't have recognized you," admitted Dora. She got up to get Emma's lunch pail, handing it to her. With a hug, she said, "Probably no bike today. Too many people might recognize it."

"I thought of that. I'll catch the trolley this morning," Emma said as she shrugged into her dark blue jacket. "I'll see you this evening." Exiting out the back door, she walked quickly to the trolley stop and only had to wait a moment for it to appear. The trip was fast, and she jumped off as they reached her destination. The employment service was a few additional blocks from the stop, she used the time to go over her notes.

The buildings had the addresses posted clearly on the outside. She located the correct one and entered, following the signs to the agency. The agency door was painted an imposing black; she slowly turned the knob and entered the room. People were lined up on both sides of the long room; some looked bored, some hopeful—all wanting jobs.

She approached the secretary sitting at the desk. "Hello, I'm Molly Mullins. I believe Mrs. Stevens is expecting me?"

He checked his card list and said, "Yes, she is expecting you."

"Can you point me to her office?" she asked.

He looked surprised that she didn't know the way and indicated the door with his hand. "You may go in now."

Emma entered and a woman she assumed was Mrs. Stevens sat at the desk. She was an imposing figure all in black, with her hair pulled back into a tight bun. "Mrs. Stevens?" she began.

"Yes, don't tarry. What do you need?" Mrs. Stevens asked rather impatiently.

"Dora recommended I speak with you," Emma stated.

Mrs. Stevens took off her glasses, looking her over, and said, "Well, yes, that is something I wanted to discuss. I'm doing this as a favor and don't want this business to reflect badly on me."

"I understand. I am qualified for the position and I'll work hard," she assured her.

That seemed to mollify her. "I would do anything for Dora. Let me know if the situation changes. Remember, no complaints from the client," she said firmly.

"I will remember," Emma assured her.

"I have a uniform for you. You'll need to change here and

head straight over." She stood and walked to a closet, pulled out a black and white maid's uniform, and handed it to her. "You may change down the hall, the small room on the left," she directed.

Emma changed and placed her gray dress in her bag. Heading out of the building, she hailed a cab; Millie's house was a significant distance from the service agency.

As they neared the townhouse, she realized it was bigger than she remembered. It took up half a block and had an intricate stone exterior. The imposing ivory columns towered over the cab as it approached.

Service people were expected to enter from the back, so she took her bag and paid the driver before making her way to the kitchen door. She knocked and waited. A woman opened the door, also wearing a black and white maid's dress. When the woman didn't say anything, Emma said, "Hello, I'm Molly Mullins from the agency." When the maid still didn't say anything, Emma continued, "I'm here to bake and assist with the cooking."

The maid reached out her hand and said, "Do you have your employment card?"

Emma reached into her pocket and handed it over to her. The kitchen-maid did not smile or show any expression at all. Her figure, if you could call it one, was more of a rectangle shape-seeming to come to a point at her head and wide at her hips. Her overall demeanor gave her an air of doom. *Not a great way to start this job*, Emma thought.

She waved her in without comment and finally said, "You can put your things in that closet there," indicating the small door behind her. "I am working on lunch. You can help with the afternoon tea. I will need two types of desserts: a cake and small pastries."

Emma nodded and asked, "Where would you like me to set up?"

She looked at her for a long moment. "Roger will want to see you first. Stay here," she warned as she exited the kitchen.

"I guess she went to get Roger," Emma mused as she looked for supplies to place on her workstation. One of the cabinets she tried had what she needed. The kitchen door opened as she started to pour the flour. She hesitated and placed the bag on the station, waiting for him to speak.

He was a tall man with a trim waist. He appeared to be in his late thirties; he had thin black hair and a small mustache. "It says here," he said reading her card, "that you bake and will assist Mrs. Miller?"

Remembering Savannah's instructions, keeping her voice and eyes lowered, she answered, "Yes. I've worked in many households as a baker and assistant cook."

That seemed to satisfy him. "You will not be allowed outside the kitchen without an escort. Mrs. Miller will brief you. If you cannot adhere to these rules, you will be replaced." With that, he turned and exited the room.

Kind of an odd duck, Emma thought. She looked at Mrs. Miller and asked, "Rules about leaving the kitchen?"

"Yes. You must be escorted to the lavatory and you are to be accompanied if you take a tray outside of the kitchen. If you want to stay, you will pay attention to my instructions," she warned softly, but not unkindly.

Emma started working on the cake, wondering about the other household help. "Isn't there anyone else working here?" she asked.

Mrs. Miller sent her a look and said, "Roger brings in people to clean as needed. I'm the only one allowed to deliver the tray to Mrs. Landon."

Emma decided it was best to work and not ask any more questions.

The cake came together quickly and she moved on to the pastries that would be needed for the afternoon tea. The rules about exiting the kitchen were strictly enforced; each time she needed to visit the lavatory, she was escorted by several men located in the hallway outside. *There is no way I am going to be able to access the study with all of the security here.*

Suddenly, she heard yelling outside the backdoor; it seemed Roger was very angry about something outside. Looking through the window, she realized he was yelling at Jeremy.

"What do you think is going on?" she asked Mrs. Miller.

"The garden is off-limits to anyone but the gardener, Mrs. Landon, or Roger," stated Mrs. Miller in a firm voice.

Roger slammed in the door and Jeremy followed behind him, his head lowered. "You are only to work on the things I tell you to and you are to leave other areas as they are. Do you understand?"

Jeremy nodded and said, "Yes, sir."

"I still don't understand what happened to the last gardener and how you happened to take the job," he muttered as he left the room.

Jeremy sent Emma a crooked smile and asked for some water. He raised his eyebrows in a silent question, making sure she was okay. She nodded to him that she was fine. When he exited, she was told by Mrs. Miller, "Go down to the basement to get some preserves for me."

Finally, thought Emma. Trying to remember the last time she had been in this area of the house. She turned on the gas lights as she made her way down the stairs. *First the preserves.* She moved several jars to the stairs and walked toward the narrow door leading to the hidden staircase. A lock had been added to it; it appeared to be a new addition. She reached for a small pin from her wig to open it. It sprang open quickly and she peered in, the stairs were caked in dust; clearly, they hadn't been used recently.

"Are you lost down there?" Mrs. Miller called from the top of the stairs.

"On my way up," she called back. She picked up the preserves and went back upstairs.

Over the next few days, Emma worked hard and didn't do anything suspicious, trying to gain Mrs. Miller's trust. The plan seemed to be working, she gave Emma a key and asked that she come in early the next day to make the bread.

The next morning, Emma entered the house in the early hours. The grounds were very quiet, and the men were already stationed in the hallway. She notified them she was in the kitchen and started the bread, leaving it to rise as she went down to the basement to access the hidden stairs again. This time she entered and made her way slowly up the winding stairs. Her portable gas lamp lit the way.

There were several landings. At the final one, she accessed the switch that allowed her entry into the study and extinguished the lamp. The door swung open and surprisingly the room was not dark, the curtains on the windows were open, letting the early morning light in. She started searching for anything that might tell her what was happening in the house. The desk drawers were all unlocked but contained only blank papers.

The door to the hallway rattled and she heard a scraping noise, like a key being inserted into the lock. This forced Emma back into the hidden staircase. With a deep shuttering sigh, she made her way down the stairs in the dark. She exited into the basement, secured the lock, and turned to head back upstairs to the kitchen. *Wait -the last time I was here I saw the dumbwaiter. Where was it?* She looked around and saw the sliding doors on the far wall.

Do I have time? Emma asked herself and went to stand in front of it. *I have to try.* It was locked, but she easily picked it and slid the two panels open. She lit her lamp and used it to illuminate the interior; slowly putting her hands inside to feel around. There was something in there, she touched it briefly and pull her hand back out. Her palm was covered with a white powder. She put it to her nose and thought, *What's that smell? Lime? Why would there be lime here?*

More information is needed, she thought and climbed into the space, her lamp in front of her, she came face to face with . . . *a man?* A scream got trapped in her throat and she crawled backward, almost falling back into the basement. Taking two steadying breaths, she forced herself to move closer to and touch him. Slowly raising her hand, she ran her fingers down his face, curiously it didn't feel like skin, it felt like leather. *The lime must have reacted with the body. Could this be the missing Mr. Landon?* She pulled her hand back and placed it on her chest, as though to prevent her heart from leaping out. *Out! Out! Out!* she thought and pushed herself out and back into the basement.

Beginning to feel faint, she bent over, trying to catch her breath. *You have to pull yourself together. I need to know if it is him. How . . .? The ring,* the one she admired at the wedding. Forcing herself back into the dumbwaiter she tried to find his hands. His arms were twisted behind him, grimacing, she leaned him toward her to get the access she needed. They were stiff and didn't come loose from their position easily. "Please don't break off," she muttered. Then she heard a sound that she didn't want to hear, it was the sound of paper tearing. She tried to ignore it as she continued to pull on his arm.

The hand became visible and she saw the ring was still in place. Pulling on it, the paper tearing got worse until the finger broke off. The ring slid off quickly and she placed the finger into his hand. Pocketing the ring, she climbed out, closed the dumbwaiter, and put the lock back on with a shaky hand.

The preserves! She immediately went to get some preserves and headed upstairs to the kitchen. The room was empty as she entered and moved them to the counter. A wave of nausea engulfed her and she barely made it to the kitchen sink before she threw up. She washed her face with shaky hands and recovered enough to go to the lavatory in the hallway to fix her makeup and put a cold compress on her neck. The guards there escorted her to and from the lavatory, they didn't seem to notice her distress.

Back in the kitchen, she began to put the loaves in the oven. The rolls were next, she had them ready to go in as soon as the loaves came out. Taking a break, she sat down, breathing deeply to settle her heartbeat as she tried not to dwell on what she had seen. Once she felt steadier, she got up to start work on the pastries for breakfast.

Mrs. Miller entered soon after. She looked over at Emma and said approvingly, "Smells good in here." She didn't notice anything out of ordinary with Emma appearance, the heat of the kitchen had helped with her color

"Thank you," Emma said quietly, not making any further conversation.

Mrs. Miller sent her a look but didn't try to engage her.

Jeremy came in for water about an hour later and sent her a look. She shook her head and mouthed, *Later.*

He nodded as he drank and went back to work in the garden. The day went by quickly, she stayed busy, trying not to think about what she'd seen.

Walking home, almost in a daze from the day's event, she noticed someone was following her. She ducked into an alley and waited for the confrontation. The shadow could be seen hesitating and she took the opportunity to nab him by the collar, pulling him into the alley. It was Jeremy. "At least there's no knife this time," he commented wryly as he kissed her.

"Jeremy," she tried to get in between kisses.

"Yes," he murmured as he moved to her neck.

"I found Mr. Landon," she said quietly.

"Really, where is he?" he asked curiously, not stopping his kissing.

Emma placed her hands on his face, looked him in the eyes,

and said, "Concentrate. Mr. Landon is dead. I found his body in the basement dumbwaiter." She let her emotions take over and cried tears she'd had to stifle earlier.

"His body! Oh, Em," he said incredulously, pulling her in for a hug. "Are you sure?"

She put her hand in her pocket and fingered the ring. "I'm sure."

"Okay, let me think a moment. This has moved into dangerous territory. I'm not sure we should continue and put you at risk."

Once she had cried herself out, she said passionately, "I'm not at risk and I would like more time to find a way to get Millie out of there."

"Let me discuss this with Cole and make sure he's on board with continuing. I'll stop by tonight," promised Jeremy.

"All right, please let him know I want to continue. We need more evidence."

"I will," he said reluctantly. He pulled her close and walked her home.

That night he came by and talked with the concerned family. "Cole agrees with you Emma, but he wants you to check in with me more often with updates on how you are doing."

"Will you be safe?" asked a worried Dora.

"I won't take any unnecessary chances, but I want to continue. We need to find out what is going on there," said Emma.

Everyone agreed to move forward with the case.

CHAPTER 39

The next morning, she was up early again and made her way to Millie's house to make pastries for breakfast. Opening the door to the hallway, she let the men stationed there know she had arrived for the day. They seemed more relaxed with her than they had previously and even waved when they saw her. She completed a set of pastries and took them out to them, she even managed to get a smile out of them.

Mrs. Miller arrived and, as usual, started her work without much talking. The day went well, with baking filling most of Emma's hours. She was thinking that tomorrow, she would check out the hidden staircase again.

With her day over, Jeremy walked her home and kissed her before parting. Once inside the boarding house, she went into the dining room and made notes for tomorrow's activities.

A smell wafted by her and she headed to the kitchen to check on dinner. She pushed open the door and could see Dora and Amy were working on preparing a stew. Amy was industriously working on cutting carrots and onions and Dora was peeling potatoes. Emma sliced off a piece of bread and added some butter to it.

Dora asked in a worried tone, "Well, how did it go today?"

"Fine, just a lot of questions. More questions than answers at this point."

"Is Millie safe there?" she whispered.

"I think she's more valuable to them alive, at least right now," she whispered back.

Dora whispered back furiously, "Can we just go get her out of there?"

"That's easier than it sounds. There is no overt abuse and Millie has a reputation for being a bit silly. I think I'll just keep researching and try to figure out what is going on. Want some help with dinner?"

"Definitely. Start the dumplings so we can add them to the Eintopf stew." Emma got to work on making the dumplings.

Narrator: Eintopf is a one-pot stew using unused ingredients so no food goes to waste. The stew would go a long way to feed the boarders. Broth, vegetables, potatoes, and beef.

Emma set the dumplings into a bowl and covered them with a cloth. Next, she helped pull the chocolate pies out of the oven, that Amy had put in earlier.

"Emma, we got word today, Chloe had her baby, a small girl, healthy," said Dora with a bright smile.

"Oh, that is wonderful! What is her name?" asked Emma, looking over at her.

Dora's face softened and she said, "Mary."

That was their mama's name, the news made Emma's eyes well up with tears, she let them fall and went to hug Dora. "That is lovely, I will make her a christening gown," she promised.

"I plan to take some food over tonight if you would like to come with me," Dora suggested.

"I would," she said, happy she could put the case out of her mind for a little while.

After dinner, she and Dora went to visit the Baby Mary. They carried the Eintopf stew and bread for the new tired parents. Chloe and Cousin's mothers were there when they arrived.

"You brought dinner!" they exclaimed.

"There is plenty for everyone," commented Dora.

"Thank you," they said and moved it to the kitchen.

"How is Chloe?" Emma inquired after them.

Before they could answer, Cousin stepped out of the back room with a swaddled baby in his arms. "Would you like to see Mary?" he asked, pulling the blanket away from her face.

"We would," said Dora, and they approached slowly, as not to scare the baby.

"Oh Cousin, she is beautiful," commented Dora.

"Well, she had to live up to her namesake," he commented.

That comment caused the girls to tear up again. "Can I hold her," asked Dora.

"Of course," he said as he carefully handed the baby to her.

When she was in Dora's arms, Emma reached over and touched the tiny hand. "How is Chloe?"

"She is fine, just tired. This little one wore her out."

They knew they needed to let them rest, so they headed home with a promise of a return visit in a few days. Dora was quiet on the way home and Emma let the silence settle around them.

As they entered the kitchen, the case was back on Emma's mind again. She looked around to see if Jake had gotten home yet. He hadn't been at the table with them that evening. He sometimes worked late, as cases demanded. The front door opened and she could hear scuffling steps going past the sitting room. Dora smiled and went to the kitchen to help him get his dinner. Emma let him eat before approaching him.

"Jake," she said as she sat next to him at the kitchen table.

"Yes," he asked, not looking at her.

"I need your camera for my current case. The smaller one."

"Okay, when?"

"I'd like to use it tomorrow and get you the pictures to develop as soon as possible. I'll see if Jeremy can drop the camera off tomorrow at your work."

"That will be fine."

She smiled and said, "Thank you." And headed back to the sitting room to work on her lace projects. The amount of time it took to create it, was the reason she only accepted two or three jobs a year. Though this particular job was more of an investigation, she didn't want to disappoint her friend and owner of the dress shop.

She worked for the first hour, setting up the initial pattern that would be repeated with the additions of scallops. While her fingers were busy, she listened but stayed out of the group conversation. She heard absently that the twins had a long day in school but enjoyed recess. Tim joined the group, sitting close to Dora, making her blush with his teasing.

Emma thought to herself, *What is going on at Millie's? How do I find out?*

She paused a moment, set her lacework down, and said, "Tim, could you meet me in the study?"

"Sure," he said and kissed Dora before standing to follow her.

They entered the study and he closed the doors. Pulling out her notebook, she asked, "If this is some type of con to take Millie's money, what types of documents should I be looking for?"

Tim thought for a moment and commented, "Logbooks, I think. Even illegal activities need to be documented."

"Where would they be? In the desk?" she asked.

"No, somewhere hidden, I think. You would be looking for a safe. Probably not anything obvious. Look for something heavy and probably big."

CHAPTER 40

The next morning, she was once again alone when she started her pastries. *This would be the best time to access the staircase and enter the study.* Finishing her work, she headed to the basement and made her way there. *If there are logbooks, they would be here.*

She remembered what Tim had said and looked for the safe or something that might house one. The desk caught her eye. *Too obvious, and it's not locked,* she thought and continued her search.

She looked past a large globe several times but then thought about what Tim had said about the size of hidden safes. Going over to it, she found it met the requirements, large and heavy. Twirling it around, she looked for a compartment or opening of some type. Her hand encountered a small indention, and she used her fingers to open the panel, revealing a combination lock.

Dear-one: How does Emma know how to open combination locks?

Narrator: She lived with two amazing women (Miss Amy and

Miss Marjorie) who were accomplished burglars. Emma worked with them to get an understanding of different types of locks and how to open them.

Emma worked the combination, leaning her head close to listen for the click as she found each number. The safe sprang open on the final one. Reaching in, she discovered Tim was right—the logbooks were inside.

She pulled them out. There was just enough sunlight with the shades open and her portable lamp to allow for the pictures to be taken. Leaning them against some of the large books on the bookshelves, she grabbed the camera, taking as many pictures as she could. They were written in some kind of code; she would get with Tim to try to decipher it.

She replaced the books in the safe, took her camera, and made her way back down the hidden staircase to the basement and then up to the kitchen. Hearing voices, she hid the camera under her apron and slowly opened the door. Mrs. Miller wasn't alone; Roger was also there.

"And where have you been?" asked Roger when he saw her enter. "You're not allowed out of the kitchen without approval."

"I sent her to the basement to check the inventory for preserves so I can determine when we have to start canning again," Mrs. Miller said, covering for her.

Though shocked at the help she received, Emma said, "Yes, we're running low on fruit but have enough vegetables."

Roger looked at them both, but since he had no reason to doubt Mrs. Miller, he said, "Just make sure you don't go where you aren't supposed to," and left the kitchen.

Emma moved and had her back to Mrs. Miller as she placed the camera in her bag before she started pulling the ingredients for a streusel. "Thank you," she said quietly to Mrs. Miller. She nodded to Emma and went back to peeling potatoes.

Emma waited another moment before saying, "Why did you do it?"

"I'm here for reasons of my own," she explained simply. Not sharing anything further, they went on cooking together companionably.

Jeremy knocked at the door and Mrs. Miller found a reason to remove herself while he was there. Emma slipped him the camera and said in a low voice, "Get this to Jake at the police station and ask him to develop the pictures by this evening."

"I will. Is everything okay?"

"Yes, I think we have an ally in Mrs. Miller. She covered for me just now."

"Interesting. I need to get moving so no one realizes I'm not in the garden." He looked around and gave her a quick kiss before he exited the room. Mrs. Miller returned and didn't ask any questions. They continued to work together in a companionable manner, the rest of the day.

On her way home, Emma slipped into an alley and removed her wig, and wiped her face. She kept her coat closed and slipped back out to return to the boarding house. Emma met Jake and went up the stoop with him. "I was able to get those prints ready for you," he said.

"Great, are they readable?"

"Yes, I could make out the individual line items," he said as he handed them over.

She clutched them to her chest. *This could be it*, she thought and carried them into the house.

She called, "Tim, can you meet me in the study?"

Tim called back, "On my way."

Emma had spread out the pictures for Tim to evaluate. "Pull the door shut behind you." He did so and walked over to the desk.

"It's definitely a code. Give me some time to look at this," he said absently. Tim continued to pour over them that evening and into the night. When Emma woke the next morning, she found him in the dining room. He had his jacket and vest off and his shirt sleeves rolled up.

"Have you been up all night?" Emma asked incredulously.

"Yes. I broke it a couple of hours ago. They're using a simple replacement code, but it was hard to tell what they were replacing." He had the photos with him and pointed to one, "Here, you see that they are importing units much bigger than they are selling. The profit margin appears quite high."

"Do you have any idea what it is?"

"Based on where it is coming from and the quantities, I think it may be opium."

"I think we should turn over the information on the drugs to Cole. He'll need to investigate further." She paused. "Tim, can we tell when the next shipment will happen?"

"That, I can tell. It looks like the ships dock about every four months and one is due to arrive soon. I think we can set up a sting to see who meets the ship and takes custody of the drugs."

"Do you think the main people will be there?"

"I think the person behind this is very controlling and will want to make sure their product is delivered. Do you have an idea of who it is?"

"Roger is the best suspect at this point. I think it's also time to get Millie out of there," she insisted.

"I agree. Can you approach her at the house?"

"That will be the hard part. Millie rarely comes out of her room. But Mrs. Miller could help me with that. She delivers her meals. I'll see if I can talk with her tomorrow."

"Emma, are you all right staying in the house until we can check it out?"

"Yes, this is too important not to follow through on. I will give Jeremy an update this morning."

CHAPTER 41

She briefed Jeremy and Cole before going to work. Cole had prior experience with drug shipment and knew who to contact about the ships that were coming in. Emma and Jeremy headed to the house to begin their day.

Emma had not seen Millie in all the time she had been in the house. There was only one way to get access and she needed Mrs. Miller's help. "Can I take the tray up today?" Emma asked her.

She sent her an odd look but answered, "Yes, you can. I'll let the guards know."

Emma set up the lunch tray and headed out of the kitchen. The men looked at her questioningly and Emma said in response, "Mrs. Miller asked me to take Mrs. Landon's tray up today."

They glanced over her shoulder and Mrs. Miller said, "Yes, she can go up." They nodded and let her go ahead.

As she headed upstairs with a guard, she had the tray perched on her right hand and shoulder. She knocked lightly and was told to come in. The guard stepped back and waited as she entered. Millie sat at the desk in her room, her back to the door. She was dressed in a light afternoon tea gown.

Emma started to say, "Millie. . ." but before she could get it out, she noticed the book Millie was writing in. The shock made her freeze; it was a logbook, just like the ones in the safe.

It was Millie! She's in charge! How could I have missed that? Women can be criminals, too, Emma reminded herself. She had been naïve on this one.

"Yes, why are you still here?" Millie asked without turning around.

"No reason, madam," she murmured, as set the tray down, and left. She immediately started downstairs to the kitchen.

This isn't about saving Millie anymore. It's now about stopping the illegal activities and taking Millie into custody, she thought.

Someone grabbed her arm and turned her around. Fighting against her instincts to react to the attack, she found herself face to face with Roger.

"What are you doing up here? You know you're not allowed out of the kitchen."

She didn't struggle but instead behaved in a docile manner and lowered her eyes. "Mrs. Miller told me she was busy and that I should take up the tray for Mrs. Landon."

"You will come with me to talk to Mrs. Miller," he demanded.

He half dragged her downstairs. Emma didn't see Mrs. Miller as she was thrown into the kitchen, but she did hear a bang and saw a pan hit Roger's head.

As Emma took in the picture of Roger splayed across the floor, she looked at Mrs. Miller in amazement. "Wow," she said, she took the offered hand and pulled herself up from the floor.

"Grab his ankles," said Mrs. Miller in a low voice, as she lifted him and put her hands under his arms. They moved him toward the basement door and down the stairs.

She pulled out a rope, handed it to Emma, and said, "Make yourself useful."

Emma tied him up and pulled out a handkerchief to tie around his mouth.

"Who are you?" she asked in amazement.

"I am Donald Landon's mother, and I know these people have stolen my son's money and probably killed him," she said grimly.

"Mrs. Landon—" started Emma.

"Hannah," she interrupted.

"Hannah, I'm so sorry, but they have killed your son. I found him more than a week ago," she said gently.

"Where?" Hannah asked in a shaky voice.

She indicated the dumbwaiter with her head. Hannah started to go over and Emma said, trying to stop her, "Please, don't look. He isn't what you remember."

She hesitated, wanting to see her boy but decided Emma was right. Instead, she asked, "How can you be sure it's him?"

Emma put her hand in her pocket and pulled out his ring.

Hannah took the ring, studied it, and asked quietly, "Are you here to stop them?"

"I am, and I think we finally have enough to get Millie and take down her operation," she said bracingly. "But now, since we have Roger, I expect we need to move a bit faster."

"Agreed," Hannah said, wiping her tears, as she slipped the ring into her pocket.

"Let me check in with the gardener. He's working with me."

Hannah and Emma headed upstairs to the kitchen. Jeremy was there, looking around when they came up from the basement. He started to talk but stopped when he saw Emma had company.

Emma saw the look and said, "It's okay, you can talk in front of her. She is Mr. Landon's mother. Mrs. Landon, this is Jeremy

Tilden. He's part of the team helping to bring this illegal operation down."

Jeremy was shocked but shook himself out of it. "Em, we got word the ship is coming in tonight."

"Well, that's a relief, because there's an issue." She went on to describe what they had done to Roger.

He looked resigned and said, "I'll get the team organized. We don't want to arouse any suspicion, so don't change your schedules and leave at your normal times."

"Oh, and one more thing. . ." Emma said, delaying his exit.

He raised an eyebrow and waited.

"Roger isn't the one in charge," she said.

He frowned, "He's not? Then who is?"

"Millie," she said simply.

He looked nonplussed for a moment and then said, "Women are moving into everything these days." He started out of the kitchen.

"I'd like to be there," said Mrs. Landon, that stopped him.

Jeremy started to say no, but Emma said, "She deserves to be there. I will bring her with me." When he looked worried, she said, "We'll stay in the background."

Jeremy headed out to get everyone in place. Mrs. Landon and Emma followed Jeremy's directions and left the house at their regular time. They had checked on Roger and he was still secure in the basement. Once Millie left to go to the ship, the Pinkertons would have him picked up.

Millie watched them leave the house. *Finally*, she thought. Getting dressed, she organized her logbook for the delivery and exited her room. "Roger!" she called from the top of the stairs. When no one responded, she started down and ask the guards at the base of the stairs where he was.

"We don't know. He hasn't been around for a while," one responded.

She frowned and thought, *This is my enterprise, after all, and my money. I don't need him.* She said out loud, "Fine, we'll go without him."

The two men gave her an odd look but followed her orders. Normally, Roger directed all things in the house, but it looked like that was changing.

"Get the buggy ready. We will be leaving at 10pm to go to the docks," Millie said.

She returned to her room until it was time to leave. At the appointed time, she exited in a dark dress and a hat covering her hair and made her way downstairs.

The guard stepped up and said, "The carriage is waiting for you."

"I'll need both of you with me and bring your guns."

They did as they were told and climbed on the top of the carriage. Millie rode by herself inside. She wasn't worried; the men with her had been through this process many times. She thought, *It's probably time to get rid of Roger. I can run this operation on my own.* She sat back, feeling very confident and in charge of the situation.

They pulled up to the predetermined position and waited for their contact to appear. She heard a knock at her carriage door and opened it to descend. A lanky man with a cap pulled over his eyes was there. She said curtly, "Well, don't just stand there. We need to confirm my items are here and ready to be transported."

Jeremy pushed up his hat, pulled out a gun, and pointed it at her, saying, "Yes, your items are here and the delivery people are now in our custody." At that moment the Pinkerton detectives surrounded them and took the two men on the carriage into custody.

Millie tried to slip into her previous persona and started to cry. "These men have kept me locked in my house and I had no one to turn to. Roger forced me to do this, all of it."

"This Roger?" Cole asked, pulling the tied-up man out of the shadows.

Millie seemed stunned to see him there. She wanted to demand where he'd been, but couldn't. She kept crying to cover her anger.

Jeremy was called over by Cole to bring Roger to the police detective. He looked at the young officer assigned to Millie and said, "Watch her. I'll be right back." The officer nodded and stayed where he was.

The issue, thought Emma as she observed Millie being taken into custody, *is that the officer appeared to believe everything she is saying to him.* She just shook her head when he gave her his handkerchief. *Good grief*, she thought and kept a sharp eye on Millie.

As Millie reached into her bag, Emma knew what would happen next. Grabbing her clutch knife from her skirt pocket, she threw it. The blade pierced Millie's hand, causing her to drop the gun she was in the process of pulling out of her purse.

Jeremy was on his way back and immediately grabbed the gun in one hand and the moony officer's collar in the other. He glanced toward Emma and sent a silent, *Thank you*.

Emma responded by saying, "I was never one to stay out of the fray."

Millie heard the comment, looked her way, and asked, "Just who are you?"

Emma took off her wig and wiped her face with her arm, Millie recognized her immediately and said, "You bitch!"

Emma looked at her and said softly, "So, now you know."

Once Millie was finally in cuffs and Emma's knife safely returned to her pocket, things started to calm down. The Pinkertons completed the final roundup of the drugs and people.

Millie just couldn't wait to rip into Roger when he was close to her again. "You are so incompetent. I have to do everything myself."

"Does that include killing my son?" interrupted Hannah, coming out of the crowd of detectives.

"Your son? What do you have to do with this? What is she talking about? I don't know the cook's son," Millie snapped, bewildered.

"Actually, you do," commented Emma. "She's Donald Landon's mother."

Going pale, she said, "His mother? But he said she was dead."

"He chose to tell people that. We didn't have the best relationship, but that doesn't mean I didn't love him. Why did you have to kill him?" Hannah asked.

"I didn't kill anyone," she said defiantly.

"They found the body, Millie," commented Roger laconically.

Millie blinked, she immediately changed her story, and said, "That wasn't murder. That was an accident."

"We'll see," said Jeremy.

"She did it!" blurted out Roger. "She was behind everything."

"You keep your mouth shut!" she shouted.

"I just did as I was told," he said. "We knew each other from her honeymoon. She knew I was moving this merchandise and she said she had a deal that would benefit us both. She said we just had to take care of one thing. That thing turned out to be moving her dead husband into the dumbwaiter and placing a lock on it in the basement. He was already dead when I got there, at the bottom of the steps."

Millie sneered and said, "Well, it just figures you would turn out to be a worm of a man." She turned her ire back to Emma. "I knew you were trouble when you started asking me questions at the dressmaker. It was Grandfather, wasn't it? The money. He always kept a tight hand on my money, and I knew it would be worse as I got closer to my inheritance."

Emma didn't answer and watched as they took Roger and Millie away, both preoccupied and glaring at each other.

Cole, Jeremy, and Emma stood together, watching them leave. "What will happen now?" Emma asked.

Cole responded, "Millie killed Donald and was the leader of a drug-smuggling operation. Prison is the least of her worries."

"So," Emma said contemplatively, "how should we word the telegram to Mr. Carlyle?"

That made Cole and Jeremy laugh out loud and Cole said, "You are my kind of agent."

They left the area together to head home after a long day.

CHAPTER 42

A few weeks later, Emma was at the courthouse; she was there as support in the trial. Benches lined both sides of the long hallway, and she was startled to see a wheelchair positioned nearby. Looking forward, she made eye contact with Mr. Carlyle. She had known he would be there to support Millie, but she hadn't expected to speak with him.

He indicated for his helper to roll him over to her. As the helper pushed him closer, Emma felt trapped, but she knew she had to face him. "Hello, Mr. Carlyle," she said quietly.

"Emma," he said. He waved off his helper; he wanted privacy for this conversation. "Emma, I want to speak with you." She waited for him to start yelling at her or accuse her of framing Millie.

Instead, he said in a quiet but firm voice, "Emma, I do not blame you for anything you found at the house or Millie's arrest."

She gave him an incredulous stare as he continued. "When I brought you in, I had my suspicions that Millie was involved in something nefarious. Why?" he asked when he saw her look. "Millie has always had a dark side. She could hide it under that rather silly surface, but I had reports of bad behavior from the help working at the house. I had hoped her marriage would redirect her."

"Well, it did that," she said.

"Yes, I am afraid she is a throwback to my father. He was not a good man. He benefitted from many illegal activities. When he died, I was finally able to move us into the legal side of things. Millie's parents died when she was about twelve, and I just found I couldn't say no to her."

"How did they die?" she inquired softly, sad this man had lost so much.

"They were on a family holiday at our country house. Millie enjoyed running around in the fields and collecting flowers. I got notified that her parents had eaten something bad and died."

"What did they ingest?" she asked curiously.

"White Amanita bisporigera mushroom, it is deadly if ingested. They died so quickly; we didn't know what had happened initially. The local doctor thought to check the leftovers from the dinner and found the poisonous mushrooms."

"Did Millie eat any of the mushrooms?" she asked without expression.

"No, she doesn't like them at all and has always refused them. After that, she seemed to change. Outwardly, she was the same cheerful, silly girl, but when she was home, she was quiet and very studious."

"What did she study?" Emma asked curiously.

"Herbs mostly. She carried the *Culpeper's Complete Herbal* book with her everywhere, making notes in it."

Something clicked in Emma's head. "Mr. Carlyle, I have to see someone. Will you be okay here?"

"Yes, my man is nearby."

She left him to find Cole. He was at the courthouse observing Millie's case and had checked in with her earlier that day. She found him around the corner and said to him in a low voice, "Cole, I think we need to speak to David. I have some information that is pertinent to the case."

He saw that she was serious and said, "I saw him in a side room, preparing for today." They walked over and Cole knocked on the door. A voice called for them to enter.

"Emma, Cole," greeted David Williams, prosecuting attorney for their case.

"David, Emma has some information to share with you." He nodded at Emma to begin.

"I was speaking with Millie's grandfather just now and he mentioned something that made me feel we weren't seeing the whole picture. I think Mr. Landon's death means more than we thought. Remember," she said as she looked at Cole, "when I told you I was invited to her house for a weekend when I was a kid?"

"Yes," replied Cole.

"Well, what I didn't mention at that time was that Millie was very pushy about what I ate, so much so that I stopped eating that weekend. I had to sneak some bread and butter from the kitchen."

"What was she trying to get you to eat?" asked David curiously.

"Well, she kept saying she had picked herbs just for me, herbs she would add to my dinner once it got to the table. The pressure was intense, and her personality would change when I said no. If her parents hadn't come home, I'm not sure I could have held out. About a month later, I heard her parents had died. We didn't know it at that time, but Millie's grandfather just confirmed that they had accidentally been poisoned by mushrooms that were in their dinner."

Making up his mind, David said, "We need to get the doctor to check for poison in the husband." He left the room immediately to get that started.

"Good job, Emma," Cole said as they waited to hear the results.

David also contacted the court immediately and ask for a continuance. He also took the time to amend the charges to add the murder of Donald Landon.

Donald's mom, Mrs. Landon, was at the court and was notified that the additional charge was being added. She looked satisfied that her son would get his justice.

Emma pulled out her notebook and said, "Cole, I think we also need to check to see if the staff who 'disappeared' actually went on to other jobs. It always bothered me they weren't around to be questioned."

"Emma, do you think she. . ." Cole felt this couldn't have happened and no one noticed.

"I don't want to think that, but now I'm wondering why the garden is so protected. Did the help 'disappear' there? Could you ask Jeremy to meet us at Millie's house, in the garden?"

Cole sent a note over, and the three of them arrived at the house within the hour.

"Over here," she said when she saw Jeremy approach. They gave him the background on the case.

Jeremy said, "I think I know where to start. If I'm right, we'll need shovels. Also, I know where the mushrooms are located."

They sent word to David and made their way to the beautiful rose bushes located at the back of the property. "This location is perfect for covering up fresh dirt around the bushes. Also, there's plenty of room if she wanted to add more bodies," stated Jeremy grimly.

Cole sent a runner to get some Pinkerton detectives to join their group and bring shovels. The men were digging and, after a few moments, found something. "Over here!!" One of the policemen called. Emma, Cole, and Jeremy ran over. Bodies, one after another were uncovered. It looked like most of the household staff had met their end in that garden. The police chief was notified immediately to come to the house to take over the investigation.

While they were waiting for him, Jeremy pointed to the hidden spot where the mushrooms were being grown. It was the only overgrown section in the garden. They examined the area and Cole squatted down, using his handkerchief to break off some of the mushroom caps.

"We'll have to have these tested, but I believe this will be what killed those people."

Emma hesitated when they were ready to depart. "Emma, are you ready?" asked Jeremy.

She leaned into him and said, "Jeremy, I need to check Millie's room for that book."

"Do you know where she has hidden it? The study?" he asked, knowing she had found the logbooks there.

"No, I think it is probably in her room," commented Emma. "Millie wouldn't want that out of her control."

"Let's go up," he said. As they entered the house, Emma glanced around and took an umbrella from the stand. He didn't ask why she needed it, and they made their way to Millie's room.

They entered the room and Emma said, "I have an idea." She used the tip of the umbrella to tap on the wooden boards. Jeremy realized what she was doing; she was listening for a hollow sound, indicating a hidden compartment. As she tapped under the desk, she heard what she was looking for. "Here," she said, pointing to the floor. They knelt and Emma pulled out her clutch knife to pry up the board. "Ah-ha," she announced. The board lifted to reveal a hollowed-out spot. She put her hand in and pulled out the book.

"We need to get this to David," said Jeremy, impressed that she had found it so quickly.

"Agreed," she said as they exited the room and headed to the police station. They got there in time to meet Cole. Jeremy asked, "What's going on?"

"David is in the interrogation room waiting for Roger. We will wait out here while they question him," he said.

They would have liked to go in to observe, but they understood that wasn't possible.

As Roger was brought into the interrogation room, he looked around and said, "Are we having a party?" The prosecutor, police chief, and assortment of policemen filled the small space.

"Roger, we have some additional questions for you," David said.

"Okay," he said warily.

David watched him closely as he stated, "We've looked under the rose bushes in the garden."

Roger couldn't decide whether he wanted to stand or to sit. He finally sat and said in a pleading tone, "I really didn't know what was going on. I know that sounds odd, but I would go on a trip to set up opium buys and another member of the staff would be gone when I got back. I was told they took other positions. By the time I understood what was happening, the only person I could save was the cook. That's when I set up the protocols for exiting and entering areas."

"Why did you stay if you knew she was a murderer?" asked David.

"We were making too much money. I kept thinking one more score and then I would get out. I also thought I could control her," he admitted.

"Would you be willing to testify about the additional bodies?"

"Do I get the same deal for limited jail time?"

"About that, we'll need to add some time for not reporting the crime in a timely manner."

Roger nodded, understanding he had to take responsibility

for his actions. He thought, *Maybe the cook will say some positive things about me. After all, I saved her life.*

The charges were amended for a second time to include the additional murders. Millie's defense attorney appeared stunned at the amendments. He looked at her, but she just stared forward and would not answer his questions.

David submitted a new witness list to the court:

- Gardener: Jim Brown was found at a family member's house. He was also arrested for disposing of multiple bodies.
- Jeremy Tilden: for his knowledge of the mushroom and rose bushes.
- Dr. Knight: doctor who examined the body of Donald Landon and confirmed poison as the reason for his death.
- Dr. Morison: retired doctor who examined Millie's parents and determined their death was from poisoning.
- Miss Grisham: previous housekeeper for information on disappearances.
- Roger Smith: accomplice of Millicent Landon.

Cole and Emma entered the court and made their way to the seats on the prosecutor's side. The judge had yet to enter and the jury was out on a break. David nodded when he saw them and was about to say something when the judge appeared and the jury took their seats. The case started again with Jim Brown, the previous gardener, as a witness.

Prosecuting attorney David Williams asked, "Mr. Brown, can you tell us if you kept the white Amanita bisporigera mushroom growing in Mrs. Landon's garden?"

Mr. Brown looked very nervous and avoided looking at

Millie. "Yes, I tried to tell her they needed to be removed, but she said she wanted to develop and oversee them."

The prosecutor asked, "Did she harvest them?"

Mr. Brown answered, "She did. She told me it was for experimentation purposes."

The prosecutor asked, "Can you tell us about the bodies we found under the rose bushes at Mrs. Landon's home?"

"She just told me they died and we should bury them," Mr. Brown said lamely, clearly not sure how to answer the question.

The prosecutor continued, "Mr. Brown, you didn't think that was suspicious, not notifying the police that someone had died?"

"Well, yes, but she was an upstanding lady. I thought she was being nice, burying them there," said Mr. Brown, looking uncomfortable.

The prosecutor gave him an incredulous look and asked, "She was such an upstanding lady that she just needed to get rid of bodies?" Mr. Brown didn't respond to the question; he just sat and stared at his hands.

The judge asked the defense attorney, Jeffery Cumming if he wanted to question the witness. He had a few questions, but there was little that could be done to contradict the gardener's testimony.

The prosecutor asked for the next witness. "Jeremy Tilden, please."

Jeremy was escorted into the court and took his seat next to the judge. The prosecutor started his questions. "Mr. Tilden, you were the gardener for the last week. Did you notice the mushrooms there?"

"Not initially," admitted Jeremy. "I was there to monitor activities inside the house."

The prosecutor continued with his questions. "What types of conversation, if any, did you have with Mrs. Landon?"

"Very little at first," he said. "She contacted me when she

found out I was a short-term replacement for the gardener. She was adamant about the garden; she didn't want it touched."

The prosecutor followed up, trying to confirm he had seen the mushrooms. "Was one of these a patch of mushrooms?"

Jeremy answered, "When I brought up that she had a patch of bad mushrooms, she said they were pesky and should probably be removed at a later date."

The prosecutor asked, "Did she mention the rose bushes?"

Jeremy nodded. "She mentioned I was to trim them only and not disturb the beds."

The defense attorney said, "I choose not to question this witness at this time."

The next witness called was Dr. Knight, the doctor who had examined Mr. Landon's body. He was an older man and slowly made his way to the stand.

The prosecutor waited patiently for him to be seated and asked, "Dr. Knight, can you tell me what you found when you examined Mr. Landon's body?"

The doctor glanced at the judge and then the prosecutor and asked, "May I use my notes?"

The judge asked to see his notebook. He reviewed it and handed it back. "You may use them."

The prosecutor prompted, "Doctor?"

"Yes," he said, reading, "I noted that he had excessive drool that had dried from his mouth, leaving a trail to his shirt. I also noticed an abnormal skin color that is similar to when the liver fails."

The prosecutor had a follow-up question. "Doctor, what was this color?"

"Yellow."

The prosecutor continued the same line of questioning. "Doctor, did you examine the four bodies buried in the garden?"

Dr. Knight confirmed, "I did."

"What did you find?"

Dr. Knight glanced back down to his notebook. "The same as I found when I examined the husband's body. Once we cleared the bodies from the flowerbed, the yellow coloring was obvious."

"What did you deduce?" asked the prosecutor.

Dr. Knight closed his notebook with a snap. "Poison. By ingesting mushrooms, in all five cases. "

"Thank you, doctor."

The Judge looked at the defense attorney and asked, "Would you like to question the witness?"

The defense attorney looked at a loss for a moment and leaned over to ask Millie a question. She shook her head vehemently in response. He looked at the judge and said, "No, I do not have any questions for this witness."

The judge said, "You are excused." Dr. Knight stood and exited the courtroom.

Dr. Morrison, the retired doctor who had examined Millie's parents after they passed away, was called next.

The prosecutor asked, "Doctor, what did you see when you examined Mr. and Mrs. Carlyle?"

Dr. Morrison stated, "Excessive drool, abnormal skin color, and complaints of severe cramps."

"What did you deduce?"

"Poison, by ingesting mushrooms," answered Dr. Morrison.

The defense attorney stood and asked, "Dr. Morrison, can you tell us how the mushrooms got into their food?"

"No, the cook said there were no mushrooms served with the meals that day," he answered.

"Thank you," said the defense attorney and sat down.

The previous housekeeper, Miss Grisham, was called next. She entered very nervously and sat in the witness stand. The prosecutor asked, "Miss Grisham, you were the housekeeper when Mrs. Landon was first married?"

Miss Grisham replied, "Yes, I was the housekeeper for Mrs. Landon for a long time, since she was a girl."

The prosecutor continued, "What can you tell us about Mrs. Landon's interests as a young girl?"

"Well, she was always in the garden and always bringing in clippings to include in the dinners," she commented.

"Did you include them in the dinners you were preparing?"

"Only if I recognized them. Otherwise, I told her it might be dangerous," she answered honestly.

"Your witness," said the prosecutor.

The defense attorney stood up, walked around his desk, and asked, "Did you ever see her put anything into the food, something you told her not to?"

"No," Miss Grisham stated simply.

"Thank you," said the defense attorney and sat down. Millie leaned over to whisper something to him. He smiled and patted her hand reassuringly.

Roger Smith was called as the next witness. He walked in and was escorted to the stand by an armed policeman. He did not shy away from Millie's gaze and actually smiled at her. The prosecutor asked, "Mr. Smith, how did you get involved with Mrs. Landon?"

"We met on a cruise. It was her honeymoon," Mr. Smith stated, continuing to smile.

"Where was Mr. Landon during this meeting?" asked the prosecutor.

"Mrs. Landon said that he was sick and confined to their room," said Mr. Smith.

"Did you ever see him?" asked the prosecutor.

"No, I did not," Mr. Smith stated quietly, his smile slowly fading.

"Why were you on the ship?"

"I was setting up some operations overseas."

"Were these illegal operations?" asked the prosecutor, looking at the jury. They looked both fascinated and repulsed.

"Yes," Mr. Smith admitted. "Drugs."

"You willingly admit you were involved in illegal activities?" asked the prosecutor in a deliberate manner.

"Yes, I am going to prison for these activities."

"And you were involved with Mrs. Landon?"

"Yes, we got very close on that cruise and I shared my business enterprise. She wanted in on the deal and said we could use her house as a base of operations."

"What about her husband?"

"She said he wouldn't get in their way, that she would take care of it."

"Did you know what she meant by that?"

"No, I didn't. A few weeks later, she notified me that I could move in and said she needed help cleaning something up. When I got there, her husband was lying at the bottom of the steps."

"Were the servants in the house?"

"She had told them they could have a holiday."

"Did she tell you what happened to him?"

"She said he was beating her and fell down the stairs."

"He would never do that!" stated Hannah Landon, jumping up from her seat in the gallery.

The judge looked annoyed and said to the gallery in general, "We can't have any disturbances from the courtroom while proceedings are taking place." Hannah sat back down next to Emma and held her hand.

"Did you think she was telling the truth?" asked the prosecutor.

"Objection, this man is not a doctor," stated the defense attorney forcefully.

"Judge, Mr. Smith can provide his observation of the man, the general condition, without being a doctor," answered the prosecutor calmly.

The judge said, "Yes, he may provide his observations as to what state the man was in when he arrived. Please, continue."

The witness did so. "He had a yellow color to him and he seemed to have liquid coming out of his mouth."

"Did he appear to have any broken bones?"

"Not that I could see," he said simply.

"You also mentioned in your statement that, at this time, there was additional staff in the house and you noticed they started to disappear."

He shook his head. "It was odd. No one gave notice; they just went away. I started to get suspicious when Mrs. Landon thought nothing of them leaving."

"You told the housekeeper, Miss Grisham, to get out of the house in a rather abrupt manner. Why?"

He looked toward Millie and then back at the jury. "I was standing by the back windows and was watching the garden when I noticed something odd. I looked closer and saw the gardener moving something that appeared to be a body. That night, after he had gone home and Millie was in her room, I went out with a shovel. I dug until I found the body. It was the upstairs maid, Renee." Crying could be heard coming from the gallery.

"Thank you. Your witness," said the prosecutor to the defense attorney.

The defense attorney stood and asked, "IF you saw this happening, why didn't YOU notify the police?"

"I felt I was stuck. There was no way to get out of the arrangement without turning myself in. I stayed," he said honestly.

The defense attorney sat down, showing no expression.

The prosecutor had a follow-up question. "Mr. Smith, what measures did you put in to protect the household staff when you realized there was a danger?"

"I put in special precautions that no one was allowed with

Mrs. Landon alone at any time. I also reduced the staff to only four persons and limited their access to the house." He looked at the jury and said beseechingly, "I protected them as best I could."

The judge called for a ten-minute break and Millie seemed to be looking around the courtroom for someone. Emma followed her gaze to where her grandfather normally sat; it was empty. Emma wondered where he was. Millie asked her lawyer something and he nodded.

Cole walked up to where Emma was sitting and sat down next to her. "Have you seen Mr. Carlyle today?" she asked.

"No, not this morning, but I can have one of my men find out if he will be here."

Emma nodded.

Cole called over to one of his men, "Go to Mr. Carlyle's hotel and check on him." The man nodded and headed out of the courthouse.

The judge looked at the defense attorney and asked, "Do you have any witnesses?"

"I had one witness," said the defense lawyer. "I call Millicent Landon to the stand."

Millie stood elegantly, her pink lace dress providing an innocent picture. Emma smirked briefly and thought, *She is wearing my lace today.*

Millie made her way to the stand confidently, certain they would believe everything she said.

The defense attorney asked, "Mrs. Landon, what are your current interests?"

"Currently, I am interested in fashion."

"Were you also involved in the illegal operation with Roger Smith, that he testified to earlier?"

"I didn't have a choice after my husband died." She took a moment to deliberately wipe a tear off her face. Emma watched the jury and could see she was getting to them, that they were buying "the poor helpless girl" act.

"Do you have any knowledge of mushrooms or other flora or fauna?" asked the defense attorney.

"No, none at all. I don't like to get my hands dirty," she said directly to the jury. They laughed in response.

"I rest my case, judge," the defense attorney said and sat down.

The prosecutor stood and asked, "Mrs. Landon, you indicated you have no knowledge of mushrooms or other flora or fauna?"

"Yes," Millie answered, knowing she could convince these men of anything and get out of the trouble she was in. She could see she was winning in the jury's faces. Even with the evidence presented, she could still come out of this.

The prosecutor saw the look on her face and knew she thought she had won. He was about to prove her wrong. "Judge, I have something to put into evidence," he said as he walked back to the table and pulled out a book from his briefcase.

"Judge, I have no prior knowledge of this evidence," the defense attorney protested.

The prosecutor answered, "I just received it this morning."

"Please, hand it to me." He handed the book to the judge to review. He examined it closely, handed it back, and said, "It is fine. Please enter it into evidence."

"Judge, may I confer with my client for a moment?" asked the defense attorney.

Millie had paled considerably when she recognized the book. The defense attorney walked over to her; he whispered questions she refused to answer. She just stared straight ahead.

He returned to his table and sat, unsure what Millie would say next.

The prosecutor asked, holding up the book. "Is this your book?"

Millie didn't answer the question and just stared forward. The judge leaned over and asked the question for him. She glanced at her attorney; he nodded that she had to answer.

She realized she had no choice and stared back at the prosecutor. "Yes, that's my book."

The prosecuting attorney nodded and proceeded to open it. "As I see here, there is writing in the book. Is this your writing?" he asked and showed it to her.

She stared at it and slowly nodded and said a quiet, "Yes."

"Thank you. Now, if I look further into the book, I see you have marked multiple pages for different types of mushrooms, including those found in your garden. We have your gardener on record saying you asked specifically for these mushroom clippings. You also mention recipes. Can you tell me what these recipes are for?" Again, he showed her the book.

"Different types of soup recipes," she said in a low voice.

"What types of soups?" he prompted.

"Mushroom."

The court hushed at that final answer, knowing she had murdered those people. The prosecuting attorney knew he had completed his case and stopped with his questions.

There was nothing more that could be said, so her lawyer didn't try. Millie stood and made her way back to the table. She didn't seem as elegant and grand as she had when first taking the stand.

The prosecuting attorney started his closing statement. "You have seen here through witness testimony that Millicent Landon was not only involved in the drug smuggling as testified here by her house manager and assistant Mr. Smith. We have also presented evidence that Mrs. Landon murdered her husband and four household staff members with poisonous mushrooms. The evidence showed she has poisoned before and gotten away with it. I implore you to find her guilty of all charges presented."

The defense attorney stood. "Mrs. Landon is a young, innocent woman who was taken advantage of by men who coerced her into participating in illegal activities after they killed her husband. Mr. Smith is trying to use an innocent young girl to hide his illegal activities and the fact that HE murdered those four people and placed them in the rose garden."

The jury was instructed to deliberate and return with a verdict. Emma, Jeremy, and Cole sat on the hallway benches outside of the courtroom. They only had to wait about three hours. The judge returned, along with the jury, stating, "You have reached a verdict."

"We have," said the jury foreman. Millie stood, looking straight ahead. "We find her guilty on all counts."

The judge nodded and said to the jury, "Thank you for your service." He looked down for a moment and raised his eyes to look at Millicent. "Millicent Landon you are sentenced to be hung by the neck until dead." Millie's hand fluttered lightly around her neck at that remark.

Cole told Emma later that Millie's grandfather died without knowing the final verdict.

Emma chose not to attend Millie's hanging. Some of the victim's families did attend. Emma had the closure she needed at the trial. She and Jeremy did appear at Millie's funeral, though no one else was present.

Millie's grandfather had requested no services for himself.

On the day of the funeral, Emma received a note from Mr. Carlyle's lawyer that he would like to see her that week. She sent back a confirmation of the time and date she could meet him.

"What do you think that's about?" asked Jeremy when she told him.

"I don't know. It could be anything."

Jeremy just smiled when he saw her drumming her fingers on her lips. *Planning*, he thought.

NOTEBOOK MYSTERIES ~ BOOK 3

CHANGES AND CHALLENGES

Notebook Mysteries

Changes
and
Challenges

KIMBERLY MULLINS

CHAPTER 1

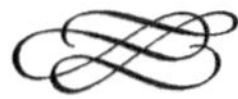

1885 PRESENT DAY, CHICAGO

*E*mma rolled over in the bed and reached out to brush the brown curls off his forehead. "Dear-one, you need to wake up sleepy head."

"Sun's not out yet," he said in a muffled voice, lying on his stomach with his face turned toward her, partially buried in the pillow.

"What has that got to do with anything?" she teased.

He opened his eyes and turned on his side, pulling her to him, murmuring, "Good morning, Emma."

"Good morning, Jeremy," she said as he turned on his back, pulling her on top of him. She sank into him with a sigh; a little while later, they came up for air.

"You need to get moving," she reminded him.

"I thought I just had," he commented wryly.

"Oh, you! Out," she said as she pointed at the bookcase and not the door.

She stayed in bed and watched him rise slowly, wrapping his long lean body in a robe. He leaned over to her and said, "See you at breakfast."

"Definitely," she said. He moved the bookcase aside to reveal a door to his room.

CHAPTER 2

*T*hings *have definitely changed in the past two years,* thought Emma as she settled back on her bed. It began with a request from Mr. Carlyle to protect his granddaughter, Millie. He believed she was being taken advantage of financially. The case had turned suddenly. Millie was discovered to be the mastermind of a smuggling organization and was responsible for multiple murders. Her death by hanging had brought the case to a dramatic end.

"Unfortunately, or maybe, fortunately," Emma mused, "Mr. Carlyle died of natural causes before he could hear his granddaughter's guilty verdict."

Then, a surprising thing happened after the funeral; a lawyer contacted Emma to attend a reading of Mr. Carlyle's will. *The will,* thought Emma, *offered many complications and opportunities.*

The day of Mr. Carlyle's funeral, after they returned home, Emma had been working on lace designs in the sitting room when Dora called her from the foyer. "Emma, a note was delivered for you." She walked into the foyer to take the note, reading it quickly.

"What is it?" asked Dora curiously.

"It's from Mr. Burns, Mr. Carlisle's lawyer. It looks like I'm invited to the reading of the will tomorrow," she said absently.

"Why is it so soon and why invite you?" asked Dora, perplexed.

"The timing must be at Mr. Carlyle's request," Emma murmured thoughtfully. "He might have left me a little something. I did adore his library and it would be nice to have something to remind me of him."

CHAPTER 3

1883 LAWYERS OFFICE

*E*mma woke early that morning, determined to be on time for her appointment with Mr. Burns. She rode her bike over to his office, placing it on her shoulder as she entered. She saw a large man in a blue suit speaking to a gentleman sitting at a desk. *Mr. Burns*, she thought.

The large man straightened when he saw her, folded his hands in front of him, and assumed a solemn expression. "Miss Evans?"

"Mr. Burns?" He acknowledged her with a nod of his head. "Call me Emma, please," she offered.

"Call me Andrew." Mr. Burns looked at the man sitting at the desk and said," Jason, please help Miss Evans."

Jason stood up, motioned toward the bike, and said, "I can take that for you."

She thanked him as he took it from her and moved it to another room.

Mr. Burns offered his elbow and escorted her into his office. As they entered, she found it was a very sober room, with a heavy desk, leather chairs, dark floor rugs, and official-looking framed documents on the walls. She looked around, curious to see who else would be at the reading. When she saw she was alone, she looked at Mr. Burns and asked, "Will anyone else be here?"

"No, I've already notified persons that have small bequests. They will not be here for this communication," he said absently, putting on his glasses as he moved to sit behind his desk. "Please, have a seat."

Emma sat in the heavy brown chair facing the desk. Her eyes darted around the room and finally settled on the lawyer. She watched him pull paperwork from his top desk drawer and was a bit startled when he abruptly began to read.

Emma didn't understand what she was hearing at first. Something about her being the sole inheritor.

She shook her head and asked in astonishment, "I was left what?"

The lawyer removed his glasses and rubbed the bridge of his nose. "Mr. Carlyle contacted me after Millicent's arrest and made the changes to his will at that time. He left the bulk of his estate to you."

"But why me? I'm the one who caused Millie's arrest. I would have thought there would have been some animosity," she said, shaking her head, not understanding.

"When Mr. Carlyle started the investigation, he was suspicious and believed his granddaughter was involved in something nefarious. I think he sent you in to uncover if she deserved her inheritance. There at the end, he had a feeling things were not going to turn out well and wanted the money to go to something positive," he said patiently.

"Okay," she said, rolling her shoulders. "I never turn down a challenge. Where do I sign?"

Mr. Burns smiled, glad there wouldn't be an argument. He stood and shuffled the papers to her side of the desk. As Emma signed, he commented, "There will be some time before the money is officially released. There will be a probate hearing and, once that is completed, I will contact you about the dispersal."

She thanked him and left the lawyer's office in a daze, walking her bike instead of riding it. As she made her way down the sidewalk, she kept thinking, *So much money and so much responsibility.*

"Hey, Em!" a voice called.

Emma didn't hear it; she was wrapped up in her thoughts. "Emma," Jeremy said, touching her shoulder.

Startled, Emma whirled to defend herself and grabbed the hand placed on her shoulder. When she realized who it was, she said, "Jeremy, sorry. I was distracted."

He pulled her in close and murmured, "I could tell." He stepped back and looked down at her. "What happened at the lawyer's office? Get a nice book or small gift?" Emma had told him she was invited to the reading of the will.

She leaned close and tilted her head to speak into his ear. "He left me everything. Don't get too excited," she added when she saw his expression. She explained how the inheritance would work. "It is an added responsibility. I will have to set up a charity to manage the money. He wants me to give it away to people who need it."

"It's still amazing," he said, dazed at the size of the estate Emma now owned.

"Yes," she agreed, not thinking about the money, but about the responsibility.

"Any plans yet?" he asked, knowing her propensity to be organized.

She smiled wryly. "I'm working on it. Can you and Cole come by tomorrow night to meet and discuss the inheritance with the team?"

"Only if I can get you alone after," he said as he leaned in for a kiss. They both enjoyed the interlude.

"Want me to see you home?" he asked.

"No, I'm okay. I think I'll ride the rest of the way," she said as she climbed on her bike.

"I'll be on my way, also. I'm working a case at Citizens bank downtown. I'll be there all week if you need anything," he said.

"Okay, see you tomorrow," she said.

He leaned in for another kiss. "See you tomorrow," he confirmed and waved her off.

She rode to the boarding house, parked her bike in the back, and entered through the kitchen door. Dora heard her coming and ran over to hug her. "Sister, how did it go?"

Emma shook her head and sat down at the table with Tim. He had his books opened and looked up. "Hi, Emma." He noticed she looked distracted and asked, "Everything all right?"

Looking at them both, she said, "Well, looks like we have another opportunity to bring the team together." She went on to explain her conversation with the lawyer. "I think a team meeting to discuss forward steps would be appropriate."

Dora and Tim looked at each other and then at Emma before nodding in agreement. "I asked Jeremy if he and Cole could be here tomorrow after dinner," Emma said.

Making notes, Tim said, "That should work. We'll let Jake and Thomas know to be here."

Emma went to bed early, thinking about the new responsibility and what it would mean. One team member was on her mind, someone who hadn't been around for a while, because of her. *I miss him*, she thought decidedly. *It's time to bring him back to the team.*

She got up extra early to make his favorite treat: strudel. She was sliding the trays out of the oven when Dora entered the kitchen, wrapping a headband around her hair.

"You're up early this morning," she commented.

Emma glanced over. "Yes, I thought we might need a dessert tonight and, since I invited everyone without telling you, I thought I'd help out."

"Thanks for doing that. I appreciate it," Dora said sincerely as she started to get breakfast organized. There was a soft knock on the door and Dora let in a yawning Amy, who greeted them and quickly began to get organized for the day. Dora noticed the box sitting on the table. "Hmm, dessert for tonight, you say? If that's so, who's the box for?" Something occurred to her as she waited for the answer. "Is it for Tony?" She knew it was his favorite.

"It is," Emma said as she added strudel to the box and used a string to hold it closed. "I want to approach him about coming back to help with cases and be an active part of the team."

"Does he know you're coming?" Dora asked suspiciously. She had concerns about Emma's abrupt way with Tony.

"Yes, I sent him a note and asked to see him before work this morning," Emma said, finishing up the box.

Dora exhaled a breath she didn't realize she was holding. Another thought occurred to her. "Does Jeremy know about this?"

Emma frowned over at her. "Jeremy knows Tony and I are still close."

"You haven't been close for a while," Dora reminded her.

"Well, that last case was involved," she said wryly. "But I plan to change that, with this," she said, indicating the box.

"You're putting a lot of faith in a pastry," Dora said with a laugh. "You might mention it to Jeremy," she suggested.

"I might," she said as a compromise.

Emma cleaned up her work area and stored the extra strudel for the evening meeting. She helped get breakfast on the table and spent the morning working on some lace designs, watching the time so she could meet Tony at the museum before they opened. The clock chimed, she gathered up her things and headed to the kitchen. "I'm headed out to see Tony." She kissed Dora on the cheek on her way out.

"Don't forget your magic pastry," Dora teased.

Emma grabbed the pastry box and sent her a grin as she headed out to get her bike. The wind was refreshing on her face and she enjoyed the ride. She was lifting her bike on her shoulder when she saw Tony sitting on the steps.

She put it down and rolled it over to where he was sitting. "Hi, I thought I would meet you inside," she said, taking extra time to settle her bike against the stairs and adjust the pastry box. When she finally glanced back and saw he was smiling, his hair falling into his eyes. Her fingers itched to adjust his hair instead, she just stared for a long moment and lifted the box in her hand. "Your favorite."

"Yes," he said quietly. She didn't notice he wasn't looking at the box. He averted his eyes when she looked toward him.

"Why don't we walk over to the park?" he suggested.

"That would be nice," she said with a quick smile.

"I can walk the bike." He stood and took it from her as they moved onward. A comfortable quiet settled around them. They found an empty bench to sit on and opened the box of strudel.

She let him eat one before starting a conversation. "Tony, we miss you and the team would love to have you participate as a full member."

"I miss seeing and talking to you, and I miss the family. I also miss the excitement," he admitted.

She laughed at that and commented, "We're never short on that!"

"I guess the question is, can we be as close as we once were, but not be together?" he asked laconically.

"Tony," she said, touching his hand and looking deep into his eyes, "I want to be close. I want to share what's happening in my life and hear what's happening in yours."

He set his other hand on top of their clasped hands and squeezed. "I do, too. I've missed this so much." For over an hour, they sat and talked about their lives and what had happened since their breakup.

"So, Mrs. Smith?" she teased.

He turned red and said with a smile, "I like her. She's taken me to her tailor and shown me how to dress. I'm enjoying her company."

"I've noticed," said Emma, touching his new collar. "Very dapper. She seems good for you. I don't see her missing an event because of an ongoing mystery."

"No," he murmured. "She wouldn't do that."

"You never mentioned what's up with Mr. Smith?" she asked consideringly.

"He passed away some time ago," he said simply.

Emma looked worried and Tony noticed, saying, "Now, stop that. He died of natural causes; he was older and had a heart condition."

Emma smiled brightly. "Well, I am a bit busy, so I may not be able to investigate that."

He laughed and continued. "I've also been studying art history and the museum is paying for school. I'm learning how to tell if paintings are authentic—the types of paints used, the cracking and wear on a picture which could indicate when it was painted. I'm especially excited about eventually traveling and seeing Paris. Philip and I have been invited there this year to authenticate some paintings."

"Paris, oh, that's wonderful! I hope to get there one day. You must tell me everything when you get back," she said wistfully.

"I will," he promised. He turned serious for a moment and looked at her searchingly. "I assume that you and Jeremy. . ." His voice trailed off.

"Yes, we're together now. Tony, it was after we broke up, I promise," Emma said softly.

He nodded, believing her, and asked, "Do you see it going long term?" He knew how she felt about marriage.

She thought about that and said, "Right now I do, but I try not to think that far ahead."

"This is true. Have you told him you're inviting me to rejoin the team?" he asked.

"Tony, you were always welcome," she said, distressed.

"I know, but I needed some time to find out what I wanted, separate from you."

"Yes, we operated so much as a couple, it was hard to find where we started and stopped as individuals," she said.

"To get back to the initial question, will you tell him?" he asked, feeling he needed to know the answer.

"I'm a little confused about that," she admitted. "Dora brought it up, too. I just don't typically run things by him, work- or case-related. We do have some overlaps when additional resources are needed by us or Pinkertons, but no communications like that."

"Emma, I think you should realize that this will go past work issues; it's personal. I would rather not have any drama tonight at your meeting," he stressed.

"There is that," she conceded. "Okay, I'll head over after and mention it to him. I won't be asking permission," she warned.

"I didn't think you were," he murmured, watching her. *I can do this*, he thought. *We can be friends again. What the future holds, I just don't know.*

"Tony, are you happy?" she asked, concerned by his intense expression.

"Me? Yes, I am. I feel I'm on the path I am meant to be on," he replied in a steady voice.

"Yeah, me, too."

They finished the pastry, enjoying their time together. They talked quietly as they walked back to the museum. Before leaving, she asked, "Tonight?"

"Tonight," he confirmed, and they parted.

She didn't look back as she rode off, so she did not see that he waited until she was out of sight before slowly climbing the stairs to the museum.

CHAPTER 4

As Emma was riding to the Pinkerton offices, she thought absently, *I'll need to confirm that I can go by and see Jeremy at the bank.* She was also thinking about her and Tony's conversation. *How to approach this topic with Jeremy?* She arrived at the Pinkerton office and placed her bike on her shoulder, climbed to the top of the stoop, and entered the office building.

She set it down to close the door behind her, noticing how quiet it seemed. It was close to lunch and there wasn't anyone at the outer desk. She started down the hallway as Cole exited the office, in the process of putting on his black jacket. He glanced toward the door and saw her standing there. "Emma, what can I do for you?"

"I hoped to stop by and see Jeremy at the bank, but I wanted to be sure it is safe to do so," she said.

"I don't see why not. We are trying to be preemptive, so we have extra people stationed and there's not a confirmed threat of a possible shooter or robbery. Just don't distract him," he warned, shaking his finger at her, then spoiled the severe words with a smile.

She blushed and grinned. "I'll try not to." She picked her bike back up and accompanied him down the stoop.

She waved at him, watching him go, and climbed on her bike to head toward the bank. As she approached the building, she rode close to the windows, peeking in. Jeremy stood inside, speaking with an older gentleman. Three other Pinkerton employees were posted nearby, watching the bank area. They noticed her in the window and called over to Jeremy. He glanced her way and waved her in.

Emma nodded, heading toward the door. She jumped off her bike and parked it in the bushes to the left of the entryway before entering and waiting while Jeremy completed his conversation. He walked over to greet her and leaned in to kiss her cheek, saying, "Hello, Em. What's going on?" He added quietly, "Don't stay around very long. We're expecting some action this afternoon."

"Just something quick, I invited Tony to rejoin our investigation group. I wanted to let you know," she said, unsure of what tone to take.

Jeremy gave her a long look and said, "Emma, I know you and Tony would like to stay close and I know you're committed to me. I appreciate you telling me, but you don't need my permission to add members to your team."

She smiled. "I love you, Jeremy."

He said back softly, "I love you, too, but you need to go now!" He walked her swiftly to the door.

"Jeremy," one of the men called, indicating a man just coming in, armed. Jeremy pulled Emma to the right side of the door.

Emma drummed her fingers on her lips. "Jeremy, I have an idea." He listened quietly and nodded, then motioned to the men to spread out. The tellers and manager were told to duck behind the counters. The gunman burst through the door with his weapon drawn. Emma was ready for him; she leaped from a crouched position, wrapping her arms around his legs. As he collapsed in surprise, Jeremy used his arms to strike downward, forcing him to drop the gun to the floor. The Pinkerton men jumped on the now unarmed man and restrained him. Jeremy retrieved the gun and helped Emma to her feet.

"Great response, Emma. Thanks for the assist." He grinned and offered her a hand up.

She accepted it and bounced a bit as she was pulled to her feet. "Glad I could stop by," she said, grinning back. "Coming over tonight?"

"Wouldn't miss it," he said and went back to directing his men to remove the assailant from the bank. Emma retrieved her bike as she exited and headed home to arrange the meeting.

Dora met her at the kitchen entrance from the dining room. "I heard you come in. How was Tony? Will he be joining us tonight?"

"He will," Emma confirmed.

"Good." She paused before continuing. "And Jeremy?"

"Oh," Emma said nonchalantly, "I went by the bank. He said it was my team and my decision." She didn't mention what happened after the conversation. Dora was a worrier and Emma didn't think she needed the additional stress.

CHAPTER 5

That evening, Emma was sitting with Dora, Tim, Thomas, and Jake when they heard a knock at the front door. "I'll get it," she offered. She went into the foyer and opened the door to find Jeremy and Cole there. As she invited them in, Jeremy leaned in for a kiss, while Cole waited patiently.

Cole gave them a minute, then cleared his throat. Jeremy stepped back from Emma with a smile.

Cole said, "Emma, we appreciate your help today at the bank. I understand," he said looking at Jeremy and then back at her, "that the takedown was your idea."

"I just thought catching him unawares would make it less likely someone could get hurt," she explained. She leaned into their group and said, "Let's keep that between us." They nodded, understanding she didn't like to share all of her adventures with her family. "Follow me, we're in the kitchen."

As they joined the others at the kitchen table, there was a knock on the kitchen door and Jake said excitedly, "I'll get it." Dora smiled as he answered the door.

Tony entered the room, hugging an enthusiastic Jake as he

smiled at the group. "I hear there is strudel available at this location."

That made everyone laugh and any tension caused by his presence melted away.

"Tony, hi." Jeremy made the first move, standing and sticking out his hand toward him. There was only the slightest hesitation as Tony accepted the gesture. They weren't friends, but they could work together. Tony sat by Jake, who excitedly began chattering about the pictures at the museum until Emma commented, "Let's get started." She went on to explain how the inheritance would work. "It will be a self-supporting charity. We have enough money to set up a management company can choose projects to support."

Tim was making notes as Emma discussed the money, other properties she'd inherited, and how Mr. Carlyle wanted it distributed.

He looked up and said, "Emma, I think you'll need to meet with his business manager and find out how the money is currently being managed. I'd also recommend a thorough audit of all of the money and property."

Emma was drumming her fingers on her lip and Jeremy noticed with a tilted smile. She looked at Tim and asked, "Who would you recommend for the audit?"

"I have three New York City companies I can recommend," he said, jotting down the names and handing her the paper.

She was studying it when Dora asked, "Emma, how are you thinking the money should be managed and distributed?"

The amount of money left to her was more than she could handle alone. "The manager I mentioned would report to a board to vote on different projects to be funded. Then I think a vote from the group and finally a co-signature from the manager and me to release the money."

"Who are you thinking of for the board?" asked Dora,

although she already had an idea of who would be asked to participate.

"I was thinking of," she looked around the room at each person, "Jeremy, Dora, Tim, Jake, Tony, Thomas, and Cole."

"Speaking for me and Dora," commented Tim, holding Dora's hand, "we would be honored."

Jake looked on and said, "Emma, you really want me on the board?"

"I do, Jake. You bring a lot of positive things to our team, and I think it'll be the same on the board. Will you join us?" she asked in a serious voice.

"I will," he said, looking very happy at being included.

She glanced over to Tony and asked, "Tony?"

"It sounds like an amazing project. I want to be included," he said.

She turned to Thomas, who nodded. "I've always looked out for you, and I think looking out for more people is a good thing," he said.

"Last but not least, Cole and Jeremy, will you be joining us?" asked Emma.

They looked at one another and then to Emma, with Cole responding, "We will do it."

Emma flashed a grin at the whole group, knowing her team was amazing.

With that, the board was in place, and Emma said, "I'll be approaching the person I think will work as a manager soon. If they accept the position, then I'll schedule my trip to New York to meet with the business manager, Mr. Beeker. Agreed?" They all agreed on the path forward.

CHAPTER 6

The next morning, Tim and Emma met separately in the study to review what she would need to speak with Mr. Beeker about. Reviewing his notes, Tim looked up to comment, "Emma, I'd like to participate in the audit. I know you can take care of the initial meeting, but I think you need someone you can trust to help guard the charity's interest."

After a moment, she said, "I agree. I'll go to the initial meeting in New York with Mr. Beeker and get the auditors set up."

"That will allow me to get organized here so I can make the trip," confirmed Tim.

"You'll be able to stay at Mr. Carlyle's house," she suggested.

"That sounds good. I'll review my schedule and give you some dates," he said, wondering if he could get Dora to come with him.

As they completed their business, Emma headed out of the study and up to her room, mulling over the candidates to lead the charity.

We'll need an extremely efficient business person who is personable and honest, she thought. She opened her notebook to review the list of potential people who could fill the role The one person who kept coming to the top of that list was Clair. She already operated a charity that was making a difference in women's lives by protecting them from abusive men. *This would give her a new direction in her life, but is it something she wants?* Emma asked herself.

Clair had become a very close friend of Emma's over the years. They were two very different people—Emma, the daughter of an engineer, business owner, and detective, and Clair, who didn't know her father and owned and operated a bordello. What brought them together was their shared past event and their common goal of helping people in trouble. Emma thought decisively as she marked other people's names off her list. *There's no better person to sift through the many requests and know which are truly deserving of help than her.*

A few days later, Emma arranged to meet Clair at their regular restaurant, where they discussed business monthly or just enjoyed each other's company. She entered the office space of the restaurant; management allowed them to use it for their private conversations. She saw Clair across the room, sitting at the round table set up with an afternoon tea. She wore a beautiful light blue afternoon dress with a bustle and a white lace shirt peeking out of the jacket opening, giving the appearance of a very lovely lady of leisure. Seeing Emma, Clair stood and circled the table to embrace her. "Emma! I was so worried about you after reading the news and hearing from Thomas about what went on in your last case."

"Yes, I was worried about me also," she said wryly. She got to the point quickly. "Something has come out of that case that I wanted to talk with you about."

Clair raised her eyebrow questioningly.

Emma smiled and continued. "That's actually why I asked you here today." She recapped Millie's case for her and said,

"Mr. Carlyle left me his entire estate and asked that I do something of value with it. I started thinking about you."

"Me? What could I have to do with this?" Clair asked in astonishment.

"Let's sit and discuss it. I see you ordered a lovely tea," said Emma warmly.

Clair nodded distractedly. They moved to sit at the table, enjoying their tea before Emma continued the discussion about the inheritance.

"I'll need to set up a trust to manage the money and determine what causes we want to help. I also need a manager to guide that trust and communicate with board members." She reached over and touched Clair's hand. "I would like that person to be you."

Clair was stunned at Emma's request. She sat for a long moment taking in what this could mean. What it could mean for her and Thomas.

"We would, of course, work a salary out and continue investing so the money can build and continue to be used for good," stated Emma.

"What about my current business?" asked Clair, taking the offer very seriously.

"It's your business, but my suggestion is that you hire a manager—someone you trust—and give them the opportunities you were given. You wouldn't have to sell it, but you could start limiting your time there."

"You've given me a lot to think about." Suddenly worried that Emma might be ashamed of her business, she asked, "Would you want me to hide my past in this new role?"

"No, not at all," said Emma, looking Clair in the eye. "This is about taking chances on people and giving them opportunities. I think you'll be the perfect person to offer them the help they need. I also think you would be able to tell the sincere proposals from those that are not."

Clair teared up and could not speak for a moment. She cleared her throat and said, "I'll need to discuss this with Thomas, and I may finally say yes to his question."

Something occurred to Emma, and she said in an excited voice, "Would that question be 'Will you marry me?'"

Clair blushed. "Yes."

Emma jumped up and went around the table to hug Clair. "Where will you have the wedding?" she asked excitedly, planning.

Clair interrupted her with a grin and a laugh. "I should probably tell Thomas first."

They sat back down and continued discussing their men.

After a few moments, Emma ventured a question that had bothered her. "Can I ask you something personal?"

Clair smiled and waited. Their relationship had always been close.

"How were you able to own your business and the house? You had mentioned a benefactor when we first met."

"Well, that is a very personal question, and I was just thinking of him when you mentioned giving a chance to someone. It was my father."

"But I thought. . ." said Emma, remembering what Jeremy had told her he'd learned from the census records.

"Yes, it's true I didn't know who he was most of my life. A lawyer contacted me to let me know my father was dying and he had no other children to leave his estate to. He wanted to help me get what I wanted, and what I wanted was to purchase the house and run my own business. I was able to work out a deal with the previous manager. She was eager to move on."

"And the shelter you run?" Emma asked.

"It was his house," she said simply. "I kept it and turned it into something useful."

"It's that kind of thinking we'll need to build the charity," said Emma, knowing she had chosen the right person.

"How soon until we know if the charity will happen?" asked Clair, wanting to make plans of her own.

"I will be headed to New York to confirm the money and the selling of large assets," Emma said.

"Alone?" Clair teased, knowing who Emma was seeing.

"Well, no," Emma admitted. "I thought of asking Jeremy to come with me."

Clair stopped teasing and asked in a more serious voice, "Do you have any questions for me?" Emma knew she meant questions about Jeremy and their private time together.

"I do." They spoke in low tones, sharing secrets.

CHAPTER 7

*E*mma met Jeremy later that evening at a nice restaurant for dinner. She brought up the subject of New York. "Jeremy, I have to go to New York to get the final settlement for the will. I'll also need to review the list of assets and the house in New York."

"When will you be leaving and where will you stay when you get there?" he inquired, thinking about the trip.

"I'll be setting it up for next week, and I'll stay at Mr. Carlyle's house. I need to meet with staff as well as Mr. Beeker. I told them to retain the staff until we can work out the next steps."

Jeremy reached out his hand and covered hers. "Emma, I'd like to go with you." Before she could say anything, he continued, "This time, I'd like to share a compartment with you."

"With you, as a couple," she murmured. She tilted her head at him, considering his suggestion. "I want to have you go with me as a couple, but you are aware that I do not want to get married."

"I do know that," he acknowledged. Emma had always been honest with him.

"And you still want to be with me as a couple?" she asked, knowing it could be a dealbreaker.

"I do. Emma, I love you in whatever form that takes, married or not married. It doesn't matter to me as long as we're together," Jeremy said.

"But if we get involved that way and you change your mind about marriage or kids. . ." she said with downcast eyes, worried she'd hurt him.

"Emma, look at me." He waited until she met his eyes. "I won't. I love you and we'll be on the same path together," he promised.

"Jeremy, I love you, too. I would love for you to go with me to New York," she said, tears welling up in her eyes.

He laughed and said, "Now that's settled, let's eat." They finished out their evening with a long walk home.

CHAPTER 8

$\mathcal{E}$mma contacted Andrew Burns, the lawyer for the estate, and had his office arrange the tickets for her trip to New York City. She sat down with her family the night before leaving to discuss her plans.

Dora commented, "It's remarkable that Mr. Carlyle left the money for such a wonderful purpose."

"Yes, and I think Clair is wanting to change her life. This could do it." She had told Tim and Dora her choice for manager and Clair's response.

Tim said seriously, "She certainly knows how to deal with money." He asked, concerned for Emma, "I know you've made this trip previously, but would you like some company? Someone, to go along with you to speak with Mr. Beeker?"

"Jeremy is coming with me on the first trip for introductions and review of the New York City property," said Emma evenly, not displaying any emotion.

Dora squinted at Emma; she knew that tone. Emma was hiding something. She gave her one last long look but decided to not interfere, for now.

"Good. I know this is your project, but I think taking someone is a good idea. He could also offer observations of Mr. Beeker," said Tim, relieved Jeremy would be accompanying her.

Emma wanted to tell Dora that Jeremy was going to share her compartment but decided it was better to keep quiet.

CHAPTER 9

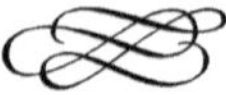

"You are going to New York with Emma?" asked Cole, pacing by Jeremy's bed.

Jeremy watched him out of the corner of his eye as he answered. "Yes, to help with the business side of things from Mr. Carlyle's will." He continued working on folding his shirts and putting them into the suitcase

"Hmm, is that the only reason?" Cole asked, finally standing still.

Jeremy smiled absently and continued to pack. "No, I like being with her."

"Jeremy," Cole said rather forcefully, waiting until Jeremy looked at him. "I don't want her hurt."

"Honestly, Pops," he dropped down on the bed beside the carpet bag, "she's the strongest woman I have ever met. Nothing happens to Emma that she doesn't want to happen."

"She is a rather independent woman, isn't she?" Cole said thoughtfully

"She is that. Pops, I love her so much. I would never hurt her," stated Jeremy simply.

"Maybe I should speak with her about you," he gently teased. Jeremy smiled a crooked grin in response.

CHAPTER 10

The next morning, Jeremy helped Emma down from the hired cab and handed the carpet bag to her. They made their way to the train and into their private compartment. As they closed the door behind them, Emma removed her hat and patted her hair. Before they could sit, a knock sounded at the door. She answered, finding the steward outside.

"Is there anything you need?" he asked.

"Right now, just privacy," she said as she slipped him some money.

He recognized her from previous trips and grinned. "That shouldn't be a problem."

Emma turned back to Jeremy after she closed the compartment door, leaned against it, and said, "Off on another adventure we go."

Jeremy grabbed her and pulled her to him for a long, thorough kiss. When they came up for air, she placed her hand on his chest and pushed back playfully. "Well, enough of that for now. Let's get settled." They unpacked in the compartment and pulled out books to relax with on the long train ride.

Jeremy patted the seat and said, "Come sit with me."

She sat and leaned into him. As the train started to move, she sat up to remove her jacket. "Would you mind if I remove my boots?"

"No, go ahead and get comfortable," said Jeremy, who had already opened his book to read.

One day turned into another, with Jeremy and Emma sharing the compartment, food, and books. They got to know each other more intimately and, as they pulled into the Buffalo station, Jeremy leaned over and kissed her, saying softly, "I love you."

"I love you, too."

They exited the train, carrying their bags, and moved to the daily train that would take them to New Jersey. They settled into their new compartment, with Emma laughing at Jeremy's antics. They completed the trip with a prearranged carriage ride from New Jersey into New York City. Jeremy looked over at Emma and asked, "Do you find it odd we're staying at Mr. Carlyle's house?"

"No," she said, shrugging. "It's mine until I sell it. Mr. Burns mentioned that some of the help will get retirement pensions and others will hopefully be offered jobs with the new owners."

"Tell me about Mr. Carlyle's man of business, Mr. Beeker. You met him on our last trip. Can we trust him?" Jeremy asked, curious about the man managing such a large amount of money.

"I had Tim check him out. He has an established business and Mr. Burns didn't have any concerns with the way the estate has been managed."

"Okay," Jeremy said, pondering, and decided he would look the man over when they had their meeting.

The carriage pulled up in front of the familiar large stone home. Jeremy just shook his head; he had forgotten how big it was.

Emma smiled faintly and said in a wry voice, "I guess I don't have to go in the back door this time."

Jeremy acknowledged this with a smile as he jumped down from the carriage. "Here, let me help you down," he said. He turned and reached to assist her from the carriage. The driver handed down their bags, which Jeremy took and thanked him for. They completed the transaction and approached the door.

The butler must have been watching for her because the door opened before they could knock. He looked down from his tall height and said, "Welcome back, Miss Evans."

She said formally, "Thank you, Mr. Cummings."

"Won't you come in?"

They nodded and entered the foyer. Jeremy placed the bags on the floor and looked around. Emma glanced at Mr. Cummings and said, "We are very sorry for your loss."

"Thank you, Miss Evans." He nodded in acknowledgment. "How long will you be with us?" he asked in a solicitous manner.

"About a week. We're here to review the books for the estate. We do appreciate you staying on until we get things settled," Emma said sincerely.

"Mr. Carlyle took good care of us and we will stay as long as we are needed," he said as he cleared the emotion out of his voice. "Would you like to see your rooms?"

"Please," she said and saw the sideways look Jeremy sent her. She didn't return it as they followed Mr. Cummings up to their rooms, located next to each other. They each went into their separate rooms. Emma laid her bag on the bed and sat next to it, studying the large room. She heard a door open and glanced toward it, but didn't see any movement.

"Psst." Emma looked to her left and saw Jeremy had entered her room through a side door.

"Interesting feature," he said suggestively.

She laughed and asked, "Mr. Cummings tell you about that?"

"He was the sole of discretion," he reassured her. "He just mentioned it as a feature of the house and thought I might want to know. How can I not take advantage?" he asked as he pushed her back on the bed. He quieted her giggling by kissing her thoroughly.

They "rested" and made their way slowly downstairs for lunch. Afterward, they met the rest of the house staff in the study to let them know they would only sell the house to someone willing to take on the current staff. There were sighs of palpable relief from the younger members. Emma said to the group, "Please let Mr. Cummings know if you would like to stay on with the new owners." With that final comment, Emma and Jeremy exited as Mr. Cummings took over the meeting.

Jeremy and Emma took the rest of the day to settle in and enjoy a quiet evening at the house. The meeting with the accountant, Mr. Beeker, was scheduled for 10am the following day.

CHAPTER 11

The next morning, Emma and Jeremy arrived at the office and were met by Mr. Beeker. Emma introduced Jeremy to him, and they shook hands.

"Emma, I didn't expect to see you so soon and under this circumstance," he said in a solemn tone, offering her his elbow. "Will you both accompany me to my conference room?"

The room they entered was large and had a long narrow table surrounded by ten chairs on each side. Those chairs were empty. "Have a seat, please," he said, indicating the two chairs toward the end of the table. He sat across from them and opened his logbook, saying, "Mr. Carlyle's organization is run by agents within this office. We'll have each one come in to discuss the investments and strategies they are managing."

As the day progressed, agent after agent explained their part in the organization. Emma's head began to spin with figures. This was far bigger than she'd realized, and she knew she couldn't do it alone. She would need to be able to interact with her business manager routinely. After the interviews were finally completed, she looked at Mr. Beeker and said in a serious voice, "Our home base is Chicago, and it will be difficult to be kept apprised of the financial situation from that far away."

He looked thoughtful and said, "I have thought about that and most of my staff is willing to relocate. We would leave a small contingent here to give us access to local investments. "

"I like that," said Emma. "I've selected my charity manager, and it would be nice if the business and the charity were in the same building."

Mr. Beeker nodded his head in agreement. "I would also recommend a board to vote on the direction of the money and the accountability."

"Yes," she said, "I had thought of that, and I've selected a board I trust. I'd like to get some money released as soon as possible so I can get the offices going and an initial budget set up."

Though he was surprised at the speed of her decisions, he thought quickly and said, "We can arrange a bank account and a line of credit in Chicago. We'll also need to scout locations for our offices."

"I can help with locations and building availability," suggested Emma.

That statement made something click for Mr. Beeker and he said, "That's right, your father is Ellis Evans. I have seen some of his work here. We would, of course, appreciate the help. Purchasing or a long-term lease is what I would recommend."

She nodded, liking that idea. "I agree. We can review what's available and make the decision together. I'd also like to include the charity manager." She looked through her notebook and asked, "Can you give me an update on the status of Mr. Carlyle's property here in New York?"

"I've given that some thought and, as you asked, I inquired about selling Mr. Carlyle's house." She nodded. "The offer is here," he said, handing her the contract. She looked at it and handed it to Jeremy to review. He went through the documentation on the house and nodded that he thought the offer was good.

"I would like to remove some things from the house-books and some carpets, painting, and books. Will that be a problem?" she asked.

"No, I don't see a reason that should be a concern."

"We will also need to have access to the house until after the financial matters are settled."

"Of course."

"Could you send me a copy of the paperwork? I'd also like to review it with my lawyer in Chicago. Have they said if they will take on any staff who may not want to retire?" she inquired.

"Yes, you can take that one with you for your lawyer. As to the staff, I made the deal contingent on keeping any staff wanting to stay," Mr. Beeker replied.

"How will the money be handled once a decision is made?"

He went on to explain the sale of the house. They also reviewed setting up lines of credit for the charity and how the bills would be paid through the business offices.

"Mr. Beeker—" she started.

"Geoff, please," he interrupted.

She smiled. "Geoff, I will be arranging for a third-party audit of the books."

He looked surprised but not upset. *A good sign,* thought Emma.

Geoff commented, "That is a good idea. We're ready. Do you need suggestions on what companies you might want to use?"

"No, I have someone who can either manage the work or will arrange for the third party to manage it," said Emma.

"I am looking forward to working with you," he said sincerely.

"I am also, but I want to confirm the numbers first," she said cautiously. She was holding off on final approval until the audit was completed.

"Are you meeting with the auditors while you are in town?" he asked, curious about the timing.

"I am," she confirmed. "I'll select one and let you know the timing."

They shook hands and said their goodbyes. After they climbed into the waiting carriage, Emma said, "Jeremy, you've been very quiet. What's your impression of Mr. Beeker?"

"I didn't see anything in his behavior that showed he was hiding something. He answered your questions and seemed open to the audit," he said thoughtfully.

"Yes, I noticed that also. I'm glad you saw what I saw," she said consideringly. She leaned over and kissed him softly on the lips. "Thank you for coming with me today."

They talked about the meeting on the way back to the house. As they arrived, Mr. Cummings let them in, saying, "Miss Emma, there was a note delivered for you." He handed it to her.

Emma opened it, reading silently.

"What is it?" Jeremy asked, noticing she seemed very happy.

She looked up with a smile. "Mark's parents. I let them know we were in town. They would like us to have dinner with them." Jeremy and Emma had met Mark a few years ago when he tried to pick their pockets. Emma had offered to send him books if he stopped the criminal activities. He agreed and they started exchanging books through the mail. Thinking out loud she said, "We need to go to a bookseller before heading over."

"When are we expected?" Jeremy asked.

"Tomorrow night, so we have time to get the books in the morning," she said.

"So, we have tonight alone?" he asked, moving toward her in a vaguely menacing manner. She laughed and eluded him by dashing into the living room. "Think you are safe there? I can still get you."

Mr. Cummings smiled and quietly stepped away to give them some privacy.

Emma let him back her into a corner, saying, "Well, I could always pull my knife on you or—"

Jeremy interrupted her with a deep kiss and suggested in a low voice, "How about a nap upstairs?"

"I do think I am a bit tired. . ." They both laughed and went up to their separate rooms.

That evening, Emma and Jeremy went to dinner at Delmonico's, enjoying a good steak dinner and a quiet pleasant conversation.

CHAPTER 12

The next day, they headed out to a local bookseller to find *Twenty Thousand Leagues Under the Sea: A Tour of the Underwater World*, a classic science fiction adventure novel by French writer Jules Verne. They kept looking and found *Frankenstein; or, The Modern Prometheus* by English author Mary Shelley that told the story of Victor Frankenstein, a young scientist who created a hideous creature in an unorthodox scientific experiment.

After purchasing the books, they spent the rest of the day speaking to various accounting firms. Emma wanted to choose the best fit for the audit. She was drumming her fingers on her lips and reviewing her notebook. She looked up toward Jeremy, lowered her hand, and asked, "Jeremy, what did you think? Which one do we pick?"

"I think we saw the same things today. The companies Tim recommended are all good and appear to be very thorough. I would say when you choose, make sure the reports and findings are sent directly to you," he suggested.

"I was also wondering about the payments for this. I'll need to get the account set up to pay them myself, that way it's not coming directly from the company being audited," she commented thoughtfully.

"Yes," agreed Jeremy.

Emma made up her mind and sent a note to the companies she had interviewed, confirming her choice. She asked them not to contact Mr. Beeker. She would take care of that herself.

The evening came quickly, and they dressed for dinner with Mark and his parents. They took a carriage to the family's apartment and found it in a working-class neighborhood. It was nicely looked after, and the family lived on the third floor. Jeremy knocked and, while they were waiting, they could hear running shoes on the floorboards.

The door opened quickly to reveal Mark. "Emma! Jeremy!" he shouted.

"Mark! How are you?" asked Emma, happy to see him again.

"Mom!" he called out loudly over his shoulder. "Emma and Jeremy are here!"

"I can see that," his mom said wryly, coming up behind him. "Come in, come in."

They entered the small hallway of the apartment, following her and Mark to the living room. The furniture was older looking but in good condition. The side tables were full of novels and textbooks. She knew from Mark's letters that his parents worked for the school system as teachers. Her husband joined them, and the introductions began with Mark's father saying, "We'll start. I'm George, and this is Elizabeth."

Emma smiled broadly. She pointed to herself, "Emma," and then to Jeremy, "and Jeremy."

Mark interrupted the introduction when he saw Emma was carrying a package. "Are those books?" he asked eagerly.

Laughing, Emma held the package up. "What, these?"

"Yes!" he said in an excited voice. "What are they?"

"Give them a minute," said Elizabeth. "Let them sit down."

They moved to the sofa with the family filling in chairs around them.

Mark looked so expectant that Emma gave in and handed him the books. They watched as he tore the paper off. *Twenty Thousand Leagues Under the Sea: A Tour of the Underwater World.* "Wow. Have you read it?" he asked, already flipping through the pages.

"I have," commented Emma.

"I have also," said Jeremy.

"There is a second one," reminded George.

Mark looked like he didn't want to put the first down, but he was curious. He picked it up and tore the paper off of the second book and exclaimed, "*Frankenstein!* I have heard this is really good."

"If you notice, it was written by a female author, Mary Shelly," prompted Emma.

"Oh?" Sounding disappointed, he put it down and picked up the first book again.

"You know," said Jeremy nonchalantly, "there is a monster in that second book."

"Really?" Mark asked, starting to sound interested. He retrieved the book to give it another look.

"A very unusual monster," commented Emma.

"What is unusual about it?" asked Mark curiously.

"Well, you'll have to read to find out," she commented. "It's really good. You'll have to write me your impressions."

Elizabeth tapped him on the shoulder and said, "Why not put it away for now and you can read it later."

Mark nodded and got up to take them to his room.

"I have to admit," said George, "that I enjoy reading the books you've sent. In fact, Mark has set up a lending library for the neighborhood. He's also quick to let people know if they haven't returned the books promptly."

Emma and Jeremy smiled. She responded, "We're very glad

you found an outlet for his energy, something other than criminal enterprises."

"Did you find out anything about how he got involved in pickpocketing?" asked Jeremy, curious how a kid from a good family with money would get into trouble.

"The Whyos gang," started George as Mark came back into the room and sat on the edge of his dad's chair. "They were recruiting the local schools and this one likes adventure," he said, patting Mark on the back.

"It sounded like fun," Mark said defensively.

"Was it fun to get caught?" Elizabeth asked, an edge to her voice.

"No, definitely not," he answered, holding up his hands in response.

"Mark, has the gang approached you since you stopped working for them?" asked Jeremy.

He avoided his eyes and his mom walked over to him and took him by the chin, saying, "Mark, Jeremy asked you a question. I think you should answer it."

As she released his chin, he admitted, "They have."

"Have they been threatening you?" asked Jeremy.

"No, not really, just offering candy and other things. I didn't accept anything," Mark said, hoping the conversation would end soon.

"I'll leave the 'other things' until later. Are you still talking to them?" asked Jeremy.

"No!" He lowered his tone and continued, "No, I'm not. I stay after school and help with classroom stuff and I take my books," he looked at Emma, "to read. When I know they're gone, I leave with the teachers."

"Smart," approved Jeremy and looked over at his parents. "I'll have the local police keep an eye on the school grounds."

"Thank you," said George in a relieved voice.

The conversation went on to more casual topics as they

moved into the dining room for dinner. The food was good and the conversation was full of books. The evening wrapped up and they hugged each other as they were leaving, promising more letters and books.

"Emma," inquired Mark as they were leaving, "can I come to see you and Jeremy in Chicago one day?"

They looked at one another and nodded. "Yes, we would love for you and your parents to visit."

"We'll plan something," Elizabeth promised.

"Jeremy, could I speak with you for a moment?" George asked.

"Yes, of course," he said and they both stepped away down the hall, speaking in low tones. Jeremy and George finished their talk and shook hands.

Jeremy took Emma's hand as they said their goodbyes.

"That was lovely," commented Emma on their way to the house, enjoying their carriage ride home.

"Yes, such nice people," commented Jeremy.

"What did George want to talk to you about?" she asked curiously.

"He wanted to confirm that I'd follow up with the local police on the activities around the school," he said absently.

"That's good. Do you foresee any problems?" she asked, worried for Mark.

"No, I have several officers I trust to check into it for me," he said as he heard her breathe a sigh of relief. "There was something else."

"What was that?" she asked.

"He wanted to know if things don't get better if we could help them relocate," he said, waiting for her response to the request.

"Of course," said Emma immediately, liking the idea of having Mark and his family closer.

They went silent, each thinking about Mark and his family.

CHAPTER 13

The next morning, Jeremy headed to the police station to talk to his contacts and ensure Mark would be protected at school. He arrived back at the Carlyle house in time to pack for the trip home; they would be leaving that night.

Jeremy sat on Emma's bed, watching her finish packing. "Any problems with getting help to watch the school?" she asked, still folding her blouses.

"No. The officer I spoke to, Mac—Steven Mackenzie—will look into it. He's going to take a personal interest because his nephew goes there also," he said in a distracted voice.

"Well good." She sat next to him and said, "We've completed all of our tasks."

He nodded and seemed to make up his mind about something. He said, rather abruptly, "Emma, I love you so much, and I don't want to be apart from you when we get back home."

"Me either," she said laying her head on his shoulder. "Let me think about how that might work."

"If anyone can figure this out, it will be you," he teased.

They descended the stairs and said goodbye to Mr. Cummings and the other staff. Emma promised she would keep them informed about any new owners. She gave them her contact information, and they headed out to the station via carriage.

The travel home was bittersweet, knowing their time together would be limited. Emma would continue to work on how she and Jeremy could be together in a more permanent manner. In the meantime, they would have memories of their stolen moments together.

They arrived back in Chicago, descended the train's stairs, and walked slowly toward the waiting carriage. The trip home was made in almost complete silence. When they stopped at the boarding house, Emma found herself with tears in her eyes.

"None of that now. This isn't forever," Jeremy said, reaching over to wipe her tears.

Emma nodded. "I know. I'll see you soon."

"Yes," he said quietly and hopped down to help her out of the cab. He handed the carpet bag to her and climbed back in, waving as he was pulled away.

She was a little down as she went into the house, but she shook it off.

"Emma," called Dora from the kitchen. "Is that you?"

"It is," Emma called back.

"Come in here and tell me how it went."

"On my way," she said. She left her bag in the foyer and started to unbutton her jacket as she made her way to the kitchen. As she entered, she saw Dora was in the middle of making Brotchen rolls.

Tim sat at the table with his books opened. He smiled broadly as she entered, saying, "Emma, it's so good to have you home. It's been quiet without you." He winked at Dora.

"Tim's right, we've missed you," she said as she finished up the last of the Brotchen rolls and placed a towel over them to allow them to rise. She moved around the table to hug Emma. "Sit. Tell us about your trip."

"It went well. I was glad to have Jeremy there with me," she said, looking down at her notebook. She didn't notice the look Dora and Tim shared. She glanced up from her notes as she started to describe the financial company she had met with.

"Were you able to meet with the audit companies?" asked Tim.

She confirmed that she had met and named the company she had selected.

"That's a good company," Tim said approvingly. "You were able to confirm there is no connection between the auditors and the financial company?"

"I didn't disclose what audit companies I interviewed with Mr. Beeker. Jeremy and I interviewed each one, and the one I selected had no past audit experience or other business dealings with Mr. Beeker," she said in a business-like manner. She looked closely at Tim and said, "You're right, it's a good idea to have you there to oversee the audit."

Tim looked thoughtful and said, "I'll have one of our more experienced temporary accountants help to manage our business while I'm gone." He looked over at Dora. "Can I tempt you into going with me?"

Dora said, "Yes, but I have the same issue with coverage here."

"Well, maybe not," said Emma slowly.

"What are you thinking?"

Instead of answering her, Emma looked over at Tim and asked, "That boarding house next door. Is it still available to purchase?"

Tim nodded and said, "They haven't had any buyers."

"Make them an offer," she said decisively. "I have my money from the Baker office job, and I have all of my savings." She had already given some of her savings to help with the expansion of the bakery and liked the idea of owning more property.

Tim had the cost of the house along with their amounts in

savings. Dora sat quietly contemplating this new business venture and said, "Please include me also." They always made an effort to keep the boarding house business separate from the other business, but this decision would mingle Tim, Dora, and Emma's money.

Tim ran the numbers and said, "We can do it. If you both are okay with it, I'll make the offer tomorrow."

"Is there anyone living in the house currently?" asked Dora.

"No, it's empty and will require some repairs," said Tim. He had already investigated the details.

Emma looked at Dora and said, "I know the boarding house is your domain, but may I make some suggestions?"

"Yes," said Dora cautiously.

"I assume you'll want to manage both?"

"Yes, I'd like to use my experience to get them organized."

"There would be no one better for the position," teased Emma, knowing Dora enjoyed her work. "I think we can all pull together on this. Papa can review the structure for any additions or renovation recommendations." Something occurred to her. "Dora, won't that be too much responsibility if it requires you to cook here?"

"I hadn't thought of that. We would need double staff. And I think it's time to consider a full-time cook and helper here also." Dora seemed a bit troubled by that.

"Dora, that would mean you would manage the boarding houses, but wouldn't have the cooking or cleaning responsibilities," said Tim.

That brightened Dora up and she said, "I like that." She looked over at Emma. "Do you still have the contact information for Mrs. Spencer?"

"Yes, she's decided to stay in Chicago. She has no reason to work, but you might be on to something. The last time I saw her, she indicated she was bored," Emma commented.

"You mentioned she was a talented cook and with the case

resolving her son's murder, I hope that she might be open to working for us," said Dora, thinking out loud.

"She cooks beautifully. I think she'd like that," said Emma.

"So, that would give me Mrs. Spencer there," Dora said making notes.

"What about Bessie for Amy's role there?" asked Tim.

"Bessie? Hmm, that might work. Harold is still trying to save money and that would give them some stability." Harold and Bess were current boarders, saving to have a family. "I'll approach her," Dora said continuing to take notes. "I'll put some figures together to see what would be fair."

"What about your position here?" asked Tim.

"Let's get both houses organized and then we can get an additional cook," she suggested. *Amy might want to move into that position.* She would have to talk to her.

Tim agreed and moved forward quickly with the purchase. He went in with a lower offer than they were asking because the house would need some modifications to be converted into a boarding house. The offer was accepted readily.

CHAPTER 14

Emma took over watching the renovation details while Dora and Tim went to New York for the audit. She had arranged for them to stay at Mr. Carlyle's house. The house was still owned by the estate and would not move to the new owners for another month. Mr. Cummings had been notified of the guests and the reason for their visit. Tim would oversee the movement of items that Emma had made a list of and had also arranged an audit space with Mr. Beeker. He and Dora would be away for three weeks.

Before they left, Dora had contacted and interviewed Mrs. Spencer for a future new role and a temporary role while she was out of town. Mrs. Spencer agreed and reviewed the menus and duties with Dora and Amy. Amy would help guide her while Dora was away. Living in would not be necessary, as she owned her own home and enjoyed her privacy. Tim also had his temporary help set up. The person would work out of his apartment and keep in contact with their workers until Tim returned.

While the renovations were underway, Jeremy stopped by. Emma took him on a tour of the new house.

"Nice. Is Dora okay with the changes?" asked Jeremy.

"Yes, she's excited, and it's another investment for us," she said, looking around.

"What about the current boarding house. Any changes there?"

"I've been thinking about that," she admitted as they walked over to the original boarding house. "We have Molly moving out to the new house, and we also offered a larger room to Bessie and Harrold at a higher price. Harrold is doing well, and he and Bessie enjoyed the boarding house environment."

"So, who does that leave living here?" he asked.

"We're keeping Jake here and I was thinking we could ask Savannah if she would like to move in also."

"So, a house of specialists?" he teased.

"I think it would also allow Tim and Dora to have extra rooms for children," she commented softly.

He smiled broadly and asked, "Are there any announcements?"

"Not yet." She laughed. "They're just working on it." She opened the door, and they entered the foyer. She nodded toward her right and asked, "Sitting room?"

"That would be nice," he said. The room was empty, and it would give them a few private moments. He sat down, thinking about the changes in the boarding houses. He rubbed his chin and said contemplatively, "That leaves the room next to yours still open?"

"Yes," said Emma, looking at him. "What are you thinking?"

"Remember that door at Mr. Carlyle's house, between our rooms?" he asked in a low voice.

"How could I forget?" she whispered back, leaning into him.

"I was wondering if we could put one in your room, connecting to the one next door?" he asked.

"I'm not sure," said Emma doubtfully. "A door would be rather obvious."

"Not if," he paused and raised his eyebrows, "we hide it behind bookshelves that we could fashion to slide out of the way when we wanted to be together."

"I like that idea," she said, smiling at his ingenuity. She pulled out her notebook, saying, "I can draw up the plans for us."

Jeremy watched her draw and offered comments on how it might work. "We'll need to reinforce the wall before we add a door."

They spent the day adding to the drawings. "What type of mechanism would you use on the bookshelves—to make them slide more easily?" she asked, showing him her drawing.

"Maybe some types of wheels or rail," he suggested.

"Hmm, I'll have to ask Papa about that," she said, oblivious as to what that would entail.

"Hmm," he mocked, "maybe not your Papa."

"Oh, sure," she said, blushing. "We can work on it privately."

"What's the next step?" he asked.

"We have to be up front with Dora and Tim," she said in a firm voice.

"How do you think they'll react?" he asked.

"I'm not sure," she said, tapping the drawings in her hands, "but they know to expect surprises from me."

"This is true," he said. "Yes, that's something we should probably do in person." He pulled her close. and said, "Come here, I have something else to confer with you about."

CHAPTER 15

The renovations were going well as Emma continued to monitor and document their progress. About a week into Dora and Tim being gone, Mrs. Spencer had settled into her job as a cook at the boarding house. She and Amy were getting along very well. So well, in fact, Mrs. Spencer developed a habit of staying after dinner was cleaned up to talk with her.

After dinner one evening, Jeremy was in the sitting room reading while Emma worked on her lace designs. A knock sounded at the door and Jeremy said, "I'll get it." He put down his book and stood up to walk to the door.

He came back in and Emma looked up, asking, "Who was it?"

"Telegram, two of them," he replied, holding them up.

"Two?" she asked as he handed them to her. "Looks like one from Tim and one from Dora."

Emma opened the one from Tim first, curious about the audit. She read out loud, "The audit is going well. Nothing in the books is out of the ordinary so far." She looked at Jeremy and smiled. "Excellent news. I'll follow up with an official confirmation to Mr. Beeker. It's time to start shopping for an office location."

"That's good. Who's the second note from?" he asked.

"Dora," she said. "I wonder why two notes." She opened the second envelope and her expression changed abruptly. "Oh no!" she exclaimed.

Jeremy walked over to look over her shoulder, asking in a concerned voice, "What is it, Emma? Is something wrong with Dora?"

"No, it's not that. I contacted Mark and his family to let them know Dora and Tim were in town. I thought it would be nice if they got together," she explained, accidentally crushing the telegram with her stress.

"Yes, that does sound nice, so what's wrong?" he asked, seeing her distress.

Emma continued, "Dora said they've sent several notes to Mark and his family but have not received any contact back."

"Emma, there could be any number of reasons for that," he reasoned.

"Yes, that's true," she noted, calming down.

He could see she was still troubled and suggested, "I'll reach out to Mac and see if he can go by their place."

She took a deep breath and let it out slowly. "Okay, I guess I've been worried since we spoke with them about Mark still seeing those men at his school."

"I'm sure they're just busy and not able to answer Dora's notes. I'll send a telegram now," he said as he grabbed his jacket.

"Thanks, Jeremy," she said, relieved.

"Anything for you." He kissed her quickly on the way out. He made his way directly to the telegraph office to send the note, making his way back to the boarding house to say goodnight to her before heading home.

CHAPTER 16

It would be several days later before Jeremy's contact sent a note back. When he received the reply, he sent a cab for Emma with a note to meet him at the Pinkerton office.

Emma arrived at the office and raced up the stoop. As she entered, the agent in the outer office motioned to Jeremy's office. She nodded and went to the door, entering without knocking.

Jeremy was in a serious conversation with Cole when she entered. They stopped talking when they saw her and Jeremy walked over to greet her. "Emma, I'm glad you could come right over."

"Jeremy, what's happened? Did you find out something about Mark and his family?"

Jeremey smiled slightly; Emma was always thinking ahead. He abruptly got serious, saying, "Emma, we had Mac check out Mark and his parent's apartment. They weren't there."

She sat down heavily in a chair near the desk. "Could they tell if they left voluntarily or were taken?"

"Mac said he couldn't tell. He did say it appeared that they left in a hurry or there could have been a scuffle. Chairs were found turned over, items on the floor."

Cole asked, "Would it be normal to find their home like that?"

"No," she said and looked at Jeremy with raised eyebrows.

He nodded and said, "Agreed. They appeared to take pride in their apartment. It was very neat and clean while we were there. Also, Mac checked with their school, they haven't reported to work in more than a week."

"Jeremy, tell Mac to make sure the place is secure. We also need to find out who owns that building," Emma said.

"What are you thinking?" asked Cole.

Looking over at him, she said, "I'm not sure, but at a minimum, we need to verify their rent is paid until they're located and their items secured." She looked at Jeremy and asked, "Was the lock broken?"

"No," he responded, "that didn't appear to be the case and the door was closed and locked when he got there."

"That doesn't mean they weren't taken," she stated, drumming her fingers on her lips.

"Agreed," said Jeremy.

"It could be either at this point," commented Cole.

Emma asked, "Jeremy, do you think the Whyos went after Mark in his home?" She didn't let him answer and continued. "Did Mac say anything about the situation at the school?"

"The Whyos gang is a possibility. It's odd," he mused, "that they're going to such lengths to get to Mark."

"Mac's note also said that, since the family's disappearance, there's no one hanging around the school," said Cole.

"Where do we go from here?" asked Emma, feeling like she needed to be doing something.

"We think," said Jeremy, nodding at Cole, "that I'll go to New York to see if I can find out what's going on."

"Okay. When do we go?" she asked, thinking ahead to what preparations they would need to make.

Jeremy turned to Cole. He got the silent message and stepped quietly out of the office. Jeremy waited until the door closed and turned to her. "Emma, I'm going alone."

"Why do think I wouldn't be going?" She was completely confused by this turn of the conversation. Jeremy never told her she couldn't do something.

He wanted her to see reason. "Because you need to stay; you have responsibilities here." His voice softened. "You know Dora and Tim are counting on you." He could see that she was going to interrupt him, and he said quickly, "We don't actually know if anything has happened."

She still looked defiant but said out loud, "What do you plan to do?"

"Go there," he said simply. "I'll look around and try to find out what might have happened." He could tell she was upset at not being included and said, "Emma, I know you care about what happened to this family. I do also, trust me to look into this."

They stared at each other for a long moment, before Emma said with a sigh, "Jeremy, I do trust you. I'll stay here." She narrowed her eyes at him and added in a mildly threatening manner, moving a hand toward her hat, "You will let me know what is happening."

"I will," he promised with a smile. "No need to pull your knife." He drew her to him and gave her a long kiss.

She pulled away and laid her head on his chest. "How long will you be gone?"

"With trains, over two weeks," he commented. When she didn't say anything, he said, "I will miss you."

She snuggled closer. "Me, too." She thought of something and said, "You can stay at Mr. Carlyle's house."

"Thank you, that would be nice," he commented, smiling

into her hair.

"I'll contact Mr. Cummings to expect you." She sat up, pulling out her notebook to take notes.

"Also, a telegram to Dora and Tim might be a good idea," he suggested.

"I'll do that," she said. "I'll head over there now."

Jeremy said regretfully, "Yes, we need to get going. I'll stop by the train station to get my tickets." They shared a long kiss and slowly separated. They walked out together and parted at the stoop.

Emma went directly to the telegraph office. She opened her notebook to read off her note, *Tim, thanks for update on audit. Good news. Renovations go well here. Jeremy will be in NY in a week. Notified Mr. Cummings to have room ready. He will be checking in on Mark and family's possible disappearance.*

They would have questions, but the note should relieve them that someone was looking into the situation. She sent a second note to Mr. Cummings: *Mr. Cummings, Jeremy will be arriving for 1-2 week stay. Please assist him as needed.*

She thanked the telegrapher, made her payment, and headed home.

That afternoon, Emma was with Jeremy at the train station. "Send me a telegram when you arrive," she reminded him. She remembered the package she was holding, "Oh, and this is from Mrs. Spencer—sandwiches and other snacks."

"Thank you," he said, grateful for the food.

As they parted, she watched him board, then turned away to go home. As she was leaving, she noticed two Pinkerton men also boarding the train. "Curiouser and curiouser," she muttered, quoting Lewis Carroll. Jeremy must be taking this disappearance more seriously than she thought.

Jeremy, though, was watching from the train and saw his men arriving. *Emma missed them,* he thought. *Good.* He had the men with him, as a contingency, to help if Mark's family was taken.

Emma was in the carriage on the way home, thinking about the agents she had seen boarding the train. Jeremy hadn't indicated he was taking Pinkerton personnel with him. "But," she mused, "it was a smart thing to do if he runs into trouble." She wasn't bothered he hadn't mentioned the agents; he was taking the lead on this case.

She did have responsibilities here, and sometimes life required one to stay home and let other people have the adventure. "Growing up," she supposed.

CHAPTER 17

This trip is less entertaining than last time, Jeremy thought, opening his book to read. He laid it on his chest, thinking of their plans. When they arrived, Mac would meet them, and...

He dozed off with the rocking of the train.

CHAPTER 18

*E*mma visited the neighboring boarding house to check on the work being completed there. Bags clanged with tools as the workers were finishing up for the day.

Hearing her name called from the stairs, she looked up and saw Mara descending from the upper floor. She was dressed in pants, a loose shirt, and had a cap pulled over her blond curly hair.

Emma smiled broadly. "Mara, how are you?"

"I'm really good," she replied, happy to see Emma. They had met when Emma was helping out Mr. Marella on a case involving Mara's family a few years before. The case ended on a positive note, and her family was happier after secrets were revealed. Marco, Tony's brother, and Mara had started seeing each other soon after the case ended.

Chicago 1883. Emma hadn't expected to hear from Mara after the case came to a close. It had been over a year since she had talked to her. The note she had sent over asked Emma to meet for lunch. Emma confirmed the date, time, and location, then went into the meeting with a bit of trepidation, wondering what Mara might want. *Was she going to be angry or confrontational?*

Emma had gotten to the restaurant first and sat at a table, enjoying the bright sunny day. The windows were open, and wind teased the curtains. The tables were set with bright blue and white tablecloths. She ordered a tea service while she waited.

The tea had not yet arrived when she saw Mara in the doorway. She was dressed in a yellow and white afternoon dress, just showing her boots as she walked. She appeared to be very cheerful. Seeing that helped Emma release some tension.

Mara walked right over and said, "Emma, thank you so much for meeting me."

She stood and greeted her with a kiss on the cheek, saying, "I was surprised to get your invitation."

"Yes, I could see you might feel that way," she said with a slight smile. "Please, sit. I would like to talk with you."

"All right," Emma replied curiously.

They both sat as the tea service was delivered. They took a moment to order their lunch. As the waiter left, Emma looked toward Mara with eyebrows raised in question.

Mara started abruptly. Emma could see she was nervous and waited to hear what she had to say. "I wanted to speak with you about working with Mr. Marella's crew. I want to learn how to be a plumber."

Emma laughed out loud. "You know, I thought you wanted to talk about what had happened last time we saw each other."

"No, Emma," she said as she reached out and touched her hand. "That's the best thing that could have happened to our family. Dad and Grandfather are so close now. They are rarely out of each other's company."

"That is so nice to hear. So many times, my cases end with someone being hurt or taken to jail. I do like this better. How is your father doing?" Emma asked, honestly interested in the wellbeing of Mara's family.

"He's so much better now that he doesn't have to hide anything. I think Grandfather has gotten him to talk about what happened in the war. It has been good for him and us," Mara stated, tearing up a bit.

"I am so glad," Emma said simply. She thought for a moment about her original question and murmured, "Okay, how to approach getting you on as an apprentice." She drummed her fingers on her lips. She thought about how to approach Michael, then looked Mara in the eyes. "I think you should meet with Michael one-on-one, without Marco. Show him this is your idea and that it's for your future."

Mara tilted her head at the comment and replied, "I see what you mean. This is for me. I always wanted to be useful and learn a skill." She considered the advice and said, "Okay. I'll try that. Thanks so much for helping me. I so want to be skilled at something useful."

Emma smiled; finding someone so like-minded was nice. They continued discussing their futures and things they would like to achieve as their lunch arrived.

Soon after, Mara took Emma's advice and approached Michael at a job near her home. Emma had indicated that it was the best place to see him about being an apprentice plumber. Michael was surprised by the request, but with Emma in their lives, he was aware girls were changing, wanting to do more. He talked to her for a long time and tried to work out if she was serious or doing this to be around Marco. He watched as he talked to her. She wasn't giggling as though hiding a secret and her clothes were sensible.

Mara stated clearly that, though she enjoyed Marco's company, that he had nothing to do with this. She suggested a trial period and, if she worked out, then she could start her apprenticeship. He considered this and asked for a few days to think about it. He also wanted to speak to Marco about how he would handle working with Mara.

That evening at the apartment, the Marella family sat around the living room, having enjoyed a nice dinner. Michael looked at Marco consideringly and called his name.

"Yes, Dad?" Marco said absently, reading the paper.

"I'm thinking of taking on another apprentice plumber," Michael said nonchalantly.

"Anyone I know?" he asked absently, not looking up from his paper.

"Marco put down your paper and pay attention. I have something important to talk to you about," requested Michael, wanting to see his expression when he told him about Mara.

Marco abandoned his paper slowly and said, "Okay, I'm listening."

"Mara came to see me today," Michael said laconically.

"Why would she do that? Is she okay?" he asked, suddenly worried.

"She's fine," he reassured him. "She wants to begin an apprenticeship to work as a plumber."

Marco suddenly smiled. "That would explain many of our conversations. She's always asking the technical details of my job."

"What do you think? Could you handle working with someone you're courting?" he asked, ready to tell Mara no if it was against Marco's wishes.

Marco considered this for a moment and said, "I would have to be professional at work. No courting?"

Dad nodded. "And there will be a trial period, so if you think you can't handle it, we can end it at that time."

Marco mulled that over and came to a decision. "Dad, I can handle it. If this is something she wants, we should help her achieve it."

Michael liked seeing how much his son had matured. He

nodded and said, "I'll send her a note now and tell her to begin working with us on Monday."

Marco checked his watch. "I need to get organized for tonight." He was meeting Mara soon to take her to the dance.

A little while later, Michael knocked before entering Marco's room.

"Come in," called Marco.

Michael entered and saw Marco getting ready to go. He said, "Marco, Mara sent a note saying she was looking forward to working with us on Monday."

"Good," Marco said as he finished brushing back his hair and did a final check on his clothes. He walked into the living room with Michael.

Mrs. Marella smiled approvingly. "You look nice."

The other boys, Enzo and David started teasing him. "Yeah, Marco, you look SOOO nice."

"Thanks, Ma," he said, pointedly looking at his mother, ignoring his brothers.

"Don't stay out too late," she cautioned.

"I won't." He leaned in to kiss her on the cheek on his way out.

Marco headed to get the wagon so he could pick up Mara for the dance. He pulled the wagon to the front of her house, jumped down, and walked to the door. Before he could knock, Christopher pulled open the door, asking excitedly, "Marco, how are you?"

"Is Mara ready?"

"Christopher, let Marco in," called Mara's dad, James Saunders. He entered the door and met Mr. Saunders in the Foyer.

"Mr. Saunders, hello," said Marco, watching how he seemed to smile more easily.

"Mara will be a moment. Would you like to come into the sitting room?" he asked.

"Thank you. Mara mentioned you're working in the garden

much more lately," said Marco, showing a genuine interest as he sat down opposite Mr. Saunders.

"Yes. We're evaluating new fertilizers, looking at what a plant needs, such as nitrogen and phosphate, to flourish."

"Where are you getting your information from?" asked Marco, wondering about this business of working with dirt.

"We are looking at these," Mr. Saunders said, indicating the stack of magazines and books next to him. The pile included the magazine *Amateur Gardening*, the books *British Apples* by A. F. Barron, *The Garden: Its Art and History* by Jacob von Falk, and *Handbook of Tree Planting* by Nathaniel H. Egleston.

Marco heard a soft voice call his name and turned around. When he saw Mara, he stopped and didn't say anything. "Marco, are you okay?"

"You're beautiful," he said simply.

She blushed prettily and turned to her mom, who stood at her side, to kiss her goodnight. They said goodbye to her family and went out on the porch.

"I was expecting pants," he teased as he walked her to the wagon.

She stopped and turned to him. "Marco, I'm sorry I didn't tell you, but I wanted to do this on my own."

He nodded and said, "I love that independent spirit in you, Mara. I just hope there'll be a place for me also."

She leaned in to kiss him. "Always," she murmured. They kissed for a long moment.

They broke apart laughing and Mara said, "We should head to the dance."

"Yes," he said, feeling content as he helped her into the wagon.

Mara started her trial with them the following Monday. She worked hard and was professional. Marco took the situation seriously and kept his attitude professional as well.

At the end of the three-month trial period, Michael decided it was time for a meeting with Mara. He asked the boys to head back home, saying they would follow behind.

Mara entered the room where Michael was working. "Did you want to see me?" she asked, nervously pulling off her hat.

Michael smiled, trying to put her at ease. "Mara, I wanted to speak with you about your work."

"Yes," she said, afraid to say anything more.

"You've been doing a wonderful job, and I want to take you on as a full-time apprentice," he said warmly.

She opened and closed her mouth, before saying, "You do?"

"I do," he confirmed. "So, we'll need to sit down and map out our plans for you to learn the business." He cautioned, "It won't happen all at once. There will be steps to follow."

"I'm ready," she commented, eager to begin her new career.

"I want you to come by on Sunday evening, and we'll begin

setting up our strategies and learning opportunities. You'll watch and learn, the next steps will include you doing the work with supervision, and then you'll work independently," he explained.

"I understand," she said in a serious voice.

"Now, we need to talk about Marco," he added. "I won't interfere with your being together, but we want to keep the same atmosphere we have had the last three months at work," he said in a kind but firm voice

She replied in the same tone, "I agree, Mr. Marella. I appreciate this opportunity."

"You know," he said, giving her a long look, "you remind me so much of Emma. I just had to give this a chance."

That made Mara smile since Emma was her role model. They walked out together, heading home, talking softly.

Marco and Mara continued to work together for the next two years and were together when they were off of work.

They were sitting quietly in the park one day when Marco turned to her and asked, "Mara, I waited to ask you to marry me, I know you wanted to complete your apprenticeship before we made any plans. Will you marry me?"

She looked at him, wanting to blurt out a yes, but she hesitated. "I know the wait was hard. You understand that I want to continue to work?"

"Yes," he said, knowing how important that was to her. There had been too many times in her life where she felt helpless, unable to support her family. She didn't want to be put in that position again.

She continued to ask questions. "And that cooking and cleaning will be split between us?"

"Hmm," he said with a smile. "I figured that might be the case. I spoke to Emma about a room in the new boarding house we're working on, to see if there was space for us. She said there was."

She grinned and asked, "Thinking ahead?"

"Of course," he said, still aware she had not answered his question.

She looked up at him, eyes shining, and said simply, "Yes."

"Yes!" he said exuberantly. He pulled her over for a long kiss. He pulled away and grabbed her hand and they headed home, almost running to tell both families. They were overjoyed with the news.

Marco sent a note to Emma confirming that they would take one of the extended rooms when it was ready.

CHAPTER 20

1884 BOARD HOUSE RESTORATION

"How is it going up there?" Emma asked, pulling out her notebook.

"Really well. The water piping is just about done. They're removing and reinforcing some walls up on the second and third floors," Mara said professionally.

"For the extended rooms," commented Emma, watching Mara turn red. She followed up with another comment. "I hear there's a wedding coming up."

Mara was still blushing but appeared to be very happy. "Yes, as soon as the boarding house is completed, we'll have the wedding at my family home and then move in here. We'll be sending out invitations soon and would like you and your family to attend."

"We will be there," Emma said sincerely.

"I'm so happy that your family bought this boarding house. It will be lovely to live here," she said, thinking of Marco and their future.

"I'm glad we'll have you and Marco as tenants. It'll be nice to have friends close by."

"Well, back to work," Mara said, picking up her tool bag and heading to the kitchen. Dora had left definitive instructions about the renovations in that area. Emma followed to make notes and sketches to send to Dora for her review and approval.

CHAPTER 21

NEW YORK CITY

Jeremy exited the second train in Buffalo with the two Pinkerton employees following. He had prearranged a carriage to take them to New York. They arrived and stopped by the Carlyle house to drop off their bags.

Mr. Cummings greeted them at the door. "Mr. Jeremy, we are happy to have you back. Will all of you be staying with us?" he asked, looking at the men accompanying him.

"No, just me. The men will be at a local hotel. Would you mind if we leave our bags here? We need to look into something that can't wait," Jeremy inquired.

"Yes, I will take them and put them away until you return. Should I tell Miss Dora that you have arrived?" Mr. Cummings asked.

"You may tell her and let her know I'll see her this evening."

"Of course." Mr. Cumming gestured to the two-footman standing in the foyer to move their bags.

"Could you also see that Officer Mackenzie at the 3rd precinct gets this note?" Jeremy asked.

"Of course, sir," he said and took the note from him. "I will have it sent over now." He snapped his fingers and the footman across the room walked over quickly to take the note.

Jeremy and the Pinkerton men left immediately. Their carriage stood waiting for them, and Jeremy gave him Mark's apartment address. He also notified Mac to join them there.

As they arrived, Jeremy told the driver he would no longer be needed and paid him. He and the two Pinkerton men climbed down from the carriage and headed into the apartment building, finding Mac waiting outside the unit.

He saw them approaching and he put his hand out in welcome, saying, "Jeremy, good to see you."

"You, too, Mac. Can we go in?" Jeremy asked, shaking his hand firmly.

He turned and opened the door. "Yes, I had it re-keyed so it would be secure until the family returned."

"Thank you for thinking of that," Jeremy commented as they entered the apartment. He looked around the long hallway and into the living room. It was much different than the last time he'd been there. Mac was correct when he said it was in a disarray; chairs were turned over, and papers lay scattered on the floor.

One of the Pinkerton men took the time to evaluate the door. "Jeremy, this doesn't appear to be a break-in. There was no splintering of wood on the doorframe." He looked over at Mac and asked, "Do you still have the original lock set?"

"I do." He pointed to a side table. The Pinkerton detective looked at it, saying, "There are no scratches that would indicate it was picked and no other damage."

They continued through the rooms, looking for anything that might tell them if the family was taken or if they had left of their own free will. Jeremy wished he had looked closer when they were last there.

Emma would have remembered everything, he thought wryly. He checked the closets and saw that their clothes were gone. If the family didn't leave of their own volition, then their abductor was smart enough to make sure the clothes appeared to be taken from closets and drawers.

Jeremy moved down the hall and into Mark's room and immediately noticed the one thing only he and Emma would have known to look for. He scooped up the incriminating items and rushed back into the living room. "They were taken."

"How do you know?" Mac asked curiously.

"These," he said, indicating the books he carried. "Mark would never leave his books, especially ones he hadn't read." Jeremy knew this was the one thing that would have gone with them. He wondered if Mark had done this deliberately, knowing he or Emma would not miss that detail. *Smart kid.*

"Okay, so what next?" asked one of the Pinkerton detectives.

"First," said Jeremy, "I need you and Paul to go door to door asking if anyone heard or saw anything. Also, find out who they pay rent to. Hopefully, that leads us to the owners."

As they left, Jeremy turned to the officer. "Mac, is that person still hanging around the school trying to recruit kids?"

"He's back since I last checked for you. I've been keeping an eye on him and, so far, he hasn't done anything I could take him in for," he commented.

"When is he usually there?" asked Jeremy.

"Early, when school starts."

"Okay, so we meet with him first thing tomorrow. Until then, let's keep it quiet. Agreed?" Jeremy asked Mac.

Mac agreed readily as they waited for the Pinkerton agents to complete their sweep of the building.

After Paul and Joe returned, Mac asked, "Did anyone notice anything out of the ordinary?"

"Not much. They didn't hear anything unusual."

"Interesting. This is definitely a professional kidnapping and not a spur-of-the-moment event," Jeremy said thoughtfully.

Paul opened up his notebook and said, "We did get the

manager's name and went down to his apartment, but he didn't answer."

Jeremy said, "We'll check in with him tomorrow." They formed a plan for the morning and split up. "Mac, thanks so much for your help."

"When a family is involved, I want to help," said Mac sincerely. "I'll meet you tomorrow morning near the school, the alley at Barnard Street." With that, he headed back to the police station.

Jeremy hailed a cab to return to Mr. Carlyle's for their bags. Once there, he turned to Joe and Paul. "Be here at 9am. You have the location of your hotel?"

They confirmed the time and the location, then made their way out of the house with the assistance of Mr. Cummings.

After Mr. Cummings showed them out, he returned to Jeremy and said, "Miss Dora would like you to see her after you get settled."

"Thank you, Mr. Cummings. Is she in the sitting room?"

"No, sir. She is in the kitchen," stated Mr. Cummings.

"Kitchen?" inquired Jeremy with a smile. He should have known.

"Yes, I believe she is working on different recipes with our chef," he said.

"Of course. I'll go see her as soon as I put my bag up and wash my face," said Jeremy.

"Follow me to your room," said Mr. Cummings.

Jeremy did as he was told. After he was refreshed, he went downstairs to see Dora. *It is a large house*, he thought as he strolled down the grand staircase.

When he reached the foyer, Mr. Cummings reminded him, "Through the dining room."

"Thank you," commented Jeremy and he headed to the kitchen. As he opened the door, he noticed the room was large and white. He immediately saw Dora and someone he assumed was the chef sitting at the table.

Dora was in a conversation about how to make macarons. "Jeremy," she said, seeing him enter. "Come here."

He went over and kissed her on the cheek as a hello.

"It's so good to see you," he said. He looked around and inquired, "Where's Tim?"

"The audit takes up most of his days. He'll be here this evening," she said matter-of-factly.

"How is it going?" he asked, hoping to avoid delving into any questions about Mark and his family.

"Really well, from what I understand. Tim says the investments are sound. They're sending out runners to the companies being invested in, to confirm facts. It takes time," she said.

"Yes, I can see that," he said thoughtfully. "Emma said the boarding house renovations are going well."

"I got a telegram from her detailing them and some other news." She pulled the note from her pocket and read aloud, *"Marco and Mara are engaged and want a double room at the boarding house."*

"That's great!" exclaimed Jeremy.

"Jeremy, this is Chef Jacques Bernard. We've been sharing recipes," she said with a smile, indicating the man sitting beside her. "This is Jeremy Tilden; he is visiting with us for a few days."

"So nice to meet you. Your food is wonderful," Jeremy commented sincerely, remembering the meals from his prior visit.

Chef Bernard bowed his head politely. "Thank you."

"Jeremy, let's move into the sitting room," Dora said in a tone that brooked no denial.

He nodded and followed her out of the kitchen. She kept her serious expression as they sat down and asked expectantly, "Why are you here? Are Mark and his family in trouble?"

"I can't share much," he said, and she looked trouble at his response. He qualified his statement by saying, "I don't know much yet. I have two men here with me and an officer from the police department. We're investigating and I promise I'll share information as soon as it's safe to do so."

"You sound like Emma," she muttered. "I understand and will try to be patient."

Hoping to distract her, he said, "Tell me about your trip. What have you seen since you've been here?"

Dora's face changed immediately, and she said excitedly, "Jeremy, they finished the East Street Bridge! We were able to walk across it. It's amazing!"

"You know, when Emma and I were here last, we didn't think to check on its completion. You'll have to show me," he suggested.

"I wish Jake were here so he could photograph it," she said.

"That would have been wonderful. I'm sure we can get him a visit soon," Jeremy suggested.

"Yes, I'll have to bring him back here at some point," she said, liking that idea. She missed seeing him daily.

"Would he be okay with the change in schedules?" Jeremy asked, knowing that Jake liked things to be in a certain order.

"If I keep his schedule about the same, with food and sleep, he should be just fine," Dora commented.

They continued to enjoy each other's company until Tim came home that evening. They were helping set up dinner in the dining room when they heard someone in the foyer.

Tim entered quickly, saying hurriedly, "Sorry I'm late."

She went over to him and asked, "Long day?"

"Long enough," he said, rubbing a hand on his neck.

He noticed Jeremy and walked over to him. "Welcome. Nice to see someone from home. Emma let us know you would be arriving. Anything to share on Mark and his family?" Tim knew some parts of the investigation process were kept quiet to protect the people involved.

"Nothing in particular yet," Jeremy said. "We have some leads to follow up on in the morning."

"How did you prevent Emma from coming with you? I can't imagine she was happy about it," Dora said with a smile.

"No, not at first, but she realized she had responsibilities to you both and your businesses," he explained.

Tim started asking questions about the renovations. Before Jeremy could answer, Dora put her hand on Tim's and said, "Let's eat first and talk about that after."

He nodded, realizing how hungry he was. They sat down at the table as Dora let Chef Bernard know they were ready for dinner. The macarons were brought out for dessert.

With dinner over, they moved into the sitting room. Tim couldn't wait any longer and said, "Tell us about the renovations."

Jeremy smiled. "Emma has Michael Marella's team working on water and gas piping. As I understand it, the larger rooms are almost ready."

"How many?" asked Tim. He didn't know about this development.

"It looks like two. Emma sent a telegram over this morning. It seems Marco asked Mara to marry him and would like a joint room," explained Dora.

"Like ours," said Tim. Jeremy wished he could bring up the idea for him and Emma, but this wasn't the time.

Dora smiled. "Yes, it'll work well because Mara doesn't want to have to cook and clean with her current workload."

"I understand that. They'll be good tenants. The second boarding house is filling nicely," Tim said.

"Yes," said Dora, "one less worry."

They talked about the audit and then relaxed with their books. It was a nice, quiet evening.

The next morning, Jeremy woke early and was able to get breakfast from the chef before Paul and Joe arrived Standing, he started to the foyer, when Mr. Cummings entered to announce that Paul and Joe were waiting in the foyer. Jeremy thanked him and exited the dining room. He greeted them and said, "Let's head out." They climbed into the waiting carriage and went to meet Mac at the school.

They arrived about a block away from the school at the predetermined location. Mac stepped out of the alley and gave them a description of the man they were looking for. He was disreputable-looking, with a rumpled brown jacket and badly cut hair.

"What's the plan?" asked Jeremy as they got a visual on the man.

Mac looked over and said, "I'll get him." He did just that; he had him by the collar before the man in question knew Mac was there. He hauled him over, asking Jeremy, "Where to?"

"The Sutherland's apartment," said Jeremy. "It's the best place for this discussion." Everyone nodded in agreement. They transported the now quiet man in a carriage to the apartment.

"Recognize this place?" Jeremy asked as they entered.

"Why would I?" he asked belligerently.

"Because you know where Mark and his family are," stated Jeremy.

CHAPTER 23

CHICAGO

Clair arrived at the boarding house for the first time in her and Emma's association. Emma had some guilt over the fact she hadn't invited her there before now. She thought she was watching out for Clair's feelings and those of the people at the boarding house. But that was probably not true; if she was honest with herself, she felt uncomfortable with Clair's occupation. It was fascinating but only from a distance. It was time to have her at the house.

Emma was making notes in the dining room when she heard a knock on the door. "I'll get it," she called out. She made her way to the door, knowing who was there. She opened the door and said graciously, "Clair, please come in."

Clair smiled and looked a bit nervous as she entered. She wore a lovely deep green dress with a matching hat. She removed it, patting her hair. "Emma, it's so good to see you. Thank you for inviting me over."

Emma looked her in the eyes and said sincerely, "No, I should've made this happen much sooner." She reached out and touched her hand. "Clair I'm sorry this invitation wasn't made long ago."

Clair hadn't realized the meeting would affect her emotions and had to wipe a tear off her cheek. "Well, I'm here now, that's what's important."

"Papa's in the study waiting for us. He has a list of buildings and properties for us to review." She saw Mrs. Spencer come out of the dining room as they passed. Emma paused, looked over, and said, "Mrs. Spencer, could you bring the tea service into the study?"

"I'll bring it in a few moments," she said quietly

"Thank you, Mrs. Spencer. This is Clair Edwards. Clair, this is Mrs. Spencer. She will be our cook at the new boarding house next door," Emma said. She noticed both Mrs. Spencer and Clair were very tense. *What is wrong between these two?* Emma asked herself. "Clair is our guest, and we will be polite to her."

"That's okay," said Clair, visibly upset. "Maybe I should leave."

Mrs. Spencer said to Clair, "I'm sorry, you are welcome." She looked down at her feet, seeming bothered by something. She looked up at Clair and said, "You don't recognize me?"

Clair blotted her eyes, ready to say no, but she took a moment to look at her more closely. "Aren't you Susan Single-ton?" she asked in amazement.

"I was," Mrs. Spencer confirmed quietly.

Emma was confused and looked between the two. "Do you know each other?"

Mrs. Spencer said, still looking at Claire, "In a previous life, when I was much younger."

"So was I," said Claire ruefully. "I believe you had a son?"

"Yes, I left the life because I wanted to keep him. He was murdered."

"Was that one of your cases, Emma?" Clair asked.

"Yes," Mrs. Spencer answered for her.

"I am sorry for your loss," said Clair sincerely.

"Thank you," she said graciously. "I'll go get the tea now."

"Thank you, Mrs. Spencer," said Emma quietly.

As they watched her go, Emma turned to Clair and asked in a low voice, "Was she?"

"One of the girls? Yes. She was already a bit older when I started and had her son by that time. She was always in the kitchen helping out. It looks like she turned that into a way to get out. Good for her," Clair said sincerely.

"Yes," said Emma. *People are so complicated*, she thought to herself. She motioned to Clair to follow her. As they entered the study, they saw Papa bent over his desk, reviewing drawings.

"Papa," Emma called. "Clair has arrived."

He looked up and smiled. "I finally get to meet you." He strode over and took her hands in his. "It is so very nice to meet you. I've heard so much about the things you have accomplished."

Clair seemed shocked at the statement but responded calmly. "I've heard about you also. It's very nice to meet you. I understand you have some recommendations for the location of our new venture."

He smiled and said, "I do. Come over and see. Emma, you know most of these buildings." They eyed the drawings and Papa started going over the list.

"Emma and I figured you needed a space with a large meeting room, an office for you, and a secretary. Clair, have you thought of what other staff you may need?" Papa asked.

She looked consideringly over at him and said, "I was thinking we would need at least two secretaries and an assistant to help me and one to help with scouting charity investigations in the field."

Papa said admiringly, "Clair, that's perfect thinking. You're right, all requests must be investigated to make sure they are deserving of the help."

"Papa, how about a space with two floors? We'd be able to have the financial people with us, too," explained Emma.

He nodded and said, "I like that idea. Clair, what do you think?"

"Yes, I think that's the right idea. Is there a building we could own outright that maybe had four stories?" asked Clair, thinking ahead.

"Yes, I think I have the one." Papa flipped through his list. "The address is 3339 Smith Street. Would you both be interested in seeing it?"

Emma looked at Clair and back at Papa, saying, "We would."

"Great. Let's go." He started out of the room just as the tea service was delivered.

"Papa," Emma suggested gently, "how about we have our tea first?"

"Oh, sure, we can do that," said Papa, looking a bit distracted. They went back into the study, sat down, and enjoyed their afternoon tea and cakes.

As they finished, he asked impatiently, "Now may we go?"

"Now we can go," Emma acquiesced.

They toured four buildings that day, but the last building Papa had picked was a new one with four stories located downtown. He had been involved in the building design and pulled the structural drawings to review. He wouldn't let them pick a building unless it had been reinforced to withstand a fire.

"Can we go in?" asked Clair.

"Yes, I've notified the owner we would be here today," he said, opening the main door. They examined it from top to bottom, letting Clair take the lead.

"We would need to remove some walls and move a few things around," said Clair.

"Yes. You'll also need a kitchen space on the two floors," said Papa.

"Yes, that is a good idea," said Clair thoughtfully. "I like this building. It has everything we need and is in the right location."

"You will have an assortment of art and rugs. I am having

these shipped from the Carlyle house. You will have first choice for the space here," said Emma.

"That is wonderful," she said thinking of all of the design choices in front of her. She looked over at Emma. "What about the financial people? Will they have to approve this before we purchase?"

"I think we should notify Mr. Beeker to come and review it. But I say, if we think this is the one you want, we make an offer today," she said firmly. Clair must be able to make decisions for the charity.

"Papa, can you send the financial information in a telegram to Tim?" asked Emma. He nodded and she looked to Clair for confirmation. "And ask the owners to hold it for us?"

"It shouldn't be a problem. I know the man," said Papa, pulling out a piece of paper to make a note.

"I'll also send a note to Mr. Beeker to come to Chicago to review the building," said Emma.

"What if he doesn't like it?" asked Clair, worried.

"I think he'll like it, but if not, we can rent the other floors out," Emma pointed out reasonably. "Okay?" she asked, looking first at Clair, then Papa.

They both answered, "Yes."

Papa had arranged for their carriage to wait for them. "Can I drop you off, Clair?" he asked.

Emma replied for her. "You can drop off both of us, Papa. I want to speak with her."

"Okay, I'll see you at home," he said absently as he helped them both down at Clair's stop.

They waved bye to Papa, Clair and Emma walked together arm in arm down the street. Emma stopped and asked, "Well, did you say yes?"

"I did," she admitted.

"That is wonderful," Emma said sincerely. They continued to walk. "Have you figured out where you and Thomas will live?"

"We've thought about it and I'm thinking of a house near the business, once we make the offer for the building," she said.

"That sounds like a plan, and it would put Thomas close to the bakery," observed Emma.

"He still enjoys the work, and I would never ask him to stop," Clair said.

"It sounds like things are coming together for you."

"Yes. One other thing I've decided: I'm selling my business to my general manager. She'll pay me monthly until it's paid off. It will remove me from the day-to-day running and allow me a fresh start."

Emma hugged Clair's arm. "I'm glad you made that decision. It sounds like the right thing for you to do."

They hugged and parted ways with Emma to the telegraph office and Clair to her business.

CHAPTER 24

NEW YORK CITY

As they entered the apartment, they sat the man down, and Jeremy moved over to start securing his arms and legs to the chair.

"Hey, that's too tight."

"Yeah, a friend of mine taught me how to make sure you can't get out of these." Thinking of Emma, he said, "You're lucky she isn't here. She's rather fond of knives." Jeremy moved in front of him and said, "Who took them?"

"Took who?" he asked, not looking him in the eyes.

"We are not playing that game. We'll start with the facts." He ticked off on his fingers. "One, you hang around schools to entice children to join your pickpocket teams. Two, I know you continued to hound Mark, but he told you he wanted out. Three, you wouldn't take no for an answer."

"So, what? That doesn't mean I took the three of them," he muttered.

"Three?" Jeremy jumped on that. "We didn't say there were three."

Cornered, the man started talking. "Listen, I'm a low man on this operation."

"What operation?" asked Mac, stepping closer.

"The kids are just part of it," he admitted. "They're the lowest level and, as we spot kids that we can move into other things, then we take them."

"Why Mark?" Jeremy asked.

"He was a problem; that could lead to other kids telling us no. We wanted to grab him as an example to any others trying to get out," he said.

"Why take his parents?" asked Mac.

"He was too protected. He was always with someone," complained the man.

Smart kid, thought Jeremy.

"So, we followed him here and planned to sit on him and get him to listen to reason," the man continued.

"What went wrong?" asked Jeremy quietly, knowing something must have to move from intimidation to kidnapping.

"The parents fought back, and we couldn't take the kid without them."

"Why move them to another location? Why not use this one?" asked Mac, knowing it would take planning to move them without being seen.

"A note arrived saying visitors were coming," the man said simply.

Tim and Dora, Jeremy thought.

"We had to get them out before anyone else got involved."

Jeremy was losing patience and raised his voice. "Where are they? Are they okay?"

"Define okay," the man muttered. When he saw their expressions, he admitted, "They are pretty banged up."

"Where are they!" Jeremy demanded again.

"I can't say," the man said plaintively.

"Can't or won't?" asked Mac.

"I honestly don't know where they are."

"Who would?" Jeremy demanded.

The man mumbled.

"What was that?" asked Mac.

He shrugged.

"Okay," said Jeremy, taking a deep breath. "Where do you think they are?"

He looked away, not answering.

"Hey! Answer him!" demanded Mac.

The man finally said, "Listen, I didn't have anything to do with this after they were moved. But I think I know where they might be."

"We're listening," said Jeremy.

"They probably have them in the East Street Bridge," he said, staring at Jeremy.

"What do you mean in the bridge? The bridge is a bridge, not a room," said Mac.

"Well, my brother-in-law worked on the building of the bridge and he worked on this room they called an anchorage. It has spaces that are 50 feet tall," the man said.

"Stand him up," Jeremy said to Joe. "You're going to draw out a map to this location and then you are going to sit here with this nice man," indicating Paul, "until we retrieve the family."

"Oh," he added casually, "and any moves to escape, Paul has authority to shoot you. Understood?"

"No-no problem," he stuttered.

They untied him, keeping their guns aimed as he drew up the location to the anchorage and how to get there. "It's located inside the base of the East Bridge at Cadman Plaza West at the intersection of Hicks Street and Old Fulton Street in Brooklyn. To get there, walk down Cadman Plaza West toward the river, past the overpass. The anchorage entrance is to the right."

He handed it to Jeremy, who looked at it and then at Joe, saying "Tie him back up and use the method from earlier. We don't want him escaping."

Jeremy folded up the map up and nodded to Mac and Joe to

go on their way. They took a carriage across the bridge to the location indicated on the map. As they were dropped off, they pulled their hats low over their faces. Mac had removed his police jacket and hat. They made their way to the entrance and stayed out of sight.

"Okay, how do we handle this?" asked Joe.

Jeremy said, "We wait for someone to come out, then grab them. We're unsure how far they are into the anchorage."

They didn't have long to wait; a man was approaching a door carrying a bag that looked to have food in it. Mac made hand signals for them to spread out and, as the figure walked up, Mac put a gun to his head and said, "Where are you headed?"

"Nowhere," he said, standing very still.

"Now, why don't I believe that? You have a family locked in there?"

"How do you. . ." he stuttered in surprise.

"How do I know that? I just do. Tell us who's in the space, how far in they are, and if any are armed."

He took a long look at Mac and then at the three guns pointed his way and gave all the details. They put cuffs on him and tied him to a tree. As Jeremy was about to place a gag in his mouth, he said, "Wait. There is a password." He told them and the three approached the door; they knocked and gave "hidden" as the password in a low voice.

The man who answered didn't look at who he was letting in and said absently, "Got the groceries? People are getting hungry in here."

Mac grabbed him from behind and held him with an arm around his neck. Jeremy and Joe had their guns drawn, and Jeremy asked, "Where are they?"

"Down there." The man pointed with his hand.

Jeremy nodded and Mac knocked the man out with the butt of his gun. They laid him down and approached the back of the area quietly. They could see two men and the family there. George and Mark were tied up and Elizabeth was lying on a cot. Mark saw them enter and averted his eyes so as not to give away their position.

Jeremy gave a hand signal to have the men spread out. They had the two men guarding the family covered. There were guns, but they were abandoned on the table and not close to the men. They must have considered the area well protected.

Once Mac and Joe were in place, he said loudly, "You are surrounded! Put your hands up."

The men went for their guns, but Jeremy shot the leg on the table. When the table collapsed, the guns scattered on the floor. The men froze where they were and lifted their hands above their heads.

Jeremy kept his gun trained on the men as Mac and Joel collected their weapons and moved them out of reach. Once all were securely tied up, Jeremy directed them to untie Mark and George. George immediately went to check on Elizabeth.

"How is she?" asked Jeremy.

She opened her eyes, moaning, holding her bruised face. "Are you okay?" asked George softly.

"Yes, I was very dizzy when they first hit me, but I'm mostly okay now. I figured it was better to pretend to be worse than I was," she explained, sitting up slowly.

"That was smart," said Jeremy, watching them hug each other.

Mac stated, "We need to get everyone out now. I'll take these men in for kidnapping and you'll be questioned at your home. Do you understand?"

They nodded.

"I'll escort the family," Jeremy said.

Mac had arranged for two carriages—one to transport the kidnappers and one to move the family. As they rode home, Elizabeth cried softly in George's arms, relieved to be safe.

Mark waited as long as he could before asking, "How did you figure it out, Jeremy? That we were taken and hadn't run away?"

Jeremy looked over at him and said, "Your books. You left them behind."

He grinned. "I hoped you would notice that. "

"I did and I found it very clever, but I think Emma would have found it faster than I did," he teased.

"I think you're right," Mark said seriously.

"Jeremy, I think we're ready for that move to Chicago," George said firmly.

"I agree. I'll take care of your tickets and see about getting your belongings shipped."

"Jeremy, can I get my books to take with me?" asked Mark anxiously.

That made him smile. "Yes, I think we can arrange that," he commented.

Jeremy would provide protection for them while they packed up their apartment and made their statements to the local police.

CHAPTER 25

CHICAGO

A telegram arrived at the boarding house late that afternoon from Jeremy. Mrs. Spencer opened the door and took the message from the waiting delivery boy.

"Emma, there's a telegram for you," she said as she walked into the dining room, handing it to her.

Emma was working at the table on the documentation for the building they had chosen for their office space. She took the telegram and said absently, "Thank you, Mrs. Spencer."

Emma opened the envelope and started to read. "It looks like we have company coming."

"Is there room here?" Mrs. Spencer asked, wanting to help.

"Yes, we can set up something in the third-floor rooms," Emma said.

She sat drumming her fingers on her lips. She would like to have more details, but those would have to wait until they arrived. *Funny, I thought I would be upset not to be involved in the adventure, but what I am is relieved that everyone's okay.*

Emma continued reviewing the two boarding houses, knowing it would be another few weeks before the renovations were completed. Water and gas pipes were just about done upstairs, and the kitchen remodel had started. The kitchen was the biggest project and was driving the schedule because of the delivery of a new stove and the building of new cabinets. There was also additional support and wall removal for the expanded rooms.

She made a list of the new housing situation that would be in place once the boarding house was available.

<u>New Boarding house</u>

2nd floor: Harold and Betsy, Marco and Mara

3rd floor: Mark, Mr. and Mrs. Sutherland and two open rooms.

4th floor: Molly, her boys, and two open rooms

<u>Current house:</u>

2nd floor: Dora and Tim and two for future

3rd floor: Jake, Thomas (Temp), Emma and one open room

4th floor: Savannah, Papa and two for future

We'll have some openings, thought Emma, *even with Mark and his family. We will have to put notices in the local paper to fill those rooms.* She would have to review that with Dora. She closed up her book, thinking it had been an active day. So many good things had happened.

A few days later, Emma got another telegram from Tim. They would be in New York for another week to finalize the details and head home. She could expect them in about two weeks.

The house should be completed at just about that time.

CHAPTER 26

She spent the next few days working with Amy and Mrs. Spencer to get the rooms ready for Mark and his parents. They opened the windows and aired them out. The sheets were changed, furniture dusted, and floors mopped.

A week later, Emma had a wagon waiting at the train station. She stood inside the station and watched the train arrive. When she saw Mark and his parents disembarked, she called, "Mark!"

He looked around when he heard his name, saw her, and ran toward her. She grabbed him in a tight hug.

"Mark, I am so glad to see you," she said, pushing back his hair on his forehead.

"Me, too. You should hear how Jeremy found us," he said excitedly, wanting to share the story.

"Let's talk about that at home, okay? Right now, I bet your parents want to get settled," she suggested, standing with her arm on his shoulders, waving at them.

"Emma, we're so glad to see you," they said as they approached her.

"As am I," she said sincerely. "Hi, Jeremy," she said softly, kissing him hello. She turned back to the group and said, "I have the wagon with me, so we can get everything at once."

"Where is it?" Jeremy asked, wanting to be on their way.

"Thomas has it over there to the left."

They spotted him and waved. He moved the wagon closer and they put the family trunks and bags into the back.

"Mark, can you ride back here with me and Jeremy? George and Elizabeth, why don't you climb up with Thomas?" Emma suggested.

When all were settled, they started on their way to the boarding house.

"Are we staying with you, Emma?" asked Mark.

"For now. I have rooms set up. We'll talk with your parents to see if you want to stay at the boarding house or find an apartment of your own."

George heard the question and turned to say, "We'll make that decision once we find jobs."

They sat quietly the rest of the way. All were grateful the family had made it safely to Chicago.

Once there, everyone helped take the bags up to their assigned rooms. George and Elizabeth exclaimed how nice it was.

Emma said, "We have breakfast, lunch, and dinner for the family. That includes you."

"Emma, we don't expect to live here for free," George protested.

"Why don't you get settled and we can talk about the long-term plans. Okay?" she suggested.

"Yes," they said gratefully.

She showed them the lavatory and told them snacks were available in the kitchen until the dinner hour. Mark's family convinced him to wash up and rest a bit before dinner. He would have liked to tell Emma all about their adventures, but it would have to wait. They knew Emma wanted some time alone with Jeremy.

Once their door was closed, Emma looked at Jeremy and said, "Want to go to the study for a bit and discuss things?" she asked with a smile.

"That would be wonderful," he said, liking the idea of some time alone with her. They headed downstairs and she closed the door of the study before running into his arms.

"I missed you," she murmured.

"I missed you too," he said, and they kissed long and slow. It would be a while before they came up for air. They finally broke apart with a laugh.

"Okay, tell me about the adventure," Emma said as she sat on the couch, eager to hear what happened.

"Emma, I'm sorry I had to go on my own," he said, sitting down next to her, hoping she wasn't mad she had been excluded.

"No, Jeremy I'm not upset," she assured him. "I realize I have responsibilities here and there will always be more adventures."

"True," he said and started to tell her what had happened and how they found the family.

"Really, a room inside the bridge? I'd like to see that," she said, awed.

"You will. We'll go back sometime and I'll show it to you," he promised.

She got serious. "We have the family out of harm's way here, but what about the kids still there?"

"Mac has made it his personal goal to give those kids an opportunity to get out," he explained.

"How will he do it?" she asked.

"He's planning a watch and raid, where they take the kids for indoctrination," he explained.

"Will it work?" she asked, concerned.

"For a while," he admitted. "The Whyos are integrated

enough to look like they support the cleanup, but I expect it will start again. Gangs like them depend on the lower part of the organization to eventually move up into the other jobs."

"I hope it works out. Maybe some afterschool programs through the charity? I'll ask Clair to look into it," Emma suggested.

Jeremy nodded, settling back on the couch, and asked casually, "Have you given thought to our living situation?"

"Oh, yes. I've mapped out the houses. Let me show you." She went to retrieve her maps from the desk drawer and laid them out for him to review.

He examined the plans and asked questions on how it would work. "This is doable. I think I can do this myself with some help."

"We'll have to get approval from Dora. The boarding house is her domain," she cautioned.

"Then we speak to Dora," he agreed. They settled down and enjoyed each other's company.

Dinner that night was full of stories of Mark and his family's adventures.

After dinner, George said in a grateful tone, "Jeremy, we need to thank you for notifying our school about our family emergency."

"It was that," said Jeremy wryly.

"Will you look for work teaching?" asked Emma.

"Yes, my administrator said he would send a letter of introduction for me. I'll go over to the local school administration tomorrow and find out what my options are. I'm hoping they approve Elizabeth working also," said George.

"Do you expect trouble getting Elizabeth approved?" asked Dora.

"They don't normally let married women work as teachers. I was able to convince them to let me continue working in New York," commented Elizabeth.

CHAPTER 27

Things worked out for George and Elizabeth; both found jobs in the Chicago education system. Jeremy arranged for their furniture and other belongings to be sent down by train. They wanted to make sure the family was happy with the forced decision. They would store the furniture in the new boarding house until their future living arrangements were settled.

Another week went by, Dora and Tim had sent a telegram saying the audit was completed and they were on their way home. Emma was relieved. Dora's job was harder than she'd thought it could be, and she didn't even have to cook.

She went to the train station with Jeremy, this time in a carriage to pick up Dora and Tim. They got off the train—Tim first, followed by Dora. She appeared happy to be home. She ran up to Emma and said, "I'm so glad you're here to get us. I just want to get home."

"How are you, Tim?" inquired Jeremy.

"Good, really good. We can discuss more information later," Tim said, wanting to get them moving. They kept the conversation light on the ride home.

"Mr. Cummings says to send his regards," Dora told Emma. "I also got recipes from the Carlyle's chef to try here."

"Wonderful, you'll have to show me," Emma said.

Jeremy commented with a laugh, "Just make sure you make those macarons!"

"I will," said Dora. She looked over at Emma and explained, "They are wonderful little cookies."

As they arrived at home, Tim kept looking at the boarding house under construction. Dora noticed and said, "Tim, why don't we get washed up and change clothes, then we can take a peek at all of the changes."

Tim was reluctant and finally agreed. "Emma, can we meet down here in twenty minutes?"

"Definitely," she agreed.

They all met downstairs and headed over to review the changes in the new boarding house. Emma brought her map to show them the room layout. Tim was eager and said, "Let's take a look."

It had been over a month since Tim and Dora had seen the house. When they left, the walls were damaged and the floors were covered in debris. What they saw when they entered was a finished house. Floors polished and clean, walls painted and finished.

Emma looked over at Dora and said, "Kitchen first?"

"Please," said Dora readily.

Tim smiled at Emma and nodded. They followed Dora into the kitchen. Dora pushed the door open and stood still for a moment. Emma cast a worried glance toward her through the continued silence.

Dora abruptly turned around and gave Emma a long hug. "It's perfect."

"I'm so relieved you like it." Emma knew it was the one room that had to be right.

Dora walked around, looking at the cabinets and long

expanses of workspace, and observed, "We'll still need a kitchen table and. . ."

As she continued to list out their needs, Tim and Jeremy indicated they were heading upstairs to observe the work that had been completed up there.

Tim yelled down from the top of the stairs, "Emma, can you explain the layout up here?"

Emma yelled up, "I have a map! I'll bring it up." She headed upstairs with Dora.

She showed them the layout she had selected, and Dora and Tim reviewed it closely.

"I like the idea of making some of the rooms bigger and having more long-term people in residence, but if it's two rooms, the rent will be higher," worried Tim.

Emma nodded, saying, "I've asked the boarders about an increase and they agreed. They would like the extra space."

Dora was thinking about the next steps. "We'll need furniture. A dining room table, couches, and chairs for the sitting room and beds."

Tim said, looking at the budget Emma had provided, "We have that covered since the house was abandoned."

"Dora, we can hunt through thrift shops and redo the furniture instead of buying new," suggested Emma.

"I like that idea; it would be a mix of things," said Dora.

They continued the tour, testing the gas lights and plumbing. All were working well. "The Marella's did a good job," said Tim.

"They always do," commented Emma. "And just think, we'll have Marco and Mara living here if something comes up." The group laughed and continued with their review.

Mrs. Spencer and Amy made a nice dinner, and the group met in the study afterward to discuss business. Emma asked the first question, as she pulled out her notebook. "The audit?"

Tim had his accounting books for the charity out. "It went

well. I sent runners out to every investment to confirm they were in place. We certainly didn't want a Little Dori here."

"No," agreed Jeremy, "I'm glad you had the runners go and investigate, so many investments were paper-only businesses."

Tim continued, "We went over the paperwork in detail and met with bank officials. The investments are solid. I've also arranged for the capital we need to start the charity. I have the books organized and I believe we're ready to set up a meeting and a one-on-one review with Clair."

"That's wonderful. Papa, Clair, and I have toured several buildings and found one we would like to make an offer on. Papa has the owner waiting for us to do a final walkthrough, which we saved for when you both got back home," said Emma.

"Mr. Beeker should be here in a day or so to confirm the building arrangements," Tim added.

Dora said with a serious expression, "Emma, we appreciate you staying and helping keep the projects moving forward." Emma smiled and reached for her hand.

Mr. Beeker arrived a few days later and confirmed the space would be fine for what the staff needed. He met with Clair and discussed the charity and how it would run before heading back to New York to start the relocation.

CHAPTER 28

*L*ater that week, after Tim and Dora got settled back into their normal routines, Jeremy and Emma asked them out to dinner. It was a pleasant evening that ended at Jeremy's house. Cole had gone to visit Papa at the boarding house.

They were telling stories to one another and enjoying the evening. Jeremy nodded at Emma, indicating for her to bring up the topic. "Jeremy and I would like to discuss something with you," she started.

Dora looked excited and squeezed Tim's hand in anticipation.

Emma noticed and said bluntly, "It isn't that kind of topic. We aren't planning to get married." This statement caused Dora to go still.

Emma took a deep breath before she continued. "What we want," she looked to Jeremy, "is to be together and we want your support to have him move into the boarding house."

Jeremy took it from there. "We're very committed to one another and know we'll be together for a very long time, and I would like to move into the room next to Emma."

Tim laughed suddenly and said, "Is that all? That will be easy to arrange. We will have the room once the new boarding house is open."

"Well," said Jeremy, "we would also like to make a few changes between the two rooms."

Emma chose that moment to pull out her drawings and showed them the design of an additional door and a bookcase to hide it on both sides, allowing access to Emma's and Jeremy's rooms.

Dora looked confused and then blushed profusely when she understood what they were saying. "But if you do that, what if. . ."

"I get pregnant?" Emma completed the question for her. She was ready for it. "We talked about that," she said. Jeremy took her hand. "We agreed we would get married if it comes down to that. I don't think it will; I just don't feel that I'm meant to have children."

Dora touched her stomach, wishing she was pregnant. It had been years and she was unsure if they would ever have children.

Emma noticed and said sincerely, "It will happen for you. It just takes time."

Tim was looking at the drawing. "We'll have to do this work ourselves to keep it quiet."

"Yes, I thought of that. I'm pretty handy with tools." Jeremy would do anything to protect Emma's name.

While they worked on the design, Dora pulled Emma to her side and said, "What if someone finds out? You know it could be bad, you would be ruined."

Emma tilted her head and said, "From what I have seen, marriage seems to be a fix for things like that. If we get caught, we will consider our options. I am not worried for me but I do not want to affect our businesses."

Dora nodded and didn't say anything further. Once Emma made up her mind, there was little that could change it.

"I can help with some of the final touches. I worked with Tony's family on the job," Emma said.

The two couples agreed. Jeremy would move in and they would keep it quiet. They also chose not to tell Papa or Cole what the actual arrangements were, only that Jeremy was moving in.

When Papa heard this, he decided it was time to give his girls their space. He mentioned his idea to Cole, and he agreed that Papa would move in with him. The "brothers" were together again.

Tim and Jeremy worked on strengthening the wall between the rooms before adding the door. Tim looked at the design again and asked, "Jeremy, what gave you this idea, to attach the rooms?"

Jeremy said, "Well, in Mr. Carlyle's house, they had connecting rooms and it seemed convenient."

"It is that," said Tim, chuckling.

They got the wall strengthened and started cutting a space for a door. Once completed, they finished the woodwork around the entrance and added the door. The bookcases were stationed in each room and Jeremy moved in. Papa moved out at the same time.

Everything was coming together; the new boarding house was completed. Mark and his family had decided to make their home at the boarding house, selling the furniture they weren't using to Dora. Dora and Emma bought additional furniture as well: couches and chairs for the sitting room, dining room table, buffet, kitchen table, and assorted beds and desks.

Tim, Dora, and Emma continued to run the boarding houses, their temporary business, and also kept taking on cases for both the Pinkertons and private clients.

CHAPTER 29

1885-BACK TO THE PRESENT

*E*mma shook herself out of her memories and could hear Jeremy moving around in his room, getting ready for the day. She moved to the side of the bed and stood up. She immediately sat back down, feeling dizzy. *I got up too quickly, that's all,* she told herself.

She tried again and felt a sharp abdominal cramp that made her sit back down again. She took a moment and breathed deeply until the dizziness passed. She tried a third time and, when she did not feel any additional pain, she moved to the lavatory to wash her face. She put the experience out of her mind as she returned to her room to get ready for her day. Cole had contacted her last night and asked her to stop by to review a case with him.

She and Jeremy met in the hallway and descended the stairs. "I think we should get a carriage to the office, that way you have your bike after the meeting."

"I agree." They ate quickly and walked her bike to the street to hail a cab. When they arrived, handed off her bike to one of the Pinkerton staff. Jeremy went to his office and she went directly to Cole's office. She knocked and was called in.

As Emma entered, she was surprised to see a nun sitting by Cole. The woman wore a gray habit with a black hood. *I'll need my best manners for this meeting*, she thought.

When Cole saw her, he said, "Emma, hello. Please join us."

Emma walked over and sat in the chair opposite the couch. She looked over at Cole as he started the introductions. "Sister Catherine, this is Emma Evans, one of our detectives."

"It's very nice to meet you. We do need help with this matter," said Sister Catherine quietly.

"Sister, why don't you describe your concerns and the support needed?" Cole encouraged.

Emma pulled out her notebook.

"The concern involves the Sisters of Charity hospital. We believe someone on our staff is stealing our medication; specifically, our morphine and laudanum," said Sister Catherine, sounding disappointed.

Emma looked up from her notebook to ask, "Do you have a medicine control system in place?"

Sister Catherine answered, "We keep the drugs in a closet, and it's locked. There is a sign-out sheet, and we inventory weekly."

"Who has access to the drug closet?"

"All the doctors, nurses, and some aides have access to the key," she admitted.

"Who has actual custody of the key?" asked Emma.

"Our medical secretary keeps it."

"Where's it kept when he's off of work? I would assume you need access to the drugs twenty-four hours a day?"

She looked a bit embarrassed at this question. "It's kept in a drawer and people that need it, know where it is."

Emma felt a bit exasperated at that answer but kept her tone civil. "Do you have any suspicions?"

"I hope it's not one of our sisters. Honestly, though, given the system, it could be anyone," answered Sister Catherine. "We would like you to come in undercover and observe the activities going on at nighttime. The hospital should be on lockdown with only the Sisters and staff in place."

"We can't make any assumptions at this point. I can be there starting tomorrow evening. What type of job are you thinking of for me?" asked Emma.

"I was thinking of a volunteer; they assist the nurses," she suggested.

"That should work," said Cole. "It will be a physical job, but at night you'd be able to observe staff activities without much notice. Will you do it?"

"Yes, of course," Emma replied as she sat drumming her fingers on her lips, thinking ahead. "Is there a uniform I'll need to wear?"

"Yes, there is a uniform top, but you can wear clothes under it. I'll have that delivered to you," said Sister Catherine.

"Who will I report to?"

"Sister Mary Faith. She's the head nurse at night and runs the staff."

"Is there anything I should know about her?" asked Emma.

"She's very efficient at her job and is good with the patients. She won't know you are there for any other reason than volunteering," said Sister Catherine.

"Do you suspect her in this?"

"I hope not," the woman said.

Sister Catherine finished confirming the information with Emma and Cole before departing quietly.

Emma looked over at Cole consideringly and said, "Cole, this case seems simple, catch the person stealing the drugs, but I am wondering if there is more to it. What are the drugs being used for? It seems more than one person's addiction,"

Cole was stroking his goatee. "Yes, I think there is more to it."

"Do you think the sister knows?" she asked, bewildered.

"I don't think so but we will keep her informed," he said. "Any issues with starting tomorrow?"

"No, I'm between assignments right now. I can do it and I've never worked in a hospital before," Emma commented.

Cole nodded and said, "Keep in contact with me. Hopefully, this is a short-term job, a week at the most. Keep it as observational only and no interaction."

"Are you sure?" she teased.

"Only if necessary and in defense of life," he said seriously, knowing how things could change. "Take your knives with you."

"I'll start tomorrow night," she said as she closed her notebook and headed out, her head down.

Jeremy stepped into her path. "Hi, I thought you would stop by after your meeting."

"Oh hi, Jeremy, just thinking about the new case and I got distracted. It's always nice to see you," she said sincerely.

"I saw the new client. Very solemn."

"Yes, could be interesting, though," she said.

"Share the details at dinner tonight?" he asked.

"Out or at the boarding house?"

"Out. Let's have some quiet time. Alone," he suggested.

"Definitely." She kissed him sweetly and left to work some courier jobs that afternoon.

He watched her go, tapping the folder in his hand. He had just been notified that Zeke Jones had escaped from prison in Washington State. The information did not indicate he was on his way to Chicago, but he would have to put a protective order in for Clair and Emma. He planned to tell both as soon as he got an idea of Zeke's direction. Emma went about her day and stopped by the museum to see Tony. She carried her bike in and the security guards at the door took it for her.

One of them indicated, "Mr. Marella is in his office."

She thanked him and headed that way. As she reached to

knock on his door, it opened. She laughed when she came face to face with Tony.

"I didn't know you were stopping by," he said as he hugged her.

"Well, I couldn't let you head overseas without seeing you. When do you leave?" she asked, walking in.

"In a few days," he responded.

"Do you have time to review the trip with me?" she asked, interested where he would be going and what he would see.

"Of course," he said, pulling out his itinerary. He sat next to her on his office couch. "First, we take the La Bretagne and arrive in Havre before traveling by day train to Paris."

"Where will you stay in Paris?" she asked.

"The Saint Laurent. We have a suite reserved with multiple bedrooms. We'll need to store any artwork we purchase to be shipped home," he said.

"Will you mostly stay in Paris?"

"Yes. But there might be day trips to see various artists in other provinces."

"Will you get to see some sights?" she asked.

"Philip said there would be time to see some palaces and other historical locations."

Emma had a dreamy look in her eyes, imagining it all. "Oh, Tony, I can't wait to see Paris. Are you excited?"

"Yes, definitely, though there will be a lot of work, learning about the different art techniques and such. So much is going on in the art world, and Paris is the center of it all," Tony said.

"How long will you be gone?" she asked.

"More than a month," he responded.

"Wow! You will send me letters and let me know how things are going?"

"Of course. One day, you'll have to visit Paris with me," he said casually.

Emma smiled sincerely at the offer, thinking she would love

to go one day. They talked for more than an hour before she stood, patting her courier bag. "I still have some deliveries to make today."

"Will I see you before we head to New York?" asked Tony.

Regretfully, she shook her head. "I have a new case starting tomorrow night."

"I'll send you a note when we reach Paris," he offered.

"I'd love that! I'll miss you. Enjoy yourself and see everything," she said as she stood and gave him a long hug.

"I'll miss you," he said. She didn't see him wipe at his eyes as she got organized to leave.

Later that night at dinner, Jeremy was asking questions about Tony's trip. "A month? Will the museum here be closed all that time?"

"It'll stay open. They have a business manager for these situations where Philip or Tony aren't available," said Emma.

Jeremy admitted to himself that he was using Tony to delay any communication about Zeke. He would wait to tell her until he knew for sure there was a worry. The conversation turned to her new case. As she described it to him, he was frowning.

"The case seems a bit light."

Emma nodded and said, "I agree. I'm going to approach this as more observation and less action. This could be resolved in one night if a staff member is involved."

"True. Would you like me to meet you to walk home after your shift?" Jeremy knew Zeke wasn't in the area yet, but he did like spending as much time as possible with her.

"That would be nice," she commented, knowing she wouldn't be seeing him at night.

When she and Jeremy arrived home, she found her uniform shirt and confirmation of a time to start work from Sister Catherine. She and Jeremy took advantage of their last night together.

CHAPTER 30

The next morning, she heard Jeremy wake and leave the room quietly, letting her sleep. He knew she needed to rest as long as possible. She didn't want to be too tired on her first night at the hospital.

Much later, she climbed out of bed, dressed, and made her way downstairs for breakfast. *Well*, she thought, looking at the time, *it's after 2pm. It's more like a late lunch and I'm starving.* She opened the door to the kitchen and saw Tim and Dora sitting at the table.

They looked up and Dora said, "We didn't know if we would see you before this evening."

"I slept all I could. I hope I'm able to make it the entire night," Emma said as she yawned.

"Tell us more about the case," encouraged Tim.

"There isn't a lot to share right now. The first night is for observing more than anything. I report at 6pm and should be off around 4am," Emma said yawning as she sat down.

"Will you need to wear a disguise?" Dora asked, handing her a sandwich and an apple.

"No, I can be just myself," she said as she started to eat.

She read and relaxed the last part of the day, getting dressed at 5pm.

"Emma," called Dora, "your meal and snacks are in the kitchen."

Emma went to the kitchen and got her food. "I'm headed to the hospital," she called back.

It was 6pm when she arrived. Even though she wasn't undercover, she didn't want to call attention to herself, so she walked rather than rode her bike over. She had on her white uniform top, a black blouse, and a black skirt underneath it. She also wore a jacket over the top. She saw a Sister at the reception desk and approached her.

As she approached, the Sister said in a commanding voice, "Well, what are you here for? Speak up."

The tone caused Emma to fall silent a moment. She finally said, "I'm here about the volunteer position. Sister Catherine told me I could start my temporary job here tonight."

The sister frowned at her and checked her book. "Yes, I see here you're expected. They're letting girls do this work now?"

Because it didn't seem like a question, Emma waited for her instructions.

"You may go up to the second floor. Sister Mary is in charge there. Get with her and find out what your duties will entail."

Emma nodded and placed her hat back on her head. She made her way up the stairs. A woman was cleaning the floors. As she walked past, Emma sent her a quick smile and got one in return.

She exited the stairs into a long hallway and followed it down to the nurses' station. Several Sisters were working at the desk. As Emma approached, one stood and asked quietly, "Yes?"

"I was told to report to Sister Mary about a temporary job as a volunteer. Sister Catherine set it up," Emma explained.

"I'm Sister Mary," she said. "You may put your things in there." She indicated the small room used for breaks. "I'm glad you have your hair tied up. There will be physical labor, changing beds, and preparing for the morning. Taking water or other needs to patients. You must not take food or water to a patient without asking. At night, when a patient can't sleep, we like to keep an eye on them. Can you read?"

"Yes, I can read," commented Emma.

The sister paused a moment in her directions and sent her an appraising look. "You may read to them if they would like you to. If you have any books, you can bring in, we would appreciate it. Now, let's go through the ward. The patients are kept in one large room. Children and adults are kept together in the same ward."

There was some moaning and crying as they entered. Emma looked around. There was so much to take in. The large ward was filled with so many beds. Sister Mary explained her job duties and sent her on her way.

She spent the first few hours of her shift helping distribute food to the various patients. She moved bedpans and brought blankets. Nurses distributed medication and changed bandages.

It was much later in the night when the ward settled down. She sat with several children, talking to them quietly and telling them silly stories. A Sister came up to her and told her to take a break. She nodded and winced as she stood. The pain was brief and stopped as soon as she started moving.

She made her way into the break area for orderlies. They were sitting talking together. She took her seat and ate her snack of German pancakes and fruit.

Emma finished her snack and sat back in the soft chair, listening to the orderlies talking about their weekend plans. She stood, put away her lunch pail, and left the area. Looking around, she pulled out the map Sister Catherine had sent over with her uniform and made her way around the floor.

She reviewed the areas listed: the main ward, offices, nurses' station, and finally the long hallway to the supply closet. After ensuring she was alone, she nonchalantly tried the lock, which appeared intact. *Well, that's good,* she thought. Quickly, she pulled a pin out of her hair and kneeled to pick the lock. As the tumblers clicked, she turned the knob and entered the small room.

She pulled the door shut behind her and secured the lock. The small room didn't have any lights, she reached into her pocket and pulled out a small portable gas lamp. Once lit it, she held up the light to see the drugs lined up in vials and bottles. Labels identified each one. She shook her head. *The first thing I'm going to recommend is a stronger lock.* As she looked around the small room, she noticed the closet was just big enough to have several shelves on her left. There was also a table with some storage underneath. Suddenly, the sound of shuffling steps and a rattle of keys sounded. She dove under the table, shoving blankets in front of her.

It was one of the Sisters. She watched the Sister gather supplies, checking off things from a piece of paper as she gathered items from the shelves. Emma stayed where she was until she exited. *They a list of approved people allowed to enter the room,* thought Emma. Emma came out from under the table and checked what the Sister had removed. The gaps showed at least 4 containers of laudanum and 4 containers of morphine had been taken. It seemed a lot, but it might just be for patients that evening. She extinguished the light and opened the door slowly, glancing around to make sure no one saw her. When it was safe to exit, she headed back to the ward. *Where is the sister I saw in the closet?* The wards were quiet and she walked around and identified each one. *She wasn't there!* She made a note to get detailed information on each staff member. This case might take longer than she'd expected.

She finished up and was walking home when Jeremy approached her. She stopped and gave him a slight smile. "Hey, thanks for coming to meet me."

"Tired?" he asked.

"Yes. Long night."

He took her arm, and they made their way home. He gave her a minute, then asked, "Did you find anything out?"

"Well, one thing is for sure, we need to add them to our charity list. They're working with so little money and doing so much." She went on to describe things she had seen.

He looked over expectantly, but she still hadn't mentioned the case. "Will you be back tomorrow night?"

"Yes, I'll have to be. The only person I saw getting drugs was one of the Sisters, or I think it was a Sister. I documented what she took to compare with Sister Catherine tomorrow."

"You mean today," he teased. He got a small, tired smile in response. He asked, "You think she might not be a Sister?"

"I'm unsure. I didn't get a good look, as I was under a table," she stated wryly. "I don't think she was one of the sisters working that night."

"Were you able to follow her?" he asked.

"No, I thought she'd be in the ward, so I didn't. I'll keep a closer eye on her tomorrow night. Can you give Cole an update for me?" she asked with a yawn

"Yes, of course. Is there anything else?" Jeremy asked, knowing Cole would like the information.

"Yes, Sister Catherine needs to confirm the inventory. Here are the amounts of medications I saw removed," she said as she tore the page out of her notebook and handed it to him.

As he took the note, he pulled her in closer for a long kiss. "Want to head home?" he asked, looking deep into her eyes.

She knew that look. "Definitely." They made their way to the boarding house.

CHAPTER 31

$\mathcal{E}$mma slept hard that day and returned to the hospital in the evening. She thought about the Sister from the night before and pulled out her notebook. *What was different about that Sister?* she asked herself, evaluating her notes *She was not wearing an apron over her dress. The Sisters I have been working with wear these routinely to protect their habits. I had not seen her previously, either in the ward or at the nurses' station. A count was needed of all of the sisters on duty at night. Was it an imposter?*

She started gathering names as soon as she arrived. She found that the Sister at the desk was very friendly and talkative, offering nearly all the information Emma needed. On her break, she studied the list and made notes about each Sister. *2nd floor: Sister Mary, the talkative Sister, has delicate features and is slight of stature, appears to be in her late 20s or early 30s; Sister Magdalene is just the opposite, tall and commanding, appears to be about 40; Sister Anne is very quiet and average, appears to be in her 50s; Sister Maura is a hard worker and very pretty, the youngest in her early 20s and a novice Sister.*

What surprised her was that they were women like her aunts or friends. They talked, laughed, and occasionally argued with each other. These women were not subjugated. They were smart and seemed very happy with their lives. She had wondered about that. *Were they forced to be in the Church or was it a decision they made on their own?* These women showed her that it had been a higher calling.

She closed her notebook and returned to following the Sister's orders. She started with delivering water and other items, reading books she had brought in, and comforting as best she could.

CHAPTER 32

The next few days were routine, with no more unexplained visits to the drug closet. One particular evening was very quiet when she had finished checking on patients. Emma was making her way to the break room when she saw the strange "Sister". She ducked into a side room, watching, positive she was an imposter.

The other Sisters moved with a certain grace. This "Sister" was doing a quick step to the closet. She wouldn't find any changes to the locks. Emma had asked that the closet locks and process remain the same, so no one would suspect they were investigating the matter. As she opened the closet, Emma noticed she didn't stop to get the keys from the drawer. *Hmm,* she thought, *she has her own keys. It does lessen the chance someone from the hospital isn't involved. The keys are easily accessible, and she could have made a clay impression of the key. That would have allowed her to make a copy and not have to chance using the one kept in the drawer.*

Emma stayed where she was and let the "Sister" get the drugs she was after. She wondered about the quantities being taken, thinking to herself, *She's smart and must have been running this scam for a while. She probably got away with more over the long term than she would have with a one-time theft.*

The "Sister" also seemed to know the other Sister's schedules of when they would be out of the area. Emma waited in hiding, as the "Sister" made her way to the back staircase. Emma took off her shoes to follow her silently. She hung back and let her exit the building. She could see through the windows that the "Sister" went to the right.

Emma slipped off her white uniform top and threw it behind her in the stairwell. It would help her blend into the shadows as she trailed behind her. She kept following until she saw her enter an apartment building. Before the door shut the "Sister" glanced behind her. Emma ducked into an alley to avoid being seen.

After waiting a few minutes, Emma approached the building. The door creaked as she pushed it open slowly. There was no one in the area, she stepped in, listening for the sound of steps on the floors above. She looked up and could see the habit through the rails on the third floor. The sounds of feet kept moving to the next floor. She heard a banging and a door open and slam closed. *Fourth floor*, she thought.

She approached the floor and stayed on the stairs. From that vantage point, she could see each of the doors. *Which door?* The question was answered when a man stepped out one and Emma got a good look inside. The sister was there, she had pulled off the hood and her blond hair stood in stark contrast to the habit.

What now? She was unsure how to approach this. *Barge in, wait for her to exit, or go for help.*

Emma stayed put, slipping on her boots as she continued to watch the door. She was trying to get comfortable by leaning against the wall when the door opened abruptly; she barely had time to get out of the way of a man descending the stairs.

He had a small child with him, who couldn't have been more than five. The boy had red hair and a slight body. Emma looked at the boy carefully, he was walking sluggishly and appeared to be drugged.

The "Sister" stuck her head out the doorway and yelled, "Get him moving! They're waiting for him!"

"Yeah, yeah," he called back. "I'm on the way." He pushed the boy roughly down the stairs. "Get a move on."

Where are they taking the child in the middle of the night? She asked herself. Emma watched and worried. The child took precedence over the drug theft. She followed the man and the sluggish boy, deliberating what to do. She had to make sure she wasn't interfering in a family matter. She could hear him muttering, "I want my mama."

She listened intently. *He's Irish.* The accent was a familiar one, she had heard she'd heard while delivering to Chicago's Little Hell. She thought about the conversation between the man and the "Sister"; they weren't Irish. She stayed at a safe distance and watched as the man pulled the boy by his small arm into the street. Her decision was made for her when he raised a hand and slapped the child hard across the face.

She pulled her clutch knife and rushed them. *I really should have put together a plan,* she thought. Executing a flying kick, she planted her pointed boots into the man's soft stomach. He went down hard, the breath taken from him. She had the knife to his throat before he could recover. "I'm taking the boy and you'll forget you saw me."

He was panting, staring at her with wide eyes. She let the knife tip his skin to show him she meant business. The blood dribbled down to his shirt as he stuttered, "I won't say anything."

"If I hear you do, I'll come after you. Do you understand?"

"But—" he started

"Yes?" she interrupted, showing him her bloody knife.

"Nothing, nothing at all." He put his hand up to his neck and pulled it back covered in blood. "What did you do to me?"

"I'll do much worse if you come after us," she threatened.

She knelt by the boy. He had laid down on the ground when she attacked. While she checked him, she kept a wary eye on the man. She said loudly, "You need to go now." When he didn't move, she yelled, "I said *now!*"

He did as he was told and ran off thinking, *When I tell this story later, I'm going to say it was two large men.* He believed her when she said she would find him. He ran; he would hide out and not report in until later.

Emma watched him run off and then reached over to pick up the now passed-out little boy. She hugged him close as she knelt on the ground and thought about what to do next. The best thing she could do was to take him to the hospital.

She stood up with him in her arms. The streets were quiet as she made her way back to the hospital.

When she arrived, Sister Mary confronted her. "Just where have you. . ." She then realized she was carrying a child. Her demeanor changed immediately to one of concern. "What's wrong with him? Where did you find him?"

Emma spoke in a low voice, saying, "Sister Mary, we need to keep this quiet."

She frowned but did lower her voice. "We have a private room we can use, this way." She motioned for Emma to follow her to the room.

Seeing Emma look around with a frown on her face, Sister Mary commented, "The other Sisters are making rounds. We have some time."

Emma hugged the boy close, wanting to protect him. "Put him down please," requested Sister Mary. Gripping him tighter she didn't want to relinquish him, but Sister Mary needed to examine him. Emma laid him down on the bed and brushed his dark red hair off his head.

"What happened?" Sister Mary asked quietly.

"I think he was kidnapped from his parents," she said quietly back.

"How did you get him?" Sister Mary asked.

Emma kept looking at the boy and didn't say anything.

Sister Mary looked resigned. "Okay, keep your secrets." She looked him over and said, "He's bruised but nothing appears to be broken. He should be all right once he sleeps off the drugs he was given."

"Can you tell what they gave him?" she asked worriedly.

"It appears to be laudanum. He'll have to sleep the medication off. He'll also need to stay here, under observation, until he wakes up," she said firmly.

"Yes, I agree," said Emma, as she pondered what to do next. She came to a decision and asked, "Can you watch him while I get some help to manage this situation?"

Sister Mary looked again at her and said wryly, "Not a normal volunteer, are you?"

"No, not really," Emma said as she headed to the door. She turned back to Sister Mary and said, "I'll be back soon. Please, stay with him. Someone dangerous might be looking for him." She didn't wait for Sister Mary's answer as she turned and left the room.

She headed out, ran down the stairs, and didn't stop until she reached the boarding house. Letting herself in, she went up the stairs to her room. There was no hesitation as she crossed over to the connecting door.

"Jeremy, wake up," she said and jostled him.

"Emma, are you home already?" he asked, yawning. "Did I forget to get you?"

"No, Dear-One, I need some help. I need you to go get Cole and wake Tim and Dora to meet at the hospital. Oh, and tell Cole to bring Sister Catherine."

That woke him abruptly. "What's happened?" he asked, catching her hand as she turned to go.

"There's a child in danger," she said simply. "Please, get everyone there. I don't want to be away from him for long."

"All right," he said, already up and pulling on his pants. She headed back out through her connecting door, secure in the knowledge he would get everyone together.

She ran back to the hospital, hoping the child was going to be okay. She thought about his accent and hoped Tim might have an idea of where to find his family. He was on her mind as she reached the second floor. She glanced at her watch and saw it was 4am. *It should be quiet for a while longer.* She could see two Sisters sitting at the nurses' station.

Sister Agnes frowned and said, "Where have you been?"

"Something came up," replied Emma in a firm voice and looked her in the eyes.

"Well, if you want to volunteer here, this has to be. . ." Before she could finish, Sister Mary stepped out of the private room where the child was located.

"Emma, please come here." She didn't look at the other Sisters and closed the door after Emma entered.

"He's sleeping peacefully," she said as Emma immediately went to the bed and took his hand.

"He does seem better," she said in a relieved voice, looking over her shoulder at the Sister.

"Yes, he's been calm."

"Was he given too many drugs?" she asked worriedly.

"I think he was given too much for his size, but I believe he'll be able to sleep it off. What are we going to do now? "Sister Mary asked, clearly worried.

"I have my team coming," Emma assured her.

"You have a team? You're definitely not just a volunteer. How is it you have a team that could address this?" she asked.

"Well, the truth is," Emma started and was stopped with a knock on the door. Sister Mary opened the door and found Sister Agnes there.

"Sister, there are a lot of people here who want to see our volunteer. What should I tell them?" asked Sister Agnes, clearly bewildered.

Sister Mary came to a decision. "Show them to the meeting room and I'll need you to come in and sit with this child." When Sister Agnes started to interrupt, she stopped her by saying, "No questions, please."

Emma stepped out of the room. Cole was waiting there. "I have one of my men here," he nodded to a Pinkerton detective, "to watch the room while we talk."

Emma smiled, grateful for the forethought. He offered her his elbow and they walked together to the meeting room.

Emma and Cole entered the room and she saw that her team had assembled with little information provided. It brought tears to her eyes, but she quickly wiped them away.

Cole directed, "Emma, fill us in on what's happening."

Emma started, "As you know my current case involves tracking the morphine and laudanum losses at the hospital. I was able to determine that the thief was a Sister." She noticed Sister Catherine frowning and reassured her, "Not to worry, Sister Catherine. She was an imposter. She wore a similar habit to yours but was not wearing an apron. I followed her out and stayed a good distance back. I followed them into an apartment building. I waited in a stairwell, still planning only to observe, but then a man exited the apartment with a small boy. He was pulling him by the arm and pushing him downstairs." She finished up with, "I believe the child had been kidnapped."

"What led you to that conclusion?" asked Jeremy.

"I did hesitate, at first, but I kept observing them. The man and the child didn't have the same accent. Also, the boy kept asking for his mama."

"What made you decide to take the child into custody?" asked Dora hesitantly.

"When the man started hitting the boy," she said and shrugged. "I just had to stop it. So, I intervened."

Jeremy held his tongue on that one, knowing he would get the whole story later.

"How is the child now?" asked Cole.

Sister Mary spoke up and gave his status. Sister Catherine looked on in approval.

"Tim." Emma looked at him thoughtfully. "I believe the child is one of the kids living in the Hell's Irish sections."

Tim nodded. "Very probably. I can ask around and find out if a small child is missing. Do we know his name?"

"Not until tomorrow; he needs to get some rest tonight. The earliest he'll be able to answer questions will be in the morning," stated Sister Mary.

"Will he be safe here?" asked Dora, looking at Tim. "Should we move him to the boarding house?"

Sister Catherine spoke up, "Before any decisions are made on moving him, I would like to keep him here until he wakes. If at that time he responds well, I see no issue with him being moved."

Cole looked over at Sister Catherine and said, "Sisters, thank you for your support. Could you give us some time alone?"

"Yes, of course," Sister Catherine said as she and Sister Mary quietly exited the room. Jeremy closed the door behind them and took his seat.

"Emma," Jeremy asked, "what do you think is happening here? What's the big picture on this?"

"I believe I may have stumbled onto a kidnapping ring," she answered simply.

"For what purpose?" asked Dora, perplexed why children, especially poor children, would be kidnapped. "There would be no money in taking them."

Jeremy answered, "I think I can answer that. We're hearing

more cases like this throughout the country. They're using them for pickpocketing and prostitution rings."

Dora had such a soft heart and started to cry softly. Tim pulled her in close. She looked up with tears streaming down her face and asked, "Can we see him?"

Emma said, "Yes, of course. Dora and Tim, I wanted you so you could be here for him until we find his parents."

"Of course, poor little boy. We'll go over now," said Dora. Tim guided her from the room.

Emma, Jeremy, and Cole were the only ones left. Cole asked, "Emma, do you have any idea where they might be keeping the kids?"

"No, I meant to follow the man to the location, but when the abuse started, I felt I had to intervene. I'm sorry if I did so at the wrong time and prevented the larger case from being solved."

Cole said immediately, "No, you did the right thing. I'll have some detectives cover their movements."

Jeremy asked, suddenly worried, "What about the man you took the boy from? Will he tell them about you?"

She smiled rather evilly. "No, I think we can rely on his vanity for that. I don't think he'll say someone like me beat him up and took the boy."

"No, I wouldn't think so," murmured Cole, wondering how she'd managed it. He would have to ask Jeremy for details later.

Jeremy took the conversation from there, saying, "We can have men in place, watching the path to the apartment, and when the false Sister comes back for more drugs, we follow her to the final location. Hopefully, we'll find any kids who may have also been taken."

"Cole, we had planned to add new locks and security measures to the management of the drug closet. Do we add the security to the closet as we had planned?" Emma asked.

Cole thought a moment and said, "Let's call Sister Catherine back in."

Jeremy did so. Sister Catherine entered the room gracefully and stood in front of Cole.

"You asked to see me?"

"We would like to be able to keep the current security measures in place so we can track the drugs back to the kids."

"Do you think she'll be back?" Sister Catherine asked, suddenly worried about her staff.

"We do, but she's never approached anyone here. They should just go about their normal schedules. Once she has the drugs, we'll have her tailed."

When she looked doubtful, Emma said softly, "We'd like your help with this Sister."

Sister Catherine nodded and said, "If it will help get children home, we'll do what we can to help."

Cole said, "Jeremy and Emma will take the lead on this and keep me informed on the progress." He wiped a tired hand on his neck. "I'm heading home; this early hour is wearing." He exited the room with Sister Catherine.

Jeremy and Emma stayed in the room, sitting quietly for a moment before Jeremy said, "I'll have men stationed covertly to watch for the 'Sister.'"

Emma confirmed, "I'll continue to work here as a volunteer."

"You've been here when she's come in. What are you thinking about how often she appears? Do we wait for a night or have everyone set up just in case?"

"I've been thinking about that. She's pretty routine with her times," she said, looking at her notes from Sister Catherine on dates when shortages were noticed. "If she follows the schedule, it won't be for another three nights."

Jeremy thought about what she had said and responded, "I'll get the men in place tonight. That way, in case their schedule changes, we'll be ready."

"Let's go check on the boy," Emma suggested.

They made their way down and found Dora and Tim sitting

with him. He was sleeping soundly. "Dora, Tim, you can head home now," Emma said softly.

Tim looked at Dora and back at Emma, saying, "We want to stay with him until he wakes up."

"That could be a long while," cautioned the nurse, sitting next to him. "I don't expect he'll wake until well into tomorrow."

Jeremy took in the room and said, "I'll have a Pinkerton detective, in plain clothes, sit with him and that will allow you both to get some rest."

Tim squeezed Dora's hand and said, "That sounds like a good idea. Let's head home and we can come back refreshed tomorrow."

Dora looked hesitant but nodded. "We can wait for your detective, Jeremy."

"Cole has already notified them, and he should be here soon."

They heard a knock on the door; Dora looked worried. Jeremy went to the door, opened it a crack, and saw it was his detective.

"Come in," Jeremy opened the door to let him in. He started giving introductions, "This is Detective Kilroy. He'll be here through tomorrow." Jeremy introduced him to each person in the room.

Kilroy nodded his head and said quietly, "I won't let anything happen to the boy."

Jeremy said to him, "Come with me, and I will introduce you to the other Sisters working tonight."

When everyone felt the security was in place and that the boy was well protected, they headed home. It was after Emma's shift and she accompanied them home for some sleep.

CHAPTER 33

She and Jeremy got back into bed at 5am and slept until 10. They heard a knock on the door and a voice said, "Emma, we're going to the hospital soon. If you're coming with us, you need to come down now."

Jeremy said in a low voice to Emma, "Have you had enough rest?" He was concerned because she would have to go back that evening.

Emma yawned broadly. "I'm tired, but I would like to be there when the boy wakes up."

"So, we go?" he asked, sitting up in the bed.

"We go," she confirmed.

Jeremy retired to his room to get ready for the day. Emma did the same. They met outside their rooms on the staircase to head down to the kitchen.

Dora was there and had breakfast ready for them. She saw Emma and said, "I'm sorry I woke you."

Emma hastened to assure her, "No, no, I want to go with you. It's okay, I'll get a few hours' sleep this afternoon."

They ate their breakfast and headed down to the hospital together. They made their way up the second floor, passing people on the stairs. Emma looked around, thinking, *It's so different in the daytime. I wonder what kind of security is in place during the day? I'll have to follow up on that with Sister Catherine.*

They exited into the hallway and Emma noticed the day Sisters were in place. She would have to get their names. Sister Catherine was already there waiting for them outside the boy's door.

She smiled as they approached and, before they could ask, she said, "He's fine and he's awake. Follow me, please."

Tim and Dora had wide smiles on their faces as they approached the door. What they found when they entered was an animated little boy. His face was flushed almost the color of his bright red hair.

Doesn't even look like the same boy, Emma thought to herself. *The drugs really changed his personality.*

Jeremy looked at Detective Kilroy and inclined his head for him to follow and give them a debriefing. Emma motioned to Tim and Dora that she would be following behind Jeremy.

On his way out, Kilroy said to Tim and Dora, "Oh, his name is Patrick. His mom calls him Pat."

Dora nodded, not taking her eyes off of Patrick. They wanted to get him moved to the boarding house to keep him safe. They also wanted to find out more about his parents so he could go home.

Emma motioned to Sister Catherine. "Could you let Tim and Dora know if Patrick is okay to go home with them?"

Sister Catherine acknowledged the question with a nod of her head, knowing he would be safer away from the hospital. "I'll let them know now."

"Sister," Emma reached out a hand toward her, "thank you so much for helping Patrick."

Sister Catherine took her hand and said, "We're here for him as long as he needs us." She gave Emma's hand a brief squeeze before walking toward Patrick's door. She knocked and Tim immediately answered.

"Could I speak with you and Dora for a moment?" Sister Catherine inquired.

Tim nodded and called back to Dora, who joined them out in the hallway.

"Would you accompany me to my office?" Sister Catherine asked.

"Of course." Tim waved to Kilroy to come back into the room. Jeremy and Kilroy had completed their meeting and were waiting in the hallway. "We need to meet with Sister Catherine," said Tim.

Kilroy nodded and returned to his post.

Tim and Dora followed Sister Catherine to her office. Tim inquired as the door closed, "Were there any problems after we left last night?"

Sister Catherine started. "No, completely quiet. I wanted to speak with you about Patrick." Dora sucked in her breath, afraid of what might be coming next. "He seems in perfect health. There appeared to be no effects from the drugs he was given."

Dora released the breath she was holding, crossed herself, and sent a silent prayer in thanks. Tim reached out his hand to her.

Dora took it and said hopefully, "Does that mean we can take him to the boarding house?"

She smiled. "It does mean he can be moved."

Dora said, with tears in her eyes, "Thank you so much. We'll work hard to locate his parents."

"I have faith in you both and pray for the safe return of his family." With that, she stood and showed them to the door. They headed back to Patrick's room. Emma and Jeremy were waiting outside for them.

Dora rushed up and said, "Emma, Sister Catherine says we can take Patrick to the boarding house."

"Good," she said, relieved. "It will be easier to protect him there."

Jeremy said, "I'll arrange the transport. We should be ready to go in about an hour."

"I'll stay here and help with the move when you are ready," said Tim. He looked at Dora and said, "We need to tell Patrick what is happening so he won't be scared."

"Yes, all of us together," said Dora.

As they entered the room, they saw Patrick talking with a Sister. "Dora! Tim! You're back!"

Dora smiled brightly, covering up her sadness. "Patrick, yes, we're back and we would like to talk to you about something." He looked curious and waited for her to continue. "We would like you to come stay with me, Tim, Jeremy, and Emma. We have a house where we all live together."

"But what about Mom and Dad? Will they come there also?" he asked, puzzled.

Dora clarified her statement. "We would like you to stay with us until we can locate your mom and dad. Would you like that?"

"I would love that! Can we go now?" he asked excitedly.

They laughed at his exuberance, but under the surface, they were sad he wasn't coming with them for happier reasons.

Jeremy stuck his head in the door and said, "We're ready."

"Okay then." Emma looked at Dora and Tim and asked, "Can you get Patrick dressed?"

"I think we can handle that," said Tim, grabbing Patrick's pants and tossing them at the laughing boy.

"Okay, we'll be in the hall waiting for you," Emma said as she exited. She wanted a final meeting with Sister Catherine, to confirm she would be back that night.

When everyone was ready, they exited the room and the group headed out. They had arranged for two cabs to be waiting outside for them. On the landing, Dora knelt in front of Patrick and said, "Patrick, we need to be as silent as a mouse. Can you do that for me?"

He seemed to understand that he needed to listen and follow their direction. He nodded and took her hand. Kilroy and Jeremy checked the alley before allowing them to exit the building. Once it was confirmed to be clear, they covered Patrick with a blanket and placed him on the floor of the carriage. Jeremy had arranged for Pinkerton detectives to be the drivers, in case of trouble.

Arriving home, they moved Patrick quietly into the house. Emma was very grateful they no longer had boarders who were not team members. Dora had cautioned the team that they must keep quiet about Patrick living there.

The minute Patrick was in the house and the blanket was removed, he wanted to see everything. Dora could tell they weren't going to get much information at that time and said, "Let's have lunch first, and then we'll sit and talk with him." She thought of something and asked Emma in a low voice, "Emma, do you have any of our old toys?"

Emma thought for a moment and whispered, "I have some blocks and a dancing man toy."

"Bring them down and we can talk with him in the library after lunch," Dora said.

Tim, Emma, Dora, Jeremy, and Patrick sat down for lunch. Once they finished, they moved to the library to speak with Patrick. Dora planned to take the lead in the questioning; she sat on the floor with the toys and said, "Patrick, I have some toys here if you would like to sit down and play with me."

He had seen the toys and hoped they were for him to play with. He nodded eagerly and sat on the floor with her, picking up the blocks.

As he played, Dora asked, "Patrick, do you know your last name?"

"Blake," he said as he stacked the blocks.

"Do you know your mom and dad's first names?"

"Da's is the same as mine," he said proudly, tilting his head up. "He is senior, and I am junior."

"Wonderful. Patrick. Can you tell us when you last saw your parents?" Dora asked casually as she added blocks to his building.

He didn't answer. Instead, he picked up the dancing man and tried to operate it. Emma knelt next to him and showed him how to make it dance. It made him smile, and they let him play with it for a moment.

Dora tried again. "Patrick, can you remember when you last saw your parents?"

This time, he answered. "We were at the fair. They had ponies and fun games."

Emma jotted down the information. She edged closer to Tim and asked, "Is that enough for you to look into his background?"

Tim said in a low voice only she could hear, "Yes, I'll ask around this afternoon."

"Quietly," she cautioned in a low voice.

"Yes, of course," he said, watching Dora with Patrick.

Dora wasn't finished with her questions. "Patrick, one more thing. Does your Da work?"

"He sells fruit," he said proudly. "He gets all the fruit we want to eat. "

Tim waved to Emma and Jeremy to step into the foyer. "I'll head there now."

"Tim, do you need someone with you?" asked Jeremy.

"It couldn't hurt, but you'll need to change," Tim commented, looking at Jeremy's nice suit.

Jeremy looked down and smiled. "I think I have some things I can wear. Meet you downstairs in five?" He went quickly upstairs and changed into an older set of clothes and went back down to meet Tim.

Before Jeremy left, he turned to Emma and reminded her, "You need to get some rest."

"I will," she promised.

She headed upstairs as soon as they left.

Dora spent the afternoon with Patrick, playing and showing him how to make pastry.

CHAPTER 34

*J*eremy and Tim took the wagon to the outskirts of the Hells. Tim directed, "We'll walk from there."

Tim saw a boy he knew hanging out nearby and called, "Hey, John."

"Hey, Tim. What's up?" John asked as he walked over.

"Can you watch the wagon and horse for me?"

"What's in it for me?" he asked, knowing Tim.

"How about this much?" he asked and counted out 50 cents. The boy's eyes went wide, and he tried to be nonchalant, saying, "I can only be here for a little while."

"Okay, we'll be back." They headed down the main road, where most of the vendors had set up booths to sell their goods. These included fruit, vegetables, meat, and other types of items. The smells and the people's accents made them pause occasionally to take it all in.

"Where are we headed?" asked Jeremy.

"I know one of the fruit vendors who might know Patrick's parents."

They continued further down the street, avoiding pickpockets and many offers from vendors. When they reached the booth Tim had been looking for, he called out, "Sean!"

The man heard his name and looked their way. He came over when he saw who it was. "Tim! So good to see you. Got any pies with you?"

"Not today," Tim said regretfully. "Jeremy, this is Sean O'Connell. Sean, we're looking for someone, actually a family. The name is Patrick Blake. I don't know his wife's name, but they have a five-year-old son."

Sean heard the request and replied in a very quiet voice, "Yes, I know where you can locate them." He looked over his shoulder and asked loudly, "Hey, Tom, could you watch my stand?"

"Sure, don't be long," Tom commented as he walked over from the stand next store.

"Come with me," said Sean. They accompanied him into an alley over a few blocks and into a business. Tim and Jeremy realized where they were; it was a mortuary parlor.

"What happened?" asked Tim quietly.

"Little Patrick went missing. Patrick senior and Adeline, that was the mama's name, went to find him," said Sean.

"When was this?" asked Jeremy.

"A few days ago. Their bodies were found yesterday morning, just tossed in a ditch. Sadly, they had no money and will have to be buried in potter's field."

Tim muttered, "I think I can manage the funeral cost."

"Make that both of us," said Jeremy.

Sean's eyes teared up, and he was not embarrassed to let them fall. Once he got his emotions under control, Jeremy asked, "Does Patrick have any other family here?"

"No, they were first-generation from Ireland. Most of their family died in the potato famine. I understood there were no other relatives. Were you able to find little Patrick?" he said, hope in his voice.

"Yes, but don't mention that to anyone. We're trying to figure out who took him," requested Jeremy. He continued, "Do you know if any other children have gone missing?"

Sean sat down heavily on a chair, saying in a weary voice, "I don't know how many, but yes, we have children missing. People are scared to go to the police, and they are keeping their children close." He looked over at Tim and asked, "Is there something you can do?"

"There might be. Where were the kids taken from?" asked Jeremy.

"We aren't sure. They just didn't come home from school," Sean said. He gripped his knees and stood. "I need to get back."

Jeremy broke the silence on the way home. "Can you get us a list of the children?"

"Yes, I can put it together now—if you have time," Sean said.

"We do." Jeremy and Tim said at the same time. He nodded and they followed him back to his stand.

Tim took out a piece of paper and a pencil and said, "I am ready."

Sean listed the names that he had heard. They thanked him and went to retrieve their wagon.

"So many," said Tim, shaking his head.

"There are at least 20 names here and he said he wasn't sure he had all of them. I need to see Cole about what we learned. Keep the information about other kidnappings quiet for now. We need to form a plan."

"I will. Can I share the information about the parents with Dora and Patrick?" asked Tim.

Jeremy sighed. "Yes. What about Patrick? Who will he end up with?"

"I think Dora will have an idea on that," he commented, certain she was already falling for the boy.

Jeremy nodded and said simply, "I'm glad."

They made their way back to the wagon and thanked John

for watching it. Tim dropped Jeremy off at the Pinkerton office to review the current status of the case with Cole. He then went home, in a deliberately slow manner, thinking how to tell Dora about Patrick's parents. He entered the boarding house via the kitchen. He saw Dora wasn't there and when Amy saw him, she said, "She's in the dining room."

"Thanks, Amy," he said and headed there. Dora looked toward the door as he entered and started to go to him. The expression on his face caused her to sink back into her seat. "Where's Patrick?" Tim asked.

"Papa took him downstairs to show him some experiments," Dora said quietly, searching his face for information.

"Has Emma left yet?" he asked, delaying the inevitable conversation.

"Yes," she said slowly, "she left about thirty minutes ago. I did get her to eat and to promise to rest if there's time." She couldn't wait any longer and said pleadingly, "Tim, tell me!"

"Let's go into the sitting room," he suggested. She nodded and followed. She sat down and watched as he sank heavily onto the couch and put his face in his hands. He finally lifted his head and gazed at her, saying simply, "Dead."

"Dead?" she asked incredulously.

"Yes. Patrick's parents tried to find him on their own and were killed. Their bodies were tossed in a ditch," he said, his voice turning hard.

Dora was thinking ahead. "Is Emma in danger?"

"No, she has what Patrick's parents didn't—a team behind her, who won't let anything happen to her."

"What will happen now?" Dora asked.

"We found out other children are missing. It might all be connected with the drugs and the hospital. Jeremy said they would continue to the investigation."

"You say, children? So, it's bigger than just Patrick?" she asked.

"Yes, Sean provided a list of at least twenty who have disappeared."

"So many, will they find them all?" "Even if we find where they are holding them, they all might not be there."

"No. That many children would be hard to manage."

"They may have moved them already."

Dora didn't cry this time; she knew she needed to be strong. "Did you find out if Patrick has family he can go to?"

"There's no one. No family either here or in the old country."

At that moment, Patrick raced in and jumped into Tim's lap. He was such a lovely child.

"What about us, Tim?" asked Dora, watching him pull Patrick close to his chest. Patrick giggled and struggled to get out of the hold.

"I would love that," he said and reached out a hand toward hers. She took it and they sat wondering if this was their new family. They hadn't expected Patrick to need them as parents; they only wanted to care for a lost child. Tim cleared his throat and took Patrick off of his lap so he and Dora could talk to him.

Dora started, "Patrick."

"Yes, Dora?"

"Do you know what heaven is?"

Patrick suddenly smiled and said, "Yes, my grandma and grandda are in heaven. God watches out for them."

Dora forced the tears back and Tim cleared his throat. "Patrick, you know I went to look for your parents today? We told you that earlier?"

"Yes," Patrick said, going very still. Children always seemed to have an awareness of sad events.

"We spoke to your neighbors and friends. Do you know Sean? He works next to your Da's booth and sells fruit?"

Patrick didn't say anything; he just waited with wide eyes.

Dora said softly, "Patrick, today we learned your parents have gone to heaven to be with your grandparents."

"Why would they go? Was I bad? I didn't mean to be taken," he said plaintively, wiping tears from his eyes with his sleeves.

Tim hastily assured him, "No, Patrick, that was bad people doing bad things."

Patrick sat down on the floor, picking up loose blocks. He finally looked up at Dora and said in a heartbreaking voice, "I want my mama."

He started to cry, and Dora gathered him up with her on the couch. Tim moved closer and they sat there together for a long while. They would give Patrick time to adjust to the news before suggesting he stay with them permanently.

CHAPTER 35

Jeremy strode up to the Pinkertons offices, saying over his shoulder to the staff, "Be prepared for a meeting in a few minutes," and entered Cole's office.

"Hey, Pops," he said as he sat in the guest chair in front of the desk.

Cole started, "The boy's parents?"

Jeremy sat forward, a frown darkening his face, and said, "Dead. Probably killed by the same group we're trying to locate."

Cole pushed back his chair. "Horrible. Do you think there are other children involved?"

"Yes, we got a list of kids who have gone missing." He handed it to Cole. "We have to stop them."

"Agreed," Cole said firmly.

"Are the men in place for tonight?"

"Yes. We want to keep a low profile. We don't want to spook them," directed Cole.

"Do you think she will try again so soon?" asked Jeremy.

"I think she will. They had a child get away and the medicine was probably for that child. They'll have to make up for losing him," Cole said, understanding the children were part of a plan in a very ugly business.

"I'll notify Emma about our plans and what we found out," Jeremy said, standing. "I told the men to meet in the conference room for an update."

"Good, let's head in now," Cole said as he accompanied Jeremy out.

Jeremy was thinking about the meeting as he headed back to the boarding house. He found out that Emma had already gone to the hospital and headed there to inform her about what was going to happen that evening.

As he entered, he went directly to the second floor. The Sisters saw him approaching and motioned him toward the patient ward. He walked to the large room looking around, finally spotting her sitting next to an elderly lady holding her hand and reading to her. They both seemed to be enjoying the company.

He walked up quietly and tapped her on the shoulder.

She looked up with a smile on her face. "Jeremy, hi. This is Martha."

He took Martha's fragile hand in his and leaned over to say, "It's very nice to meet you."

Martha was an elderly woman with white hair and a pale complexion. She blushed when the good-looking gentleman paid attention to her. "Can I steal her away from you?" Jeremy asked kindly.

"You may, young man," she said and looked over at Emma. "Come back to see me?"

"I will," Emma promised, leaning down to kiss her cheek. She got up and followed Jeremy out of the ward and into the hallway. "Visiting?" she inquired.

"Yes and no." He briefed her on Patrick's parents. "We think the 'Sister' will be back tonight."

"Yes," she said, trying not to think about Patrick's loss; she followed his train of thought. "If this does involve a certain number of children, she will be short, with the loss of Patrick. That means an additional kidnapping and more drugs to keep them subdued."

"What time did you see her access the closet?" Jeremy asked.

"3:30am. I expect she'll follow the same schedule since she's gotten away with it up until now."

"Okay, so we wait," he agreed.

She nodded.

"I'll be outside watching, and we'll tail her," he suggested.

Emma was drumming her fingers on her lips and asked, "What if you miss her coming in?" A thought came to her, and she pointed to the window facing the road. "I know! I can use my portable gas light to signal you from that window there. When she's headed down."

"Good idea," he said. "I'll be close and will keep an eye on it." They parted ways with a soft kiss.

The evening went along quietly with Emma completing her rounds and helping the Sisters. She looked at her watch and realized it was nearly 3am; she hurried to finish wrapping bandages and put them into the cupboard. Rushed footsteps sounded, giving her just enough time to crawl under the nurses' station. Emma had made sure all of the Sisters stayed in the ward during the hour she thought she might arrive. She didn't want them in harm's way. The door closed, and she lit her lamp quickly and went to the window.

A creak could be heard as the door opened, she extinguished the light and dove back under the nurses' station. Staying still she waited for the door to the stairway to open and close. She stuck her head out and looked tentatively around. Once she confirmed the 'Sister' had left, she quickly went to the ward door and waved at Sister Mary.

She approached Emma and said, "Yes?"

"She was here. I'm going to follow her," Emma said quickly.

Sister Mary nodded and said quietly, "Careful."

"I will be," she said and headed down the stairs. She caught a glimpse of Jeremy's team tailing the "Sister" and stayed back, letting them take the lead. She caught up with them as they surrounded the apartment building, waiting for someone to exit.

They waited 20-30 minutes and, this time, two men in working-class clothing exited the apartment building. They had another child with them—a little girl. She was noticeably drugged and one of the men carried her loosely on his shoulder.

Jeremy had cautioned everyone to remain unemotional and follow the men and child to the drop-off location. They walked a few blocks and climbed into a waiting carriage. Jeremy had planned for this contingency and had transportation nearby. His men followed on foot to get the direction the men were headed in.

Jeremy waved for Emma to join him and the two detectives. When she got in the carriage, he commented, "The others will follow."

They were able to catch up to the two men and kept the carriage within view as they made their way toward a warehouse at the dock. The carriage pulled over, they moved past and pulled out of site into an alley. They approached the warehouse, Jeremy had the men divided in half to enter from the front and the back. "We need to approach this silently and do not draw your guns unless there is no other choice," he directed.

Emma had her large knife out and followed the direction of the agents entering the front of the building. Their group made their way through the mostly empty space. As they approached the back, they saw a room with a single door. Jeremy signaled the team to hold back and waved at Emma to approach. She glanced in the room through the window in the door. Ducking down after a long glance, she signaled to Jeremy, holding up four fingers, and mouthed, "Four men and the kids are there."

Jeremy got the message and signaled the men to hit the door hard with guns drawn. The men knew there were children in the room, and they were instructed not to fire unless fired upon.

It was a mad rush, the men inside, not expecting the ambush, were easily subdued. As they were taken into custody, another man walked in casually from the back, wiping his hands. When he realized what was happening, he grabbed the nearest child to shield himself and started yelling, "You're going to let me out of here or I'll kill her!"

All of the agents had their guns directed at the man, but they didn't want to hurt the child.

Jeremy glanced around, saw Emma, and motioned to her. The man holding the child would expect a gun but not a knife. She gripped it in her hand and waited until he was looking at the guns. He was continuing to talk, demanding to be allowed to go.

Emma took the opportunity to throw her knife. She had a clear path to his right shoulder. As soon as the knife hit, he dropped the child and an agent rushed to grab her before she hit the floor.

As he collapsed to the floor, gripping his shoulder, Emma walked over, put her boot on his neck, and pressed down as she reached for her knife. She pulled it out and wiped it on the man's shirt, saying laconically. "Well, Harry, we meet again."

He looked at her in surprise. "You again!"

"You think I wouldn't know you? You're the same as you were before, a coward. You have a thing for kids, don't you?" She pressed harder on his neck with her boot and said in a low voice, "You don't involve children. Ever. Do you understand?" She leaned down while examining her blade, thinking she would have no problem plunging it into his chest and ending him.

Jeremy saw the emotions across her face and took charge. "Nick, take him."

"Sure, take the scumbag away," Emma said. Jeremy sent two of his guys to get Cole to provide transport wagons for the criminals and the children.

"Jeremy, we need to get them out of here fast," she said, referring to the children.

"What do you suggest?" he asked, looking at them lined up on the floor in two rows of 15 total.

"Let me check each one first," Emma said.

She had learned how to take pulse rates at the hospital. She checked each, trying to not look too closely at them. Emotions need to be removed from the situation until they had them in a safe location.

Emma called to Jeremy as she finished with the last child. "They are breathing. If we each take a child, we should be able to get them out of here and to the hospital."

They had the fifteen men they needed. Each took a child and exited the building. Cole had sent wagons over immediately and asked that they meet a few streets over, going through the alleys.

They made their way to the waiting wagons, each agent staying with their assigned child. The trip to the hospital was handled quietly. Emma went up and notified the Sisters that they would need temporary space for the children. The Sisters used a portion of the ward not occupied by patients and started making pallets on the floor for them.

The Pinkertons moved the kids upstairs and helped roll out blankets for each child. It was a very crowded space, but it was warm.

Sister Catherine had been notified and arrived to help. She just shook her head when she saw them. "I'm relieved we found them before further harm could come to them. "

The nurse was checking pulse and heartbeats. "God was with you," she said, crossing herself.

Jeremy wanted to get to the apartment to see if Cole needed help and said to Emma, "Can you keep an eye on the situation? We'll leave guards here."

"Yes, I'll be here," she said, wanting to stay with the children.

"Thank you," Jeremy said before leaving.

Sister Catherine came over to stand next to her. Emma looked over at her and gently teased, "I guess we need to discuss increasing the security on your drug closet now."

"Yes, but if she hadn't stolen from our less than secure drug closet, we wouldn't have had you here and these children may not have been saved," Sister Catherine said, looking at the bright side of things.

"Yes," agreed Emma.

"Prayers were answered with your intervention tonight."

Jeremy had rushed out to see if any help was needed for the takedown at the apartment building. He got to the location as they were bringing out a very angry woman. She was still wearing the habit but had taken off the coif. While Cole lead her out, she didn't look defeated; she still looked defiant. Cole was aware she thought she had won and said to Jeremy so she could hear, "Did you get them?"

"Yes, we have them all and the crew is in custody. Oh, and surprisingly, Harry Simpson was involved in this," commented Jeremy.

That caused a reaction from her. She opened and closed her mouth, the false bravado visibly sliding away.

"You're going away for a long time," said Cole, pushing her forward.

She dug her heels in and said, "What if I can give you someone else?"

Cole stopped pushing and looked at her consideringly. "We will listen, but because you involved children, there will be no special deals." He handed her off to a police officer to place into the wagon.

As they watched her go, Cole asked, "How are the children?"

"Sister Catherine seems to think they will just sleep it off. I left the men there to guard them. Do you think they will come for them again?" asked Jeremy.

Cole was contemplative about that. "I wouldn't think so. This type of operation only works if no one suspects it's happening. They will probably disappear for now."

"Will she give us a name?" Jeremy asked curiously.

A shot rang out and, as Cole and Jeremy dove for cover behind the carriage, they saw the 'Sister' go down. Cole waved at his men to investigate where the shot came from. They watched and all stayed quiet. They made their way to where she lay on the ground. She had a hole in her head that exited out the other side." I guess they didn't want her to talk," said Cole wryly.

"Doesn't look like we will get much information out of her," responded Jeremy in a similar tone. "What about Harry? Do you think we will get a name out of him?"

"He probably only knows her name and not the mastermind. I'll be surprised if we find out anything more from tonight's activities," said Cole.

CHAPTER 36

POLICE STATION

The police chief walked in, immaculate as always, and said, "Well, what do we have here?" Cole listed the information they had, the arrest they had made, and where the body was located. "Any idea who the woman was?" he asked his assistant.

"Several of the people we got from the warehouse have said Beatrice Purvis," he replied.

The police chief asked Jeremy, "The kids?"

"They're okay, but we'll need help locating their families."

"Of course. I'll send some officers over," said the police chief.

They continued discussing how they might get the kids home when a delivery boy came into the station stating, "Note for Jeremy Tilden."

Jeremy took the note, opened it, and read. He suddenly started laughing and folded the paper up before saying, "Emma has an idea that could help identify the kids in a faster manner. She would like to use Jake to take pictures of them and put their names on them to make the identification easier. She recommends setting this up for early afternoon tomorrow when the kids are expected to be awake"

"Jake Cooper is our forensic photographer," reminded the police chief's assistant Jim. "He's very good at his job."

"Yes, he's also a team member of Emma's and lives at their boarding house," commented Jeremy.

"Interesting," said the police chief, thinking of the young man who kept to himself. He nodded decisively and said, "That is a good idea. Jim, send a note over to Jake to work with Jeremy on the pictures." Jim was taking notes and nodded.

CHAPTER 37

HOSPITAL

Jeremy came back to the hospital to sit with Emma. The kids were on pallets and a guardian sat next to each. He murmured, "The police chief likes your idea of utilizing Jake."

"Good," she said quietly. She asked, feeling too tired to go herself, "Would you mind contacting Tim to let him know about our plans and Jake's involvement?"

"I will." He kissed her head and went to find Tim at the boarding house. It was about an hour later when she felt him return to her side.

"What did Tim say?" she asked, dropping her head on his shoulder, fatigue making her voice lower.

"He agreed to make sure Jake was on board in the morning," he said. "Try to get some rest. I will watch." She was so tired, she didn't argue.

It was a long night sitting with the kids and everyone was very tired, but no one wanted to leave until the first child woke up. The morning was slow in coming but when the first child awoke, the entire ward became invigorated.

CHAPTER 38

BOARDING HOUSE

Tim waited until early morning to have a conversation with Jake about their plans for identifying the kids.

Jake wasn't sure overall. "But I'm supposed to be at work."

Tim had dealt with Jake on many occasions and said in a reasonable voice, "Jake, listen to me. The police chief wants you to take the kid's pictures as part of your job. You saw the note."

Jake was unconvinced. "This isn't part of my normal duties. I'm not sure."

"Jake, I promise that, as soon as we get the pictures developed, you can go to your work and print them."

He seemed reluctant but finally agreed to take his camera and accompany Tim to the hospital.

They found Emma still there. Tim saw her wince as she stood.

"Emma, we can handle things from here; you should go home and get some rest."

She waited a moment until the pain subsided. "I'm okay. I was just sitting funny," she insisted. "Though I could use some sleep," she admitted.

"Is Jeremy still here?" asked Tim.

She shook her head and said, "He wanted to see if Harry had told the police any additional information last night."

Tim nodded. "We'll get the pictures and names of the kids so we can meet with the community leaders."

He started to turn back to Jake when Emma said in a low voice, "Tim, I need to speak with you."

Before he walked with her, he said, "Jake, I'll be right back. Wait for me here." Jake nodded, not looking up from his equipment. Tim glanced around and said, "Over here." They retreated to a small alcove where they could have some privacy.

Emma started, "The police investigating the warehouse came by this morning; they found some kids who didn't survive. They must have been experimenting with how much of the laudanum and morphine to give them."

Tim froze at the news; he didn't move until Emma called his name, concerned.

He shook his head and said, "I need just a moment." He gathered himself and wiped his eyes as he tried to be unemotional. "I think we need to have pictures of them also."

"Yes. Jake should be okay with those. Taking pictures of the dead is part of his normal job."

"I'll get him started. We'll get both sets of prints completed," said Tim.

CHAPTER 39

*E*mma felt another pain in her abdomen as she headed home. She stopped and put her head down, the dizziness became overwhelming. She sat on the sidewalk and waited until the dizziness had gone away. *Did I strain something when I lifted the children?* She pulled herself up and forced herself to her home. She slowly made her way home and entered the front door.

Dora was waiting for her in the dining room. When she saw her, she said, "Come in here, you need to eat."

"Yes," Emma said, her voice strained. She noticed Patrick playing nearby. "Dora, can you have Amy watch him for a moment? I need to talk to you."

Dora could tell Emma was serious and did as she asked. "Amy, could you come get Patrick?" She looked at Patrick and asked, "Would you like to help Amy ice a cake?"

He nodded eagerly and when Amy came out, he rushed to grab her hand and headed into the kitchen.

"He seems to be doing pretty well," commented Emma, watching him leave the room.

"Yes, I think it affects him mostly at night—nightmares, crying," said Dora.

"That sounds familiar," said Emma.

"Yes," agreed Dora. "I hope we can be here for him like you and Papa were for me. Let's move into the sitting room."

They walked arm and arm into the room. Emma sat down on the couch and let her head fall back.

Dora waited as patiently as possible and finally said, "Emma, tell me."

Emma sat for a moment, staring off into space, then stated abruptly, "Dora, they killed five of the kids. We think they were experimenting on the number of drugs to keep them quiet."

Dora covered her mouth, tears streaming down her face. Emma just felt too tired to cry. Dora came over and sat next to her. She pulled herself together and said, "You need to eat and go to bed."

"But—"

"No! We have plenty of people working on this, and I don't think working yourself to exhaustion will help anyone."

"Yes, Mom," she teased.

"Can you make it upstairs by yourself?"

"Yes," she said, though she felt another twinge of pain.

"Are you okay?" Dora asked, concerned with the pain Emma appeared to be in.

"Yes, I just lifted too much today." She headed upstairs, washed up, and changed into her nightclothes. As she was climbing into bed, Dora brought a tray up to her.

She helped settle it on Emma and said that she had prepared her favorite things: chicken soup and fresh bread. Dora sat quietly as she finished her meal.

She took the tray and said, "Get some rest."

Emma settled down to sleep. Just before she nodded off, she heard the side door open and the bookcase shift away. A cold body slid in next to her. They didn't talk; they just slept.

CHAPTER 40

BACK AT THE HOSPITAL

Tim and Jake worked with each child to get their names and pictures. The older children helped supply names for kids who were either too scared or too young to answer.

When they had finished, Tim addressed the group. "Listen, we'll be developing the pictures today and meeting with your parents to have you picked up. Until then, the Sisters and these gentlemen will continue to watch you."

Jake and Tim took the camera to the police station to develop the pictures.

Jake worked through the afternoon to get the film developed and Tim worked as his assistant. The time was fast approaching for a meeting with the parents.

Cole and Jeremy picked up Tim to go to the meeting. They had told the families of the missing children to be there at 8:30pm. It was very crowded when they entered, and the masses surged toward them. Everyone seemed to be demanding, "Did you find them? Where are they?"

"Let's quiet down!" A local policeman from the area stepped between the crowd and Tim, saying, "If you sit, we can begin."

Some looked like they wanted to argue, but they took their seats and waited.

The officer introduced Tim, Cole, and Jeremy to the group. Tim stepped up to the podium and said bluntly, "We have found some of the kidnapped children."

That statement caused the group to start speaking all at once. Tim responded by holding up his hands and saying, "Please, be patient. We need to tell you how we're handling this."

"How long will we have to wait?" shouted one of the parents, desperation evident in his voice.

"Just overnight. We'll have the pictures and names all organized by that time." People were murmuring when the mention of pictures came up. "We need you to keep quiet for now, until we can get you the pictures for you to identify your child," Tim continued.

"Why can't we go identify the kids in person?" one woman asked, bewildered at their methods.

"We don't think we got everyone involved in this, and we want to make sure kids get back to their actual parents. What we would like from you are your first and last names. For the children, that should include names, descriptions, and ages."

They agreed to provide the needed information and kept the news about the dead children quiet. The families started to line up to provide the information.

The man who had asked the earlier question asked, "You are sure we'll see the pictures in the morning?"

"We're working on them now. We'll all meet here tomorrow at 10am," Tim confirmed to the group. Most nodded and agreed to be there to view the pictures.

As they were leaving, a woman came up, crying heavily. "My Shannon, have you seen him?"

A man rushed up to take her in his arms. "Doireann, let them get the pictures to us. We'll see them tomorrow." He tried to take her away.

"Are they safe where they are?" she asked, not willing to move.

Cole confirmed softly, "We have protection in place for the children."

"Thank you," she murmured. She visibly calmed down and allowed herself to be led away.

As they were headed home in the wagon, Cole said, "That went well, or as well as it could have."

Tim said, "Now, we wait for Jake to complete the pictures."

CHAPTER 41

That evening, Emma returned to the hospital and started reading to the children. She noticed her audience included some of the more mobile adults as well.

After she completed her story, Emma was giving out crackers to the children when the familiar pain on her right side flared up again. Only, this time, it seemed to be spreading to her lower back and belly. The pain became so intense, she doubled over. When it passed, she stood and took two steps before falling to the floor. She didn't hear the children calling for help.

She didn't know how much time passed before she woke, but she realized she was in a bed. A doctor was leaning over her, pressing on her stomach, making her cry out in pain.

"What's happening?" she asked in a dazed voice, realizing she was laying on her back. She looked around and saw she was in one of the private rooms.

The doctor ignored her question and asked one of his own. "How long have you been having this pain?"

"Off and on for a few weeks," she admitted.

"Shut the door, please," the doctor requested, and a Sister assisting him immediately did so and returned to the bed.

"Emma, are you having amorous congress?" the doctor asked.

"Yes," she said, aware of what the term meant. She refused to show any embarrassment.

The sister's color deepened a bit, but she did not offer any judgment.

"I will need to check your breasts. Is that okay?" he asked.

"Yes," Emma said, trying not to be uncomfortable.

He then pressed on her breasts and noticed her moving restlessly. "Turn on your back, please." He moved his hands down to her lower back and belly. She yelped in pain. "When was your last menstrual cycle?" he asked, attentive to her pain.

"I'm late," she muttered. "I didn't think anything of it."

"How late?" he inquired intently.

"About four weeks, though I've had some abnormal menstruation-just off and on."

"Have your breasts been tender?" he asked, watching her response as he touched them.

"Yes," she admitted.

"Cramping?" he inquired.

"Some, but light," Emma said. She was usually the one asking the questions and had to know what he was thinking. "Doctor, what's your suspicion?"

He looked at her for a long moment and said, "Your symptoms are leading to a diagnosis of ectopic pregnancy." He watched her and she didn't react, waiting for more information. "Your symptoms include all three of the main signs: a missed period, vaginal bleeding, and belly pain."

"Well, I certainly have those symptoms," she gasped out as the pain returned and she bent over. She took a deep breath as it passed and asked, "What do we do now?"

"I have some good news on that. There has been a successful surgery for an ectopic pregnancy performed by Doctor Lawson Tait in 1883."

"Can you perform the surgery?" she asked.

"I can," he acknowledged. "I trained with Dr. Tait in England."

"Is it dangerous?"

"It can be, but the survival rate is quite high for this procedure."

"Please, go into detail," she requested, trying to breathe through the pain.

"I will remove the affected tube along with the embryo. You may not be able to have children, but the surgery could save your life," he said seriously. "This will need to be scheduled—" He cut off when she doubled up in pain again.

The door opened and Jeremy rushed in. "Emma, are you all right? What happened?" he asked, panicked. Emma was his rock.

She was in too much pain to answer. His eyes searched the room, looking for answers.

The doctor stepped closer to the bed. "Are you her friend?" he asked. His tone indicated he was asking if Jeremy and Emma were more than friends.

"Yes," answered Jeremy, aware there could be judgments about their arrangement. "What's wrong with her? Why is she in so much pain?"

"She has an ectopic pregnancy," he said.

"She's pregnant?" Jeremy asked, dazed.

"Not in the way you mean," commented the doctor.

"Can the baby survive, Doctor?" asked Jeremy. He wanted to have all of the facts.

"No, I'm afraid not. It's not where it should be and it could kill her," he said regretfully.

Watching her, Jeremy was concerned that she was almost doubled up in pain and couldn't talk. He said, "Doctor, she's getting worse. What can you do for her?"

"Right now, we need to start preparing her for surgery. We'll give you some privacy." He and the Sister left with that comment.

Jeremy could do nothing but sit with Emma and hold her hand as she continued to struggle with the pain. He had never felt so helpless in his life. The door opened with a slam and the Sisters rushed in to move her and her bed out to surgery.

Jeremy sat in his chair, watching them move her, unsure what to do next. He got up and walked dazedly into the hall. Dora and Tim rushed down the hallway toward him.

Dora reached him first. "Jeremy, what happened? Where's Emma? Sister Catherine notified us that she collapsed."

"They took her to surgery," he said in a hoarse voice.

When he realized Jeremy wasn't able to share what was happening, Tim said quietly, "Dora, I'll go get a Sister to talk to us." He strode away, leaving Dora to comfort Jeremy.

A few minutes later, Tim and a Sister walked up. She said, "If you will accompany me into Emma's room." They nodded and followed behind her. Jeremy went to the nearest chair and slumped down as the Sister quietly explained what had happened.

"Oh goodness," Dora said, going white. "Will she be okay?"

"I'm sorry, we don't know at this time. We're hopeful, and she has the best doctor for this type of surgery," said the Sister compassionately.

"They don't know if she'll be okay!" Dora cried and buried her face into Tim's chest. He could only hold her and worry.

The Sister understood they needed some time, but asked that they move to the waiting room. Cole and Ellis arrived together to join the family waiting for word on Emma.

Ellis went to Dora. "Dora, what's happened to Emma? Was she in an accident?"

Dora said, "Papa, let's go sit down for a moment." They went to a quiet corner of the waiting room and she started to explain what had happened.

Papa listened and tears started to flow down his cheeks. "Will she be okay?"

Dora tried to keep her tears back. "They don't know, Papa. We need to pray that Sister comes through this."

Papa wiped his face and said, "Emma has always enjoyed a challenge. She will come through this." He took Dora's hands and they prayed for Emma to come through the surgery.

The time seemed to drag. Cole tried to get Jeremy to eat something, but he just stared forward.

The doctor finally appeared hours later, tired, and pulled off his cap.

Jeremy stood and waited. He shook himself out of his haze. "Is she okay?"

"Yes."

"Oh, thank goodness," Dora said, grabbing Papa's hand. He squeezed it and waited for the doctor to continue.

"Unfortunately, we had to remove the tube where the embryo was located. It will have long-term effects on her fertility."

Jeremy didn't care about anything at that moment but Emma's health. "How is she?"

"She'll be tired, and it will take time for her to recover."

"How long will she need to be here?" asked Dora.

"Just a few days, if you can get her to stay in bed for at least three weeks at home."

Jeremy smiled wryly and said, "That will be the hard part." Everyone laughed.

They all waited until Emma was moved back to her room. Once they had her settled, the group moved quietly to her side, staying until here her eyelids fluttered.

Emma said as she awoke, still not able to focus. "Dora, are you here?"

"Yes, Sister, I'm here," Dora said, squeezing the hand she was holding.

She closed her eyes and said, "Papa, Jeremy?"

"We're all here, little girl," Papa replied.

"Good," and she went back to sleep.

Emma slept through the next few days. Jeremy sat at her bedside the entire time. He didn't want to budge from that spot.

Papa and Dora took turns coming to visit, bringing food and drinks.

CHAPTER 42

On the third day since her surgery, Emma was fully awake and was asking to get up. The doctor came in and cautioned her to take it easy. "You don't want to ruin my good work, do you?" he teased.

"No," she said grumpily. "How long until I'm back on my feet?"

"You're healing well, but it will be three weeks before you'll be allowed up," he murmured as he checked her incision.

"Three weeks!" she exclaimed.

"Emma," Jeremy started, "you have to listen, or you could hurt yourself."

"Okay, but I can go home?" she wheedled.

"Yes, this evening if you like," stated the doctor.

"Really?" asked Emma.

"Yes, I'll leave directions for your care with the Sisters. However, if you don't follow my orders, you'll end up back here. Do we understand each other?" he asked, looking her in the eye.

"Yes, I understand. I'll do as I'm told," she said earnestly.

Jeremy muttered something under his breath and Emma shot him a look that said for him to be quiet.

"I'll leave you now," said the doctor as he exited the room. He believed her when she said she'd listen and take it easy at home.

Emma was being very quiet and drumming her fingers on her lips. Jeremy knew she was planning. He grabbed that hand and said, "Emma, you know you have to rest."

"That doesn't mean bed, though. I could work on projects," she said evenly.

"Yes, and I'll be there to keep you company," he said firmly.

"Hmm." She started to think about the case. "Jeremy, I've been so out of it. Could you tell me about the children? What's happened?" she asked.

He started explaining. "We weren't able to get any further information from Harry other than to confirm Beatrice was his main contact."

"So, a dead end?"

"Yes, unfortunately," he said.

"What about the kids?"

"Jake got the pictures ready and we were able to identify the parents. We had some happy reunions."

"What about. . ." She trailed off.

Jeremy knew what she was asking. "The dead children?"

"Yes," she said steadily.

"We were able to narrow down who they were and identify them by clothing and hair. Those meetings were not fun," he admitted. "Cole and Tim did most of the communication."

Emma asked tentatively, "I understand you've been here with me all this time?"

"Where else would I be?" he asked, looking at her unwaveringly.

"Nowhere else," she acknowledged quietly. "Jeremy, let's go home."

"Let me get a Sister and make sure we don't do anything to hurt you."

He left the room and returned with Sister Anne. The

instructions were simple: rest for at least three weeks and then light walking.

"No bathing and no activities of a physical nature," the Sister said, turning a bit red.

Jeremy and Emma understood, and both said, "Yes, Sister Anne."

"I'll bring you some water and help you wash up before you leave," she said and exited to retrieve a washbasin and towels. She came back in as Jeremy was helping Emma sit on the side of the bed.

As they washed her, Emma pushed her hair back and said, "Ugh, I'm going to have to wash my hair."

"Just no full baths until the doctor releases you officially," Sister Anne reminded her.

Emma nodded.

"We can wash your hair at home. Maybe you can sit in front of the fire to dry it," he said, tempting her.

"That sounds like a plan," she said, wanting to feel clean again.

Sister Anne left to allow Emma some privacy to dress. Jeremy helped her pull on her skirt and top. She watched him struggle with her boots and said, "Could be worse. I could've had knives that popped out," she teased, referencing a previous case where the villain had knives as weapons in his shoes.

"Yes, well, this was hard enough," he said as he gave the boots a final tug.

A knock sounded at the door. "Come in," said Emma.

The doctor walked in with a smile on his face and said, "You look anxious to leave."

"Yes. I'm ready," Emma commented.

"We've had some problems keeping your visitors low. It will be way quieter for us with you gone," he joked.

Emma smiled and said, "I agree."

Jeremy stood and bent down to pick her up.

"Jeremy, I'm too heavy," she protested.

He just gave her a look; she saw it and stopped arguing. He carried her out of the room.

Papa met them at her hospital door saying, "Ready to go home, little girl?"

"Yes, Papa," she said, looking around. "Are Dora and Tim here also?"

"No. They're at home waiting for you. We didn't want to give the Sisters more people to deal with," he said softly. "Let's get you home."

They exited the hospital and Emma saw a carriage had been arranged to pick them up. Papa climbed in the conveyance and Jeremy handed her to him. As Jeremy climbed in, Papa carefully moved her to Jeremy's lap and put her legs over his.

Papa gave instructions to the driver, "Please, pull off carefully. We'll be taking it slow."

The driver nodded and started them off at a slow, steady pace. As they arrived home, Emma was again handed down to Jeremy. They climbed the stoop to the boarding house and saw Tim and Dora waiting in the foyer as they entered.

Dora rushed forward, kissed her on the cheek, and said, "You're finally home." She could tell how tired the short trip had made her and said, "Jeremy, take her upstairs. She'll need to rest."

"But—" Emma tried to protest.

"No. You're under my watch now." She saw Emma's face drop and said consolingly, "If you're good, I may let you sit downstairs with me later."

"You need to listen, little girl," said Papa.

Emma realized she was too fatigued to fight and acquiesced. Jeremy was worried; he had never seen Emma this tired.

"It's okay," mouthed Dora when she saw his expression.

He nodded and noticed Emma drifting off.

"Okay, let's get her upstairs," said Dora. Jeremy followed her up with a now sleeping Emma and laid her carefully on the bed. They removed her boots and loosened her collar. She didn't stir as they pulled her blanket over her.

They exited the room quietly. Dora was concerned about Jeremy; he had been at the hospital constantly since Emma had been ill.

"Jeremy, are you all right?" Dora inquired

"Yes. I think I'm just really tired also," he said, pushing a hand through his curly hair.

"Why don't you get a nap. too? I'll wake you both later," suggested Dora.

"You know, that's a good idea." He nodded, going into his room.

Dora smiled and watched him go into his room. Tim came up behind Dora, wrapping his arms around her waist, and asked quietly, "Are you going to tell her?"

Dora frowned at the question. "I'm not sure. I don't want to hurt her."

"I'm sure she will be happy for us," he tried to reassure her.

"Let's give it some time," she suggested.

"Not too much," Tim laughed and rubbed her slightly protruding tummy, "or the news will be obvious."

CHAPTER 43

eremy locked his bedroom door and walked through the secret door into Emma's room. He locked her door, as well, before slipping into the bed.

"Hmmm," she murmured as he embraced her. "So nice to finally be back here again."

"Yes," he agreed, quietly allowing himself to drift off to sleep. That was the last word spoken until they heard a knock on the door.

"Emma, are you ready for something to eat?" Dora asked through the door.

Emma said loudly, "Yes, I'm hungry. Will you ask Jeremy if he'll join me?"

Jeremy unlocked Emma's door and slipped through the secret door to his room. Dora was aware they were together but went along with their ruse to protect their privacy. She knocked on his door and said, "Jeremy, Emma would like to eat with you in her room. I'll bring up some food in a few moments."

"Thanks, Dora. I'm up," he called.

He changed his shirt and went to the washroom before

going to Emma's door. As he reached it, he knocked softly. "Come in," Emma called. Jeremy entered and saw she was sitting up and trying to move to the bedside.

Jeremy rushed over. "Emma, you still need to take it easy."

"I will," she promised, knowing she had to follow the doctor's orders to get well. "Can you help me to the washroom?"

"Oh! Sure. Let me help you," he said as he lifted her and carried her there. He waited patiently and carried her back to her room when she finished.

"Dora's bringing your tray up here. You don't need to get up," said Jeremy.

"Could you ask her if I can go downstairs? I promise to take it easy."

He thought for a moment and said, "I think I can arrange something," He bent down and scooped her back up. "I'll set up two chairs, one for your bottom and one for your feet." He juggled her to grab a pillow and placed it on her stomach.

They made their way downstairs to the dining room. Papa was with Patrick at the table, playing with his blocks. When he saw them, Papa immediately jumped up and pulled out a chair for her.

"Grab a second chair for her feet," Jeremy directed. "Emma, hand Ellis the pillow."

Once she was arranged, Jeremy went to the kitchen to tell Dora they had moved to the dining room.

Emma looked over at Patrick and said, "Patrick, how are you?"

He turned his big brown eyes on her. "You disappeared. You weren't here."

Emma felt so sad for the little boy who had lost so much. She held out her hands to him, saying, "I didn't go away on purpose. I got sick. I'm back now. I just have to take it easy."

"Did they hurt you, too?" Patrick asked in a low voice.

"Oh, baby, no," she said and held open her arms. He walked

over to lay his head on her chest. "I was sick before that, but I didn't know it. I was lucky to be at the hospital when it got worse." She asked teasingly, "So, are you living here now?"

"Yes, Dora and Tim asked if I could be their little boy now," he said, quietly looking at her.

"And what did you say?" she asked, knowing his answer.

"I said yes. Tim and Dora are my new mommy and daddy now," he said proudly.

Dora and Tim stepped into the room and heard the last statement. Dora buried her head in Tim's shoulder.

Tim stroked her hair and said, "Patrick, since you've finished your lunch, Amy said she'd love to play ball with you outside."

"Really?" He took off running, shouting, "Amy!"

They heard Amy reply and the back door open and then slam shut.

The group in the dining room smiled. "Patrick seems to be settling in," commented Emma. She was happy he had a family.

The conversation moved to the topic of children. "The funeral planning is still ongoing for the kids," Tim said

"Who's paying for them?" asked Emma.

"I'm unsure," admitted Tim.

There was a knock on the door as Dora headed toward the kitchen. She glanced toward Papa and said, "Papa, could you get the door while I make Emma's plate?"

"Yes, of course," he said, putting down his paper.

They heard a female voice and Papa saying, "Clair, welcome. Come in."

"How is Emma?" she asked, her voice tinged with concern.

"She's doing well. She's in the dining room getting some lunch. Won't you join us?"

"Please," she responded.

She entered and immediately to Emma's side. "Emma, I was so worried about you. I tried to come to the hospital to see you, but they limited your visitors."

Emma smiled broadly. "Clair, I'm glad to see you. I'm feeling well. Now, I just have to rest." Emma saw Jeremy nodding out of the corner of her eye. She focused back on Clair, saying, "We were just talking about the children's funerals and the cost to the parents. I'd like us to review taking care of that. They've already been through so much."

Tim added, "I'll have to check with the families, but that area is very poor and I doubt most have the money to pay for proper funerals."

Clare was aware of the children being kidnapped and knew some had died. She pulled out her notebook to take notes. "Do we know the family names?"

"We can get them. Cole has a list of everyone," Tim stated.

Jeremy was grateful Tim had been helping Cole and said, "Thanks so much for your assistance, Tim."

"We're family," he said. "You do for family."

Emma warmed at this comment. She teared up and tried to cover it with a statement to Clair. "Claire, I'd like you to speak with them. Find out about each child and what they would like." She looked around at the group and said, "I assume my board members would approve this?"

"We'll have to make it official," said Clair, "but we can move forward and get all the details. I'll have a formal vote sent out to everyone."

"Wonderful," said Emma, relieved to be able to help those families who experienced loss.

"Would you like something to eat?" Dora asked Clair.

"That would be nice," she responded.

They all settled into lunch. After they ate, Tim said to Clair, "If you would like to come with me, we can go get the details from Cole."

"I would appreciate that," she said. "As soon as we finish?"

"Yes, we can do that," Tim confirmed.

Dora said, "Clair, you and Thomas need to come by this weekend for dinner. It's been a little while."

"That would be lovely," she said and looked toward Emma, "if you're up for company?"

"I will be," she said.

Tim had gotten his jacket and asked Clair, "Ready?"

She held up a hand. "Tim, just a moment. Dora, could I have a word with you?"

Dora immediately nodded and asked, "Kitchen?"

"Yes." She stood and turned to Tim, saying, "I'll be ready in just a moment."

Emma frowned as she watched them leave the room. *What's going on here?* she thought.

Jeremy said to Tim, "I think I'll come with you and check-in at the office. I have a few cases that might need my attention. If you're okay with that," he said to Emma.

She smiled. "I'm fine now that I'm home. You do what you need to do."

Dora and Clair came back out quickly. Dora's cheeks were red, and Clair was smiling. She bent over and kissed Emma on the cheek. "I'm very happy you're home."

"Me, too. Let us know if you need any help with the details for the funerals. I could help from here."

Clair looked at Jeremy in askance. "As long as she takes it easy," he cautioned.

The afternoon wore down slowly. Emma worked on her lace designs after being moved by Papa into the sitting room.

Mark and his parents joined her there before dinner. She briefed them on what was happening with the children. "It is so terrible," said George.

"Yes," Emma agreed.

He looked at Elizabeth and back to Emma before saying, "Have you looked at who else might be involved in the kidnappings?"

"Do you mean other than the people we caught?" asked Emma.

"Yes, I think that the investigation should also include the people who targeted them."

"Who would that be?" asked Emma.

"You would be looking for people that are already in the kid's lives," said George.

"Why makes you say that?" asked Emma curiously.

Elizabeth responded. "Kids wouldn't normally go with someone they don't trust. Well, the older ones anyway"

Emma thought about that.

CHAPTER 44

PINKERTON OFFICE

"How is Emma?" asked one of the detectives sitting in the outer offices as Jeremy, Clair, and Tim entered.

"She's home and being forced to take it easy," Jeremy commented.

"Not easy for her."

Jeremy smiled. "No, definitely not."

Cole heard his voice and stuck out his head. "Jeremy, come see me."

When he saw Clair and Tim had accompanied him, he stepped out into the hallway. "Welcome, what can I do for you?"

"We'd like to have a list of the children who died so we can inquire about helping with the arrangements," said Clair.

"That's wonderful. Allen," he called, "can you assist Clair and Tim?"

Allen came up and said, "Why don't we meet in here?" He escorted them into the conference room to help them with the information request.

Cole and Jeremy watched them follow Allen down the hallway. Cole looked at Jeremy and said in a serious tone, "Jeremy, come into my office."

"On my way," Jeremy said. He knew that tone.

"How's Emma?" Cole asked as he entered.

"She's good. We both finally got some rest today. It was good to be home," he said.

"Are you okay?" his father asked, knowing the stress Jeremy had been under.

"I am now. I was so scared," he admitted. "I thought I was going to lose her. She was in so much pain. She is better now and will be herself soon."

"I'm happy to hear the charity will be helping the families."

"Yes, the money will be helpful."

"Sit, please," Cole said, indicating the couch.

Cole sat down next to him. He looked very serious and said, "We finally think we found him.

"Where?" asked Jeremy, knowing who he was referencing.

"We know Zeke was in prison in Washington State. He was transferred there after New York and was tried for an outstanding warrant. He escaped and we have had word he has been spotted in Montana and Wyoming."

"Heading east," Jeremy said, thinking. "Do we know his final destination?"

"I think here," Cole said, sounding resigned.

"Is he after Emma? Or Clair?"

"We can't know for certain."

"I'd like to go after him," stated Jeremy in a tone that didn't invite argument.

"Let's work on finding him first," Cole suggested.

They made a plan to find Zeke.

CHAPTER 45

BOARDING HOUSE

Papa had moved Emma back to her bed. "Thank you, Papa."

"Anything for you, little girl. Get some rest," Papa murmured. He stood looking at Emma and started to cry.

"Papa? Why are you crying?" Emma asked.

"Oh, my little girl. I was so afraid I was going to lose you."

"I'm fine now. You won't lose me," she said.

Papa wiped his face and hugged her. He caressed the side of her face, smiled, and exited the room, leaving Dora and Emma together.

Dora fussed with Emma's blanket and averted her eyes.

"Dora?" Emma inquired quietly.

"Yes," Dora said absently.

"Are you avoiding being alone with me?" she asked, watching Dora's reaction closely.

"No, of course not," Dora said as she kept her eyes averted.

"I think you are," Emma said and started to get out of bed.

"No, don't get up on your own," Dora said, reaching for her.

As she got close, Emma grabbed her by the arms and said triumphantly, "Got you."

"Fell for that, didn't I?" Dora asked, knowing it was impossible to keep anything from her.

"Yes," Something occurred to Emma. "Dora, are you disappointed in me for having this happen outside of marriage?" she asked referring to the pregnancy.

"What? No!" She looked her in the eyes and assured her, "Never."

"Then what's wrong?" Emma asked, bewildered. Before Dora could answer, Emma took a long look at her, noticing things she hadn't before. Her rounder face, fuller hips, shiny hair, and lastly, her breasts. "Dora, you're having a baby!"

"Yes," she admitted, turning red.

"Why didn't you tell me?" Emma asked. Something else occurred to her. "Clair knew, didn't she?"

"Yes, she figured it out also. I didn't tell you initially because you were involved in the case. Then you had your procedure…I just couldn't tell you, knowing you might not ever be able to have children." She felt so miserable knowing she would have something Emma could not.

"Dora, I mean it when I say I don't want kids. I don't want that, but that doesn't mean I won't be a good aunt to your baby." She reached out and said, "May I?"

"Of course, I felt a little something earlier today," she said as she lifted her shirt to show a small rounding of her belly.

Emma reached over and felt the firm skin. "What does it feel like?"

"Tiny butterflies," she said placing her hand over Emma's.

Emma asked, "Wow. How do you feel?"

"Good. Scared. This is something Tim and I have wanted for so long," she admitted.

Emma grabbed Dora's hands and said, "Please don't keep anything from me."

"I won't," she promised. "Tim is so happy. He already wants to start decorating the nursery."

"I'll make you a cover for the bed with a lace trim," she promised.

"That would be lovely." Dora hugged her suddenly and said, "I'm so glad I can share this with you."

"Have you told Patrick?" asked Emma, knowing Dora was protective of him.

"We told him he was going to have a little sister or brother. He was happy," Dora said softly.

Emma was thinking aloud, when she said, "I would guess she has seen the symptoms in her girls." Clair had run a bordello and pregnancy would have been a normal occurrence.

"Did she say what they did in those cases? Did they keep their babies?" asked Dora curiously.

" I've heard about the ways women can get rid of the baby," commented Emma.

"Get rid of?" Dora asked, not understanding.

Emma explained that herbalists or apothecaries carry the herbs that seemed to encourage miscarriages, such as tansy and pennyroyal. The herbs would be made into a tea or infusion and taken by the patient in the hopes of encouraging uterine contractions.

"How do you know about this?" Dora asked, astonished at the information.

"Clair shared it with me when I was thinking about being with Jeremy," she explained.

"I don't understand it. A baby is. . ." she said, holding her stomach protectively.

"A miracle," she said with a smile.

"Yes."

They talked into the next hour about baby names.

CHAPTER 46

$\mathcal{A}$s Emma convalesced at home, she spent time thinking about the children and what George and Elizabeth had said the day before. She made a list of who could be around kids: parents, teachers, preachers, and older sibling's friends.

My team, she thought, *we need to bring them in and talk about this. We also need to have George and Elizabeth there. They can share their reasoning for this theory.*

Emma hadn't been allowed to walk yet, so she called loudly, "Dora!"

Dora walked out of the kitchen, wiping her hands on her apron as she made her way into the sitting room, asking, "Emma, do you need something?"

"Yes, sit here with me for a moment. I want to ask you something," Emma said, patting the seat beside her. Dora sat and waited for her to continue. "The case we are working on, with the children. . ." Dora nodded. "Cole has Pinkertons working on leads for the case, based on the fact Harry was involved. They're also trying to check out the background of the 'Sister,' but I think those leads aren't going to get us to the main person involved."

"What are you thinking?" Dora asked curiously.

"I'm thinking about a conversation I had with George and Elizabeth," she said and went on to describe the new theory.

Dora said thoughtfully, "You know, they're right. Kids are rather insulated from most adults."

"I was thinking of calling a team meeting after dinner, and including George and Elizabeth," said Emma, continuing to make notes.

"Yes," agreed Dora. "If we can help find out who did this to Patrick's parents and those poor children, it is the right thing to do."

Later that evening, Tim, Dora, Jeremy, Cole, Jake, Emma, Elizabeth, and George were sitting at the kitchen table. Emma started, "I invited Elizabeth and George because they might have some insight into our current case." She looked over at Cole and asked, "Could you update us on the current status?"

Cole nodded. "We looked into the Harry connection first. He was a visible connection between the child murder found by Mr. Marella and the dead children now. We questioned him and he only admitted to involvement once the kids were delivered. He was also in charge of administering the drugs; he's confessed to experimenting on the amounts. He will hang for those murders."

He paused, as he needed to clear the emotion out of his voice. He started again, "He said he reported to the 'Sister' and her name is Beatrice Purvis. She was the only one who knew who their contact was in this area."

Emma asked, "Has anyone interviewed the children to find out if they are aware of who initially took them?"

Cole answered, "We did interview them before sending them home from the hospital. They weren't able to communicate much. Their memories were affected by the drugs."

Dora's thoughts were about the children's well-being. "That is a blessing."

Jeremy looked at Emma and said, "You mentioned a new theory?"

"George," prompted Emma, "could you explain to the group what you were saying about who might be taking the kids?"

George sat up straighter and said, "Elizabeth and I work with children in our jobs as teachers, we have a special bond with them. They see us every day and know their parents trust us. We believe the people behind this might have thought of the same thing."

Jeremy was pondering that and said, "So, teachers, preachers, parents."

Emma was checking off her list and added, "Also older sibling's friends."

Dora said, "We don't want to forget about community people, people they see every day: grocers, store owners, ones who tend to have a lot of kid traffic."

Cole was taking notes. "That does help with direction. I can have people watch the more open places: grocers and stores with kids." He looked up and said to the group, "Does anyone know the priest or preachers in that area?"

Tim suggested, "Father Cavanaugh, our parish priest, he could help with that and any rumors."

Elizabeth spoke up, "George and I have an idea about the school."

The group looked on expectantly as she continued, "We've talked about teaching at the school there. They need teachers and we could be used to keep an eye on what might be happening."

Dora asked surprised, "Would that mean you'd move?"

"We'd hoped to stay, but we would need transportation to and from the school each day. We'd need help on that."

Tim raised a hand. "We can help with that, we have several couriers who could take you in the wagons and bring you back."

Cole asked, "How hard would it be to move over to the school?"

George looked at Elizabeth and said, "We've already inquired, and they said we can start as soon as we can get released here. We expect to be able to move over next week." Their jobs here hadn't been made permanent yet and there was some flexibility.

Jeremy frowned. "My only concern is your safety. We'll want you to observe and report anything you see."

Cole cautioned, "This may be long-term. We may have driven them underground."

"We're okay with that. We plan on staying permanently. We feel this is where we're supposed to be teaching," said George.

"Okay then, we'll get everyone in place. If something is needed to be reported, send a note to the Pinkerton's office. We'll have a weekly group meeting to discuss updates," stated Emma.

CHAPTER 47

The next day, Cole and Jeremy had the teams set up to watch the stores. "I thought we'd have fewer kids to worry about on the streets," he said, watching the children play and run around.

"You have to remember these are working families and they do the best they can. There isn't always money for people to watch them. They do seem to be hanging around in groups and not individually," said Cole thoughtfully.

That week went by quickly, and they were soon sitting down for their first group meeting at the boarding house. Emma looked toward Cole and Jeremy and asked, "Anything to report?"

"There are more kids out than I would have thought, but they seem to have group leaders. I haven't seen any of the owners approaching them, except to have them leave if they get too rowdy. We'll keep watching," he promised.

"Tim?" Emma continued around the table.

"Father Cavanaugh said there are several churches in that area—Catholic and Protestant. He knows both men. The priest is quite old and may not have the mobility required. The Protestant preacher has been on a missionary trip for the last few weeks."

"What about their replacements?" asked Emma.

"The Protestant church is just meeting for prayers as a community, so I think we can discount them. The priest does have a younger replacement, but he only started about a year ago."

Emma mulled that over, *The first child abduction I was involved in was six years ago. If this is part of that original case, it would involve someone who lived in the area at the time.*

"George, Elizabeth?" Emma inquired.

George looked at Elizabeth and she started. "We're just getting to know everyone. Most are married men or unmarried women."

"What about single men?" Jeremy asked.

"There are a few," she admitted.

"Are they close to the kids?" asked Tim.

"Two of them work on special programs helping them after school. Albert Chastain and Lee Jones," George said.

Jeremy said, "I can find out from the parents if any of the children taken were in these programs."

Emma closed her notebook and said, "Good work. This will take time."

Cole said, "We need to be aware that, if the person is still here, they might try again. We know that the money involved would be hard to turn down."

"Yes," they all agreed.

Elizabeth spent the next week paying particular attention to the two after-school groups she'd mentioned to the team. She went to the schoolroom where the students would be that afternoon, pretending to look through her papers. She noticed Albert preparing drinks for his group; it seemed to be some type of punch.

"What do you have there?" she asked curiously from the doorway.

"Just a little punch to help the kids make it through an extra hour of teaching," he said, giving her a sideways glance.

"Oh," she said trying to be nonchalant. She had seen him make these drinks before and knew the kids would grab the cups quickly as they entered. She excused herself to go find George.

She found him and said in a low voice, "George, I'm going to stay around a bit today to grade some papers. Could you let Lester know?" Lester was their driver to and from school each day.

"Sure, I'll wait," he said, reading the stress in her eyes.

"Okay, I'll meet you." She quickly went back to Albert's room and stayed in the hallway watching the kids enter. Her tally was twelve of various ages. They seemed to be settling into their lessons and she went down to get the papers she needed to grade. As she returned she sat in her chair, positioned near the room. She glanced in the windows and the first thing she did was count the children. *Eleven. Weren't there twelve earlier?* She frowned.

She waited for the program to be completed for the day and, as the children left, she said to a tall boy, "Are you all here? Did someone leave early?"

He shook his head. "Maya was a bit sick, so she laid down in the large closet." He didn't say more and just walked away.

She continued to watch the room and saw Albert locking up and turning off the lights to his room. She had to act; she couldn't wait for help, so she stuck her foot out and tripped him as he exited. He fell face-first on the floor and looked at her accusingly. "You tripped me!"

George was just coming around the corner, saw Albert on the floor, and asked, "What happened?"

"I fell," he said, still looking angrily at Elizabeth.

"George, I think we need something out of his school closet," she said.

George took the hint and said, "Albert, can you open your closet for us? We need to borrow a book from you."

"What book?" he asked belligerently.

"Does it matter? Why don't you open the closet for us?" George asked, stepping toward a still sitting Albert. "Why don't I help you up?" As Albert put out his hand, George grabbed it firmly and pulled him up and toward him. "Now, that closet."

Albert nodded and turned toward it, seeing George was serious.

"I think one of the girls in his class is missing," Elizabeth murmured as they followed.

Albert opened the closet and Elizabeth went in.

She came out and said, "She isn't there."

Lester walked into the classroom and asked, "Ready to go?"

"Not yet. Could you go get Cole and Jeremy for us? Tell them we need help," George requested.

Lester got serious quickly and said, "Yes, on my way." They could hear his steps as he ran down the hallway.

As they watched him leave, they noticed Albert trying to sneak away. Elizabeth looked him in the eye and asked, "Albert, where is Maya? I heard she got sick."

He looked a little evasive but muttered, "She didn't feel well so I sent her to the nurse."

Elizabeth said, "Hold him." George took him by the arms and restrained him while she ran to the nurse's office. She saw her leaving and yelled, "Wait!" The nurse looked wide-eyed at her office, then at Elizabeth, and started running toward the exit.

Elizabeth didn't go after her; she was more concerned about Maya. She tried the door to the office and found it locked. There was a small window on the door; she broke it and managed to get the door open. She glanced around and was about to leave when she heard a small moan. "Maya!" she said dropping down to look under the desk. The girl was there. Elizabeth crawled under and wrapped her arms around her and pulled her out. Holding her close, she rushed back to the room with Maya in her arms and said, "The nurse is gone."

"Thank god she didn't take Maya," George said fervently.

"Yes," she said, holding her tightly. "She ran out the back when I was coming up."

"Well, we have him," George said, nodding at Albert. "We'll wait for Cole and Jeremy."

Albert slumped to the floor, knowing he was left with all the blame.

CHAPTER 48

Cole, Jeremy, and several Pinkerton detectives arrived. Cole and Jeremy immediately wanted to question Albert. He sat straining at his bonds and sweating profusely. Elizabeth and George had briefed them on his and the nurse's activities.

"Lester, could you take Elizabeth and George to the principal's office and see if we can contact Maya's parents?" Cole asked.

Lester nodded. Elizabeth continued to cradle Maya as she and George followed him to the office.

Jeremy bent down and got face-to-face with Albert. "Come on, you know you want to tell us what's happening here."

"No, I don't want to talk," he muttered, looking away.

Jeremy came at him harder. "So, you like to hurt children?"

"No, no, of course not. I'm a teacher," he stuttered.

"What was in that punch, Albert?" Cole asked quietly.

"Nothing."

"Want to try that answer again?" Cole asked, his voice low and dangerous.

He looked mutinous but saw Jeremy was carrying a gun. "I won't go down for her."

"Her?" asked Jeremy.

"Yes, Christy Black. She's the nurse here. This was all her idea," he said.

Principal Harrison stood at the door and said, "She's a traveling nurse, going to schools here and on the east coast."

"Allowing her to set up networks to remove multiple children," commented Jeremy.

"Yes," Albert admitted.

"Why did you do it?" asked the principal, not understanding.

"Money. There's always a need to have more," he said quietly.

"But they were children!" the Principal said.

Albert looked down, knowing it was over for him.

Cole looked at the principal and said, "We need the records for where she lives in the area and what other schools she works for."

He nodded and said, "I'll get the information immediately."

CHAPTER 49

BOARDING HOUSE THAT EVENING

Cole and Jeremy brought a chalkboard to the boarding house to demonstrate the extent of the missing children case. The team was in the sitting room, watching Jeremy document the nurse's schools. "We have information showing she was working at four schools in Chicago and six in New York State. We also have her in Boston and other cities up the east coast."

Jeremy drew out the information, showing she had access to kids all over.

"Have you contacted the schools in those areas to ask about any missing children?" asked Emma.

"Yes," he said. "I got the telegrams off and hope to hear something soon. I also gave them warnings about the nurse."

Cole added, "I've notified the Pinkerton offices to send detectives to the schools to see if they can find her. I also mentioned the punch and to apprehend anyone serving it to children."

"So, what happens now?" asked Tim.

"We wait. We can't get to the areas to help, so we have to check our schools here," said Cole.

"Frustrating," said Emma.

"Yes, but we have to trust they're doing everything they can," said Jeremy.

CHAPTER 50

NEW YORK STATE

"They know who she is?" the older man asked quietly.

"They do," the younger man answered in the same tone.

"You took care of Beatrice?" he asked.

"Yes. We had a man in the area, and he prevented any information exchange."

"Should we worry about the people they have in custody?"

"No, they only knew Beatrice and no one else. We're well insulated," he said calmly.

"Good," said the older man. He looked thoughtful and said, "It's time to shut this operation down. Can you take care of it?"

"Yes."

"Make sure she's found quickly. It needs to be a statement."

"Of course."

"Terrible business. I never should have allowed it to happen," the older man said regretfully.

"It was very profitable," the other man murmured.

"Yes, but hugely emotional. It could have taken us down. This should remove all connection to us."

"I'll take care of it now."

He waved him off and said, "We'll talk later."

"Yes, sir," the man said as he stepped back and pulled the cell door closed with a loud clank.

John Hardin sat thinking about how his operations were running very smoothly from prison. He mulled over how the current enterprise had ended. *Emma, we will meet again.*

CHAPTER 51

PINKERTON OFFICE

A telegram was brought in.

Cole read it and then looked at Jeremy. "Miss O'Brien has been found."

Jeremy smiled and asked, "Good. When can we get her here for an interview and trial?"

"Never, I'm afraid," Col said without expression.

"Why not?"

"She's dead. She was found in a very public place, outside of town hall in New York City. She was tied up and shot in the head. Someone wanted an example made of her. I'm assuming this was a statement they're done with this business."

Jeremy frowned. "Do we believe it?"

"I'm sure it will stop for a while. It would seem rather risky at this time."

"Do we have the numbers of kids taken from each location?" asked Jeremy.

"Each precinct is working on that now. We should have the final numbers soon."

"Is there a chance to find them?"

"There will be raids on bordellos that have underage children, but they could be anywhere," Cole said regretfully.

CHAPTER 52

The funerals were set for that day. In all, five children died. The families decided to have the services together. Emma and Jeremy were in her room at the boarding house, discussing the event.

"Emma, it will be a long day," he started.

The event would be long, but Emma did not want to be kept home. "I think—"

"Emma, if you would let me finish," he interrupted, arching an eyebrow at her. "I would agree it's time and you should be there. You weren't able to save those five, but fifteen went home to their parents."

She took a deep breath, admitting, "It is going to be a long day."

"Yes," he said as he helped her get dressed. Their clothing was sober, a stark contrast to the sunny day.

Tim, Jeremy, Cole, Dora, and Emma moved to the carriages. Patrick would remain with Papa for the day. Patrick had attended his parent's funeral and they wanted to protect him from more sadness.

When they got to the church, they saw Thomas, Clair, and

her assistant Sam. Clair walked over, saying quietly, "Everything is arranged. I have places reserved for you all." She'd had the charity set up and paid for all the children to have services and be buried.

As she walked them in, Emma asked, "Why are we going toward the front? That is for the families of the deceased."

Clair stopped and turned back to their group. "The families requested it."

Emma nodded, not knowing what to say, and continued to follow her up the aisle. *There are so many people. Children's funerals are always crowded*, she thought. Her condition had prevented her from meeting with the families, so she didn't know they were eager to be introduced.

As she approached the front, she noticed several women nodding toward her. They broke away from their group and started toward them.

"Miss Evans?" one asked tentatively.

"Yes. Call me Emma, please," Emma asked, unsure how they would react to her. She was the one who had found the location of the children, both dead and alive. *Do they hate me?* she wondered. She waited for someone to talk.

The other ladies gestured at one to start. "Emma, we wanted to thank you for bringing our children home." Emma didn't realize she was crying until Jeremy handed her a tissue. She smiled at him gratefully.

Jeremy was watching her and saw her energy dwindling. She was white as a ghost. He leaned over and said, "We need to sit you down." He turned to address the others. "Ladies, she shouldn't be standing too long."

"Yes, of course. We would like a chance to speak with you later," the leader of their small group requested.

Clair interceded and said, "There'll be time after. We'll have a wake, with food for everyone. I've arranged a hall."

The women nodded and returned to their families.

Jeremy and Emma made their way to their seats. Thomas nodded toward Clair as he sat with Emma and the family. Clair and her assistant Sam approached the priest to discuss any last-minute issues.

Emma looked around and noticed that a large number of Sisters from the hospital were present. She saw Sisters Catherine, Ann, Mary, and others. Catching Sister Catherine's eye, she nodded toward her. Sister Catherine acknowledged her, nodding in return.

Emma turned back to the front of the church. Flowers overflowed atop the church altar. The priest stood in front of the pulpit to read the Gospel. It was a traditional service—prayers were said; families cried.

When it drew to a close, the fathers of the dead children stood. The priest had agreed to let them make a statement, and their speaker stepped forward. "We want to thank you for being here for us and our families today. We have lost something that can't be replaced. We love and will always miss Christopher, Michael, Cindy, Evelyn, and Katherine." His voice broke and he stopped a moment; he took a deep breath to clear his voice and continued. "We can't stop blaming ourselves for not being able to protect our children. We are at this lovely service today because of the charity. We've also been informed that they want to set up a location for children who are home alone. Mrs. Callahan, could you come up?"

"Yes, thank you," Clair said graciously. "We want to make a safe place for the kids to be kids. We are looking for a location in your areas where they can get to safely after school. My assistant, Sam Peterson, will start having community meetings to discuss the progress."

At that final statement, the fathers and men in the audience surrounded the caskets and raised them on their shoulders. The small size of the caskets affected everyone. All movement was done in silence.

They were moved to waiting wagons and would be transported to the local cemetery. They'd chosen a close one so the families could walk.

"Will you be able to make the walk?" a concerned Jeremy asked Emma.

"I can take her to the hall," volunteered Sam. "I need to check on the arrangements."

"We'll both go and meet everyone else there," suggested Jeremy.

"Yes, let's do that," she said and followed him to the carriage.

The hall was both sober and beautiful. Food was provided on side tables and arriving families talked together quietly. The services were completed and the mourners arrived at the hall. The mothers of the lost children wanted to have some time with Emma, and she followed them to a side room. They allowed her to sit down and one of the ladies started. "We appreciate you finding our children so they could be buried properly."

"I'm just sorry we weren't able to save all of them," Emma said helplessly.

"No! You're not responsible for that. Other people are. Without you, we would never have known what happened to them."

They were all crying at that point. Several of the men came in and one spoke up. "Okay now, let's break this up. We're sure Emma is getting very tired."

Emma realized she was tired, but not exhausted. *I'm better,* she thought. She returned to the hall and Jeremy. He raised his eyebrow at her and she said, "Later."

When they were heading home, alone in their carriage, she told him what the ladies had wanted.

"They are amazing people," Jeremy commented

"Yes, I think they have to be," she said. She looked over and stated, "Jeremy, I am getting better. I can feel it."

He smiled and said, "We could start with a short walk this evening and build up your energy each day."

She smiled, happy as always that they were on the same page.

On the way back from their walk that evening, she saw a courier ahead of them near the boarding house. They followed him up the stoop and got to him before he could knock.

"I can take that," stated Emma.

"Do you live here?" the courier asked.

"Yes, who's the telegram for?" she asked.

He looked down and read, "Emma Evans."

"Well, that's me," she said with a smile.

He had her sign for it and went on to his other deliveries.

"Who's it from?" asked Jeremy, always curious about a telegram.

"Tony," she said simply as she opened it.

"Oh, the world traveler," he said lightly. "What does he say?"

"Oh no!"

"What is it? "

"The museum curator, Philip Johnson, has gone missing. Tony's requesting my help."

"Help where? Overseas?" Jeremy asked incredulously.

"Yes," she said, tapping the letter on her hand. "I could go by boat and be there in a few weeks."

"Be where?" Jeremy asked, bewildered.

"Paris. It shouldn't be a problem, and it would give me time to rest and walk before I get there," she said, planning.

Jeremy thought at first to say it was too soon, but then he thought of Zeke. The latest intel continued to indicate he was heading straight for them. *This might not be a bad idea. It would get Emma out of the way,* he thought. "I think that sounds like a plan. Tony could use a friend there," he said positively.

She frowned. "Jeremy, aren't you angry about this?" She had expected a very different response.

"You going to Paris? No," he answered firmly.

"By myself? To see Tony." She didn't know why she kept questioning if he had no objections.

"Well, you are not one-hundred percent yet. Do you need someone to accompany you?" he asked, thinking.

"I don't think so, but couldn't you make time to come with me?" she asked hesitantly. It would be a long separation.

"I have several cases at critical points. I have to be here for them," he explained.

There's something more, thought Emma, but she couldn't read his face. "Okay, I'll send a telegram to Tony and tell him I'll be going over to see him." She wanted to be excited, but she was unsure why Jeremy was acting this way. She looked at him thoughtfully and wondered if she was worried about nothing.

"I'll go with you to send it."

As they made their way to the telegraph office, Emma was still contemplative. She thought to herself, *I need to refocus. I'm going to Paris to help Tony.*

CHAPTER 53

The next morning, she took a carriage to the office to get tickets for the ship. She would be going to Havre, France—a port city—and catching a day train to Paris. The initial trip would be about six days on the La Bretagne if there were no delays. They got Emma reserved in 1st class. That would allow her some privacy on the trip.

As she was making her travel plans, she worried about leaving Dora.

"Emma," assured Dora, "my doctor said I'm doing well and have a long way to go before the baby is born. I'm not due until well after your return."

"You're sure?" Emma asked. "I can have a Pinkerton detective go over for me."

"Emma, it's Paris. You've always dreamed of traveling, and you know you wouldn't want anyone else to help Tony," she said, understanding Emma still cared deeply for him. She looked at Emma consideringly and said, "You'll need clothes for the trip, and fast."

"Yes, the seamstress we work with might be able to make me some travel clothes. We can go see her today." They both went that afternoon. Luckily, there was an order almost completed, then canceled. The clothes were fitted to Emma and promised to be delivered in the next few days.

She confirmed her ticket and arrival data via telegram to Tony, remembering their conversation before he'd left. He had been so excited about learning more about the masters in Paris. His eyes had lit up as he talked about what he and Philip would see. Tony had raved about the main innovation of the era—the collapsible tin paint tube, invented in 1841 by American painter John Rand. This revolutionized the color palette and technique of Plein Air oil painting by offering a range of pre-mixed colors in a convenient, portable medium. This was a major factor in the emergence of Impressionism. He couldn't wait to see the paintings in person.

CHAPTER 54

Jeremy planned to accompany her on the train to New York and drop her off at the ship. He was withholding the information about Zeke until the last possible moment.

Everything came together quickly, and they left a few days later on the train to New York. Their time together was very pleasant, except for Jeremy's continued concern about her reaction to his deception.

They switched trains and moved into a carriage for the final leg of the trip. They went directly to the ship; it would be leaving that evening.

As they pulled up, Jeremy removed her luggage and waved over a porter to move it onto the ship. They followed him on board and found her cabin assignment. The porter stowed her bags while Jeremy and Emma stood at the rail to say goodbye. Jeremy looked pained when he said, "Emma, I have to tell you something."

She frowned; he sounded upset. "What is it Jeremy?" she asked, concerned.

He pulled her close, laying his head on her shoulder. "I really want to go with you."

"You still can. I have a private cabin. Would you like me to change the arrangements?" she asked and tried to step back to see if she could do so.

He pulled her back and looked her in the eyes. "No, you don't know what is going on. Zeke Jones escaped from prison and has been tracked heading toward Chicago."

"Zeke," she echoed, going white.

Jeremy replied, "Yes. We found out he had escaped a little while ago, and we've been getting reports he's been seen traveling East."

"Going after me and Clair," she said, finishing his statement. "I need to stay and help catch him," she said, trying to move toward the gangway to disembark.

Jeremy pulled her to a stop. "No, Emma, you're going to stay on this boat and stay safe."

Emma thought of Tony and asked, "Is Tony's telegram a lie?"

"No," he insisted. "I love you so much and, just this once, I want to be the one to protect you. Can you let me do that, please?"

Tears filled her eyes. "If you get him—"

"When," he interrupted.

"When you get him, can you make sure we don't have to deal with him again?"

He got her silent message and promised, "I'll make sure." He wanted off the topic. He didn't want their last moments together to be about Zeke. "Will Tony meet you in Havre? Or in Paris?"

Emma let him change the topic and responded with, "He said he would be in Havre, and we'll take the train to Paris together. He can brief me on the details before we arrive."

A loud voice sounded, calling for visitors to leave the ship. Jeremy looked like he didn't want to leave her.

"Get some rest, please. Send me a telegram when you arrive in Paris," he requested.

"I will," she said softly. "When I return, we will be together again." Her cheeks flushed.

"I look forward to that," said Jeremy, enjoying her embarrassment.

They called a second time for visitors to leave the ship. "I have to go."

She grabbed him and kissed him hard, then broke away to say, "Jeremy, I love you. Be safe."

"I love you, I have to go now."

She walked him to the gangplank, and they kissed softly. She watched him walk down and then waved as they got underway. She waited until she couldn't see him anymore and headed to her cabin to rest before dinner.

As she entered her cabin, she looked around and was surprised at how nice it was. The floors were darkly stained wood with rugs throughout. She had a sitting room and a small bedroom.

She turned and locked her door before going to the bed to lie down.

CHAPTER 55

She slept hard and woke in time for dinner. The ship had sent an itinerary to the rooms dictating the time and location. She would need to get dressed and go straight down. Since it was the first night, the itinerary also indicated that the dress for dinner would be casual. Her outfit of choice was a black skirt and a red blouse. Carefully making her way down, she passed many couples on the walk down and nodded politely. The dinner line was short as she waited to be seated by the host.

"Your name?" he inquired

"Emma Evans," she supplied.

He looked down at his book and looked back up to say, "Yes, we have you sitting with a group. Is that okay?" he asked politely.

"That would be nice." She followed him to the assigned table. It was a large room with burgundy carpet and white tablecloths covering round tables. The chairs were painted a gold color and seemed to sparkle in the evening light. They reached the table and the host pulled out her chair. Her gaze fell on those she would be spending the next six days with. They were a friendly bunch and were already talking animatedly about their destination.

An older woman across from her was saying to the group, "Paris, can you imagine? I understand many artists are working there now."

"And the food is supposed to be wonderful," responded a young woman next to Emma.

"Yes, but can you speak French?" asked the older woman.

"I hadn't thought of that, but I'm sure they speak English," the younger woman responded.

I wouldn't be so sure of that, Emma thought. As soon as Papa learned Emma would be going to France, he'd had a specialist come to the house and practice pronunciations with her. Her advice had been to keep as quiet as possible and try to speak French, never to assume they spoke English. *Thank goodness Tony took French lessons for months to prepare for his trip,* she thought to herself.

The older gentleman opposite Emma suggested introductions. *Hmm,* she thought, *this will allow me to put my observational skills to work. I'll need to document who's at the table. There are eight people in all.*

"Young lady, would you like to start?" he asked, indicating Emma.

"Yes. I'm Emma Evans, and I'm on my way to meet a friend and see Paris." She kept her information simple. No need to share why she was going there.

"Are you traveling alone?" asked the older gentleman's wife.

"I am," Emma responded.

"Aren't you nervous?" she asked.

"No, not really. My friend will meet me when we dock," she said casually.

"Well, just let us know if you need anything," her husband responded.

"I will, thank you," said Emma sincerely.

The older gentleman continued with the introductions and looked at the couple sitting on Emma's left. "Would you like to introduce yourselves?"

"Yes," the gentleman answered for them. "We are Scott and Meghan Bauer, and we're on our honeymoon."

"Congratulations," said the group.

Emma watched them closely; something about them made her uneasy. She noticed Scott spoke for both of them and Meghan kept her eyes down. Emma noted the rings Meghan wore. Evidently, she'd married into money.

The couple on Emma's right was next. They were an older couple, probably in their mid-fifties. "We are Richard and Susan Billings, and we're traveling after selling our business to our son and his wife. We are also celebrating our thirtieth anniversary."

"Congratulations," said the group.

The gentleman seated next to her was next. "I'm Walter Garber. I'm not married and I'm on my way to Paris on business." Emma noted his age to be about thirty. "And," he teased, winking at the two ladies who had spoken earlier about the French language, "you should practice your French. The trip will be more entertaining for you. I can help you if you would like."

The older gentleman who had started the introductions went next. "We are Lloyd and Merry Jackson. Merry has always wanted to see Paris, and I just couldn't say no. So, we're off on an adventure."

Emma noticed Merry seemed to have tremors in her hands, and she kept them hidden in her lap when she wasn't using them. *Would medical issues be another reason for the trip?* she wondered.

Dinner was then served. The main course was Beef Wellington with carrots and peas. During dinner, there were conversations with Walter on his business. The group wanted him to give them details about what they might see in Paris

Walter continued to talk at length about castles and other lovely architecture. Emma was fascinated and she could tell her fellow tablemates were also.

The one outlier was Meghan. She seemed distracted. She didn't say a word and let her husband continue talking for her. Emma wanted to speak with Meghan and mention she had options if she needed them.

When Meghan got up to look at the dessert display, Emma followed and said in a low voice, "If you need help or want to talk, I can assist you."

Meghan replied in a low voice, "I can meet you after midnight. Scott is normally passed out drunk by then, and I should be able to sneak out. Meet by the railing by the lifeboats?"

"I will meet you," Emma promised and moved away. Emma noted Scott watching, but he didn't seem concerned.

CHAPTER 56

*L*ater that night, Emma left her cabin and made her way to the prearranged meeting location. Nearing the lifeboats, an argument made her pause. It was Meghan and Scott.

She continued toward them and saw they were struggling with one another. *What is going on? Is she ...* Before she could finish the thought, Scott went over the side and of the ship! Emma ran to the railing to see if she could see him. She noticed immediately that Meghan was not looking and had not called for help. Emma started to yell when she heard someone else call out, "Man overboard!!" The boat started slowing as the search teams were sent out.

Meghan's mood was oddly calm. She didn't cry or even seem upset as she stood with Emma. That all changed when the captain strode up to them.

She immediately started crying. "My husband fell overboard! He was trying to push me off and he fell instead. I don't know why he would want to kill me! Emma saw him attack me!"

Emma watched her, not knowing what to believe. Something about the struggle she witnessed was bothering her but she was unsure what it was.

The captain said, "We can get into that later, the rescue is our priority currently."

The crew sent out boats all night and into the next day. Scott's body was not found. An emergency station had been set up within a conference room, near the captain's cabin. Meghan and Emma waited there as the search took place. When it was called off, Meghan was notified and promptly fainted. They transferred her to the doctor's office and Emma accompanied her.

Meghan came to as the doctor was examining her. Emma stayed to help her take off her shirt and skirt, revealing bruises on her forearms and the front of her legs. Emma noticed there was no bruising on her back or areas that would be unreachable by Meghan herself.

Emma had worked helping women who were actual victims of physical abuse and knew what self-inflicted wounds looked like. They weren't as deep as wounds inflicted by assault, due to the difference in the force applied, and were often found on forearms or legs, less vital areas of the body.

She might be faking it, though she couldn't be for certain that she did this to herself, Emma thought. *Her husband had been insensitive and selfish. Was he also a wifebeater?* She helped Meghan dress and sit up. The captain joined them and immediately Meghan's behavior changed. She ran to him and her body shook as she cried in his arms.

Meghan could turn the grieving wife display on and off at will. The captain was solicitous, patting her on the back and saying, "Madam, I'm so sorry, but we must keep our schedule. We've put out notices to passing ships to watch for him." He seemed at a loss as to how to comfort her.

Emma took that moment to step in and say, "Captain, I'll take care of her."

He looked at Emma gratefully and said, "Miss Evans, we appreciate your help in this matter."

"I'll accompany her back to her cabin," Emma said, offering Meghan a hand up.

When they reached her cabin, Meghan turned to her. "I'm just so tired. I would like to rest now."

Emma wanted to get into the cabin to look around and said, "Why don't I come in for a bit. We can talk?"

"NO!" Meghan shouted. She realized how shrill she sounded and said in a calmer voice, "No, I really want some time alone."

Emma looked at her and thought, *There's no place for her to run, and I can confide in the captain concerning what I believe happened.* She said out loud, "If you need to talk, just have a note sent to my cabin."

"I will," she said softly. "Thanks for trying to help me."

Emma frowned, and finally said, "Okay then, get some rest and I'll see you in the morning." The door closed and stood in the hallway for a long time. She was suspicious and felt they needed to look at the wife's role in this event. The captain needed to know of her suspicions. She headed toward his cabin. A ship's officer was stationed outside of his door and she asked as she approached, "Does he have time for me?"

"Just a moment," he said. He knocked on the door and stepped into the cabin.

He stepped back out and said, "You may enter."

The officer pushed the door opened and she stepped in. The captain was there sitting in a heavy brown chair. He stood, walked to her, and said, "Yes, Miss Evans? Is Mrs. Bauer okay?"

"Yes, I believe so," she said.

"Would you like to sit down?" the captain asked.

Emma nodded and took a seat on his couch. She stated, "Captain, we haven't had a chance to talk since I boarded your ship."

He looked at her consideringly and replied, "No, I've been busy."

She smiled at that and said, "Yes, well, I'm an investigator. I work investigative jobs for my business and the Pinkerton Detective Agency."

The captain knew the Pinkerton name well. "Isn't that unusual for a woman?"

She thought, *One day, I hope that won't be a question when I talk about my investigative work.* Out loud, she answered, "Yes, it is."

"Does this have something to do with Mrs. Bauer?"

Emma figured being blunt was the best option for the disclosure of this information and started, "I believe Mrs. Bauer has murdered her husband."

He frowned and sat forward in his chair. "I think you'll need to explain yourself. As I understand it *you* saw Scott try to force *her* from the ship."

"I did see them grappling with one another," she confirmed. *I need to think about what I saw.*

The captain continued, "And from interviews with fellow passengers, we determined he was abusive and controlling. Out doctor said there was evidence of abuse in the form of numerous bruises."

Emma pulled out her notebook and opened to the page where she had documented the bruises. "I believe those bruises might be self-inflicted."

"Explain yourself," he commanded.

She showed him the notebook and explained the injury locations and intensity. "It's very unusual that a beating would only occur in areas she could reach."

"Hmm," he said, reviewing the notes.

"Also," she continued, "what we saw was merely the appearance of abuse. For instance, he answered for her, and she was very quiet and didn't say anything. I believe that was also an act."

"Why would she do it?" he asked, at a loss.

"I believe the motive might be money. Her husband appeared to be quite prosperous," she stated matter-of-factly.

"But she appears so young. . ."

"Yes," Emma commented.

"We won't have access to background information until we reach France."

"I'll have to get her to talk to me," she said.

"I don't think it would hurt anything, and if nothing comes of it, we don't disclose the investigation," stated the captain, unsure what to believe.

"Agreed."

She made her way back to her cabin to get some rest. She slowly undressed, missing Jeremy. As she lay down, she thought about her plans to investigate Meghan. Her thoughts went back to what she witnessed before Scott went overboard. Something clicked and she smiled. *I've got you! Meghan believes she has me fooled, that I think she's the victim. I need her to keep talking to me to keep up that façade. I have four more days to figure out how to get her to admit she killed Scott.*

She fell asleep pondering the case.

CHAPTER 57

DAY 3 OF 7 ON THE LA BRETAGNE

The next morning at breakfast, Emma saw Meghan sitting alone at their group table. She made her way forward, saying casually as she sat down, "Good morning, Meghan. I hope you're doing better this morning." She watched her closely and didn't notice any evidence that she had been crying.

Meghan looked her in the eye and said, "I'm fine."

"Have you heard anything more about Scott?" she asked.

"No, the captain said was presumed dead and that he would notify the authorities once we reach Havre."

"I'm so sorry," said Emma, reaching out. Meghan looked at Emma's hand but moved hers to her lap to avoid the touch.

"You saw what kind of person he was, what he did to me," she said accusingly.

"Your bruises? Yes, I saw them. Are you saying when he fell overboard, did you plan it as punishment?" Emma asked innocently.

"No, what I am saying is he was going to hurt me again, and we fought. He tried to push me overboard. You saw!" she said with a frown.

"Yes, I saw something," Emma said cryptically. She continued, "You had mentioned that he normally was asleep from heavy drinking at that time." She made a mental note to find out if he'd had drinks at dinner or in his cabin.

"I thought he was passed out, but he must have followed me when I went to meet you last night," she explained.

"Hmm," Emma murmured.

Meghan fell silent and began eating again. Emma waved to the waiter and ordered breakfast. As they ate, the quiet settled around them.

Meghan finished her meal, folded her napkin, and said abruptly, "I'm going to the upper decks for some sun."

I'll use this time to check out her story. Emma nodded to Meghan. "I'm going to get my book from my cabin, and I'll join you in a little while."

Meghan looked so relieved that she wouldn't insist on joining her, Emma had to hide a smile. She watched her leave and was thinking about what she'd said about Scott's drinking. She asked the waiter, "Can I speak to the main steward?"

He inclined his head and said, "Yes, madam." He walked over to the main desk and spoke in low tones to the man there, gesturing to Emma.

The man walked over and inquired, "Madam, you asked to see me?"

"Could I inquire about the alcohol set up for the cabins?"

"Yes, these are set up at the guest's request. Would you like us to have something delivered to your cabin?"

"What? Oh no." She laughed. "But thank you."

"If you will excuse me." He bowed slightly and turned to leave.

Emma sat by herself, thinking over her next steps when her other tablemates arrived. They started to eat while discussing the day ahead when Emma asked Walter casually, "Did you happen to notice if Scott drank a lot last night?"

He sat back and considered her question. "No, in fact, he didn't drink at all. He said his stomach was not doing well and the alcohol would just cause him more problems."

As the group moved on to other topics, Emma considered his answer. *I need to get into Meghan's cabin,* she thought.

She excused herself, saying she wanted to lie down for a while. She was heading toward her cabin when she noticed Meghan's door ajar and the maid service rack in the hallway. She quickly stuck her head into the space and, when she did not see the maid inside, hurriedly went inside, searching for the alcohol setup. She found it almost immediately on the table beside the dresser.

She examined each bottle. They appeared to be untouched. She looked around the rest of the cabin quickly and opened the closet. It seemed to only have Meghan's clothes inside. *She certainly didn't waste time,* thought Emma.

She exited the cabin without being seen and headed to her room thinking to herself, *What do we know?*

She went over the facts so far. *Scott didn't drink in public, and the alcohol in the cabin was unopened, despite Meghan saying he'd indulged. Most likely, no additional alcohol had been ordered for their room, though that needed to be confirmed with the ship's bar. The bruising on her body appeared to be self-inflicted. Scott was wealthy, and they had been married for just a short time.*

Emma drummed her fingers on her lip, thinking, *Is it possible she's done this before? I need more background on her to figure that out. She does seem rather practiced at this type of deception.*

She documented her studies in her notebook; only four days left (including today) to figure this out. She headed to her cabin to get some more rest, wanting to be as healthy as possible for Paris.

After her nap, Emma went back to Meghan's cabin to walk her to down to dinner. She knocked, hearing a scrambling from within as she pressed her ear to the door. *There was someone else in that cabin.*

"Who is it?" Meghan called.

Emma didn't have time to think about it when the door opened suddenly. "Is everything okay? Did you have company?"

Meghan frowned severely. She didn't like being questioned. "No, I was just reading and was startled."

"Oh," Emma said, putting on a concerned tone, "I thought I heard someone else's voice in your cabin."

"No," Meghan said forcefully, "you would be wrong. Let's get going." She grabbed Emma's arm and pulled her away from the cabin.

Emma let herself be yanked down the hall, thinking, *This is getting interesting. Who's involved in this? Another passenger? Someone working on the ship?* She would watch tonight and see if anyone got special attention from Meghan or, alternatively, who is she pointedly ignoring.

As they made their way to dinner, Meghan commented she was worried but still had hope Scott was alive. Emma nodded and said she hoped so as well. "Where did you and Scott meet?"

"Could we not talk about that? It just upsets me," Meghan said shortly.

"You brought him up. I thought I'd inquire, in case you wanted to talk about him," she said reasonably.

"Well, I don't!" she nearly screamed.

Emma dropped the topic and they didn't say anything further until they arrived at the dining room. They sat with the group, filling out the last seats at the table. They had removed Scott's chair so it wouldn't be obvious someone was missing. Everyone was initially quiet when the ladies sat down.

Their companions seemed to be waiting for someone else to start the conversation. Mr. Jackson, who had introduced everyone the night before, took over and said to Meghan, "My dear, we are so sorry about your husband."

Meghan was clear-eyed as she said, "Thank you for that, but let's not talk about it. It upsets me."

"Of course, my dear, of course," he said consolingly.

Everyone started to talk, trying to fill the quiet by sharing stories of their day. Emma listened and participated in the conversation, all the while observing Meghan's behavior. She seemed to be specifically avoiding Walter. He also seemed to be animated with everyone but her. He was even working on the other lady's French accents.

Emma waited until dinner was being served before asking him a question. "Walter, how many times have you been to France?"

"Oh, many," he said.

"What business do you have there that takes you so often?" she asked curiously.

He waved his hand vaguely. "Oh, buying and selling."

"Buying and selling what?" she pressed.

"This and that," he said, clearly wanting her to accept his answer and end the conversation.

Emma let it go and continued to watch everyone at the table, conscious that time was running out to solve this mystery.

She followed Walter to his cabin after dinner, hanging back at a distance. She paused around a corner, waiting to see if Meghan would turn up. A lady with a shawl covering her face eventually appeared and knocked softly on the door.

Got you, thought Emma, ready to step out and surprise them. She hesitated a moment to see how Walter would react to the woman. As he opened his door, he saw who it was, and a wide smile spread over his face. The woman's shawl slipped and Emma ducked back in surprise. It was not Meghan, but Susan Billings!

She pulled herself further away and thought, *I'll have to rethink my list of suspects. Who do I still have on the list? I need to head to Meghan's cabin NOW!*

She hurried there and stayed around a corner to ensure she was not seen. Meghan's door opened and the captain stepped out, holding her hands. Emma narrowed her eyes. Was the captain involved in this? She watched their body language. *No, not him. He's there to reassure her, but not in a romantic way.*

She watched him leave and waited to see what would happen next. She thought about her list of suspects, *It's not Walter or the captain. Who else is there?*

Just as she was ready to head back to her cabin for some much-needed rest, a cabin steward knocked on Meghan's door. She heard him inquire, "Miss, would you like some additional towels?" Emma yawned, not expecting much. A surprising thing happened next; Meghan placed her arms around him and pulled him into her cabin.

Emma smiled. The steward. The same man who had "looked" for Scott when he went overboard. *I'll bet that, even if he had seen him, he wouldn't have said so. Now, I have the who, what, and why.*

She closed her notebook and thought, *It's time to meet with the captain. Not much can happen tonight. I'll tell him my findings tomorrow.* She headed to her cabin to sleep.

CHAPTER 58

DAY 4 OF 7 LA BRETAGNE

*E*mma dressed and went to the captain's cabin before breakfast. The officer saw Emma approach and asked, "Would you like to see the Captain?"

"Yes, if he has time," she responded. "Wait a moment," he said and went in to check. He returned a moment later, saying, "You may go in."

The captain was donning his jacket as she entered. He looked over at her and said, "Miss Evans, please come in. Have you completed your investigation?" he asked and smiled at her, not expecting much.

"I would not say completed but captain, I have some things to share," she confirmed. She detailed the information she had found. "I never saw Scott drink, so I checked with our meal steward and he confirmed Scott did not order any drinks. The only drinks in their cabin were unopened. I also checked with the bartender and no additional drinks were ordered for the cabin. That, along with the self-inflicted injuries, leads me to believe she planned this. I didn't mention it before, but she set me up to witness their struggle; we had planned to meet there at midnight."

"Why were you meeting with her at that late hour?" he inquired.

"I work with a group of people who help women at risk," she explained.

"So, you believed she was at risk," he stated.

"I did initially," she admitted, "but I believe I was used to be a witness to prove she was the one being attacked."

"Are you sure about this?" he asked, with a frown.

"When looked closer I saw discrepancies in her story. Captain, I think your issue here is how could a woman do this. Don't underestimate us; women can be the bad guys. I want to show you something. Could you stand here with me?"

He looked like he might say no, but he complied.

She started, "Okay, if Scott was trying to throw Meghan overboard, I think his arm placement would have been different than what I observed when I came onto the deck."

"How so?" the captain asked, curious where this demonstration was headed.

"Watch," she said as she grabbed him by the shoulder; his response was to grip her back. "Look down at the hand placement."

He did so. "My hands are under yours."

"Yes. But, when I saw them, I expected that his hands would be higher if he was trying to push her overboard; however, hers were higher. It's also possible she drugged him to make him easier to manipulate."

"So, you think she drugged him and pushed him overboard. But why?" he asked.

"There's one more fact I have to share. I was observing her cabin last night and saw one of the stewards join her."

"What's unusual about that? The stewards work in the cabins at all hours. Maybe he was just there to do his job," he said. He was, understandably, being protective of his staff.

"This steward was kissing Meghan, and she gave an enthusiastic response before pulling him into her cabin. I also heard a man and a woman's voice in her cabin that morning," she explained.

Shaking his head in disbelief, he said, "So, you think she did all of this to get with a steward she just met?"

"I think it's more than that. I think they planned this together, and I believe they murdered her husband," she stated firmly. "Do you have any background on this steward? Where did he come on board? Is he one of your regular crew? Do you have access to that information?"

"My dear, I am the captain," he said, straightening his white jacket. "It's my ship and all of the information is mine."

She saw his serious expression and reacted in kind saying, "Of course."

"Come with me."

As they exited the cabin, he told the officer where they were going and ordered him to stay put. They made their way downstairs to the administration office. He produced a key, opened the door, and turned back to her saying, "They won't be in until after 9am."

He immediately went to the drawers containing the personnel information. He pulled the steward's employee file, saying, "Hmm, he is a first-time crew member."

"Do you normally have new employees working alone?" she asked, surprised.

"No, normally customer service is crucial, and a new member would shadow another member on their first trip," he explained.

"How are members hired?"

"We have a pool of available people. If someone wanted to become a member, we take recommendations from another crew member."

"Is there someone listed for him?"

"Yes," he said quietly. "My main steward who is in charge of this area. It appears they have the same last name."

"Brothers?"

"Yes. It would have been easy for him to slip in unnoticed. A boat this size, I wouldn't have noticed a difference in staffing at this level."

"No, of course not," she said, understanding the complexities of his job.

"We're still more than three days out. Do we confront them now?" he asked earnestly.

"No, I would wait until the morning we arrive at the port. Make them believe their plans are coming to fruition," she suggested.

"I like the idea, but that is my busy time."

"Yes, but I think we'll have a worse time trying to figure out how to keep them under control if we take them into custody now."

"Yes, I think we can make that work. What do you suggest?" he asked.

She went over her plans.

CHAPTER 59

DAY 5 AND 6 OF 7 LA BRETAGNE

These two days went by quietly.

Meghan thought she had gotten away with her plan and had dropped the sad act altogether. She seemed to be enjoying herself. Emma stopped asking questions and Meghan was even friendlier to her.

CHAPTER 60

DAY 7 FINAL DAY ON THE LA BRETAGNE

The morning the ship was to dock, Emma had access to the dining room. She had requested that the captain bring his senior crew members and the brother of the steward there. The steward under surveillance was harder to locate because it appeared he'd begun sleeping in Meghan's cabin.

The captain accompanied Emma to Meghan's cabin and knocked briskly on the door. From the noise, it was obvious there were two people in there. Meghan finally answered, pulling her robe tight around her, and said, "Captain, this is such a nice surprise."

"Mrs. Bauer, we request your presence in the dining room," he commanded.

"Oh, okay. I need to dress. I'll meet you there," she said.

"I think not," he said, his tone stern.

She frowned, not understanding.

The captain continued, "I'll wait until you dress and escort you."

She noticed another officer was with him. After a minute, she nodded and started to close the door when the captain put his hand on it to stop her.

"And tell Steward Beardsley we'll be expecting him as well."

Meghan's mouth opened and closed several times. She tried to act like she didn't know what he was talking about when a voice sounded behind her.

"Yes, sir, I will be there."

Meghan's expression changed, her mouth tuned downward and her eyes closed. Emma had seen that look before; she knew she was caught.

The captain allowed her to shut the door and get dressed. There was nowhere for the two to go.

Things were very quiet within the cabin, and they wasted no time getting dressed and exiting. The officer went to stand by the steward, and the captain accompanied Meghan. She saw Emma watching and said, "I knew you were trouble."

"Not the first time I've heard that," commented Emma. She motioned to another senior crew member to enter the cabin and search it as they made their way to the dining room.

The ship had docked early, and the gangway was lowered. The captain's assistant had gone for the police. As they entered the dining room, they found the French police waiting.

Meghan seemed to shrink when she saw them. They put her and Steward Beardsley in chairs at the center of the room.

The captain stood in front of them and said, "We have some things to talk about." He looked over at Emma and said, "Miss Evans?"

Emma was talking to the person who had just searched Meghan's cabin. She thanked him and turned to the captain.

"Yes, I'll take it from here."

As she stepped forward, she pulled out her notebook and started going over her observations. "You're having an affair with Steward Beardsley. When you left your cabin just now, we were able to search it. As I understand it, Scott didn't have any alcohol on the ship. Comments from other passengers indicated he had said he couldn't drink due to a stomach condition. We found this in your cabin, hidden in your closet," she said, holding up a vial. "I will confirm with the doctor, but I expect you used this to make your husband appear drunk. I would assume you haven't had a chance to get rid of it."

"No one would leave me alone," Meghan said bitterly, knowing she was caught. "What made you suspect me?" she asked, curious.

"It was when I saw you struggle with your husband," Emma explained.

She looked confused at that statement. "Why's that?"

"It looked like he was struggling to get away from you, not you away from him."

The steward's brother, Charlie Beardsley was brought into the room, accompanied by another of the ship's officers. His brother, Nathanial, hung his head, not saying anything. Charlie immediately confronted him. "You just had to be with her, didn't you? You said this was all planned, and we wouldn't lose anything."

Nathanial grimaced. His brother was acting like all of this was his fault! He lashed out recklessly, "It worked great last time!"

"Nathanial! Shut up!" Meghan whispered fiercely.

Emma glanced between them. "So, there are other people involved in your scheme? I'm sure the French police can work that out."

The captain waved to the officers. "Take them away." He looked at Emma and said, "Emma, thank you. They would have gotten away with it had you not been here."

Emma smiled and said, "Thank you. Hopefully, they will also find out who else was involved in this. If you will take custody of this vial, I believe they will tell you it is what I suspect." She handed it to him.

"I'll send this and the details of which ships the Beardsley's have worked on and information about Mrs. Bauer, too. We have your hotel information in Paris if there are any further questions. You had best get moving, Emma. We've arrived at your destination," he said as he smiled broadly.

"Yes, you're right. I'll go get my bags now," she said, anticipating seeing Tony.

She had a porter carry her bags and they made it just in time to exit the ship ahead of the police escorting Meghan, Charlie, and Nathanial.

Tony stood at the bottom of the gangplank, watching her descend. He frowned, concerned when he saw the police. "Emma, is everything okay?"

"Oh, this isn't about me." She nodded toward Meghan, Charlie, and Nathanial, who were being led off in handcuffs.

"Did another adventure come your way on the ship?" he asked knowingly.

She smiled. "It is nice to see you, Tony."

He smiled back, looking strained, and said, "Emma, thank you so much for helping me locate Philip."

"Should we be going?" They were being jostled by passengers trying to leave the ship.

"Yes, sorry. I'm distracted. I have a carriage to take us to the train station. Come with me," he requested.

"My bags?" she asked. indicating the porter.

"Yes, please, follow us," Tony directed, his hands shaking as he indicated where the steward should go.

Tony was more rattled than she had ever seen him. They would have to talk on the train.

They made their way to the carriage, and Emma started noticing the voices around them. *Lovely language,* she thought.

CHAPTER 61

NEW YORK

*J*eremy climbed into his carriage after dropping Emma off. He looked around the area and thought, *New York isn't someplace I want to be without Emma. She'll be gone for at least a month if the case goes well. I'm going to miss her.*

He shook himself out of the melancholy settling over him and pulled his paperwork from his pocket. He glanced at it and then looked at the driver and said, "Please take me to the local telegraph office, located on Market Street."

"Yes, sir," the driver said and clicked at the horses to move on. When he pulled in front of the telegraph office, he looked back and said, "Sir, should I wait for you?"

"Yes, please," said Jeremy absently as he exited. He walked into the office and said, "I should have a telegram to pick up?"

The operator checked the stack in front of him and looked up at Jeremy. "Your name, please."

Jeremy looked him in the eye and said in a clear voice, "Jeremy Tilden."

He looked through his files. "Yes, this is it here." He reached out to hand the telegram to Jeremy.

Jeremy accepted the message and stepped back from the desk to read it. *Zeke found, but not apprehended. He appears to still be on a trajectory to Chicago. Witnesses in several states have said he was on his way to finish a personal vendetta.*

Jeremy thought about that information. Zeke was originally placed in the McNeal Island prison in Washington state. The penitentiary system had taken over the running of the prison in 1875. It was surrounded by Puget Sound. *He took a long, cold swim,* thought Jeremy. *It couldn't have been pleasant. He must be desperate to go through this much trouble to wreak his vengeance on Emma and possibly Clair. I'm very glad we kept it quiet that Emma has left the country.*

He started tapping the telegram against his hand. He nodded and thought decisively, *Time to head home and wait for him.*

He asked the driver to take him to the rail station. He was going to head home on the next available train. He arrived at the New Jersey rail station in time to take the day train to Buffalo. Once in Buffalo, there was a wait until that evening. As he boarded, he felt some frustration at not being able to arrive sooner. The only good thing was that Zeke was experiencing the same travel limitations and he had a greater distance to go.

CHAPTER 62

Jeremy spent the next week on the train thinking about the best way to handle Zeke's return to Chicago. They would need to get the word out to the bakery staff that, if anyone asked, Emma was working the morning shift. They would put extra men at the bakery and Clair's house for protection. Cole was already guarding Clair at the charity but not at her house. They had time to get everyone in place before Zeke arrived.

There was also the boarding house to think about. They would need men there as well. Tim would be called upon to make sure Dora never went out alone. *And I can't forget about Amy,* he reminded himself.

What's the best way to let people know to be on the lookout for Zeke? he asked himself and remembered Dora's accounting books. She often drew pictures of her desserts and he had also seen a sketchpad around the house with family members drawn in coal and pencil.

That's what we need. A drawing of Zeke that we can distribute; Clair would be the best to help describe him, he thought to himself.

"Finally," he said as the train pulled into the Chicago station.

He exited and looked around. Jeremy spotted Cole waiting in a nearby carriage and waved.

Cole said, "In my boy, we have a lot to discuss."

"Yes," said Jeremy and he climbed on board. "Do we have any idea if he's closer now?"

"We've sent men along the route to Washington, but he must be taking alternate transportation. That will allow us more time to plan."

"I was thinking, no one should be told Emma's out of town. We should ask the bakery personnel to tell anyone inquiring that she still works there."

"Good idea, misdirect," commented Cole.

"I was also thinking of Dora. I believe she could provide a drawing based on an interview with Clair. That way, if Zeke does show up, people will know to avoid him."

"We've gotten word that he's already beaten up several ladies in bordellos on his way here," said Cole

"Okay, so we have Clair and Thomas distribute the drawing to those businesses. We'll make sure places where Emma has worked will have copies of the drawing and are notified to be extra cautious."

"Would you like to go home first?"

"No, I like the idea of seeing Clair as soon as possible," said Jeremy, wanting to put their plans into action.

"Good idea." Cole gave the charity address to the driver. They felt a tug as they started moving.

CHAPTER 63

Clair heard a light knock on her door and when it opened, she saw it was her assistant, Sam.

"Cole and Jeremy are here to see you."

"Show them in, please," she said, closing the books she was working on. She stayed at her desk and waited for them to enter. *I wonder what this is about?* she thought, watching the door.

Cole entered first, followed closely by Jeremy. They greeted her warmly.

Jeremy leaned over to kiss her on the cheek. "Clair, it's so good to see you. I appreciate you making time for us today."

"Anything for you, you know that. Would you like to move over here?" she said, indicating her couch surrounded by heavy chairs. Once they sat, she looked over and said, "Jeremy, it is good to see you back." She glanced at Cole and asked, "Is this about the charity?"

He didn't answer. Instead, he nudged Jeremy. "Jeremy, why don't you start?"

Clair's mind raced and, suddenly concerned, she asked, "Have you heard from Emma? Are there any problems with her health or her trip?"

"I expect to hear soon. The ship should dock in a few days. You haven't mentioned her trip to anyone?" asked Jeremy

"No, I kept it quiet, as you asked," she confirmed.

Jeremy was glad Emma was away from this. *Now, how to protect Clair?*

"Clair," he began, "We came here to share something serious with you. Zeke Jones has escaped." He hesitated when she let out a small scream, then continued. "We're getting intel that he might be on his way here."

She stood, needing to walk. "Do you think he is after me?"

"And Emma," confirmed Cole. "We need to get organized for him. We have time to put things into place before he arrives."

Clair asked him curiously, "Did you tell Emma about Zeke?"

He grimaced, saying, "I did."

"Was she upset to not be in on the action?" she asked, knowing how Emma felt about him.

"I think so, but honestly, she seemed more concerned that no one gets hurt." He smiled crookedly. "And she said to take care of him this time."

Cole smiled coldly and said, "Oh, we will take care of him."

"Yes," agreed Clair with a similar expression.

"Can you accompany us to the boarding house? I have an idea of where we can start," requested Jeremy.

She nodded and said, "Yes, of course." She called out, "Sam, please come in."

Sam did so and she said in a businesslike tone, "I'll be closing the office for today. I have personal business to attend to."

"Yes, of course. I'll continue to work and lock up at the normal time," Sam said, taking notes.

"Thank you," she said gratefully as she gathered her things. Sam brought her coat and assisted her in putting it on.

They made their way downstairs to the waiting carriage and headed to the boarding house. They arrived and climbed the stoop; Jeremy opened the door and held it for Clair. As they entered, he heard humming coming from the dining room. He spotted Dora working on her books at the table.

"Jeremy!" She jumped up as soon as she saw him. "I'm so glad to see you. Did Emma get off okay?"

"Yes, she should be there in a day or two," he confirmed.

"Funny. Just think, you can cross an ocean and it's the same timing as the trip from New York to Chicago," she said wonderingly.

"It is amazing," he agreed.

She noticed Clair and Cole behind him. "Oh, company! How is everyone? Would you like something to eat?"

"We're good," Jeremy answered for them. He looked around the dining room and nodded at her accounting books. "Dora, I noticed that you draw."

"Yes, documenting my desserts and for fun," she commented, wondering about this turn of conversation.

"Can I see your sketchbook?" he inquired.

"You're sure? It's just drawings I've done of the family," she said, confused.

"Please, it's important," he requested.

"I'll get it." Reading the seriousness in his expression, she went to the buffet and pulled it out, handing it to him for review.

He started flipping through the sketchbook and, after looking at each drawing carefully, he was sure it was the right decision. He looked up at Dora and said, "We'd like your help on a case."

"Shouldn't you be speaking with Emma?" she asked with a nervous laugh. She held her hand protectively on her stomach.

"No, you're the right person. Is Tim around?" Cole spoke up from behind Jeremy.

"He's in the kitchen," she said.

"I'll go get him," said Jeremy.

She frowned as she watched him go. He returned a

moment later with Tim walking behind him, frowning. Tim looked at the group and suggested, "Why don't we move to the study?"

Everyone nodded and followed him. As they entered the room, Tim pulled the doors shut to allow them more privacy.

"What is this about?" he asked.

"Zeke Jones is back," Jeremy answered bluntly.

Dora sucked in her breath and clutched Tim's hand. Tim's face went dark.

Dora thought about Emma and said, "Oh, Emma's leaving, that worked out well."

"It did actually. I waited to tell her until we were at the ship," he admitted.

"Was she angry?" asked Dora, worried about her sister.

"No," he said, "she understood, and she knows Tony needs help."

"Yes, that's true," she acknowledged.

Tim commented in a serious voice, ready to protect his family. "What is it you want Dora to do? Not fieldwork?"

"No." Jeremy smiled, understanding his concern. "We want her to sketch Zeke."

Cole looked over at Clair and said, "We brought you here to help us with the sketch. We would like to get a picture of Zeke plastered all over town. It'll help limit his movements if he makes it here."

Clair had gone pale, but she looked Cole and Jeremy in the eyes before saying resolutely, "I'll do anything to make sure he isn't free ever again."

"Dora, can you get your drawing pencils?" directed Jeremy.

Tim said, "I'll get them for you" and patted Dora's hand before he stood. He exited the study and closed the doors on his way out.

Clair took the opportunity to ask, "Dora, how're you feeling?"

"I'm good, though the morning comes up a bit faster than they used to."

"Crackers work," she commented. Jeremy missed the twinkle in her eye.

Dora saw it and said, "Clair, are you and Thomas?"

She blushed and nodded.

Jeremy noticed the nod and put things together. "Hey, what's this? Another baby?"

"Yes," she said, blushing again.

"Congratulations!" said Cole and Jeremy at the same time and laughed.

"Thomas must be overjoyed," said Dora.

"He is and he's trying to do everything for me," commented Clair.

"Tim is the same," she murmured as he approached. He not only brought her pencils; he also had her shawl.

"In case you get chilly," he said.

Clair laughed out loud. When Tim looked at her askance, she just smiled back.

Dora motioned to Tim and, when he bent down, she whispered in his ear. He turned to Clair with a wide smile. "Congratulations, Clair! You must send Thomas our congratulations as well."

Jeremy said, "Let's get started."

Dora opened her book and readied her pencils. "Clair, we'll work through this together. Let's start with the shape of his face; is it long and narrow, short, round?"

"Long and narrow," she said, trying to keep emotion out of her voice.

"His eyes, can you remember their shape?"

The only sound in the room was the scratching of the pencil.

"Yes," she said a bit shakily, "they're brown and the shape is. . ." She looked at Jeremy and Tim. "Smaller than Jeremy's eyes."

She watched Dora draw and commented, "No, there's a further distance between them."

Dora adjusted the eyes and asked, "Like that?"

"Better."

"How about his forehead—high or low?"

"High."

"His nose?"

"Straight and a bit turned in at the bottom."

Dora drew an exaggeration initially. It made them all laugh. She erased it and drew another. "Is that close?"

"A bit narrower here," she said, pointing to the bridge of his nose.

She corrected the drawing and asked, "What about ears?"

"Just regular, they didn't stick out much."

She added ears and Clair confirmed, "Yes, you're getting there."

"What about the hair?"

"Oh, that hair. He loved his hair. Thick black and he always wore it a bit longer than he should."

She added the hair. "Did he have bangs?"

"No, he took pride in it and had it combed back."

Dora took a moment to move the sketch pad toward her, completed the details, and asked the group, holding up the sketch for them to view. "Is this the man you remember?"

Clair went white. "Yes, you got him."

"Jeremy, Tim?" inquired Dora, turning it for them to view.

"He looks right to me," commented Tim.

Jeremy nodded.

"Okay, so how do we get this out for everyone to see?" Jeremy asked.

"Papa," suggested Dora. "He has a process to make copies."

Cole looked over at her and asked, "How does that work?"

At that precipitous moment, Papa opened the door and walked into the room. He answered their question himself.

"There is an ability to copy. I have the required hectograph, gelatin duplicator, or jellygraph. The printing process involves the transfer of an original, prepared with special inks, to a pan of gelatin."

"Papa, how did you know we needed you?" asked Dora, getting up to kiss him on the cheek.

"Cole mentioned I might need to come by," he said laconically.

"Did he tell you—" Dora started to ask tentatively.

"About Zeke?" he interrupted. "Yes. He knows if my girls are in danger, then I will be involved."

Jeremy handed him the paper to copy and Papa looked at it closely. "Good job, Dora. This looks just like him." He gestured to Cole and Jeremy. "The chemicals are in my lab. I have the setup down there."

"How long will the process take?" asked Jeremy, thinking ahead to distribution.

"If I get them started now, overnight to dry. We'll need paper to get us started."

"I can get that," indicated Tim.

"Okay, let's get going."

Tim got the paper to Papa, and they worked through the night, with Zeke's image spread all over the house to dry. Papa checked them and said they would be ready to go out the next afternoon.

Cole and Jeremy met early the next morning and discussed where the copies should be handed out. Thomas stopped by with information on the distribution. "Clair wanted me to give you a list of the houses he might frequent." He handed the list over to Cole.

"Hmm," said Cole, "good idea. We don't want anyone hurt in this. Thomas, thank Clair for us."

"We'll cover the bordellos, the bakery, the office, here at the boarding house, and next door. I'll also give these to our men on the streets," confirmed Jeremy.

They agreed and Papa, Cole, Jeremy, and Thomas headed out to distribute the copies. The more people who knew Zeke was in town and dangerous, the better. Tim wanted to help and started to leave with the group.

Papa stopped him. "Tim, I think it's best if you stay here."

He looked like he wanted to argue, then looked at his lovely Dora playing with Patrick. He realized his priority was there. "You're right, my place is here."

"Thomas, are the guards with Clair?" asked Cole.

"Yes, we also got two more for the charity."

"Good," Cole said.

They left taking different carriages to get the papers were distributed. Pinkerton agents were also placed in strategic locations around town.

CHAPTER 64

It would be another week before any information about Zeke started coming in. "We have a sighting," commented Jeremy, reviewing the note just delivered to their agency.

"Where?" Cole said, immediately standing and walking over to review the note.

"Where else? The Bordello on 5th," Jeremy commented.

"Is he still there?" asked Cole, ready to head over.

"No." He chuckled suddenly.

"Why is that funny? This man is dangerous."

"The lady he grabbed recognized him immediately and screamed. The others went on the attack. He barely made it out of there alive."

Cole laughed. "Did they say what direction he went in?"

"Just out. They managed to give him a limp and a black eye."

"Hmm, that also may make him more desperate to get to Emma and get out of town."

"I'm going to the bakery," Jeremy said, "to join the men there."

"Okay, keep me informed and I'll send over any information that comes in," Cole promised.

Jeremy headed over in a carriage and had them drop him off a few blocks away. He saw the Pinkerton men, some hanging out in the front of the bakery, others disguised as delivery drivers in the back.

Jeremy joined the men in the back. He pulled his hat down over his eyes and leaned again the wall, waiting. *So much of investigation is waiting,* he thought. He kept his head down but was watching the door closely. Several female bakers were exiting at the end of their day. He was worried; they appeared to be alone. He didn't have to wait long. Thomas ran out behind them saying, "Hey, wait for me. You promised I could see you both home."

They looked back and a small blonde said, "Oh, sorry, Thomas, we would like your company tonight." He stepped between them and they linked their hands into his elbows as they were leaving. Thomas saw Jeremy and walked past without any acknowledgment. He wouldn't give him away as undercover.

They were there through the evening until the last employees left for the day. As the final person cleared out, Jeremy told his men to get going and he started to make his way home. As he walked to the back gate of the bakery, he didn't feel the hit on the back of his head.

He woke up slowly and realized he was in a chair with someone tying his hands behind him. He was able to pretend to still be asleep as he flexed his arms to allow for a loose tie on the ropes. He continued to sit still, pretending to wake up at that moment.

He tried to figure out where he was without opening his eyes. *The room smells familiar.* He could smell baked goods. *The bakery. I didn't go far,* he mused. Pain radiated from his head and his arms were very sore. *He must have pulled me inside by my arms.* He let his eyes open slowly and saw Zeke pacing the office. He noticed Jeremy had woken up and was watching him.

"We got the nose right," Jeremy said, indicating the drawing Zeke held.

"This!" Zeke snapped, wadding up the paper and throwing it at Jeremy's face. "This is causing all of my problems! I can't go anywhere or do anything because of it."

"I did hear you went somewhere and. . . what was it?" he said consideringly. "That's right, you got beaten up by a bunch of women." He laughed.

Zeke looked like he would explode and used his arm to knock everything off the desk. The sounds were loud in the small office.

"Where is she?" he screamed.

"And who would that be?" Jeremy asked, taunting him.

Zeke's face went dark as he said in a low, menacing voice, "Where is she?"

"Far, far away from you."

Zeke used his fist on Jeremy's face in response. Jeremy let his head fall back, then he straightened and gave him a twisted smile. "We have you; you just don't know it yet."

"I have everything under control," Zeke said with false bravado.

"Why come back here?" Jeremy asked, keeping his voice light.

"To get her and that other one," Zeke answered.

"Other one?"

"The redheaded whore. She's going to get what she deserves, too," he threatened.

"Think so? I don't." Jeremy knew something Zeke did not. There were safety measures in place: all agents must check-in after leaving their final assignments for the day. He knew the

Pinkerton staff would notify Cole of his last location and check out the bakery first. With a head wound like this and Zeke being smaller than Jeremy, blood and drag marks were probably apparent in the dirt outside.

I would also assume, he thought, *the lock was broken when he entered the bakery. Just a matter of time now. The best thing I can do is keep Zeke talking.*

"Where to next after you take care of the two women?" he asked, not saying their names.

"I have plans," he said importantly.

"Plans?" he inquired.

"Yes, I have someone who'll help me. Someone important."

Jeremy nodded like he agreed. He heard something out in the bakery. The sound stopped their conversation.

Zeke said triumphantly, "They're early for the baking. Emma's always early. This will be easy."

"That's true," Jeremy said, going along with him. "She's always early to the bakery."

He listened and could hear a familiar female voice. Jeremy knew Zeke wouldn't know what Emma's voice sounded like. He said, "That does sound like her."

He didn't think he was putting anyone in danger. He knew that, at this hour, it was highly unlikely a bakery employee had entered the store. He suspected Cole was behind this visitor.

Zeke looked conflicted; he wanted to find out if it was Emma, but he didn't want additional people to monitor. He came to a decision and pulled out his gun, pointing it at Jeremy. "You, I will deal with you later." He opened the door slowly and looked out, listening.

"She's probably in front preparing the counters," Jeremy said innocently.

Zeke didn't think as he nodded and headed toward the front of the store.

Jeremy undid his hands and reached for the clutch pistol he kept in his boot. He was expecting that Cole had men scattered around the bakery, and he was right. As he made his way out of the office, Pinkerton men seemed to come from all sides. Zeke was not in the mood to go back to jail and started firing his pistol.

Jeremy realized he had the perfect shot, and he did not hesitate to take it. Zeke dropped to the floor, not moving.

He looked around and saw a woman standing nearby and said, "Savannah, I thought that was you. Were you in the bakery?"

"No," said Cole, coming up behind her, "not a chance. With her theatre training, I knew she could throw her voice. She never left my side at the door."

"Cole, if you don't mind, I'm going to head home for some rest. We, theater people, don't like to get up before noon," said Savannah, yawning broadly.

"Thanks for the help," said Cole.

"No problem," she said as she headed out.

"Dave," he called to a detective standing nearby. "Please escort Savannah home."

Dave nodded and followed her out.

Jeremy nudged Zeke with his foot; there was no movement. "No loss there," he said.

"No," Cole agreed. "Alan, let the police chief know we'll need help with cleanup. Also, before we move him, we need Jake to document the scene." He looked over at Jeremy and said, "You can head home and get some rest." He noticed the wound on his head. "Do you need to be checked out? The Sisters could probably do it for you."

Jeremy grimaced, touching the lump on the back of his head. "I might need to stop over there before I head home."

"Do you want me to send a carriage with you?"

"No, we're close by. I can walk," he said as he headed out into the night. Something was bugging him. *Zeke mentioned a benefactor, someone who had promised to help him. Is it someone we know?* He would have to think about it.

He made his way to the hospital and climbed the stairs. The Sisters remembered him and were immediately concerned with his appearance. Sister Mary said, "Sister Ann, please see to Jeremy. The rest of you, back to work." She motioned for the Sisters to disperse.

Sister Ann gathered up her medical tray and told him to sit down on a side chair by the nurses' station. "Jeremy, what happened?"

"Head got hit with something hard," he said simply.

"Let me take a look." She cleaned the wound, saying, "I don't think I'll need to put in any stitches. It looks worse than it is."

"Thanks, Sister, good to know," he said, grimacing as she finished and applied a bandage.

She was tidying up the bandages and replacing her equipment when she said, "You'll have a nice bump that you'll need to watch. Put cold compresses on it to help with the swelling."

"I will," he said as he pressed gently against the bandage.

"I do recommend that you have a ride home; you might still experience some dizziness. One of our volunteers can take you," she offered.

Jeremy realized how tired he was and said sincerely, "I would appreciate that."

"It shouldn't be a problem," she said. She called out, saying, "Dan, could you take Jeremy home?"

Jeremy told Dan the address and he said, "Sure, I know this neighborhood. I'll get the wagon ready to take you. Meet me downstairs?"

Jeremy nodded. They only had to wait a moment for the wagon to pull up in front of the hospital.

Jeremy looked at Sister Ann and said, "Thanks for helping me."

She reminded him, "Be sure to rest tonight and tomorrow."

"I will. Thank you again." He climbed into the wagon and thought to himself, *I'll go to the charity in the morning and confirm that Zeke is no longer a threat. We owe it to Clair and Thomas to let them know they're safe.*

CHAPTER 65

The trip home was uneventful. Jeremy climbed into his bed and slept hard. When he woke the next morning, he had a small headache, but it wasn't something that would stop him from spreading the good news that Zeke Jones was no longer a threat.

He headed downstairs and went straight to the kitchen, where he found Dora and Amy preparing breakfast.

Dora saw his bandage and immediately said, "Jeremy, what happened? Were you attacked?"

"Oh this," he commented, reaching up to touch it. "It's nothing." Before she could ask more questions, he said, "Dora, can you call Tim in? I need to speak with you both."

"Of course." She looked at Amy and said, "I'll be right back."

When Dora left to get Tim, Amy asked, "Should I step out?" She knew some cases were private and didn't want to intrude.

"No," said Jeremy. "You can stay for this news." He looked around, saying, "Where's Patrick?" He knew how much the boy loved to be in the kitchen with Dora.

"He's with Ellis. I believe they're performing some experiments," Amy commented, going back to frying her sausages.

Tim came into the kitchen with Dora trailing behind him. He asked, concerned, "Is everything okay? Dora said you've been hurt?"

Jeremy smiled reassuringly and said, "I'm good. Please, sit down." He waited for them to sit and said, "We got him last night."

Dora immediately put her hands together to give thanks. "You have him in custody."

"Better than that. He's no longer a threat," Jeremy said.

Tim looked at him shrewdly and said, "He's dead." It was not a question, but a statement of fact.

"Yes," Jeremy said.

"Good," said Tim, with no remorse. He was glad the threat had been removed from their lives.

"What now?" Dora asked.

"First, I'm going to see Clair when she opens the charity and give her the good news. Later, I'll send a wire to the hotel Emma's staying at and give her all the details."

"Not before you eat and put some cool water on that cut," said Dora.

Jeremy smiled. It was nice to have family taking care of him. He ate breakfast and let Dora minister to the wound before heading over to see Clair.

As he arrived at the charity, he noticed something odd. The two bodyguards Clair had added were not in the outer office area. Odder still, the two secretaries normally in position were also missing.

Jeremy frowned, looking around. He noticed Sam's office was open, but he was not there. As he approached Clair's office, he heard arguing—Clair's voice was raised, and he could tell from the tone something was wrong.

He knocked, saying, "Clair, it's Jeremy. I have some news to share with you."

More arguing ensued. Clair opened the door and said in a

strained voice, "Would you like to come in?" Her eyes were bright with tears and very red.

He mouthed to her, "*It's okay.*"

Her eyes got wider and they darted to the right. She mouthed, "*Gun.*"

"Sam, where are you?" said Jeremy in a clear voice.

Sam stepped from behind the door, behind Clair, waving a gun. He grabbed her by the hair and pulled her back with him.

Jeremy started forward, but Sam had the gun steady on him.

"Don't hurt her," Jeremy said. He looked around and asked, "Where are the guards and secretaries?"

"I told the guards they were no longer needed," he sneered.

"And the secretaries?"

"I sent them on a fool's errand to review some property for Clair."

"Why the subterfuge? What are you trying to accomplish?"

Something occurred to him; Zeke had mentioned a benefactor, and Sam had access to the charity accounts.

Jeremy asked softly, "Sam, are you waiting for someone?"

"What do you mean?" he asked nervously, looking out the side window.

"Maybe Zeke?" He narrowed his eyes, ignoring Clair's start at the name.

"What, what are you talking about?" he sputtered.

Jeremy said, "Sam, I know you're working with Zeke."

Clair looked shocked. She had hired Sam and trusted him.

Sam groaned and asked. "Where is Zeke? We were supposed to meet here this morning, get the money from Clair, and then make our escape."

"Bad news on that front. We got him early this morning," Jeremy said with an evil grin.

"Where is he?" Sam was still thinking he could get him. "I'll trade this whore for him."

"Well, I can't say I know where he is right now, but tomorrow he'll be six feet under," commented Jeremy.

"That Emma bitch! I tried to get her for him, but you kept her too well protected."

"At the funeral, you tried to get her alone at the hall," Jeremy recalled.

"Yes, I thought I took care of her. He just couldn't leave her alone!" Sam finally realized what Jeremy had said. "You killed him! But we were going to leave together." He wiped his hand over his eyes, growing more desperate by the minute. He didn't understand what was happening.

Jeremy was waiting for that moment when he loosened his grip on Clair. He yelled, "Clair, get down!" She immediately dropped out of the way.

Jeremy leaped forward and latched onto Sam. They wrestled on the floor. Sam was reaching for the gun when he was stopped by Clair. She put her heel on his wrist and pressed down. He screamed as she kicked it away. Jeremy jumped up to grab the gun. He put Sam's gun in his pocket and pulled out his own, pointing it at Sam. "A few questions for you, Sam. Who was Zeke to you?"

Sam didn't answer, just kept screaming. Jeremy looked at Clair and said, "Hand me some rope."

She kept some in a drawer for packages that might need to be sent out. Jeremy immediately grabbed Sam's wrists and tied him tightly. When he tried to allow some room in the ropes, Jeremy put a knee in his back and pulled back hard, saying, "I know that trick."

"Jeremy, sit him down. I would like some questions answered," stated Clair.

Jeremy did as she asked and guided Sam to a chair facing them. He had finally stopped screaming and was just sitting there, looking into space when Clair stated, "What did you and Zeke want?"

"What? The money, of course. You're handing it out. You can hand us some."

"The discrepancies, that was you!" she accused.

"It was," he admitted. "I wanted to see how much I could take without you reporting it to the board."

She looked at Jeremy and said, "I had the accountants reviewing the losses and I was going to share it with the board at that time. I didn't have a chance to review with Emma before she left."

Jeremy nodded, unconcerned; he trusted Clair. Jeremy continued to watch Sam and wondered what he was missing. There was something about him, his mannerisms, and then he remembered the hair pulling.

Jeremy said smoothly, "Sam, are you related to Zeke?"

"What are you talking about?" Sam asked, not looking him in the eye.

That's it, thought Jeremy. "How did he find you?"

He looked defeated. "He didn't find me. He wasn't even looking. I found him. I knew I had to come from someone better than my mother. She was a whore like you," he said with disgust toward Clair.

"So, it's better to be related to a monster than a whore?" asked Clair, anger in her voice.

"We were going to have a good life, away from here. But he just had to settle the score with Emma. He just wouldn't let it go."

They heard someone enter from the outer office and a voice called, "Clair!"

"It's Thomas!" said Clair. "We're in here," she called out.

"Where is everyone?" he asked, staring at them in astonishment. What he saw was Sam tied up, Clair's hair down around her shoulders, and Jeremy with an injury.

Jeremy took over and said, "Thomas, could you get Cole and tell him we need a team here?"

"Yes, but I want to check on Clair first." He went over and kneeled in front of her. "Are you okay?"

She started to tear up and said, "I am now. Jeremy, can I go with Thomas?"

"Of course, you can," he replied.

On her way out, Clair looked at Sam and said, as a parting statement, "Why is your family always pulling hair?" She didn't wait for a response and headed out with Thomas.

Jeremy sat with a very quiet Sam, thinking about what his telegram to Emma would say.

CHAPTER 66

FRANCE

$\mathcal{E}$mma was struggling to remember her French as a porter retrieved her luggage. She said hurriedly, "Merci."

"Di rein," he said and inclined his head as he picked up her bags.

Tony noticed and said, "You've studied."

"Not as much as you," she said with a grimace. "I have a few phrases and will be relying on you for the rest."

It was quiet between them, but it was not an uncomfortable silence as they followed the porter to the waiting carriage that would transport them to the train station. "We're just in time," said Tony, walking swiftly, carrying Emma's bags to the train. They made their way to their cabin and got settled just as it started to pull out.

As it picked up speed and moved them toward Paris, she looked at him and asked quietly, "Tony, what's happened?"

He shoved off his hat. As it fell to the seat beside him, he answered, "We were involved in reviewing special works of art to determine their age. Philip has been working on putting together books about painting authentication. He began talking to various artists about a catalogue raisonne, a book that would provide a reliable method to examine the age of paintings."

Tony continued, "We've been examining paintings and documenting the smell of oil in the paintings. They should have an oily smell for many years until the oil fully dries. If you're looking at investing in an oil painting more than a few years old, it shouldn't have this smell. Next, there was the evaluation of age, the cracking of the paint on canvas."

He realized he was sharing too much detail. He tried to be clearer. "We were working on reviewing the age of paintings. We'd been here a few weeks and I was seeing so many great artists."

"So far it sounds great. What happened?"

"We received an invitation from the Laurel Museum to authenticate an important exhibit. Philip was very excited that the curator, Monsieur Martin, had invited us because he had known him since the beginning of his career. He was instrumental in helping Philip learn about art," Tony explained.

"Did something go wrong during the authentication?" asked Emma, trying to put the facts together.

"No, just the opposite. We reviewed the collection in detail and met with each artist to confirm the authentication. The job was completed with positive results," said Tony.

"Why do you think that museum is involved in Philip's disappearance?" asked Emma.

"On the night he went missing, we received a note from Monsieur Martin. They had received a late shipment and wanted Philip to see it before it was displayed," he explained.

"Did he go alone?" she asked, taking notes.

"Yes, I was tired. We'd been working all day. He said he wouldn't be long, so I retired for the night. When I woke the next morning, he hadn't returned."

"What did you do first?"

"I waited and went to our first morning appointment without him."

"Was it at the same museum?"

"It was. I headed there after breakfast, thinking I might find a very tired Philip."

"What did you find?"

"They were closed."

"Closed?" she exclaimed.

"Yes, the day before they were fully operational, with a staff in place and art on the walls." He appeared to be at a loss as to what could have happened.

Very odd, thought Emma. She continued with her questions. "Did you try the door?"

"I did, and it was locked," he confirmed.

"Windows?" she asked.

"Galleries typically want more wall space, so no windows," he explained.

"Okay, let's stop by. I can get us in," she said in a firm voice.

Tony smiled. He was glad she had come to help him. "I thought you'd say that."

She smiled back. "Tony, it is good to see you."

He looked at her for a long time before replying quietly, "You, too."

That long moment made Emma want to talk about something else. She requested, "Tell me about Paris."

He happily started talking about the location that was fast becoming his favorite place. "Paris is a place of extremes. There's so much art that you just can't take it all in. The food is amazing, with pastries that make your mouth water. Then there's so much poverty and so many dirty areas. The children pickpockets are worse than in New York."

"It's disappointing to hear that. I'll have to get some information on charities in the area for Clair," she said, making a note to follow up. She looked over at him and said, "I can't wait to see it. Tell me about the art," she added, knowing he wanted to talk about it. "Who have you seen?"

"Claude Monet, Edgar Degas, Pierre Auguste Renoir, and others. They're doing something called Impressionism. This group chooses the depiction of modern life."

"Impressionism. Interesting term. Where did it come from?" Emma asked curiously.

"Claude Monet says it is the visual impression of the moment. Emma, when you look at it, how he uses color and light, you feel something go over you. It's an emotional connection."

"Wonderful! Who else have you seen?" she asked, wanting to hear more.

"Women painters. Mary Cassatt, she is an Impressionist also." Remembering something, he said, "Emma, do you recall the John Singer Sargent painting you saw at the museum back home?" When she frowned, uncertain, he reminded her with one word: "Venice."

She suddenly exclaimed, "Oh, my. I would love to see more of his paintings."

"There is a wonderful portrait of Madame Pierre Gautreau, known as Madame X, currently on display. We can go see that."

"Who else?" she asked, fascinated.

Tony continued on his favorite topic. "Paul Cézanne is very interesting. He seems to be turning away from Impressionism, more objects and landscapes, going to their geometric forms: the cube, cone, and cylinder."

"Are these works of art from Cézanne very expensive?"

"Right now, the art world isn't keeping up with all of the changes. We believe their future value will be very high." They continued talking about art until they reached Paris.

"I have arranged a carriage for us," he said as they exited the train.

"My bags?" inquired Emma. They had taken them off the train and had them sitting next to her.

"I have them being picked up," he said as they approached the hired carriage.

"Bonjour, nous aimerions aller au musée s'il vous plait," Tony greeted in flawless French, greeting the man and asking to be taken to the museum.

He helped Emma into the carriage, from where she took in the sights. "Tony, there is so much building going on. Papa would love it here."

"There is The Basilica of Sacré-Cœur on Montmartre, built-in neo-Byzantine style. It was begun in 1873, that we can see. It won't be completed for a while, but the architecture is amazing."

"That would be lovely," she said, peering at the buildings as they drove.

Tony commented, "Some interesting history about the neighborhood organization: a guy named Haussmann had a gigantic building project, and it may have caused some social dispersal. He relocated thousands of families and businesses and had their buildings demolished for the construction of the new boulevards. He was also blamed for reducing the amount of housing available for low-income families. In the old design, the higher level of apartment buildings was stratified to have higher classes and lower classes occupied lower floors. The new design didn't allow that, so many had to move to lower-income areas."

Emma thought about that as they neared the museum, located on the west side of Paris. There were new boulevards, stewards, water supplies, schools, and gardens. She marveled at the many stone buildings and wide streets.

They pulled up to the museum and Tony climbed down first, reaching up to help her down. "Merci et pouvez-vous revenir dans une heure," he offered to the driver, requesting him to return in an hour.

The driver nodded and clicked at his horse to move on. As they watched him leave, Tony commented, "We should start looking around."

She glanced at the front of the museum. It had the appearance of not being occupied. The door was braced, with a chain and lock attached. Looking around the sides, she saw that Tony was correct; there were no windows to peer into.

The front was too exposed. "We need to go around the back and away from any prying eyes."

He agreed and said, "Follow me."

He started around the building and she followed. They exited the alley into the back of the museum. Emma saw that it butted up against another structure with no windows. There was an element of privacy that would allow Emma to access the locks. At the back door was another heavy lock and chain. She knelt and pulled out her kit, placing the tools inside the lock. She quickly manipulated the tumblers until she heard it open. She smiled as she opened the lock and removed the chain, handing them to Tony. He carried them as he followed her inside.

Emma looked around the rooms and said, "Whatever happened here, they left in a hurry." Art had been removed from the walls; wires and hangers were still in place. Packing papers were strewn all over the floor. "Tony, have you been in all of the rooms of this building?"

"Yes," he said as he laid down the lock and chain. "The authentications we were invited to perform involved a large group of paintings that had been recovered from a theft."

A memory stirred. "I read about that. It made news back home. They recovered the paintings, but they didn't know who took them."

"Yes. Finding the collection stopped a massive manhunt."

"How long was the current exhibit supposed to be here?"

"I believe the agreement was a limited time."

"But not this limited." Emma started looking around. "Was Philip suspicious of anyone here?"

"I didn't think so, but now I'm not so sure. He did take notes while we were walking around," he said, thinking back.

"Hmm, do you know where his notes might be?" she asked, thinking they would help tell them what Philip was thinking.

"I'm not sure, but he would have kept them in his room. We can check when we go to the hotel," he suggested.

She continued with her questions. "How many times have you been to this museum?"

"More than a few," he admitted.

"What was going on during those visits?" she asked, trying to get a mental timeline together.

"Initially, we walked around and introductions were made," he said. "After that, we spent time evaluating each painting. It took a few days. Even after the authentications were complete, we would continue to come back here, just to see the Vermeer painting," he explained. "It was one of the older artworks that did not have the artist to authenticate it."

"Was there something odd about the picture? Something that Philip saw?"

"I didn't think so at that time, but now I'm wondering," he said consideringly.

"Think back to that night he went missing. Did you talk?"

"Yes, Philip was discussing how Paris had changed and that it was the center of the art world now. He also discussed how troublesome it was to authenticate art here, especially with the new artists. They were creating part of the problem with authenticating pictures."

"Why is that?"

"We've found that the new artist will sign their art, but some have also signed good copies. It just makes it harder to authenticate."

"The Vermeer wouldn't have that issue?" Emma looked at her notebook, circling Vermeer several times.

"That's right. An older painting, such as those by Vermeer, is much harder to duplicate. The one on display at the museum was *The Concert*. It was a depiction of a man and two women performing music."

"Tony, could they have taken the other paintings to cover up the Vermeer theft?"

"It's possible."

"Tell me about the initial theft. Was the art in this museum?"

"Yes. The entire exhibit was missing for more than a month. Once it was found, the artists came in and verified their work. We reconfirmed that during our authentication."

"Is it possible there were forgeries in the museum after your authentication?"

"I don't think so, but we kept coming back for something. Something was bothering Philip."

"You said he knew Monsieur Martin?"

"Yes, they've been communicating by mail for the last ten years."

"Do you happen to have any of the letters with you?"

"Not with me," he admitted, "but they might be at the hotel."

"Okay. Let's finish looking around here and we can head back to check that out."

They went through each room, searching for anything out of the ordinary. They found more debris and wires. As they completed the viewing rooms, she looked at Tony and said, "We need to check the storage rooms."

He nodded and indicated to the back with his hand. "They're this way."

As they entered the door at the back of the room, they found extra crates and little else. Tony noticed something and bent down to examine the floor. "Odd," he said as he brushed two fingers against the ground. "There's paint here, on the floor."

"It is a museum. Wouldn't they have paint around?" she reasoned.

"Not this museum. The exhibit should have only been the recovered paintings. None of those were freshly painted."

"Rub some on my page here," she said and handed him the notebook. The paint was still tacky and allowed him to smear a small segment in her notebook. He handed it back to her and she documented the paint in her notes.

"Do you think Philip thought there was a con going on?"

"He may have, but he didn't share it with me."

"You mentioned Monsieur Martin and Philip were friends. He would have trusted him. So, he would go if Monsieur Martin requested him in the evening or the middle of the night?"

"Yes, he would have gone with no hesitation."

"Okay, so our theory is that someone here has forged art and is possibly holding Monsieur Martin and Philip somewhere."

"Yes. I hope Philip's all right."

"I know how much he means to you. We'll stay until we find him," she promised.

"Thank you." Something was bothering him, and he asked, "Emma, can I see your notebook?"

"Of course," she said, handing it to him.

He studied the paint color and said slowly, "Emma this paint. . ."

"The blue?" she asked.

"Yes, it is very similar to the ultramarine used on the Vermeer."

"Similar? Not the same?" she asked.

"The paint used in the Vermeer was made from an expensive mineral blue pigment extracted from the semi-precious stone lapis lazuli, which was imported into Europe via Venice from Afghanistan. This is similar but not the same," explained Tony.

"So, that color could confirm the painting might be a forgery?" asked Emma.

"Yes, it could," Tony confirmed.

"What have you done to find Philip this week?"

"I talked to the agents de police and reported him missing. They said they would make a report, but it didn't sound like an emergency."

"That's when you notified me," she finished for him.

"You were the only one I could think of to help," he said a bit helplessly.

She reached over and touched his hand. "I'm glad you contacted me." She glanced around and said, "What's that on the ground?"

"Just a piece of paper. It probably came from the packing boxes," he said as he reached for it. As he straightened, he noticed she seemed a bit unsteady. Alarmed, he went to her and said, "Emma, are you okay?"

She stood still a moment to catch her breath, taking a deep breath. "I'm just getting fatigued."

"Are you all right?" he said, immediately concerned. She was always full of energy. "Was there an accident?"

"No accident. I'm fine," she assured him. "I just get tired sometimes."

"Okay, we can go," he said, looking at his watch. "The driver should be waiting."

He drew her hand into his elbow and guided her out. He stopped as they exited and put the chain and lock back on. They made their way to the front of the museum to meet their carriage. "Hôtel Saint Laurent s'il vous plait," Tony said to the driver as they climbed in.

Tony let Emma rest against him as they made their way to the hotel. He had to tell himself to give her some time to tell him why she was feeling weak. As they arrived at the hotel, he nudged a sleeping Emma. She woke with a start.

"It's okay, Emma. We're here," he said, gesturing at the hotel.

She glanced up and saw the majestic hotel. "This is a nice place," she said as Tony helped her down from the carriage.

"Je vous remercie," he said. Emma looked at him askance. "Thank you," he said to her with a smile.

She nodded and they made their way in. The attendant saw him enter and said, "Monsieur votre coffre a été livré à votre chamber."

"Je vous remercie," he responded, then turned to Emma. "Your bags are in the room."

"Wonderful," Emma said, happy her things had made it there.

"Monsieur votre compagnon a un télégramme," called the desk clerk.

Tony stopped and said, "Emma, just a moment. I need to get a telegram from the desk." She nodded and he left her to go to the desk for the envelope. He brought it back and they headed up to their room.

They were on the third floor in a corner room. He opened the door and showed her in. When she entered, she saw a large room with a sitting area and a dining room. He directed her to an inner door, saying, "You'll be in here. This is the room we were using for an office. I've moved the books and papers out of it for you."

She opened the door and found a small clean room.

"Bathroom?" asked Emma.

"Shared," he said ruefully. "We have a key for it. It's down the hall. Be sure to knock first. I can have fresh water brought up for the basin."

"Thanks. I'd like to wash up and lie down. Can we review Philip's room later?"

"Yes, of course. I'll go check on the water now."

"Je vous remercie," she said to him teasingly.

He smiled. "It's great to have a friend here."

She used the washroom down the hall and was happy to see the wash water in her pitcher when she returned to her room. Tony was nowhere to be seen and probably in his room. She closed her door and laid down on the bed thinking, *Telegram. Don't forget to send Jeremy a telegram.*

CHAPTER 67

$\mathcal{E}$mma woke and, for a moment, forgot where she was. She looked around and remembered with a smile, sinking back on the bed. *Paris.* She was here on a case, but there was no reason not to enjoy it.

The sun was up, and she felt so much better than she had the previous day. She lay there thinking, *What did we learn yesterday? The curator received a note to meet his friend, owner of the museum. Later the same evening, he went missing. The next day, Tony found the museum empty and all the art removed. A blue color similar to the Vermeer painting was found on the floor of the storeroom. Still, just pieces that need to be organized.* She lay quietly until she heard a knock on her door.

"Emma, breakfast is here," called Tony through her door.

"I'm getting up," she called back. She pulled herself to the side of the bed and took an inventory of any weaknesses. When she didn't notice any, she thought, *I'm finally feeling like myself.*

She stood and washed her face in the basin. She dressed in a black skirt and red shirt with a white lace collar. She pulled her hair into a bun and laced up her boots before leaving her room.

As she entered the main room, she saw the food set up but

no Tony. She left the room and went to the lavatory. On her way back, she noticed a small, nervous-looking man in the hallway. She eyed him curiously, wondering why he was there. He ducked his head and shuffled past her, entering the staircase.

Hmm, something to think about, she thought.

As she entered the room, Tony called from the dining area, "Breakfast is set up over here."

"Thanks, Tony," she said as he pulled out the chair for her. She noticed he continued to wear nice suits; he had developed a style. She smiled, happy he was doing so well.

"I'm starving," said Emma as she settled into eating some of everything: croissants, eggs, bacon, and fruit.

"I did try to get you up last night, but you didn't stir," commented Tony.

"Yes, well, I just needed some extra rest."

Tony started eating also. He finished before Emma and said, "That telegram delivered yesterday was for you."

"Oh. May I have it?" she asked, hoping it was good news.

He pulled the envelope out of his pocket and handed it to her.

She opened it and read silently. *We've gotten him. Zeke is no longer a threat. I'll explain when you return. We miss you. Let us know how Tony is. Love Jeremy.*

"What is it?" Tony asked.

She set the telegram down and looked at Tony, "Tony, Zeke Jones returned to Chicago. Jeremy says they have taken care of him, permanently."

His face went white and said, "Emma, why are you here? I would've thought you'd be in the middle of it. Why aren't you?"

"That's a complicated question. You needed help, and I wanted to be here for you," she explained.

Tony frowned severely and said, "There's more to it than that, isn't there? Emma, I've never seen you without energy, but yesterday you seemed to just fade."

She tried to dodge the second part of the question by saying, "It was a long trip, between the ship and the rail. We also went to the museum."

"Yes, but even then, I wouldn't have expected you to be so tired," he said reasonably.

She would just have to tell him what happened, maybe not all the details, but enough that he was aware she was still recovering. "Tony," she stated, looking him in the eye, "I had surgery a few weeks before I boarded the ship."

"Surgery! Are you okay?" he asked.

"I'm okay now. I was lucky that I was working in a hospital when they found I needed help."

Tony teared up a moment, then something came to him, and grew angry. "Jeremy thought it was okay for you to travel here alone when you were in a weakened state?"

She saw his anger and knew it was because he cared so much for her. She started gently, "Jeremy wanted me out of harm's way because of Zeke's reappearance."

Tony was very silent and then finally said, "So, he made the safe decision to get you away."

"About that," she said, "he didn't tell me until just before I boarded the ship in New York."

Tony saw the humor in what had happened. It was impossible to stop Emma from being in the fray unless she didn't know about it. He laughed out loud at that.

Emma understood the humor and joined him.

"He knows you very well," Tony said.

"Yes," she acknowledged. "He knew I was committed to coming here, and it worked with his plans for Zeke."

"Will you be all right? Can you tell me what the surgery was for?"

Emma turned a bit red, not wanting to admit the full truth. "It was a female surgery, and I was working with the Sisters at the hospital when I collapsed. They immediately took care of me." She saw he was still concerned and said, "I'll be fine."

"Promise?"

"I promise."

Tony looked satisfied and said, "Would you like to move into the living room?"

"Yes," she said, relieved to be moving on to another topic, and followed him into the living room and sat down. She pulled out her notebook to review her notes, then looked up and said, "Tony, what bothers me is why he went out so late and didn't ask you to go with him."

"He felt he was seeing a friend; I don't think he thought there would be any danger. Would you like to review his room?"

She nodded and moved to the room down the hallway from hers.

She looked at him and said, "Do we have a key?"

"Do we need one?" he teased.

"No," she replied, as she reached up to pull a hairpin out and walked over to the door. She knelt in front of the lock, standing after the telltale click. "It's opened."

He smiled and said, "I expected that." He pushed the door open to enter.

As they went in, she could see the room was identical to her own. There were several pieces of furniture: a desk, bed, and dresser. Tony opened the curtains to allow light into the room. It was a bright shiny day and the light flooded all corners of the room Emma looked around, noticing the bed was made, and asked, "Has the maid been allowed in to clean since he disappeared?"

"No. He would only allow cleaning if he was here. I made sure no one was given access in case you needed to examine it."

"Thanks for that," she said absently.

She noticed a large package against the wall and glanced at

Tony. He had opened the closet and was looking around. "Tony, what's that package there?"

"Package?" he asked, stepping out of the closet.

"Yes, over here," she said, kneeling in front of it.

Squatting down next to her, he said, "It looks like a painting. Do you want to open it?"

"Yes, please," she requested.

Tony picked up the picture and laid it down on the bed, then untied the strings holding the brown wrapper closed. "Oh," he said.

"You have seen this before?"

"Yes, as a matter of fact, this is a copy of the Vermeer painting The Girl with A Pearl Earring."

"Why is this one important?" she asked, having to rely on Tony for his expertise.

"It demonstrates the artist's technique for copying Vermeer's. I think Philip saw that. This also gives us the copier's name." He indicated the righthand side of the painting. "It's Charles Allaire."

"Do you know him?"

"Yes, we actually went by his studio. He's very talented; he makes money making copies of other works."

"Interesting. Why would Philip want a copy of a piece of art?"

"Let me look at something," said Tony, moving the picture into the light, looking for something Philip may have seen. He remembered all of the rules for determining if the pictures were fake.

He started talking out loud, detailing his thoughts. "The age of the fame wouldn't be applicable here; the one in the museum was determined to be the proper age. The cracking here is expert and would be hard to tell the difference between an older and newer version of the picture."

She was quiet as she waited for his evaluation.

He continued, "It must be the color. Emma, do you have that example we found in the museum?"

She flipped her notebook back to the aquamarine paint sample. "Yes, here it is," she said.

He took the notebook and compared it to the color used in the picture. "It is an excellent forgery, but the color in this painting is made from more current paints."

"Tony, is it possible Philip noticed the Vermeer in the museum was a fake?"

"The first one we saw was the original, but later when we went back, Philip saw Allaire in the museum storeroom. He was visibly agitated and followed him."

"Did he tell you what he saw?"

"No, he asked me to leave and meet him at the hotel later."

"Do you have any idea what he was planning to do?"

"No, I just followed direction. We often separated to allow us to review more art."

"Tony, we need to go see that artist."

"Yes, I know where his studio is located," said Tony.

"Let's finish this room and we can head that way after."

They continued studying Philip's belongings, finding no other clues.

"Tony, have you seen his notebook or letters?"

"No, but he would probably have taken it with him."

They finished the room and locked it behind them. Tony suggested, "Let's head out. We'll need our coats. It's chilly this morning."

They headed downstairs to their waiting carriage, heading to Monsieur Allaire's studio.

"Tony, do you think Monsieur Allaire is involved in Philip going missing?"

"I think he might be someone with a piece of this puzzle," said Tony firmly.

Emma fell silent as she watched the scenery passing by.

The area changed as they drove and Tony commented, "We're going into a poor area on the west side."

"I thought he was successful."

"He is, but he's had the space for a long while and I think it keeps him from being too visible."

She watched the elegant homes be replaced by rundown buildings and apartments. The roads also appeared to be less taken care of.

"This is what I mentioned about two sides to Paris. The well off and the not well off," said Tony.

"Yes," she said softly.

When they arrived, they exited the carriage, thanked the driver, and headed toward the doorway of what appeared to be a warehouse. He guided her to the side door, then reached up and banged on it. It was only a moment later when a rather stooped older gentleman opened the door. Funnily, Emma had seen him before this. He was the man in the hallway at the hotel!

"Tony, what a surprise to see you," commented Monsieur Allaire in English.

Emma was watching him carefully and noticed he wasn't surprised to see them. He seemed to be avoiding looking at the painting Tony held. "What can I do for you?"

"You can let us in," Tony said pointedly.

"Both of you?"

"Yes," he said, nodding at Emma.

"Yes, of course." But instead of letting them in, he tried to shut the door. Emma anticipated that move and put her foot in the door to block it from closing. She had also pulled her very large knife out of her hatband. Holding it toward him threateningly, she said, "I think you could step back and allow us in for some questions. You will cooperate, right?"

Monsieur. Allaire looked confused at the little girl with the large knife. He nodded slowly, backing up and letting them in.

"I knew it was a good idea to bring you," muttered Tony out of the side of his mouth as he followed her in.

Emma stayed close to Monsieur Allaire and kept her knife drawn so he would know they were serious. They made their way into a large room full of easels. She assumed this to be the main work area. She couldn't look around much until he was secured. "Tony, I think we should tie him up before we ask our questions."

"Yes," he said, looking around for rope. He saw some piled in the corner, probably used to secure the paper wrapped around the frames. He grabbed a chair and Emma motioned with her knife for Monsieur Allaire to sit down. She watched Tony tie him up and said, "Wait a moment, I know that trick," when she saw how he stiffened his arms. She gripped his shoulders and squeezed so Tony could get the rope tighter around his wrist.

"Tony, also tie his legs to the chair," she directed.

Tony nodded. Once Monsieur Allaire was secure, he backed away.

Emma ran her finger down the length of the knife. "I know you don't want me to use this on you." She was fully prepared to do so if needed.

"No, I want to talk. What's the topic?" he asked innocently.

Tony yanked off the paper on the picture he was carrying. "What about this as a topic?"

"I don't know what you are talking about." He avoided looking at the painting.

Tony continued, anger noticeable in his tone. "This painting has striking similarities in technique to the Vermeer painting. I think Philip Johnson saw you at the museum and thought the same thing we did. You supplied a forgery of the Vermeer to the museum. I think you knew this painting, showing your technique, could give you away."

Emma interrupted, "Tony, he was at our hotel. I saw him in

the hallway. I think he wanted this painting back and he tried to get it from our hotel room."

Tony frown. "Why did you let Philip buy it if you were just going to try to steal it back?"

Monsieur Allaire admitted, "I was careless and did not think when I sold it to him. It wasn't until later when I heard he was authenticating the exhibit, that I knew I'd made a mistake." Emma took a step closer, and he gulped. "Okay, Mon Dieu! I will tell you. Yes, I painted a copy of the Vermeer for the museum and, yes, Philip did see me delivering it."

"Why?" asked Tony.

"The people who originally stole these paintings realized there was no way to escape with the art, much less sell it, so they set up the story that they had recovered the art and became heroes."

"So, Monsieur Martin was involved," Tony concluded.

He didn't want to answer, and Emma nudged him with her boot. "Yes, he was losing money. His museum was not doing well," he said grudgingly.

"Why the duplicate pictures? If he had the originals?"

"He wanted to see if he could fool experts. It would allow him more time to sell for higher values."

"Yes, the authentication would stop any further question about the exhibit," Tony muttered.

"What happened to Philip?" asked Emma.

"I don't know. I just know I told Monsieur Martin that we had not fooled him and he had seen the painting." He shrugged and said, "After that, I was not involved."

Tony looked at Emma and asked, "Do we believe him?"

There was no hesitation in his voice, and he held direct eye contact. "Yes. I think he's telling the truth, at least partially."

"Okay," he said, trusting her.

"But," she said, "I still think he knows more than he's saying. Do you mind if I take over?"

"No, please." He waved at her to start.

Emma stepped closer and said, "Monsieur Allaire, you've told us of your involvement in the forging."

"Copying," he interrupted.

She gave him a look and raised her eyebrows. "Monsieur Martin had to leave in a hurry. What was your role in this?"

"I had no role. I only provided the copy; I was not involved in any of the rest," Allaire muttered.

"It occurs to me that Philip would have been a loose end, a person creating a muddle for this enterprise," commented Emma.

He was quiet and she watched him closely. She went to the big question, wanting to see his reactions if he gave anything away in surprise.

"Charles, where is Philip?" she asked unexpectantly. His eyes darted to the wall and back. He bowed his head and did not respond. She turned immediately to Tony, saying, "That wall."

Tony didn't hesitate and ran over, tapping on it. "It's a fake." He started tearing the facade with his hands. Emma ran over to help. It only took moments to take it down and reveal a door.

Tony reared back once to kick it; it gave but did not open. He kicked it again. The lock flew off and the door splintered. They pushed the debris out of the way and saw the tiny room beyond.

Emma said, "Wait, I have my portable light." She pulled it out of her pocket and lit the small gas lamp. Walking ahead of Tony, she saw a huddled figure against the wall.

Tony ran over to the figure. "Philip." He turned him over. His appearance shocked Tony. He was at least 10 lbs. lighter and appeared to also be dehydrated. He started to untie him, saying over his shoulder, "Emma, get something for him to drink and eat! Hurry!"

Emma left the small room, walked over to Monsieur Allaire, and gripped his neck, saying in a low, threatening voice, "You deserve to be hurt for what you did to that man." He didn't move; he was too scared of her to say anything.

"Where are your food and drink?" she demanded.

"Over there," he said, careful not to move his neck.

She released him and immediately found the baguette and cheese, along with some wine. She ran over to where Tony had moved Philip into the main room. He was coming to, saying, "Tony, I am so glad you found me."

"Tony, get him to eat," Emma encouraged as she tore off some bread, added cheese to it, and opened the wine for him to take a long drink.

He sat eating and trying to gather strength. He had been left in the room with almost no contact and very little food for weeks. The last few days, he had been left completely alone and tied up. After he finished eating, Tony helped him stand and took him to confront Monsieur Allaire. "I have nothing to say to you. You tried to kill me, and you didn't succeed. You did this for money."

Monsieur Allaire was completely defeated at this point.

"It will be prison for you," Philip continued. He sat down; he was still very weak. "There is a schedule of the trip, listing the cities where the art will be shown. We will need to interview some of the rail personnel for storage and location."

Emma watched him, thinking, *Philip will need time to recover.* She looked over at Tony and said, "Tony, you have been in contact with the police about Philip being missing. Could you have them come here to pick up Monsieur Allaire?"

"I can. I will go immediately." He knew Emma could handle herself and didn't stop to question her. He headed out the door, calling, "Emma, lock it up behind me."

"Good idea," she said. After doing so, she returned to the two men. Philip did not want to talk about what had happened to him, but he was curious about other topics. "How did you get involved in this mess?"

"Tony. He knew immediately that something was wrong. He contacted the police, but there was no indication of foul play; they also didn't know you. Tony checked in at the museum and found it abandoned. He knew he needed help and contacted me."

"I appreciate your aid in this. I am not sure I would have made it out alive," Philip said gratefully.

Emma nodded and let the silence settle around them. Much time passed before she heard a pounding on the door. She jumped up and went to answer it, letting Tony and the police in.

As she opened the door, she heard Tony explaining what had happened there. The words forgery, kidnapper, and rideau de mur reached her as they walked to the room. The story unfolded as Philip described the last few weeks. They were pointing at Monsieur Allaire and then at Emma.

"Mademoiselle," the officer said in English. "We have some questions. How did you know the man was hidden in that room?" he asked, pointing at the wall that had been torn down.

"I had a feeling this man was hiding something and, when I asked, he looked in that direction. We investigated and found Philip," she explained.

Philip said, "She is a trained detective. She works with the Pinkertons in Chicago."

The officer knew of the Pinkertons, gave her an appraising look, and thought, *A woman detective?* The officer marked down that information in his notebook. He stopped his writing and said, "We will be taking him in for processing." He motioned toward the officer who had Monsieur Allaire in cuffs. They left with him, saying there would be follow-up questions.

Tony said to Philip, "We have the carriage waiting. We should get you a doctor."

He stood, a bit shaky, but said, "No, I just need out of here. Along with a bath and some more food."

CHAPTER 68

*E*mma and Tony ignored Philip's objections and went to each side of him, supporting him to the carriage. The ride over was quiet as they each thought about what they had learned. They reached the hotel and helped him inside. Tony assisted him to the lavatory, where he could bathe. After they got him settled onto the couch with a tray of food, he looked like he was feeling better. He asked, "Where do we go from here?"

Emma said, "I think we check in at the rail station and find out where the paintings were shipped. I would assume they had to arrange for the boxes to be loaded into rail cars."

Philip nodded in agreement.

Tony said firmly, "Emma and I will follow up. You need to rest."

"What I need now is not rest. I will stay here and compile my notes for us to review."

"Good idea. Tony, we should get going," Emma said as she gathered her notebook and jacket. They headed downstairs and arranged for a carriage to take them to the rail station. After they arrived, they looked for the office that handled shipping in boxcars. They knew that pictures in that amount and size would need to be on a separate rail car. Approaching the counter, Tony asked for the manager. The man waved him to the side office.

They thanked him and went to knock on the door. Tony called out, "Bonjour."

An older man with dark blond hair walked up, greeting them. "Bonjour, puis-je faire pour vous?" Tony explained the paintings they were looking for.

The manager gave them a surprised look and said, "Oui," as he pulled out his files and confirmed the shipment. "Ils sont sortis il ya deux semaines."

"Pouvez-vous nous dire la destination?" Tony asked.

"Dijon to Lyon, Marseille, and Cannes." He indicated that their tickets had delays scheduled for two weeks at each stop to show the painting locally and continue from there.

"Cela les rendrait maintenant en route vers Lyon," the manager said.

Tony thanked him for the information. They now had a heading: Lyon. He turned to Emma. "Let's go." As they headed to the carriage, he explained what the manager had told him.

Emma nodded and said, "Yes, that confirms it. They are using a tour to change out the painting for the fakes and sell the originals. The artist is lead to believe that their originals will still be returned at the end of the trip."

"Do you expect him to return when the tour is over?" Tony asked.

"No, I think it is an elaborate cover for a long-term theft. I expect he will disappear a very rich man."

They mulled this over and returned to the hotel. As they entered the room, they saw Philip was doing much better. "I guess a few meals made the difference?" asked Tony.

"And lots of water. A bath did not hurt either," Philip said wryly.

As they sat down, he asked, "Did you confirm the stops?"

"Yes, they detailed the locations that the pictures will be on the rail," said Tony.

Philip checked his notes and said, "Okay, he is staying to his schedule, trying to act like nothing is wrong."

"We need to keep it quiet that Monsieur Allaire was arrested and you were found," suggested Emma.

"Yes," they agreed.

"I will notify the police of our plans," said Philip.

"Could we notify authorities at those stops?" asked Emma.

"We could," Philip acknowledged, "but they would not be able to hold Monsieur Martin. They would have to release him since there is no proof that he has done anything wrong."

"What about Monsieur Allaire?"

"They are not sure about him; they think this could just be the work of a sick man. Monsieur Martin is well respected in this community."

"What would make him do this?" asked Tony.

"Money, I think. I sent a note to the bank to ask about the building and ownership. He was way behind on his payments."

"Why handle it this way? Was he involved in the original theft of the artwork?" Tony asked.

"The theft was from his museum initially and, when 'found', it made him a hero. It also made the artist/owners of the art believe he would do anything to protect their paintings."

"Why was the Vermeer included in the show? It seems all the other art is more modern," Tony commented.

"Yes," Philip said, considering this. "I believe the Vermeer is the main prize here. The other works are part of a cover and will get lots of money, but the Vermeer is the one that will allow him to disappear."

"So," said Tony, "we think that, at each stop, he will probably be selling one work of art and replacing it with a copy?"

"I think so," he acknowledged.

"And since the Vermeer is the most valuable piece, it will

probably be the last sale in Cannes," Emma stated, studying at the schedule.

"And from there," finished Tony, "he will disappear."

"Okay, so we go to him, right?" she asked.

Philip and Tony laughed. Philip commented wryly, "Yes, I believe we do."

Tony asked, "Philip if the forgeries are that good, how will we be able to show them to the police?"

"Two things," said Philip. "One, the forgeries will be located somewhere nearby. I assume he wouldn't keep them on location."

"And the second?"

"The second," he said contemplatively, "is based on Allaire's vanity."

"Vanity?" asked Emma.

"Yes, Tony could you bring the Vermeer forgery from my room?"

"I have that out already," he said, indicating the wrapped painting against the wall by the door.

Philip did not look toward the painting. "No, not that one. There is another one. Pull up my mattress, you will see it."

Tony got up to retrieve it. He brought it back to the room and uncovered it. "You had the picture from the museum!"

"Yes, that day I told you I would join you later at the hotel, I had seen Allaire and knew he might be up to something. I found this in the storeroom."

"What made you take it?" asked Emma.

"Instinct, Allaire's behavior, and my wanting to protect Monsieur Martin."

"Which is it the original or the copy?" asked Emma.

"Let's take a look," Phillip said.

"Where do you want it?" asked Tony.

"Over here on the table. Emma, open the curtains," directed Philip. "Tony, take a good look and tell me what you see."

Tony looked at it again, marveling at the detail. "The cracking in the aged paint is amazing; the colors, though a different medium, pass for the original at first glance." He looked at Philip and asked, "What am I looking for?"

"It is a tiny thing, but you are looking for something that should not be there. Mr. Allaire is a very vain man and, when I saw this in the storeroom at the museum, I knew I had to take it and evaluate it. They really should hire better security," he said wryly.

"Taking the painting was what got you targeted? Then why go when Monsieur Martin called that night?"

"I'd thought we were friends. I hoped he wasn't involved or, at the very least, I hoped to talk him out of his plans."

"And when you got there?"

"He was waiting, I tried to talk to him, but he kept demanding to know where I had taken the painting. I wouldn't tell him; he had men hiding in the shadows. We didn't talk much after that," he said ruefully. "Next thing, I woke up in that tiny room."

"So, what did you see on the painting?" asked a curious Emma.

"Look here," he said, pointing to a faintly-stroked AA, barely distinguishable.

"What is it?" Emma asked, squinting.

Tony smiled when he located what Philip was referencing. "Allaire's initials."

"Good eye, Tony," offered Philip, proud he had seen it. "That's it exactly, and that was the reason I knew they were forgeries."

Tony said, "I had thought it was the color blue; it is not an exact match to Vermeer's blue."

"Tony, I knew you were perfect for this work. Yes, that is also another tell, but most people don't know to look for it. It will be easier to show the authorities the initials."

"So, we need to get to Monsieur Martin and locate the forgeries?" asked Tony.

"Yes," said Philip." I have arranged for tickets. We will keep these rooms and take smaller bags with us. We will go by train first to Dijon and then Lyon. Train travel should put us in Lyon while the exhibit is there."

"When does the train leave?" asked Emma.

"We leave at 4:00pm."

She looked down and saw it was 2:00pm and said, "Let's get packed and meet here in twenty minutes?"

They nodded, looking at each other, and then headed to their rooms. Philip had arranged for a carriage to the train station. He exited his room and saw Tony but not Emma. "Is Emma not ready yet?"

"She needed to send a wire in the lobby. We'll meet downstairs."

They joined her there as she was finishing up her message. It contained an update of her plans and that they had found Philip. She also sent her relief and gratitude that Zeke was caught, as well as confirming her return in another one to two weeks.

They left the hotel and took a carriage to the train station. On the way there, Emma tried to see everything. Philip saw her straining out of the carriage and promised, "Emma, we'll show you around as soon as we return."

She smiled. "That would be wonderful."

They reached the station and found their cabin. They would need just the one due to the fact the trip to Dijon would only take a day. They settled in and Philip said, "We'll be getting off at Dijon and going to the museum there."

CHAPTER 69

They spent a pleasant morning on the train and got organized as they entered the station at Dijon.

The museum they were looking for was located in one of the grand mansion houses. Philip had the address and gave it to the carriage driver.

They stopped in front of one of the more imposing buildings —beautiful and so much older than anything Emma had ever seen. They paid the driver and approached the entrance. There was a painted sign turned toward the wall. Tony turned it toward them and read it out loud. "It says it's a limited one-week exhibit." It was an open museum and seemed quite popular.

They entered the door and asked for the curator, giving his name and title. Philip did not know him but hoped he would be able to tell them something about Monsieur Martin's behavior.

They waited for a moment when a man with black hair and dark brown eyes came up, saying, "Je comprends que vous êtes ici pour me voir à propos d'une exposition antérieure?"

Philip nodded, glad he was open to discussing an exhibit not currently featured, but they needed privacy. "Oui est-il quelque part où nous pouvons parler?"

The man looked at him consideringly and said, "De cette façon s'il vous plait."

They followed him and entered a rather large office filled with stuffed furniture, an imposing desk, and lovely artwork on the walls.

"S'asseoir s'il vous plait," he offered, gesturing to the seats.

They sat. The curator started, "Vous avez mentionné votre nom est Philip?"

"Oui. Et voltra nom?" asked Philip.

"Claude Bernard. Je te connais vous avez authentifié les peintures qui étaient dans notre exposition la semaine dernière."

Philip's eyes widened, surprised the man knew his previous work authenticating paintings. He went on to explain that he had been tricked and the paintings were being switched out as they were sold.

Mr. Bernard looked at Emma and Tony. "Would you like me to switch to English? So that we may include your companions?"

"Please."

"So, tell me what we can do to prevent this theft from continuing. I am ready to help. People like this man make our business difficult," said Monsieur Bernard.

"Do you have additional storage other than the pictures on display?" asked Philip.

He frowned and said, "Now that you mention it, he did ask if we had an offsite storage location beside the one here."

"Do you?" Philip pressed.

"Yes, we do. We change out our displays and have a controlled area for the works of art not on display."

"We believe he is keeping the forgeries at those offsite locations," said Tony.

"It is empty now, and they have made their way to Lyon for the next part of the exhibition," said Mr. Bernard.

They nodded and Emma asked quietly, "Can we ask you not to mention our visit to anyone?"

"Oui, of course." He was also thinking out loud. "I might also have the person who purchased the picture that was replaced with a copy."

"Who was it?" Emma asked.

"That is hard. It is a political thing for me. If you allow it, I will look into this while you go after Monsieur Martin," he requested.

Philip studied him, then looked at Emma, knowing she would see something he didn't. She saw his gaze and nodded that he should continue forward. He turned back and said, "Okay, we have a deal."

"You will contact me about your progress?" Mr. Bernard inquired.

"We will and please let us know the progress here," stated Philip firmly.

"One more thing. Do you know the museum curator at the museum in Lyon?" asked Tony.

"I do. He is an honest man. He will work with you once he realizes he is involved with a criminal. I will write you a letter of introduction," Mr. Bernard said.

"Thank you so much. We're heading out by train this evening," said Philip.

"I will have it to you at the station before you leave," he promised.

"Thank you so much."

"No, thank you. We must stand together to stop people like this."

"Agreed." They all shook hands and left the office.

They didn't have much time, but they did take a moment to eat a nice dinner before heading back to the train.

The promised letter of introduction arrived just prior to them leaving. Philip read it as they discussed their learning on the trip to Lyon. He put it down and asked, "How do we want to handle this? It could be confrontational if we go straight to the museum."

"We'll need support before we go. We should talk to the local police and explain the situation. We should also get the curator to meet us there," suggested Emma.

"Agreed. We don't want anyone hurt, but we want to prevent any more theft," said Philip.

They arrived in Lyon late at night. They agreed to stay at a local hotel and go to the Sûreté in the morning. They met early and went straight there, asking for an officer who could speak English; it was getting complicated, and they needed to make sure there were no misunderstandings.

The Sûreté looked at them and said, "I will have to confirm this information with the office in Paris."

"Yes, I understand, but we need to move as soon as possible," Philip said and remembered the letter. He took it out of his pocket, handing it to the officer. "This might help."

The Sûreté read the letter and said, "I will still send the note to Paris, but with this, we can contact the curator to come over." He looked behind him and called, "Julian, I will need you to ask Jules Borde, the museum curator, to join us for a talk. You must keep it very quiet and do not wear your uniform. Pretend to be a friend and hand him this letter."

"I will change and head over now."

The officer directed them to a conference room down the hall. "You may wait in that room there; I will also get the note to the Sûreté in Paris."

Once they entered the room, Tony asked, "What do you think, Emma?"

"I think we have to trust that he's doing as he says. We have no reason not to at this time."

"That's true," he agreed. All they could do is wait.

It turned out that it didn't take long, A knock sounded at the door and a man they assumed was the curator appeared.

"Bonjour, I am Jules Borde, the curator for the museum," he said in very hesitant English. "I have read that you must speak with me and I cannot tell anyone about this."

They introduced themselves and went over everything in detail with Mr. Borde.

"You are sure that Monsieur Martin is involved in this, this criminal enterprise?" he asked, surprised he had such a man's exhibit in his museum.

"We are," stated Philip firmly.

"Before you come into my museum with such accusations, I will need proof."

Tony looked at Philip and said, "I think I can do that." He had the Vermeer with him and removed the paper to reveal it. There was a gasp from Monsieur Borde. "But that is the Vermeer we have in the museum exhibition. IIow do you have this?" he asked incredulously.

"It is not an original. This is a copy that was made to replace the original," explained Philip.

"How do I know this is a copy and not the actual picture?"

Philip understood that this man did not want to be involved in something nefarious, so he was responding defensively. He acted calmly, pointing to the addition of Allaire's name. Mr. Borde knew that name and how talented he was at forgery. "I will need to check the painting in my museum, but I am believing more and more that we have a criminal running an exhibit there."

At that moment, the Sûreté entered and said, holding a telegram, "Mr. Boarde, I can also confirm that Monsieur Allaire is in prison awaiting trial for kidnapping and attempted murder of Monsieur Johnson."

Monsieur Borde looked resigned and said, "It looks like we need to work fast and get these people out of my museum."

"Agreed. Can you tell me if you have another storage location Monsieur Martin was using?" asked Tony.

"There is," he acknowledged and shared the location.

"Do you think it's watched?" asked Tony.

"I think he would have a person assigned," the Sûreté said, looking at Monsieur Borde. "We can handle that. You will need to go to the museum with Monsieur Johnson and his group to confirm the paintings."

"Can you send an officer with us as well, to stop him from leaving?" asked Emma.

"I will need one of you to come in and identify the forgeries," stated Mr. Bernard.

Tony said, "It will have to be Emma. She's the only one of us he doesn't know."

"That's right, she would go unnoticed," confirmed Philip.

When they arrived at the museum, Tony and Philip waited outside with the officer. Others were guarding the back entrance. Emma went in and was being walked around the new exhibit with Monsieur Borde. "There it is over there," he said to her.

"Let's not rush," she cautioned.

"You are right. Let's look at some of the other paintings." She went to each one, using her observation skills to find the added initials. She made a mental note which one had been replaced. "If you'll notice," she said, trying to keep it brief, "this painting has Allaire's initials. We need to move on, or we'll be noticed." She had seen Monsieur Martin in the room with them. He seemed to be taking special notice of her.

"Yes," Monsieur Borde said, feeling troubled but trying to be nonchalant. "We have another exhibit going on I think you would like to also see." He escorted her to the next exhibit. That seemed to relax Monsieur Martin, and he went back to studying the book he was holding.

Emma reached the window and sent the prearranged signal. It was the right time and there were few people in the exhibit. The officers came into the back room as Tony and Philip were escorted in the front door. Monsieur Martin looked incredulous at the sight of Philip. "But you are dead!" He didn't seem to notice the police officers arriving.

"Turns out Allaire is better at forgeries than he is at murder. You should have gotten a professional," commented Philip in a dry tone.

Monsieur Martin looked at a loss, not understanding the conversation he was trapped in. An officer tapped him on the shoulder, and he jumped. "What?"

"You will need to come with us," the officer said in French.

He didn't seem to know how to respond.

"Emma, did you find the painting that was forged?" inquired Philip.

She nodded toward the wall across from them. "It's that one."

Monsieur Martin blanched at the identification, stuttering, "I don't know what you are talking about. These are not forgeries and, if they are, I was not aware."

At that moment, the lead officer entered and said, "We have the other forgeries; they are secure and the gentleman watching them is in custody."

Monsieur Martin kept arguing that he didn't know what they were talking about.

"We will need to take custody of the painting and shut down this exhibit," stated the officer.

Monsieur Borde said, "I understand. We will have them taken down."

"I will leave several officers here to help you. The other paintings are being delivered to the station."

They took Monsieur Martin down to the station and placed

him under arrest. He just didn't seem to believe that his operation was over and that his well-thought-out plan wasn't going to work. When they arrived, they escorted him to the interrogation room, where he kept arguing they were wrong and he wasn't aware of any of this.

The Sûreté let him talk, not asking any questions. Another Sûreté came over and whispered, "The room is set up for your convenience."

Feeling he was finally being treated with the respect he should have been given all along, Monsieur Martin stood and wrinkled his nose at them as he passed. *I knew I was smarter than these people. I will be released soon,* he thought as he moved to the next room. What he did not expect to see was the art from his exhibition lined up around the walls. It was not just his art; the forgeries were also there next to their originals. *They think they have me,* he thought. *I can explain this.*

The Sûreté started with their questions. "Monsieur Martin, can you tell me why you have two of each painting?"

Feeling very much in charge, he said, "As any seasoned museum curator will tell you, you need to have copies on hand in case one of the originals is on loan to another gallery or a private party."

"Hmmm, that is an explanation," he said as he slowly reached into his pocket. "Except that I have a wire here from Paris that states Monsieur Allaire has said he was paid for forgeries and further implicates you in Monsieur Johnson's kidnapping and attempted murder."

"Bah," Monsieur Martin said loudly. "Allaire is a villain. Whatever he did, he did of his own volition."

"Hmmm, that may be," commented the Sûreté, "and I might have given you the benefit of the doubt. But then I received another wire from the gallery curator in Dijon. It was sent to Monsieur Johnson; I hope you don't mind if I read it aloud."

"Please do," said Philip.

"It says here that the original of that painting," he pointed to the one standing on its own, without a copy, "was sold to a city official. The official says he was unaware that his provenance was falsified. I believe, if we also check with the artist, that this work of art is on loan and not for sale."

"Well, mistakes could have been made. I thought I sold him a copy not an original," he blustered.

The Sûreté looked down on him from his imposing height. "A man with your experience could not tell a copy from an original?"

"Allaire is very good," he said lamely, for the first time looking defeated. That seemed to finally make Monsieur Martin stop talking. They took him out of the room for further processing.

The officer jotted down Emma, Tony, and Philip's statements.

"What will happen to the art?" asked Philip.

The officer looked up from his notes and said, "It will be held until the trial, along with the originals and forgeries. We will notify the owners of the situation and the location of their art. Thank you so much for your help in capturing this man. What do you believe the plan was?"

"My theory was that Monsieur Martin had planned to sell the originals along the route and replace them with the forgeries," said Philip.

"How would that have worked with the Vermeer, since you had the forgery?"

"Interesting question," said Philip. "I have thought about that; it would have to be the last one sold. I think he didn't plan on returning. You will probably find out that he let go of his Paris apartment."

"So, just disappear," the officer stated.

"He would have had plenty of money," said Tony.

"Do you plan to stay in Lyon? We have some wonderful buildings and museums to view," the officer asked with a smile.

"I think we will stay for a few days and then head back to Paris; I owe someone a tour there," Philip teased as he looked at Emma.

CHAPTER 70

The Sûretés arranged a hotel for them and they stayed for three days. While they waited to give testimony, they toured and saw La Basilique Notre Dame de Fourviére. Emma read that Fourvière is dedicated to the Virgin Mary, to whom is attributed the salvation of the city of Lyon from the bubonic plague that swept Europe in 1643.

Next was the Vieux Lyon, the largest Renaissance district of Lyon. There are three distinct sections: Saint Jean, Saint Paul, and Saint Georges. In the Middle ages, the Saint Jean quarter was the focus of political and religious power. The Cathedral of St. Jean, seat of the Primate of Gaul, was a good example of Gothic architecture.

The Saint Paul section, predominately Italian banker-merchants in the 15th and 16th centuries, had moved into wonderful urban residences called hôtels particuliers.

Lastly, they saw the Cathedral Saint-Jean-Baptiste. It was founded by Saint Pothinus and Saint Irenaeus, the first two Bishops of Lyon, located in the heart of Vieux Lyon, and backed up to the Saône river.

After they had completed their final statements to the police, they caught the train back to Paris. It would take a full day, but they were eager to return. When they arrived at the hotel, they found a message for Emma from the local police. They wanted her to meet with them. "I wonder what this is about," said Emma.

"I am sure it's okay," stated Tony. "We can head over together and ask in the morning."

"Yes," agreed Philip.

Emma thought about that and said, "You know, I'll go on my own. I'm okay."

"If you're sure," said Tony.

"I am," she stated.

They started to head up to their room but were stopped by the manager. "I would like to accompany you to your room. If you do not mind."

Philip frowned but said, "Yes, that would be fine."

As they were finally entering their room, they were surprised at what they saw. Numerous paintings lined the walls. "Where did these come from?" asked Philip.

The manager spoke from behind them. "Monsieur, all of Paris heard what you have done for our artists. This is their thanks. Some of our best artists are sending their work to your museum. On loan," he cautioned, with a chuckle.

As Tony and Philip immediately began looking at each painting, the manager silently exited. Emma was sitting quietly and said, "I think we should all head home. I think it's time."

"But I have promised to show you Paris," protested Philip.

"I know, but I want to get back. I have responsibilities there," she said.

"Okay, I will start the arrangements," Philip promised. It turned out that they did have time to see the sights; it would take at least four days to organize the paintings for shipment. They took her to see the Arc de Triomphe, a massive triumphal arch that Napoleon Bonaparte commissioned in 1806 after his great victory at the Battle of Austerlitz.

Next, they saw the royal residence and the Palais du Louvre had been hosting the Louvre Museum since 1793. Lastly, they saw the Notre-Dame de Paris, the location of Napoleon Bonaparte's coronation in 1804.

Emma took a carriage to the Sûreté. They had heard about her experience with Pinkerton and wanted to spend some time showing her one of their methods called signaletics or bertillonage. This method identified an individual by measurements of head and body, shape formation of the ear, eyebrow, mouth, and eye. It also included markings such as tattoos, scars, and personality characteristics. They applied this information onto cards that included photographs. The cards were systemically filed and crossed indices so they could easily be retrieved. Emma took lots of notes to share with Cole and Jeremy. She thanked them for their time.

The ship pulled into the port in New York, and Emma was the first person waiting for the plank to be lowered. She took off at a run and was in Jeremy's arms before anyone else could leave the ship.

"Welcome home, Emma," Jeremy said as he kissed her forehead and held her tight.

Notebook Mysteries

Kimberly Mullins

ABOUT THE AUTHOR

Kimberly Mullins is the author of series of books titled "Notebook Mysteries". Her stories are based on historical events occurring in 1800's Chicago. She holds a BS in Biology and a MBA in Business. She lives in Texas with her husband and son. When she is not writing she is working as a Process Safety Engineer at a large chemical company. You can connect with her on her website www.kimberlymullinsauthor.com.

Photo Credit: Blessings of Faith Photography

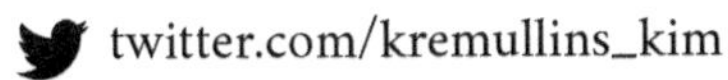 twitter.com/kremullins_kim

www.ingramcontent.com/pod-product-compliance
Lightning Source LLC
Chambersburg PA
CBHW070656010826

48975CB00014B/1339